Harriet Smart was born a[...]
ham. She attended the University of St Andrews,
specializing in the architecture and applied arts of
the eighteenth and nineteenth centuries. The
research for her degree thesis into a firm of church
furnishers in Birmingham inspired her first novel, *A
Garland of Vows*, which fulfilled a life-long ambition
to write historical fiction. After graduating in 1988,
she married a fellow student and they now live in
Edinburgh.

Also by Harriet Smart

A Garland of Vows

Green Grow the Rushes

Harriet Smart

KNIGHT

First published in 1992
by HEADLINE BOOK PUBLISHING PLC

First published in paperback in 1993
by HEADLINE BOOK PUBLISHING PLC

This edition published 1997 by
Knight an imprint of Brockhampton Press

10 9 8 7 6 5 4 3 2 1

ISBN 1 86019 6209

Typeset by
Letterpart Limited, Reigate, Surrey

Printed and bound in Great Britain by
Mackays of Chatham PLC, Chatham, Kent

Brockhampton Press
20 Bloomsbury Street
London
WC1B 3QA

For Julian

Part One
1900
1

As she took off her hat and gloves, Jessie MacPherson looked around the kitchen with a mixture of satisfaction and sheer terror. So this was her new empire. It was not that she was unused to large kitchens – she had worked in such places since the age of thirteen when she had left her home in Kirkcaldy and come to Edinburgh, to work as a scullery maid in a house in Randolph Crescent. But there, and in her subsequent places, she had always been at the beck and call of the cook, merely a humble assistant learning the craft. But now she was the cook, faced with a kitchen maid and a scullery maid who were eyeing her with the same nervous suspicion that she had once extended to her sometimes tyrannous overseers.

It looked to be an efficient kitchen, but first appearances could be deceptive. It felt reasonably cool, which was a good sign considering it was a June morning of dry heat outside. The walls were painted a strange but pretty shade of blue-green which set off nicely the copper ware that was arranged on open shelves and racks about the the room. Carefully she noted the size and extent of this collection of pans. Everything seemed to be there from the great triangular kettle for poaching a turbot to the tiniest pan for heating a spoonful or two of sauce. The range was not smoking, she noted with relief, and seemed adequate for the size of the house. But ranges were tricky animals. She had never come across one which did not exhibit strange foibles, peculiar to itself. Above the range, on the brick chimney breast, was inscribed in dark letters the moral: 'Waste not, want not'.

'You'd think it was a workhouse!' exclaimed Jessie. The

maids looked startled, as if they did not understand what she was speaking about. 'That motto – it's like something out of a poor house, isn't it?'

'I suppose so, missus,' murmured one girl uncomprehendingly.

'Oh, just call me Jessie,' she said, throwing her hat and gloves on a chair. 'I may be the cook, but I'm no going to be pompous about it.'

The girls looked even more surprised, for the custom was to address the cook as if she were a married woman of mature years. But Jessie, who had just turned twenty-three, could not yet resign herself to the idea of being thought of like that.

'What are your names?' she asked.

'Effie, missus – I mean, Jessie,' said the elder girl. 'And this is Annie.'

'Well, I shall need you both to help me get my bearings. Where are the store rooms?'

'Through there – off the scullery.'

She walked through the open door that Effie indicated into the scullery. Compared to the kitchen it was primitive with a gloomy view of brick walls from its window and that faint smell of damp dish rags, endemic to sculleries, hanging in the air. The lowest rack of the drainer was filled with breakfast plates, and stacked none too neatly by the sink were some unwashed dishes. Her arrival had obviously interrupted Annie in her first washing up of the day. With annoyance she saw there was no way of heating up water in there. All the hot water would have to be carried through from the kitchen.

So much for the scullery, she thought, and pushed open the door in the corner which apparently led to the larders. She found herself in a barely lit passageway with three doors facing her. The first, conveniently nearest the scullery, appeared to be the dry larder, with broad stone shelves bearing cheeses coyly sheltering under gauze domes, baskets of eggs, and, most strikingly of all, a vast white bowl grandly bearing the family device: a large black 'L' with some sort of crest above it. The bowl, she discovered when she lifted the beaded muslin cover, contained nothing more exciting that some weary-looking milk which had been left to separate and had, by the look of it, been somewhat forgotten. But that grand 'L' struck her, for now as she looked around the shelves she saw it was everywhere, even on the humblest butter dish. It was family pride taken to a ridiculous degree. The Lennoxes of Quarro obviously thought a great deal of themselves! She wondered what they were all like.

She turned to find that Annie had followed her into the larder.

'This milk is off,' she said. 'You'd better get rid of it. In a few hours in this heat it'll reek.'

'Yes, missus,' said the girl and staggered into the scullery with the great bowl.

In the next larder the meat and fish were kept and from these essential items she could begin to construct the evening's menu. She took out her pocket book and made a few notes. There were some fine-looking sweetbreads and a handsome loin of lamb which would provide an entrée and roast. But what of the fish? She looked inside the ice chest and found residing in solitary splendour a large salmon, wrapped in damp sacking, which seemed an ignominious fate for such a beautiful fish. She lifted it out and felt the weight and stiffness of it, for looks could sometimes be deceptive. But this fish was fresh and firm, muscled like a prize fighter from struggling against the wild torrents of the Tweed. Monsieur Auguste, the French cook for whom she had worked for the last three years, had never been able to decide whether he thought Tay or Tweed salmon the finest, but Jessie could only imagine that the best fish in the world was the one caught within walking distance of the kitchen. She had seen the river, for the road from the station had run alongside it. It had flashed and sparkled in the early morning sun, running swiftly over rocks which looked as though they had been tossed in by some careless hand. She had thought of salmon then, and now she held one in her hands, precious and heavy, like some great piece of silver.

She placed it back in the ice chest and wiped her hands on

3

her handkerchief. She took up her pencil and wrote in her pocket book: 'Saumon Poëlé – beurre Montpellier?' She queried the sauce, because she had not yet inspected the vegetable store and kitchen garden. Herbs, those magic ingredients which could transform the simplest dish, had been both Monsieur Auguste's delight and despair – the latter because of the reluctance of Scots market gardeners to grow the range of herbs that he had known in his mother's sunny garden in Provence. In the end he had been forced to cultivate his own, growing neat tubs of sorrel, tarragon, rosemary and parsley in the tiny basement yard of the house in Randolph Crescent.

The vegetable store smelt sweet. It was easy to see why, for there were several large baskets of over ripe strawberries flooding the place with their unmistakable scent. Strawberry ices? she thought, for these strawberries were not pretty enough to send to the dinner table. They would have to make jam as well, to preserve what they could of this glut. It would be a disagreeable job on such a day. It was too hot for boiling cauldrons of sugar syrup but a few dozen jars of strawberry jam would be welcome in the bleak days of winter when the taste of fresh strawberries was a faint memory.

She turned her attention to the other vegetables. It was a reassuring sight. The kitchen garden was obviously in skilled and fastidious hands. There was asparagus, thick green and white fingers of it, touched with pink, as if they were blushing from the knowledge of their own quiet perfection. There were tiny carrots, tied up in elegant bundles like posies. There were lettuces, just unfurling their leaves and as complex as any rose. There were currants: black, white and red, beautifully presented on beds of leaves, like the many coloured blocks of annuals in a garden parterre. But most promising of all was an earthenware jug, stuffed to overflowing with parsley so that it created a neat green sphere, like a miniature piece of topiary. If there was such parsley, there was a good chance there would be other things and she decided to make a visit to the garden when she had a chance.

But now she would have to go and get changed. The mistress would be expecting her upstairs to discuss the day's menu.

Effie showed her to her quarters which lay not in the attics as she might have expected but up a flight of stairs adjacent to the kitchen. Such were the privileges of being an upper servant, for there was privacy, even a certain luxury, in such an arrangement. It was true that the furniture was old-fashioned and plain, that the drugget on the scrubbed and stained boards was fraying in places and that the chintz curtains were so faded that it was impossible to guess what exotic colours they might once have displayed. But the fact they were bleached meant but one thing – that the room caught the sun. And it was full of sunlight now, for the light flooding though the tall sash and pretty circular window above it had shone right in her eyes when she had opened the door. It bore no resemblance to the chilly attics or the stuffy box beds she had endured in the past. It was big enough to pace about in. It had a bed broad enough for two and a little desk with a fretwork bookshelf above it. There was only a Bible on it at present but Jessie mentally filled it with her own small collection of books.

'Oh, I shall be happy here!' she exclaimed as she opened her box. At the top, carefully wrapped in tissue, was her favourite working dress that she had laundered and ironed at the end of a brief holiday in Dysart. It was nothing special, a plain blue-and-white-striped washing cotton, but Monsieur Auguste, who had an eye for such matters, had complimented her on it and had called her 'ma belle cuisinière' when she had first worn it. She needed that glow of self-confidence now as she stood at the looking glass, buttoning on a fresh white collar and cuffs, for she had not yet seen the mistress, Mrs Lennox, and the idea of an interview with her made Jessie nervous. The consultation with those upstairs was something of which she had no experience. Her previous employers had been remote figures who never penetrated into the depths of the kitchen. But she was now the cook and was expected as soon as possible in the boudoir. A final glance in the glass

5

confirmed that her cap was straight and she smoothed her apron with a gesture that was ineffectual but calming.

When she had written out her menu, she went downstairs in search of someone who might point her in the right direction. She looked into what was presumably the butler's pantry and found a white-haired old man bent over a table covered in various pieces of silver, one of which he was polishing intently.

'Er, excuse me, sir . . .'

He turned round and smiled.

'Welcome to the Quarro, lassie,' he said, laying down his polishing rag. 'I'm sorry I wasn't there to meet you at the door but I was upstairs giving Sir Hector his coffee. You must be Mrs MacPherson.'

'Jessie,' she said. 'And you are Mr Maxwell?'

'Aye, that's right. Well, you'll be wanting to go upstairs and see the mistress, won't you?'

'Yes – if you've a moment to show me where to go.'

'Come with me, lass,' he said taking off his green baize apron and pulling on his tail coat which had been hanging over the back of a chair. 'You've got your menu, then?'

'Aye – do you need to see it?' she said, reaching into her pocket.

'Oh no, lass,' he laughed. 'I was just checking you hadn't forgotten. You wouldn't want to get off on the wrong foot now, would you?' And he winked and smiled in such a kindly way that Jessie felt reassured about the forthcoming interview.

Mr Maxwell took her up a flight of dark oak stairs that were dangerously well polished.

'That's the dining room through there,' he said, indicating one door as he opened another. 'You'll want to see that, I expect, when you've finished with the mistress. This is the saloon. This is where they have dances and such – it's a fine room, isn't it?'

The vast room was in semi-darkness as all the holland blinds were firmly down to keep the sun off what Jessie presumed was some very fine furniture.

6

'Very grand, yes,' she said. 'But I wouldn't feel comfortable sitting in here.'

'No, no, it isn't used much these days. It's a shame – you should have seen it when it was all lit up for a ball. Aye, that was a sight worth seeing . . . Here we are,' he said, for they had reached a door on the far side. 'I'll just announce you.'

She heard him say, 'The new cook is here, madam.'

'Send her in, Maxwell,' said a woman's voice and Jessie, summoned by a smile from Mr Maxwell as he came out, stepped into the boudoir.

Jessie knew at once that Mrs Lennox was a fraud. She did not quite know how she knew, for she did not count her experience of the world or of human nature to be very great, but in her bones, in those first few moments, she knew that this employer of hers was not at all what she pretended to be.

It was true that like a well-dressed stage set all the props of gentility surrounded her as she sat at her little desk. The panelling was an attractive faded cream and there was some pretty china carefully displayed on the shelves on either side of the fireplace. It was a mixture of Chinese and famille rose as far as Jessie could judge, for one did not work in smart Edinburgh houses without washing up a fair amount of valuable porcelain. There was a pair of old armchairs, covered in pink and gold tapestry, and the flowers in the room had been carefully picked and arranged to reflect these colours. Mrs Lennox herself, perched on a chair at the desk, was as beautifully arranged, the striped white voile of her skirts falling in an elegant serpentine curve in a manner which struck Jessie as altogether too studied.

It took Mrs Lennox a full few moments to bother to turn and look at her new cook. When she did it was with a long, scrutinizing gaze which did not at all become her undeniably pretty face.

'MacPherson, is it?' she asked, glancing at a letter which she held and which, Jessie presumed, contained her references.

'Yes, ma'am.'

'Your references seem quite in order – but I see that this

7

is your first post as a professed cook.'

'Yes, ma'am, but for the last three years I have been first kitchen maid for a French cook. I'm quite used to advanced work.'

'We shall see,' said Mrs Lennox in a tone which made Jessie quite mad. 'We entertain a great deal here, MacPherson, very distinguished people who are used to high standards. I hope you appreciate that.'

'Of course, ma'am. I'm sure you won't be disappointed.'

'Well, I shall give you a month's trial. I think that is quite reasonable in the circumstances.'

It will be quite mutual, thought Jessie, wondering how she was to bear the high-handedness of such a creature. Why, she's no different from me, except she's done well for herself! For as she had spoken, in a drawling, affectedly languid manner, Jessie had heard quite clearly the remnants, although carefully suppressed, of broad Scots, the undeniable accent of small-town Scotland, a world which Jessie knew well for she had grown up in it. Mrs Lennox was, she judged, perhaps the daughter of a clerk or small shopkeeper who by her wits, her face and sheer good luck, had managed to marry well.

'Very good, ma'am,' she managed to say. 'What are your orders for today?'

'We will be eight at dinner. We have guests coming down this afternoon. I have the menu here.'

Jessie glanced at it and suppressed a smile. It had the look of being copied straight out of Mrs Beeton, dull and entirely lacking in finesse. She decided to disregard it. She would make this jumped-up Mrs Lennox grateful to have her working there.

'Can you manage that, do you think?'

'Well, if you'll forgive me for a moment, ma'am, I've already visited the larders and made up some suggestions. If you don't mind my saying, this menu is not really suitable for what's in season. I suggest, for example, potage à la jardinière, followed by . . .'

'Jardinière?' interrupted Mrs Lennox, repeating the phrase awkwardly in an accent which made Jessie wince.

8

Monsieur Auguste had not only taught her how to make French sauces but how to pronounce them properly.

'Yes – it's much nicer on a hot day than a brown soup like consommé, wouldn't you say, ma'am?'

'Perhaps,' she said, sounding somewhat piqued. 'What else do you suggest then, MacPherson?'

'Well, ma'am, for the fish – saumon poêllé au beurre Montpellier, for the entrée – ris de veau a l'oseille . . .' Mrs Lennox's face was blank. 'That's sweetbread with sorrel, ma'am,' said Jessie, confident now in her own knowledge and this woman's utter ignorance. She carried on: 'Then sorbet de champagne. For the roast – loin of lamb with rosemary. Vegetables – petit pois au laitue, pommes dauphinoise. And finally tartes de groseilles à l'alsacienne, crème aux fraises and a soufflé à la vanille.' She was tempted to add 'Ça va, madame?' as Monsieur Auguste had always said to her when she had looked puzzled. But such a joke could not be shared with Mrs Lennox.

'If that is what you regard as suitable, MacPherson,' the mistress said after a moment, 'I can only hope that your ambition does not outstrip your capabilities.' She turned back to her desk. 'That will be all. You may go.'

Outside Jessie did not know whether to curse or to cry. What an impossible woman! I hope it wasn't a mistake to come here. She looked again at Mrs Lennox's menu which she still held, examining the neat copperplate hand which was not very far removed from board school copybook. She recognized it, for her own had once been as regular, but years of scrawling recipes on scraps of paper in order not to forget some gem had made her writing less than legible. She would have to make an effort with that; it was another of her responsibilities to write out menu cards for the dining room.

Before she went downstairs again she went into the dining room to see where her food would be presented. She hardly noticed the grandeur of it as she considered the practicalities. At one end of the room was a door to a small servery, and beyond that, an ominous flight of steps up which all the food had to be carried. She went that way back to the kitchen, measuring the distance, a perilous draughty

9

distance which could cool a dish or take the height from a soufflé. She would have to be careful about that.

A few hours later, she began to feel she had made good progress with the day's work. Effie made a creditable job of the staff dinner while Jessie cooked asparagus and cutlets to send upstairs for luncheon. The stock pot was simmering gently, the sorbet was in the ice chest, and when the time came for the staff dinner, Jessie felt quite happy to take her place in the servants' hall and relax.

The other servants returned to their work directly after dinner but Jessie remained in the hall with Mr Maxwell, enjoying for the first time the small pleasures of being an upper servant. Effie fetched them a pot of tea and while Jessie poured, she let Mr Maxwell elucidate the mysteries of the family 'upstairs'.

'Of course,' he said, 'things aren't as they used to be. When I first came here there were fifteen indoor staff – now we have to struggle along. It's a great shame that a grand old place like this can't be kept up properly these days.'

Certainly the size of the servants' hall, a large white-washed room with a ceiling shaped like a barrel and a long oak table with places enough for twenty, suggested that the Quarro had seen better days. Mr Maxwell gazed around him at the empty places with the look of a man who has seen the glories of Rome and now sees only ruins.

'No, it's not the same,' he sighed. 'Not with Mr James away all week in Edinburgh working – it isn't right that the eldest should have to work like that. Mr Andrew, yes, but the heir as well . . . I suppose he has to keep that wife of his in petticoats,' he added with a certain contempt.

'Mrs Lennox, you mean?'

'Yes – Mrs James. I think he could have done better for himself than that, but the girl obviously got her hooks into him. It wouldn't have happened when the master was young – things were better managed. People knew their place then.'

'And who else is there?' she asked.

'Well, there's Miss Elizabeth, the master's sister – she's been like a mother to Mr Andrew and Miss Celia since their

10

mother went. A very religious lady, she is, very proper – a better lady you couldn't ask to work for, unlike some I could mention.'

'I see,' smiled Jessie, organizing the ramifications of the family in her mind. 'How old are Mr Andrew and Miss Celia then? Will I have visits to my kitchen for cakes and lemonade?'

'Well, Mr Andrew always has a good appetite – but he's away at present, staying with some school friend in England. They're both seventeen – twins, you see.'

'Do they look like each other?'

'Oh no, not at all. You wouldn't know to look at them that they were brother and sister. I'll show you a picture,' he said, getting up and going over to a large Scotch chest at the far end of the room. 'Now, where did I put it . . .' he mused aloud, as he rummaged through a drawer. 'Ah, here we are. This was taken on Mr James's coming of age.'

The photograph showed a family group, with Sir Hector and Miss Elizabeth seated on chairs on a strip of carpet, the two children cross-legged on the ground in front of them, and standing behind, the young heir, the first growth of a moustache decorating his upper lip.

'No, they don't look alike at all,' she said, for the boy was fair and ruddy-looking while the girl had straight, dark hair and an intense expression on her slender face. 'I should reckon that she's grown up bonny,' she remarked.

'Oh, aye,' said Mr Maxwell with great satisfaction, 'she's the image of her mother and she was a real beauty.' There was real wistfulness in his voice, as if he had once extended to his lovely mistress a more than ordinary respect.

She glanced up at the clock and laid down the photograph.

'I'd better get started if we've visitors. I shall want to impress the mistress – she didn't seen quite convinced that I was up to the job.'

'I shouldn't worry about her, lass,' said Mr Maxwell. 'If Sir Hector likes what you send to the table, you'll be all right. He's still the master here.'

In the kitchen that afternoon, Jessie began to settle into a

11

routine. Effie was not entirely the liability that she had first suspected her to be, for like many girls she had learnt to bake at her mother's knee and if she knew no culinary refinements, she had a skill with cakes and pastry. Jessie showed her Monsieur Auguste's recipe for madeleines and it was not long before there was a rack of fragrant little cakes cooling on the kitchen table, each plump, golden and scallop shaped. She broke one in half to let Effie taste it and watched with a certain pleasure as the girl ate it greedily.

'Not bad for a first try,' said Jessie. 'I'll show you a lot more before I'm done with you.'

'Oh, would you?' asked Effie. 'Last cook we had wouldn't tell me anything and wouldn't let me do anything important. All I was allowed to do was make toast. Apart from the scrubbing, of course.'

'Why did she go?' asked Jessie, taking up the mandoline slicer and beginning to slice a cucumber.

'Mistress sacked her for giving her lip.'

'I shall have to watch what I say then,' said Jessie, 'I'll take my tempers out on this, or the meat pounder, instead of her!'

'Oh, aye, so long as you don't take it out on me,' said Effie with the first show of real spirit that Jessie had seen her display.

'I'll try not to,' she said. 'Now, I think you'd better get on with the vegetables for dinner. The peas need shelling and I want you to put on one side all the big tough ones. Nothing bigger than your littlest thumbnail, mind.'

'Can we brew up a pot of tea, Mrs MacPherson?' said Maudie, the younger of the housemaids, coming in. 'Just to catch our breath before the folk arrive. The mistress has been right fussy today. Anyone would think it was the Prince of Wales who was coming to stay.'

'Of course you can – any time you like. I like the company when I'm working. And please don't call me Mrs MacPherson – I hate that. Plain Jessie does for me.'

'You're a strange one, aren't you?' said Jean, the head housemaid. 'What are these, then?' she said, surveying the table where the plates for tea were laid out and pointing at the madeleines. 'Awful queer shape for a queen cake.'

'They're madeleines.'

'French, eh? I don't know what the master will say to that,' she said, shaking her head and walking away.

Jessie did not rise to the bait. She knew that people were notoriously conservative about what they ate, and that a middle-aged Scottish baronet would be no exception. Monsieur Auguste had once told her that when he had first come to Scotland, he had found a kitchen maid boiling cabbage for several hours. 'Mon Dieu!' he had exclaimed. 'What a wicked thing to do. So I asked her, "Ma petite, what 'as that poor chou done to you that you are so unkind to it?" When he had first told Jessie that story, she had been too young and ashamed to admit that her mother had taught her to do just the same.

While Jean and Maudie, the housemaids, sat and gossiped over their pot of tea, Jessie set up the tea trays. Over this she exercised a certain artistic licence, watching the quiet amazement of Jean as she placed a rose on top of a sponge cake and put a few flame-coloured nasturtium heads amongst the wreaths of parsley and watercress on the sandwich plates.

'Voilà!' she announced, when she had finished. 'That should show madam upstairs what I can do! Is there any tea left in the pot?'

2

It was a slow train down from Edinburgh, a slow afternoon train with an almost Mediterranean sense of languor as it toiled through the heat, which was intense for June and had taken them all by surprise. Alix sat impatiently in the compartment, bereft of intelligent company for her brother had fallen asleep over his book of French poetry and Sholto Hamilton, their travelling companion, who was no companion at all, had vanished, probably to smoke a cigarette. She had a book of her own, but she had not bothered to open it. It had been recommended by Ralph and she often found his taste too erudite. And today it had proved too much, even for him, for he was lost in the depths of sleep, his head lolling back on the antimacassar and his mouth hanging open in a manner which did little for his looks. He looked more like a vulnerable child than the fashionable young man that his pale suit and artistic tie suggested. His hair, thick and dark, and far too long for their father's taste, was well disordered and fell over his eyes in an ungainly shock. No one, seeing him then, would have called him handsome.

She fidgeted and cursed her own uncomfortable clothes. Her dress was a recent acquisition, but to her it seemed unbearably childish. Her mother did not seem to realize that she would soon be eighteen, and made no concessions to Alix's burgeoning womanhood except to decree that she was to have slightly longer skirts and always wear her stays. She felt, in that quantity of white starched muslin, like nothing so much as a lamb cutlet crowned with an absurd paper frill. The plain comfort of lawn tennis clothes would have been better for a day like this than ruffles and ribbons and gloves.

She got up and tried to force the window open a little further to catch the breeze, getting smuts on her gloves and waking Ralph by accidentally kicking him.

'Oh, I'm sorry,' she said, as he slowly gained consciousness.

'Are we there?' he asked, in a startled voice.

'No, I'm afraid not.'

He rubbed his face and yawned.

'Oh, what a day to be stuck in a slow train. I shall be glad to get some fresh air.'

'But we'll have to sit in the drawing room and have tea,' said Alix.

'If Lennox's wife has any sense, she'll have them serve it in the garden. Where's Sholto?'

'I don't know. He disappeared a while back.'

'He's probably fortifying himself in the buffet. I would,

too, but I'm under strict orders from Mother not to let you out of my sight.'

'How do you know what I've been doing when you were asleep?' she said provocatively, annoyed by this injunction of her mother's.

'Well, you haven't been reading that book I gave you,' he said, reaching forward and taking it from the seat beside her where she had abandoned it. He turned it lovingly in his hands, as if it were a precious bronze rather than a commonplace book. 'You should try this, really you should, Alix. It's wonderful stuff.'

'I can't manage it in French,' she said. 'I'll get a translation.'

'But you can't trust translations,' he said, opening the book at random and smiling at what he saw. 'Just listen to this . . .'

'No, Ralph, not now please,' she said, jumping up with exasperation and snatching the book from him. 'Must you be so pretentious?'

'Your trouble is that you are a philistine,' he said, 'like the rest of our family.'

'No, I'm just practical, Ralph. I don't want to live my life with my nose stuck in a book or glued to a painting. I want to do things!'

'That's because you have nothing to do,' said Ralph, with a smile. 'For me, this stuff is my only escape from the tedium of that dreadful office.'

'I'd work for Father if he would let me.'

'Pigs would have to fly first. But you wouldn't like it, really, Alix, it's a deadly, dirty business. No, if you'd been a boy, I could imagine you running away to sea or distinguishing yourself in some border skirmish in the farflung corners of the Empire. You wouldn't settle to dogsbodying for Father as I have had to.'

'Then why do you do it, if you hate it so, Ralph?'

'Because I am a spineless individual who wants a quiet life. And, I suppose, I've found I'm not incompetent at it. That pleases the old man, doesn't it? And God knows I please him little enough.'

'What, has he been telling you to get your hair cut again?' she laughed. 'Or is it that new tie he doesn't like? I must say, it is a little outré.'

'Well, it won't show the marks if I spill something down my front, when I get my usual attack of nerves. I hope all these Lennoxes aren't as crusty as James. He always makes me feel that I'm back in the third form.'

'Well, Celia is very sweet. You'll like her – she's desperately pretty and not the least bit crusty.'

'You'd better keep Sholto away from her then. He has an eye for pretty girls.'

Which is why he has ignored me, I expect, thought Alix, who had not been brought up to think of herself as even remotely beautiful.

'Is he a lady-killer then?' she asked.

'In a mild way. He's always in love with someone. I think he must have Italian blood in him somewhere.'

'Who has Italian blood?' said Sholto Hamilton, returning to the compartment.

'You do, Mr Hamilton,' said Alix.

'I was just warning her to hide her pretty friend from you.'

'Yes, sound advice, Ralph,' said Sholto, sitting down opposite her. 'You see, Miss Erskine, I eat women – devour them even. They are all the food and drink I need.'

'So you haven't been drinking tea and eating penny buns in the buffet,' said Alix, 'but making eyes at the attendant.'

'Unfortunately, no. He was bald and very married.'

'I hope you two are going to behave,' said Ralph, laughing. 'These are very nice people, as my mother so elegantly puts it, that we are going to stay with.'

'Oh, don't worry, Ralph darling, we shall be very, very nice,' said Alix. 'I think we must be nearly there. This train seems to have slowed even more than usual.'

She got up and turned to the looking glass which hung between the sepia views of highland scenery, with the intention of adjusting her hat, but there was a sudden jolt as the train drew to a stop. She found herself thrown across the

16

compartment and, somewhat embarrassingly, fell into the arms of Sholto Hamilton who had been getting up from his seat.

'Careful now,' he said, smiling down at her, and she realized he was enjoying this unexpected embrace, for his arms were more firmly about her than she supposed was strictly necessary in the circumstances. She had never been looked at quite like that either, with a disturbing quantity of pleasure in his eyes and his words of a moment earlier flashed through her mind: 'I eat women, devour them even . . .'

Be careful, Alix told herself, disentangling herself as soon as she could. That man is a Don Juan.

She could not rid herself of that impression, rather everything began to confirm it, and she looked at him surreptitiously in the carriage as they drove towards the Quarro, imagining him, with his elegant, curling beard and flashing brown eyes, clad in a black velvet doublet and hose; in short, appearing so devastatingly handsome that even the most virtuous and chaste of women could not possibly resist him.

The road to Quarro was long and dusty, but there was a magic in it, in the wonderful hilly scenery and the freshness of the air, which made Ralph, often nervous at the prospect of meeting new people, relax. No harm could come to him here, no petty social embarrassments could besiege him in such a landscape. When the old house came in sight, he felt as if he had entered an enchanted world, where perfection might truly exist. The grey stone house, absolutely and austerely classical, its roof of pewtery coloured slate unpunctuated by any grandiose portico, had all the charm of an old Scottish melody, unspoilt by modern arrangements. Decline was in the very air as they went up a drive lined with heavy hanging chestnuts, but Ralph was sickened by the modern world and here breathed the air of a more romantic past. Behind the house lay a mountain, dark with green pines but topped at the summit by rough red moor where nothing would grow, and he resolved at once to climb it and lie on the bracken at the top and let the wide skies wash over him.

The carriage left them in a forecourt where the air was hot and still. Bright borders of pinks, wallflowers and snapdragons trimmed the yard, like strips of gaudy braid and the sweet scent of vanilla and cloves from the flowers reverberated about them. He stood, startled by it, lost for words, drinking it in deeply, feeling his soul shake at the beauty of it all.

And then, through the open door at the top of a double sweep of steps, came a girl who made him forget whatever else he had seen. She leaned over the railings for a moment and then ran down to them.

'Celia,' said Alix, kissing the girl on the cheek. 'How lovely to see you.'

Love at first sight is nonsense, Ralph told himself, but the moment he saw Alix kiss her, he wished that privilege might have been his, for the girl had such a face as he had only dreamed a woman might have. He had seen such a face in profile in a Renaissance portrait, crowned with a cap of brocade and pearls, with a many-towered Tuscan city in the distance beyond. But he had not hoped such a face might live, might grace the earth in these dreary times. He had thought that the creature who had sat for the painting had been made beautiful by virtue of the painter's genius. But here she stood, in the blazing sunlight at the foot of those steps, dressed, not in Florentine velvet, but in a white sailor dress, and her face was lit up with the pleasure of seeing her friend in a manner that was entirely human. But, as Alix introduced him and she put out her hand to him, he felt that to shake hands was an unthinkably banal gesture and that he should have been better falling to his knees and kissing the hem of her skirt. He had no such courage and shook her hand, and, with his usual embarrassment, was quite unable to look her in the face. Then with agony, he watched Sholto, with his aggressive self-confidence, kiss the girl's hand with effortless gallantry so that she blushed delightfully, her cheeks resembling for a moment the petals of an old rose in their subtle washing together of ivory and pink.

As they went into the house, Celia and Alix linked arms, their heads bent together in some girlish confidence, and Ralph walked behind them up the steps, trying to get a grip on himself for he felt quite drunk.

Halfway up she turned and said, 'You do play tennis, don't you?' And before he had a chance to answer, continued, 'It's been such marvellous weather and I've had no one to play with. James doesn't, you see.'

'Well, I think Hamilton has been known to cut an impressive figure at tennis,' said Ralph, without quite knowing why he was prepared to praise Sholto when he feared his rivalry.

'Oh, you won't get a decent game out of Ralph, Cissy,' said Alix, scathingly. 'He's hopeless.'

'I have been known to try,' was all he managed to offer in his defence, for he was increasingly aware, as Celia pushed open a handsome, panelled door, that he would soon have to confront a room full of unfamiliar faces, and felt again the nerve-twisting grip of his shyness, which he had never been able to cast off. Not for him the happy, assured manner of his sister who sailed into the drawing room ahead of him with the poise of a duchess and who managed in some way to command the attention of all. No, he was left in her wake, quaking at the prospect of the back-slapping bonhomie of James Lennox and his father, Sir Hector, a flamboyant six-footer who stood, one elbow on the mantleshelf, gesticulating with a whisky glass. And then there were the two female occupants of the room: one a pale, thin husk of a creature whom Ralph suspected subsisted entirely on tracts and weak tea; the other a voluptuous contrast, in a shimmering hyacinth-coloured tea gown, artfully draped on a little sofa like a coquette, just showing satin slippers and silk-clad ankles. Presumably this was James Lennox's wife. Ralph found himself surprised. He had imagined a far less glamorous creature – a tweed-clad, county girl with a passion for horses, not a siren with golden hair and a smile which was unerringly constant.

'Do please sit down, Mr Erskine,' she said, indicating a fragile little chair close at hand. 'You will have some tea?'

She evidently enjoyed the business of pouring tea, for she performed the ceremony with something of the studied grace of a geisha. Ralph could guess that it gave her an opportunity to show off her pretty white hands, in a quintessentially feminine activity, and found himself quite understanding how James Lennox had been ensnared. This was a woman who liked to be the object of every man's attention, and she had almost succeeded, for James and his father gazed fondly at her, with bland smiles, while Sholto made amusing talk and made her laugh a silvery laugh. But Ralph could not be ensnared; he had been captured already by the girl across the room who sat with a large tabby cat on her white lap, stroking its velvet fur with a quietly sensual hand.

The cat stirred and jumped off its mistress's lap. Ralph stretched out his hand and tried to attract it. To his surprise, it accepted the advance and he was able to pick it up. Its hot, plump body felt charged with Celia's own erotic presence and he felt that this was a good omen. Certainly, she smiled at him as as he planted the cat's front paws on his shoulders and embraced it like a child.

'What's his name?' he asked.

'Tam,' said Celia. 'Not a clever name, is it?'

'Well, it is just a common tom cat,' said Mrs Lennox, disparagingly. 'I wonder why you let it in here, Celia. It's really just the kitchen cat.'

'Oh, he's too handsome a beast for the kitchen,' said Ralph.

'We have always had cats in this family,' said Sir Hector. 'Upstairs in the library there is a portrait of my ancestor, the second baronet, Sir Archibald, with his cat Mondbuddo.'

'After the judge?' laughed Sholto. 'Perhaps you should re-name this one Stormonth-Darling!' he said, alluding to the judge then presiding over the exchequer cases in Edinburgh, where James Lennox's advocacy was put to the test.

But Celia Lennox obviously had no stomach for such intellectual jokes and said simply, 'I don't think so. It would be silly to change his name now.' She got up from her seat and came across to where Ralph was sitting. 'Might I have him back?' she asked, rather in the fashion of a mother who wishes to comfort a child who has started screaming in some stranger's arms.

'Of course,' he said, detaching the claws which had tenaciously hooked into his lapels. He noticed that the cat seemed to relax in her arms and when she sat down again, he was soon asleep, purring gently. You lucky beast, thought Ralph, and wondered if he might ever lie, his head in her white lap, feeling the soft caress of her hand in his hair.

After tea Celia showed Alix to her room. She was in an eager and confiding mood, for once they had shut the door and before Alix had had even a moment to get her bearings, she said, 'Now we can talk properly!'

Celia, released from the constraints of the drawing room, had become a different person. Amongst her family she had showed a well-bred languor. Now the enthusiasm of her age flooded her face. Alix knew exactly how she felt. That drawing room had not been a place in which one could be oneself. The soft heat of this pretty bedroom was a better place for confidences.

'Oh, I've so much to tell you,' said Celia, taking Alix's arm and making her sit beside her in a pool of sunlight on the faded chintz squab in the window seat. 'You'll never believe what's happened . . .'

'Not a man?' said Alix eagerly, caught up in her friend's excitement. 'Are you in love?'

'Madly, wildly!' she said, with a dramatic gesture.

'Who, Cissy? Anyone we know?'

'No, nobody knows him – and that's the beauty of it – I met him when I went for a walk one night. He's a poacher!' she finished in triumph.

'Oh, come on, Celia, you're pulling my leg . . .' said Alix with delight at this outrageous revelation.

'I'm not, I swear it,' giggled Celia. 'His name is Hamish and he's so handsome you'd think he was an angel at least.'

'How old is he?'

21

'Eighteen. He's got fair hair, blue eyes, and he's about six foot tall.'

'Oh, he sounds really braw . . .'

'Oh, yes, he is. He makes me feel weak just to look at him.'

'Is that how it makes you feel then? Tell me exactly how it feels. I want to know everything about it.'

'There's so much to tell, I don't know where to start . . . oh, I know. Well, it was about a week or so ago – that's why I haven't written to tell you about it – I decided to go for a walk at night, like Andrew and I used to when we were little, and I went down through the woods there, those ones at the bottom,' she explained, pointing out the woods which terminated the view from the window. 'There's a stream in there – it feeds the canal – and I was walking along it when I found him. He was kneeling on the bank with his hand in the water, tickling for trout!' She laughed at the memory of it. 'And he looked up and saw me and he really stared at me as if I was something out of the grave – perhaps it was because I had a white dress on – I don't know why, and I just stared at him, because I couldn't think what else to do.'

'And then what happened?'

'Well, I was going to say something, but he just put his finger to his lips, so I didn't say anything, and a second later he pulled out a fish, just like a conjuror! It was wonderful!'

'And then?'

'He said, "You're not going to tell on me, are you?" and I said, "Of course not", and he said did I want to share it with him? He was going to cook it and did I want some? So we walked to the ruined bothy and he made up a fire. And we talked a bit about this and that and he cooked the trout. It was so delicious and we ate it with our fingers, and he gave me some beer, and then, it just happened . . .'

'What happened?'

'Perhaps I've told you too much already,' she said with affected coyness.

'You can't not tell now, you rotter,' said Alix. 'What happened?' But there was silence from Celia. 'You don't mean . . . he didn't . . . not just like that?' Celia nodded slowly. 'He kissed you?'

She nodded again and then they both exploded into giggles.

'Oh, Celia, how wonderful, how absolutely wonderful! You lucky devil. And you love him, love him utterly?'

'Absolutely – 'til I die, I'll love him!' declared Celia, jumping up from the window seat.

'Celia Lennox, allow me to offer you my congratulations,' said Alix, shaking her hand. 'I hereby award you the most dignified order of the corrupted woman,' she added, getting up and taking the pin tray from the dressing table. 'You are now a first-class savant!' And she knelt and handed it to Celia.

'Thank you, m'dear!' she laughed, and in a moment they were both on the floor, convulsed with helpless amusement.

The door opened and Alix raised her streaming eyes to see Mrs Lennox standing in the doorway. She looked down at them disdainfully and burst the cloud of hilarity with a mere glance.

'Having fun, darlings?'

'You should knock, Olivia,' said Celia calmly. 'Alix might have been getting changed.'

'I did knock,' she said, 'but you wouldn't have heard me. I only popped up to see that everything is all right, Alexandra.'

'Yes, thank you. It's a charming room.'

'So glad.' She smiled. 'Perhaps you should let Alexandra rest, Celia. She's had a long journey.'

'Oh no, I'm quite all right, really I am,' said Alix. 'In fact, I was just about to ask Celia to show me the gardens, if we've time before dinner?'

'I should think so,' said Mrs Lennox. 'But take your hats, dears, the sun is still quite strong.' And she drifted away.

Celia stepped forward and pushed shut the door.

'Vixen!' she said. 'Never knocks and never shuts doors. What a damned vixen she is! I hate her – I wish Jamie hadn't been so stupid as to marry her. She's always snooping, you know.'

'That's why I said we were going into the garden. She can't interrupt us there and I haven't had the full, gory details yet . . .'

'Very well, darling,' said Celia, imitating Mrs Lennox's languid manner. 'Shall we descend?'

'Oh, she isn't that bad, surely?' laughed Alix.

'She's worse if anything,' said Celia, and then added, seeing Alix pick up her hat from the bed, 'Leave that. You shouldn't listen to a word she says. Come on, I'll race you to the bottom of the canal.' And before Alix had a moment to think of objecting she was hurtling down the back stairs in pursuit of Celia.

Leaning back in his chair and inhaling the intense bouquet of his glass of claret, Ralph decided that it had been a memorable dinner.

It had not been the conversation that had been so satisfactory – in fact, there had hardly been any real conversation for the table had been dominated by Sir Hector. He was fond of the sound of his own voice and would seize any opportunity to recount a lengthy anecdote, usually about one of the Lennox ancestors. But Ralph, who would normally have been irritated by such behaviour, found himself quite prepared to listen in a half-hearted way to the old man's recitative, nodding and smiling where appropriate. There were compensations enough in that dining room to make him tolerate the windiest oratory. There were Ramsays and Raeburns on the walls, there were clove carnations mingling their scent with sweet wax candles, and there was wine – such good wine – which had been brought to Leith harbour over forty years ago. They were drinking the final bottles from that bin in the cellar, Sir Hector had explained so that they might treat it reverently. 'I believe in the old hospitality,' he said, 'and when the house is full of lawyers, one must bring out the best claret, to honour their noble profession.' The stuff itself was little short of heavenly, served in heavy eighteenth-century glasses with delicate spirals and twists caught in the stems like wisps of smoke might be caught in aspic. And running like a contrapuntal melody through all this was the food, which took even the Lennoxes by surprise, for there was a new cook, quite untried until that night. No, the conversation did not matter in the least, he decided. He had never felt less like talking, for to talk would have been to distract his senses from all those exquisite sensations which reverberated about him, flooding over him, like so many colour washes on a water colour, each fresh impression building a deeper, more resonant whole.

Most wonderful of all, as he ate ambrosia and sipped nectar, was to look across the table to where Celia was sitting. It was fortunate she was not opposite him or beside him, for he did not yet know what he wanted to say to her. To watch her was enough that evening.

She was dressed in a pale pink silk dress, the colour of the inside of a shell; a dress which was not quite that of a woman but was no longer that of a young girl, for it fell slightly from the shoulders, revealing a neck and chest as soft and pale as the silk itself. At her throat was an amethyst and pearl cross held simply by a length of ribbon, and in her smooth hair, to perfect this artless toilette, a full-blown rose which might have shed its petals at any moment. These simple decorations struck Ralph as almost sublime, for they did nothing to distract the eye from the faultless lines of her face and figure. A painter could not have arranged things better.

He watched her eat with an action which was both delicate and sensuous, as she dug her silver gilt spoon into the crystal depths of a sorbet glass. He watched her pluck off the little arrangement of frosted red currants that drooped over the side of the glass and saw her mouth pucker a fraction as their sharpness registered on her palate – he knew that sensation exactly for he was enjoying their bitter-sweet taste himself. All her movements which were slight and self-preoccupied, mesmerized him and he was startled to hear Mrs Lennox, who was sitting beside him, say as she got up from her chair, 'Well, gentlemen, if you'll excuse us . . .'

He wanted to reach out across the table and put his hand

on her arm and say, 'Don't go yet – stay for me, please . . .' but Celia, in an instant, for she was as fleet-footed as she was beautiful, had moved to the dining-room door as if she was eager to be gone.

'Don't be long,' said Mrs Lennox as a parting shot.

They resumed their seats when the door was shut and there was that sudden sense of relaxation which always accompanied the departure of the ladies and the appearance of the port. But Ralph, unlike his fellow drinkers, did not feel that same benign mood. Now Celia was gone, the bubble of his pleasure had been pricked and he was returned to that cigar-smoking, bluff-talking, masculine world in which he felt ill at ease. He did not want to talk politics or sport or business but these things were inescapable. Sir Hector, as he passed the decanter, seemed determined to break Ralph's silence.

'My son tells me you're in steel, Erskine,' he said.

Steel! The spectre of it haunted him. It shackled his name with fetters as invincible as anything which came out of the great press mill in Lanarkshire. How often would he have like to avoid being 'in steel' and be anything else: Ralph Erskine the scholar, Erskine the collector, Erskine the poet; anything but to be Ralph Erskine 'in steel', heir to one of the largest industrial concerns in Scotland. He knew that a hundred men would have killed for such an inheritance and he was bitterly conscious of his own ingratitude, but he could not bring himself to be anything more than a dutiful son working for his father. He could not love the business as his father did.

'Er, yes, amongst other things.' He wished his father could have been there. He talked about steel like a revivalist minister. When he spoke of it he made it seem as if Erskine steel was the very backbone of the universe.

'Interesting business, I should think,' said Sir Hector.

'Well, I suppose so. My father gave up the law for it.'

'Did he?'

'My great-uncle started the mill in Lanark, and when he died he left it to my father because he'd always been so interested in mechanics and engineering.'

'Don't you make ships as well?' interjected Sir Hector.

'Yes. Yes, we do. We've a yard on the Clyde and one at Dundee. My father patented a new marine engine just last year – a triple expansion turbine – I don't know if you know about these things . . .' He finished, aware that his throat was dry and that Sir Hector was looking blank. He took a swift gulp of port, treating it like cough mixture.

After a pause, Sir Hector said in measured tones, 'There must be a bit of money in all that I imagine.'

Ralph felt faintly shocked but also amused. He had scarcely expected Sir Hector with his rarefied ancestor cult to be so frankly curious about money. His mother had always maintained it was supremely vulgar to talk about money and here was Sir Hector, head of what she would call 'a fine old family', breaking the ultimate taboo.

'We make a living,' said Ralph, and made the old man choke on his cigar with laughter.

'Ah ha! I'm sure you do! Here, have some more port, Erskine,' he said, getting up and slapping him on the shoulder with a jolly, drunken gesture. 'Are you sure you won't smoke?'

'Quite sure, thank you.'

Sir Hector strolled down to the other end of the dining room, carrying the decanter.

'Who's for billiards?' he asked, interrupting Sholto and James Lennox who had been deep in conference.

'But what about the ladies?' said Sholto.

'They'll live without us. Erskine?'

'No, thank you, sir – it's not my game,' said Ralph, wondering if to refuse was to offend the man.

But Sir Hector went on cheerfully: 'Good. I can't bear to have incompetents trying to graze the table. Hamilton, can I tempt you?'

'Of course, sir.'

'He'll give you a good game,' said Ralph. 'I think I'll take a turn in the garden, if I may?'

'Of course, of course,' said Sir Hector. 'Jamie, show young Erskine the way to the garden.'

Ralph hoped as they emerged on to the steps from the

french windows of the saloon, that James was not intending to walk with him.

'Well, here you are, old chap,' he said, going down the steps. 'Quite a sight, don't you think?'

'Oh, yes, it's very beautiful,' said Ralph, trying not to sound too gloomy, for James was hardly the companion he would have chosen for a moonlit stroll.

'Of course,' James went on relentlessly with his hearty voice, as if the moon in the violet sky meant nothing to him, 'the old place is not in such good order as it could be. We could do with a bit of spare capital really. We're down to three gardeners. It isn't as it used to be. You know, my pater worries about money all the time now. He thinks I should have married money, still rags me about it – but who in the world could have resisted a girl like my Livy? Isn't she just a peach?' he said proudly.

'Yes, she's lovely.'

'Isn't she? Of course, her people aren't all one could want, but girls from the right families these days aren't what they used to be. They all smoke and talk about women's rights – ghastly, don't you think? Women like that should be horsewhipped.'

'Isn't that rather extreme?' laughed Ralph.

'Not in the least. Just imagine if your sister got like that.'

'My sister is her own woman. I shouldn't dare to interfere.'

'Exactly the problem, Erskine. It's gone too far already. If we don't look out, they'll end up running the show.'

'Why not? They might be better at it than we are.'

James laughed, taking Ralph's remark to be nothing but an absurdity.

'You always were a droll one,' he said. 'Well, if you don't mind, I think I'll go back inside now. Livy will be fretting if I'm not back soon. Little angel – she does miss me so. Are you coming in?'

'No, not just yet,' said Ralph, settling down on the stone bench at the head of the canal.

It was pleasant at last to be alone, to take stock of the day. He felt tired for he had been swinging, pendulum-like, between high emotion and social agony. But now he felt comfortable and peaceful, with the canal glittering faintly at his feet and the trees rustling in the slight breeze. He took off his coat and rolled up his shirt sleeve, tempted by the water. He sat down on the edge of the canal and dipped his hand into it, bringing up a handful and letting it rush through his fingers. He bent forward and splashed his face which was flushed with wine. He closed his eyes for a moment, and when he opened them again saw a reflection in the water below him. Someone was standing over him.

'Celia . . .' he said softly as he looked up, not quite believing that it could be her. But it was, as pale as the sky, except for her dark hair and eyes. She stood as motionless as a ghost. 'Celia . . .' he said it again, relishing the sound of her name on his lips.

For a moment she looked back, piercing him with her calm gaze.

'I'm sorry,' she said, 'I thought you were someone else.' And then she ran away.

He struggled to his feet and pursued her for a few yards. But she had vanished and Ralph stopped in his tracks for on the grass before him lay the rose which had been hanging so perilously in her hair at dinner. He stooped to pick it up and it collapsed in his fingers.

3

Jessie ranged through the kitchen garden with scissors and basket in search of herbs. Although the etiquette of the below stairs world made it more customary for the gardener to send his boy up to the kitchen with the produce, Jessie wanted to see her materials in their natural state, away from the artificial titivation of head gardeners. In Edinburgh she had been accustomed to get up early and walk to the fruit and vegetable market with Monsieur Auguste, and had learnt from him to pick out the finest quality ingredients.

This kitchen garden, bathed in morning sun, was more interesting than a market with its beautiful functionality. The elegant espaliered fruit trees running like a frieze on the grey stone walls, the bright flowers of beans and peas, the luxuriant boughs bending under the weight of currants and berries; all was ordered and yet without severity. Jessie felt again, as she knelt and plucked a handful of purple-tinted sage, the full pleasure of her chosen craft. There was a simple poetry in the shape of every leaf, in the sensual swelling of every vegetable, in the very smell of it all, and it inspired her to new heights of creativity.

She filled her basket with sage, parsley, chervil, and her favourite, sorrel, with its subtle lemon tang. The fishmonger had come from Peebles that morning with an irresistible crate of Dunbar crabs and succulent lemon sole which needed only to be fried in a little sweet butter and scattered with fines-herbes to make a dish fit for the gods. To cook in summer time, when plenty tossed her cloak with careless generosity across the land, was hardly to work, despite the heat and toil of the kitchen. The smell of freshly chopped herbs or the beautiful sight of raspberry purée being folded into cream, making for a moment a patch of precious marble – these were compensations enough. And that morning, when she had taken up the menu to Mrs Lennox, she had even got a grudging compliment from her: 'I have been asked to convey Sir Hector's satisfaction.' She had wanted to laugh when the mistress had said that, but she managed to accept with some grace, for she suspected that Mrs Lennox would not give many compliments and she had better be content with the few she would get, no matter how pompously expressed they might be.

She gazed into the undergrowth, resting back on her heels, contemplating for a moment the events since her arrival. In amongst the humming insects, she reflected that it had not been a mistake to come to the Quarro. *Perhaps in the winter, I'll regret it, when I've chilblains and nowhere to go on my evening off. But now* . . . And she looked up into the the cloudless blue depths of the sky for a minute, as if in appreciation of the fates who had brought her there. Such was the heady pleasure of that fragrant garden on such a morning.

' "Gin a body meet a body, coming through the rye . . ." '

A man's voice behind her made her jump and twist round, still half kneeling, to see who had spoken. She found herself staring, without meaning to, for the man matched the voice, which had been relaxed and confident and undeniably attractive. He was tall (or perhaps he only seemed so as Jessie looked up at him from the ground), with dark hair swept back from his forehead, and most strikingly a neat black beard which set off a fixed and hypnotic smile, like that of the Cheshire Cat. Bright blue eyes accompanied it, eyes which scrutinized her at their leisure. It was disconcerting, but she was conscious that she was looking at him with equal frankness, as if locked there by some force beyond her own reckoning. And the words he had spoken, the first line of a couplet which she knew well, were so provocative that for a long moment it silenced her. But at length, grabbing hold of herself, she managed to blurt out: 'And what do you think you mean by that?'

'An excellent question,' he said, not the least put out. In fact, he tossed his jacket, which he had been holding over his shoulder, down on to the ground, and sank to his knees beside her. 'What do you think I mean? Do you think I am being impertinent?'

'Of course I do,' she said, attempting to get up, but he grabbed hold of her skirt and would not let her rise. 'Do you mind – I have work to do, you know!'

'No, don't go, not yet – please,' he said. 'I've been watching you. You're so bonny, lass, I can't bear to let you go just like that, not without doing poetic justice. "Gin a body, kiss a body . . ." '

'If you think you can do any such . . .' she protested, but it was too late for the stranger, evidently well practised in these matters, had enfolded her in a strong embrace from which she could not free herself.

' "Need a body cry?" ' he said softly, and with a gentle, surprising hand brushed a lock of hair from her forehead before planting a delicate kiss there. She felt herself relax with relief but felt also a sharp pang of disappointment that he had not kissed her on the lips. That would have been too much, too audacious, and yet his restraint annoyed her. If one was going to kiss a girl on sight, acting in the spirit of Burns, as this man pretended to, then what a half-hearted way to do it! She knew enough of Burns to know that he meant a kiss on the lips, and probably more. Why else would the prim minister's sister have refused to let her have a volume of Burns as a Sunday School prize? And so it was with real irritation, partly at his effrontery and partly at his cowardice, that she struggled to her feet.

'You're angry,' he said.

'Of course!' she exclaimed, incredulous. 'What do you damn' well expect?'

'I've never done that before,' he said, 'not at first sight. But it's not often that I see such a beautiful face, such an exceptional face . . .'

'Oh, aye, and the moon is made of blue cheese!' she retorted.

'Believe me,' he said. 'And forgive me – although I must confess, I should have done more, been more impertinent, but something in your face deterred me.'

'Perhaps you were afraid I would hit you.'

'And I deserve it. Come on, slap me now, make me suffer for it.' And he proffered his cheek for her to slap in such an absurd gesture that Jessie at once burst out laughing.

'Ah, that's a sight,' he said. 'That's better than I thought it would be. You should laugh as much as you can – it makes you even prettier.'

'For God's sake, man!' she exclaimed, suddenly angry with him again. 'Are you mad, or what?'

'Most probably,' he smiled.

'I don't know why I'm even bothering to talk to you! My time is more precious than a fine gentleman like you could know, and yet here I am, wasting it quarrelling with a fool!' And she snatched up her basket and made as if to go.

'But you don't want to go, do you?' he said, catching her wrist with a deft gesture.

'You know nothing about that. Let me go!'

'Perhaps I should have kissed you on the lips,' he said. 'To see you angry makes me want to . . .'

'You *are* mad.'

'Yes, and why not? Perhaps this is one of those moments when the ordinary rules are suspended and sanity flies out of the window. Divine madness – perhaps that's it. I come out into the garden for a smoke and I see you, in your white dress, lost amongst all this, and I think – I must, I cannot resist. "But to see her was to love her, Love but her and love for ever",' he quoted again.

> ' "Beware a tongue that's smoothly hung,
> A heart that warmly seems to feel!
> That feeling heart but acts a part —" '

'Tis rakish art in Rob Mossgiel!' she said in response, pleased that she had remembered such an appropriate verse.

He whistled softly when she had finished and said, as if quite amazed, 'What are you, lassie? *Who* are you?'

'Just a cook,' she said with a smile, somewhat amused by his manner.

'No, you're something the earth conjured up just to tantalize me. You're a trick of the light on a hot day – something I never saw the like of before, but you're flesh and blood, I know that . . .' And he reached out and caressed her cheek.

'You've the devil's own gall, haven't you?' she said, not angrily, for she was past that. Rather, she was caught up in the charm of it all, as if reality had in fact transformed itself for a moment, crowning the porridge bowl of common-place life with a spun sugar coronet. She knew that she should not have given this man a moment of her time, still less permit him to kiss her, but now it was done and as they talked in that bright sunshine, the scent of herbs and flowers drifting around them, she could not find any more indignation.

'You're not really angry with me, are you?'

'I should be,' she said. 'But why bother? You're like a

river with all your fine words – you can't fight against a torrent like that.'

'My nurse always did say that I chattered like an Irishman,' he remarked.

'Are you Irish?' she asked, for she had heard of the dangerous charm of the Irish.

'Good God, no. Would an Irishman know Burns, eh? No, I'm from Perthshire, from a long line of ministers whose sermons always exceeded the hour.'

'But I don't suppose you're a minister!' she laughed. 'God help the Church if you are.'

'You're too sharp to be just a cook, lass,' he said. 'Let me guess, you're the governess – and it's a great shame that they don't let you eat downstairs with the rest of us.'

'If they did, there'd be no dinner,' she said, 'and there'll be none tonight, if I don't get back to work, Mr . . . what is your name?'

'Sholto, Sholto Hamilton,' he said, putting out his hand.

They shook hands which felt oddly formal after that earlier moment of intimacy.

'Then what's your name?' he said, gripping her hand with both his before she had a change to break away.

'Jessie MacPherson, Mr Hamilton,' she said.

'Now don't you "Mr Hamilton" me, lass,' he said. 'I won't have you putting up walls. You're mine now and I'm not going to let you slip away. You'll call me Sholto, now that I've kissed you, Jessie.'

'Instead of calling you names as I ought to?' she said. But this did not make him release her.

'When is your afternoon off?'

'What is it to you?'

'I want to take you out.'

'I don't suppose Mrs Lennox allows followers.'

'She needn't know, need she?'

'I suppose not,' said Jessie, quite unable to comprehend how she could be accepting an invitation from a total stranger, when it might mean losing her place. But this man was so compelling, so exciting, that she reckoned that only a woman entirely lacking any sort of curiosity could refuse to meet him.

'Good. You'll meet me then? When are you free?'

'Wednesday afternoon and Sunday evening.'

'I can't wait until Sunday,' he said. 'Wednesday it'll be then. I'll meet you here, after luncheon. Do you promise to come?'

'All right – I've nothing to lose, have I?'

'No, my pretty Jessie – nothing to lose, but everything to gain.' And he brushed her cheek lightly with his hand. 'Oh, let me kiss you again, will you?'

'I don't think I have much choice in the matter,' she said for he had pulled her into his arms again and she felt relaxed, compliant and quite unafraid.

She did not know how long that embrace lasted; an eternity, a moment, she could not say which. She only knew she was drowned in it, sunk utterly and without hope in his power. And she had waded in quite willingly, thrown herself into it, stayed when she could have escaped. But she knew in the midst of those kisses, so recklessly given and taken, that she had longed for years for such a moment without ever daring to finds words. For if she had looked beyond the dreary walls of basements and attics, if she looked up from the work to which she had devoted herself, the whole edifice would have come crumbling down around her, destroyed by dreams which were too potent, too heady for anyone in her position to bear. For those forbidden to have followers, love was an impossibility. Some of the other girls had read novelettes and gloated over the fashionable engagements in the newspapers, but Jessie had put on a face of indifference, preferring to concentrate on that which she knew she could achieve, on becoming a professed cook with the handsome prospect of £60 a year for it, instead of pipe dreams about footmen, policemen and post office clerks! And she had reached her goal and was in command of the kitchens of a country house. It was what she had always wanted, and yet here she was wrapped in the arms of a man who was answering and awakening deeper, more dangerous desires in her.

'I have to go,' she said, managing to wrest herself from him. 'I can't, not now, not any more . . .' But it was hard to speak. His hands not only captured her body but her voice as well. 'You'll no have any luncheon if I don't get back to work . . .'

They drew apart and Jessie hastily smoothed her apron, suddenly acutely aware her hair was in disorder. But he still looked at her with those burning, admiring eyes, his arms folded, while she made useless little adjustments to her hair.

'I shall remember the way you look now, for ever,' he said. 'Now run along before they miss you.'

So she left him, almost running along the brick path which crossed the garden, not fleeing from him but forcing herself away from him, as if by running she had created a momentum which her will could not counteract.

By the time she reached the little yard which opened off the kitchen, she had begun to wonder if she could control herself. She felt so exultant, so full of life, that she felt she could have danced a jig on the kitchen table. But she would have to go in and behave quite normally.

The kitchen was hot and calm. Through the high windows the light flooded, illuminating Annie's blonde hair as she stood hulling strawberries at the kitchen table. Her movements were regular and self-absorbed. Madness in gardens might not have existed, and certainly nothing as base as bodily passion, for she stood there looking faintly seraphic, like a Virgin Mary unaware that the angel was hovering with extraordinary news. But Jessie had more sense than to announce her news, although she longed to pour it out to someone.

'Still on those strawberries, then?' she said plucking one from the basket and eating it.

'Aye,' said Annie, 'I'm right sick of them. They go on forever. An' then it'll be all the rasps. Did you find what you were after in the garden?'

It was an artless question, but for a moment Jessie was startled. She felt herself flushing and to distract herself tipped out the contents of her basket onto the table.

'Yes . . . I did,' she said, reflectively, breaking a mint leaf in her fingers and smelling it. 'I certainly did.'

'I have just met a stunning creature in the kitchen garden,' said Sholto, coming into the room so noisily that Ralph felt that his head, which was already throbbing with the intensity of a steam turbine, might explode altogether. Usually Sholto would have been a welcome guest, for he always had enough amusing talk to charm away any amount of time, but that morning, as Ralph lay in the stuffy heat of that old-fashioned bedroom with a raging migraine, he was hardly the visitor he wanted.

He had dreamt, almost feverishly, that Celia might drift in and press cool, white hands to his forehead with the quiet countenance of a healing angel. But when, after breakfast, he had been forced to retreat to his room, he had seen only Alix and the elder Miss Lennox. Alix had been briskly unsympathetic, complaining that he had scuppered everyone's plans for tennis, while Miss Lennox had come with a cold poultice and a glass of some vile cordial. She had forced him to drink it with a dictatorial gentleness which reminded him of his own mother. He was half convinced that she would begin to scold him kindly, as his mother always did, when he failed 'to look after himself' and had brought on migraines, feverishness, coughing fits or stomach cramps which comprised his peculiar affliction. She would scold him for his stupidity, for his own ridiculous inability to accept what all those wretched doctors before whom she had paraded him, had always confirmed – that he was 'delicate'.

Now here was Sholto, bursting with rude good health. He pulled up a chair to the bedside and sat astride it, evidently most pleased with himself. In fact, his grin was more than Ralph could bear and he closed his eyes to it. But Sholto was without mercy.

'A real woman, Ralph,' he continued. 'Not one of those waif-like creatures you are so fond of, but a nice, plain woman . . .'

'I'm sure she wasn't plain,' Ralph managed to say.

'Oh, no, not plain like that. I mean straightforwardly womanly, no artifice about her, none of those ghastly prudish manners you get in middle-class women. No, this girl is real, Ralph old man, so real that you can almost smell her blood. And she's the cook, would you believe!' He laughed. 'Well, we said the food was exquisite. Now we know why – it's cooked by a damned goddess!'

'I thought you said she was real.'

'Diana was real to Acteon,' said Sholto. 'But this lass, she's no cold Diana. By God, she's not!

'What the hell have you been up to?' asked Ralph, struggling up on to his elbows. But seeing Sholto's face, he added, 'On second thoughts, don't answer that. I've imagination enough . . .'

'But she defies imagination. She quoted Burns – would you credit that? A cook who quotes Burns! God, Ralph, she is magnificent, absolutely magnificent. I cannot wait to get her into my bed!'

Ralph sank back on to his pillows, exhausted by Sholto's bravura. He felt faintly shocked and then ashamed at his own hypocrisy, for had his own mind not raced to the same inevitable conclusion only a few minutes after seeing Celia Lennox? He would never have admitted it as frankly as Sholto, but the desire was there, as keen and as graphic. But with it went despair, for he had no more hope of sleeping with a girl like Celia than he had of flying to the moon. Girls like Celia were not to be enjoyed like ripe fruit that fell into one's lap by sheer chance, like Sholto's garden goddess. No, they were elusive as hares to a hunter. They needed pursuit and promises, firm promises, before they would give an inch. Celia Lennox would want an engagement ring before she would permit a kiss.

It was not such a bad idea, and for a moment the thought of the intimacy marriage would bring intoxicated him. He almost forgot his migraine as he imagined Celia wearing nothing more than her nightgown, sitting curled up on the faded armchair in his dressing room, watching him as he dressed to go to work, with some sweet, sleepy expression on her face.

'She's agreed to meet me on her afternoon off,' Sholto was saying, 'but I don't know if I'll be able to wait until then. I wonder where she sleeps – but that's too risky,' he reflected. 'I should end up blundering into Lennox's room!' He laughed. 'He might get the wrong idea, especially if he still has the same inclinations you said he had at school . . .'

'I shouldn't think so,' said Ralph, 'not with a wife like that.'

'Yes, she is a stunner, isn't she? No one could resist her. But they've no children, have they? Married three years and no children, eh. Perhaps he does still prefer . . .'

'You are perfectly incorrigible,' said Ralph. 'You've spent too much time with your nose stuck in the *Police Gazette.*'

'But that's where the real world is,' he said. 'Not in your poets and painters, Ralph, who can't bear the thought of a speck of dirt in the ointment. You can't have the world without the dirt, can you?'

'No, but you don't have to revel in it, do you?' said Ralph. 'Especially when I've got this bloody head.'

'I suppose I'd better bugger off then,' said Sholto. 'I promised your sister and Celia Lennox I would umpire for them. Ah, what an onerous duty!' And he winked significantly.

'Christ, Sholto, leave them alone, for God's sake. They're little more than children.'

'Oh, Ralph, it's you who is the innocent, not they!' he laughed. 'Well, you'd better get well again soon so you can come down and protect your sister's honour.'

And with that he left, leaving Ralph annihilated by his boisterous presence. For a man who was supposed to be a friend, Sholto could sometimes be little better than a torturer.

'Where are we going?' Jessie asked, for he had tucked away the tickets in his pocket.

'Must you know everything?' said Sholto Hamilton.

'I only want to know that my clothes are all right.'

'You look divine,' he said. 'More than a lady.'

'Don't think you can get to me that way. I'm not as stupid as you think I am.'

'I know you're not stupid,' he said. 'Would I take you out if you were?'

'I must be daft to be here anyway,' she said, as they stood on the platform in the dry heat. 'This is bound to get back to the house – it's such a small place.'

'What you do on your day off is your own business,' he said. 'Besides, wouldn't Mrs Lennox be pleased that you have such a respectable follower?'

'Ha ha!' She had to laugh at that. 'You, respectable? I don't think so.'

'In fact,' he continued, 'I rather think she would be jealous. She likes the gentlemen to dance attention on her, I think.'

'That I can imagine,' said Jessie, 'from what I've seen of her. But she is very pretty.'

'Oh, yes, desperately. That's how she got stupid old Lennox, by sheer beauty and feminine wiles.'

'Well, I'm sure you know all about that. I bet you've resisted a few.'

'Me, resist? Dear lady, how little you know me . . .'

'I wasn't being serious,' she said with a smile. 'Is this our train?'

To her surprise, he flung open the door of a first class carriage and handed her in with all the gallantry he might have given to Mrs Lennox.

'I've never been first class in my life,' she said, unable to conceal her delight at the comfortable privacy of the compartment with its luxurious upholstery.

'This is where you start.'

'Oh, I don't think so,' she said, regaining her composure. 'It'll be third class again when I lose my place, or shanks's pony, even.'

'No, no,' he said, sitting down opposite her and taking both her hands in his. 'Destiny meant you to be a carriage woman.'

'Don't be daft, Sholto Hamilton!' she laughed. 'I've earned my own living since the age of twelve – what's going to change now, eh?'

'We shall see about that.'

'I wouldn't trust your promises.'

'Oh, but you're sharp,' he said.

'Careful,' she said. 'I've been to the melodrama. I know that the gentleman is always wicked.'

'Do I seem wicked?'

'Absolutely!' she said, and wondered if she had enjoyed talking so much in years. For once she felt that her words were not misunderstood or being deemed impertinent. After years of being quiet and obedient, it was suddenly all right to talk, to let the voice in her head, which had for so long been her only true companion, speak out and give her a definition quite separate from that of Jessie MacPherson the servant girl. The dominie at Dysart had told her she might be a pupil-teacher if she applied herself, but her mother would have none of it, as if 'book-learning' might rot the brain, instead of improving it. She had been forced from the house, her mother nagging her to go until the drudgery of that first awful year as a scullery maid had seemed like blessed relief! Since then those modest intellectual ambitions had been put on one side, indulged in only in her few moments of leisure when she had not been too tired. Instead, she had thrown her energy into becoming an excellent cook, not just a mediocre, plain cook, but a professed cook who could command a high wage and hold a household to ransom with her skill! For good cooks, exquisite cooks, were courted and cajoled by employers . . . but here she was, throwing all of that away, without so much as a backward glance, as she rattled away from normality in a first class carriage with a man whom she scarcely knew. The only certainty she had with regard to Sholto Hamilton was that he was too attractive and too amusing for a prudent person to become involved with.

But suddenly she was sick of prudence. She twenty-three years old and her life had been little more than a dried out husk. Where was the richness, the fragrance, the sheer sensuality that she put into her food? Was it not about time she tasted some of that for herself?

'Here we are,' said Sholto, when the train stopped at Peebles. 'Quaint hydro town. What do you want to do? I believe they have such dissipated amusements as tea dances here . . .'

She had cooked for those in the past – salmon sandwiches, lobster salad, eclairs, champagne cup – but she had never imagined she might go to one.

'Does that appeal to Miss MacPherson?' he asked, handing her out of the train.

For a moment she worried about her clothes. It was a very plain spotted voile she was wearing. It had seemed expensive to her once, and yet suddenly it felt obviously cheap when she mentally compared it to Mrs Lennox's elegant confections. But the way Sholto looked at her, the way he offered her his arm, made her take confidence in herself. After all, if that Lennox woman could dupe the world, so could Jessie MacPherson!

Peebles was a pretty town and the air was as fresh and as bracing as all the advertisements proclaimed it to be. As they strolled about, she felt quite at home amongst the discreetly well-dressed women. The speed at which one walked seemed to be the key to it all. One walked, not aimlessly, but not with any discernible or workaday purpose. Glancing into a plate glass window, she saw a fine couple, and it took her a moment to realize that it was herself and Sholto Hamilton who looked so handsome, so leisured, indeed so middle-class!

'We make a braw pair, don't you think?' he said, also observing their reflection.

'I hardly know myself,' she said.

'That I can't believe,' he said. 'You strike me as a creature who *does* know herself.'

'How can I, when I know so little about anything?'

'You are ruthless with yourself, Jessie.'

'I have to be. There's no point in having silly notions in my place.'

'Silly notions – what do you mean by that?'

'I mean that I can't pretend to hope for anything better than the things I've worked for – for anything more than the things within my grasp.'

'Your grasp, eh? Would you seize them all by the neck, if you could, and throttle them all, Jessie? Are you so ambitious?'

'I have to be. What else can I do but try and better myself. Oh God, how I hate that expression, but I've lived by it for long enough, so I can't really despise it . . .'

'Well, if it's any comfort, lass,' he said, patting her arm, 'I'm just the same.'

'How?'

'I've only got on by luck and hard work. True, my father was a minister, but we never had a ha'penny to spare and I only got to university through slogging for prizes. And I've no money to keep myself, except what I earn. I'm not one of your Lennoxes or Erskines. Money for me, unfortunately, is earned not inherited. But that doesn't mean I don't enjoy it – and you should too,' he finished. They had reached the portico of the Tontine Hotel, which would have intimidated her in other circumstances, but which today seemed a kingdom quite within her rights to enjoy, for he added: 'After all, we deserve it, don't we?'

The tea dance was taking place in a large room built for the local assemblies of the previous century. It was painted in green, gold and white, and great Venetian windows flooded it with sunshine. In the gallery a small band was playing waltzes for the benefit of the three sedate couples who had taken to the floor. The other guests were scattered about at tables around the room, and Jessie felt their eyes boring into her as the waiter took them to their table. She tried valiantly not to blush, and when she had sat down on the little gilt chair, she found herself (quite effortlessly) taking up a pose she had seen Mrs Lennox practise at their morning interviews. She rested her wrists close together on the edge of the table and brought together her gloved finger tips in a manner which looked elegant and stopped her hands shaking, which she feared they might in such unfamiliar surroundings.

The tea arrived, and she busied herself studying it, rather than Sholto, whom she was suddenly embarrassed to look at, even to speak to. But his hand flashed out for a moment and squeezed her fingers reassuringly.

'Will you pour, darling?' he said.

That 'darling', so unexpected and yet so exactly what she wished to hear, made her glance up and she found herself looking directly into those calm but compelling eyes.

'How I wish I could kiss you now,' he murmured.

'But you can't,' she said. 'Now, do you take it with milk or black?' she asked, feeling that she was asking some profound question. Indeed, it might be useful enough to know how he took his tea. To make a man a cup of tea was an important step towards intimacy.

'Black, one sugar,' he said, 'and quite strong.'

'I guessed right,' she said, for she had predicted his words.

'And you?'

'As it comes. I don't have time to be fussy about it.'

'I can't believe that,' he said. 'A creature with your discriminating palate.'

'I only cook the stuff. I don't get the chance to eat it.'

'No, I don't suppose you do. I noticed all the plates went back thoroughly empty. You do realize you have quite astonished that family? They are very pleased with themselves for having the taste to employ such a good cook.'

'Perhaps I ought to ask for more money,' she said, lifting the teapot lid and peering into the steaming depths. 'But I can't really complain. It's more than I could have hoped to get a few years back.'

'How much do they give you?'

'Fifty pounds a year. I should be able to save a bit with that. Anyway, enough about me. What do you do for money, if you say your family hasn't any?'

'I'm at the bar in Edinburgh,' he said. 'You are speaking to a rising star, you understand, whose brilliant advocacy dazzles even the most antediluvian members of the bench.'

Her face must have registered her lack of comprehension.

'I'm a lawyer,' he said more simply, 'who doesn't make much money yet, because I haven't made my name. It takes time to persuade the solicitors that you're the man to whom they should send their brief. But I've one or two interesting things coming up. I'm junior counsel for a lovely juicy murder – an incorrigible fellow who beat his wife so often that she died. But we shall argue that he was provoked.'

'How can you?' she said. 'A fellow like that deserves to be hanged.'

'But he's entitled to his defence. It wouldn't be fair, if he wasn't, would it?'

'It wasn't fair what he did to his wife.'

'Yes, but the law can't admit such spot judgements. One has to put each side of the case to the jury, so that they can make an informed judgement.'

'It's horrible.' She shuddered. 'How can you want to help a man like that? A jury of women would hang him and no mistake!'

'A jury of women – what a terrifying thought,' he laughed. 'If they were all as pretty as you, bar and bench would be struck dumb in admiration.'

'No, they'd all talk as cleverly as you,' she said, 'and then the women wouldn't stand a chance. We would all be terrified into silence if all the lawyers were like you, Sholto Hamilton.'

'Alas,' he said, kissing her hand, 'I am exceptional.'

'You're a monster.'

'Yes, but an agreeable one, you must concede. And a monster, in fact, who would like to dance with you, very much.'

He was not the most accomplished dancer but it hardly mattered for neither was she and the floor was almost empty. She guessed that the pleasure he found in it was similar to her own: to be comfortable in each other's arms, close enough, but not too close. This slow waltz, she sensed, was a decorous ritual, a prelude to something else. It was like all their conversation, which to any observer would perhaps have seemed immodest for two people so little acquainted with each other. But to her, its boldness was entirely permissible, because, like the great blast of a trumpet off-stage, it announced the arrival of something fine and magnificent. For there was fire here; she felt it in the pit of her stomach as his arm went about her waist, and fires did not creep over things like slow worms, but jumped up with large, greedy flames consuming everything, stripping away with hot urgency decorum, convention and sanity.

They moved about that stretch of parquet together, catching the slow one-two-three beat of the waltz, which was supposed to be sedate, but which was hypnotically sensual in its throbbing regularity. It was not dizzy, but deliberate, like a tribal dance from Africa rather than a piece of tea-room romance. Neither past nor future mattered, only the moment, the warm-breathed, steady, smiling moment, in which Jessie, without knowing how, felt the full significance of life, as if all the symbols had fallen into place and the world made sense for once!

'We have to be alone . . .' he murmured, saying exactly what her own mind was saying. She nodded and they broke away from the dance. He flung a handful of coins on the table and they walked away, leaving their tea untouched. In the lobby, Sholto led her to a leather armchair and, solicitously, made her sit down.

'Sit there a minute,' he said. 'I've an idea.'

She heard him walk to the reception desk.

'Excuse me.' His voice, clear and confident, rang through

the lobby. 'My wife has a headache and needs to lie down. Do you have a room?'

She wished she had a veil on her hat, for she found herself flushing crimson as he spoke. But Sholto's authority was undeniable, and the clerk at the desk replied, 'Of course, sir. Would you like us to fetch you a doctor?'

'Oh no, that won't be necessary. I'll go to the pharmacist and fetch her something myself.'

He was the epitome of the concerned husband and she did her best to be the fragile wife. The play-acting delighted her. It only added to the excitement, an overwhelming excitement which, along with a gale of forbidden laughter, was welling up inside her as they climbed the scarlet-carpeted stairs. She leant on Sholto's arm like a helpless invalid, but did not dare look at him in case they should both explode with laughter and ruin the entire charade. Somehow they lasted in decorous silence until the gleaming mahogany door of room 12 had closed behind them.

'You . . . you . . . rogue!' She forced out the words, as they laughed helplessly and her protest was only rhetorical.

'I didn't notice you objecting. How is your head, dear?'

'It's not my head I'm worried about.'

'Are you worried?'

She shook her head.

'Good, good,' he said. 'You're a brave lass, aren't you? There are not many who would have gone along with that.'

'Well,' she said, glancing at the large brass bedstead which dominated the room, 'I never did plan to lose my innocence in a field.'

'You are brave!' he exclaimed, obviously delighted by her recklessness. 'I appreciate your courage. There's nothing in this world I despise more than cautiousness – it destroys youth, it destroys beauty, it destroys life itself! But it doesn't touch you, does it, my pretty Jessie?' he said, putting his hands on either side of her face. 'It couldn't, could it? Oh, I've a feeling about you, Jessie, about us, about all this! This isn't just summer madness, I know it. This is something altogether more remarkable – a man and a woman coming together like this, almost by chance yet

47

as if . . . oh, but I am talking too much,' he said.

'I like to hear you talk,' said Jessie. 'It's fine talk.'

'But actions speak louder than words,' he said, and kissed her. 'Don't they?'

His actions were as fine and as practised as his words. Clever, careful hands unhooked the back of her dress, her fine, expensive dress which needed another pair of hands to put it on and take it off, unlike a working dress which buttoned up the front. Effie had hooked it up, and Jessie had not thought then that a man with cool and sensitive fingers would undo Effie's more perfunctory actions. As the dress slipped from her shoulders, he covered the bare tops of her arms with kisses, brushing them with the roughness of his beard.

'You've got skin like a duchess,' he said, as she stepped out of her dress.

'How many duchesses have you slept with?'

He laughed at that, and pulled her into his arms again.

'None until today, Your Grace.'

'Well, it will be as novel for you, Mr Hamilton, as it is for me!' she said, wondering where she found the words to be so piquant.

She felt no shame as she stood there before him in her underwear, although they had always tried to drill prudishness into her. And she did not care even that it was not Valenciennes but machine-made lace that trimmed her drawers, and that her blue washing stays had faded to grey, for she felt the triumph of being wanted for what lay beneath, for being wanted for herself, body and soul. To bare herself to him, to remove every last shred of conventional modesty, seemed to be the most liberating thing she had ever done, and the most gratifying, for she saw the real pleasure in his eyes when she took off her chemise and stood naked before him. He had been pulling off one of his boots and staggered in the action, catching sight of her, looking utterly delighted.

'You are a goddess,' he said, 'I knew it.'

'I'm just a woman,' she said, confident of the power of being just that.

They did not get to the bed, but lay on the floor together, in a pool of sunlight which drugged them into slow sensuality. He seemed to kiss every part of her, sweeping over her like some warm wave, more potent than any liqueur. And then, when she stretched out to let him into her, the pain he brought, although it made her gasp at first, seemed incidental, for something stronger mastered her, and she no longer cared. She knew that if there was little pleasure that time, her turn would come. For then, it was enough to see him struggle to his climax and then fall upon her breast, a heavy-breathing, exquisite burden that she would have borne a hundred times for the simple pleasure of such marvellous, heedless intimacy.

She wondered if she would ever forget that room, for every object in it, no matter how prosaic, became etched in her memory, and by enshrinement there gained a significance far more potent than their primary function. Such is how myths begin, how mountains become sacred, how ordinary wells and springs become shrines when they are the silent witnesses to something extraordinary and inexplicable. Thus the rose-patterned wallpaper, the red plush curtains, the chenille tablecloth and gaudy carpet of the room where she first gave herself to a man, were totems in her consciousness, raised to the memory of that afternoon when she changed the course of her life.

Now come on Jessie, lass, she told herself, sternly. Give this all your concentration. Come on now . . .

She had made hollandaise sauce a thousand times. It was one of the things she did best of all. Monsieur Auguste had always delegated the task to her, which was a great compliment for sauces were usually the sole prerogative of the chef. Normally, she could have made hollandaise standing on her head, but that evening she could feel the wilfulness of the ingredients. The whole thing was threatening disaster. She had only added two pieces of butter and yet she could see the mixture beginning to disintegrate, despite vigorous mixing. It was the sort of accident that only a novice would have, and yet here she was, with all her experience, standing by the range, watching with despair as her sauce collapsed.

Fortunately she still had the wit to take the double boiler off the heat before the eggs scrambled, for in a second they would have reached that point of no return. The sauce could still be saved. She felt herself relax at having averted disaster and also from the physical relief of moving away from the heat of the fire, which was burning with all the intensity peculiar to summer when it was not so much needed.

For a moment she leant against the kitchen table, unwilling to move, exhausted suddenly by heat and excitement. To come back into the kitchen after that afternoon with Sholto was to be like that Greek goddess (whose name she could not recall) who had been condemned to spend half the year in the depths of Hell, and half above the earth. The Underworld was the Greek name for Hell, that she did remember, and she understood the fear of it then, standing in what had so recently seemed such an impressive kitchen. That evening it seemed unbearable, like some monstrous prison, with its great vaults and shiny paintwork, its pious slogans printed on the walls – and worst of all, most prison-like of all, those windows set so high up that one could not see out. She had never noticed that before but then it struck her that had been a feature of all the places she had worked, from the dour school-room in Dysart to that grand kitchen in Randolph Crescent, as if whoever had built these places, these places where the ordinary, unfortunate people like herself were destined to spend their time, had done it with the express intention that they should never see out, never guess what a fine place the world was and in what slavery they were kept below. Because if you could not see out, you could not know what it was you were missing.

But I've seen it now, she thought, looking about her with sudden, angry despair, and I shan't be able to settle for this again! The injustice of it rose in her throat, for was she not toiling to make a beautiful sauce that she would never taste, but to which her lover would be quite at liberty to help himself as he sat at that great table upstairs! Worse still, she would never be permitted to sit beside him there, because she was trapped in a place where no one could recognize that she was just the same as them all. For one thing had been made clear to her that afternoon as she had lain in his arms: that fundamentally, they were all the same. It was not death that was the leveller, but love.

She went to the dresser and fetched a basin in order to resurrect her sauce. She cracked an egg and put the yolk into the basin and then began slowly, and with great circumspection, to whisk, drop by drop, the disintegrated sauce into it. This calmed her, and she began to feel a sense of contentment knowing that, even if they could not be together physically, he would be eating this sauce, knowing she had made it. Monsieur Auguste had always said that to cook was to perform an act of love but she had never understood what he had meant until that evening. Even if she could not sit and watch him eat her asparagus and hollandaise; even if she could not see him plunge his fork into the crisp gold surface of puff pastry round the joint of beef; even if she could not see the pleasure register on his face as he tasted the mousse au chocolat, she would know that she was not sending up her masterpieces into a room of faceless individuals whom she did not know or care about, because now there was one amongst them about whom she did care, about whom she cared very much indeed.

The sauce had returned to a state of equilibrium. Jessie dropped the basin into the top of the double boiler and went back to the range. She put in another piece of butter and stirred deliberately, watching the sauce thicken into a state of pale yellow and glossy perfection. She dipped in a teaspoon to check the seasoning. It was perfect, sharp but creamy, the texture like silk velvet. What could be more appropriate to send up to Sholto?

5

'Is that the best you can do?' asked Celia, watching Ralph as he pushed forward his draught. He nodded, not particularly caring if he won or lost the game. It was enough to be sitting alone with Celia on that low half-collapsing sofa in the entrance hall, of which the springs were so decrepit that they forced a certain intimacy upon them. Only the checkerboard balanced on a little tripod table separated them, and Celia, charmingly absorbed in the game despite her lack-lustre opponent, had been free with her hands and feet in a manner that disturbed Ralph more than it gave him pleasure. It triggered off such signals in his body that he began to wonder if he would be able to control himself if once again her foot kicked against his or her hand, as softly as a butterfly, grazed across his knees.

'I'm sorry then,' she said without the least hint of apology, as with a swift hand she darted over the board and disposed of all his pieces. 'There!' And she laughed, full of innocent pleasure at this too easy victory.

'Sorry,' he said, 'I'm not much good at it. But, look, it's served its purpose – it's stopped raining now.'

'You're right – so it has,' she said, twisting round on the sofa to look out of the window properly. 'Do you still want to go for that walk?'

'If you don't mind . . .' He hoped that what he had so carefully connived for that morning would not be destroyed by a sudden whim on her part. It had taken so much courage to ask if she would walk with him and then that wretched rainstorm had come and delayed them in the entrance hall.

'No, no, not at all,' she said, getting up. And then added piquantly, 'It would have to be better than playing you at draughts, wouldn't it!'

She pulled on her dust coat which she had thrown over a chair.

'Aren't you going to put your hat on?' she said, for Ralph was fingering his broad-brimmed Panama.

'You sound like my mother,' he said, pulling it down across his eyes.

'Oh, yes, very good,' she said. 'I do like that – your poet's hat.'

Her words, so unselfconsciously flattering, made him as nervous as her accidental touches and he hardly knew what to say.

'I am right, aren't I?' she continued, quite unconcerned, as they walked through the saloon to reach the garden front. 'You are a poet – Alix said you were.'

'I'm sure she was very disparaging about it.'

'Oh, no, not at all. She told me how brilliant you are,' she said, as they went down into the garden. 'All those prizes for Greek verse.'

'She doesn't know enough Greek to know how bad they are. And as for my other stuff, well, I haven't really shown it to anyone. It simply isn't good enough.'

'I'm sure it is,' she said, with the unshakeable confidence of the polite but ignorant. He wished he might dare to show some of it to her, for she had brought such phrases, such ideas into his mind, that he felt that with time he might do something of real value, something which he might not have to hide away.

'Do you like poetry then?' he asked, glancing at her as she walked along beside him, noting with pleasure the sensual rhythm of her regular, elegant step. But she's poetry herself, he thought.

'Some of it,' she said. 'I like little poems, you know, not those great long ones which tell stories. Perhaps I'm lazy, but I do prefer short poems – they're like little parcels with a lovely idea wrapped up in them. Like the Shakespeare sonnets – I like those very much.' Her sudden volubility and enthusiasm surprised and delighted him more than anything he had yet seen about her.

'You can't be lazy if you read the sonnets,' he remarked.

53

'Now how does that one go . . .?

' "When in the chronicle of wasted time
I see description of the fairest wights,
And beauty making beautiful old rhyme,
In praise of ladies dead and lovely knights,
Then in the blazon of sweet beauty's best
Of hand, of foot, of lip, of eye, of brow,
I see their antique beauty would have express'd
Even such a beauty as you master now.
So all their praises are but prophecies
Of this our time, all you prefiguring;
And, for they look'd but with divining eyes,
They had not skill enough your worth to sing:
For we, which now behold these present days,
Have eyes to wonder, but lack tongues to praise . . ."

'Goodness, I can't usually remember verse,' he added, embarrassed by his audacity. Suddenly he remembered why he had learnt that poem. It had been on a summer holiday in St Andrews, when he had been about fifteen. He had sat amongst the dunes on the West Sands, aching with impossible love for the outrageously pretty French girl who had come to be his sister's governess. He had been reading through the sonnets and learnt that one because it had so aptly expressed all the high flown emotion he had directed towards Mademoiselle Marie-Pierre. She, however, continued playing ball with Alix a little distance away, quite unaware of the great and romantic turmoil afflicting her charge's brother.

Then he had thought his heart might crack open, but now that seemed a mere shadow compared to what he was beginning to feel for Celia Lennox. Here lay the possibility of fulfilment, for was she not walking beside him, declaring she liked his hat, sharing his enthusiasm for Shakespeare and touching him, for God's sake, touching him! When he had finished his little recitation, she had tapped him affectionately on the arm, as if to say, 'Well done!'

Perhaps I shall kiss her today, he thought, as they walked in comfortable silence through the woodland which fringed the gardens. They were climbing up a little, on a path that was shining with mud and probably treacherous, but Celia walked confidently ahead of him, her coat swinging back in a handsome motion. And soon, we will be on that wonderful hill, he told himself, hoping he would not falter and slip. He did not want to make a fool of himself just now, not when she had listened so attentively to him. He was afraid she might laugh at him, in that unkind, heedless way that he had observed in Alix, and he did not want to have to dislike her for it.

'For an invalid you walk well,' she remarked.

'Who said I was an invalid?'

'Alix.'

'It's like the poetry – the reports are grossly exaggerated.'

'I'm sure your mother wouldn't say so,' she said. 'Is it very rotten – all those migraines and things? Alix said you were in a bad way yesterday.'

'I try not to let it bother me, but it does make me angry sometimes. It's annoying not to be properly made, like a rickety bit of furniture.'

This seemed to amuse her and she stopped for a moment to look him up and down.

'I'm just trying to imagine which piece of furniture,' she laughed. 'I always like comparing people to things. It helps one to work a person out, don't you think?'

'Put me down as a hall stand,' he said, 'and I'll topple over if you hang too many things on me.'

'Too simple,' she said decidedly. 'I shall have to think about it. I shall tell you when I think of it. Or perhaps not – you might not like it.' And she set off up the hill again.

And what would I compare you to, Celia? he asked himself and a thousand clichés jostled for attention in his mind. But he could think of nothing appropriate, for she seemed perfect in herself, more original than any image he might dredge up.

'Come on, come on!' she called, for she was going briskly now, as sure-footedly as a mountain goat, and he almost lost sight of her amongst the trees. It was an irresistible challenge and he went forward as fast as he could, no longer caring if he stumbled for he was convinced she would be lenient with him. To have her out of his sight for only a moment had become unbearably painful and he knew he must chase and chase, no matter what it cost him, to catch her and keep her.

Suddenly the trees had thinned out and he was following her over a sun-bleached, windy hill top. For a moment he stopped to catch his breath and a first glimpse of the view, but she called out again, 'Come on, come on!'

She dashed up the final crag which lay ahead of them, kilting up her skirts and displaying as she ran slender, strong legs, unprepossessingly clad in dark brown woollen stockings. He watched, amazed, as when she reached the summit, she flung herself face-down on the rough turf, like some priestess indulging in an obscure and primitive ritual of her cult. He hesitated to join her, wondering if he dare intrude upon another person's ecstatic pleasure in the raw beauty of nature. In her abandonment, she seemed to symbolize all the pleasure he had found in such lonely places, and yet she was more than that. She seemed more of the place than he could ever be, for she did not embrace the earth with her eyes but with her whole body, as if it were her lover to which she was returning.

But when he reached her, she had rolled over on to her back and was staring at the sky. He sat down beside her and tried to ignore the disturbing erotic thoughts that flooded over him, concentrating instead on the magnificent view of park and house that lay spread out in front of them. But now he could not separate nature from sexuality. He knew his exhilaration was partly from the clear air and the view, and partly from the closeness of her as she lay less than an arm's length away from him, stretched out on the ground, breathing hard to recover herself.

They sat in silence for quite some time, much to Ralph's relief, for he felt he could not have spoken without letting his whole heart pour out in a confused torrent of words. But

56

then he heard her stir (he did not dare look at her) and say, 'Do you like it, then?'

'Do I like it?' he said incredulously. 'Do you need to ask?'

'No, I suppose not. I can feel that you like it.'

He turned and looked at her, feeling his stomach jump in joyous amazement. She was propped up on her elbows, her hair wild about her face and her cheeks glowing with the exercise. She looked more animal than human, but never had he felt more tempted by her. It would be easy to lean forward and kiss her as she lay there so relaxed and available, as if she were waiting for him to do it. But something held him back, something which he cursed himself for but which he was powerless to overcome, as if to have kissed her then would have been as outrageous as pressing his lips to the painted face of an old master. He had no right to touch her. To invade her with his own desires when she was so perfectly and independently herself, would have been an act of violation. She was not a woman like Mrs Lennox who set her scale by the admirers in her drawing room. She did not need men to make her come alive – that was all too obvious. All she needed was the resources of her own soul and he could not bring himself to desecrate that with his own clumsy fumblings.

He got up and walked away a little, removing himself from the agony of this denied temptation. He felt nothing of the triumph of self-denial, only a nagging sense of inadequacy and disappointment. He wondered if his high flown reasoning was nothing but a mask for his own cowardice, and wished suddenly that she might offer herself to him, that she would urgently demand from him what he longed to give her. That would have been easier. But it was not very likely, for she lay there still, her eyes closed to keep out the sun, completely indifferent to his presence. And in a few minutes, he noticed, she had fallen into a light sleep.

'There's a telegram come for your brother, Miss Erskine,' said Maxwell, the butler.

Alix, curled up in the sunny window seat of her room, was reading Trollope, not because she had especially decided to, but it had come to hand in an idle moment, and the story had caught her. For the last few hours she had been thoroughly engrossed in the difficult choice between two men which confronted Alice Vavasor in *Can You Forgive Her?* Alix herself was half in love with John Grey but more passionate about George Vavasor, the wild man, and was really beginning to wonder if any satisfactory conclusion could be worked out, when Mr Maxwell came with Ralph's telegram.

'I'm afraid I couldn't find your brother, Miss Erskine, so I thought you had better have it, in case it was family business.'

'Thank you, Mr Maxwell, that's very kind,' she said, taking it. 'Telegrams always make one nervous, don't they? Oh, it's all right. It's just business. My father wants my brother to run back up to Edinburgh tonight. Perhaps we should look up a train for him.'

'The five-forty-five would suit, I should think, Miss Erskine. Shall I go and pack for Mr Erskine?'

'That would be useful. I wonder when they'll be back. He went for a walk with Celia . . .' And she glanced over her shoulder out of the window, in case they were within sight.

'Well, if he's with Miss Celia, there's no need to worry. She's always back in time for tea – it's her favourite meal.'

'You're right – it is, isn't it?' she said, surprised at the butler's perspicacity. But he had been with the family for years, and old servants had a habit of knowing these things.

About ten minutes later, and half an hour before tea, Ralph and Celia did return from their walk, quite as predicted. Alix handed her brother the telegram, the contents of which he received with a scowl.

'What a damned thing,' he murmured. 'I'm supposed to be on holiday, but of course he doesn't understand the meaning of that!'

She followed him into his room, and sat on the bed while he washed his face.

'I don't know what I shall say to Sir Hector,' he said, rubbing his face vigorously with a towel. 'It looks so damn rude – but Father wouldn't see that.'

'I'm sure they'll understand.'

'Well, I hope it's worth the journey,' he said, and sat down beside her wearily. 'The last thing I want just now is to get on a train. Oh, well, it's a good thing I've had some exercise today.'

'Did you have a nice walk, then?'

'Very pleasant. Celia fell asleep just like a cat when we got to the top – there was something almost pagan about it.'

'Do you like her then?'

'Yes, I do rather,' he said. 'She's a bright girl, very sensitive to things. I'm sure if she was given the opportunity, she could do something tremendous.'

'You do like her, don't you?' said Alix. 'Or is it more than liking?'

'Do you think I'd tell you that?' he said with a grin. 'When the two of you are as thick as thieves.'

'But wouldn't you want her to know?' she said. 'Can't I just hint a little?'

'No, Alix, please, I'd rather you didn't,' he said with a nervous sincerity which made her realize that he was badly bitten. 'Do you promise?'

'Of course I do,' she said, and then added flippantly, 'If you'll let me be best maid!' To which he gave her a look which could only be described as murderous.

'Someone should give you something useful to do, Alexandra Erskine,' he said, perhaps a little annoyed but still good-humouredly, 'or you'll do nothing but meddle and cause trouble.'

'Well, perhaps you could speak to Father about it,' she said brightly, and decided that this was the best moment to leave before he shied the towel he was holding at her.

As they sat in the drawing room, having tea, Alix found herself looking at Celia with fresh interest, wondering what it was about her that had managed to ensnare the hearts of two quite different men. For undoubtedly Ralph was very different from Hamish the poacher. And what if she likes them both? she found herself asking. What an extraordinary situation that will be . . . just like that novel! And felt pleased that literature could anticipate life.

6

'Here we are!' said Robert Erskine as the Victoria drew up at the mouth of a dusty wynd where weeds had pushed up between the cobbles. His excitement, which Ralph had observed fermenting gently since setting out from Edinburgh, was now bubbling over, and he sprang out of the carriage with a boyish enthusiasm inappropriate to the dignity of his morning coat and silk hat. It was endearing but a little daunting, for Ralph could tell that his father had some great plan afoot involving these unprepossessing premises, a plan which involved his own presence there.

He followed his father down the wynd, towards a pair of green gates with peeling paintwork. Hanging above them was a sign reading 'The Musselburgh Coach and Motor Works', with another sign, nailed unceremoniously across the corner, bearing the ominous words 'For sale, apply within'.

'Motor works – horseless carriages, you mean?' said Ralph. 'Surely not, Father? I thought you had decided that those things weren't going anywhere . . .'

'You sound like an old man, Ralph,' said his father, 'and your scepticism is unfounded. They are wonderful machines – perhaps a little primitive, but if we sank some money into developments, imagine where that might take the company in a few years. We have to get into this now. I've left it almost too late. The Germans are streaking ahead. It's something we really should be looking into and this is a nice little company. Wait until you see it.' He tugged on the bell chain as if he were already the proprietor.

'You've seen this already?'

'Oh, yes, I was down here yesterday. That's why I cabled you. I didn't want to make a decision without you. It is your future as well, you know.'

Ralph wondered what use his opinion would really be in

the matter. Whether or not the Erskine Steel Company acquired another subsidiary was really of little moment to him, except that some of the legal paperwork would find its way on to his desk. He knew quite well from his father's manner that the decision had already been taken. He was not offended. He knew his own business sense was woefully inadequate to make even the slightest sensible contribution to such an undertaking. It was a little annoying to be dragged away from his pursuit of Celia when his consent was only a formality. But that was typical of his father. He would not have been able to understand Ralph's indifference.

Robert Erskine collected companies as other rich men collected paintings. Where other industrialists had sold out and attempted, prodded by ambitious wives, to break into society, he had stayed loyal to his empire, behaving still as if every penny mattered and throwing himself into every technical advance as if he were still a young engineer. The motor carriage was obviously the next dream, and he would see the world filled with Erskine motors in the same way he had, with single-minded determination, seen to it that Erskine Steel formed the very ribs of the world's railways.

'They've got a clever man here,' he said, as they waited for someone to open the gate. 'A chap who really knows how to put an engine together. You'll be impressed with these machines. They're not as barbaric as you think they'll be.'

'I didn't say anything about barbarism,' said Ralph.

'No, but I know that look on your face,' smiled his father.

'Well, that contraption you had that summer at Berwick was rather . . .'

'That was French, and it was four years ago. Things have moved on.'

'I hope so,' said Ralph, remembering the irascible machine which had dominated and in fact ruined a brief family holiday. His mother had been terrified that his father would kill himself as he careered inexpertly around the forecourt of the house. That of course was when it actually worked; for most of the time it could not be coaxed into motion but still demanded the full attention of his father. He had spent hours tweaking the engine, producing from it, like some diabolical organist, a repertoire of noises that would raise the dead and which caused the neighbours, who lived half a mile away, to complain. Ralph did not know what happened to the machine because he had gone to France before his father's obsession had burnt itself out, but when he had got back to Edinburgh in the autumn for his final year at the university, it had been quite forgotten in the excitement of acquiring the steam launch company in Dundee.

'That was a dreadful machine,' reflected Mr Erskine. 'The principle of these are the same, but the design is so much better. Less explosive, you'll be glad to hear.'

'But they'll only ever be for a hobby, won't they?' he said. 'It'll never replace the railways for convenience.'

'Look at the bicycle, Ralph,' said his father sagely. 'Ten years ago, less even, it was just a sport. Now every messenger boy has one. I wish I'd seen that one coming. So we're not going to miss this.'

'I'm surprised you did miss it.'

'I was too busy developing armour plating then, you remember. That seemed more important at the time.'

'It still is, surely,' said Ralph, thinking of the large admiralty contract they had negotiated the previous year.

'Yes, of course,' said Mr Erskine. 'But I've got a real feeling about this. This is something really . . .'

In his mind Ralph saw the Erskine empire as some vast tract of seaweed which could not be contained, growing with vegetable steadiness under the sea, stretching out its tentacles to embrace everything. It would need a hero to wrestle and subdue it and he felt he had no such heroism in him. It would strangle him slowly, and most terrifying of all, collapse about him. Killed by his own incompetence. His father's touch of genius had not been passed on to him.

After an eternity the gate was opened by a wizened man in a thick tweed suit which looked unbearably hot on such a day. He took off his cap with great deference, evidently recognizing Ralph's father as the new power at the Coach Works.

'Ah, good day to you, sir,' he said. 'Mr Dundas and the gentleman from the bank are waiting for you.'

'And is MacDonald here?' asked Mr Erskine.

'No, I'm afraid not, sir. But his lady is. He's drinking again . . .'

'MacDonald's the owner – a rather feckless individual, it seems,' explained Mr Erskine in a low voice, as they followed the old man into the offices. The whole place seemed dusty and neglected. There was no noise coming from the yards that might suggest any industry at all. Ralph wondered if his father's instinct was as sharp as it had been. This hardly seemed the sort of thriving concern one would want to acquire. 'It's his wife that's selling. She needs the cash to pack him off to a sanatorium before he kills himself.'

Mrs MacDonald, a formidable-looking creature in a gaudy dress, was sitting at the desk in the office with an expression on her face that would send any man running for the whisky. She acknowledged their arrival with a curt nod.

'It's very good to see you again, Mr Erskine,' said Mr Frazer, the man from the bank. Ralph guessed that the company was in considerable debt to his bank and he was in hope of its being made good by the sale.

'Well, shall we get started?' said Mr Erskine, with his customary briskness. He put down his briefcase and hat on the table. 'We touched a little on prices yesterday, Mrs MacDonald. Now, I was thinking over this last night. I offer you two choices. The higher price, or the lower together with settlement of the debts.' So there were debts, but Ralph was surprised at his father's offer to meet them. It seemed too advantageous to the seller. He had never seen him deal so generously, and for a place that was half falling down through the neglect of a drunkard! What could he be up to?

Mr Frazer and Mrs MacDonald exchanged a glance.

'I'll take the lower price,' she said, and Ralph saw Frazer relax visibly, happy that the debts would be paid.

'Excellent,' said Mr Erskine. 'Well, you'll just have to get your husband to sign the papers. I'll have them sent to you. He will sign, won't he?'

'He'll sign, Mr Erskine, you need not worry about that,' she said, getting up from her chair. 'I don't need to stay any more, do I?'

'No, not unless you want to.'

'I hate this place,' she said simply. 'It's filthy.'

'Let me see you to your carriage, Mrs MacDonald,' said Mr Frazer.

'No, I'm quite all right. Good morning to you all,' she said, and left, her skirts sweeping the dusty floor.

'Well, well,' said Mr Erskine. 'That was straightforward enough. If you can give me a list of the debts, I can meet them for you, Frazer.'

'I have them here, Mr Erskine. I do hope you will decide to bank with us when the sale goes through?'

'Well, that's not really for me to decide,' said his father. 'You see, my son here will be managing the place. You'll have to ask him.' And he turned and smiled at Ralph, who had been standing somewhat in the background, hoping he would not be involved.

It took him a moment or two to realize what his father had said and the shock of it numbed him.

'Well, then, I hope I will have the privilege of working with you, Mr Erskine,' said Frazer obsequiously to Ralph.

He could not think what to say, for his numbness was rapidly being replaced by anger at his father. How could he spring something like this?

'I'll let you know, Mr Frazer,' he managed to say, and then emboldened, added, 'I wonder if you gentlemen might let my father and I have a few moments alone?'

Frazer and Dundas went to the door.

'Don't go far, Dundas,' said Mr Erskine cheerfully. 'Your new boss will want to see all your exciting innovations, I'm sure.'

The door shut and Ralph exclaimed, 'What are you doing, Father? How dare you!'

'My dear Ralph,' said his father emolliently, 'I know how it must seem. But I thought I'd surprise you. I thought you'd be pleased. I know this place doesn't look like much, but Dundas, he's got something, and with a bit of work . . .'

'Then why didn't you get *him* to manage it?'

'I want to keep him on the technical side. That's where he's best. You see that, surely? We can't worry him with the business side.'

'If I have anything to do with this, there won't *be* a business,' said Ralph. 'You might as well ask me to manage a slaughter house – at least I'd know what I was supposed to do there!'

'You do know what to do, Ralph,' said Mr Erskine, his manner a little sharper. 'You're going to make motors, and you're going to sell them and turn in a good profit.'

'I can't do that.'

'Well, it's about time you learnt, isn't it? Now it strikes me this place is about the best training you could get. You'll have complete control of the operation. It's the best way to learn, and you are going to have to learn, and soon. I'm not going to live forever.'

'You'll be throwing money down the drain here.'

'It's your money too, Ralph, think about that,' his father said. 'Your money. It's what pays for all your continental jaunts, for your precious old books, for your fancy silk ties!' And with a deft, aggressive movement which totally surprised Ralph, flicked his tie from out of the top of his waistcoat. He looked quite disgusted. 'So you are going to run this place,' he said with a firmness that Ralph found disturbing, 'and turn it from a wreck into something viable. It's what I had to do with the mill, and I don't see any damn' reason why you shouldn't be able to do it too.'

'What an ultimatum,' said Ralph caustically, for he could not think of any adequate counter-argument. It felt like a death sentence, to look about that dreary office and know he must make something of it.

'If you've any sense, Ralph, you'll turn this to your advantage,' said Mr Erskine. 'Most young men would be pleased to have such an opportunity.

'Don't shovel on the guilt, Father, it's bad enough as it

is!' snapped Ralph. And then suddenly conscious that he had been unkind, added, 'Oh, I'm sorry. I just feel daunted, that's all.'

'Well, what do you think I felt when Uncle John left me the steel mill? But I tried. For his sake, I tried. And I found I liked it after all. You never know. . .'

'I think you are being optimistic about that,' said Ralph. 'But if you insist, I will try. I haven't really got any choice, have I?'

'I knew you'd see it,' said his father with a conciliatory smile. 'Your mother's pleased about it. She was worried about your travelling so much – she thinks it will be healthier for you to work nearer home.'

'Why didn't you consult me?'

'Surprise is a good rule of business,' said his father, picking up his hat from the desk. 'Now, let's go and find Dundas.'

The entire place was desolate and torpid in the heat. But Mr Erskine was undaunted, as eager for the venture as if it had been his first. Still Ralph felt he had been handed a white elephant. It was all very well to dream of progress, to see the horseless carriage as the transport revolution of the next century, but to imagine it might come from here, where the old porter and two witless-looking apprentices were hanging about like lost souls, while Dundas, a wiry little man, poked and oiled the engine of the most infernal contraption that Ralph had ever seen, seemed little short of ridiculous!

'This is our latest model,' said Dundas proudly, 'a six horsepower run-about. Top speed 20mph.'

'Mph? What's that?' asked Ralph.

'Miles per hour, sir,' said Dundas. 'If you'd like to have a look at the engine, you'll see it has certain novel features – the two cylinders, for example, arranged in such a way as almost to eliminate vibration; hot tube ignition; two brakes, hand and foot; and a steering wheel. All the finest innovations up to this time, with a brougham body.'

'Marvellous, isn't it?' said his father, while Ralph, in silence, attempted to digest this incomprehensible informa-

66

tion. 'Look at those crankshafts, Ralph, they rotate in opposite directions – it's a beautiful piece of design.'

'Whatever you say,' murmured Ralph who could not make the least sense of the mass of valves, tubes and pistons. 'Twenty miles per hour, you say?'

'That's right, sir,' said Dundas.

'And this is the only one of these?'

'We've made three over the last year and a half,' said Dundas.

'And sold them?'

'No, no, unfortunately not . . . no, we've had to fall back on the coach building side to keep it going. Mr MacDonald has been rather disillusioned about the whole enterprise, but I think you'll agree, sir, it's the coming thing.'

'Don't worry, Dundas,' said Mr Erskine, 'you'll be quite free to carry on your excellent work. My son and I are in complete agreement that these little beauties,' and he tapped one of the cylinders appreciatively, 'are here to stay.'

Ralph returned to Rothesay Terrace with an orange box full of documents, ledgers and technical drawings. Mr Erskine had decided that the first priority was to secure the patent for the two-cylinder, rotating crankshaft engine and Ralph, as he staggered in with his load, predicted the rest of his summer would be occupied with the legal complications relating to that. But he was determined to get back to the Quarro tomorrow, for he had been invited for the week, his father had granted him the time off months ago and he was not going to be cheated of that. Rotating crankshafts, whatever they were or did, could wait.

'Ralph dear, is that you?' said Mrs Erskine, coming out on to the landing from the drawing room. Typically she stood and waited to be kissed, her cheek a little inclined. He put down the orange box, the momentum of rushing upstairs with it quite interrupted, and kissed her as she expected.

'Oh, you're hot, dear,' she said, brushing his forehead.

'It's a hot day, Mother,' he said, disentangling himself.

'Are you sure you are all right?'

67

'I'm fine, Mother, honestly,' he said. 'Apart from being saddled with this motor carriage business, I'm fine.'

'Oh, that,' she said. 'Your father thought you would be pleased. It will be a very good thing for you.'

'I dare say,' said Ralph wearily, 'but he might have warned me.'

'Come and have some tea,' she said, going back into the drawing room.

'I'd rather have a gin and soda,' he said, following her in.

'It's not yet one o'clock, Ralph,' she said reprovingly. 'You shouldn't drink spirits at all really. Remember that Dr Bannerman said that . . .'

'Please, Mother, not now,' he pleaded. 'Can't you see I've had an annoying morning?'

'Oh, my poor love,' she said. 'I know you're angry, but you must see, your father doesn't do these things deliberately to torment you. He wants you to do well.'

'Well, we'll see about doing well. The place looks to me to be heading for disaster as it is. It turned the last owner into a drunkard. I wonder what it will do to me.'

'Ralph, really,' said Mrs Erskine. 'Don't get so cross – it doesn't help your ulcers.'

He flung himself into an armchair and tried to control his temper, not for the sake of his ulcers but to stop his mother's nagging.

'Really, my dear,' she continued, looking him up and down as if he were a piece of cattle come to market, 'you don't look at all well. I wonder if you shouldn't go upstairs and rest. This weather is really too much. I hope you haven't been overdoing things in the country.'

'Mother, I told you, I'm fine,' he said, wishing he could push her away in a brutal movement, for she was bending over his chair determined to discover some slight sign of debility in him. But to be brutal with her was unthinkable, as if she were the one with delicate health.

She always reminded him of a rare orchid, with her pale, slender face, her softly coloured, softly draped, crêpe-de-chine dresses and her fine gold hair, dulled subtly with the first signs of grey. And like an orchid, her appearance was deceptive, for orchids only seemed fragile and exotic because they were seen to bloom nursed in the luxury of a winter garden. Who was to know, except the plant collectors who had trekked over mountains and across torrents to find such oddities, that *there* they were not in the least fragile, but as persistent and as vigorous as any common weed in an ordinary Scottish garden? So it was with his mother, who the world in general perceived as a yielding, shy and gracious wife, while to Ralph it was clear that she had a will of iron which equalled, if not surpassed in its limited sphere, that of her determined and dynamic husband.

'Well, if you are sure,' she said, with such a lack of conviction that Ralph wondered if there was any point refuting her and whether he should simply submit now, rather than later, to her suggestion-cum-order that he should rest. But to his surprise she said nothing further, busying herself with the tea things, and he watched her from the languor of his armchair, performing the ritual with all the precision of a chemist in the laboratory. The room was shrouded in silence and still heat, for outside only an occasional carriage rumbled across the cobbles, and inside, as always, reigned a decorous quiet, as if the place was a temple to domesticity rather than a house inhabited by real human beings. There was nothing that his mother disliked more than raised voices, and even his father, who could explode with fiery wrath at the office, observed this rule scrupulously. This house was her empire, not his.

She would not let Ralph get up and fetch his tea cup but brought it over to him, sitting beside him on a low chair like an attendant nurse to make sure that he took the proper dosage. It was weak and very hot, heating up the small, twiddly handle of the cup, making it almost unbearable to hold.

'I think,' she said, after a while, 'that perhaps you had better not go back down tonight. It really is too hot to travel.'

'But I said I would be there for dinner. It really looks bad enough as it is – as if I'm only treating the place like an hotel . . .'

'Of course it doesn't look like that. If you send them a wire, I'm sure they'll understand. Perhaps I should do it . . .'

'No, Mother, please. I'm not a schoolboy who has to be excused by his mother now,' he said, a little exasperated by her manner. 'Besides, I want to go back. I was enjoying myself.'

'Wearing yourself out, no doubt, being silly and drinking too much and running around as if you were . . .'

'As if I were perfectly all right, which I am, Mother, don't you understand that? I haven't felt so well in years, you know that.'

'And why is that, Ralph?' she said. 'Because you had started to be sensible and do what you were told. That's why you feel better. But if you insist on carrying on like this, running around in this silly way, you will be back to how it was when you were at school.'

It was impossible to argue with her. There was not an argument in the world which would make her change her mind. She had decided she wanted him to stay, for she was possessive about her children. She had been somewhat piqued when the invitation had come for them to go to the Quarro, as if they were independent beings, like other people's children but not her own. Ralph knew too well she could not imagine they would want to begin a life separate from hers. She used his illness and Alix's sex like fetters to keep them near her, for he was incapable of looking after himself, and a daughter's place was with her mother. She pretended to act for their own good, but the selfishness of it was sometimes too bitterly obvious, like the rank taste of some beautiful but poisonous fruit. She had not questioned his father's decision to summon Ralph back from the country, to an Edinburgh labouring under a heat wave, and to pile him with responsibilities which might prove more detrimental to his health than a game of tennis or too many glasses of claret. It would not have occurred to her to question that, for it acted in her favour and brought him

70

back to her, albeit for only a day or two. But Ralph was not going in to give in to her pressure. He simply would not tell her whether he was going or staying, but would go. There would be tears and recriminations from her later, but he was prepared to bear them. At that moment it was more important for him to get back to Celia.

Celia . . . The sudden remembrance of her brought on a sense of supreme well-being which, however, only lasted a moment, until he glanced again at Mrs Erskine. She would probably greatly dislike the thought of his marrying, and would certainly not approve of any girl he happened to choose, for no matter how self-effacing the girl, she would still be a wife, and a wife steals from a mother the lion's share of intimacy. If he told her he was thinking of marriage, he could imagine that she would find some dreadful doctor to advise against it on the grounds that 'intimate relations' were inadvisable because of his weak heart. At least I know that's not true! he thought, and found himself laughing at the thought. His mother stared at him and asked, 'What are you thinking about?'

'Oh, just something that Sholto said the other day . . .'

'Then I don't wish to hear it,' she said tartly. She disapproved of his friendship with Sholto. 'I can't imagine why the Lennoxes asked him to stay.'

'He's the perfect guest,' said Ralph. 'He plays tennis and billiards, flirts with all the women, even the old ones, flatters all the men, and is generally the life and soul of the party.'

'Ralph, really!' she said. 'Perhaps these Lennoxes aren't as nice as I thought they were. But Celia did strike me as a very well brought up girl, despite the circumstances – poor child, having no mother.'

'Well, there is James's wife, and her aunt,' he said, wondering how he was going to talk non-committally about Celia.

'But it's not the same as one's own mother, is it?' she reflected. 'But she is a charming girl, all the same. I should imagine you would find her rather pretty. She reminds me of some of those engravings in your room – the Italian ones.'

'You're right, Mother,' he said, as if it had not occurred to him. 'I suppose she is rather nice-looking.'

'But a little young still,' she said, patting his knee as if she had guessed at his true feelings despite his evasive words. 'Just a little too young . . .'

'I didn't expect to see you, Ralph,' said Finn O'Hara, coming out of the back of the shop. 'I thought you'd gone off gallivanting to the country, to stay with some grand folk.'

'I did,' said Ralph, 'but my father called me back on supposedly urgent business, which wasn't the least bit urgent.'

'I see,' said O'Hara, 'it's like that, is it? You look as though you could do with a drink.'

'I could, indeed. Why do you think I've come here?'

'I might have guessed you didn't want to buy anything.'

'Well, you might be able to help me,' he said, glancing around the shop which was, as usual, well stocked with a bizarre mixture of old and unusual objects. 'I'm looking for something to give to a . . .'

'To a woman?' cut in Finn, with exuberant delight. 'Now, we *will* have a drink! Come through and sit down, man, and tell us all about it.' And he drew back the tapestry curtains which divided the front from the back of the shop. 'Nancy, my darling, look who's here.'

Finn's wife was sitting at her embroidery frame in a pool of sunlight at the far end of the room. She was heavily pregnant and dressed in a flowing blue dress with a broad white collar, making a picture as serene as a Vermeer. Ralph, in the past, had been inclined to be somewhat jealous of Finn and his beautiful Nancy, but today, with his mind full of Celia, it did not trouble him in the least to see this happy, young marriage, for he had hopes of being happy in the same way. He was determined to be.

'Hello,' he said, going over to her and kissing her fraternally. 'How are you feeling? This weather must be an awful nuisance.'

'Well, I wouldn't call it perfect,' she smiled, 'but I shall survive.'

'I'm sure you shall. How long is it now?'

'Two months,' said Finn proudly. 'And it's kicking like a champion. I've felt it myself.'

'We were about to have some lunch,' said Nancy, indicating the table where on a white cloth a loaf of bread, a large piece of cheese, a basket of strawberries, a blue and white jug of milk and some bottles of Younger's Ale had been placed, as if to compose a still life rather than provide anything as simple as luncheon. 'Will you join us?'

'Of course he will,' said Finn, opening one of the bottles of beer and handing it to Ralph. He drank out of the bottle – Finn did not generally run to such refinements as glasses when it came to beer. 'Well, sit down then and tell us all about her.'

'Oh,' said Nancy, obviously interested, 'you've met someone nice have you, Ralph?'

'Someone nice? Nancy, really, what a bland way of putting it,' said Finn, swigging vigorously at his bottle. 'If Ralph's eye for women is the same as his eye for pictures, she'll be supremely ravishing, an exquisite beauty – oh, you're the poet, Ralph, you tell us what she's like.'

'She's very nice,' said Ralph, and they all laughed.

'Come on now, the truth,' said Finn.

'What you are asking me to do,' said Ralph, 'is quite impossible.'

'Oh, for God's sake man, try – you are in love with the girl, aren't you?'

'I rather fear so,' he said, with a touch of mock-pomposity which made Nancy giggle.

'What's there to be afraid of?' she said. 'Do you think she doesn't like you?'

'I simply don't know whether she does or not.'

'Why don't you ask her to the Studio Ball?' said Nancy.

'Oh, yes, what a good idea,' said Finn enthusiastically. 'Then if she says yes, you'll know she likes you.'

'Yes, but I'm not sure that her people would let her go,' said Ralph, feeling sure that the Lennoxes would frown on such a bohemian debauch as the Studio Ball.

'It is for charity,' said Nancy. 'No one could object to a charity dance – and if they are that fussy, you can say that I'll chaperone her.'

The thought of Nancy, who was not much above twenty, as a chaperone was amusing, but Ralph knew that she would not take her duties too seriously. Rather, she was offering him a name, a respectable married woman's name, which would act as a guarantee that Celia would not be getting into a scrape with a young man.

'Yes, I will – thank you.'

'Well, hadn't you better ask me how much the tickets are? We've been trying to sell as many as we can,' said Finn.

'Of course – I forgot you were on the committee,' said Ralph. 'How much then?' he added, reaching for his wallet.

'Two guineas for a pair,' said Finn. 'A fiver for half a dozen – it's for the orphans, remember.'

'Here,' said Ralph taking out a five-pound note and handing it to Finn.

'Ah,' he said, holding it up appreciatively, 'what a thing it is to have a private income!'

'I have to work for it, you know,' said Ralph. 'My father's latest scheme is that I should manage a motor carriage works in Musselburgh.'

'A what?' exclaimed Finn, highly amused.

'Motor carriages – you know, those self-propelling, exploding contraptions that they say are the transport of the future.'

This amused Finn so much that he rolled back in his chair and laughed helplessly for several minutes.

'Your father is either wildly optimistic or utterly insane!' he said. 'Why, you'll never be able to do anything like that!'

'Do you think I don't know that?' said Ralph, more rueful than amused.

'You're not going along with it, I hope?' said Finn, suddenly serious.

'I don't see what choice I have,' Ralph said.

'You should get out of all that. It's no business for you. You're wasted there. You should come in with me on the picture dealing – we could be partners. Now wouldn't that be grand? A man with your eye – we'd make a fortune.'

But Ralph shook his head.

'No, I couldn't do what you do, Finn. I couldn't trade in beautiful things. I'm too sentimental, I suppose, too much of a collector myself to be able to sell what I'd discovered. I don't know how you do it – how you can bear to do it. Doesn't it break your heart sometimes, to sell something you've really fallen in love with?'

'But I could never have had the thing even for a minute if I wasn't selling it on. It's the only way I'll ever get to own such things, even if only temporarily,' said Finn, getting up and taking a key from his waistcoat pocket. He stooped down and unlocked a cupboard in the large desk that stood against one wall. 'Take this, for example. I should never have been able to hold such a thing if I wasn't going to sell it,' he said, taking out a large jewellery case and putting it on the table. 'This is for Lord Fergusson. At least, I hope he wants it or I shall be in trouble – well, not really, because quality like this will always sell – but he'll give me the price I want. I found it in Carcassonne last month.' And he opened the lid, and lifted out from a shabby black velvet ground a small, delicately wrought golden crown. 'Now, that's something, isn't it?'

Ralph was lost for words for a moment. The thing was so exquisite that he could not quite believe it was real, but when Finn put it in his hands, and he felt the cool gold against his fingers, he had to concede it was. The utter simplicity of it was stunning: a circle of golden oak leaves, intertwining so naturally that it seemed that the goldsmith had merely dipped a real wreath of oak twigs into a pot of molten gold.

'It's quite extraordinary,' he said. 'How old is it?'

'Well, hard to say really, but it came from a family of French nobles in the Languedoc. They believe that it came into the family as part of an Italian bride's dowry – it might be a wedding crown.'

'It could be fifteenth-century,' said Ralph, lifting it up to the light to catch the subtle vibrant glow of that ancient red gold. 'Doesn't it make you think of Botticelli? I'm sure there are crowns like this in the early Italian masters. Good God! Think of that. Made in Italy at the time of Botticelli and Ghirlandio!' And he stepped forward and crowned Nancy with it. Resting on her thick, chestnut-coloured hair, it looked even more magnificent. 'Now you can't say it will be easy to sell that to Fergusson! It makes you like an expectant madonna, Nancy – you look quite wonderful.'

'Yes,' she said, lifting it out of her hair and returning it to her husband, 'but the profit on that will pay for the baby clothes.'

'More than that, I hope,' said Finn, putting it back in its case.

'But must you sell it to Fergusson?' said Ralph. 'He hasn't even a wife to wear it. It will just stay locked up and no one will ever see it.'

'It's just the sort of thing that he loves,' said Finn, pragmatically. 'He spends more on jewellery than anything.'

'How much is it?' said Ralph, suddenly inspired to mad enthusiasm by the thought of Celia wearing it.

'I couldn't sell it for less than two thousand guineas,' said Finn.

'You didn't tell me it was worth that much,' said Nancy, faintly shocked. 'Shouldn't it be in the bank?'

'No, nobody knows it's here,' said Finn.

'It's a shame my father has no taste,' said Ralph, wistfully, gazing at it again.

'Tell him it's an investment,' said Finn.

'No, it's not the sort of investment he understands,' said Ralph. 'If it were a steel mill, or a rundown brass foundry, he'd understand that, but not something like this.'

'So you don't think you could afford it?' said Finn.

'Not really, unfortunately. After all, I have to be pragmatic too. With you it's baby clothes – for me, well, I shall need some capital to furnish a house.'

'Oh, you're that serious about her?' said Finn.

'I think so,' he said.

'Well, we shall expect to be invited to the wedding,' said

Finn. 'Shan't we, Nancy? And if you want a little something for her,' he continued, reaching down into the desk cupboard again, 'I've some pretty little seventeenth-century rings here . . .'

7

Jessie hesitated outside the drawing-room door. It was slightly ajar and there were obviously people inside, for most alarmingly she could hear Sholto's dark brown velvet voice, waxing lyrical about something, producing little ripples of amusement. It was not that she did not want to see him. There was a scarcely a minute of the day that she did not long to feel his arms about her, but she did not want him to see her now, in her plain working clothes, having to be so obviously a servant as she delivered the day's menu to Mrs Lennox.

Usually the drawing room was empty and Mrs Lennox alone, but that morning, because the weather had broken, the guests had stayed indoors. She wondered if she should go in. Mrs Lennox might not wish to be disturbed just then. The thought of provoking some sharp or dismissive word from her, and being humiliated in front of Sholto, was too awful to contemplate. She had a feeling that he would not spring to her defence – and why should he? That would destroy their secret, and it was too good a thing to be ruined by a piece of boyish chivalry. One had to be pragmatic about such things.

'What, lass, are you frightened to go in?' said Mr Maxwell, tapping her on the shoulder and making her jump.

'Oh!' she exclaimed involuntarily, and then added, 'I wasn't listening – I was just wondering whether the mistress will want to see me now, as usual, seeing as she's busy with folk . . .'

'Well, she's just rung for me, so it must be all right.' He

smiled. 'Shall we go in together?'

He went ahead of her, unfolding the double doors decorously, almost as if she were someone important. She tried to come in inconspicuously, but she knew at once *his* eyes were on her, and a blush was stealing over her face. She managed one brief glance at him. He was lounging in a chair, his legs crossed, a newspaper half unfolded on his knees and his appearance quite respectable. He raised one eyebrow as if to say 'hello' and then returned to his newspaper. His sang-froid amazed her, but she knew she had to match it. She had to try and forget that only a few hours ago he had been lying naked in her bed, propped up on the pillows, watching appreciatively as she got dressed.

'You rang, madam?' enquired Mr Maxwell, but no answer was forthcoming, for Mrs Lennox's attention was engaged elsewhere and it was clear that they would have to stand and wait by the door until she was ready.

'It's just a charity dance, Mrs Lennox,' a young man was saying, his manner noticeably nervous. He was tall and thin to the point of gauntness, with a pale complexion that was not helped by dark hair falling across his forehead. By comparison, Sholto looked robust and handsome. 'For the orphans, you know. And I can assure you Celia will be well looked after. Mrs O'Hara will be there to make sure . . .'

'Oh, I don't know,' said Mrs Lennox. 'Celia is awfully young.'

'Nonsense!' said a bluff, commanding voice which belonged to a man who had been hidden behind a newspaper but who had laid it down to remonstrate with Mrs Lennox. Jessie guessed that this must be Sir Hector, for no one else in the room could match the formidable character which had been ascribed to him. 'Of course you may take her, Erskine,' he said with great magnanimity. 'It's about time my little Cissy went up to town and had some fun,' he added, getting up from his chair and going over to the sofa where Miss Celia (who Jessie recognized from Mr Maxwell's photograph) was sitting with another girl. 'Isn't that so, my dear?' he said, ruffling her hair as if she were a spaniel.

'Thank you, Papa,' she said. 'Oh, it will be fun, won't it, Alix?'

'Thank you, sir. I promise to take good care of her,' said Erskine. 'It's a fancy dress ball, you know. The theme is the Renaissance.'

'How charmingly artistic,' drawled Mrs Lennox, obviously piqued that Sir Hector had over-ruled her. 'Ah, Maxwell, you're here – good. And what have you for us today, MacPherson?'

Jessie stepped forward, but to her surprise Sir Hector intercepted her.

'If I may?' he said, plucking the menu from her hand.

'Of course, sir,' she said, and dropped a half curtsey as she was expected to do in the presence of her master.

'You see, young woman,' said Sir Hector, scanning the menu with considerable interest, 'I've been very impressed by the standard of your work – very impressed. For a while, I thought we'd got a Frenchman downstairs. That lamb last night – well, I haven't tasted lamb like that since I was in Paris on my wedding journey.'

'Thank you, sir,' she said. 'I am glad you are satisfied.'

'Very satisfied – delighted, indeed,' he said. 'Tell me, m'dear, did you learn from a Frenchman?'

'Yes, sir, I did.'

'Ah, it shows, it shows,' he said, and then continued expansively, as if addressing the room at large: 'My grandfather kept a French cook, you know. He was an emigré, came over in the revolution. He had been cook to the Marquis de Montalambert, until he went to the guillotine. Ah, well, Montalambert's loss was the Quarro's gain! But I'm sure he wasn't as pretty as young MacPherson here. You'll have to keep Jock and the grooms out of the kitchen, Maxwell, or we shall be losing the best cook we've had in years!' And he laughed heartily at his own joke, glancing around him as if he expected everyone else to join in. Jessie for her part scarcely knew what to do and stared pointedly at the floor. A furious storm of conflicting emotions was brewing up inside her. She felt both elated and humiliated, both angry and triumphant! To be exhibited like an object by this odious old man, and to hear herself declared a prey for stable hands and gardeners, when her lover was sitting there right in front of them, a perfect gentleman. It was galling. But her pride was awakened as well, for she knew the master liked her work, that he was greedy to know what he would be fed that night and she could not deny the satisfaction that brought.

She wished that Sholto would look up from his newspaper and give her a reassuring smile, but she knew that was quite impossible. She also saw for the first time, with a clarity that terrified her, the ambiguity of the situation into which she had so willingly thrown herself. She was no longer simply Jessie MacPherson the servant, but she was not one of them; she would never be permitted to sit with them in that drawing room. She had entered a twilight world where she was neither one thing nor the other, and she began to understand that her situation would never again return to simplicity.

'A garden party,' said Mr Maxwell, as they went down the back stairs together. 'Well, that's a fine thing. It's been a long time since we've had one of those.' His enthusiasm was childlike, but Jessie could only think of the work.

'A hundred is a lot of people to cater for,' she said.

'Aye, but you've the master's confidence in you to help you along,' he said. 'He's a grand gentleman, don't you think?'

'He was very kind.'

'That's breeding for you,' said Mr Maxwell. 'Ah, it's good to see him so pleased. He hasn't been so cheerful for a long time. I think it's due to young Mr Erskine.'

'Why, are they good friends?'

'No, no, it's not that. No, he's pleased because Mr Erskine has taken such a fancy to Miss Celia. There'll be a wedding here before the year's out, if things carry on like this . . .'

'Is he a catch then?'

'Oh, yes, very much so. No title, but a good family and

very wealthy,' said Mr Maxwell, with particular emphasis on the last phrase.

'Oh, I see,' said Jessie.

'Yes, he'll do very well for Miss Celia,' continued Mr Maxwell. 'He's been properly brought up, not like some I could mention.' She thought for a moment he was alluding to Mrs Lennox, for whom he had little respect, but he went on: 'You saw that gentleman with the beard in there – well, I say gentleman, but if you ask me, that Mr Hamilton's no more a gentleman than I am.'

Just about concealing her astonishment at this little tirade, she said, 'Oh, is he not?'

'No, lass, that man is a trouble maker. I knew it the moment he walked through the door. Not the sort of person who should be under this roof at all. Aye, it's a good thing he's going today, if you ask me.' And he walked away in the direction of the wine cellar.

She stood in the passageway, unable to believe what she had just heard. Leaving . . . he can't be . . . he wouldn't, not without telling me . . . But he had said nothing to her, not the slightest word. She had somehow imagined his stay to be indefinite and that he would be coming to her room every night and capturing her again with his passion. Perhaps he forgot to tell me, she told herself, as in a rising tide of panic she walked back to the kitchen. But that seemed too unlikely and she began to be convinced that he had meant not to tell her, that she was to be abandoned, just like a common whore who had provided a diversion for him in a dull country house.

Oh God, please don't let that be true! Don't let it be so! How can it be, he was so, so convincing . . .

She stood at the kitchen doorway, feeling all the sweetness evaporate and bitterness flood over her. She wanted to cry, to shout, to let out, in some form, the inexpressible anger and turmoil that was inside her. She had been a fool and she had been used! She had seen all the warning signs but ignored them. She had believed this to be different – and yet it was just like every other story of girls getting mixed up with gentlemen. She had thought herself above such snares, and here she was trapped and helpless. He was going away and had not breathed a word of it to her. The bastard!

She wished suddenly that she had the courage to rush upstairs to that drawing room. She wanted to snatch the newspaper from him and hit him about the head with it – no, better, use her hand; it would hurt him more – for he deserved all the pain, all the rage she could unleash on him. The bastard!

But then she would certainly lose her place and any chance of a reference. It would be even more stupid than giving in to him, and she was disgusted enough already with her own foolishness. She looked across the empty kitchen, which was plunged in gloom. Above her, rain hammered on the roof like an insistent refrain of mockery.

'Well, damn you!' she exclaimed, going to the kitchen table where a bowl of minced veal for a galantine was waiting to be pounded. It was generally a job for a scullery maid, but Jessie could not be bothered with etiquette. She only wanted distraction, and tipped the meat into the pounder. With considerable force she brought the pestle down and began to pound the meat vigorously, gaining a certain grim satisfaction from it.

'Someone's in a temper,' said a voice across the kitchen. She let go of the pestle and turned to see Sholto, leaning on the kitchen door post. He was wearing his hat and coat.

'Are you bloody surprised!' she exclaimed. 'Why the hell didn't you tell me you were going? Did you think I wouldn't notice?'

'What do you think I am doing here?' he said, coming over to her. 'Oh, there's no need to be angry, my sweet. I didn't want to tell you this morning – I couldn't bear to. I didn't want to upset you, to upset myself, because I don't want to go, I really don't want to go . . .' His words were sweet and quiet and he stood close to her, his hand resting lightly on her arm. She felt herself reduced to a pulp by his words, she could not resist their sincerity.

'You are impossible . . .' she managed to say, for he had begun to kiss her neck, with such tenderness that it made her throw back her head, desperate for more. He could catch her with the slightest touch, the least word, for she was utterly in his power and always would be.

'But I love you,' he whispered between kisses. 'Don't be angry with me, please. I can't bear the thought of that.'

'You love me?' It was the first time he had said that.

'Yes, of course. You have transfixed me, Jessie. I can't get you out of my mind, not for anything. That's why I couldn't bear to tell you I had to go, because it hurts me. God, it hurts me!' And he pulled her into his arms and clung to her with desperate strength. 'I shall think of you every minute of the day.'

'When will I see you again?' she said breathlessly. 'When?'

'I'll be back as soon as I can. If they don't invite me, I'll stay in the village. No, no, don't cry . . . it's not like you to cry.'

But the tears had come quite involuntarily and she found herself burying her face in the rough tweed of his jacket to hide them.

'I'll write to you – you'll let me write to you?' she said.

'I'll treasure every line,' he said, digging in his pocket and giving her his handkerchief. 'Dry your eyes now, love. Crying doesn't suit you.'

'No, I guess not,' she said, managing a smile. She wiped her face and handed him the handkerchief.

'Keep it,' he said. 'A souvenir d'amour.'

'That sounds too romantic for a handkerchief,' she said. 'Where do I write?'

'Here's my card,' he said. 'Now, one last kiss and then I have to go . . .'

And he pressed his lips to hers.

When he released her, she did not watch him go. She could not bear to. The sound of his steps, echoing into the distance, was enough. She stood and twisted the handkerchief in her fingers. Only when she had heard the door close did she notice that in one corner he had knotted a little gold ring, set with a small pearl.

He must have guessed I would cry, she thought, and

pressed the handkerchief to her face, trying to catch from it
the last remaining warmth of his body.

8

'Come on – are you ready yet? We shall be late,' Ralph was
saying outside, banging on her door.

'Oh, isn't he impatient!' giggled Celia, who was still at the
dressing table.

'Go away, Ralph,' said Alix. 'We shall be ready when we
are ready.'

'It's a quarter past, you know,' he said.

'Yes, yes – now go and wait downstairs. We'll be down
soon.'

They heard him go downstairs and then they both
laughed.

'Poor Ralph!' said Alix. 'Anyone would think it was his
first dance – not ours! I suppose it must be because of all
this Renaissance nonsense. He's always been silly about
those sort of things. It must be a dream for him to make us
dress up all à la Botticelli. I still think it's daft, though!' she
added, taking off her dressing gown and pulling over her
head the vast white nightgown which was to form the base
of her costume. 'You really shouldn't have encouraged him
so, Cis.'

'But it *is* a good idea,' said Celia, pinning a final elaborate
braid in place.

'I still feel an idiot,' said Alix, flapping the tent-like folds
of the nightgown. Celia, having studied a few engravings,
had gone to the draper's in Peebles and bought the two
enormous nightgowns with their overlong sleeves. She had
then persuaded the sewing maid who came up to the Quarro
once a week to mend the linen, to run up tunics cut from old
curtains which had been retrieved from the attic. Finally,
she had made Alix sit down and help embroider them – a
disastrous move, in fact, and she had been swiftly delegated

to sewing on ribbons and braid. They had only just finished the costumes in time and had not yet dared show them to a soul, because they were somewhat outlandish.

'Right then,' said Celia, 'will you do me up?'

Her enthusiasm for Ralph's wild schemes had surprised Alix. Celia and Ralph had almost formed a sort of conspiracy about it and had insisted she go along with it, when she could think of nothing more absurd than being so serious about fancy dress! But she had submitted and wondered if Celia felt any of the attraction to Ralph that he so obviously felt for her. For he scarcely attempted to conceal his devotion, and was never far from her, like a faithful dog. Celia did not seem annoyed by it, not in the way Alix felt she might have been annoyed if she had sworn blindly that she was in love with someone else! Perhaps Celia did not know her own mind on the subject – and that made Alix uneasy, for she imagined that one should be clearer on such an important matter.

Celia had put on her tunic now, which was cream damask, embroidered with large green swirls of chain stitch and trimmed with gold braid. Alix helped her do up the sleeves, which she had contrived, by use of tapes, to look slashed, so full puffs of the nightgown sleeves were pulled out in a fashion which was surprisingly effective.

'There,' said Celia, tying up her girdle. 'What do you think of that? The image of Sandro's Pallas, don't you think?'

'Is that who you are supposed to be?' said Alix, noting that Celia had picked up Ralph's annoying habit of calling Botticelli 'Sandro', as if they were acquainted with the man, rather than the paintings.

Celia tilted her head to one side and assumed a sweet, vacuous expression.

'Oh, won't he love that!' she said, laughing.

'I expect so,' said Alix. 'He likes most things you do.'

'You think so?' she said with sudden earnest interest. 'Really?'

'More than likes, I should say,' said Alix, aware that she was betraying Ralph's confidence, but wondering if it was not best to let Celia know that his feelings were not to be trifled with. For Celia had suddenly struck Alix as dangerous as she stood before the mirror, aware of her own devastating beauty and the exciting power it gave her over men.

'Do you like him then?' Alix pressed. 'I mean, in the way you like Hamish?'

'I love Hamish,' said Celia thoughtfully as she gathered up her green velvet cloak. 'But I do like Ralph, in a funny way, which is more than plain liking. Do you think that's wicked?'

'No, no,' said Alix hurriedly. She did not wish to appear critical. 'It's just, well, Ralph feels things so deeply . . .'

'Yes,' said Celia, 'I'd noticed that. It's part of what is so nice about him. It's almost irresistible, that sensitivity. It's so unusual in a man!' And she shrugged her shoulders as if to imply she did not know the answer to this problem.

'You might have to give one up, you know,' said Alix, lifting up from the bed her own heavy tunic of printed velvet. 'I mean, you should really, to be honest.'

'Why can't one be in love with two people at the same time?' asked Celia, a trifle defensively. 'It must happen all the time – and if I choose, well, I shall only hurt the other. Why shouldn't both of them be happy? If they both want me, let them both have me!'

'But you can't live your life like that!' exclaimed Alix. 'It's so deceitful.'

'I'm sure men do it all the time,' said Celia tartly. 'Now are you putting that on or not?' she added. 'Or are you going to lecture me instead?'

'I didn't mean to lecture,' said Alix. 'I was just wondering, that's all.' She was shocked by Celia's easy solution to her dilemma. It was too simplistic to be safe.

'Don't worry, Alix,' said Celia, with supreme confidence, arranging the folds of her tunic. 'I know what I'm doing.'

I hope so . . . thought Alix as they went downstairs.

Ralph was waiting for them on the drawing-room landing. He jumped to his feet at the sight of them as they processed downstairs at a stately pace, for their skirts were deliberately long to give the effect of the sculptural drapery in the paintings. (How they were to dance in them, Alix could not not begin to imagine!) He looked striking in a dark crimson doublet, trimmed with black velvet. He wore soft red leather boots with spurs and a large golden sword was hanging from his belt. Alix had feared he might look ridiculous, as so many men did in fancy dress, but he was very convincing. His face, she realized for the first time, was not the least bit modern and it was as if his ordinary clothes hid the primitive cragginess of his features. As he stood and stared at Celia, his face wore a look that she could not read, like those strange faces in the crowds of the paintings he so admired and she so little understood. In a moment however it passed, and she saw the face of a man quite lost in a woman's beauty. She had thought of warning him, but saw that it would be quite useless. He stepped forward and took both of Celia's hands, and, with a lack of inhibition which she knew to be quite unlike him, kissed them fervently. As he did this, Alix saw their mother come out of the drawing room, a vague, troubled expression on her face, as if she too sensed the danger Ralph was in.

'My goodness!' exclaimed Celia, laughing. 'How gallant!'

Her words seemed to embarrass him and he dropped her hands at once.

'Here,' he said, 'I have something for you both,' and he indicated two striped florist's boxes which were lying on the table. 'Yours first, Alix.'

She opened it slowly, for there was clear disapproval in their mother's eyes. It was soon obvious why, because the box did not contain the modest corsage which she would have deemed appropriate for the occasion but two extraordinary wreaths of flowers: daisies, lilies, roses and sprigs of bay.

'Two?' asked Alix, puzzled.

'But of course,' said Celia, who was looking over her shoulder. 'Flora! Oh, how clever you are, Ralph – how absolutely perfect! Come on, Alix, do put them on. One round your neck and the other for your hair.'

As Celia garlanded her, Alix had the strange sensation

that she had become a heathen idol rather than a human being. The flowers round her neck were heavy and their scent overwhelming. She wondered if she could bear to wear them all night and was suddenly intensely angry with Ralph's romantic follies. To give her flowers was only an excuse to make it decent for him to do the same for Celia. She had no doubt about that, because she knew she looked nothing like the Botticelli except for her fair hair! No, it was Celia who was the Botticelli, and how well she knew it, throwing back her head to show off those waves of dark hair, while Ralph took from her box two more crowns, not of flowers this time, but of long-leafed, dark green, glossy myrtle. She bent her head to let him put them on her, in an elegant, submissive gesture which Alix realized would be impossible for most men to resist. It was as if she had been put on the earth simply to please men, an idea Alix found abhorrent, because there was in it a sort of slavery, not just for the admirer, but the admired herself.

'Now you will be good,' said her mother, as they were about to leave. Ostensibly, the remark was directed at Alix, but she knew that evening her own conduct would be the last thing her mother would be worrying about.

It was the last dance before supper – not a sedate waltz but a wild bout of reeling into which everyone had thrown themselves with gusto, as if to build up a really good appetite for the food. Ralph had Celia as his partner in the set, and watched with intense, half drunken pleasure as she stood in the centre of the ring, dancing with each man in turn. She no longer looked like Pallas, for her face was flushed, her crown awry, and no one in the elegant, languid world of Botticelli had ever danced with the vigorous passion that she displayed. No, she was more potent and dangerous than a painted beauty as she lifted her skirts to jump all the higher, flashing her legs before them all as if she cared not a whit what the world thought. And when it came to his turn to hold her again, he felt the fiery heat of her hands and saw her dazzling smile, heard her shout with a wild uninhibited voice as they spun round in the centre of the ring, hands crossed, as if into a vortex, while the others about them clapped in time to the music. Ralph felt that not a woman in the room could match her in that moment, and that all the men must envy him for having as his partner that most dazzling creature!

The music grew faster and faster, the dancing less and less disciplined. People slipped and shrieked on the well waxed floor, but Celia and Ralph were sure-footed, weaving round the ring until they met again for a brief clasp of the arm, when suddenly and miraculously the music stopped: miraculously, it seemed, to Ralph, to be caught there together – it was like an omen from the gods. Such omens could not be dismissed lightly, and he, exhilarated, could not resist her a moment longer and bent forward and kissed her, placing his hands on either side of her glowing cheeks and tilting her face to meet his lips.

She did not resist. Not in the least did she resist! Ralph, incredulous at this success, would have thrown his arms about her, but someone shouted out 'Woah!' and, startled, he released her.

'I think people are staring,' she said, not critically but as a bald statement of fact.

'Let them,' he said. 'They're only jealous.'

She smiled and said, 'Shall we go and eat then? I'm so hungry!'

She took his arm and they followed the crowds down the stairs to the supper room. They were jostled somewhat and Ralph, confident now, put a protective, steering arm about her shoulders – and still she did not resist. Rather she pressed up to him, taking the shelter he offered. Suddenly it was the most normal thing in the world to have her so close beside him. He did not feel worried because he might lose control, because control had vanished long ago. He had crossed the threshold of restraint with that kiss. He was not an invader but a welcome conqueror, of that he was sure now. She was giving herself to him, just as he had hoped she might on that frustrating day on Quarro Hill.

It was an agony to leave her while he fought his way to the buffet table, but she wanted food and so he was bound to fetch some. He piled a plate with enough to feed a farm hand, tucked a bottle of hock under his arm and returned to her.

'There are no seats,' she said. 'Let's go upstairs, shall we?'

The stairs were now full of magis and madonnas forming a very earthly conversazione, with plates on their knees and wine glasses in their hands. Ralph spotted Alix in a corner, squashed between two young men. They were all laughing and eating strawberries. My God, what would Mother say? he asked himself in mock-alarm, pleased that Alix, who had been dubious about the occasion, was enjoying herself. But she can't be as happy as me . . . no one could be that happy.

Celia was dashing up the stairs into the darkness at the top of the old house. Ralph felt his excitement double as he followed with eager steps. She wants to be alone with me. Alone . . .

'What are you looking for?' he asked. They were on a dusty landing.

'A way on to the roof,' she said, pushing open doors at random. 'It's almost a full moon tonight. I want to see it – I want to eat in the moonlight.'

'What about this one? 'he said, opening a door. 'How's that?'

It was an old lumber room, flooded with moonlight.

'How clever you are!' she exclaimed, rushing to the window and pushing up the sash. 'There she is.'

'Is it a she?' said Ralph, coming to the window and looking out.

'Oh yes – well, I always think so.'

'You little pagan,' he said, putting down the food on a rickety table. 'Goodness, it's hot in here . . . do you mind if I take my jacket off?' The room was very close, despite the fresh draught of air from the window, and Ralph found suddenly that the weight and warmth of his velvet doublet were unbearable.

'Of course not,' said Celia, who seemed determined to be quite at home and was pulling an old day bed from one wall so it faced the window. 'Now we can sit down,' she said, kicking off her shoes with a swift, delicate action and, settling herself on one end of the day bed, stretched out her legs along it. Ralph unbuckled his sword and unloosened the ties at the front of the doublet.

'That's better,' he said, as he struggled out of it. 'That was like a strait jacket.'

'You looked very handsome though,' she said, regarding him. 'Come and sit down then. You must be tired. All that dancing.'

'It was a pleasure,' he said. 'Especially with you.'

'Yes, it was fun, wasn't it?' she said, reaching out and taking the plate of food. 'What have we here?' she said peering at the contents.

'You'll have to taste it and see,' he said. 'A surprise.'

'You've probably got everything I hate,' she said. 'Things in aspic . . . ugh!'

'I don't think I got any of that,' he said, perching on the end of the day bed, wishing she would move her legs. But then a better idea occurred to him and he moved up, simply lifting her legs so that they rested across his thighs. She smiled her assent and waved a fork, upon which was dangling a large piece of roast beef, under his nose.

'Do you want some?'

'I'd rather kiss you again,' he said, emboldened.

'You're very sure of yourself tonight. I thought you were supposed to be shy.'

'Well, I'm not tonight,' he said, and took a swig from the bottle of hock. 'I wonder why . . .'

'You should eat something,' said Celia, her mouth half full. 'Then that stuff won't go to your head.'

'I could get drunk on moonshine tonight. In fact, I probably am.'

'That's the moon for you. I could quite easily worship things like that, you know. Much easier to believe in, don't you think? Not like stuffy old God, who never shows himself.'

'So you don't believe in him?'

'No, I don't think so. Do you?'

He shook his head.

'I'm afraid I don't believe in anything much.'

'I bet you do,' she said, taking the wine from him. 'I think you believe in life, and love, and beauty, and all that sort of thing. Am I right?'

'Perhaps. But I don't think it is so simple. Life is not just a question of pleasure . . .'

'I wish it could be. Why do we have to be so complicated about things? Why don't we just do as we wish and be happy?'

'I'm not sure that would always make one happy.'

'That's because no one ever tries. They're all too stuffy about things . . .'

'Just like the stuffy old man up there?'

'It's all his fault, if you ask me,' she said decidedly and took a deep draught of the wine. 'Oh,' she shivered. 'That's sharp!'

'Don't you like it?'

'I don't know,' she said, and drank again. 'Perhaps it will grow on me.'

'Perhaps . . .' he said, as she took yet another gulp. 'You'd better leave some for me, you know.'

'Why should I?' she said, playfully. 'You're drunk already.'

'But I'm more used to it than you,' he said, attempting to snatch the bottle back from her. But she stretched the hand she was holding out of reach and he was forced to lean across her to retrieve it. In that moment, as his body pressed against hers, the wine was forgotten. She had been giggling, and then, when he looked into her eyes, she became still and serious. He heard her put the bottle down.

'Do you want to kiss me?' she murmured.

He did not bother to answer but put his arms round her and pulled her towards him. She yielded instantly, melting against him. She grasped at his neck and shoulders with feverish fingers, and returned his kisses fiercely with a desire which seemed to match his own.

'Do you want me?' she asked breathlessly. 'Do you?'

'Of course, of course – I love you, Celia . . . I love you . . .' he said, kissing her bare shoulders which rose out of the disordered folds of her broad, ruffled collar. She grabbed one of his hands and pushed it up under her full skirts. As he fumbled to loosen her clothing and touched the soft private skin of her thighs, she shook with desire, her head lolling back on the arm rest, her lips parted. Incredulous that she was permitting him to do it, he pushed back her skirts to reveal the dark triangle of hair at the top of her legs. She bent them up, now quite abandoned to the pursuit of her own private pleasure.

'Take me then . . . for God's sake,' she said in a hoarse whisper.

It did not take him long to comply with her demand. She groaned with deep pleasure as he entered her, and the sound seemed to echo through every fibre of his being. He could not have guessed at such ecstasy and yet here, on a shabby sofa in a forgotten lumber room, she was fulfilling the nightly fantasy which had been haunting him for weeks. He had always hoped that such a woman might exist, but had never believed it could be true. And yet here was Celia, gasping at his every touch, desperate to be loved most passionately by him.

She urged him to be faster and stronger, and before long her passion reached its climax. His own climax followed a moment later, triggered by the sight of hers. They lay together in silence, exhausted and astonished by the power of their own bodies. Downstairs, he suddenly noticed, the music had resumed.

'They'll be wondering where we are,' she said.

Reluctantly he crawled off her.

'I don't want to go down again. I don't want normality,' he said, drying himself with his handkerchief. He wanted to sleep and wake to find her lying in his arms, in some great white comfortable bed. But she had got to her feet and was shaking out her skirts almost as if nothing had happened. She put her shoes back on and adjusted a garter which had gone awry.

'Listen,' she said. 'They must be dancing again – shall we go down and dance?'

'How can you think of dancing, my sweet?' he said,

reaching out and taking her hand. But to his surprise she pulled her hand free. 'Celia?'

'Oh, I could dance for hours,' she said, going to the window. 'For hours and hours . . .' And she stared out at the moon, as she had been doing earlier. Ralph looked up at her and felt as if the last ten minutes had not happened but had been some freak imagining by his disordered brain. For she was suddenly alien to him as she had been that day on the hill, entirely absorbed in her study of the moon, as if nothing of the least significance had happened. It was extraordinary to see her, so calm and quiet by that window. She did not look in the least like the girl who had behaved so recklessly only a few minutes previously.

'What are you thinking?' asked Ralph.

'Nothing,' she said, in a voice which was almost cold.

'Are you angry with me?' he asked, worried by her dispassionate manner. 'Have I done something I should not?'

'No, of course not,' she said sharply. 'Whatever made you think that?'

'It's just that you seemed a little distant just now . . .'

'Oh, did I?' she said. 'I was only thinking.'

'I thought you were thinking of nothing,' he said.

'I hope you don't think that I must tell you everything now!' she said.

'But Celia,' he said, getting up and going to her, 'surely you understand, things are different now.'

'Why should they be?' she said.

'Because . . . because . . . oh, isn't it obvious why?' said Ralph, astonished at her strangeness. 'We can't be just friends now – it's gone beyond that. I love you, Celia, and I want to marry you.'

'Oh,' she said, as if surprised. 'You do, do you?'

'Of course I do,' he said, taking her hands. 'I love you and I want you with me always.'

She looked at him very earnestly for a moment, and then looked away.

'Can I think about it?' she said quietly.

'Of course,' he said, trying to sound as serenely reasonable as he could and disguise the keen sense of disappointment which had flooded over him when she had not at once said yes.

'I'm going down to dance now,' she said, after a pause. 'Are you coming too?'

'In a minute,' he said. 'It will look better if we go down separately.'

She smiled, and pecked him on the cheek with flinty lips – a kiss very different from those passionate ones she had given earlier. When she had gone, Ralph felt a curious sense of relief, for she had so confused him that he needed a few minutes to sort out exactly what was going on. But the more he thought, the more it defied any explanation. She had given herself to him and then rejected him in the space of half an hour. It was as if they were playing some game where he was blindfolded and in complete ignorance of the rules, while she was mistress of all its complexity.

But at least she did not say no, he consoled himself, at least she must consider me now . . . especially now that she's let me seduce her. Or had he? Had he really seduced an innocent or was she, in truth, a woman even more unconventional than he had imagined?

9

'Mr James wants another kipper,' said Mr Maxwell coming into the kitchen, 'and Miss Celia's rung for her breakfast tray. Is it ready?'

'It's on the table there,' said Jessie. 'Effie, will you go and get another kipper from the store.' She wondered how she would bear to cook it. The smell of smoked fish, usually appetizing, had become utterly nauseating to her. The very remembrance of it made her reel and she grabbed at a chair back to steady herself, as her stomach jumped up into her throat. Christ – she thought, this isn't just a bad stomach. This is something worse, much worse.

All about her work in the kitchen went on as normal. Mr Maxwell was distributing the mail amongst the breakfast trays, while Annie carried a can of steaming water into the scullery to start the washing up. Effie seared the kipper on the hot plate to remove the skin, adding the scent of burnt fish to that of singed toast. They were all carrying on quite as normal, unaware that Jessie, standing by the range, supposedly watching that a pan of milk did not boil over, was not watching it at all but was beginning to realize that she had committed the ultimate imbecility – that she had fallen pregnant.

The milk foamed up and over the sides of the pan with spectacular turmoil, cascading on to the freshly leaded range, undoing all Annie's hard work.

'Hey, look out there!' exclaimed Effie, grabbing the pan. 'Are you still asleep?'

'I don't know . . .' said Jessie, staring blankly at the pan, and then felt again that revolting gripe inside her, this time assailing her with such force that she had no option but to clap her hand over her mouth and dash out of the kitchen and into the privy which lay in the yard beyond.

She had expected to vomit but could only retch, because she had nothing to vomit up. She had taken only a little black tea and some dry toast for breakfast. She knelt on the brick floor, grasping the rim of the lavatory bowl, her head bent over it, determined to rasp out whatever impurities she could. But it brought no relief, and she sank back on to her heels, hugging her sides to bring some sort of comfort, and stared up at the cracked ceiling of the privy, wishing she might let out some animal scream of rage and despair. But although she felt the tears starting in her eyes, she would not give in to them, no matter how much she wanted to. She would not give in to this thing, she would not let herself drown in a sea of remorse because that was how they would want her to feel. She remembered a girl from Dysart, a few years older than herself, who had come back in disgrace, having fallen pregnant while in service in Glasgow. Diseased dogs were treated better than that poor creature had been by her neighbours and Jessie had watched them squash every last drop of pride from her with their sharp comments and wicked gossip. Then she had said, 'Never, never, will I let that happen to me!' But now she had a sudden, horrible vision of herself staggering along the market gate at Dysart, swollen with the child, the object of everybody's censure. I won't go back there, she told herself resolutely. But where will I go? What will I do?

She got slowly to her feet, and pulled the lavatory chain. She tried to think clearly. Above all, it was important to be practical and sensible about this thing. Being hysterical would not solve anything. I'll have to go and tell him, she decided. He's not going to like it, but I'll have to tell him. After all, it's as much his fault as mine, though I'll have all the trouble of it. Meanwhile, I shall carry on here as if nothing was amiss. I don't want them all to think that I'm a fool . . . even if I am.

She went back into the yard and washed her hands under the standpipe in the corner, splashing a little cold water on her face to remove any traces of tears. She looked up and saw Effie staring out of the open scullery window, dish mop in hand.

'Are you all right?' she asked.

'Of course,' she said. 'Just something I ate. Must be the hot weather – you have to be careful when it's like this.'

Effie, unsuspecting, returned to her washing up. Jessie took a couple of deep breaths of air and returned to the kitchen. It would be unbearably hot, but somehow she must bear it. And tomorrow, she told herself, I will go to Edinburgh and see him, and sort this thing out.

'Another letter?' said Alix, coming into Celia's bedroom. 'I never realized Ralph was such a prolific correspondent.'

Celia, propped up on mounds of white pillows, her hair falling about her shoulders, looked a picture of girlish innocence. She had only just woken up, and seemed delicately indifferent to the breakfast tray that the maid had brought in, and to that fat envelope, addressed in a familiar hand, which was leaning against the tea cup.

'Aren't you going to read it?' asked Alix.

97

'Later,' said Celia, stretching and yawning. 'You're up early.'

'No,' said Alix, perching on the end of the bed. 'You've slept late.'

'I suppose I have,' said her friend, quite unconcernedly.

'Did you see him last night?'

'Mmm, I did,' she said, with an air of pleasant recollection. 'We went for a bathe.' And she reached out and took the breakfast tray from the side table. 'Goodness, I'm hungry.'

'You're always hungry, Cissy.'

'Yes, I know. It must be all that fresh air.'

Alix took up the envelope and looked at it, while Celia spread a roll with apricot jam.

'He has nice handwriting, don't you think?' she said. 'What does he write, though?'

'You can open it if you like,' said Celia, her mouth full. 'The usual romantic stuff, but I must say he does do it rather well.'

'I don't think I should. He'd be very angry if he knew.'

'He doesn't need to know, does he?' said Celia. 'Go on, open it – you can read it to me.'

'You do take these seriously, don't you?'

'Of course I do. They're lovely letters. You should see.' It was impossible to tell whether she was being artless or heartless.

'Are you sure I should open this?'

'Of course, Alix. I have no secrets from you. Open it now.'

It felt awful to open that letter, as if she was betraying Ralph in the worst possible way. She knew his reticence was not lightly conquered, and this lengthy letter, for there were three dense pages of it in her hand, would have been written with drops of his soul for ink. She glanced at the first page, which began 'My dearest girl . . .', and then put it aside, unable to bring herself to read any more.

'I can't,' she said. 'I simply can't.'

'Coward,' said Celia, taking up the letter and scanning it rapidly. But as she read, she began to look disconcerted and

Alix began to feel very glad she had resisted the temptation to read on.

'Oh how impossible! How impossible they all are!' exclaimed Celia with sudden annoyance, throwing the letter down with an angry gesture. She sank back on to the pillows and stared at the bed canopy above her. 'What am I to do?' she said after a pause. 'What on earth am I to do?'

'I thought you knew what you were doing,' said Alix. 'That's what you said at the ball.'

'That was different. It was simpler then, much simpler.'

'I did warn you that you might have to choose . . .' Alix said quietly.

'Oh, don't moralize,' said Celia sharply. 'It may seem simple to you, but you don't know how I feel. You don't have the least idea of what it feels like to be in love.'

'No, perhaps not,' said Alix. 'But I think I know what's right – it isn't right to keep two men on a string like this!'

'But I love them, Alix, don't you understand that? I'm mad about them both. Yes, mad, quite mad, for how else would I find myself in this ridiculous situation? He wants to marry me, you know, and I don't know whether I want to or not.'

'Who? Which one?' said Alix, exasperated.

'Ralph, of course.'

'Of course,' she said flatly. Things had gone very much further than she had thought. She had thought Ralph was only infatuated but not in love enough to want to marry. 'How can you love both of them, Celia?' she said. 'How can you possibly. Surely the whole thing about being in love with someone is that you can only love that person.'

'That's just in novels,' said Celia. 'Life seems to be a great deal more complicated, doesn't it?'

'Only because you've made it so.'

'Do you think I did it deliberately? Do you really think I would do this deliberately?'

'I don't know, but you have done it, and you've got to sort it out or you will all get hurt,' said Alix firmly.

'But I can't choose,' said Celia, with angry desperation. 'I can't! I need them both. It's like asking me to choose between the moon and the sun. I can't do without either. I need them both, I love them both, and I'd give my whole soul to either if I could.'

'But you can't, can you? You have to choose, Celia, you have to.'

'What, and split myself in two? I'd rather die first. I need them both, don't you understand?'

'I understand quite well,' said Alix coldly. 'You're a greedy little bitch who can't bear the thought of being unselfish, no matter how it might hurt other people. I'm warning you, if you hurt Ralph, you'll have me to answer to. I won't have you messing him around, just because you can't make up your silly mind!'

Alix had intended to shock and she saw her friend blench at her words.

'I know,' said Celia, quietly and with some contrition. 'But I still don't know what to do.'

'Choose,' said Alix, getting up. 'That's what you must do. For the sake of everybody.'

Jessie stood in the dusty darkness of the close and waited for someone to answer the door. She felt not a little afraid and wondered if she should not have written first. But letters were easy to ignore, and she feared he might ignore her unless she confronted him with the truth. Men had a habit of running away from such responsibilities, and although in her heart she did not wish to believe that Sholto Hamilton could be one of those sort of men, she had to prepare herself for the fact he might be. And she needed to speak about it. The silence of her secret was becoming unbearable. To be able to confess it would have to help in some way, and, although she knew she was perhaps grasping at a slender straw, there was in her some vague hope that he would know what to do, that he would solve everything in that marvellous, mercurial way of his.

She had expected he might live in a more respectable-looking tenement, but she had found herself climbing high up a gloomy common stair with peeling paint and a vile, stuffy smell. But his door, with its engraved brass plate, was reassuring enough to look at while she waited that little eternity for someone to answer.

At last someone did. It was not Sholto but a fair-haired young man in shirt sleeves, with a cigarette in one hand and a faintly supercilious manner.

'Is Mr Hamilton at home?' she asked.

'Sholto,' the young man called out, turning back into the hall. 'There's some woman here for you!'

'Typical!' shouted someone else within and there was a gale of laughter. There was obviously quite a crowd in there.

An inner door, which had been slightly ajar, was pulled wide open, letting through a brilliant shaft of light which for a moment obscured the fact that Sholto was standing there. He did not see her at first, but when he did perceive who it was, she saw the pleasure on his face at the sight of her, and felt such relief that she hardly knew what to say.

But, as usual, he had no trouble finding the words.

'Why, my darling!' he said, rushing forward and pulling her into his arms. 'What a wonderful thing! What brings you here?'

'We've got to talk,' she managed to say, overwhelmed by the sudden comfort of being so close to him. 'We're in a mess . . .'

'A mess, my sweet?' he said, not sounding too concerned.

'Something serious . . . can we go somewhere, please?' she whispered, for they were still in that little hallway and she was very keenly aware that the young man was staring at them.

He took her down the hallway into a room which might have been described as a kitchen, but which was so squalid that Jessie would not have recognized it as such. There was a table piled with dirty plates and pots, there were newspapers and books on most of the chairs, and in the scullery which opened off the room was a large block of ice in the sink which smelt very obviously of fish.

'This is disgusting,' she found herself saying. 'You don't really live like this!'

'My daily woman has come down with something,' he

said. 'And we've been having a bit of a party.'

'I can see that,' she said, observing the empty bottles which had been haphazardly pushed into an empty wine crate. Then the smell of fish assailed her and she discovered once again that the term 'morning sickness' was a distinct misnomer. 'I'm sorry I can't stay in here,' she said, making for the door. 'That smell . . .'

'Shall we go out?'

'I think we'd better.' But they did not get much further for Jessie found she was suddenly gasping for breath, her head swimming, her legs collapsing under her, as she fell to the floor in a heavy faint.

She came round to find herself lying in an unmade bed, half clothed. The air was warm and still, the light golden, speckled through lace curtains. At the end of the bed Sholto was sitting, a glass in his hand.

'I'm pregnant, Sholto,' she said. The calm quiet of the room made it easy to say. She wondered what he would reply, but instead he got up and went to the window, standing with his back to her so that she could not read his expression.

'Did you hear me, Sholto?' she said. 'I'm pregnant.'

'I wondered if that wasn't the case,' he said quietly.

'Well, it does happen when folk . . . you know. I suppose we should have known better. But what's the point of regretting it now?'

'None,' he said, turning back to her. '"Sweet fruit o' monie a merry dint", eh?'

'But what are we going to do?' she said, struggling up from the bed. 'What are we going to do?'

He seemed to think for a moment and then his face broke into a broad smile.

'We'll get married,' he said. 'I should think that will solve everything.'

This she had hardly expected. She had thought he might try and keep her as a mistress but not offer marriage. That seemed almost ridiculous, and she found herself laughing.

'Don't laugh,' he said, 'I'm serious.'

'Is that what you say to your other wives?' she said, and that made him laugh and kiss her.

'Oh, Jessie – I'd be a fool not to marry you. I need a housekeeper, you can see that, and I can't think of a better bed fellow.'

'But are you sure?' she said. 'I mean, I'm not what your family will want for you.'

'Oh, don't you worry about my family, Jessie,' he said. 'They aren't worth listening to. No, the more I think of this, it will be a damn' good thing. If I'm the father of a boy, I don't want him coming into the world "asklent", as dear Rabbie would put it.'

'I can't believe you're saying this,' she said, leaning back in the bed again.

'Do you always think the worst of people, Jessie?' he asked, sitting down next to her and putting his arm around her shoulders. 'You have to learn to trust me, eh? I'll look after you, I promise. I'll be the husband you always dreamt of.'

'I never thought I would marry,' she said.

'That would have been a dreadful waste,' he said, putting his hand on her stomach. 'So that's our child in there, is it? Our son, eh?'

'You can't say that for sure.'

'I've got a feeling about it – just like I had that feeling about you. There's a judge in there, Jessie, or a prime minister at least.'

'Now you are being daft!' she said. 'I'm just a servant girl . . .'

'No, you are engaged to an advocate, Jessie, and you mustn't belittle yourself any more. I forbid it. A woman takes her social status from her husband. With your wits, you'll fool them all.'

Just like Mrs Lennox, she found herself reflecting. I hope I won't go like her – I'm determined I shan't!

10

'Well, this is a fine time to give notice, I must say,' said Mrs Lennox. 'I hope you don't expect a reference.'

'I don't need a reference,' Jessie cut in. 'I'm not looking for another place – I'm getting married.'

It was very pleasant not to have to beg for a reference, to be able simply to say 'I am leaving in a week's time' and not have to care what Mrs Lennox thought. There was an added pleasure, albeit a little malicious but irresistible all the same, in springing the news on her on the morning of the garden party! But Jessie had decided that Mrs Lennox deserved it, for in the week preceding the party she had been thoroughly ill-tempered and autocratic, finding fault with everyone and everything and constantly changing her mind over the arrangements. If Jessie had not had to give notice, she would seriously have considered quitting, for to work under the yoke of such maddening behaviour was insupportable. Telling her on the morning of the party that she wished to leave was justifiable and made a very pretty revenge.

Mrs Lennox had summoned her upstairs to her room that morning, and received her lying in bed like some eighteenth-century grandee. Presumably she was resting in order to prepare herself for the rigours of the afternoon ahead. Alice, the poor, quiet creature who had the misfortune to be her maid, was padding about the room, putting things in order as if she were attending a deathbed. It was as quiet as a sick room in there, but it did not take Mrs Lennox long to disturb the peace and break into her characteristic, hectoring whine which had become far too familiar of late.

'I want the complete menu,' she had begun and Jessie had had to list it all, although they had been through it several times before. Mrs Lennox was unable to accept that the situation was under control. She clearly imagined that servants, if left to their own devices for a moment, would forget some crucial item or unleash some chaotic train of events. She had it fixed in her ignorant mind that: 'Servants could simply not be trusted!' It was by far the most objectionable thing about the woman: her utter inability to recognize that those who worked for her had any skills worthy of note, let along worthy of praise. Despite the fact that she had no idea how to starch and goffer iron the elaborate frills on her nightgown or how to make the simplest sauce, she behaved as if she were quite the mistress of all these skills and that she had a perfect right to pronounce how things should be done. At first her attitude had both angered and amused Jessie, but now she found it vaguely alarming, for she could guess that at its root lay a well of insecurity, an insecurity which she, soon to be an advocate's wife, could appreciate.

She must live in fear of being thought not to be a lady – that's what makes her so high-handed. It must be difficult for her, thought Jessie, sympathetic in spite of herself. It must be difficult keeping up the act – and she's got no bairns to make them proud of her. For she knew now how important that was to such a family. Sholto had given her a hint of it, for he had become immensely proud of the fact she was expecting, that there would be another Hamilton, and that the dynasty would flourish. If Sholto, who was only a minister's son, could feel like that, what would a baronet's son feel? And Jessie felt a profound sense of pity for her mistress, for she had something Mrs Lennox had not, and probably longed for: a child, growing quietly inside her.

She might have had the luck to marry into all this, thought Jessie, but I wouldn't change Sholto and this child for anything, even if we do have to struggle. For it was clear that they would. Marrying Sholto was not marrying into leisured ease, for he was still young and was certainly not earning enough money to marry a girl of his own class, although he seemed to expect that was how they must live, as if Jessie was coming from some modestly comfortable home. He had taken the lease on a large flat in Marchmont, with two bedrooms, a drawing room, a dining room, a kitchen, and most luxurious of all, a bathroom with a window! She had tentatively suggested that she would be quite happy in something half the size, but he would have none of it, as if it was impossible for him to imagine himself, as a married man, living in any less comfortable surroundings. She had a suspicion then that she would have to practise economy, if they were to meet that formidable monthly rent.

It took Jessie some time to convince Mrs Lennox that all was in hand downstairs; that the joints and raised pies were already in place under muslin shrouds in a firmly shuttered dining room; that the ice chest was obscenely filled with ices; that in the still room were legions of fancy cakes and tartlets, and that in the kitchen Effie and Annie were busy carving roses from radishes and carrots or threading attelêtes with diamonds of aspic, peeled crayfish and quartered mushrooms: in short to convince her that the least paper frill had not been forgotten.

'What about the band?' she said, determined to find fault with something.

'There's bread and cheese, pickles and plum cake for them in the servants' hall, madam, and Mr Maxwell has brought up two casks of small beer from the brew house.'

'That should be more than adequate – I don't wish them to be tempted into over-indulgence. Now, MacPherson, you understand that I require you and the head kitchen maid to be in the dining room from three o'clock? I want you to make sure that the girl is very neat and tidy and that her hands are clean.'

'No one has dirty hands in my kitchen,' said Jessie, needled by this imputation. In a few minutes, she promised herself, I shall tell her I am going . . . and noticed that her remark had made Mrs Lennox pucker her lips in annoyance. But surprisingly she did not comment, and for a few minutes they had continued to discuss various things connected with the party. Then, when she looked about to dismiss Jessie, for Alice was coming in with a copper of steaming water, Jessie decided she must give her momentous news.

'You're getting married?' said the mistress. 'This is very sudden. Have you been engaged for long?'

Jessie had been prepared for such a question.

'Oh, yes, madam, for three years. We've been waiting until he got a steading before we could marry.'

'A farmer's wife – well, that will be different for you, a fine thing for you. You are a fortunate girl.'

How dare she call me a girl! thought Jessie. Why, there's no more than a couple of years between us! But she managed to say, in a tone of suitable humility, 'Thank you very much, madam,' which seemed to satisfy Mrs Lennox. Jessie was astonished by her own capacity for self-abnegation. It is probably impossible to argue with her – nothing will change her, but I wish I could give the jumped-up minx a piece of my mind just once, to show her that I know what she is!

Alice was hovering at the bedside with a pile of towels and a plate of cucumber slices. Mrs Lennox was presumably about to undergo some elaborate beauty treatment and as she did not wish to appear ridiculous in front of her cook, hastily dismissed her. Jessie found herself outside the bedroom door, vaguely cross with herself for not having had a proper run-in with the woman.

Before she went back to the kitchen, she went into the dining room, just to check that everything was indeed as perfectly under control as she had assured Mrs Lennox. It was – and she felt not a little proud, for the effect was magnificent, even though not all the food had been brought up yet. The table had been opened to its full length and covered with a great white linen damask cloth which had been starched until it was as stiff as pasteboard. On the skirt of the cloth, long swags of greenery and knots of lemon coloured ribbons had been fixed, and the same pretty garlands had been suspended between the three épergnes, heavy with scented fruit, which were spaced along the table. The largest of these, at the very centre, resembled, as it sailed above the fleet of ashets, the flagship of a great navy. She went to the sideboard and lifted a cloth, revealing a regiment of silver cutlery, which glittered with such freshness, even in that half light, that it looked as if it had all just been taken out, for the first time, from the tissue paper wrapping of a wedding present.

I don't suppose we'll ever give such a fine junket as this! thought Jessie, looking about her with some satisfaction. Not unless Sholto becomes a judge . . . But the thought of that was too wild a fantasy to contemplate further. There were enough astonishing changes in her life for her mind to deal with already.

'Hats!' exclaimed Alix, as she stood in front of the dressing mirror, wrestling to fix at a satisfactory angle the elaborate confection, the triumph of some milliner's art, which their mother had sent down from Edinburgh. 'I think it is ridiculous – utterly ridiculous. How on earth is one expected to do anything in this?'

'I thought you would be pleased that Mother has decided to let you go into long skirts,' said Ralph, who was watching this performance from an armchair in the corner. 'You did nag her about it.'

'But I wanted to choose!' she said. 'And I wouldn't have chosen this or this awful dress. I feel like a rhododendron bush!'

Although she might not have been pleased at her graduation into adult clothes, Ralph was certain she would make quite an impression in them. He had never really looked at Alix objectively until the night of the Studio Ball, when she had surprised him with a certain statuesque beauty. And now, exquisitely dressed in another, very different fashion, her handsome looks impressed him once more. He cared little for the style of the day, which seemed to distort women's bodies, but Alix, in embroidered muslin the colour of an unripe peach, made a pleasant picture. The detested hat, which was indeed ridiculous in size, being over a foot in diameter, was wreathed in silky orchids and foamed with tulle, and made, despite itself, a very charming addition.

'There . . .' she said, in the voice of one who has just swatted an irritating insect, 'I think that will do.' And she leant out to grab a hat pin. 'And if it falls off,' she continued, through gritted teeth as she drove in the pin with such force that Ralph feared for her skull, 'I simply shan't care!'

'You look magnificent,' he said, getting up and standing behind her in order to put his arms about her waist.

'I'm glad you think so,' she said, still regarding herself in the glass as if she were not the least convinced.

'Is there something wrong, Alix?' he asked, releasing her, for it seemed to him that her mood was not entirely connected to her awkward clothes. He had noticed when he arrived the previous evening that she appeared to be vaguely troubled.

'No,' she said, rather too quickly for comfort. 'Why? Should there be?'

'Well, if there is, don't be afraid to tell me, eh? That's what brothers are for, you know.'

'That's very sweet of you, Ralph,' she said. 'But there's nothing wrong, honestly there isn't. I can't imagine why you think there is.'

'You looked worried just then, that's all,'

'Just about keeping my hat straight,' she said very brightly, 'and managing this silly train! Come on, hadn't we better get downstairs?'

'Where's Celia?' he said.

'Oh!' she said, as if exasperated by his remark. 'There's no point waiting for her – she always takes hours to dress.'

'There's plenty of time. It's only a quarter to three,' he said, sitting down on the window seat. 'Why don't you go and see how she's getting on?' he added, indicating the little door which he knew led to Celia's room. That had been one of the reasons he had come upstairs to see Alix, in the vague hope that Celia would run in and he would have the chance of seeing her in relative privacy, for it was privacy that seemed to elude them now. Although last night she had behaved adorably, with a shy, tender friendliness, like the

109

most innocent girl, they had not contrived to be alone for more than a moment. A moment was not long enough even to begin to tell her what he felt or to begin to press on her those thousand kisses which he longed to give. But he shouldered his disappointment with good grace, encouraged by her manner and by Sir Hector's hearty welcome. Perhaps she had hinted at his proposal – his letters could not have gone unnoticed. He had a strong impression from Sir Hector that his suit was unlikely to meet with any objection from that quarter; indeed, that the old man was offering Celia to him, whether he wanted her or not.

'Well, I am going down,' said Alix, taking up her parasol, 'and you had better come too. If you wait for Celia here, you will probably wait for ever. For all I know, she's downstairs already.' She put out her hand to him. 'Come on, Ralph. What would Mother say if she knew you were skulking around in women's bedrooms?'

'You're a wretch, Alix, you know that?'

'Yes, a perfect wretch,' she said, 'in a ridiculous hat!'

Celia was not downstairs – at least he could not see her, and tried earnestly to suppress a suspicion that she might be hiding from him. For even when he felt most confident about her, there was always a nagging fear of failure, which, like the various irritations that from time to time afflicted his body, he never completely succeeded in ignoring. That afternoon, he was stern with himself. Don't be a fool, Ralph. You've come this far – it must happen now – you must succeed – you will get her. She will say yes this very afternoon! Fortified by this reassurance, he went into the dining room to find fortification of another, more liquid variety.

As the party had only just begun, the dining room resembled the buffet of a great station at the beginning of the day, before any passengers have arrived to disturb the display or the composure of those in attendance. A number of maids were standing at their posts waiting to begin serving, one of whom he recognized as the cook whom Sholto claimed to have seduced. She was certainly a very handsome woman, with dark, well-curled hair, the beauty

110

of which the uniform cap and streamers enhanced rather than concealed. He noticed also, rather in the way that one might appreciate a statue, for she was standing very still and quiet in a plain black dress which draped her figure almost classically, that she had very fine white hands that were neatly clasped together and gave the impression both of strength and elegance. Her face was set in the supposedly unseeing mask of a well-trained servant, but he sensed she observed him as much as he observed her. It rather unnerved him, for he felt she looked at the very core of him, which was of course impossible, but Ralph had an impression of the inviolable strangeness of women, as if they were privy to some supernatural skill and could, at times, see into the very heart of a man's soul, and yet retain an opaque layer about themselves, through which no man could ever perceive more than a glimmer of the secret, feminine essence within.

As the butler offered him a glass of claret cup, he dismissed this idiotic train of thought. It is only my self-love that wishes she were looking at me, he decided, as he walked out on to the terrace. She is probably thinking of Sholto. Poor girl – I hope she isn't too unhappy when she discovers what he is like with women . . .

Presumably, by some quirk of heavenly justice because the Lennoxes had been so audacious as to decide to have a garden party, the hot weather which had dogged and delighted them for the last month or so looked as though it had reached the point of burning itself out. If the Lennoxes had hoped for the brilliant sunshine and still air of recent days they were unfortunate, for the sky was hazy and a muggy wind disturbed the air. Ralph settled himself in a basket chair. There was no point attempting to circulate as there was hardly a soul with whom to talk. This was a relief for had not Celia been there, he would have trawled up any excuse to avoid such a function as Mrs Lennox's garden party.

There's going to be a storm, he thought, staring up into the sky, and shivered in anticipation. He had a passion for thunderstorms because of the spectacular light and noise they produced and that senseless release of pure energy which drove against all the rational systems of the world beneath. He had hated it when as a boy his father had carefully explained to him the physical laws behind the storms, and had in his heart steadfastly clung to the childish belief that such things could not and should not be explained, because to explain was to destroy their elemental power.

He leant back in the creaking wicker chair and shut his eyes, enjoying the taste of the claret cup, feeling that slight suggestion of alcohol relax his whole body. He would have slept easily then, had it not been that somewhere in the distance a wind band began to play, not exquisitely by any means, but not as badly as he might have expected. With his eyes still closed, he focused his hearing on the music, which although in a major key, had that melancholy timbre peculiar to wind ensembles, as if beneath their external show of jolly tunes and pleasant harmony lay some quiet and private tragedy. He would have continued to muse on this as the strains of 'The Lincolnshire Poacher' drifted over him, had not a pair of gloved hands suddenly clapped themselves over his eyes.

'Well, well, thou art a lazy beggar and no mistake, Ralph Erskine,' said his assailant, in an assumed, gruff voice. But he was not deceived for a moment, for every fibre in his body knew it was her without having to see her. When the sight is blocked, the other senses are keener and he knew her smell at once. He remembered it from when he had held her in his arms. It was a mixture of rose water and something more earthy but no less sweet for that, because it was entirely her own, the very scent of her passionate spirit.

'Celia,' he said, smiling broadly, and stretched his hands into the darkness, hoping he might draw her down into a kiss. But she eluded him, although her hands still covered his eyes.

'No, lad, no,' she continued in the same manner as before. 'I'm no your Miss Celia, I'm her maid, and she's sent me down to tell ye she'll no be coming to the party.'

'Then tell her,' said Ralph, amused by her silly deception

which was worthy of the most inept amateur company, 'that I shall be up to join her, and that I shall carry on where we left off . . .'

The hands flew away and the pretence dropped.

'Shush!' she said frantically. 'What if people hear?'

'I don't care,' he said, catching her hand and pulling her towards him. 'What does it matter anyway, since we are going to be married?'

'We are, are we?' she said, with mock defiance which did not disturb him in the least. For the instant he had guessed it was her, he had been launched into a state of complete self-confidence. Her impulsive little trick seemed to him nothing less than a show of exuberant regard for him. He was at once convinced that she loved him, exactly as he loved her.

'Yes, we are getting married,' he said, pulling her down into his lap. She shrieked but did not resist. 'I have decided. You've had long enough to make up your mind so I have decided to make it up for you. You are going to say yes, do you understand?' And he shook her, pretending to be stern and angry with her.

'Yes, yes!' she laughed, protesting and struggling in his arms. 'Yes, Anything, Ralph, but stop – you are making me feel sick!'

'Never let it be said that you agreed under duress,' he said, putting his hand under her chin and kissing her. 'Will you marry me, Celia?'

'Yes,' she said. 'Haven't I just said so?'

She slipped her arm comfortably about his shoulders, as if she had done it a thousand times before, and pressed her cheek against his. And Ralph clung to her, like a man in a shipwreck clings to a floating bark, because at last he knew for sure and he had not been disappointed.

'Well then,' he said, after a pause in which the full, sweet realization of the moment had flooded over him, 'I suppose I had better go and have a word with your father . . .'

At about half-past four it began to rain, and the house was suddenly inundated with people who looked surprised, if

113

not slightly outraged, that the weather should be so discourteous as to spoil their pleasure. Jessie, although hard at work dispensing tea and cakes (for the rain had sharpened everyone's appetite), could see, by taking the occasional glance out of the window, that the rain was descending with all the force one expects of spring and autumnal rain, but not of summer showers. In the greying distance, she could see figures, who had been making an elegant, slow-paced promenade along the full length of the great canal, breaking into an undignified trot, which was all their fancy clothes permitted in the way of speed. When these bedraggled revellers reached the house, all dignity washed away, a different atmosphere came over the party. Previously it had been stately and somewhat dreary, but the storm, which soon appeared to be freakishly wild, loosened everyone's tongues and relaxed their manners. Soon the place was ringing with laughter and noise. The drink flowed freely: the claret was no longer drowned in the cup but taken straight to warm the bones of delicate ladies, while the gentlemen sent for drams.

A spirit of jolly fortitude in the face of adversity possessed them all. Jessie watched with amusement as that fine assembly lost all their polished manners and began in a bluff way to enjoy themselves! She even observed that Miss Elizabeth Lennox, usually so pale and shy, who had taken a particularly bad soaking, was downing drams, protesting that they were 'purely medicinal', while her cheeks glowed with roses and her eyes sparkled as if she were a girl again.

Ralph had not intended to get drunk, but it seemed his future father-in-law expected him to prove his worth by matching him glass for glass. Since he had broached the subject with Sir Hector, who had responded like a man who has just been acquitted from some heinous crime, his glass had not been allowed to remain empty for a moment.

'Come along, my boy, drink up!' urged Sir Hector, beaming with manic delight. 'This is such splendid news that it deserves the noblest of drinks to celebrate – and

114

you'll be needing it too, I should imagine. It's damned hard work proposing!' he added, nudging Ralph with his elbow. 'The little beauties take a lot of convincing. Mind you, I always knew that my little Celia wouldn't be such a fool as to let a fine young chap like you slip through her fingers. If she had, she'd have had me to answer to!'

Ralph, overwhelmed by drink and this excessive bon-homie, found himself wishing that Celia was an orphan, bereft of relatives. But, unfortunately, relatives were something she appeared to have in profusion and he resigned himself to them all, accepting that for the glory of getting the girl, one had to tolerate, and even learn to like, her family. It was the least one could do for her, and so, like a lamb to the slaughter, he submitted to Sir Hector.

'We'll announce it today, of course,' said his host, rubbing his hands in anticipation. 'I suppose you will be wanting to get married as soon as possible?'

'Well, yes, if you don't mind, sir . . .'

'Mind, Erskine? Why should I mind? If it's her age you're concerned about then don't bother, my boy. I think it's better for a girl to marry young – and seventeen is not so young by the standards of this family. My great-grandmother, Euphemia Fordyce – the daughter of Fordyce of Fordyce, you know? – well, she married my great-grandfather, the first Sir Hector, when she was just fifteen. And she had nothing but sons . . .'

Ralph, in all his wild fantasies about Celia, had not considered the matter of children in the least and felt a sense of shock to be confronted with a man who considered marriage in severely dynastic terms. He's probably a frustrated grandfather, thought Ralph, a suspicion which was confirmed by Sir Hector's next remark.

'We'll see if you two can't put young James to shame before next year is out, won't we? Ha! You never know, she might give you twins, being a twin herself. They say it works with people as it does with cattle, you know.'

Ralph had hardly expected such bluntness, but he was fast realizing that the mere word 'marriage' acted as a sort of magic password to make topics that were unacceptable in normal conversation, strangely permissible. Marriage licensed the highest intimacy between a man and a woman; indeed, marriage glorified it, and he remembered a line from Beaumarchais which seemed to express this paradox so elegantly: 'Grâce à la douce cérémonie, ce qu'on vous défendait hier, on vous prescrira demain!'

They had come into the large entrance hall now, where a fire had been lit and a crowd had formed around a still smoking fireplace. There was also a crowd round the piano, because one of the guests, a young man whom Ralph did not know, was thumping out the tune of a vulgar and raucous modern song. Amongst the singers was Celia, who was leaning over the young man's shoulder to read the words. It pained Ralph to see her hand resting on his shoulder, ostensibly to steady herself, and he told himself firmly that he must trust her. After all, I should loathe it if she was not spontaneous like that. It would not be Celia at all. I would not love her if she were prim and modest.

This little declaration of faith was rewarded, for when the song had finished, she glanced up at him. When she saw he was with her father, her face broke into a radiant and reassuring smile. A moment later, she had come over to them, a frank, excited, questioning expression on her face, as if to ask: 'Well, what does he say?' Ralph would have answered but Sir Hector stepped in between them, taking both her hands, and with a gesture which seemed to Ralph to date at least from the Middle Ages in its measured courtliness, placed them in Ralph's. This act, so flamboyant, attracted the notice of everyone, and Ralph watched Celia blush and felt his own cheeks redden as the company fixed interested eyes upon them. The meaning of the action was so transparent that Ralph thought no announcement would be needed and that the women were already turning over in their minds what they would wear to the wedding. But Sir Hector was not the man to let the opportunity to make a speech pass:

'My lords, ladies and gentlemen . . .'

It struck Jessie that the master was a man very fond of the

116

sound of his own voice. She was glad to be in the dining room and therefore not quite able to hear what he was saying at such length, for she had a suspicion it was probably far worse than the driest sermon. When he finished, there was some muted applause and a sudden rush of people into the dining room, all of them in need of refreshment to counteract the sobering tedium of their host's speech.

'What was that all about?' she murmured to Maxwell. 'I couldn't hear.'

'Well, that's a shame,' he said, 'for it was a fine speech. He really knows how to speak does the master. He was announcing Miss Celia's engagement to Mr Erskine – so it looks like you'll be cooking that wedding breakfast after all.'

'I don't think so,' said Jessie, feeling that this precedent was enough for her to make her own small announcement. 'I'm leaving next week – to get married myself.'

'Is that so?' said Mr Maxwell, a little amazed but not out of his depth. 'Well, I suppose a pretty lass like you would have plenty of fellows dangling after her.'

'Just one, Mr Maxwell.'

'Well, he's a lucky chap,' he said. 'We'll all miss you, Jessie. You've brought a bit of life to us all.' And before she could thank him for this tribute, he was summoned away by Sir Hector who was calling for champagne for the toasts.

At the other end of the room the young couple were being kissed and congratulated as if this were the wedding already and not the engagement. Mr Erskine, whom Jessie remembered as being pale, now looked flushed, as if feverish, and there was about the line of his shoulders something which suggested exhaustion. But his smile was set in a broad, entirely contented grin, giving him the appearance of an athlete who has just triumphed in some strenuous race. Celia, on the other hand, was perfectly animated, running from person to person, laughing, talking constantly; in fact, she was overflowing with life, like a roman candle in a firework display, throwing sparks of energy about her, regardless of where they fell and whom they touched.

117

'Well,' she heard one lady say to another, in a dry, disapproving voice, 'I'm sure he'll have a busy time keeping a girl like that in line.'

'She may calm down,' said her companion. 'A lot of girls do, when they marry. And, besides, what will it matter to him if she behaves extravagantly? It will take more than a few dressmaker's bills to make a hole in that young man's fortune.'

They moved away out of earshot, leaving Jessie wondering. She knew now that Ralph Erskine was a friend of Sholto's and thought it likely that their respective marriages would make them less intimate. For would Celia Lennox want her husband to be friends with a man who had been so déclassé as to marry the cook from her old home? It was most unlikely, and Jessie found herself wondering if she were not dragging Sholto down in some respect. Probably the noble, proper thing to have done was to have refused him and to have taken the burden on herself alone. But she wanted her child to be born respectable so that bastardy would not taint it for the rest of its life. And more than that, she wanted Sholto. She knew now she could not endure life without him, and that to be his wife, and the mother of his child, was the one thing she desired above all others. That feeling, so powerful within her, must justify any social unorthodoxy, she reasoned.

At about six o'clock most of the guests had gone away and the servants were finally dismissed from their posts. Feeling exhausted suddenly, she made her way to the servants' hall with the others, to eat the cold high tea which had been laid there hours before.

'Eat up, everyone,' said Mr Maxwell. 'Get your strength up. There's still the clearing up to be done.'

Jessie leant back in the chair and stared into her tea cup, thankful that, as the cook, she would be excused that part of the work at least. She would not have to stir for a while. The family wanted a light, hot dinner at eight-thirty, and she knew plenty of elegant little dishes which took only moments to prepare.

11

Night came on, and Celia, like someone caught in an ancient enchantment, stood at the window as the landscape shrouded itself in velvet black, and felt herself become that other Celia, who was not the Celia of the day but a nameless, silent-footed creature, who stalked through the forest in search of her strange lover. She had no control over this transformation now; it had simply become necessary for her, as it is necessary for the moon to rise and the sun to set. To have gone without seeing him, without being held in his arms, without indulging in that fierce passion which spontaneously kindled between them, would have been impossible. Every assignation they made, like a dose of opium to an addict, only made the thought, let alone the act, of ending the affair unimaginable.

Well practised now, she slipped through the glass door on to the terrace. If she had opened it a fraction further, it would have screeched upon its hinges. She pulled her dark cape around her, blotting out the whiteness of her dress, and vanished into the dark shelter of the hedge which surrounded the parterre.

The grass was still very wet from the storm and her feet and ankles were soon soaked. She did not care. Like a plant with dry roots, thirsty for water to renew life, she felt the cold caress of that wet undergrowth. It awakened her senses, those senses which were dull and confused by day but which, at night, vibrated at the slightest breaking twig, at the smallest drop of water, at the faintest scent of wild garlic. I am alive . . . alive again, her heart sang, for her mind had no distinct thoughts as she ran into the woods, her face up-turned to accept the brush of the wind.

Of Ralph she did not think; she would not, could not indeed, because he was to her now only a vague memory, a pleasant faded scent which had no strength to compete against the fresh and compelling sensations which assailed her with such rough intensity that there was almost pain in it. She felt the moment stab her with such violence that the past had no meaning, for she was now in the thick of the woods and could see in the distance the glow of a storm lantern through the entrance to the old bothy. And in that light, so pure and yellow that it cast a veil of gold, she saw him sitting on the ground, his knees tucked under his chin, watching her approach, his posture and gaze as still and as inscrutable as an oriental idol.

She paused for a moment in the doorway before going in, feeling that mixture of fear and joy which seemed to attend her whenever she saw him. It was as if he was not human but something else stranger and more powerful, like the incarnation of an age-old spirit which inhabited those woods, indeed all woods, and showed itself from time to time in mortal form. If now he called himself Hamish, and wore the rough, unkempt clothes of a working man, and spoke the broadest Scots, Celia felt that there was more to him than that; that his power over her was supernatural. Perhaps he was Pan himself – a young, beardless, blond-haired Pan, but with all the passion and experience of love and lust of that ancient goat god. The thought of it made her shiver and she lingered still on the threshold, anxious to be near him but suddenly afraid. To sleep with a man was one thing, but a god? What could be the consequences of that? For in that instant she truly believed that he was not mortal. It seemed as if a thousand strange notes which had echoed separately over the years were now playing together; feelings which had been inexplicable were now explained and vindicated. She had always hoped and desired that she might comprehend that spirit of nature which had so often moved her, stirred her sometimes to tears by its intensity, and here, she was convinced, it sat before her, incarnated in that handsome body, exerting such a power over her that she knew she could never escape.

He stretched out his hands to her with a gesture that commanded rather than implored. She went to him and sank to her knees, so that their eyes were level. He put his arms about her and held her very tightly, pressing her against his body. He said nothing but she knew what his gesture meant: You are mine, you will be mine, always . . . and for herself she wanted nothing else but that embrace. Gladly would she have lost herself in it, drowning herself in the strong, earth-like smell of his body, languishing under his touch, but something kept her back. A claw in her mind caught up her daytime consciousness, and she was unable to forget that only an hour or two ago she had been fast in the arms of another man who had been kissing and holding her with equal fervour, a man who that very afternoon she had agreed to marry. Now in Hamish's arms, this action of hers seemed incomprehensible, and although she tried to put it out of her mind, like a nightmare the memory of it persisted vividly. How could she have done it? How could she betray him for a mere mortal? Suddenly she felt such guilt, such disgust at her own ingratitude, that she broke away from him, convinced she must not deceive him any more. Into her mind sprang terrible stories of what befell those foolish enough to attempt to hoodwink the gods. No, she had to be straight with him, but the fear of his anger tied her tongue.

'Celia lass, what is it with you tonight? You're as stiff as a corpse in my arms. What's amiss?'

His words were soft-spoken, as caressing as his fingers, and she wanted to blurt out: 'Oh, forgive me, forgive me – I've done a dreadful thing.' But she could not – not yet at least. So she hung her head, not wanting to look at him again, feeling unbearably ashamed of herself.

'What is this?' he asked, when she again rejected his embrace.

'Oh, nothing!' she said, as brightly as she was able. 'I just feel restless tonight – why don't we go for a walk?'

'Och, no, I'm too damn' tired to walk,' he said. 'Some of us have to work, you ken,' he added with a grin. 'Come on, lass, come and sit beside me. I can't bear to see you flitting about like this.' For she had been walking idly about the bothy in a vain attempt to elude his grasp. He pulled her down beside him, rather roughly. In a moment he had straddled her and had pinioned her arms with his hands. The action was playful enough but his strength, which had previously impressed her, now frightened her and she was torn between honesty and deceit – to see him angry would be unbearable. Surely it would be better to say nothing, she reasoned, and smiled up at him and let him kiss her.

But she knew, as she felt him release her arms, that he was not deceived. He read her like a book, he knew her secret trouble, for he asked again, this time in a voice which seemed to her to be horribly accusatory: 'What is it, lass?'

He looked down at her with eyes which burnt into her soul. She opened her mouth to speak but her throat was dry and her tongue seemed frozen to her palate.

'You look as though there's something you want to say to me,' he went on, and Celia felt convinced that he already knew her wickedness but that he wanted her to confess it. 'Is that it?'

She nodded, slowly.

'You're no in trouble, are you?' he asked. 'I mean, there's not a bairn coming, is there?'

'Oh, no!' she exclaimed, relieved that he was not perhaps as omniscient as she had feared.

'Thank God for that!' he said, sinking back on his heels. 'Christ knows what we would have done. What is it then, Cissy, what's making you so cold and frightened?' And tenderly he reached out and caressed her cheek. 'Oh, you are an unco' bonny quean, Cissy. I wish I could have you for my ain . . .'

'I am yours,' she said. ''Til I die, I swear it.' And she caught his hand and kissed it fervently. 'I don't care about anything else, what anyone thinks, anything. I care about you, and only you!'

'Hey, hey!' he laughed at her protestations. 'Do you think I don't believe you? I know you're not the sort that plays with a fellow's heart. I only have to look at you to know that.'

You know, thought Celia as he spoke. You know, don't you?

'I know you wouldn't do anything as cheap,' he went on cheerfully. 'Christ, I must be the luckiest man on earth to have a girl that'll be true, come what may . . .'

His sincere and touching faith in her was more disturbing than anything he had yet said, and yet it compelled her to be honest. If she were not she might lose him, and seated there so close to him, she realized that was what she feared the most.

'You asked me what was wrong,' she began, after a little silence in which she mustered the courage to speak frankly. 'Well, I think I should tell you, if that is how you feel about things. I think I should tell you that someone asked me to marry him today.'

'Well, what's wrong about that, Celia love?' he said. 'You're a bonny creature and I'm sure you've turned down a dozen offers in your time . . .'

'No, Hamish, the point is . . . the point is this . . .' It was so hard to speak, and when she finally did, the words came out desperately quickly, perhaps in a vain hope he might not hear them. 'I said yes.'

'You what?'

'I said yes,' she said again. 'That's what I've been trying to tell you – oh, Hamish, I'm sorry, so dreadfully sorry. I don't know how it happened – he was so persistent.'

'You don't know how it happened?' he repeated, his voice very cold and astonished. 'What do you damn' well mean by that?'

'I mean I had no choice, really I didn't. My father wants the match very badly. You see he's very wealthy . . .'

She would have gone on, but suddenly he dealt her a stinging, heavy blow across the face which made her cry out with pain and surprise.

'That's the least you deserve, you two-faced, lying whore!' he exclaimed, his voice dry with anger. 'Christ! I couldn't believe that anyone could be so damned . . .' But words failed him, as he stared at her with those terrible eyes of his, full of wrath.

123

'But I don't love him, not in the least.' she blurted out, tears in her eyes. 'I love you, I told you. I love you, Hamish!'

'Shut up!' he said and hit her again, with more force, so that she fell backwards on to the floor. He got up as if to go, but she struggled up on to her knees, grabbing his legs to prevent him.

'No, no!' she begged. 'Please, let me make you understand, let me explain. I couldn't do otherwise. You can't know how difficult it is for me. I do love you so, Hamish, you're the only thing in the world for me.'

'I wonder why you bothered coming down here tonight.'

'Because I love you – I can't live without you, believe me!'

'How the hell do you expect me to believe anything you say?' he hissed.

'Because I've told you the truth. Isn't that something? I had to confess because I felt so bad. So please forgive me, Hamish, please. I know I don't deserve to be forgiven but . . .'

'No!' he cut in. 'You bloody well don't! And if you think that just because you've told the truth now that I'm going to trust you again, then you can think again, lassie, you can think again!' And with a powerful kick, he disengaged himself from her grasp and made for the door.

'No, no, Hamish!' she cried out. 'Don't leave me, don't go. I love you – I can't live without you – I can't . . .'

'Well, you'll have to damn' well try,' he said, turning and looking at her malevolently. 'Won't you?'

Then, in an instant, he was gone, vanishing into the darkness as if he had been only a phantom conjured up by the shadows. But that was not how Celia felt his going. She felt that in leaving he had torn out her heart and left her body bleeding, pained, and without enough true life to struggle on. Truly, the revenge of the gods was terrible.

12

Ralph woke about five o'clock that morning, and finding himself unable to sink back into sleep, got up and decided he would walk up Quarro Hill before breakfast. He thought of waking Celia and making her come with him but then considered it would be better to let her sleep. The party and the excitement had exhausted her. Last night she had apologized profusely for yawning and had struggled vainly to stay awake. Although he wanted her by his side all day and night, he felt in too good a humour to be anything but magnanimous. Therefore he had insisted she go to bed. This little show of firmness of his and her sweet and docile compliance had amused those around them. It was as if they were actors in a new play which had only just opened and of which everyone anticipated a long run. That first night of their engagement was the first night of a play called *Marriage*, with Ralph playing for the first time the husband and Celia the wife. So, when he had said: 'Won't you turn in now, my sweet? You look quite exhausted', he sensed his drawing-room audience nodding with approval, as if to say he was shaping up well for that demanding role.

He dressed in that grey but promising light of morning, glancing out of the window at the silvery-green, dew-soaked lawns with anticipation. Seeing, as he finished dressing, that sizeable patches of blue now streaked the sky, he thought suddenly of bathing, grabbed the bath towel from its rail and hung it round his neck. Celia had showed him an inviting bathing pool in the forest on one of their walks and he only hoped he could find it again. The thought of plunging into its icy depths, albeit faintly masochistic, was an exhilarating one. For that morning, he felt, deserved such a baptismal act. Was it not the beginning of the end of his solitary life? In a matter of months he would be married and then would have no reason to spring out of bed. Rather he would want to stay there, cradling in his arms that adorable creature who had, by some miracle, agreed to marry him! So that morning he would taste the pleasures of independent young manhood, conscious that their day was passing and that new responsibilities and pleasures would soon be his.

As he walked down through the gardens his mind raced through the possibilities for the future. If they married in September, which was about the longest he reckoned he could bear to wait, they could be in Florence for the autumn – and it would have to be Florence, for he so much wanted to see her there. If only we could spend the whole winter there . . . But it was most unlikely that his father would let him go. There was the Musselburgh Coach and Motor Works to worry about after all. Well, damn that, he thought, I don't suppose six months will make the slightest difference to that torpid establishment, but I'll have the devil's own job persuading Father of that . . . But I will try! he decided, remembering how successful his bout of self-confident assertiveness had been with Celia. Six months alone with her in Italy was the nearest thing to Paradise he could imagine. We'll take a floor of a palazzo – one of those extraordinary old places with red damask hangings and collapsing gilt furniture . . . He could see her in such a room, shining amongst shabby Florentine grandeur as she shone amongst the faded treasures of the Quarro, for she seemed to him like some fabulous incandescent lamp who not only brought light to all she looked on but was the very spirit of life itself. He felt well. So well, that he could scarcely believe it.

It's as if she has cured me! he thought, as he reached the bathing pond.

It was as idyllic as he remembered, set in a glade that was bright with the early sun. The water, fed by a burn, sparkled enticingly and he began to undress, regardless of the slightly sharp breeze which lingered about him. He felt strong and hardy in a way that he had scarcely ever felt in his life, and although, as he waded into the water, he felt the agonizing cold of it against his bare flesh, he knew it could not really damage him, despite all the dire warnings of his mother and the doctors about such 'foolish behaviour' which still rang in his ears. He was somehow free of all that. At last – at last! he thought in triumph as he sank into the depths, enjoying the icy embrace of it as if it were a woman's.

Suddenly, I am invincible! he thought, and remembering how Achilles had missed being immortal because his mother had held him by the ankle and had not fully submerged him in the River Styx, took care to get himself thoroughly wet, ducking his head under the surface for a second or two. When he came up again, gasping for air, he laughed aloud at his own superstition. But even a sense of his own idiocy could not displace the conviction that he did feel better and stronger, as if magically renewed.

He climbed out of the pool and sat on its edge in a patch of sunshine, drying himself, feeling a delicious warmth creep over his limbs as his circulation began to work in earnest. The feeling of well-being was so intense that he felt half drunk with it. His mind could scarcely accept that the rickety structure in which it was encased was suddenly behaving like a well-oiled machine. And it's all because of her, he thought, picturing how she must look at the moment, her head on the pillow, her features still and serene in sleep, her eyes closed but her lips slightly parted, demanding with unconscious provocation a kiss . . .

Ralph, seized by desire, struggled quickly into his clothes, not half dry but uncaring of it, because he was suddenly desperate to see her. I'll go and wake her up with a kiss, he decided, a decision which he knew the Ralph of a month or two ago would have been unable to reach. But that person was dead. He had determined it should be so, and it was a bolder, more reckless man who crashed back through the undergrowth to the house where his lover lay asleep.

'Ralph?' said Alix, realizing that the noisy visitor who

roused her from sleep was not a clumsy housemaid but her brother. 'What are you doing here?'

'Shush . . .' he said, putting his finger to his lips.

Alix propped herself up on her elbows and stared at him. It was somehow very unlike Ralph to behave as if he were a character in a second-rate farce, but that was how he appeared. His clothes looked as though they had been thrown on in a hurry, as if he had been escaping from some compromising situation.

'What have you been doing?' she asked more quietly, noticing as he sat down on the bed that his hair was wet.

'I've just been for a bathe,' he said. 'And I was about to go in and see Celia but there was a maid hovering about, so I ducked in here instead. It looks slightly more respectable.'

'You're insane, Ralph,' said Alix, still thinking about the bathing. 'It must have been freezing.'

'Bracing,' he smiled.

'Well, don't tell Mother,' she warned.

'I shan't,' he said. 'Don't you worry. Besides, I have decided that all her nonsense is going to stop – I've decided that, no matter what she and all those damned doctors say, I am quite healthy. That in fact I am going to sire a dozen children and die in bed at the age of eighty!'

She felt pleased by his mood of resolution and relieved that Celia had come sufficiently to her senses to accept him. Her strong words had not been in vain, and now here was Ralph, looking so gloriously happy that she wondered when she herself would feel so transformed by love and when she might meet someone who would change her as radically as Celia appeared to have changed Ralph. That morning he seemed as bold and as vigorous as an unbroken horse.

'You'll get into trouble with Sir Hector,' she said as he went to the door which led to Celia's room, 'if he catches you in there.'

'Oh, I don't think so,' he said cheerfully. 'The man would eat out of my hand if I asked him to, he's so grateful that I want to marry Celia. From the way he goes on, one would think she was fifty and extremely plain,' he added, and opened the door. For a minute or two he said nothing but stood in the doorway, presumably looking appreciatively at Celia as she lay asleep, for Alix recognized his stance. She had seen him in that state of peculiar stillness before, when in some picture gallery he had been transfixed by the sight of a painting. And then he went in, leaving the door open behind him.

Quickly, because she did not wish to hear their conversation, Alix slipped out of bed in order to shut the door but found herself looking in at Celia's room without meaning to. For at once she could see what had kept Ralph in the doorway. The picture the room presented was exceptional.

The curtains were not properly drawn and a great, strong beam of sunlight, as brilliant as the light from a magic lantern before a slide is put before it, cut across the darkened room, illuminating the extraordinary sight at the centre: namely the bed, which was not the least bit extraordinary in reality, but which that morning, with Celia lying in it, seemed to Alix to be both sinister and compelling. Sinister, because she was lying on her back profoundly and stilly asleep . . . like a corpse! The phrase jumped into her mind from nowhere, and she shuddered at this irrational thought. But it would not go away. Like a corpse . . . a beautiful corpse, she thought, fixed in this horrid impression, observing with strange detachment her friend's pale complexion, her dark hair flowing out across the pillow, and her hands shining white against the dull red chintz of the counterpane.

She watched her brother step forward, take up one of those pretty hands and raise it towards his lips as if he were going to kiss it. But to her surprise, he suddenly let it drop and it fell with a dull, lifeless thud. And Celia did not stir, not in the slightest . . .

'My God!' Alix said involuntarily, and Ralph turned towards her with such a look of dumb confusion on his face that she found herself coming at once to his side.

'Her hand,' he said, 'it's cold, so cold . . .' And suddenly

129

he seized her shoulders in a rough movement and shook her, quite violently, for several minutes. But nothing happened. Celia did not stir, did not wake up. Instead her head flopped forward in such a fashion that the only conclusion that Alix's mind could reach was hideously proved. She's dead. Oh, my God, she's dead!

'Wake up, wake up!' said Ralph, shaking Celia again. 'For Christ's sake, wake up!'

'She won't,' said Alix. 'Can't you see, she won't? She's dead, she's dead, she must be . . .'

'No!' he cut in sharply. 'Don't be stupid, Alix. It's a faint or something.' He pulled Celia on to the edge of the bed and pushed her head between her knees. 'Get some salts!'

Alix went quickly to the dressing table, happy to obey him. Perhaps he knew better . . . perhaps. She could not see any smelling salts but a large, unstoppered bottle caught her eye. She picked it up, seeing it was empty.

'Some salts, for God's sake, Alix,' said Ralph, coming over to her. 'What's that? What are you doing?'

'Look,' said Alix, pointing to the label. 'Read that – look, it's empty.'

'Nicholson's patent sleeping draught,' he read aloud and Alix saw in his face that he had reached the same conclusion as herself. 'You don't think, do you . . .' he said, slowly.

'There was a full bottle of this stuff in the bathroom last night. I think Miss Elizabeth takes it.'

'Well, I damn well hope it's still there,' he said, making for the door. In a moment they were dashing towards the bathroom. Alix saw at once that the bottle she had seen there at about half-past eleven the previous night, was gone.

'Celia must have drunk the whole bottle,' she said.

'Why?' said Ralph, but it was obvious in an instant he wanted no answer. He turned sharply away from her as if he had been struck. She saw him cover his face with his hands, concealing features which had creased into an agonized grimace. She heard his breathing become shorter and more ill-controlled, and soon it was replaced by that dreadful, wheezing rasp which she knew too well from past experience meant the onslaught of an asthma attack.

She knew what to do, she had seen her mother do it, and now she instinctively loosened his collar and rubbed his back and chest as vigorously as she could. But although she said calming words to him and tried to guide his breathing back into some normal pattern, she felt no such calmness. She only felt the start of a deep burning pain in her stomach as the awful reality of death, of which she had been innocent before, now consumed her for the first time.

13

Accidental death . . . That was what the doctor had put on her death certificate, but Andrew Lennox could not rid himself of the conviction that there was more to it than that. But his family were being oblique about it, giving him the disagreeable impression that they were hiding a great deal from him. It was as if they had lifted up a stone for a moment, and, seeing a seething mass of insects crawl out, had dropped it again, anxious to forget what they had seen there. But, damn it, why should they keep it from him? He had a right to know, needed to know, and yet the truth was eluding him. He was given platitudes and euphemisms instead. But these could not comfort him. He felt he could not begin to be rational and resigned about her death until he had found out exactly what had gone on.

On the night before his father's telegram had come, he had dreamt about her. This in itself was not so odd – he had often dreamt about her – but that dream had been particularly strange and vivid. He had woken in the morning still thinking of it. He had been walking with her in the woods at the Quarro in this dream, but she had been a child and he grown up. They had come to a certain point and she had refused to go any further, becoming suddenly very frightened. 'Why are you frightened?' he had asked, but she would not answer him, or at least she seemed to speak, for her mouth opened, but not a sound came out, as if she were dumb. He had tried to make her come, pulling her along, but she seemed fixed to the ground like a statue . . . and he had woken up the next morning with his mind full of this dream and a deep, grinding sense of unease because of it. When he had seen the telegram a few hours later, he had known and feared, even as he opened it, that it concerned her.

Jack's people had been wonderful, of course. By some subtle means he did not understand, they had transformed themselves from genial, if somewhat distant, hosts into the most understanding and sympathetic friends, without whom he did not know how he would have got through that first harrowing day. When he had run away to hide the first onslaught of tears, which had conquered him when shock had given way to realization, Jack's mother had sought him out and put her arms about him. How she had known he needed someone, that he needed the warm comfort of an embrace and kind words which he would not have dared request, he could not say. He only had a strange sense that he was glad (if glad was a word which could be applied to these appalling circumstances) that he had first heard the news in that quiet parsonage in Derbyshire. Since he had returned to the Quarro, he had been struck by the stark contrast between his own family and Jack's. If he had suspected it before, he was now certain of it, and he felt another terrible burden of grief. For, with Celia gone from it, he realized how little the Quarro and its occupants now meant to him. When Celia had been alive, there had been meaning in the place, but now it was like an empty stage and his people appeared like the cut-out, pasteboard characters on sticks in a toy theatre. He felt like a stranger amongst them.

The funeral party was larger than Andrew considered decent, but he knew his father would have been unable to resist making a public show of it. His ridiculous pride meant her funeral had to be conducted with as much ostentation as her wedding might have been. And this should have been a wedding . . . thought Andrew, looking across the room at the young man who had been her fiancé. He had never met Erskine before and had known nothing of the engagement until he had got back. That had been an extra, shocking circumstance for him – to hear that she had been so happy and in love the day before, and then was found dead the following morning because she had accidentally taken too much sleeping draught! It appalled him, for he could not imagine Celia even contemplating taking that concoction. She had always laughed at their aunt's patent medicines and he had never known her prone to sleeplessness. Rather, he had always thought it remarkable the way she went to sleep so easily, like a cat.

If that's the truth of all this, he thought, reaching for one of the whisky decanters which had been placed along the length of the dining table, if she took her own life, then . . . then . . . But he could not think how to conclude, for a black cloud of confusion had come over him and only the fiery spirit could distract him. He sat down on one of the chairs which were ranged about the walls and stared into his glass, sniffing the whisky and trying to stifle the angry tears which he felt could not be far away. Why did you do it, you stupid, stupid girl? Why? What could have made you so unhappy to unleash all this misery on us? Why didn't you tell me what was wrong? You always did before . . .

He glanced up and saw that his father was talking to Erskine, or rather talking at the poor chap, who looked as blank and as bleak as an icy day in the depths of winter.

'You and your people will stay for dinner, won't you, Erskine?' he was saying.

'I really don't think so, Sir Hector.'

'Oh, but you must, I insist on it. It would be a great comfort to me if you did. For I should hate the connection – no, the friendship – between our families to be dissolved because of these tragic circumstances. Rather, I think we owe it to Celia to remain as intimates . . .'

Andrew leant back in his chair, sickened by what he heard. Christ! If he had another daughter to offer him now, he would. Perhaps Celia didn't want to marry that chap at all, but he forced her. I wouldn't put it past him, he thought malevolently. Then it would be all his damn' fault! He wished this were perhaps true. His father made a most convenient scape-goat, upon whom Andrew had no qualms about heaping much of his present anger and ill-feeling. After all, he had always heard it said that it had been his father's behaviour which had driven his mother to an early grave. Andrew had been five years old at the time of her death, and had enough memory of her to sense that there had been some very real injustice. He remembered her tears, and the indifference of his father to them and to her subsequent death. He knew also of the little house in Peebles which had housed a succession of expensive mistresses, and remembered the hypocritical scorn with which Sir Hector had greeted James's decision to marry Olivia. 'One doesn't marry a woman like that, James. One keeps her perhaps . . . but not marriage,' he had said.

If marrying Olivia had perhaps been a foolish thing for James to do, it had taken, Andrew had to concede, considerable courage. It had surprised him that James, who was so indolent in many respects, could be stirred by such passion, and he respected him better for it. And if Olivia was not the kindest, nor the cleverest, nor the richest woman in the world, she surely did not deserve the treatment that his father had given her. She deserved courtesy, surely, because James loved her. But, of course, that was not how his father would see the thing at all. She was a failure in too many things to gain any respect with him. If she had been wealthy and frequently pregnant then she would have been deluged with the same odious charm with which he was now covering poor Erskine: a noxious slick of fine, hollow words.

Fortunately for Erskine, rescue was at hand. His own father came up to them. Erskine Senior seemed to Andrew to be a most impressive figure, especially when he compared him to his own father, who reminded him of nothing so much as a comic undertaker with his crest of white hair, his whisky-reddened cheeks and his old-fashioned mourning coat which had done service for too many funerals. Mr Erskine, on the other hand, was a model of dignified decorum. Anyone looking at the two old men might have guessed in fact that Mr Erskine was Sir Hector Lennox, for in appearance he seemed far more blue-blooded than the man who set such store by his fine ancestry. But was not Mr Erskine, for all his lack of title and lands, the true aristocrat, with the power of a renaissance prince over his great companies? His own father lived, or rather leeched, on memories of past glories in which he had had no hand. Mr Erskine had built and now ruled a small empire in a fashion which, Andrew imagined, his more distant and warlike ancestors would recognize. At least, they would understand it better than the present Sir Hector's worship of them.

'Now, Mr Erskine,' his father began, 'perhaps I can persuade you to stay to dinner? Your son seems unaccountably reluctant.'

'It would be an honour Sir Hector,' said Mr Erskine, 'but one which I am afraid we must decline. I have business in town tonight which cannot be put off.'

'Ah, business . . .' said his father, making a show of deference. 'Then I shall say no more on the subject. I quite understand that a man in your position . . .'

Andrew decided he would not stay to hear any more. Nobody would notice he had gone, he knew, for he was not exactly an important member of the funeral party. He might have been her closest relative, but according to the hieratic rules which governed affairs at the Quarro, he was just a younger son and therefore a person of slight consequence. This did not bother him unduly, for it gave him a measure of independence which James had never had. It meant he could slip away without being noticed, while James must talk on dutifully with the local Duke, Celia's godfather, who had honoured them with his lugubrious presence.

He went upstairs by the back stairs, taking care to avoid the drawing room which was as full of women mourners drinking tea as the dining room had been full of men drinking whisky. For some reason he did not understand the sexes did not mix at funerals, nor had the women come to the graveside. So he had only seen that black-gowned congregation very briefly as he had stood with his father and James in the entrance hall by the bier upon which her coffin rested, receiving the guests as they arrived. They had looked very strange – familiar faces were rendered almost unrecognizable by the broad dark hats and quantities of heavy veiling. He had watched them file decorously into the drawing room, like some order of nuns, and had remembered that there was nothing that Celia had disliked so much as mourning clothes.

Upstairs, the house was warm and very still. As he walked along, he pulled off his jacket and loosened his tie. He was about to begin to wrench off his stiff high collar when he noticed, as he reached the gallery which ran like a transept widthways across the first floor of the house, a woman seated very still on the low ledge which ran under the window at one end of it. She made him stop and stare for a moment, his hand still on his collar stud, for she seemed extraordinarily composed as she sat there, her head outlined by a nimbus of black veiling which stood out stiffly where she had folded it back over her head. The sun shone very strongly through it, casting her features into shadow so that they were unreadable.

'You look like a ghost,' he said involuntarily, for she did not move, no matter how he stared.

But now she did, inclining her head to see him better.

'Are you Andrew?' she said.

'Yes, yes, I am,' he said, coming towards her. 'Who are you then? I'm afraid I can't guess.'

'I didn't expect you to,' she said, adjusting her skirts so that there was room on the stool for him to sit beside her. 'I'm Alexandra Erskine – Alix?'

'Oh, you're Alix,' he said, looking at her properly as he sat down. 'I see. So you couldn't face it downstairs either?'

'No, I'm afraid not. They all expected me to cry, and I won't, not in public at least. I have cried though – if not today – so I can't be so heartless, can I?'

'I don't know how you could even think it,' he said, anxious to reassure her. If those harpies in the drawing room had been making her feel bad, it made him angry to know it. For he felt strangely protective of her – as Celia's friend, she deserved his protection and friendship. Besides, she did not look the least bit heartless with her grave, ghost-like demeanour. 'I hate this whole business, you know, this whole damn' burying business. It isn't like her at all – it makes me furious that my father could think such a thing appropriate.'

'What do you think she would have wanted, then?' asked Alix.

'Oh, I don't know – but not this, I'm certain of it. And certainly not these.' And he pulled at the dull black silk of her skirt. 'You shouldn't wear black, you know. It doesn't suit you at all.'

'That's exactly what my brother said.' And she smiled.

He suddenly felt embarrassed by his own frankness, and apologized.

'There's no need to,' she said, interrupting him. 'I wasn't the least bit offended. I quite agree with everything you said. It makes me angry too. But people have such fixed ideas about these things, don't they? What can you do? My mother thought it would help us to come, especially my brother, although he didn't want to in the least. But she insisted, which I think was cruel of her – not cruel to me, because I can bear it, but to Ralph. He's so cut up, but won't admit it.'

'Might I ask you something, Miss Erskine?' he said, encouraged by her frankness. 'You were here when she died – won't you tell me exactly what happened? They won't give me the truth of it, and I have the most terrible suspicions . . .'

'I can give you the truth,' she said, 'but I'm afraid there isn't much comfort in it.'

'I'd rather have the truth that hurts than lies. I have to know what happened.'

'You should know, I suppose,' she said. 'I am convinced she meant to kill herself. It wasn't an accident.'

Only this girl had been brave enough to tell him that! Only this beautiful, pale-faced creature, for whom at that moment he would quite readily have risked everything to save her from the slightest unpleasant circumstance, had been able to say the awful thing that others, older and more world-weary, had sought to conceal.

'That's what I thought,' he said. 'That's why I had to know. I don't suppose you know why?'

But here she shook her head at once.

'No, I'm afraid I can't tell you. That's the worst of it, isn't it, not knowing that?' He nodded. 'I suspect we shall all go to our graves wondering whether it wasn't something we said or did.'

He wanted to beg her to elaborate but she was getting up as she spoke, as if to signal that their conversation was at an end. He glanced along the gallery and saw why. Mr Erskine, silk hat in hand, was coming towards them.

'Ah, there you are, Alix,' he said. 'Come along, we must be going now.'

'Yes, of course, Father,' she said, pulling on her gloves. 'Goodbye, Mr Lennox,' she said rather quickly, and in a moment had set off down the passageway with her father. He was obviously not a man one could keep waiting.

14

Was this flat really so enormous, or was it only the lack of furniture which made it appear so? Jessie stood alone in the centre of the vast room with its bay window, which Sholto had blithely called the 'drawing room'. A drawing room, she thought, staring at the expanses of freshly painted wall. What on earth am I going to do with a drawing room?

There had been a room in her parents' little house in Dysart of which the door had always been kept firmly shut. One entered it only on pain of death, because it was the best room, and was always kept in a state of sanctified cleanliness in case some important person, such as the minister or his sister, should call. It had not bothered her in the least that she was not allowed to go in there as she pleased, for she had always hated the look of it with its aggressively shiny furniture. Of those rare occasions when she had had to sit in there, she could only remember the discomfort of the high-backed, horsehair chairs which were her mother's pride. Was that what she was supposed to do with this room?

She thought of the drawing room at the Quarro: of its great windows hung with curtains of some softly shining stuff and trimmed with silvery fringes; of those large, inviting-looking sofas and easy chairs where the guests had lounged with newspapers and tea cups; of the miniature worlds displayed in the paintings on the walls, which she had only glanced at but had longed to study at her leisure. She remembered how utterly at ease Sholto had been amongst all those fine things, taking them quite for granted. Did he expect a room like that in his new house? Looking at that great blank space, she could not begin to imagine how it would be achieved. She had saved fifty pounds in a Post Office Savings account. That had seemed like a fortune to her once but now, faced with this space and grandeur, she did not think it would be enough to set up house on.

That morning Sholto had met her at the station and brought her here in a hansom cab, a luxury to which she imagined she might eventually become accustomed. He had given her the key to the flat, pressed two five-pound notes into her hand and had told her to go and buy a dress for the wedding. 'I have to go now,' he said, 'I'm expected in court within the hour.' And she had been left, with her box, at the bright red front door of her new home, feeling bewildered but excited. She had carried her box up the three flights of steps without difficulty, knowing that in a few months she would not find it so easy. However, she would not complain, because she knew that top-floor flats were the cheapest to rent.

The flat was all Sholto had promised: there was the miraculous bathroom with its window, its water closet and its hot water geyser; there were the two bedrooms, one large and one small and cosy, in which Jessie at once imagined the bairn; there was the kitchen, with a shiny new range, a box bed, should they ever employ a maid, a built-in dresser painted in cheerful green enamel, and a deep white sink and wooden draining board. As if this were not enough, there were the two big rooms at the front, with views from their vast windows over what seemed the whole city, for she could see the Castle if she looked one way and Blackford Hill the other, while in front stretched another broad street of impressive tenements, fronted with gardens. One room had a plaster cornice of vines and ears of corn, which signified it was a dining room. The other, in which she now stood, had in its cornice such fine and elaborate scrolls and twists that she was reminded of the lace flounces beloved by Mrs Lennox.

Marchmont Road. She relished the sound of her new address, as if the words, like the area, had nothing mean and shabby about them.

She went over to the marble fireplace where the two five-pound notes which Sholto had given her were lying, ostentatiously large. She would have to go to the post office and change them. She hoped they would not stare at her when she handed them over, afraid that they might think she had come by such a sum of money dishonestly. I shall just have to do it with confidence, she decided, and took a turn up and down the grand room, relishing the sound of her heels on the bare boards. Even if they had nothing to cover them, they still looked smart enough, being brightly varnished. I shall go and buy him a present, she thought. I couldn't possibly spend all that just on a dress. But what can I give him? For he seemed well furnished with possessions. In the dining room there were several large crates and boxes which formed, apparently, only a small portion of what he had in his flat in the Old Town. She had nosed a little into them and found mostly books. I can't give him a book, she thought, but then changed her mind. She took up the notes with decision and folded them into her purse. She fetched her best Sunday hat and found a pair of fresh gloves (for one has to feel smart to spend money). The latchkey, still with the house-agent's paper ticket attached to it, completed her toilette and Jessie set out to buy a volume of Burns and her wedding dress. It was not quite how she might have imagined such an occasion, but she would not have changed it for the world.

Part Two
September 1900
1

It was clear to Alix the moment that they stepped into the dining room at the Badischer Hof Hotel that they were, despite it being only eight o'clock, by the standards of the place, late. It was not the waiters who gave her this impression, because they were faultlessly polite, ushering them to an empty table with perfect good grace. No, it was the other diners who had decided that Alix and Mr Erskine were late. They had all finished their soup and were using the interval between courses to assess the new arrivals. Some only glanced up covertly as the newcomers crossed the room, but others stopped talking and gave them a good, frank stare as if their arrival was the most interesting thing that had happened in several years.

This Alix found embarrassing, and would quite gladly have turned on her heel and fled, but her father was quite impervious to it all. He addressed the waiter in fluent, rather loud German, and had the guests all exchanging glances. She knew that they were attempting to place them, for people living in hotels become extraordinarily curious about each other, crediting fellow guests with fanciful histories on the slightest evidence. They will think we are German, she thought, and reflected that at least was better than being at once stamped as English. That most of the people in the room were English was at once obvious to her. Their English stuffiness hung in the air like a faint, dusty smell which could never be removed because one could not possibly do anything so ill-mannered as open a window! Thank God, we are Scots, she thought.

'Are you hungry?' Mr Erskine asked.

'A little,' she said, watching as the waiter set down a wine cooler with a tall, elegant brown bottle of wine in it. It looked wonderfully cool and refreshing, the glass spotted with condensation. 'I should think Ralph would like some of that,' she remarked.

'Yes, I should think so,' said Mr Erskine, dismissing the waiter and pouring out two glasses himself. 'But doctor's orders are doctor's orders, aren't they?'

She was a little surprised that her father gave her the wine. She was quite sure if her mother had been there, she would not have been allowed any, but dining alone with her father, a thing she had never done before, she found a different set of rules applied. When she saw him at home in Edinburgh, seated at the head of the table in the dining room at Rothesay Terrace, she was inclined to forget that he was anything else but her father. Now, as she saw his complete ease in this strange dining room, she realized how much of his time was spent amongst unfamiliar things and faces, that he lived a far more public life than she was capable of guessing at. The way the hotel staff had responded to him when they had arrived, how his every command had been granted at once, he had seemed immediately a frequent and favoured customer. But she knew for a fact he had never stayed here before. It was extraordinary that he should command such authority, so easily, without arrogance. His dignity impressed her, and she felt suddenly very proud of him.

The waiter put down in front of them two plates of fish, a pair of sole, very white and neat upon the plate, flecked gold a little from the frying. The only decorations were slices of lemon, of which the skins had been grooved with a knife to appear white against the yellow. It looked and smelt very appetising, and as she sipped her wine from her green-stemmed glass, she thought of Ralph upstairs who usually would have relished such food, but who now had no appetite.

That had been the first sign of his breakdown, and she remembered too well the look of alarm in her mother's face as in the days succeeding Celia's death, he had pushed away

144

plate after plate of food. Gradually he had ceased to appear at meals at all, leaving for the Musselburgh works before breakfast and coming back after dinner. Her mother would waylay him in the hall when he got back, and force him to eat. But he would only take a mouthful or two, complaining that it was painful to eat, that the slightest amount of food made his whole body feel like lead. 'Besides . . .' he had protested on one occasion, thrusting under his mother's nose a bursting attaché case '. . . I'm too damn' busy to be bothered with food.' And he had gone upstairs, demanding that no one should disturb him.

When she had fetched the doctor, he had refused to see him and had locked the door of his room. Alix had stood for an hour outside it, pleading with him, because Mrs Erskine had thought he might listen to her. But he had not listened, and after a while did not even answer her. She had rushed downstairs in a panic, suddenly terrified of what might have happened. In the end, Mr Erskine and the doctor had forced the door with an almighty crack which might have raised the dead. But it did not raise Ralph, who had collapsed at his desk, surrounded by papers.

The next day the nerve specialist arrived, and declared, after what seemed too short a time, a diagnosis of visceral melancholia, brought on by Celia's death and overwork. 'A complete mental rest is absolutely necessary – and hydropathic treatments. I suggest Baden or Homburg. The Germans have these things so well organized.' He had pronounced it like sentence of death, in a deep, perfunctory voice.

The week which had followed, and now found its conclusion in that first dinner at the Badischer Hof, had been harrowing to say the least. The pleasure of a first visit to the continent and the exciting luxury of the wagon-lits had been obscured for Alix by Ralph's condition. She had not noticed France as the train passed through, for she had been too preoccupied by the sight of him, so feeble and thin, propped up on a pile of pillows to prevent an asthma attack. Every jolt of the train pained him, and he was restless and hot, occasionally delirious, constantly demanding liquid.

That was fortunate at least, for it meant they could get a little nourishment into him.

And now here they were in Baden Baden, in a white stuccoed hotel which was clinically pretty, as spotless as a hospital, with neat pink geraniums at every window. She hoped to God that the cure the specialist had so confidently prescribed would work.

'Now, don't you get gloomy,' said Mr Erskine, observing that she had fallen into a thoughtful silence as they ate their fish. 'We don't want you going into a decline as well.'

'No, I won't, I promise.'

He smiled and squeezed her hand.

'That's the sprit,' he said. 'Have some more wine. You can drink a glass for Ralph.'

'Do you have to go so soon?' she asked. 'Can't Berlin wait a few days?'

'Berlin can wait,' he said. 'But I don't think His Highness will. I've been told he's a rather impatient individual.' He had been asked to make some railway bridges for a tiny German principality, somewhere to the east of Berlin. 'And the Board of Trade will never forgive me if I let this one slip through our fingers. It will be quite a coup for a German to buy Scottish steel. It will ruffle a few feathers here, I'm sure – and when I get back, I expect to find Ralph eating three meals a day again. I'm sure you and your mother will work wonders.'

'We didn't have much success before, did we?'

'Nobody could have done anything about that,' he said, leaning back in his chair. 'You know, Alix,' he continued in a confidential tone which was new to her, 'I think Ralph is a great deal stronger than we give him credit for sometimes. He'll pull through, just you wait and see. I must say, it was very brave the way he took that dreadful business. He didn't break just like that. No, he tried to put it behind him, just like a sensible man would. He made some good efforts at the motor works, you know. He's more of a gift for business than I'd thought.'

'But it made him ill,' said Alix, a little astonished by her father's line of reasoning. 'Surely it would have been better

146

for him to admit a month ago how cut up he was, instead of letting himself get into this wretched state.'

'Perhaps,' said her father. 'But I still think it was brave – it was spirited to try, don't you think?'

She could not answer, for she thought Ralph had been foolhardy. It would have been better if he had cried with her and let his grief out rather than letting it poison his mind and body the way it had. But perhaps that was impossible for men. They were not allowed such a weakness as weeping and she remembered he had once told her of some school-boy code in which one of the greatest sins had been to cry out when one had been hit. But I should have thought you had more sense, Ralph, she mused, and then wondered if it was not something more complicated than the sheer manly guts that her father ascribed it to. Perhaps the pain was too great for him to contemplate, too frightening for him to acknowledge.

After the swaying railway carriage, the room was white, and clean and very still. It was dusk, that much he knew, for the light which filtered through the gently flapping muslin curtains was soft and grey. It relieved him to know that he would not need to move again from the comfortable, linen-wrapped haven of this bed. There was no need to worry about being in Germany, which he had always disliked, in this room, for although the things in it seemed peculiarly German in shape and colour, the overall effect was so neutral that it did not disturb him. If it had been France, he would have wanted to jump out of bed and get into the streets of the place, to savour every smell and sound that was special to France. But because it was Germany, he was quite happy to stay in this bland little room and enjoy the comfort of clean sheets on his feeble body.

The door opened and Mrs Erskine came in, with her silent, sickroom step. She had changed out of her travelling dress into cornflower blue cotton, somewhat old-fashioned in style, which she wore when she wanted to be comfort-able. She carried a tray and Ralph felt the moment of calm he had experienced, vanish. She would want him to eat

147

something and his stomach turned at the mere thought of food. He had drunk a whole cup of beef tea on the train that day – wasn't that enough for her? The tray was one of those contraptions with legs, and in a moment she had set it down in front of him. He wished he had the strength to kick it away, but could only lie there hopelessly while she spread a napkin over his chest and lifted the lid of the little tureen.

'Look, Ralph,' she said. 'Carrot soup. You always liked carrot soup.'

He shut his eyes, not wanting to look at it. But the stench of it filled his nostrils and he felt his throat constrict. He knew he should eat, that he must eat, but how could he, when everything they put in front of him, beyond water and coffee, seemed as if it were made from his own vomit?

'I'll try . . . just a spoonful,' he said, and reached out for the spoon. He grasped it, feeling the clumsiness of his own fingers, and plunged it into the soup. He saw his mother smile encouragingly and lifted up the spoon again, full of soup. But as he guided it towards his lips, his arm began to shake uncontrollably and he spattered soup across the white napkin she had carefully spread out. He let the spoon go without caring where it landed.

'What's the damned point!' he said, hoarsely and despairingly. 'I don't want the bloody stuff anyway.'

She, as ever, was undaunted. She took up the spoon and put her arm around him, bending him forward so that he was nearer the dish. Gently, she lifted a half full spoon to his lips.

'Come along now, Ralph. Just a little, yes?'

He submitted, but a mixture of this humiliation and the vile taste conspired against him, and he felt tears start in his eyes. That increased his misery the more for it seemed he had no remaining shred of self-control. He had not even the strength to howl out his angry frustration. He could only sit there and let the tears run down his cheeks, while his mother fed him like a child.

Why don't they just let me die . . . why don't they just let me alone? He no longer cared about life. He would happily have been confined to an empty cell in an asylum and left to die. He did not believe he could get better, although that was what everyone kept saying. How could they know? They did not know what he suffered.

He took six or seven spoonfuls of the soup and that seemed to satisfy her. She let him rinse out his mouth with a glass of water, but would not ring for coffee, to which he had apparently become addicted and which was, they said, a dangerous stimulant. He hated the injustice of it. The one thing which tasted normal, which tasted pleasant indeed, was denied him. She suggested instead that he take a glass of goat's milk.

'They make a speciality of it here in the Black Forest,' said his mother, putting the glass beside his bed. She sounded as if she was quoting from Baedeker. 'Besides, Dr Shairp mentioned it particularly.'

'That man only wants to torture me,' said Ralph, petulantly. 'What am I being punished for anyway?'

'It's not punishment, it's treatment. It's to make you better, my darling,' she said. 'Just remember that. I know it may seem hard for you just now, but it will work, and you'll be glad of it then.'

In a day or two, his strength permitting, he was to begin the hydropathic treatments, a series of ordeals which he hardly dared contemplate. He had seen the directions (although he was not supposed to have read them, since he was not allowed to read anything) and wished he had not. The very names – cold douche, Swedish Massage, sitz bath and inhaling chamber – frightened him. It was like a medieval description of hell.

Mrs Erskine had sat down on the other side of the room and taken up a piece of embroidery.

'Can't I read something?' he said. He didn't want silence or the least opportunity to contemplate.

'No, you know you can't,' she said.

'Couldn't you read to me?'

'You should try and sleep. Tomorrow will be tiring.'

'I won't sleep, you know that. Just a novel or something? Just for a while . . .'

'I'll read to you if you think it will help,' she said. 'But

149

not your sort of book. Something light, I think.'

'Whatever you like.'

She disappeared for a few moments and returned with a book.

'*Pickwick Papers*,' she said, sitting down and opening it. 'Will that be all right?'

Ralph, to his amazement, found himself laughing. He could not quite believe how but he was, and he saw his mother's astonished delight.

'What is it, dear?' she said, but he knew he could not tell her. It had just struck him as absurd that amidst all the chaos that his illness must have caused, she should have thought of packing the *Pickwick Papers*, a novel which none of them liked! It was the first normal, unmorbid thought he had had for days and he felt a wave of sheer relief flood over him. Then, without thinking about it particularly, he reached out and drank a little from the glass of goat's milk. It tasted almost bearable.

'Oh, my dear,' said his mother, stroking his forehead with a fond hand. 'Didn't I tell you it would all be better soon?'

2

'Good morning, my dear – and how is your brother this morning?'

Alix, who had managed to secure a London newspaper and a quiet sunny bench on the far end of the hotel terrace, had hoped she would not be interrupted. But after three weeks of hotel life she had begun to realize that the sort of privacy which one took for granted at home was impossible here. At the Badischer Hof, when one spoke to a fellow British guest, one could not expect to escape with a few words as if they were only slight acquaintances, because the fact they were all staying under the same roof automatically made them intimates. Shared domesticity (if that was how the luxurious arrangements of the hotel could be described) made everyone forget British reserve and plunged them all into a sort of holiday friendliness which, although pleasant enough in principle, could on occasion be extremely annoying. The Misses Lewis, who now addressed her, generally fell into this category. It was not that they were unpleasant or rude. Rather it was their excessive gentility, their heartfelt kindness, their interest in the slightest trifles about her family, which was so infuriating. They were like a pair of lap dogs which she could not shake off, especially since her mother had encouraged them so, deeming them to be 'thoroughly nice people'.

'Oh, he's much better thank you, Miss Ada.'

'I'm so glad, dear,' she said, sitting down beside Alix. 'You see, we were so worried when you and your mother didn't come down last night. We thought he might have had a relapse.' She whispered the word 'relapse' as if it were too dreadful to say aloud.

'Oh, no, nothing like that. We just ate together, that's all. He ate a whole trout last night.'

'A whole trout! My goodness – did you hear that, Evie? – a whole trout!'

'Well, you must be relieved, dear,' said Miss Evie. 'But I knew we could have confidence. Now if you had gone to Homburg, I should not have felt the same. But here, well. . . .' She sniffed the air. 'There is something in the air here. It is so refreshing, so healthful. We tried Homburg once but it was quite exhausting.'

'So now we always come here,' chimed in Miss Ada.

Alix, who had found Baden distinctly dreary in the first week, wondered what there was to fascinate the two spinsters, year after year.

'I wonder if your brother shouldn't try the grape cure,' said Miss Evie. 'I can thoroughly recommend it.'

'Goodness no, Evie,' said Miss Ada. 'You can't possibly recommend something like that. Only a physician can recommend a cure. What would George say if he knew that you were trying to do his work for him?'

'I was not prescribing, dear, only suggesting,' said Miss

Evie. 'It's such an invigorating cure, and so delicious.'

'What is the grape cure then?' asked Alix, folding up *The Times*, knowing she would now have no opportunity to read it.

'Well, it couldn't be simpler, could it, Ada?' said Miss Evie. 'One simply eats six to eight pounds of grapes a day. It really does work miracles.'

'I can imagine,' said Alix, trying very hard not to laugh.

'It's the minerals in the grapes, you see,' she continued. 'They soothe the mucous membrane and act as, well, as a . . . you know . . .'

'Evie, must you be so frank?' cut in Miss Ada. 'What will Miss Erskine think of us? By the way, dear, did we tell you that our nephew George is coming tomorrow?'

She had mentioned this at least half a dozen times previously, but Alix managed to feign interest. The thought of the nephew George, the physician as they pompously called him, a masculine version of the Misses Lewis, was too horrible to contemplate.

'Yes, he's coming from Vienna. Isn't it exciting – he's such a dear boy. We thought we might take a carriage and make an excursion to the Alte Schloss. The view there is so charming. Perhaps you would like to join us?'

Alix could think of nothing more dreadful than a long carriage ride with them, but she knew her duty.

'How kind. I should love to – but I must see if my mother can spare me, you know.'

'Of course, dear. We should not dream of taking you otherwise. It is a shame that your mother could not come as well, but the patient can't be left, can he?'

'Perhaps she could go in my place,' said Alix. 'I'm sure I can look after Ralph just as well.'

'What a good girl you are,' said Miss Evie, appreciative of this piece of self-sacrifice. 'You must ask her if she would like to go, then.'

Alix hoped she would agree to the scheme, for she knew that Ralph would be glad to have some time to himself. He had said to her last night that the only thing which would kill him now was their mother's fussing.

★ ★ ★

Alix was waiting for him outside the Friedrichsbad. He was glad to see she was alone, for his mother usually came, full of anxious questions which quite destroyed the sense of relaxed well-being that the bathing now produced in him.

At first it had been agony, just as he had predicted. He had been so weak that two burly bath attendants had propelled him from treatment to treatment as if he was some criminal imbecile in the worst sort of asylum. The first sitz bath he had taken, which they had said would only be tepid, had been so painfully cold as to make him almost pass out. But now that he was stronger, he found it strangely refreshing and had fallen asleep in it the other day, which was apparently a very good sign. 'You are making excellent progress, Herr Erskine,' his masseur had said that morning, and it was true that he no longer felt the daily massage to be a vindictive battering designed to break every bone in his body, but an invigorating experience which made him realize that his body was alive after all and not just a piece of bed-ridden, weary flesh. He had even come to like the salty, sulphurous water at the Trinkhalle. And now, on the steps of the the Friedrichsbad, he felt quite distinctly a pang of hunger.

'Alix,' he said, crossing the street to where she stood, 'you'll never believe this but I actually feel hungry, just like I used to! Isn't it extraordinary?'

'Really? But, Ralph, that's wonderful!' she said, kissing him.

'In fact, I want to eat now. Let's go and have kaffee und kuchen.'

'But you're not supposed to have anything too rich yet, Ralph . . .'

'Don't be stupid. You've all been trying to make me eat for weeks. Don't you dare say I can't eat when I want to. Mother has been getting to you, hasn't she?'

'No, it's just that it would be foolish to ruin things by being silly.'

'You have been listening to Mother too much,' he said. 'It

153

doesn't suit you, Alix – you were made for better things than fussing.'

'Well, I haven't had much chance to pursue them yet, so you'll just have to take me as you find me,' she said. 'Are you really so hungry that you could eat German cakes, Ralph?'

'Yes – I'm not quite sure how I am, but I am. That taste in my throat – it's gone. And I should love a cup of coffee. Now come on, Alix, let's go to one of those places in the Lichtenhaler with a garden, and watch the world go by.'

'But Mother will be expecting us back. I know she won't scold you, Ralph, but she will me. I'm supposed to be responsible for you.'

'You don't need to feel you are,' he said, taking her arm as she was about to turn in the direction of the hotel. 'Let's go to the Lichtenhaler.'

Alix knew she should be pleased by Ralph's sudden burst of high spirits, but it disturbed her. There was a restlessness about it which reminded her of how he had been in his feverish pursuit of Celia. He carried her along to the confectioners in the Lichtenhaler Strasse as if she were the reluctant invalid who had to be fed up. It was too great a change coming on too suddenly. She could not quite believe that the treatments could be so effective. It was not exactly characteristic of Ralph to be so at ease, and yet he was – he got them a good table, despite the place being crowded, and he ordered with relative confidence in reasonable German.

'Your German is better than mine,' she said.

'Don't you remember that Father made me learn it – for the business?'

'Of course,' she said, 'and you hated it.'

'Well, I was furious because he said that it was pointless my spending so much time composing Greek verse. He was right as well, I suppose. Greek verse is not much use when you want to tell the masseur that he's just wrenched your shoulder!'

'That's not like you,' she said. 'You used to live for poetry.'

154

'And now I just live,' he said, a sour note in his voice. 'All I think about is my stomach or my bowels or whether my head aches or whether I can get to sleep. My mind is quite dead, I think. My body may be working again, or at least getting stronger, but my head – well . . .'

'Well what?'

But he did not answer her and began looking about them, as if he expected to see someone they knew at the other tables.

'Don't do that, Ralph,' she said, embarrassed. 'It looks so very rude. Who are you looking for anyway?'

'It's just that when we came in . . .' he said, still searching the faces of the other customers 'I thought I saw . . . ah . . .' and he got up and went towards a table on the far side of the garden some yards away where two women were sitting with their backs to them. At first Alix could not understand what he was doing and then, as she looked at the women for an instant longer, she knew why. The appearance of one of them struck her like a blow across the face: the dress, the hat, the way the hair was arranged in that thick pleat at the nape of the neck, even the manner of sitting, all conspired to give the appearance of Celia. For a moment she was half convinced, and then, collecting herself, knew she must stop Ralph. But he was walking towards her like a man hypnotized and Alix only had time to rise half out of her seat and call, rather feebly, 'Ralph, no . . .' because he had tapped the strange woman on the shoulder.

She turned and looked up at him. She was probably a handsome woman but the look she gave Ralph was ugly and hostile. Alix saw his shoulders droop and he stepped back quickly, muttering some apology. Then he turned back towards his sister, his face not red with embarrassment but set in a far grimmer mask. He paused for a moment at their table, thrusting a few marks into her hand.

'I'm going,' he said, and marched away.

Alix, terrified by his manner, paid the bill as quickly as she could. But the waiter was slow bringing the change, and by the time she left the restaurant Ralph was several

155

hundred yards ahead of her in the Lichtenhaler Allee. Not caring that this was one of the most elegant and dignified promenades in Europe, at that moment thronged with people, Alix caught up her skirt in one hand and ran towards him, dodging bath chairs and astonished flâneurs who had never seen the like of it. She managed to catch up with him.

'Go away,' he said. 'I want to be alone.'

'Where are you going?'

'Where do you think?'

He's going back to the hotel, thank God! she thought.

'I shan't say anything,' she said. 'Just let me walk with you.'

He gave a curt nod of agreement and they walked back to the Badischer Hof in silence.

Now he knew that the real crisis had come. The floodgates had opened and he knew all the traumas of the past weeks had only been distractions, desperate attempts to defend himself from the truth. His mind had numbed itself into forgetfulness, but now memories of her rushed over him like a savage army determined to batter him into submission, into the final acknowledgement of what had really happened.

It seemed he stood in that room with her ghost, so vividly did she appear to him in a thousand shards of recollection. He could smell her skin and feel the warmth of it; he could hear her footsteps and her laughter; he could see her handwriting on the brief, scrawled note she had once sent him as if he held it in his hand; but worst of all, he could see her face, still and very beautiful, as it had lain on the pillow that morning. The morning when he had found that she was . . . 'No!' he exclaimed aloud, and began to pace about the room, wringing his hands together, determined that he would not think that terrible thought. Not yet – please God, not yet. I can't face it yet. I'm not strong enough . . .

Still she danced around him. He felt her lips against his, but the sweetness had gone. Each kiss he remembered cut him like a whip. And every embrace led to that final, futile time he had held her, shaken her, desperate to revive her.

But she is dead. She would rather die than have me. The words slipped into his brain quietly and unbidden. It took him a moment to realize that they had come, but when he had, he knew that he could no longer ignore the truth of them, no matter how painful it might be.

He felt his body shake with the sobs he had so long suppressed. His mind collapsed into a whirling vortex of misery and he sank to his knees in the middle of the room, choking on tears so painful that they seemed to be drops of his own blood.

3

One of the Misses Lewis had just said something rather disturbing.

'Of course, Mrs Erskine,' she had said, 'Ada and I have only been able to travel since our dear mama died. She was such an invalid, you know, she could not be left. Not that we minded – we should not have let anyone else nurse her. I mean, it is the least thing a daughter can do for a mother, don't you think?' And Alix had a vision of herself, at some indeterminate age like the spinster sisters, telling someone how she had devotedly nursed her parents; how it had been no sacrifice at all: 'But simply the least I could have done for them . . .'

She had seen such cases many times: the middle-aged daughter who remained at home and acted as an unpaid companion to her mother, usually because she had been the plain daughter with neither the wits nor the good fortune to find a husband. Alix had always scorned such females, but now she had a curious premonition that if she did nothing about it, it could very easily happen to her. Her life was so limited, so rooted in domesticity, so absolutely regulated by her mother, that she sensed that soon she might be hopeless. Now she was strong and independent-willed, but sometimes that flame guttered dangerously. It was too easy to behave as her mother wanted.

That morning, for example, when Ralph had told them that he thought he might ride to the Alte Schloss with them, she had asked if she might ride also rather than go in the carriage.

'But there's a place for you in the carriage,' Mrs Erskine had said. 'Besides, Dr Lewis and Ralph will only feel obliged to keep to your pace, which will spoil it for them.'

'Alix can ride as well as a man,' Ralph had interjected. 'And we shan't exactly be steeple-chasing. Lewis says he's no horseman.'

'Then why doesn't he go in the carriage?'

'If Ralph is going to ride,' said her mother, 'then I should rather it was with someone responsible.'

'Let her ride, Mother, for goodness' sake,' said Ralph. 'I am not going to break my neck, you know. I'm supposed to get all the exercise I can, remember!'

'Ralph dear, now don't get excited . . .' she said in a warning tone, and Alix had thought, she treats us as if we were children still. 'In fact, I wonder if we should be going at all. After your treatments you need to rest, you know. Perhaps we had better stay here – but you can still go in the carriage, Alix. The Lewises would like you to go – they're very fond of you, you know.'

'Mother, I want to ride,' Ralph had said doggedly. 'I'm sick to death of being cooped up. I don't want to have to sit here in this damned hotel and brood for the rest of my life. How on earth can I sort myself out unless you let me out of this invalid's cage, eh?'

Since the incident in the cafe, which was now three days ago, Ralph seemed to have come back to life in a rough-edged, belligerent fashion. He was frequently gloomy, frequently short-tempered but she had heard him crying in the solitude of his room, as if he were going through some personal catharsis. Those tears, which should have been spilt months ago, seemed like water on parched earth; he seemed to feel and think again because of them.

'And if Alix wants to ride, let her,' he had continued.

'She's had little enough fun since we came here. I may be a damned nuisance to you all, but I'm not so bloody-minded as to spoil all your pleasure. I think we should all go – you especially, Mother. You probably need the fresh air as much as I do.'

'Oh, very well then,' she had at last admitted. 'But you will be careful, won't you?'

Alix knew that had not Ralph stepped in, she would not have been able to resist her mother. It was invariably easier to submit to her than to argue, for when one did, even in the mildest terms, she looked so pained and offended that one could not continue without feeling profoundly guilty, no matter how justified one's complaint. And now, as she saw her mother nodding in agreement with Miss Evie as they sat amongst the ruins of the Alte Schloss, she felt she was in danger of losing her will.

I shall have to stand up to her more – no matter how bad it may make me feel, she decided. And I must find something to do with my life. Something useful. Ralph has always said I should do something or I'll become nothing but a nuisance. I wonder if he has any ideas . . .

Ralph was lying under a tree a little distance away from the others. His eyes were closed and Alix wondered if he was not pretending to be asleep so that he would not have to be sociable. If he had not been a convalescent he would never have been allowed to do it. Their mother would have scolded him for lying like that, so relaxed and abandoned to the warm day, his jacket and waistcoat rolled into a pillow and his shirt tails falling out of the top of his breeches, plainly displaying in places the bare, white flesh of his stomach and back.

Perhaps he is asleep, she thought.

'I wonder if Ralph might be thirsty,' she said, casting round for an excuse to get away and talk to him.

'No, dear, don't disturb him,' said her mother.

'Miss Erskine has a point, you know,' said Dr Lewis. 'In this heat there's quite a chance of dehydration.'

'Oh, well, if you think . . .' said Mrs Erskine, taking a bottle of mineral water and a cup from the picnic basket.

'I'll go and give him some of this.'

'No, Mother, don't get up,' said Alix, scrambling to her feet before Mrs Erskine had a chance to rise. 'You look so comfortable there.'

'Yes, Mrs Erskine,' said Dr Lewis, who was proving an unexpected ally, 'rest is as important for the nurse as for the patient.'

So Alix was dismissed on her errand of mercy.

When she reached Ralph's tree, she was glad to see that she could not hear what the others were saying. It was a relief to be out of earshot of their banal conversation. She knelt down beside Ralph and said, 'Well then, are you really asleep?'

'How did you guess?' he said, without moving.

'You fell asleep too quickly – so you had better wake up slowly. You've got to have some mineral water – doctor's orders.'

'That Lewis fellow plays straight into her hands,' he said, propping himself up on his elbows. 'Still, I can't say this is unwelcome. I'm sure you were glad to get away from all that wittering.'

'Of course,' she said, pouring out the water. 'I find it terrifying, you know. I keep imagining that if I don't look out, I shall end up just like them.'

'I doubt it,' said Ralph, gulping down the water.

'But things like that happen so easily. People get trapped – you said so yourself this morning. Sometimes I think I shall never get away from her.'

'From Mother, you mean? Yes, I can understand that.'

'But what on earth should I do about it? If I were a man it would be obvious, but what am I fit for?'

'Some women these days do get educations, you know,' he said. 'It would be a good thing, I think, if more did. If more bright girls were decently educated then they wouldn't be so . . . so . . . well, you know.'

'You mean like Celia?' she said tentatively. This was not a subject she had ever dared broach with him since his breakdown.

'Yes,' he said gloomily, peering into his empty cup. 'Like

Celia. For such a naturally intelligent girl, she behaved stupidly. Perhaps, if her mind had been trained a little, given something to do, not wasted like that, then . . . but what's the point of speculating over a thing like that. What's over, is over, isn't it?'

'I shouldn't ever have said she was intelligent,' said Alix, encouraged by his calmness. She felt it would help her as well as Ralph to discuss the matter frankly at last.

'What makes you say that?' he asked.

'Well, she was not exactly consistent. She could never make up her mind about the simplest things, such as which dress she would wear. I don't think she knew how to be true to one thing. I suspect she wouldn't have made you a very good wife.'

'You're very severe,' said Ralph. 'How can you judge her like that?'

'You said yourself she behaved stupidly.'

'I meant impulsively, irrationally if you like. If she didn't want to marry me, she might have simply told me instead of . . . of . . . killing herself.' It was obviously hard for him to say it. 'Yes, perhaps stupid is the word for it,' he said. 'What did she think I was going to do to her? She can't have been afraid of marriage, of what I might do to her – not when she gave herself to me like that.'

'You don't mean . . . you didn't seduce her, did you?' said Alix, astonished at this revelation. Then she felt angry with him. 'Then that's why she said she would marry you – of course she would. She would have felt she had no choice.'

'No, Alix, I did not seduce her,' said Ralph. 'When I slept with her, she was not a virgin.'

'Then – Hamish Anderson . . .' said Alix, without thinking about it. Suddenly all Celia's oblique accounts of her nocturnal adventures became clear. That there had been more to it than kisses was obvious. No wonder she had found it impossible to choose, when she had slept with both of them! Alix found she could not imagine herself behaving like that. Celia had broken every rule in the book. No wonder she killed herself – how must she have felt!

'Hamish?' said Ralph. 'Who the devil . . .?'

161

Alix looked away. She was conscious that she had concealed an important truth from him, and she was afraid it might make him angry.

'Alix,' he said suspiciously, 'do you mean that she told you about this other man?' But she could not answer. Her throat felt choked with keeping the secret too long. 'Do you mean you knew about this other chap?' he went on. 'That you knew there was someone else and you didn't bother to tell me?' He grabbed her chin and made her look at him.

'Let me go, Ralph!' she said.

'When did all this happen?' he said without releasing her. His anger was frightening. It was so unlike him and she did not want to answer because it would make it worse.

'Let me go!' she repeated. 'You're hurting me.'

'When did she tell you about this Hamish?' he said, 'When?' And he shook her by the shoulders. 'Tell me!'

'On the first day at the Quarro,' she said, 'but you wouldn't have listened, I know you wouldn't. And I promised her . . .' She struggled free and got to her feet. 'Do you think there would have been any point telling you?' she continued, incensed by his behaviour. 'You wouldn't have listened. You were so head over ears in love that anything I said wouldn't have made the slightest difference!'

'Alexandra!' their mother's voice called out in the distance. But they were both too angry to take any notice.

'Then you knew this was going on, all the time? And you didn't tell me? I'm your brother, Alix, doesn't that mean anything to you? Wasn't it your duty to tell me?'

'I made a promise, Ralph. I'm not the sort of person who breaks her word.'

'You damnable little prig!' he exclaimed, scrambling to his feet. 'Haven't you any idea what I've been through? I've been to hell and back because of this – something which could have been entirely prevented if you hadn't been so nicely scrupulous about breaking your word. Why the hell didn't you warn me?'

'Because you would not have listened. If I'd told you she was unfaithful, you would have accused me of slander.

162

Admit it now, Ralph, you would have . . .'

'What on earth do you two think you are doing!' hissed Mrs Erskine, breaking in between them like the referee at a prize fight. 'What is the meaning of this disgraceful behaviour? They have heard every word – I don't know how I shall explain it. You will both come and apologize at once.'

'Don't think we are stopping,' said Ralph, 'we haven't even begun, have we? If you knew what this ignorant, heartless little bitch has done . . .'

'Ralph! This is unpardonable,' said their mother.

'No, *she* is unpardonable. Damn you, Alix Erskine, though you deserve worse than damnation. You deserve to suffer what I've suffered!' And he attempted to strike her but she stepped out of the way. Just in time, Dr Lewis stepped up and drew Ralph aside.

'Come now, Erskine, calm down – this isn't doing you any good at all . . .'

'Dear God in heaven!' muttered her mother, clenching her hands together. 'When will this all end? If only I hadn't let you go and stay with those terrible people . . .' And then, like a whip lash, she turned on Alix: 'I don't know what you've been doing, young lady, but I hope you're ashamed of yourself. You shouldn't have upset him like that. His nerves simply can't stand it. I should have thought you had more sense than to pick a quarrel with him. You haven't the least idea how disgraceful it looked, have you? What a stupid, thoughtless girl you are, Alexandra!'

'And why is that, Mother?' she said, more angered by this than any of Ralph's taunts. 'Because that's all you've ever allowed me to be! If I'm stupid and thoughtless, then you have only yourself to blame for it!'

She ran over to where the horses were tethered, roused the sleepy coachman to help her mount and began the descent down to Baden at a dangerously brisk trot, feeling a turmoil in her stomach of fury and self-disgust.

'Pax, Alix?' he said, putting out his hands to her.

'I don't know how you even dare say that,' she said,

turning away from him. 'You know what you said, what you did was unforgivable.'

The immaculate garden of the Badischer Hof at night was lit by Chinese lanterns hanging in the trees, giving it the appearance of a garden on a stage. Alix, in her white silk dinner dress, sitting on a bench with a mass of perfect pink geraniums around her, seemed to Ralph for a moment not to be his sister, but some heroine in a drawing-room comedy, who was mildly upset about a trifle and would soon be wooed back to good spirits by clever words from the hero. But he knew that he needed more than clever words to make her forgive him and that it was no trifling misunderstanding which made her turn away from him.

'I don't ask for forgiveness,' he said. 'I know I don't deserve that. Just peace.'

'You're very sanctimonious,' she said bitterly. 'Anyway, what are you doing out here? I thought you had been sent to bed with a sedative.'

'I refused to drink it,' he said, 'and that damned Lewis looked as if he should send out for a strait-jacket when I did.'

'You think your insanity is a fine excuse, don't you?'

'I'm not giving it as an excuse.'

'Well, that's something, I suppose.'

'Then you don't think I am insane?' he asked.

'I don't suppose it matters what I think,' she said tartly. 'I'm not a person of any importance in this family, am I? My feelings and opinions are so rarely consulted, it wouldn't matter if I thought you should be confined.'

'It does matter to me, Alix, believe me.'

'Does it really?' she said, as if unconvinced. 'Well, for the record, I don't suppose you are insane, although you've done a good job trying to convince us. Especially this afternoon . . . You tried to hit me, Ralph!' she added with genuine exasperation. 'I couldn't believe it!'

'It wasn't you that I wanted to hit,' he said. 'You must understand that. And all those words, those terrible things I said, they weren't really meant for you . . .'

'I know,' she said, after a pause, and when he put his

hand over hers, did not attempt to move it. 'You know what the worst of this is, don't you?' she said quietly. 'You did have a right to be angry. I was a fool, I should have told you, but I could never find the moment . . .'

'And I wouldn't have listened – you were right about that. Oh, I'm sorry, Alix, for all of it. I would have done everything I could to prevent it, but it was as if there was an explosive charge laid inside me and someone lit the fuse. It had to happen – it was the last explosion of my madness. It's funny, I feel calm now, not happy but calm, and almost resigned.'

'I'm glad to hear that,' she said, inching towards him on the bench. He put an arm round her shoulders, and kissed the top of her head. He felt her relax in the embrace. 'Oh, Ralph, I wish we could go home.'

'I'll second that,' he said. 'In fact, I shall tackle Mother about it tomorrow.'

'She won't hear of it,' said Alix. 'She doesn't care what we think.'

'Well then, we will leave her here if necessary,' he said.

'Oh, we couldn't – not really,' said Alix, laughing at this extraordinary suggestion.

'No, I suppose not. She'd have us pursued by half the police in Europe. But, my dear,' he said, ruffling her hair, 'I think you should get away at some time. It's right what you said this afternoon – you shouldn't stay with her for ever.'

'And what about you?' she said. 'Shouldn't you get away as well?'

'A man always has more freedom than a woman,' he said. 'I have a business to run, remember? That will keep me away. But you need to have some freedom.'

'What do you suggest?'

'Well, what we said earlier – an education. It's the least you deserve. You should go to university, perhaps.'

'But I know nothing!' she exclaimed. 'One has to study for it.'

'Well, I could help you with that. It would be a pleasure to teach you Greek.'

'Greek – could I do that?'

'Of course, there's no reason why you shouldn't, is there?'

'I suppose not. But it seems such an odd idea. The thought of going to university never crossed my mind. How can I ever persuade them to let me go? I can't imagine that they would agree.'

'If I can convince Father,' he said, 'I think Mother would fall in with it.'

'Your confidence amazes me,' she said. 'You are like a new man.'

'Well, one can't go through something like this without getting something from it.'

'And what's that?'

'That we have to push on, don't you think, Oh, anyway, I don't suppose I'm making any sense, am I?'

'You're making perfect sense,' she said. 'You know, I'm glad we're friends again.'

'So am I,' he said. 'Now, will you come down to the Conversazione Halle with me? There's a Mozart concert there tonight that will be better for me than any sedative that Lewis could give me.'

'Of course, I'd love to come,' she said.

'Good,' he said, getting up and giving her his arm. 'It's very appropriate, actually, to be going to listen to Mozart. I always think of it as the music of reconciliation.'

'Oh, Ralph,' she laughed, as they walked through the garden. 'What a ridiculous generalization!'

4

Settling on a ridge of Blackford Hill, Ralph turned up his coat collar against the wind. To recover his breath from the climb, he took deep, calming breaths of the cold, clear hillside air, finding more comfort in it than he had in the sulphurous inhaling chamber at Baden, which the doctor had so highly recommended. Perhaps there was sulphur enough in the air here, for Edinburgh, despite the clearness of the day, was partially lost in a fug of smoke, as if all the grates which had sat idle all summer, garnished with ferns or paper fans, were now in use again. However, the smoke did not prevent his picking out familiar landmarks with the same pleasure he might have spotted various friends amongst strangers in a crowded room. In the west, rising against the distant rolling line of the Pentlands, were the half-built spires of the Episcopalian Cathedral, while in the east the great craggy mass of Arthur's Seat remained block-like and resolute in the face of the city which seemed determined to expand and rival it in scale. In the foreground broad avenues of grand tenement blocks marched with great confidence, punctuated with bright and handsome church spires making the distant crown of St Giles seem delicate, quaint and old-fashioned.

He found he could not sit still in contemplation for long. The wind sliced through his overcoat and he realized that the balmy air of southern Germany had made him forget the bracing sharpness of Edinburgh air, as a man lulled by the indolent flattery of a woman forgets the brisk wit of another. He was glad to feel it, for it went with all the other signals which told him he was recovering his health. He had been supposed to winter in Cannes, but he knew that only Edinburgh, work and reality could restore him.

That morning he had gone down to the works at Mussel-burgh and had found that the various changes he had made in the fevered weeks before his collapse had borne surprising fruit. The air of torpor had gone and there were even orders in the book. The vaguely artistic advertisements which he had put in the society magazines, about which his father had been resolutely sceptical, had brought in more enquiries than even Ralph had anticipated, particularly from the owners of Highland estates. That vein seemed to be one which the company could well exploit – for were they not better placed to deliver than makers in the south of England?

As he went down the hills, he found himself searching for suitable names for the motors which would appeal to such country sporting gentleman, enjoying the distraction more than he might have imagined. When a clump of thistles by the path caught his attention, he had a moment of inspiration which had never been equalled while trying to write poetry. The Thistle Motor Company . . . that had a ring to it! The name seized him, and like a man finding his faith in a glimpse of heaven, Ralph had a vision of what the company might become – the sort of vision that he knew his father was frequently privy to but which, before that moment, he had been unable to comprehend. Yet now, he felt the sheer intoxication of it and found a hundred ideas flashing through his mind. He suddenly remembered seeing a motor at Baden carrying on the front, like the crest on the helmet of a medieval knight, a small sculpture of a bird. The thistle, which he had seen in silver on the handle of a dirk or cast in iron on a pair of gates, would sit, in gleaming brass, on the front of his motor cars. He laughed aloud at his own enthusiasm but it only held the slightest hint of self-mockery, for he stopped to pick a spray of the thistle, pushing it through his button hole as a badge of his resolution.

Good God, I feel almost cheerful! he realized, as he strolled past the substantial villas of Grange towards Marchmont, and decided, since he was in that part of town, that he would go and call on Sholto and his wife. He had not yet seen them – and had only found out about the marriage when they had got back to Edinburgh, for his mother had been discreetly holding back his letters. It was a great surprise to find his friend had actually married his kitchen garden goddess and was now living like a respectable man at a modest but highly respectable address. It was so unlike Sholto, whom Ralph had always imagined would have been the last man to marry. He had always enjoyed his freedom too much, but perhaps the charms of the woman were too much for even Sholto's resolute independence. She had certainly struck Ralph as very handsome.

Jessie, hearing the bell jangle, came out on to the common stair and pulled the knob on the landing which opened the door to the street. She was not expecting anyone, and supposed it was Sholto back early from the courts, triumphant from his case. She leant over the banister and peered down.

'Did you forget your key?' she called. 'That's not like you – did you win?' And then realized, as the person in the stairwell stopped and looked up at her, evidently rather surprised, that it was not Sholto, that the gloom of the stairway (for the gas had not yet been lit) and a dark overcoat had deceived her. Embarrassed, she retreated to the threshold of the flat and waited for the man to come up, wondering vaguely where she had seen that face before. She hoped it was no one important to Sholto's career when she had made such a bad impression. Hastily, she took off her apron, wiping her hand with it to remove the last traces of flour. Unfortunately, she did not have a chance to dispose of it, and as the man reached the landing, it was still in her hand. But her awkwardness about this lasted only a moment, to be replaced by a worse feeling. She knew now where she had seen the man before – it was Erskine, the fellow who had been going to marry Miss Lennox.

'Mrs Hamilton?' he said. 'I hope this isn't a bad time?'

'No, no, it isn't. It's Mr Erskine, isn't it? I recognized you, you see from . . .' She broke off, wondering if she should remind him of when they last saw each other. She remembered the occasion quite distinctly. It had been at that garden party, when she had been on duty in the dining room. Then he had been immaculate, in light trousers and a frock coat, but she had still thought him gaunt and somewhat ill-favoured. He looked worse now, far thinner, like a bag of bones and skin, despite thick winter clothes. 'You look cold,' she said, without thinking about it. 'Come in, there's a fire in the kitchen.'

She did not stop to think whether barristers' wives received visitors in the kitchen or not. Rather she was moved to compassion by the sight of him, as if he might suddenly crumble to dust if he was not sat down and fed at once. Besides, the kitchen was the only room for which they had acquired any furniture, excepting of course the large brass bedstead which Sholto had bought.

He did not object to her insistence that he come and sit by the fire.

'Do you want a cup of tea?' she said. 'You look as though you could do with one.'

'I should love some tea, Mrs Hamilton,' he said, rubbing his face with his hand. 'I hadn't realized I'd got so cold. I was just up on Blackford Hill, you see.'

'Oh, aye,' she said, setting the kettle on the range. 'That's a lovely spot. I was up there the other day. But I got told off by Sholto. He thinks I'll make myself and the bairn ill if I walk too much, but what harm can it do?'

'I didn't know that you were expecting – congratulations.'

Sholto had obviously been discreet about it and she was glad of it. With luck, only ill-minded wives would count back when their child was born, and then in time, what would two or three months matter?

As she made the tea, she noticed he was looking about him with interest.

'I can't believe how tidy all this is. You must have reformed him, Mrs Hamilton. When we shared digs, you always had to fight your way through the mess . . .'

'Well, you should see his room through there,' said Jessie. 'It's supposed to be a dining room – although, we don't have a stick of furniture for it – but you can't get in there for the books.'

'And thousands of old copies of the *Police Gazette*?'

'Yes,' she laughed. 'But I must confess, Mr Erskine, I've used one or two of those to light the fire.'

'You're a brave woman, Mrs Hamilton,' he said, with a smile. 'He's very attached to those, you know.'

'Don't I just!' she said. 'Now, what will you have to eat? As you can see, you're in luck because it's my baking day,' she added, indicating the racks of cooling cakes on the dresser. 'You can have anything except the seed cake, which is too fresh to cut.'

It was strange how comfortable it felt. Perhaps it is because we both like Sholto that we get along, she reflected,

170

and felt very pleased to be entertaining her first visitor, even if he had been unexpected. For she realized how quiet the last few months had been. She had hardly spoken to a soul above Sholto and a few tradesmen. She had not felt lonely though, for Sholto was all the company she felt she needed. However, that there was pleasure in talking to someone fresh, and seeing someone else enjoy her cakes, could not be denied.

'So you've no furniture, you say?'

'Not much. I don't even know what we need for such a grand place as this. Sholto says that if he wins another two cases we can go and order some things for the drawing room from Brown's.'

'Goodness, you don't want to go there,' he said. 'Don't buy modern furniture, Mrs Hamilton, it's dreadful stuff. Old pieces will cost half the money and look much better.'

'Do you think so?'

'Absolutely,' he said. 'I'm surprised Sholto hasn't taken you to see Finn O'Hara's yet – but then, perhaps it isn't surprising. I think if the wine and the conversation were good enough, he wouldn't notice if he was sitting on an orange box! But you should go – you'd be interested to see his shop, I'm sure.'

'Oh, but I don't know anything about that sort of thing . . .'

'It isn't a question of knowledge,' he said. 'It's a question of natural artistic taste, which I'm sure you have. Anyone who could put a garland of nasturtiums on a plate of cucumber sandwiches, could pick out a good piece of furniture.'

'Did you notice that?' she said, astonished.

'Of course,' he said. 'Surely we were supposed to notice it?'

'Well . . .' For a moment she could not think what to say. When, in the past, she had sent dishes upstairs, beautifully garnished, it had been rather for her own gratification, an attempt to balance the appearance of the dish with its flavour. She had hardly thought that anyone would have paid great attention to it, rather as the ribbon about a parcel

171

would be hastily torn off in the excitement of discovering the actual contents. It would have been unthinkable to send a dish up ungarnished, because that was what etiquette demanded, but it had never occurred to her that anyone would have noticed what she had been doing, let alone remembered it. 'The man who taught me to cook used to say that in his country, cookery was an art, not simply a necessity. I suppose he said it to make me put my whole heart into it.'

'He sounds very inspiring, your mentor.'

'My mentor!' That made her laugh. 'No, Mr Erskine, only grand folks like you and Sholto have mentors! And you wouldn't have called Monsieur Auguste inspiring, if you'd seen him in a filthy temper on a Monday morning.'

'No, perhaps not,' he said with a smile, and then added, as if seized by an idea, 'Perhaps you'd let me take you to O'Hara's, Mrs Hamilton, if you feel nervous about going alone – not that I'd want to intrude.'

'No, no, I'd enjoy that. As I said, I don't know a thing about it, so I'd be glad to have a guide. Sholto told me you were quite a collector, you see.'

What strange things this new life of hers threw up! She could not quite imagine what this Finn O'Hara's shop might be, but it had to be exotic if the name was anything to go by.

'Would tomorrow be too soon?' he asked. 'It's just that I'd arranged to go anyway – that's what made me think of it.'

'Tomorrow will be fine,' she said. 'I'm not exactly busy these days – I've no furniture to polish yet, you see.'

'Well, well, what's all this then?' It was Sholto, bounding in like a large black Labrador. 'What? Is my wife already entertaining strange men?' he said jocularly. 'No – but it's Ralph Erskine! My God, man, I scarcely recognized you. You look as though you have been at death's door,' he added, pumping his hand.

'In a sense,' said Erskine. 'But you're looking magnificently well, Sholto. Marriage obviously suits you.'

'Oh, it does, it does!' he said, pulling Jessie over into his arms and kissing her briefly but intensely. 'Well, this is a piece of luck. To win a case and then to find you here – I'd almost given you up for dead, you know.'

'I've been in Baden Baden, which isn't so different,' said Erskine. 'I'm sorry I haven't written but I didn't know. My doctor ordered I wasn't to read so they hid all my post.'

'Good God, you have been through it, haven't you?'

'Well, I'm past it now,' he said with a dismissive gesture. 'But I should like to make amends for my discourtesy even if it wasn't deliberate. Why don't we all go and dine somewhere? If you've just won a case . . .'

'No, no, I insist you dine here, with us. That's no trouble is it, Jessie?'

'Oh no, there's plenty to go round.'

'Then I'll go and get some wine, shall I?' Ralph said, getting up.

'I'll come with you,' said Sholto. 'There's a grocer on the corner who knows a decent bottle of claret.'

'Well, don't come back too soon,' said Jessie, looking about the disordered kitchen, for she had not cleared up her baking things. She wanted a chance to arrange things properly for this first, impromptu dinner party.

'Then perhaps we'll go across the Links to the Golf, for a dram – that'll give us a decent appetite.'

'Yes, you'll need it. It's pigeon pie.'

'My goodness, Jessie,' exclaimed Sholto, kissing her exuberantly, 'what a genius you are! What man could ask for more – pigeon pie and claret!'

When they had gone, Jessie lit the gas and tried to make the kitchen appear as festive as she could. She covered the table with her only tablecloth, which was a trifle too small but cheerful enough, as it was worked with clumsy cross-stitch roses. The plates did not match and there was nothing remotely grand about the cutlery, but a few flowers in a cracked jug in the centre of the table seemed to turn the eye from these imperfections. Certainly it lacked the magnificence of the buffet table she had arranged at the Quarro, but she felt equally pleased by it, if not more so. It was like a seedling from which would grow some greater hospitality, but a hospitality which would still be the same in its essentials, namely to do with friendship, good humour and love. Perhaps one day she would preside over a large table, with a crowd of friends and children all about it, but she determined she would never forget the peculiar contentment she found in preparing this table.

After they had eaten and drunk their fill, they pulled their chairs around the range and sat basking in the intense heat. Ralph felt like an intruder then, for Jessie sat on a low footstool, leaning against her husband's legs, while he stroked her hair in a careless but affectionate manner. Their comfortable sensuality was not overt, but he sensed its presence with the acuteness peculiar to those who do not share it. He felt his melancholy return as they sat in that quietness (for they were too indolent to speak) and remembered how he had imagined himself in such domestic idleness with Celia. Fate had given that to Sholto who had scarcely looked for it, while he had been denied it. But he no longer felt bitter and could only feel very mildly jealous of their evident happiness. He decided that he must look for happiness in other forms, that it could come only if he was alone and untroubled by the dictates of the heart. The tragedy with Celia and his own mental inability to cope with it, showed him that he could not trust himself to love wisely or well. If he had chosen so badly once, how on earth could he trust his judgement? It was safer to leave well alone and find his pleasure in paintings, music and poetry.

It was odd that when once perhaps he had thought his own appreciation of women was more subtle than Sholto's, that Sholto should choose well (despite the strangeness of his choice, according to conventional standards). Ralph could not have invented a better wife for him than Jessie MacPherson. She seemed to encourage in him all those traits which were charming, but which in the past had been considerably dimmed: his buoyant optimism, his good humour and sheer high spirits, which had intoxicated Ralph more than his first magnum of claret when they had met.

He noticed that Jessie was getting sleepy and so got up from his chair.

'I really ought to go. Just because I scarcely sleep, I shouldn't keep you good people from your beds.'

'One for the road?' asked Sholto.

'No, I mustn't,' said Ralph. 'Thank you, Mrs Hamilton, for a delightful evening. I haven't eaten so much in months.'

'I'm glad to hear that. You look as though you could do with some feeding up,' she said.

'So you must come again,' chimed in Sholto.

'You'll be sick of the sight of me,' he said. 'I shall be here tomorrow for certain – about three, Mrs Hamilton?'

'Oh, yes, to go to O'Hara's,' said Sholto. 'Well, perhaps I'll look in there later. I should be through in court by then. I'd better come to stop her buying up the whole damn' shop – O'Hara is too good a salesman, I'm afraid!'

Ralph got back to Rothesay Terrace at about eleven and was glad to discover that his mother was not waiting anxiously on the stairs but had instead gone to bed. He went to say good night to her.

She was sitting up in bed reading, as was her habit each evening, a portion of the Bible. Seeing her like that made him a little ashamed of himself, for the whiteness of the pillows behind her head seemed to accentuate the lines of age and weariness on her face. He was not the only one who had suffered. He had dragged them all down with him and it showed in her face, although her expression was the one of serene concentration which he had seen when she sat and listened to a sermon.

'Oh, it's you, dear,' she said, looking up. 'You're very late. What have you been up to?'

'I went to see Sholto Hamilton and his bride. They insisted I stay for dinner.'

'I can't quite imagine your friend Hamilton married, you know,' she said, closing her Bible. 'Though perhaps it will be the making of him.'

'Oh, I think so,' said Ralph, sitting down on the bed. 'She's a charming woman.'

Of course his mother did not know that Sholto had married the cook from the Quarro and Ralph did not think it would be prudent to mention it. She would instantly be too prejudiced to receive Jessie, for she had very rigid notions of caste. But if his mother could be persuaded to take Jessie Hamilton up, as it were, he felt it might be a good thing. Mrs Hamilton had struck him as too fine a woman to be wasted in obscurity.

'She was very kind, you know,' he went on. 'I had a seat by the fire all evening and all the pigeon pie I could eat.'

'Pigeon pie,' said his mother, faintly astonished. 'And you ate it?'

'Quite a quantity of it. It was delicious.'

'Oh, that is good news,' she said, patting his arm affectionately. 'She must have a good cook, then.'

'She cooked it herself, Mother – they can't afford a cook yet.'

'I'm glad to hear it,' said his mother. 'It's nice to hear of young people being prudent and not living beyond their means. Perhaps I should call . . .'

'I think she would like that,' said Ralph. 'She doesn't know many people in Edinburgh – she's from the country.'

'Well, I shall have to revise my opinion of your friend Sholto, Ralph. He's obviously more sensible than I thought to marry such a girl.'

5

The next morning, a great basket of flowers was delivered while they were having a late, self-indulgent breakfast. They had found, on Ralph's departure, that he had hardly touched his share of the wine which he had so kindly provided and that they, therefore, had drunk rather more than they intended. Jessie, despite being conditioned by years of early rising, had found it all too easy to stay in bed, and Sholto compounded her laziness by holding her in warm, sleepy arms until ten o'clock. It scarcely mattered, though, for he was not wanted in court until the afternoon and had prepared his brief well in advance. So they had been sitting in their dressing gowns eating oatcakes and honey and exchanging kisses and lovers' banter in a manner which was better suited to a bohemian garret in Paris than an Edinburgh tenement. When Jessie had gone to the door to collect that fabulous bouquet, her hair was still down and her dressing gown had been disarranged by Sholto's caresses. The prim spinster across the landing, on her way to the shops, stared for a moment, and then, as if embarrassed, dodged past the delivery boy so fast that she almost sent the flowers tumbling down the stairs.

'Sholto?' said Jessie, coming back into the flat with the basket.

'Mm?' he said, from the bathroom. 'What is it?'

'Tell me – it's not wrong for a married woman to get flowers, is it?'

'Depends who they're from . . .' he said, coming out of the bathroom, his face still half covered with soap. 'My God!' he exclaimed seeing the flowers, and then in a tone of mild disgust added, 'More money than sense.'

'Who has?'

'Ralph Erskine, you daft girl,' he said. 'Isn't there a note?'

She put the basket down, and bending over it for a moment, noticed that there was a small envelope almost obscured by foliage.

' "Mrs Sholto Hamilton",' she read aloud, relishing the sound of it, for she had not yet received anything addressed to her in her married name. 'Goodness!'

'Haven't you got used to that yet?'

'No,' she said, opening the envelope, feeling the thickness of the paper between her fingers. The note inside was impressively headed with solid, embossed lettering: '3, Rothesay Terrace'.

'From Ralph. I told you so.'

'Why on earth would he send me flowers?'

'Because it's considered good form to send flowers to your hostess.'

'Oh,' said Jessie, scanning the note. ' "My dear Mrs

Hamilton, I hope you will not find these an unacceptable expression of my thanks for a most pleasant evening . . ." Goodness!' she found herself exclaiming as she read. 'I never thought I should get letters like this . . . let alone flowers.' And she sank down on her knees to study them better. 'They are so beautiful.'

'I wonder he didn't send the whole rose bush,' said Sholto, stepping past her with difficulty because she and the flowers were partially blocking his way out of the bathroom. 'It would take up less space.'

She followed him into the bedroom and put the basket down on her small trunk which was sitting under the window. She perched on the edge of the bed, still unable to take her eyes off them.

'Ah, well, if he's taken a fancy to you, Jessie, you'll have to cultivate him,' said Sholto, fastening his cuffs.

'What do you mean?' she said. 'Cultivate?'

'You think I'm being improper, don't you?' He smiled. 'No, I don't mean like that – I mean, make a friend of him. He could be very useful to us. Generous wealthy men are always useful.'

'Sholto!' She found she was shocked. 'But I thought he was your friend. You couldn't ask a friend to give you money, surely.'

'Why not? If we need it and he doesn't, I can't see the harm in it, especially when he's so happy to part with it. That's the trick of it, of course. Just think, my dear, in a few years' time there will be the question of our boy's education – good schools don't come cheap, you know.'

'That would be like taking charity,' she said. 'I should have thought you wouldn't want to be beholden to anyone, like that.'

'My dear,' he said, 'we have to be practical, don't we? Beggars cannot be choosers.'

'Oh, we're hardly that,' she said, amazed that Sholto could think their life beggarly.

'You may not think so now, my sweet, but when you've dined a few times at Rothesay Terrace, you'll feel differently.' He bent down and kissed her but she took little pleasure in it, for his tone and manner seemed patronizing, a thing which she had not observed in him before. 'Just you wait and see,' he added, confirming this disagreeable impression.

'I'm not a child, Sholto,' she said. 'Do you think I'm so daft as to have my head filled with nonsense because I see a few grand folks? I know that I'm damn' lucky to have all this – I'm surprised that you could think that I could be so greedy as to want anything else.'

'My God!' he said, rolling his eyes. 'I've married a saint! So you promise you shan't be bothered when I don't bring a penny home for weeks and we have to live on boiled potatoes? You won't complain?'

'No, no, of course not!' she protested, aware she was now being teased but not much bothered by it. It brought back the Sholto she liked, the Sholto who made her laugh. 'If we have to live in the gutter, husband, so be it.' And she made a gesture of mock deference. 'But really, my love,' she added, 'you mustn't think I shall always be wanting more than I can have. I'm quite content with what I've got.'

This time when he kissed her she did not mind in the least. Rather, it was such a protracted embrace that they almost fell back into bed, until Sholto remembered that a solicitor with a stack of briefs for him (or so he hoped) was expecting to meet him at twelve o'clock. So he rushed off, leaving Jessie to contemplate at her leisure Ralph Erskine's extraordinary gift of flowers.

It took her quite a while to decide what she would wear for her excursion with Ralph. At four months pregnant, most of her old clothes were becoming unwearable, her stays definitely so. It seemed she had nothing respectable, let alone remotely smart, but remembering what she had said to Sholto about not craving pretty things, she made do with what she had: a navy serge skirt and a loose smock-blouse in plum-coloured wool which she had bought from a drapers, intending it for later in her pregnancy. Now, however, belted loosely, it looked at least neat, although certainly not fashionable. Her coat was decidedly ancient, but it had stood the test of time better than might have been expected with its silk revers giving it a class it perhaps did not fully deserve. Her hat, at least, she could be proud of. It was the plain navy felt which she had bought for her wedding. It had been expensive for such a simple hat, but she had seen that in its plainness lay all its style. Its only trimming was the broad band of satin which finished in a large bow at one side, but its chief charm came from the shape of the brim which stuck up at the back, like a man's hat. Wearing this hat, Jessie felt quite able to conquer the world. She enjoyed its effect in the little glass over the washbasin in the bathroom, not as a coquette might enjoy her reflection, but in that strange sense which one sometimes has when wearing clothes different from those normally worn; that sense of seeing an interesting stranger in the glass and not oneself at all.

The bell rang just as she was putting on her gloves, and to save Ralph the climb she locked her front door and went down to meet him. He looked startled by the sight of her, as if he was not used to women being ready to go anywhere on time. Probably his mother and his sister, with their expensive, elaborate clothes, were never punctual.

He was dressed very differently from the previous day, in a frock coat, and carried a glossy silk hat.

'I'm not late, am I?' he said, reaching for his watch fob. 'If I am, I do apologize. I've been lunching with a banker, and you know they have no sense of time.'

She did not, of course, but said, 'No, of course you aren't late. I'm just impatient, I suppose.'

'Well, I hope you won't be disappointed,' he said, handing her into the carriage. 'In fact, I'm sure you won't be.'

The carriage, like the flowers, surprised her. It was clear, as she settled in its comfortable depths, that this was the family carriage, brought because she, as a woman, could not be expected to ride in a hansom. Last night he had come and gone on foot, like an ordinary man, but now that a woman was involved, it seemed that an entirely new set of rules had to be taken into consideration. She had never thought she might be subject to this unwritten, unspoken code. Sholto's small acts of gallantry she imagined had been prompted by love, but this man did not love her, yet he sent flowers and treated her with extraordinary deference, as if she was to be sheltered from every unpleasantness.

As they drove in that carriage along the long road which dissected the Meadows, through avenues of trees in their magnificent autumn show, she began to understand the temptation of such luxuries. It would be all too easy, as Sholto had suggested, to become accustomed to them; to demand them as necessities, when they were really superfluous. She would happily have walked, or taken a tram, for it was a fine, bright afternoon and she liked to observe street life. However, she realized that Mr Erskine, for all his lack of stuffiness in many ways, would have felt himself to be reneging on his duty if she were not taken from door to door in the quiet sanctity of a private carriage. It did not matter that he knew who she was and how she had once earned her living. To him, she was the wife of a friend who therefore deserved to be treated with the same consideration as if she had been the only daughter of the Lord Lyon, King of Arms, himself! The feeling which this gave her was indescribably pleasant, and she sat back wondering quite what she had done to deserve to be so fortunate as to be the wife of Sholto Hamilton.

'Where is Mr O'Hara's shop then?' she asked, for she had only heard him instruct the driver to go to Mr O'Hara's.

'Raeburn Place in Stockbridge – do you know it?'

'Oh, yes,' she said. 'I used to walk down to St Bernard's Well sometimes, when I had an afternoon off.'

'It's lovely there, isn't it?' he said, and then added with a vague sigh, 'Yes, I almost bought a house in Ann Street this summer, you know, for when . . . er . . . we were married.' There was reluctance in his words, but also she sensed he needed to speak of it. 'It had a lilac tree at the front,' he went on wistfully. 'I should dearly have liked to have lived there but – well, you know the rest, I suppose, Mrs Hamilton?'

'Yes, and I'm very sorry. It was a dreadful thing, but I

shan't be so unkind as to say "you'll get over it" as people always do.'

'I think I shall always be a haunted man,' he said, after a reflective pause. 'But at least now I know I shall struggle on. It's been touch and go at times. My poor mother – God only knows what I've put her through with all my antics. You women have an extraordinary capacity for forgiveness, I think, and tolerance. Her patience, and my sister's for that matter, was remarkable. I'm sure I didn't deserve it.'

'It's not a question of deserving anything,' said Jessie. 'It's just that they love you, and want the best for you – that's what makes a family a family, wouldn't you say?'

'I would say that I think my friend Hamilton is a lucky fellow to have found you,' he said, and then continued in a brighter vein, 'Tell me, are you planning a great dynasty of young Hamiltons? I think he expects six or seven sons at least.'

'The wretch just wants to ruin my figure!' she said brightly, and then was conscious that it had not exactly been a ladylike remark. However, he laughed and did not look remotely shocked. How can he be, really? she told herself. He's known Sholto too long for that.

By this time they had stopped in Raeburn Place, outside a double-fronted shop. The atmosphere of the place, she could see at once as she climbed out of the carriage, was discreet and refined. She gave up any hope of bargain hunting, seeing that one window displayed only a pair of blue and white pots whilst the other held a single oil painting, displayed in solitary splendour on an easel. Ralph Erskine's idea of inexpensive furniture was evidently very different from her own.

The sparseness of the windows gave no idea of the interior. Jessie could not imagine she had ever seen such a crush of wonderful things before, not even at the Quarro, for there they had been spaced out with elegant decorum. Here everything was packed together as if it was worthless trash. Her astonishment as she looked about her must have been obvious, for Erskine said, 'Yes, it's a marvellous sight, isn't it? I don't know where he finds such things.'

'I know that voice!' said someone, coming from the back of the shop. 'Ralph, my dear fellow – it's good of you to come. Nancy's waiting for you upstairs with your godson, but I think we should have a little drop . . .'

'Later Finn, later,' cut in Erskine. 'Mrs Hamilton, may I present Mr Finn O'Hara, the proprietor of this extraordinary establishment? Finn, this is Sholto's bride, Mrs Hamilton.'

'Mrs Hamilton, indeed!' he said, taking her hand and shaking it vigorously. 'Well, well, this is a surprise. We shall be drinking toasts all afternoon.'

'I don't think the ladies will thank us if we get drunk,' said Erskine. 'Besides, we've some business with you first, if we may. Sholto, being such an impetuous bridegroom, has left poor Mrs Hamilton without any furniture to speak of. I wondered if you'd come across some good, moderately priced pieces recently.'

'I've just the thing, Ralph,' said O'Hara ecstatically. 'Do you like Biedermeier, Mrs Hamilton?'

Jessie felt a terrible pang of embarrassed ignorance. Still, it was better not to try and conceal it.

'I'm afraid, Mr O'Hara, that I shouldn't know Biedermeier from Adam,' she said, a remark which caused O'Hara to laugh explosively. Terrified lest she had said something very foolish, she glanced at Mr Erskine for reassurance.

'He thinks you've made a pun,' he murmured. 'Adam is also a style of furniture.'

'It isn't!' she exclaimed, and could not help laughing herself.

They followed Mr O'Hara into the back of the shop and across a courtyard into a large, glass-roofed warehouse at the rear. He pulled off a few dust sheets to display a large sofa, with opulent curves, a striped red and white cover and a wooden frame in a pale, bright wood that she had never seen before.

'It's Swedish – about seventy years old. Of course, some people say this sort of thing is hideous, but I like it. I like the craftsmanship. It's good work, wouldn't you say, Ralph?' said O'Hara, stroking the broad wooden expanse which rose above the cushioned part of the sofa.

'What's the wood?' he asked.

'Satinwood – isn't it a superb colour? Do you know, I think that in a dozen years' time it will be as sought after as a Chippendale-style carver is now. Everything comes back into fashion eventually – it is extraordinary, but it does.'

'Well, Mrs Hamilton, is this the sort of thing you had in mind?' asked Erskine.

'I don't think I had anything in mind,' she said. 'But I do like it. It's cheerful and . . .' She hesitated, fearing she might be committing herself. It would probably cost far more than they could afford.

'There's a desk as well,' said O'Hara. 'A nice piece for a drawing room.'

This time the dust sheets hid a high, bow-fronted chest, with pillars at the corners, all made in the same pale wood. O'Hara pulled open a drawer, which was in fact a fold down flap which made the desk top. Set at the back were a dozen or so tiny drawers with handles like ivory buttons. Jessie thought at once of Mrs Lennox's writing desk, with its little vases of flowers, its letters stuck in the slender pigeon holes and its rose-patterned ink stand. She shook her head. She could not think she would ever have a use for such a desk. She could do the household accounts just as well sitting at the kitchen table.

'Don't you like it?' said O'Hara. 'It's a strange piece, I admit. It is extremely plain but I think it has a certain . . .'

'Oh, no, I do like it, Mr O'Hara,' said Jessie. 'Don't misunderstand me – but I can't think I'd ever need a thing like that.'

'You should indulge yourself, Mrs Hamilton,' he said. 'These pieces are not expensive now, I assure you. But they will be valuable. You should follow your good instincts. It'll be a fine investment which in thirty years' time your husband will thank you for.'

'Now, Finn, don't pressurize Mrs Hamilton,' said Ralph Erskine.

'It's not pressure, Ralph, it's the truth. Now, look at this little sofa table, Mrs Hamilton. It's twenty years earlier, and

184

a mite more delicate, but I think it suits the sofa . . .'

He was like a conjuror, pulling off dust sheets and producing ever more elegant and extraordinary things. Here were a dozen tablet back dining chairs, inlaid with a Greek key pattern in brass; there, a mahogany book case with acanthus leaf carving; here, a Crown Derby dinner service in deep red and gold; there, a pair of gilt, chinoiserie girandoles . . . By the end of it, she felt overwhelmed.

'Please, Mr O'Hara,' she remonstrated. 'No more – I need some time to think.' She sank down into the nearest chair, feeling if she did not sit, she might fall. Her coat fell open, revealing the delicate but still obvious bulge of her unborn child.

'My dear,' said O'Hara, noticing it, 'I'm so sorry – Ralph, what were you thinking of? You should have stopped me. Now then, Mrs Hamilton, can you bear to climb a flight of stairs? My wife is upstairs.'

'Oh, really, I'm all right,' she protested. 'I just felt a little tired – all these lovely things . . .'

'Well, you can think about them upstairs,' he said firmly, offering her his arm. Jessie wondered if he was the sort of man who never let his wife out of the house during a pregnancy. Some men, she knew, became over solicitous.

She let him take her upstairs and found herself ushered into a large drawing room which ran the whole width of the building. Three great windows flooded the place with afternoon sun of such autumnal intensity that she felt the warmth of it embrace her and saw the occupants cast in that beautiful light as if she were looking through a golden lens. At one window a woman was sitting, holding a baby in her outstretched arms while it kicked and gurgled. It was a powerful sight and made Jessie feel a surge of joy at the pleasure which would soon be hers. For all the inconveniences and worries of pregnancy could not destroy one whit of the excitement she felt at the prospect of that new life growing inside her.

The woman, seeing she had visitors, turned towards them and smiled, drawing the child back to her breast with a gesture which Jessie understood as instinctively protective.

'Nancy, my dear,' said Erskine, crossing the room and kissing the woman on each cheek. The child, angry at this intrusion, at once began to wail. 'What did I do?' he said, stepping back in alarm.

'Now, come on, Frankie,' said O'Hara, taking the baby from his wife and attempting to pacify him. 'What sort of a way is that to greet your godfather, eh?'

'Don't worry, Finn,' said Erskine. 'I shan't cut him out of my will. Nancy, this is Mrs Sholto Hamilton.'

'Who should be sitting down,' said O'Hara, indicating a chair.

'He looks a handful, Mrs O'Hara,' said Jessie, as Finn failed to pacify the child. 'How old is he?'

'Just two months,' said Mrs O'Hara, getting up and taking the child back from her husband. 'But it's amazing how big he is – and how noisy he can be. Just like his father, really . . .'

'Something tells me, Ralph, that these two ladies are about to have a baby conversation. Do you think they would excuse us?' said Finn O'Hara.

'Yes, yes!' laughed Mrs O'Hara. 'Get away with you both – but, Ralph, make sure he doesn't drink too much.' When the men had gone, she added, 'Poor Ralph – I don't think he's ready for babies yet. He looked terrified, don't you think?'

'I suppose he did,' said Jessie, suddenly nervous to be alone with this strange woman. She did not know if she could manage drawing-room conversation and could not guess what sort of a woman her hostess might be. She was not a Mrs Lennox, certainly, for she seemed too direct to have any such airs. The charming Irish brogue, albeit refined, was reassuring but she was expensively dressed, in a fashion which made Jessie very keenly aware of her own shabbiness.

'Are you expecting?' she said, with a frankness that startled Jessie. 'Oh, I'm sorry, Mrs Hamilton, isn't that rude of me? What can you think of me? But, you know, ever since I had this little chap, I know – I can see it. It's so funny, don't you think?'

'Four months,' said Jessie.

'I knew it!' exclaimed Nancy delightedly. 'Goodness, it's like having second sight. All these things you never notice or understand until you become a mother. Doesn't it just change everything?'

Jessie found herself nodding, her anxiety vanishing. In a rush of words they talked, discussing a thousand trivialities, tallying experience with experience. They laughed, exchanged confidences, each taking turns to dandle the child. In short, they indulged in that curious freemasonry peculiar to women, which enables strangers to talk with an intimacy which would surprise any man who might over-hear it.

6

I'm like a traveller in a foreign country, Jessie thought as she looked about the drawing room at Rothesay Terrace. Yes, that's what it is – I have to remember that. I am only different from all these people, not better nor worse than them, only different. However, these brave thoughts did little to relieve her sense of intimidation. She could not quite rid herself of the conviction that her fellow dinner guests were in fact her judge and jury, who in one cruel glance would be able to condemn her as an upstart and an impostor.

Of course, she knew that to have got to this point, to be standing with a glass of sherry in Mrs Erskine's drawing room, was to have achieved a great deal. There had been certain arduous rituals to perform before the honour of a dinner invitation could be obtained. Firstly, she had had to be 'At home' on a certain afternoon, so that Mrs Erskine could pay a call. The dust had hardly settled from the delivery of the furniture from Finn O'Hara's shop when this portentous event took place, and Jessie had felt a little like a fraud sitting on that glorious sofa, rather as if she had merely hired the furniture for the occasion. She could not quite believe that it belonged to her.

Although the visit was brief, less than fifteen minutes, Jessie had sensed she was under a more intense scrutiny than she had ever been by an employer. Mrs Erskine had been calm and extremely polite, but Jessie felt that her every movement, her every word, was evaluated with a ruthlessness which the woman's dignified demeanour did not at once suggest. When she had gone, having nibbled at a madeleine and drunk half a cup of tea, Jessie had been downcast, convinced she had failed utterly. However, the grapevine brought back the news that Mrs Erskine had found her charming and unaffected. So three days later, clutching her brand new calling card case, Jessie had returned the call. That she had not committed any major faux-pas soon became evident when the invitation to dine landed on the door mat.

Sholto had been delighted, especially when he had learnt from Ralph that Lord Fergusson would be present. It was important, he explained, for aspiring Tory candidates to be in favour with Fergusson. 'He has real influence in the Party,' he had added. 'If a seat comes up, he's the man to know.' That Sholto could even consider the possibility of contesting a seat seemed to her extraordinary, but she said nothing, imagining that she still understood too little of his world and its opportunities. For he was a talented man, that was undeniable, and who knew how far he might go? It was certainly not her place to object. 'You'd better get yourself some evening dresses,' he said. 'It might be a busy winter.'

She had only ordered one – the extravagance of the single, midnight blue silk velvet dress had been shocking enough to her frugal habits. But Sholto had not blenched on being shown the bill – he had only wondered if the colour was not a little too sober. 'What, would you rather I made an exhibition of myself in something gaudy?' she had said. 'I chose this because it's discreet. I don't want to draw attention to the fact I'm expecting, do I?'

At that moment, remembering what she had said, she

wished that the generous folds of the dress might in fact be the folds of one of those magic cloaks one finds in fairy tales which make the wearer invisible. That would be discreet enough! she thought, unable now to subdue the terrible nervousness which had gripped her, for Mrs Erskine was approaching with a strange woman, doubtless the first of many to whom she must be presented. If Mrs Erskine had seemed frightening, it was nothing in comparison to the fears that this autocratic female produced in Jessie. She was tall and very broad, dressed in tight yellow satin the colour of custard. Her face was somewhat haggard and was not improved by the lorgnette which she lifted to her eyes in order to stare pointedly at Jessie.

'Miss Fergusson, may I present Mrs Sholto Hamilton? Mrs Hamilton, this is Miss Fergusson, Lord Fergusson's sister.'

'Haven't we met before, Mrs Hamilton?' said Miss Fergusson, as they shook hands. 'Have you recently come to Edinburgh – I feel sure we've met in the country somewhere.'

'Oh, I don't think so,' said Jessie, surprised at the woman's conviction. 'I'm sure I would have remembered.'

'But I never forget a face, my dear. Especially not one as pretty as yours, Mrs Hamilton,' she went on blithely. 'Tell me, do you know the Fordyces? I feel sure it was there I saw you – at their place in Perthshire.'

'No, I'm afraid it can't have been – I don't know them at all.' She hated to disappoint. Sholto would want her to make a good impression on Lord Fergusson's sister, and here she was doing nothing but point out that she was mistaken.

'Oh, well then, if you're quite sure, Mrs Hamilton,' she said, slightly put out. However, Jessie could not feel really distressed for long. Rather, she felt her confidence grow. If she resembled someone that Miss Fergusson might have met at someone's place in Perthshire (and how grand that sounded!), then she felt that her appearance and manner must be convincing enough. It was becoming almost possible to relax.

189

'Is that your husband talking to my brother?' went on Miss Fergusson.

'Yes, it is.' It had not taken Sholto long to stake his quarry.

'I hear he is doing very well at the bar,' said Miss Fergusson. 'They all speak of him as quite a rising man.'

'Well, I hope so.'

'Ah, yes, my dear,' said Miss Fergusson, 'you do appreciate that a man can only go as far as he would in his career if his womenfolk support him. I've yet to see a successful candidate without a good wife behind him.'

'I'm afraid I don't know anything about politics,' said Jessie, 'but I should like my husband to succeed in whatever he sets out to do. If I can help him, I will, in whatever little way I can.'

'You should not underestimate a woman's influence,' said Miss Fergusson. 'You would be surprised at how much of importance goes on in the drawing room amongst the ladies. I tell you, my dear, all this agitation for women's suffrage is nonsense – women have more power in the land than many realize. We don't need the vote when we have our husbands and brothers to do it for us. You should encourage your husband, Mrs Hamilton, you will find his political activities much to your taste.'

Jessie remembered Sholto's words about Fergusson: 'If there's a seat coming up, he's the man to know', and wondered if Miss Fergusson really had her brother's ear on the subject as she had implied. They certainly looked very alike; their faces so very much of the same stamp; their figures and gestures even resembled each other's with only slight variations to mark the difference in sex. No wonder they have never married. They are too close to let another soul in, she reflected, as she glanced from them to another brother and sister who had just come into the room, namely Ralph and Alexandra Erskine who, by contrast, seemed to exemplify just how different siblings could be. Although they were both tall and thin (in fact the whole family looked as if they had not an ounce of flesh to spare and that they had never had a square meal in their lives, despite the very considerable luxury which obviously surrounded them), here any similarity ended. For where he was dark and gaunt and vaguely melancholy, she was bright, fair, and winningly beautiful. Jessie had not noticed it so at the Quarro where she had been just a face in the crowd, hidden under a picture hat, but now in the simplicity of a white evening dress, as she walked amongst her mother's guests, shaking hands and smiling, she was the living embodiment of charm and poise. Jessie wondered when she might learn to walk into a room with such confidence and then decided that it must be a thing one is born with, like a talent for music.

'Now there is a girl who should marry well,' remarked Miss Fergusson. 'If her mother put her mind to it, Alexandra could be a duchess.'

'Do you think she'd want to be?' said Jessie, wondering if a girl like that could be drawn by the mere lure of a title. She looked too high-minded and independent.

This discussion went no further because Miss Erskine, who had been proceeding round the drawing room rather in the manner of a royal progress, had reached them.

'My dear Alexandra,' said Miss Fergusson, 'how well you are looking. Your stay in Baden Baden must have done wonders.'

'Oh, no, it wasn't Baden, Miss Fergusson,' she said. 'It's the brisk air of Edinburgh – Ralph and I realized that we'd been half asleep there when we got back here. I think they should make Auld Reekie a health resort. It would be so much more exciting for the invalids than Baden. And it's much more bracing.'

'Well, I suppose it was rather late in the season there,' said Miss Fergusson, 'and somewhat dull for a girl your age. Fergusson and I always go to Marienbad. Which do you prefer, Mrs Hamilton?'

'I wouldn't know,' said Jessie. 'I've never left Scotland.'

'There's patriotism for you!' said Miss Erskine with a triumphant smile, and then added, 'I'm so sorry – we haven't been introduced, have we? But I do seem to know you from somewhere . . .'

'That's exactly what I said to Mrs Hamilton,' interposed

Miss Fergusson. 'But she denies it.'

'Well, I do know you by sight, Miss Erskine,' Jessie was forced to confess. 'From the Quarro . . .'

'Oh, you know the Lennoxes?'

'Very slightly.'

Jessie found it extraordinary that Ralph Erskine had told his family nothing of her origins. Perhaps such trifles did not matter to him and his own sense of chivalry lifted her automatically to their level. But she still felt awkward. If this girl made the right connection she would be exposed.

'Yes, you were at the garden party, weren't you?' she said. 'You would have been sorry to have missed Sholto, I imagine.'

'Well, we were to be married a week after that, so I could bear to be without him when I knew I would soon be spending all my life with him.'

Miss Fergusson looked startled by this frankness, and Jessie would have been embarrassed at her own loss of reserve had not Miss Erskine smiled and said, 'It all sounds terribly romantic.'

'You should be careful what you say to her, Mrs Hamilton,' said Miss Fergusson. 'One shouldn't encourage young girls to have romantic follies – they end up throwing themselves away on worthless men.' And with that somewhat crushing remark, she went away.

'Goodness,' said Alexandra Erskine.

'I should tell you,' said Jessie, 'she thinks you should marry a duke.'

Alix laughed at this and said, 'How ridiculous she is! I think she genuinely believes she controls the entire Tory Party through her beloved brother.'

'Yes, she told me.'

'I can't think why my mother invites them – any of these people really,' added Alix. 'Well, you and Sholto excepted – but don't you think this is a terribly dull crowd? One can't have a sensible conversation with anyone.' And then she added, as a little coda to her outburst, 'I say, shall we go and sit down, Mrs Hamilton? Then we can talk properly – away from all this small talk? You see, I've got terribly strict instructions from my brother to see you are all right. And I want to know all about you and Sholto – I can't believe he was such a dark horse about getting married.'

'Well, there are various reasons for that,' said Jessie, throwing caution to the wind in the face of such warmth. They had sat down on a large sofa, covered in rose-coloured damask, with high sides which hid the rest of the room from them. It was the perfect place for confidences and Jessie had the instinctive feeling that she could trust this girl. 'You see, there are certain things about me that your brother hasn't told you.'

'Oh yes?' She seemed fascinated. 'What?'

'Well, you know you said you recognized me?'

'Mmm?'

'Well, do you remember a morning at the Quarro, when your brother asked Mrs Lennox if he could take Miss Celia to the ball . . .'

She did not need to say anything more for the girl's jaw dropped and then, after a moment, she collected herself and said: 'MacPherson! Of course – yes, I remember. Sir Hector gave you that terrible interrogation. I squirmed for you then, you know. I wanted to hit him.'

'So did I.'

'Goodness! And Sholto was there all the time. And you . . . well, I don't know what to say.'

'I hope I haven't shocked you.'

'No, no, it's the most marvellous thing I've heard for ages. I just wish Ralph had told me. He thinks I'm still a child who has to be protected. But it's so romantic. No wonder Sholto kept quiet, though. It must have been awful for you, having to keep it all a secret.'

'Well, being in love makes a lot of things bearable.'

'How brave you are!' exclaimed Alix. 'A new woman.'

'I don't think so,' laughed Jessie.

'But it's remarkable. Do you know, I've been reading so much lately and finding how much there is that's wrong with society. We're all so caste ridden and prejudiced, and then you two come along and do something magnificent like this!' And carried away by her rhetoric, she leant forward and kissed Jessie. 'I salute you!'

'I don't think we meant to start a revolution,' said Jessie, unable to prevent herself from laughing a little at Alexandra's enthusiasm. 'We just fell in love.'

'You must come to the suffrage meeting next week,' said Alix very decidedly. 'You simply must.'

'Oh, Alix, there you are.' It was Mrs Erskine, looking somewhat flustered. 'Do excuse us, Mrs Hamilton, but I'm afraid that there's been a bit of a . . . oh dear . . .'

'Mother, what is it?'

'You won't believe what's happened,' she said. 'I scarcely believe myself. That Mrs Lord the agency sent . . . the one with all those marvellous references. She's just left! Can you believe these people! Have they no sense of good workmanship – in half an hour I have to serve dinner to twenty people, if there is any dinner to serve.'

'Well, Mrs Erskine, I think I can help you, if you let me,' said Jessie.

'Thank you Mrs Hamilton, but there's really nothing one can do, unless someone can produce a cook out of a top hat!'

'She *is* a cook, Mother,' said Alexandra Erskine.

'Don't be silly, dear.'

'It's true, Mrs Erskine. I was a professed cook before I married.'

'Yes, and a jolly good one. She was the cook at the Quarro.'

'Oh!' was all Mrs Erskine managed to say, staring at Jessie with some astonishment.

'I know it's a shock, Mrs Erskine, and I'm sorry. I don't like pretending that I'm something I'm not. If you want me to go, I'll go, but I'd rather stay and help you. If it was forty people you had at table, I could cook for them.'

'My dear,' said Mrs Erskine quietly, 'I shouldn't dream of sending you away. It would be unthinkable. Thank you, I should like you to help very much.'

'Excellent!' said Alexandra. 'Then we'll go and get started. You'd better think of an excuse for Mrs Hamilton, Mother.'

'That shouldn't be difficult in my condition,' said Jessie.

'Oh, goodness,' said Mrs Erskine. 'I hadn't thought of that. Won't it be too much for you? I should hate to think . . .'

'I'm very strong, believe me,' said Jessie. 'Now can you lend me an apron?'

Alix soon realized that true cooks, like true seamen, are never as happy as when they are pursuing their passion. Mrs Hamilton had seemed diffident and quietly ill at ease in the drawing room, but the moment the challenge of cooking the dinner at such short notice was presented her, she seemed roused, excited even, at the prospect. The task in hand was daunting to Alix, especially as she realized, taking Mrs Hamilton downstairs, how unfamiliar the kitchen regions were to her, although they were part of her own home. But Mrs Hamilton looked around confidently enough at the unfamiliar layout, although she was not entirely pleased with what she saw.

'No wonder the woman cut and ran,' she remarked. 'This is pretty chaotic, considering. What's the menu, then?' she added, directing her question at one of the kitchen maids.

'I cudna tell you,' she said vacantly. 'She didna tell us nothing. She was too drunk to say.'

'Well, it looks like we'll have to do the best we can. How long has that roast been on?' she said, going over to the range. 'Too long, but I dare say we can do something with it. What on earth was she thinking of here? It's a good piece of venison almost ruined. Was it marinated?'

'I cudna say.'

'Try and remember, Jane,' said Alix. 'Mrs Hamilton needs to know.'

'I told you, Miss Alix, she never told us anything.'

'It doesn't matter, I'll find out soon enough,' said Jessie. 'Will you help me move this hastener – Jane, is it?'

'Aye, Mum.'

'My name's Jessie, all right?' said Mrs Hamilton.

Alix watched as they dragged the strange metal structure away from the range. It reminded her of a tin bath up ended, and inside, as they turned it away from the fire, she saw a large piece of roast meat suspended on a rotating hook. She was astonished. She had never seen how it was done before.

'At least with venison you've not too much fat to worry about,' Mrs Hamilton was saying. 'Now, where are your large ashets?' With complete unconcern for her dress, she lifted the rotating hook with the great joint dangling from it. The juices spattered her apron front, and Alix could not prevent herself exclaiming: 'Be careful! What about your dress – the velvet will be ruined.'

'Rather that than the meat,' she said pragmatically.

'You are remarkable,' said Alix.

'Not in the least,' she said, laying the joint on the plate. 'I've just learnt a trade like anyone else. Now, Jane, will you put some slices of fat bacon across it and wrap it in paper – cover it well, mind – and then put it in the warming oven, right at the bottom. It should be all right. We'll do a redcurrant and orange sauce for it – do you know that? No, then I'll teach you it. You'll find it so useful. Where are the larders?'

Alix felt not the slightest inclination to go upstairs and rejoin her mother's guests. Mrs Hamilton's performance in the kitchen was too stimulating. She had always imagined cookery as a lowly activity, beneath the notice of those with intellectual pretensions. But watching Jessie Hamilton take command of that kitchen was like watching a master mariner take command of a great four-masted galleon. Her enthusiasm was infectious and soon Alix found she had discarded her gloves and tied a tea towel about her waist in order to perform the humblest duties of a vegetable maid.

'No brussels sprouts larger than my thumb nail,' Jessie had commanded, and Alix, with clumsy but enthusiastic fingers, struggled to meet this requirement. She had watched with some amazement the way Jessie had chopped shallots for the fish course. She would never have tackled the job with such a large knife, but Jessie had a knack of flashing it over the vegetables with devastating rapidity. When Alix expressed her admiration, she just said, 'Well, it would be better with my own knife – but, naturally, I didn't bring it with me.'

'So cooks get attached to their knives?'

'Oh, yes. Monsieur Auguste, the man who taught me, gave me mine. He bought it in France – they don't make decent knives in this country, you know. There's never enough weight in the steel.'

'Oh, don't tell my father that,' said Alix. 'He would tell you that Erskine steel is the best in the world.'

'Let him make a decent knife, and I'll believe him,' said Jessie. 'Now Jane, how's the soup coming on?'

'Nearly done.' She had been laboriously pushing it through a sieve. 'We're no going to tammy it, are we?'

'No, there isn't time for that. So long as it tastes all right. Let's get it on the stove again. They'll be going in in a minute. Shouldn't you be up there with them, Miss Erskine?'

'I should,' said Alix, 'but I don't really want to go. I'd much rather help you.'

'You won't say that when we get to the washing up, Miss,' said Jane, and made them both laugh.

'Well, Mother,' announced Alix, as they returned to the drawing room, 'wasn't she just splendid!'

Mrs Erskine was sitting alone now, for it was well past eleven and most of the guests, Jessie assumed, would have gone home. But on seeing them she jumped up and came over to them. Taking both of Jessie's hands in hers, she said, 'My dear Mrs Hamilton, I can't think where I can begin to thank you for this. I feel quite ashamed that I let you do it, you know – it's almost unforgivable, I think, to invite someone to dinner and then expect them to cook it.'

'Oh, it was nothing, really, Mrs Erskine,' said Jessie, knowing that she had enjoyed herself downstairs far more than she would have in the dining room.

'But it was such a marvellous meal – far better than that woman could have produced, I'm sure. Your husband is a very lucky man, Mrs Hamilton. You look quite fashed, my dear. Come and sit down and have some tea. And you, Alix, you were naughty staying down there all evening, but you were quite right, I think – you couldn't possibly have deserted Mrs Hamilton. And of course,' she continued confidentially, 'with two of you gone, the table didn't look so unbalanced, so it was rather fortunate really.'

'You see then, Mother,' said Alix, 'Jessie has saved us all from social disaster.'

'It looks like it,' Jessie smiled. 'But, honestly, I should have thought it would have been the other way round. I was so frightened that I would do something wrong up here that it was quite a relief to get back to what I knew.'

'There was no need to be frightened,' said Mrs Erskine. 'You seemed perfectly poised to me. But I do understand how you feel. You see, we are not really very fond of entertaining. We only do it when we must – out of duty. That is why I was so upset when that woman packed her bags – I simply didn't know what I should do. We were so lucky you were here, Mrs Hamilton.'

At that moment, Ralph and Mr Erskine came in, followed by Sholto and Lord Fergusson. The latter was about to leave, because he had draped his evening cloak around his shoulders.

'You must forgive me for being such a stubborn guest, Mrs Erskine,' he said. 'The trouble is that the conversation at this house is always too good. One never wants to leave. Not to mention the food – truly, that was an exquisite dinner.'

'Then, Lord Fergusson,' said Alix brightly, 'you can congratulate the cook herself. Mrs Hamilton here saved the evening for us when our cook gave notice.'

'Madam,' said Lord Fergusson gravely, 'you are to be congratulated,' and shook her hand. He seemed quite sincere and Jessie felt pleased, knowing that Sholto was keen to impress the man.

'We really should be going too, shouldn't we?' said Sholto. 'You must be tired, my dear.'

Suddenly it seemed as if he could not bear to stay a moment longer, and with an almost indecent haste they left. He bundled her into the hansom with a perfunctoriness that surprised but did not greatly bother her. She still had the Erskines' compliments and kind words to beguile her. She had not imagined people who were so wealthy and powerful could be so kind, so simple; indeed, so similar to herself! I shall have to see what Nancy says about them, she reflected, for they had become firm friends. Perhaps she'd like to come to this suffrage meeting with us?

She realized as they drove home how quiet Sholto had become, how he would not be drawn on any subject. Perhaps he's tired, she thought. But she had imagined he might be more voluble, especially when he appeared to have had Lord Fergusson's ear for quite a time.

'What did Lord Fergusson say to you then?' she asked, as they drew up in Marchmont Road.

'Don't you talk to me about Lord Fergusson!' he said, sharply, jumping out of the cab. He did not wait to help her so she scrambled out after him, astonished by his sudden briskness of manner.

'What?' she said, while he paid the driver, but got no response. Rather, he made for the door, unlocked it and charged up the stairs ahead of her. Terrified by this she dashed after him, trying to think what might have upset him. She had never seen him angry before and the thought of it made her deeply uneasy, because she sensed that she had been the cause of it.

'What is this, Sholto?' she said when she had reached the flat. She was answered by his study door closing abruptly in her face. 'Sholto!' she exclaimed, provoked into anger herself now by this, and pushed open the door. 'What on earth is it?'

He was standing with his back to her in the window. He had not yet closed the shutters or lit a light and the gas lamp in the street cast an eerie yellow light across the room, making his figure seem very dark and forbidding. For a moment she was genuinely frightened lest he might turn on her, for he was suddenly quite a stranger to her and she had no idea how he might behave. She had not forgotten her father's occasional savagery towards her mother.

'What is it?' she repeated.

'Don't be stupid,' he said, without turning. 'You know quite well what it is.'

'Do I?' she said.

'Yes, you little fool!' he snapped, facing her now. He looked at her with an expression which she tried not to believe was contemptuous but which looked suspiciously like it. 'Heavens above, woman, can't you see what a fool you have just made of me!' he said. 'I would have thought you had more sense, but . . .'

'What have I done?' she said, trying to sound calm and unconcerned. 'I really can't guess.'

'Don't try and be clever, Jessie, it doesn't suit you,' he said. 'I suppose,' he went on with a devastating note of weariness in his voice, 'I should have known better myself than to think you would know how to behave. It would have been better to have left you at home – that would have stopped you disgracing me!'

'Disgracing you? What do you mean? I haven't disgraced myself – I know I haven't.'

'Christ, Jessie, you haven't the least idea, have you?' he said despairingly. 'Can't you see how bad that looked? I could have strangled that damned Alexandra Erskine. All that work with Lord Fergusson for nothing! You can just imagine him saying it, can't you: "No, no, Hamilton won't do – he married a cook!" What the hell did you have to do it for?'

'Do you honestly think I should have refused to help Mrs Erskine?' said Jessie, unable to know whether she was more angered or astonished by his words.

'Of course. You should have kept quiet,' he said. 'It wasn't your problem. If she can't keep her damned servants, that's her business. There was absolutely no reason for you to let the cat out of the bag like that. Now the whole damn' family knows, and Fergusson, God damn it! I had that man in the palm of my hand, Jessie, in the palm of my hand.'

'Let the cat out of the bag!' exclaimed Jessie, furiously. 'You make it sound as if I were a whore! And I thought you said that things like that didn't matter to you.'

'I should have had more sense than to think I could make a silk purse out of a sow's ear,' he said bitterly.

'How dare you! Sholto, how can you say that? How on earth can you say that?'

'Because it's true,' he said calmly. 'Christ, what a fool I've been. I've seen other men do this and laughed at them. I was foolish enough to think that you were different, but you're not, are you? You've no more idea of how to behave in decent society than a common whore to whom you think yourself so superior!'

'You bastard!' she exclaimed and lashed out in an attempt to hit him across the face, but he caught her hand.

'I rest my case,' he said, and released her hand, dropping it as if it disgusted him. 'I'm going to bed. I've to be in court early tomorrow, so I shall want breakfast in plenty of time.' And he strolled out of the room, leaving Jessie with the depressing conviction that he had just treated her, for the first time, with no more courtesy than he would a servant.

She could not face following him to bed. Besides, he did not deserve to share it with her, not after saying those dreadful things which had wounded her to the quick. Her sense of outrage and disillusion (which was worse) did not permit her to concede that he might in fact be right, that she had made a fool of them both. She knew she might be ignorant of his world, but she knew gratitude when she saw it and felt she was not such a fool as to take every compliment as sincere. But Fergusson had seemed sincere, she was convinced of it. Then it was Sholto who was being a fool; a damned, stuffy, snobbish fool who had not the sense to see that helping Mrs Erskine was the only decent thing she could have done. There was no way in which she could have let the poor woman fluster and flounder knowing she had it in her power to remedy the situation. Then, why could he not see that? Why was he so ashamed of her for doing what was right? That was the hardest thing to take; she had expected that he would have been proud of her, pleased that she could help such a grand lady as Mrs Erskine and make a friend of her daughter in the process.

And I thought that he loved me, she found herself

201

thinking, as she sat in the kitchen, lighting the fire. The smoke filled her eyes, but she found the tears which came were from the depths of her heart. That he loved me for what I am. And damn it, I am what I am, and nothing will change that. I can't force myself into a mould just to please Sholto Hamilton, damn him! And I thought he was different . . .

She did not know how long she sat there, but she could not stop the bitter flow of tears. Some of her fury was directed at Sholto, but most of it at herself, for she cursed her own credulity. I should have known, I should have known better!

'Come to bed, Jessie.'

She looked up and saw him standing in the doorway. He was such a comfortable, familiar figure in his dressing gown that she wanted to forgive him on the spot. However, she restrained herself. She would not give in so easily to her dependence on him, although to humble herself would have been the easiest thing in the world. But Sholto was not the dominie at Dysart School who was more lenient when his pupils confessed to their supposed crimes. Rather, he was the criminal and she was determined to make him see it.

'Don't think you can give me orders,' she said.

'You'll catch a chill,' he said. 'I don't want you making yourself ill over this.'

'As if you cared about that!'

'Oh, Jessie, Jessie my love – you are upset, aren't you?' he said, coming and sitting opposite her. He tried to take her hands but she would not let him.

'Are you surprised? After what you just said to me? I wonder that I don't pack my bags and go.'

'That would be a shame,' he said.

'A shame!' she exclaimed. 'I was right, wasn't I? You don't give a damn about me, do you? I'm just the wretched creature you felt obliged to marry because you got her into trouble. Frankly, I'm surprised you bothered.'

'I bothered because I love you, Jessie.'

'You've no more idea of love than . . . than . . .' She broke off, unable to find the words she wanted.

'Than a stupid young fool, who hasn't learnt to appreciate what a remarkable woman he has married?'

'If you think flattery will get me now, you're very much mistaken.'

'It's not flattery, Jess, believe me. It's the simple truth. When I went to bed just now, I found I couldn't face it alone. I can't conceive of life without you, my love. I felt utterly bereft without you. I hadn't realized how much I need you, and then I saw what a brute I'd been, that I was utterly pig-headed. I judged you without weighing the evidence, Jessie. I suppose what you did was really rather fine – and I'm sure Lord Fergusson hasn't thought twice about it. I was only angry because I was anxious – can you understand that?'

'I suppose so.'

'Say you'll forgive me, please, Jessie,' he pleaded and slid out of his chair so that he was kneeling in front of her. The gesture was so absurd that she could not help laughing.

'Ah, I knew you wouldn't stay angry for long,' he smiled. 'I know that you're not so hard-hearted.'

'And you?' she said. 'Can I be sure about you?'

'Believe me, I'm contrite,' he said. 'But you can give me that whack you wanted to give me earlier. I'm sure I deserve it.' He inclined his cheek, just as he had done in the garden on that morning when they had met for the first time. Again she laughed, but only for a moment because he caught her hand and pressed it to his cheek, kissing it as he did so.

'Oh, Sholto, what am I going to do with you?' she murmured as he stretched up and put his arms around her.

'Come to bed with me, of course,' he said. 'It's the best way to keep me out of mischief.'

7

'Good afternoon, ladies, I should like to welcome you all here today, whether you are joining us for the first time, or you are old and faithful members of our society. This is a most gratifying turnout and I hope you will not be disappointed by this afternoon's programme. We have, as you can see, two speakers: Miss Grant, who represents the Edinburgh Women's Medical School student society, and Miss Gore-Booth, from the Lancashire and Cheshire Women's Suffrage Society . . .'

One would not have expected a large and old-fashioned drawing room in a house in the West End of Edinburgh to be the scene of revolution, but Alix, since she had been coming to the suffrage meetings at Mrs Jameson's house, had begun to see that room as a crucible into which were tossed the most exciting ideas she had ever come across in her life. There was a dynamism about it all that the gold-spotted wallpaper and morocco-covered chairs of fifty years ago did not suggest. One would hardly take the widow Jameson herself for an ardent revolutionary, for her dress was as conventional and as severe as the Queen's whom she vaguely resembled. When Alix had seen her chairing a meeting, as confident and as lively at sixty as she had been at twenty, when she had been a beauty, she had been astonished, but now she knew that there was electricity enough in the cause to rejuvenate a thousand old women.

That afternoon she felt especially pleased with it all, for she had brought two possible converts, Jessie Hamilton and Nancy O'Hara. Miss Russell, who was coaching her for her matriculation and who had introduced her to the whole thing in the first place, had looked very pleased to see her walking in with two new faces, for she always maintained that the greatest strength came in numbers. Now they were sitting beside her and she longed to whisper, 'What do you think? Isn't it all splendid?' but restrained herself, for they had not really had time to make up their minds. Jessie, she was sure, was halfway there already, but she could not be so certain about Nancy O'Hara, for she had been reluctant at first to leave her baby, even for an afternoon. Alix hoped she would not be worrying so much about the child that she could not attend to the meeting.

It was Ralph who had found Miss Russell – a stroke of genius on his part, because she was so respectable that Alix's parents had been unable to find anything about her to which they might object. She was middle aged and lived with a bachelor brother, a schoolmaster, for whom she kept house. The coaching was, she explained, merely to earn a little pin money, a statement which did not suggest what a fine and well-qualified teacher she was. She had attended Miss Beale's training college in Cheltenham and had taught in various girls' public schools before ill health had forced her to give up. Now she lavished all her skills and attention on a few, intelligent pupils and Alix was sensible that it was quite an honour to be taught by her. Yet she had done more than teach; in the few months she had been going to her, Alix felt Miss Russell had turned her life inside out, taking her into a world which previously she had thought that women did not penetrate. Miss Russell believed that a thorough education covered more than passing the required examinations, so they went to picture galleries together, heard popular preachers and lectures in natural science, and most exciting of all, her teacher took her to the Edinburgh Women's Suffrage Society. When Miss Russell had added the surprising injunction: 'Perhaps you had better not mention it to your parents just yet, dear,' Alix had known that she was about to be involved in something dangerously radical. She had not been disappointed.

The first speaker Alix recognized. She was the daughter of Sir William Grant, the famous painter. Once, when Alix had been about thirteen, Ralph had sacrificed a whole quarter's allowance to buy a tiny painting by him which showed a white tea cup and a handful of sweet-peas. She had gone with him to the studio to collect the painting and

Sir William had asked her if she would like to sit for him. She had dutifully replied that she must ask her mother. Her answer had been intriguing: 'I might have permitted it, when Lady Grant was still living there, but now, I think not.' Alix had longed to ask her mother what she meant, but she had known that she would not have got the truth. She would not have dared ask Miss Grant either, for she was formidable-looking, despite being rather handsome. She was not a very good speaker either, although she was supposed to be a brilliant student. Her speech, or rather her paper, for she read it aloud, perhaps too nervous to stray from the written word, concerned the growth of suffrage groups amongst women students in European universities which she had visited that long vacation. It was interesting enough, but it was hardly the stuff to set people on fire. The applause when she had finished was polite but distinctly muted and she saw Jessie and Nancy exchange a bewildered glance. I hope Miss Gore-Booth proves more inspiring, she thought.

She need not have worried. Miss Gore-Booth stood up without any notes, but instead spread her hands towards the audience and began: 'Ladies, I have two questions to put to you. First – why are working women paid five shillings a week, and working men twenty-five? Secondly, why do working women live on bread and margarine, while working men eat beefsteak and butter? The answer, I am sure you all know, for why else would we be gathered here today? Working women have lower wages and scanty food because they are political slaves. They have no way of making their voices heard, because they have no representation in parliament, because they have no votes. Of course, ladies, what I am saying to you is obvious, but I am saying it again, because the scandalous tyranny of this situation cannot be stated too often. Sometimes, in our work of committees and meetings, we forget the basic facts, the sheer injustice against which we have come together to fight. I, as you all know, am an Irishwoman, and you know of an Irishwoman's love for her country. You are Scotswomen, a race as proud and independent as the Irish, and therefore I know that tyranny and injustice are anathema to you and that the sooner it is banished from our countries, the better!

'So today I am not going to speak to you of facts and figures and petitions and committees, but I am going to ask you to reaffirm your faith in this great cause. You will need all the strength and courage in your beings because the fight is on. We are in the twentieth century, with progress marching on every side, and yet we are still slaves! But we will not remain as slaves, and as this last century saw the emancipation of the Negro, so this century will undoubtedly see the full and true emancipation of women. And I say undoubtedly, because I see before me in your faces the courage and determination to see this thing through. We will not fail in what we have set out to do, because we have decided we cannot fail!'

This time the applause was tremendous and spontaneous. Even Miss Grant, who might have been put out by being followed by such a piece of oratory, leapt to her feet to shake Miss Gore-Booth's hand. In a moment the whole room was on its feet, and Alix heard Nancy O'Hara beside her exclaiming, 'By God, it makes me proud to be Irish and a woman!'

That evening, comfortably ensconced in the box bed in the kitchen, Jessie mused on what she had heard that afternoon. She had made up the bed in the kitchen because it was bitterly cold out and she was too tired to sit up in the drawing room, which was grand but hardly hospitable on a freezing night. Sholto had gone out to some dinner or other and promised not to be back until the small hours. So she had collected up the spare linen and blankets, unrolled the mattress they had bought for the maid they might one day employ, and settled herself there with a hot water bottle, a shawl and various suffragette pamphlets which she had been given at the meeting. She had stoked up the range and the room was soon deliciously warm. She simply lay there, propped up on the pillows, drowsily contemplating the events of the afternoon. All those brave, idealistic words echoed in her head: injustice, slavery, tyranny! She still seemed to see the faces of the women around her as they applauded Miss Gore-Booth. Alix Erskine had been the most fervent of them all, her face ecstatic in the moment, clapping furiously as if her life depended on it. And then, after the meeting, they had come out into the freezing darkness of the afternoon still glowing with their warmth and enthusiasm.

Nancy had said, 'Oh, I can't wait to tell Finn about this! I wish he could have heard her – he's from Donegal himself – he would have adored her!'

Some instinct in Jessie made her more reticent when her husband got home. He did not ask her what she had been doing all day – he was in too much of a hurry to bathe and dress for his dinner. While he was in the bath, Jessie pressed his evening trousers, bringing the iron down with more than usual force as she thought of tyranny and injustice. But she did not think it prudent to mention it to Sholto. One of the women there had said how much the Tories hated the thought of women's suffrage, and she knew that was where his politics lay. He was also rabidly for the Union and would probably have dismissed Miss Gore-Booth as a lunatic Fenian. It was best to keep quiet about it for the present. She decided that she would sound him out about it over a period of time.

For herself, she had no doubts. What she had heard in that room had been an inspiration. She had had a faint unease for a long time that a woman's humble place in the world was in some way unjust, but she had never found the words to prove what she had guessed at. Now, however, she had heard the arguments properly rehearsed, and had found herself nodding in agreement with every fresh point. When after the meeting tea had been served, she had found herself talking to some member of the committee, and telling her how ill treated women servants were in comparison to their male counterparts, and had been astonished when the woman said, 'You must write a paper for us, Mrs Hamilton, on the domestic servant question. Perhaps you might even speak? It would be invaluable to have your personal experi-

208

ence on the matter. I'm sure you could inspire a great many more working girls to take an interest in the matter.'

Her initial reaction was to think she must refuse, that what the woman was suggesting was impossible, but she remembered the speech she had just heard: 'You will need all the strength and the courage in your beings . . .' and she knew she could not refuse. To do so was to be a coward and she knew she would hate herself for it. Besides, she had friends to help her now. There was nothing she could not do!

'Come on, Sholto, old man, you can do it. Only one flight more.'

'One flight?' he said bleakly. 'I'm sure this damned tenement has grown since I left it.' Obstinately he sat down at the foot of the last flight. 'Just a little rest, Ralph, just a little rest . . .'

Sholto was appallingly drunk. Even Ralph, who had been through many student excesses with him, had not seen him so drunk for many years. He probably just seems more drunk because I'm more sober than I have been in the past, he decided, as he wriggled out of Sholto's leaden grasp, for he had been supporting him as he staggered upstairs.

'I'll go and open your front door,' said Ralph. 'And don't start singing again – you'll wake your neighbours.'

He unlocked the door of the flat. It was dark and quiet inside, and he assumed that Jessie was in bed, asleep. Realizing she would not be best pleased if he deposited an inebriated Sholto alongside her, he decided that he would leave Sholto on the drawing-room sofa, make him some coffee and go home. He went outside again to find Sholto crawling on his hands and knees up the last flight. It was an amusing sight and Ralph had had enough to drink to make him want to laugh loudly. But, remembering Jessie, he restrained himself.

'This is quite like old times,' said Sholto, sinking back on the sofa, while Ralph pulled off his boots. 'We should be talking about women now, you know, telling one another all those intimate details which one regrets the morning after.'

209

'Not these days, Sholto,' said Ralph. 'I think we're a little old for that. Besides, you're a married man, remember.'

'Oh God, yes,' he groaned. 'How did I let that happen? That wasn't like me at all.'

'I'll make you some coffee,' said Ralph, not wishing to stay to hear Sholto make endless expressions of regret for lost liberty.

The kitchen was warm and light because it was occupied. He hesitated for a moment, for the sight of the woman in the box bed disturbed him. He wanted to turn away and shut the door, suddenly afraid that she might not be sleeping but, like Celia, lying there dead. The fear gripped him and he could not think what to do, when she she stirred and opened her eyes.

'I'm so sorry,' he said, 'I'd no idea. I came in to make some coffee.'

'Have you brought Sholto home?' she said.

'Yes, rather the worse for wear, I'm afraid.'

'Oh, dear.' She smiled. 'Is he very drunk?'

'Appallingly so.'

'I might have known. He did warn me he would be late. Sit down and get warm. I'll make that coffee. What have you done with him?'

'He's in the drawing room on the sofa. I should cover him up with a blanket and leave him there if I were you.'

How can Sholto have any regrets? thought Ralph as he watched Jessie get out of the box bed. At least he tried not to, but he could not help looking at her, for there was something comfortably sensual about her. He had never thought that a pregnant woman would look so attractive, but as she stood there in her nightgown, her dark hair flowing down her back and the folds of cloth falling over her bulging stomach, he felt calmed by the sight of her. She had an eternal quality in that moment in the lamplight, as if she represented the best qualities of all women; tenderness and strength combined.

'Coffee then,' she said, filling the kettle and setting it on the range. 'This fire has lasted well,' she added, while she threw on a few more lumps of coal.

'You'll need it. It's a foul night. There was sleet when we came in. I sent the hansom away – it was too cold to make him wait.'

'How will you get home?' she said.

'I'm not sure,' he said. 'I might find a hansom if I'm lucky. But I don't suppose the walk will kill me.'

'You'd better stay here. You're not dressed for walking in the snow. Your mother wouldn't thank me if I sent you home in this weather.'

'I couldn't possibly. It really is no distance.'

'I shan't hear of it. There's plenty of room here, and plenty of blankets. It isn't any trouble at all.'

So, an hour or so later, Ralph found himself the occupant of the box bed which she had so recently vacated. She had put a fresh hot water bottle in her own bed, she assured him, and he had scooped up a pan of half burnt coals from the range and put them in the tiny grate in the bedroom for her so that it did not seem so dauntingly cold. All the remaining blankets had been heaped over Sholto, who had fallen profoundly asleep. She came into the kitchen with the tray of coffee, just as Ralph had climbed into bed, and they laughed together, vaguely embarrassed at this reversal of circumstances. For a moment he entertained the ludicrous notion that he should ask her to climb in beside him, but he quickly dismissed it. It would have been the most inept, selfish thing to do. She was a serenely happy, married woman and he had no place to interfere. But he could not help wondering, when he was left alone, what it must be like for Sholto to share her bed. I hope he is grateful for it, he thought. Women of that stamp are rare enough in this world.

8

By the time Andrew Lennox's train reached Edinburgh, they were in a blizzard. Andrew and his fellow travellers looked out at it with some dismay. They were hardly dressed for such weather. When they had left Wiltshire, early that morning, it had been close and surprisingly mild. It had made them forget the bitter extremes of the elements in their homeland, and so they were sitting there, dressed in their school uniforms, which had an elegant charm in the ancient cloisters of their English public school, but now, faced with a snowstorm, the silk hats, white ties and swallow-tail coats seemed absurd. Only one of them had bothered to bring an overcoat. The others had packed them, convinced the weather would hold and impatient with such prudence.

'What do you say to us diving into the station buffet for a stirrup cup?' suggested Rab Colquhoun. 'Are you game, Lennox?'

'I'm certainly thirsty,' he said. 'But what about the tugs? Their mothers won't be pleased if we send them home drunk.'

'We'll give them ginger beer. It's cheaper, anyway, and I've hardly a shilling left.'

These tugs, as the school slang described first year boys, were already in the corridor of the train. The first half at public school was a tremendous shock to the system, Andrew knew, and he remembered how eager he had been to be home that first Christmas holiday. But now, in his privileged position in the upper sixth, he could not muster the same enthusiasm. What was there to go home to, anyway? The thought of Christmas in the bosom of his family was not appealing.

'What about you, Sinclair?' asked Colquhoun. 'Will you join us?'

Sinclair, the only one who had been prudent enough to bring his overcoat, looked up from his book.

'No thanks, Colquhoun,' he said. 'My uncle is meeting us here, so that's one less tug ginger beer for your pocket to worry about.' His little brother was one of the tugs in the corridor and was probably about to get his head sliced off by leaning out in the tunnel which led into Waverley Station.

Colquhoun did not look disappointed. Sinclair would not have been an ideal drinking companion for one who was reputedly as wild as Colquhoun. Andrew only knew him through those long journeys north, for he was in another house. He had the sort of bad name that made Andrew glad they were only intimate then. During term time Colquhoun courted danger to such an extent that he had been on the brink of expulsion several times. It was not that Andrew was a model of decorum at school; rather he knew the value of keeping his head down. That was something the flamboyant Rab Colquhoun would never have understood.

The train stopped and they gathered up their belongings and climbed out. Although it was only half-past three, Edinburgh was already dark.

'When's your train?' Andrew asked Colquhoun.

'Six, worst luck. And yours?'

'There's one every hour, but I'll wait with you if you like, Rab.'

'You would? That's grand, Lennox.'

'Well, to be frank, I don't want to hurry home in the least,' said Andrew, watching one of the tugs being enfolded in his mother's arms. His only welcome at home would be a sterile peck on the cheek from his aunt. The others would be indifferent. 'There's nothing there for me now,' he mused aloud.

'You're gloomy,' said Colquhoun. 'You should have said something earlier, you know, old chap. I could have got my mother to ask you to Invernarry. That would have been fun, eh? Well, how about Hogmanay? I'm sure it can be arranged.'

'Thanks, but I ought to spend a bit of time there. I'm always avoiding them.'

213

'Thank God I don't have to avoid my family,' said Colquhoun, with real sympathy. 'We all get on very well.'

'Well then,' said Andrew, 'let's go and drink to that! To the health of the Colquhouns!'

'Cnoc Ealachain!' shouted Colquhoun, dashing ahead on the platform, waving his silk hat. It was the ancient Colquhoun war cry which Andrew had seen him use to good effect on the rugby field, to clear the opposition when he was about to score a try. Once a master had sent him off, believing that it was no war cry and he had simply been swearing. Colquhoun's expression had been memorable. It had seemed to display a whole nation's contempt at English ignorance.

The station buffet, Colquhoun decided, was not up to scratch and he assured Andrew that he knew of a capital place in Waterloo Place that was worth the dash. They left Waverly by a side entrance at the furthest end of a far flung platform and emerged into swirling sleet. In a few minutes Andrew was soaked to the skin and was hardly amused to find Rab's 'capital place' boarded up and deserted.

They made their way down Princes Street, not attempting now to shelter in doorways as some people did. There was little point – they could not get wetter than they already were. Rab remembered a snug in Rose Street, and so they turned up Hanover Street. They were about to turn again into Rose Street itself, when a carriage drew up alongside them and someone jumped out, hastily opening an umbrella, which Andrew discovered to his amazement was soon being held over him.

'By God, I was right – it is you, Lennox!' the man exclaimed. Andrew blinked and remembered.

'Erskine – well, this is a surprise,' he said, and put out his hand. It had taken a moment to put a name to the face, for the circumstances were so very different from when they had last met. Now, Ralph Erskine was wrapped up in an Ulster, a very broad-brimmed hat pulled low across his eyes.

'Come on, Andrew!' called Colquhoun and then seeing

214

why Andrew had stopped, came back. 'Oh, I'm sorry, I didn't see.'

'Let's get out of this weather,' said Ralph Erskine, indicating his carriage. 'Hop in, both of you.'

They climbed in. Andrew felt like a spaniel who has just swum for a bird. He wished he could shake out his fur before sitting down on the luxurious upholstery of Erskine's carriage.

'Can I drive you gentlemen anywhere?' he asked when Andrew had introduced Colquhoun. 'I was just going home. It strikes me that you might appreciate a warm fire and some dry clothes – or am I imposing?'

'No, no, not in the least,' said Andrew. 'We were looking for a drink between trains and Colquhoun said he knew a place in Rose Street . . .'

'But I didn't think the weather would be so diabolical,' cut in Colquhoun.

'It's been like this for a week,' said Ralph. 'To my house then?' They nodded and he knocked on the roof with his umbrella handle to signal to the driver.

'It's lucky I came along,' he said, regarding them with an amused expression. 'Whatever happened?'

They explained the business of the overcoats, the end of term desire for a drink, and Colquhoun's impossibly late connection for Inverness.

'The worst of it is,' he said, 'that if we'd stayed in the station, none of this would have happened. I'm a damned fool sometimes.' He looked down at his silk hat which was ruined. 'My mother will kill me for this. It's supposed to go to a cousin after me.'

'Aah, those damned hats,' said Ralph Erskine. 'I only wear a silk hat under duress now, you know, because of those.'

'I didn't know you were at Amesbury,' said Andrew.

'Only for a year, thank God,' said Erskine. 'But then my health gave up, so I went to Edinburgh Academy instead. That was one of the worst years of my life, actually.'

This year must have been another of them, thought Andrew, observing that Erskine did not exactly look healthy now. Presumably he had been dragged down by it all.

At first, Andrew had been pleased to see Ralph Erskine, as a man would be pleased to see any rescuer in such circumstances. Now, however, he found that the sight of him awoke a hundred unpleasant memories. He imagined that this feeling must be quite mutual and was thankful that Colquhoun was a master of ineffectual chatter, for he himself was slipping again into gloom.

Ralph took his bedraggled schoolboy charges inside and then slipped out again to tip Jock, his driver.

'Och, Master Ralph, there's no need for that,' he had protested.

'You deserve it for driving me in this awful weather. Get yourself a warming bottle, will you?'

Jock touched his hat and drove off towards the mews.

In the hallway the visitors had been caught in the act of stripping off their jackets by Mrs Erskine.

'Ralph dear?' she said questioningly as he came back in.

'Mother, you remember Mr Andrew Lennox, don't you?' He thought he saw a flicker of anxiety cross her face at the mention of 'Lennox'. 'And this is his friend, Mr Robert Colquhoun. They've had a spot of bad luck, as you can see . . .'

'I can,' she said. 'Well, I'm sure we can find you some dry clothes. Why don't you take them upstairs, Ralph? I'll have them send some tea. I'm sure you're hungry.'

'Rather, Mrs Erskine,' said Colquhoun, with the sort of frank, honest smile to which Ralph knew his mother always responded.

'Good,' she said. 'Well, off you go then.' She added, with a gesture of dismissal: 'You don't want to catch cold, do you?'

While his guests dried themselves in front of the fire in his dressing room, Ralph looked out some clothes for them. Colquhoun was no problem – he was about the same size as Ralph – but Andrew Lennox was a powerfully built young man, very tall with broad, well-muscled shoulders. That was how Ralph had known him at once in the street. It had been a surprise to find how well he had remembered him from the funeral, but on reflection it would have been difficult to forget such a striking figure. Those great hands he had recalled particularly, for as they had driven to Rothesay Terrace, he had sat twisting them together, perhaps out of unease rather than to warm them. Although his face was placid and politely smiling, Ralph sensed that he himself was not altogether the first man Andrew Lennox would like to have met.

He probably holds me responsible, he thought. And I can't blame him for thinking it, for in part I am responsible. Thank God for that droll highlander Colquhoun! He'll stop us coming to blows, at least!

'What sort of a fellow is this Erskine, then?' asked Colquhoun, as they got undressed. 'He has extraordinary taste, at any rate,' he said, looking about the small room which Ralph Erskine had described as his dressing room, but which was furnished like a study. Under the window was a desk so stacked with books and papers that it looked as though no work was ever done there. Instead, a fragile table beside the armchair seemed to serve as a writing desk, for it carried an ink stand and a jar of pencils. One wall was entirely covered in bookshelves, extending even above the door lintel, while the other three walls were so crammed with pictures that hardly a chink of wall showed through, except here and there, to give space to a small shelf carrying some precious pot.

'Do you know, this reminds me of Bouverie's study,' said Colquhoun. 'Don't you think, Andrew?'

'Yes, I suppose so,' he said, trying to form some judgement from the place about the man who had loved his sister. He looked around again and his eye lighted on a small, framed photograph which had been propped on the edge of one of the bookshelves. He reached out and picked it up, for Celia's face shone out at him, not as it had done before in the conventional photographs of her which he possessed, but with an odd, unreal beauty. She was wearing some fancy dress costume which transformed her appearance. The girl who stood beside her in the photograph was similarly tricked out, making her for a moment equally strange to him. But those features had made too much of an impression on him for him to forget them altogether. It was Alexandra Erskine.

'Who are they?' asked Rab.

'My sister and Miss Erskine.'

'Quite a handsome pair,' said Rab, appreciatively.

'Yes,' sighed Andrew. 'My sister was going to marry Erskine.'

'Oh, what happened?' said Rab. 'Did they have a tiff?'

'No,' said Andrew. 'She died last summer.'

Rab Colquhoun looked awkward. Andrew had not meant to be so blunt. It was unfair on Rab, after all. He was not to know. He had only mentioned the business to one or two of his closest friends.

'My dear chap,' Rab began, 'I'm so sorry – I didn't realize . . .'

'Don't worry about it,' said Andrew. 'Please.'

'I see now why you didn't want to go home,' said Rab. 'But then – do you really want to be here? I mean, it must be like opening up the wound again.' His simplicity was brutal, but it was hard to be angry with him, for one could not expect subtlety, only raw emotion.

'Perhaps,' said Andrew, returning the photograph. 'But one has to face these things. And the Erskines seem very decent people.'

'Yes, they do, don't they?' said Rab. 'Where does their money come from then?' he said, for there was a certain understated luxury about everything.

'Steel,' said Andrew. 'Well, I think there is more to it than that, but I know that Mr Erskine owns one of those vast foundries in Lanarkshire and a shipyard as well.'

'Of course,' said Rab, 'I thought I knew the name. So Ralph Erskine's old man is *the* Robert Erskine. I wouldn't have guessed, you know. This all looks pretty solid,' he said, indicating the room. 'But not that solid. I thought these steel men lived like princes – well, that's what my father always says, but I should imagine he's simply green, not having two farthings to rub together himself.'

This discussion could go no further because Ralph Erskine returned with some clothes for them.

'My mother has tea for you in the drawing room,' he said, 'but I imagine you might want something slightly stronger to take off the chill.' He opened the cupboard of his desk and produced a decanter of whisky and a couple of glasses.

'You're not joining us?' said Rab, amazed, as Ralph poured out two measures.

'Only in spirit,' he said. 'My doctor has forbidden me to indulge.'

'The swine,' said Rab with feeling. 'This is damned good, you know. Doctors have no consideration of what good a dram can do.'

'Or schoolmasters,' said Andrew, sipping his own dram with relish. Colquhoun was right – it was excellent whisky, the sort of rarefied single malt which his father would have liked to drink if he could afford it.

'Although that is obviously mother's milk to you both,' said Erskine, 'I shouldn't have too much. My mother has a way of spotting a breath of spirits at twenty paces and I shall get a dreadful lecture on leading youth astray. She can't help it, I'm afraid, it's being a daughter of the manse.'

'Well, Mr Lennox, this is a surprise,' said Alix, when he came down for tea. She had to suppress a smile at the sight of him for he was dressed rather strangely for her mother's drawing room, in an ancient Norfolk jacket which her father sometimes wore when he expected to get dirty visiting a mine or a blast furnace. Presumably that's all they could find to fit him – and it hardly fits him. She had never thought of Ralph or her father as particularly small men, but they were mere willow wands in comparison to Andrew Lennox. Under the Norfolk jacket she recognized one of her brother's artistic shirts in soft blue flannel. On Ralph, these hung loosely – Mrs Erskine considered them very ill-fitting – but Andrew Lennox's broad chest seemed to stretch the material, giving it the neatness that their mother desired in shirt making.

'Yes, Miss Erskine, but a very pleasant one,' he said, shaking her hand. She had expected her hand might be crushed in his, but he was surprisingly gentle with her. She might have imagined that a man of his size would be clumsy, but he seemed to have perfect control of his body, and sat down as if perfectly at ease, although she feared his trousers might be causing him agony. She wanted to laugh at that – not at him, because he did not look the least bit foolish, despite everything, but with him, for she thought she could read in his eyes some expression of amusement at the ridiculous situation in which he had found himself. She could imagine him, with his friend Colquhoun, recounting this escapade when they returned to school the following term.

Colquhoun did look foolish. It was inescapable, but he was slightly built and Ralph's suit hung off him to such an extent that it looked as if it had been bought by an economical mother who expected him to grow into it. But he had a pleasant smile and a charming manner. Soon, as he made substantial inroads into toast and Gentleman's Relish, he conquered Mrs Erskine entirely by knowing intimately her cousin who had married the minister of some remote Ross-shire parish. Alix found, therefore, that she was left to entertain Andrew Lennox.

'I'm very glad to see you again,' she said. 'I felt we didn't have a chance to talk that day at the Quarro. I've rather regretted it since.'

'Yes, it was annoying,' he said. 'We'd only just begun to talk. But how are you now? How has it been for you?'

'Difficult, of course. Ralph has been to hell and back, he says. He was horribly ill. And you, how have you managed?'

'I think I am a stoic,' he said, after a moment's reflection. 'It's been rough, I won't deny it, but I've gritted my teeth. I've had lots to distract me, of course.'

'Yes, that's the best thing, isn't it?' she said. 'I could never have managed if I didn't have something serious to do.'

'Oh, what's that then?'

'I'm preparing for my university entrance.'

'Really? That's impressive. Where do you want to go?'

'Well, my parents have decided that St Andrews is the most respectable place for women students. They think I'll get into less mischief there than in a big place.'

'I'd thought of going there, you know,' he said. 'I've always liked it. My mother was born there. But my father wants me to go to Edinburgh and read law, just like everyone else in the family.'

'So you don't want to be an advocate, like James?' she asked.

He shook his head vehemently.

'No, not in the least. I want to read engineering and chemistry.'

'Oh, I can't imagine Sir Hector will like that,' she said.

'You know him too well, don't you, Miss Erskine?' he said with a wry smile.

'Well, one can't stay under his roof for eight weeks without noticing certain things . . .'

He laughed at that and said: 'I wonder how you stood it for so long. I never can. How ridiculous it is – here I am, talking of stoicism, and yet I'm really a coward. I don't want to go back to the Quarro at all, I suppose, because she won't be there. That's why I was cavorting round Edinburgh with Colquhoun. I was putting off the evil hour.'

'I am sure my mother will let you stay for a few days,' she said. 'After all, if you're to be an engineer, you must have a good talk with my father.'

She was a little surprised at herself for making this slightly audacious suggestion. But he sounded so miserable at the idea of going back to the Quarro, she felt she must be constructive. Besides, he was pleasant company and she felt sure her father would like him.

Alix found herself moved to vanity that night as she dressed for dinner. She had a sudden desire to look her best. For Andrew and Colquhoun were staying the night. She had not even had to suggest it. Her mother, moved to warmth and charity by the awful weather, had decided it would be better if they stayed. Their luggage had been retrieved from the station and their families wired. The house was suddenly lively with high spirits, extending even to Mrs Erskine who seemed moved almost to gaiety by this disarrangement of her domestic affairs.

Alix put on her new evening dress. It was a soft silk, the colour of an old pink rose, and she had managed to persuade the dressmaker to keep the trimmings very simple. As a result the beauty of the cloth shone out, and she felt it gave her a superior elegance. She did not wish to dress frivolously now, that went against her new code, but she could not think that she was prevented by it from dressing well. As she looked at herself in her long dressing mirror, she was conscious she would make an impression on the young men downstairs, not of a pretty young girl, just out, but of an intelligent woman who did not let her clothes dominate her. At least, that was what she hoped.

'You look very nice, dear,' said her mother, coming in. She was obviously pleased at the pains Alix had taken in dressing, for she had borrowed Berthe, Mrs Erskine's Belgian maid, to help dress her hair. 'Yes, very nice,' she said, coming and standing beside her, so that she was also reflected in the mirror. Mrs Erskine also, it amused her daughter to see, was not immune to the charm of her young guests and had put on her duck egg green chiffon, with the antique lace collar. It was one of her favourite dresses.

'So do you, Mother,' she smiled.

'I couldn't resist putting it on,' she said, with almost coquettish confidentiality, 'I don't know why!'

'Yes,' observed Alix, 'it does feel very festive, doesn't it?'

'I've ordered champagne with dinner,' said Mrs Erskine, adjusting her collar. 'I think the boys would enjoy that, don't you? After all, it is their end of term.'

'Yes. Isn't it funny?' said Alix, remembering how they had always marked Ralph's ends of term. 'It's quite like the old days.'

'Yes,' sighed Mrs Erskine. 'Oh, Alix, when you marry, I'll give you one piece of advice. Have as many children as you can. I was lucky to have you two, I know, but I should have liked more.'

Alix was surprised at this revelation.

'Yes, children are the most wonderful thing,' her mother continued.

'I'm sure Ralph and I haven't been that wonderful,' said Alix.

'Oh, but you have.' She smiled. 'It's a shame you couldn't have had a few more brothers and sisters though. I've always regretted that. I had three miscarriages, you know.'

'Oh, Mother – no,' said Alix, putting her arms around her and kissing her. 'I'm so sorry.'

'You are growing up, aren't you, Alix?' said her mother, stroking her cheek. 'You understand quite how it is, don't you?'

'I suppose I do, although I'd never have thought I would.'

'It's nature, I suppose,' said Mrs Erskine. 'It has a surprisingly insistent voice. My dear, I don't want to stop you pursuing your ambitions. I think they're very worthy. But please don't forget that you're a woman. That's something very precious.'

Alix was moved by her sincerity, and longed to ask more. But this rare mood of her mother's passed as soon as it had come, for in a moment she was glancing at the clock, as if embarrassed.

'We really ought to go down now,' she said. 'We can't stand here and chatter all night, can we?'

Dinner proved to be a happy, gregarious meal. Andrew found himself thinking: This is what families should be like, and tried to imagine how Celia would have been among them, as Mrs Ralph Erskine. He did not know why he inflicted this painful exercise on himself, especially when he was enjoying himself so much, but the impulse was irresistible, because it was very easy to see her there. She would have been comfortable amongst them, as comfortable amongst them as he now was. He could see her, dressed in some expensive, glorious dress, sipping at her champagne, fingering the crystal flute and relishing each mouthful in that delicate, cat-like way of hers. It would have suited her very well indeed. Then why? Why the devil did she do it? The old question begged to be asked again, for he still had no answers, or rather any answer he might have formed was quite destroyed by seeing the Erskines like this.

He glanced across the table and caught Alexandra Erskine's eye. She smiled at him, a smile which seemed as rosy and as warm as the silk of her dress. He had been right to say at the funeral she should not wear black. To see her in the wonderful colour she wore tonight was like looking into the heart of the fire, at that pure intense flame which lay at the very centre. The sight of her awoke both desire and scruples in him, for she was lovely, but her beauty was of an untouchable kind, not because she was the well-protected daughter of a respectable family, but because he saw in her a fierce independence. She was very different in that from other girls of good family he had met. He supposed she was what was termed 'modern' with her intellectual ambitions.

When she had said she was going to try for the university, he had been surprised but had not let it show, for he had guessed she might despise those who could not accept such things. For women in their circles to express a desire for education was rare indeed. He could easily imagine what his own father would have said had Celia ever dared to express such an audacious ambition. He was surprised Mr and Mrs Erskine had allowed it, but he imagined that her will was not easily broken, that she could and would fight for what she desired. And good luck to you! he thought, taking a mouthful of his wine and mentally toasting her. St Andrews, eh? Perhaps, I'll see you there – that would be pleasant, he reflected, seeing her in his mind's eye, lighting up for him a bleak winter's day there, with a wave and a smile across a windy street.

224

9

'I don't suppose you've been to a steel mill before, Lennox?' said Mr Erskine. 'Would it interest you to go over to Garbridge with us this morning?'

'I should be very interested, sir,' said Andrew Lennox, 'if it's no inconvenience to you.'

'No, not in the least,' said Mr Erskine very genially, which made Ralph smile. He knew that his father did not extend this privilege lightly. He was usually too busy to show any but the most important visitors over the mill. Andrew Lennox could hardly be classified in the league of those Indian princes who came to order their railway lines and bridges, but Ralph perceived he had awoken more interest in his father than any foreign potentate. Their minds had seemed to interlock at once, for despite the difference in age, it was easy to see that they shared the same raw passion for iron and steel. The moment it had become clear that Andrew wished to be an engineer rather than an advocate, Ralph had seen his father extend a metaphorical wing over the young man. It was not difficult to understand why – Andrew Lennox had genuine charm, not polished, affected charm, but a real, honest pleasantness of manner, which at once convinced one that beneath lay a man made of very fine stuff.

Because of this, Mr and Mrs Erskine had at once asked Andrew to extend his stay until Christmas. That he had been glad to fall in with this plan had been all too obvious, and Ralph wondered if there was not a great deal of friction between Andrew and Sir Hector. Certainly he could not imagine a father and son less like each other. It made his own differences with his father seem increasingly trivial. Indeed, in the last few months, Ralph had felt he understood his father better and that he perhaps was not so misunderstood. That he was making an effort with the motor company, and even enjoying it, had seemed to make his father a great deal more tolerant to what in the past he had described as Ralph's 'weaknesses'. The manner in which he had acquiesced to his scheme for Alix's education had been little short of a miracle. Perhaps because the motors were mildly profitable under Ralph's nervous management, his opinions could not be so easily dismissed. He had obviously proved himself.

That morning, when Mr Erskine suggested the tour of the mill, Ralph had been planning to go over to Garbridge to see how the machine shop was getting on with the first batch of motor engines. Previously these had been hand built at Musselburgh as if time were no object. But Ralph now had over a dozen people waiting impatiently for their motors and more orders coming in each day. It was quicker and cheaper to get them made in the engineering shops of Garbridge than set up the plant necessary to make them at Musselburgh. The carriage bodies were still made there and Ralph had lured several master carriage builders from established firms in Edinburgh to try their hand in this new trade. They had taken a great deal of convincing, but Ralph had managed to show them that he appreciated their sense of craftsmanship. Indeed, that perhaps was the most satisfying part of the whole business – welding an ancient craft to something very modern. It satisfied his notions of artistic innovation enough to make the work bearable.

The Garbridge Steel Mill lay about half way between Edinburgh and Glasgow, in the heart of the Lanarkshire coal and ore fields. Ralph's great-uncle had set up a blast furnace there to make pig iron in the eighteen-thirties, within easy distance of the Caledonian Canal. He had made a modest profit but the place had been floundering badly when Mr Erskine had inherited it in the eighteen-sixties. For the next twenty years he had taken breathtaking risks, transforming the place from just another Lanarkshire pig iron foundry into one of the largest and most innovative industrial plants in Scotland. It had been Robert Erskine who had first used the Siemens open-hearth furnace for steel manufacture, and it had been Robert Erskine who had cornered the vast market for steel plates for ship building which had grown up in the eighteen-eighties. These achievements, with which any other man might have been satisfied, did not satisfy Erskine, and he ploughed back the profits into further audacious schemes, so that by the time Ralph was old enough to realize what his father was and did, he found himself under a tremendous shadow, with a destiny of steel and ships already mapped out for him.

At Airdrie station, they changed trains, crossing to a distant platform where the private line from Garbridge linked up with the Glasgow–Edinburgh line, and thence to the south. Standing at the platform, the door being held deferentially open, was the single private railway carriage coupled to one of the three engines which ran the line, usually pulling great loads of steel ingots or perhaps a giant twin-screw propeller destined for the Erskine shipyard on the Clyde.

'Good morning, Mr Erskine,' said Tealing, his father's secretary who always travelled down from the mill to meet his employer with the morning post. 'And to you, Master Ralph. I didn't know you were coming over this morning. I expect you've come to have a look at those engines.'

Tealing knew everything that went on at Garbridge and was effectively the day to day manager in all but name. When Ralph had first started at Garbridge, in the long summer interval between school and his first term at university, he had been put in Tealing's office as an assistant clerk. It had been a humiliating initiation for Ralph, still buoyant from carrying off most of the classical prizes at school, to discover that his handwriting was illegible and his arithmetic erratic. Tealing had not criticized him openly, but the facts had got back to Mr Erskine and Ralph had been subjected to a good many severe lectures, the embarrassing memory of which had not quite faded, despite the interval of seven years.

Mr Erskine introduced Tealing to Andrew Lennox, and explained that he would be occupied with him all morning.

'I'll rearrange your appointments then, sir,' said Tealing, opening up the large, black leather-covered diary which spent so much time tucked under his arm that Ralph had once thought it was welded there.

'Oh really, sir,' protested Andrew, obviously alarmed by this. 'I can't let you change appointments on my account.'

'Nonsense. They aren't important,' smiled Mr Erskine. 'Now, Ralph, why don't you take Andrew out onto the observation deck while I sort out all this post, eh?'

'I hope you don't mind the cold,' said Ralph, going to the end of the carriage and pushing open the door which led on to the little open viewing deck. 'Father had this made especially – he saw this type of thing in America. I think it probably works better in their climate.'

The snow of the past week had not entirely melted away, but lay in patches on the wasteland of the railway sidings making it appear more bleak than usual.

'Is all this part of it?' asked Andrew.

'Yes, potential for expansion. The whole area is about forty acres, and we've built on about twenty-five of those now. But the space is always useful for dumping slag and that sort of thing.'

'Twenty-five acres – that's pretty impressive.'

'I suppose it is,' said Ralph, who had not really considered it. 'I must say, I always feel overawed by it, half terrified really.'

'Because it will be yours one day?'

'Yes,' said Ralph. 'I wonder how I'll manage. My father is somewhat exceptional.'

'But don't you find it terribly exciting?' said Andrew, leaning over the rail to get a better view as one of the great sheds came into sight.

'That's the cogging mill,' said Ralph. 'I don't know. I suppose all this heroic engineering is exciting in a way, and I must confess I am quite enjoying what I'm doing at the moment. But I've always been reluctant about it.'

'What would you have done if there hadn't been all this?'

'I always think I would have been a rather pathetic schoolmaster – you know, the sort who is only interested in the classical sixth and regards all the others as a penance.'

'You are joking, aren't you?' laughed Andrew.

'Of course – but I can tell you, there are times I've been tempted to run away from all this.'

'I can't think why,' said Andrew, looking about him with satisfaction.

'It seems we both want to kick at our allotted destiny, doesn't it?'

'You mean, my not wanting to be an advocate?'

'I think your case is better than mine, Andrew,' said Ralph, watching him as he leant on the rail and stared out across the massive and dirty buildings. The scale of the man seemed to suit the enterprise. One could not see him in wig and gown, pleading some cause, but Ralph could imagine him in shirtsleeves, his face smudged with oil, solving a complex mechanical problem.

'How can you not find this exciting?' he said. 'Don't you feel that you're in the hub of the world here? Isn't this the absolute essence of progress – it just shows you what man can do! It proves evolution, don't you think?'

'Good God!' Ralph could not help exclaiming at his youthful idealism. 'You sound just like Alix.'

'Oh, do I?' he said, and grinned, as if that idea rather pleased him.

It was the great press which decided him. Ralph Erskine, as they had gone into the shed, had jokingly described it as 'Wagnerian', a remark which Andrew had to confess was wasted on him, for he was ignorant of music.

'You're lucky today,' said Mr Erskine. 'We don't start her up every day.'

'I can't really see that it's a she,' murmured Ralph, but this remark made no impression on Mr Erskine. He was rapt in the sight of his great hammer press.

'We only put this in two years ago, but it's already paid for itself. It's the largest in Britain. In the empire, I believe – 12,000 tonnes. What do you think of that, then?'

'It's wonderful!' Andrew was not exaggerating to gratify his host. This place was the culmination of everything they had seen, and they had seen a great deal that was staggering. But this great press, unique in construction as Mr Erskine

229

pointed out, which stamped out great sheets of armour plating for the navy's warships, was beyond anything he might have imagined. He could understand why it was Mr Erskine's pride and joy, why he affectionately called it 'she'. And when Mr Erskine told him how he had helped design the thing and how innovative was the mechanism which coupled the engine to the great hammer, he knew that to be an engineer would be the only thing that would make him happy. The noises: the roar of the engine and the hell-cracking clang of the hammer, which might have shredded delicate nerves, were to him musical in their intensity. They were exactly what he wanted to hear.

'That's very ingenious,' said Andrew, when Mr Erskine had finished explaining how it worked. 'I suppose you'll be adapting it for the smaller steam hammers we just saw?'

'You're sharp, aren't you?' said Mr Erskine. 'You'll make a fine engineer, lad.'

'I hope so. If my father lets me.'

'I'll have a word with him,' said Mr Erskine. 'Don't worry about it.'

Then they went to have luncheon. This was served in the boardroom in the large office block which fronted the railway siding. It was the only part of the mill which aspired to architecture, and the entrance hall, stairs and suite of principal rooms on the first floor were impressive. There was a mosaic floor, marble pillars supported the staircase, and glass cases along the passageways contained model ships and engines, beautifully made by apprentices. Each showed some important innovation such as the triple turbine marine engine or a cut away section of an armour plated ship.

'I shall want Dundas's rotating crankshaft for here,' said Erskine to Ralph, while Andrew looked at the cases. 'Do you want one of your lads to do it, or mine?'

'Yours, I think, Father. Mine haven't the skill yet,' said Ralph.

The boardroom resembled a dining room only superficially. Beyond the fact that the table was laid for luncheon, the atmosphere was still clear-headed and businesslike. There were no curtains at the window, only a view across the railway sidings, and the room was not warmed by an open fire but by a cast-iron stove which had been made in the days when pig and cast iron had been more important to Garbridge than steel. There was a solitary painting on the wall – not a portrait from life, but a copy of a daguerreotype of John Erskine, the original iron master. It was surprising to see how much he resembled Ralph Erskine. It hung in a very plain frame between the windows as if it were not a thing of great significance. The contrast between this and Sir Hector's veneration of the family portraits at the Quarro was striking. Mr Erskine, who had been forthcoming about everything else, did not bother to explain the painting. Andrew had had to ask about it. And my father will never let a guest sit down for dinner until he has seen all the Lennoxes, he reflected wryly.

After the meal, Mr Erskine was called away to the telephone, and Ralph and Andrew were left in solitude to finish their beer and cheese. (The food had been as unpretentious as the room.)

'You look at home here,' said Ralph.

'Yes, I feel that way. It's funny, isn't it?'

'Would you like to work here?'

'If they'd have me.'

'I'm sure my father would have you,' said Ralph. 'Perhaps next summer, after you've finished at Amesbury.'

'I wish I could leave there now. What use is it to me? I can study for the prelims myself. They're not that difficult. I should rather get some real experience.'

'You enthusiasm is laudable,' said Ralph, draining his beer glass. 'Did I hear my father say he would have a word with yours?'

'Yes – it's very kind of him.'

'Well, I think if anyone can change Sir Hector's mind, it is my father. He's very good at changing people's minds.'

'And my father will always listen to a rich man,' said Andrew.

'I hadn't taken you for a cynic,' said Ralph with a smile.

'Only where my father is concerned,' said Andrew. 'He is *really* a most corrupt individual. I'm sure you noticed that.

I'm sure he fairly forced Cissy on you.'

'I didn't take much forcing,' said Ralph.

'Yes, I know, but what I mean is that he would have wanted her to marry you for all the wrong reasons – because you were well-off, to be frank, rather than because you were the right man for Cissy, which I'm sure you were . . .' He broke off, embarrassed suddenly by his own show of emotion on this subject, that delicate subject which they had not broached before.

'I don't think I was,' said Ralph quietly. 'Yes, I was very much in love with her, mad with my passion for her, really, but I shouldn't have been right for her. It wasn't your father who did the forcing. I forced her into a position which was obviously unbearable for her. What else can explain it? She was in love with someone else.'

'What?'

'Yes, it was a shock to me,' said Ralph wearily, going to the window. 'If only she had been able to be frank about it, we might all have been saved a great deal of pain.'

'It's still his fault,' said Andrew angrily. 'He has never let anyone follow their instinct and yet he indulges his own very grossly! Of course Cissy wouldn't have dared to tell you that there was someone else not if he had made it so clear that he wanted you to marry her. She was afraid of him.'

'She would have been afraid to tell him what she had been up to with that man,' said Ralph. 'She might even have been pregnant, I don't know.'

'Pregnant! Christ, that isn't possible. Surely not?'

'I really don't know. It would have been a good reason for killing herself, I think.'

'But you're sure she could have been seduced by this fellow?'

'Yes, absolutely.'

'But she wouldn't have told you, surely?'

There was a long pause during which Ralph did not turn from the window.

'How the devil do you know that?' said Andrew.

'Look, Andrew, you may think after I've told you this

that I am a blackguard who deserves to be horsewhipped, but I only ask that you try and understand that these things are never as simple as common morality makes out. I was moved by the deepest love in what I did, and I thought I saw it in her too. That was my justification, and I saw nothing sordid or depraved in it. I cannot apologize for what I am or what I believe in, but if you think what I did was wrong, you have every right to believe that. I suppose you can guess what I am about to say, from that?'

'Pretty much,' said Andrew, feeling his stomach turn over. It was not that he was suddenly disgusted at Ralph Erskine, but that the image of Celia, always so bright in his mind, was now so hopelessly distorted that he could not recognize anything in it of the sister he had once loved. It was like losing her again, to know that she had not been at all the person he had believed her to be. 'I thought I understood her,' he said, 'but I haven't known her at all, have I?'

'People are never simple,' said Ralph. 'I should know that by now, shouldn't I? I'm sorry, I shouldn't have bothered you with all this.'

'No, no,' said Andrew, taking hold of himself. 'I'm glad you did. I hate lies. I hate covering up, pretending that there's nothing wrong when the whole thing is riddled with canker. That's the trouble with my family. They wouldn't have been as damned honest as you and Alix have been. That's why I want to get away. Can't you see? I don't want to get eaten up like the rest of them. I want to be free of them, independent, so that I don't have to take their tainted money!'

'All money is tainted,' said Ralph, as if he was exhausted. He had propped himself against the window frame, and the thin, winter light coming over his shoulder cast his gaunt face into shadow, increasing the impression of melancholy. 'Oh God in heaven,' he said, 'that I had one ounce of your defiance, Andrew, to give me the strength to go on. I loved her so much – I still love her – that sometimes I cannot stand the loneliness of it.' He folded his arms round himself and rubbed his forearms, in some feeble gesture of solace.

'She'll never go – we'll never lose her, you know, Andrew. She's a ghost in our imaginations.'

'But that ghost is not the reality of what she was,' he said bitterly.

'No, but it's the ghost of what we loved, and that is what it hurts most to part with. We should cherish our illusions – they may be all we have.'

10

New Year's Eve, 1900

'This time,' said Alix, glancing at the clock on the dining-room mantelpiece, 'it really will be the new century.'

'And about time,' said Ralph. 'We've been throttled by nineteenth-century notions long enough.'

'Really, Ralph, I don't know how you can be so disparaging,' said Mrs Erskine. 'I think we should be saying goodbye graciously to the old as much as welcoming the new.'

It struck Jessie that it was typical of Mrs Erskine to be so fastidious on this point. For her to let the century pass without due deference, as if it were some old and genteel person about to die, would have been a breach of good manners. If to the others this Hogmanay dinner was a christening party for the new century, for Mrs Erskine it was as much a wake for the old.

'We should remember all the important things that have happened,' she went on a trifle didactically so that Jessie could imagine her, twenty years ago, teaching Ralph his prayers in the nursery. She could picture Ralph too, for she had been into Mrs Erskine's private sitting room and seen the painting of the solemn little boy in his kilt.

'Yes, Ralph,' said Sholto, 'I thought you were supposed to revere history. Well, here you have all the history you want. The nineteenth century is about to become history – a fresh chapter for the dominies to inflict on their pupils.'

'Oh, I'm not denying that the century has brought good things, but surely everyone must agree that it has brought rubbish too, that there's plenty we should throw out with last year's calendar?'

'For example?' said Mr Erskine.

'Where shall I start?' said Ralph.

'His mind has gone blank!' said Alix in an undertone, and caused much amusement.

'Come on, Ralph, come on,' said Sholto.

'Well, I shall give you a frivolous example to begin with. What about the barrel organ? There is something which could happily be consigned to the depths of the ocean.'

'That is only because you are a musical snob,' said Alix. 'Give us some proper examples.'

'All right, madam,' he said. 'What about that despicable notion of the deserving poor? Or the fact that a man can divorce his wife for adultery but she cannot divorce him for it unless he adds injury to insult and beats her as well? Or the fact that most of the families in this country are subsisting on bread and margarine? Or that we can still justify murdering a man when he has murdered another? Aren't those all things we could well do without in this brave new century of ours?'

'You're very radical tonight,' observed Mr Erskine.

'And what about your favourite cause, Alix?' Ralph went on. 'Surely the fact that women may be doctors and teachers but still cannot vote, when lunatics and ex-criminals may, begs for change?'

'Of course,' she said. 'I'm only surprised that you agree with us.'

'All men are not tyrants,' said Andrew Lennox, a statement which seemed rather ardently directed at Alix.

'What, Lennox, have those hyenas got their claws into you as well?' said Sholto. 'Ralph has an addled brain so we can excuse him, but surely you must see that the thought of women voting is preposterous?'

'No,' said Lennox firmly, 'I only find the arguments against it preposterous.'

'Well, well,' said Alix delightedly, 'we shall have to take them to our next meeting, shan't we, Jessie?'

Of course, Alix was not to know that Jessie had not told Sholto about the women's suffrage meetings. She was not the sort of person who could think of concealing such a thing, but Jessie wished she might be a little more devious from time to time. She did not think Sholto would take too kindly to this deception on her part.

'What!' said Sholto, but his voice was not angry as she had feared. Of course, she thought with relief, he will not make a scene here. 'Oh, my dear girl,' he continued, 'you haven't been letting them fill your pretty head with their nonsense? Really, Alexandra, it isn't fair of you to involve my wife in such absurdities. She isn't to know that they are mere pastimes for old women too ugly or too stupid to find themselves husbands and families to look after.'

That was worse than anger, and Jessie felt the spark of wrath ignite inside her at this public imputation of stupidity. His malice shocked her and she found her eyes meeting those of Alix. She looked incensed, for the insult had been as much directed at her as at Jessie.

'Yes, Ralph,' said Alix, 'you are quite right. We are still throttled by nineteenth-century notions. Why else would Mr Hamilton have said something so stupid? I'm sure it was nothing to do with his intelligence, for if he had bothered to use it, he would have known what nonsense he has been speaking. It is only habit, pure and simple, which makes him think all women are fools!'

'Alix, dear . . .' murmured Mrs Erskine.

'My dear young lady,' said Sholto, not the least put out by this, Jessie was furious to see. She knew it was wrong of her to wish suffering on him, but nothing could rid her of the conviction he deserved to be treated pretty sharply for his prejudices. 'You are quite mistaken. This is a question about which I have thought long and hard. You are right, there are arguments on your side, but they are arguments which are of the flimsiest stuff – they crumple up like the pretty tulle which trims your charming gown. I am an open-minded man, I assure you, and if you will give me one convincing argument, I will become a loyal supporter of your cause.'

'Come, Sholto, you're not in court now,' said Ralph.

'Can you tell me what convinces you?' said Sholto to Ralph. 'Or you, Lennox? What puts you so firmly in the ladies' camp, beyond the attraction of their pretty faces?'

'Very well, Sholto,' said Ralph, propping his elbows on the table. 'I will tell you why I believe in their cause. Doubtless you will reject my reasons as not sufficiently logical, because I know the way your mind works, but you will have to accept it as the best my addled brain can do. I think women are entirely justified in agitating for political representation, and that they should be given it, not as a favour for nobly consenting to bear and bring up children for us, but because, like us, they are members of the human race. They breathe the same air, eat the same food and feel all the same complex human emotions. They are subject not only to the same laws and penalties, but to the same desires, follies and ambitions as us men. They are no better than us, but they are certainly no worse. To divide ourselves from them, to set ourselves up as something finer or stronger, is not only arrogance but gross self-delusion. We are, blood and bone, the same.'

'One could say that of children. No one thinks of letting them vote.'

'Of course they are not like children!' said Ralph. 'If they appear to be, it is because we have cheated them of an education. If a woman was educated as a man and put to a man's work, you would not know the difference.'

'But they simply are not strong enough,' said Sholto dismissively.

At this Jessie could keep silent no longer.

'Strong enough, Sholto!' she exclaimed. 'I don't think you've the least idea of what you're talking about. You've never done a really hard day's work in your life. If you'd watched a maid of all work or a scullery maid do her day's tasks, it would wear you out just to look at it! And she'd get half the money that a man mining coal would, for the same hard work!'

'You shouldn't excite yourself, Jessie,' he said, in a tone which was only superficially larded with concern for her. Rather, she saw it as another barbed remark to keep her in her place as 'a little woman, who knew no better', but, damn it, she did know better now! She felt herself teetering on the brink of a great explosion but saw that Mrs Erskine had gone pale with alarm at the turn the conversation had taken. So she swallowed the torrent of angry words she had wanted to hurl at him. This was not the time and place for them. Instead she sat stupefied, both by repressed anger and amazement at his behaviour.

'Perhaps,' said Mrs Erskine, seizing a moment's pause in hostilities, 'the gentlemen are growing anxious for their port?'

Jessie was glad to go, but it was obvious that Alix was not too pleased to have been dragged away from the battlefield.

'Oh, Mother, how could you!' she exclaimed as the three of them stood in the hallway after the dining-room door had closed behind them.

'I think it was better we left, dear,' said Mrs Erskine. 'Not everyone enjoys arguing as much as you do.'

'He was enjoying it thoroughly, and if you had given me long enough I'm sure I could have battered him down.'

Jessie found herself shaking her head.

'I don't think so,' she said. 'He's stubborn as a mule.'

'But you have to try, Jessie – I mean, we all must. Just think what a piece of ammunition he would be to us.'

'Alix, I won't have you proselytizing to my guests,' said Mrs Erskine. 'Mr Hamilton is perfectly entitled to hold his own opinions. It is very rude not to respect them.'

'But those opinions are wrong, Mother, can't you see that? One simply cannot let someone get away with such immoral prejudices.'

'Whether they are immoral or not, I don't know,' said Mrs Erskine, 'but I do know that it doesn't do to provoke people like that. My dear, think of Jessie's side in this. He is her husband and if you have put him in a bad humour, she will have to bear the brunt of it.'

'Mrs Erskine, it isn't really Alix's fault,' said Jessie, 'I was just as angry with him in there.'

'Yes, and that's one other reason why I thought we had better leave, Alix. Jessie shouldn't be upset – not in her condition. Can't you see that?'

'Oh, I'm all right, Mrs Erskine, please don't worry about that . . .'

'One can't be too careful,' she said. 'You're at a critical stage now, Jessie. Anything can happen. Believe me, I do know these things.'

This, for some reason, seemed to subdue Alix, and they went upstairs to the drawing room in relatively good humour. But Jessie could not rid herself of a terrible sense of unease. Sholto's contempt, his prejudice against all the things which she was beginning to discover in life, was frightening. Did it mean she was wrong to hold those beliefs, or that he was no better, for all his fine words and ways, than the narrow-minded, wife-beating, wastrel men like her father and his friends? She had hoped that she had found something better than that, but she could no longer be sure.

Alix sat in humid and exotic solitude in the little conservatory which ran along the back of the house. It was a place she had often run into as a child to hide from some unpleasantness, for it was easy to lose oneself and one's bad temper amongst the dense greenery. The very damp smell of the place was calming, and although she still felt half choked up with anger at Sholto Hamilton, she knew it was better to let it evaporate there than rage on in front of Jessie and Mrs Erskine. If such an upset could bring on miscarriages, as her mother had seemed to imply, Alix did not like to think she might be responsible for something like that.

I suppose I shouldn't be surprised that he is like that, she reflected, remembering what he had said in the train to the Quarro: 'I eat women, devour them even . . .' A man who could make a boast like that could only have contempt for women. But then, if he is a complete swine when it comes to women, why did he marry Jessie? He must love her, but what sort of love is it? I suppose she is very remarkable, but

239

I'm surprised that he should see that. I hope he appreciates how remarkable she is.

'Penny for them?'

She had not thought she would be discovered but looked up and saw Andrew Lennox standing in the doorway.

'They were all rubbish,' she said. 'Hardly worth a penny.'

'I can't believe that,' he said. 'May I come in?'

'Of course.'

'You look very private there, in your own little glade. I wonder if there's room for a great brute like me.'

'I should think so,' she said, moving along the bench to let him sit down. 'How did the argument go on? I was mad to have to go away like that, you can imagine.'

'I'm afraid it rather lost impetus,' said Andrew. 'Your brother and I don't have your authority in the matter.'

'Oh, I don't know.' She smiled. 'I think you were fairly tremendous.'

'Perhaps Ralph should go into politics. I can imagine him and Hamilton battling across the dispatch boxes.'

'Ralph would make a terrible MP!' laughed Alix. 'He couldn't possibly address a crowd. He had to give some Latin oration at his school speech day once and almost dried up in the middle of it. He was horribly embarrassed. Besides, can you imagine him being a good party man?'

'So it will be A. Erskine who's heading for the Commons, then?'

'Oh, yes, that would be something, wouldn't it?' she said, excited by his suggestion. 'With time we shall get there, I promise you.'

'I look forward to it. I shall expect to be asked to take tea on the Members' terrace.'

'Very well, I promise you that now. Oh, Andrew, isn't it so very exciting? In half an hour it will be a new century. Our century – not our parents', but ours – because we will be the ones to shape it.'

'Let's hope we do it well.'

'We will, I'm sure of it,' she said. 'Won't we?'

'Of course,' he said, and surprised her by taking her

hands. 'If everyone were like you, there would be nothing to worry about. The world would be paradise in twenty years.'

'I think you give me more credit than I deserve.'

'It's what I feel,' he said, squeezing her hand. She wondered if he was going to kiss her, something which she would not have objected to in the least, for she felt so stirred up by him. He was like an echo – he knew all her thoughts and ambitions without her having to explain laboriously. But he did not kiss her and she admired his restraint. A lesser man would have ruined the moment with a kiss.

11

March, 1901

Jessie stared again at the pile of bills on the table and wondered how on earth she could begin to meet them. She had thought she had been as economical as possible, but there was still an alarming amount owing.

She got up from her chair, slowly now, because moving was becoming more and more difficult as the time of her confinement grew nearer. The midwife reckoned that in a week or two she would go into labour. Jessie wished for a moment that the child would be tardy so that they would be able to afford to pay her. Sholto might have a good brief by then. She reached up and took down the tea caddy from the shelf over the range where she kept the housekeeping money. It felt ominously light – she had not expected there to be much there, but had hoped, in a foolish way, for a forgotten sovereign.

She sat down and pulled her shawl round her more tightly. It was a bright but still cold spring morning, and she had not lit the range in the kitchen in order to save coal. Sholto was in Aberdeen, suffering the indignity of being junior counsel to some arrogant QC (or was it KC, now the Queen had died? she wondered). There was presumably little money in the work, for he had sent her none. I should have married a man with a steady wage, she thought, opening the tin reluctantly. She tipped out its contents on to the table. Two ten-shilling notes, two half crowns and a few pennies fell out.

I would have thought myself lucky to have this a few years ago, she reflected, but the expenses of running the Marchmont Road flat were heavier than she could ever have imagined. She had tried to save a little for baby things, but the thirty shillings housekeeping that Sholto had given her had been quickly used up over a week. But for the past two months, she had had not a penny in housekeeping, and the baby clothes money had gone on food and coal. He had said she was to run up bills and pay them later, but she could not bear to do it. She hated the ill will of tradesmen, so had paid for all she could. And now, she was down to the last of her reserves, precisely twenty-five shillings and threepence, to meet bills which came to over four pounds!

I hope he's paid the rent, she thought ominously, and terrified herself for a moment with a vision of the bailiffs turning up at the door. She knew what her mother would have done in these circumstances – she would have gone into the front room and wrapped up the clock in a piece of old sacking. She would then have gone to the pawn shop on the other side of Dysart by a discreet route so that the neighbours might not guess where she was going and whisper again about those feckless MacPhersons. What could I pawn? she found herself asking, and then decided that it was unthinkable. The only things that might be of interest to a pawn broker were the silver candlesticks that Ralph Erskine had given them as a belated wedding present, and she felt to pawn them would be to spit in the face of all his family's kindness.

She picked up the first bill again – it was from the laundry. She had been quite willing to launder Sholto's white shirts and ties which he needed for work, but he had insisted on sending them out, along with all the other household linen. 'I loathe the smell of washday in a house –

I won't have it,' he had said, but he had not thought how expensive it might prove. Perhaps he had saved her hands from the carbolic and starch but he had not saved them any money.

She knew she ought to feel angry with him, but she did not have the energy for anger.

I can't pay half these, she thought, dividing the pile, and if I pay all these, I shall not have enough left to buy something for dinner. Oh well, I can manage on oatcakes and tea, can't I? Perhaps Sholto will send some money tomorrow. This last thought was uttered in the spirit of a prayer, for she felt truly desperate now, and hungry. The thought of subsisting on oatcakes and potatoes was not a pleasant one, although she felt she was ungrateful to despise the food which would have been very welcome to many people who had less than her. I still have plenty, really I have, she told herself, looking around the kitchen, If he's remembered to pay the rent . . .

She decided she would go and pay the butcher's bill. The fresh air would do her good and the exercise would warm her up. She counted out exactly what she would need, carefully leaving the excess money on the table. There was no point in being tempted to buy unnecessary sausages or bacon by having spare pennies in one's pocket.

She took off her apron and fetched her gloves and hat from the bedroom. Standing at the hall mirror, she re-arranged her hair a little and arranged the folds of her blouse as neatly as her swollen body permitted. But these actions did little to give her self-confidence and she had the depressing conviction that she had 'disillusion' written upon her forehead in large black letters.

The butcher's shop was only at the far end of Marchmont Road, two hundred yards away from their tenement, but it seemed like several miles. She found she was breathless when she reached the shop, and was thankful for the chair at the counter.

'What will it be today, Mrs Hamilton?' asked the butcher. 'We've some lovely pork in this morning.'

'No, I've just come to settle my account,' she said,

opening her bag and taking out his bill. 'It's ten and six, isn't it?'

'Yes, that's right, Mrs Hamilton. Now, are you sure you won't take some of this pork fillet for your husband's dinner tonight? It's very good – look – isn't that a fine piece of meat?' And he thrust a tray of pink, glistening fillets under her nose.

'No, really, please,' she managed to say, for the sight of it was suddenly nauseating. 'That's everything.'

She did not know how she got out of the shop so quickly, but in a moment she was propelling herself down Marchmont Road, in the wrong direction but not really caring because she was desperate to put any distance between her and that odious-looking meat. It really was extraordinary what pregnancy did to one sometimes. She had never been offended by the sight of raw meat before.

Suddenly she found herself so short of breath that she had to stop and grab hold of the iron railings which fronted one of the tenement blocks. Oh God in heaven! she thought, struck with absolute and sudden terror, for her entire body felt so constricted that she thought she might explode in the street. Damn you, Sholto! Why aren't you here when I need you? And then suddenly the tension seemed to ease and she felt able to breathe properly again. But the relief this brought was not absolute, for with it came the realization that this was the first sign of labour. The midwife had mentioned she would feel a lightening – and what else could this sudden relief from tension be? For a moment later came a stinging, stabbing pain in the small of her back at which she gasped aloud. If I have another of those within twenty minutes . . .

She attempted to straighten herself up, aware that passers-by were staring at her. For a moment she could not think what to do. Panic engulfed her and she stood there, rooted to the spot, the wind, which always swept forcefully along Marchmont Road, whipping round her with more than usual vehemence. She felt completely foolish, and yet could think of no way to begin to get home. For what could she do when she got there, when she had crawled up all those steps? There was no one waiting for her there to send out for the midwife, who lived a good mile away, a mile which she could not contemplate walking herself.

She looked up and saw a hansom cab driving down towards her. She signalled feebly to it, and to her amazement it stopped. I can't pay for it, she thought. I can't really do this.

'Are you all right, missus?' said the cab man.

'No, no,' she said. 'I don't need you really . . .'

'Whether you need me or not, missus,' he said firmly, 'I'm taking you home.' And he jumped off the box and helped her into the hansom.

'I haven't any money with me . . .' she protested feebly.

'I don't care,' he said. 'I'm no' goin' to be responsible for you losing a bairn, am I, not just because you haven't any money. Where shall I take you?'

'Oh, God!' she exclaimed suddenly, for the pain had come again, this time so sharply that tears came to her eyes. She tried to think where she might go for help. Nancy was her first thought, but they had gone to Ireland for a month to show little Frank to his grandparents.

'Where shall I take you?'

'Rothesay Terrace,' she said, hardly thinking about it. She had no idea how Mrs Erskine would react but she could not imagine she would be capable of callousness. She had showed such concern before that she must show compassion now.

'Rothesay Terrace, eh? Are you sure, missus?'

'Yes, yes . . . please. Number three.'

'All right then,' he said, shutting the leather apron in front of her. 'I'll get there as quick as I can.'

He was as good as his word, but Jessie, for all her sense of urgency, might have wished he had driven a little slower. To dash in a hansom across the cobbled streets of Edinburgh was an additional terror and eventually she shut her eyes, unable to bear looking as he wove, at breakneck speed, through the traffic in the Lothian Road, and swung round the crescents of the New Town and West End. She opened them again to see the grand doorway of the Erskine house, a door which had once frightened her but which now filled her with relief. It had the look of a sanctuary.

The cabman rang the doorbell and she tried to muster the strength to climb out of the cab, for she had just had another contraction. She saw the parlour maid, still in her morning uniform, come out to the steps. She looked dubious to see the cabman but Jessie, desperate now, leant out and signalled to her.

'Oh, it's Mrs Hamilton!' she exclaimed. 'Oh, madam, are you all right?'

'Is Mrs Erskine at home?'

The question was unnecessary for Mrs Erskine, who had presumably seen her arrival from the drawing room upstairs, came running out. Jessie had never seen Mrs Erskine move quite so quickly, she seemed to fly across to the cab, her arms extended, her pale blue skirts fluttering like a pennant.

'Jessie, my dear – has it started?' she asked in an excited whisper.

'Yes. I'm sorry, I couldn't think what else to do . . .'

'You did exactly the right thing,' she said, helping her out of the cab. 'Now let's get you inside. May,' she added to the servant, 'will you please pay the driver – and give him a good tip.'

'Thank you, missus,' said the cabbie, smiling. His charitable instincts had been rewarded. Jessie, thankful that her rescuer had not been forgotten, promised herself to give Mrs Erskine the fare when she was able.

From the moment she entered the hall, Jessie felt for the first time the excitement of what was about to happen to her. The dread vanished, and she found herself crying with sheer relief that she had reached such a safe haven. For in the moments she had stood clutching the railings in Marchmont Road she had had visions of being carted off to some workhouse or lying in hospital – terrible, alien places where women died like flies after childbirth. But here she was, being helped up the turkey-carpeted stairs at Rothesay Terrace, that quiet, solid house which always smelt so deliciously of beeswax and fresh flowers.

246

She was not allowed to get into bed at once, but was installed in an armchair by the fire in Mrs Erskine's sitting room, while the best bedroom was aired and the bed filled with hot water bottles. It was clear that Mrs Erskine thrived in a crisis and Jessie heard half-whispered instructions being given to the servants. One was to go for the doctor, the other to the pharmacist for raspberry leaf tea, and Jessie could not muster the strength to object to these elaborate luxuries which she felt she did not really deserve. Some residue of foolish pride inside her made her feel that she should not need to be throwing herself on Mrs Erskine's goodness like this, that she had in some way failed to organize things properly. She had always been proud of her independence and yet here she was, hopeless and dependent upon this woman's kindness.

'Now, now, Jessie, you mustn't cry,' said Mrs Erskine, putting her arm round her shoulders. 'It's all going to be all right now, I promise you. You'll have the easiest labour we can manage.'

'Oh, I'm so sorry . . . I didn't mean to bother anyone. It's so silly . . .'

'My dear, I'm glad you came here,' she said. 'You helped me once – I'm so pleased to be able to repay you in this small way. Besides, I love babies. It will be a great joy. So you're not to worry. Why don't you try and sleep a little before Dr Nicholson gets here?'

The best bedroom was ready and Mrs Erskine helped her into bed, lending her a nightgown made of such fine lawn that Jessie felt she was being wrapped in tissue paper. The raspberry leaf tea arrived in customary style, on a tray with a lace-edged cloth and a crystal bud vase containing a single freesia stem. She drank it and felt very relaxed although the contractions were still intense. But she lay on her side, her head sunk in a mound of pillows, and savoured the quiet of the room. She was alone for a few moments, but had been told not to hesitate to ring the bell, should anything happen, for her waters had not yet broken. But for a while everything was deliciously tranquil and she enjoyed the warmth of the bed and the soft yellow light which was filtered through lace curtains. It was as well to gather all her strength for the ordeal to come. But she was no longer afraid. She would soon have her child in her arms.

That afternoon, Ralph caused a mild sensation by having Dundas drive him back to Edinburgh in the Thistle Motor Company's latest model, a four-cylinder engine with a shooting brake body. Motors were still a rare sight in town, and the new prototype was larger than any yet seen in Edinburgh. Dundas had been working on the design all winter and it had only been taken out on the front at Musselburgh as yet. He had been delighted at the chance to flaunt his creation in town. Ralph was equally pleased at the effect they had. People simply stopped and stared, and when they paused outside a bookshop where he wanted to pick up some books he had ordered, a crowd of children soon formed round it, fascinated by the sight of such a large horseless carriage.

'We should take it to Musselburgh Races, you know,' said Ralph, climbing back into the seat beside the driver. 'If we can get the sporting set interested, I think it would be a good thing.'

'It's going to need a few more months' work still, Mr Erskine,' said Dundas. 'It's going sweetly today, I know, but we don't know what a bit of bad weather might do to it. These things are very sensitive to the cold.'

'You can have all the time you like,' said Ralph. 'It's better to get the thing right before we start selling it.' It was not his own maxim, but one his father had drilled into him and it amused him to find himself using it so confidently.

When he got home, he found the house in a state of quiet turmoil.

'What on earth is going on?' he asked, bemused, as Berthe, his mother's maid, who was usually a model of dignity, came dashing downstairs with a slop pail.

'Non, Monsieur Ralph, you're not to go upstairs,' she said firmly. 'Madame's orders.'

'Why? What is going on, Berthe?'

'It's Madame Hamilton – her time has come.' And

without another word, she pushed smartly past him in the direction of the basement. For a moment he scarcely understood what she was saying, but when he realized what she meant, he exclaimed aloud: 'Good God!' and went upstairs at once.

His mother met him on the landing, barring his way.

'Didn't you hear what Berthe said? Downstairs now, Ralph. This is no place for you.'

'She is all right, isn't she?'

'Yes, yes, of course – she is now,' she said. 'But she was in a dreadful state when she got here. Dr Nicholson said she was dangerously run down.'

'Where's Sholto? Is he in there with her?'

'I should think not!' exclaimed Mrs Erskine. 'No, he's in Aberdeen apparently.' She sounded angry.

'I'm sure he had good reason to go.'

'Oh, yes – and leave his wife alone at a time like this? It's quite disgraceful! He should have made arrangements. Any responsible man would have done so.'

'But she'll be all right?'

'We think so,' said Mrs Erskine. 'Now go downstairs – there's some tea in the library if you want it.'

'No, I think I'd better go and try to get hold of Sholto.'

'I wouldn't bother,' said Mrs Erskine. 'What can he do, after all? Men worry absurdly over these things. They are a hindrance rather than a help, I assure you. We'll let him know when it's all over.'

'You sound as if you have delivered a hundred babies,' Ralph said, but she did not answer him. Instead she gave a slight shrug of her shoulders and waved her hands in a gesture of dismissal.

The library was scarcely the most hospitable room in the house. They used it rarely, for it was rather characterless and was kept in a state of perfect readiness, in case some important client should call and wish to discuss business with Mr Erskine. It was not Ralph's idea of a library at all, and when he had spent any time amongst those glossy mahogany shelves, lined with useful books on engineering, chemistry, commerce and law, he had always felt like a stranger in his own house. Today the waiting room atmosphere seemed singularly appropriate, now that his mother had turned the place into a nursing home.

Perhaps I should go and wire Sholto. I suppose he must be up there on a case so that sending it to the Sheriff court should reach him. He thought of Sholto, on his legs in court, in full flow, about to get his client off the hook, when the clerk of the court hands him a telegram, full of upsetting news. It might ruin his nerve – he might lose the case, and turn a dozen solicitors against him. Perhaps my mother is right to keep him in ignorance. He will need all the briefs he can find now there will be a child to support.

'Dangerously run down' was what his mother had said. Ralph felt vaguely guilty. He had not seen a great deal of Sholto and Jessie since the New Year, for the motor works had been very busy, and his father, pleased with his progress there, had been moved to give him the directorship of the steam launch company in Dundee. He had not had much time for social life, and had wondered if Sholto had been going through a difficult patch. A young advocate's income was never generous at the best of times, and he knew that Sholto could be uncompromising and liable to offend those whom he should have been cultivating. He could also be a spendthrift, as Ralph knew well, having settled debts for him in the past. I wish he had asked me now, thought Ralph, suspecting that his old student penury might have reoccurred. Jessie, he could imagine, was the opposite. She is probably economical to the point of self-denial, he thought, and found himself astonished again by the female capacity for sacrifice, and the male readiness to exploit it. He had leeched on his own mother's strength enough times to recognize that it was a very general sin.

His guilt and a growing sense of anxiety made him restless. He began to pace up and down the room, trying to distract himself with thoughts of the new four-cylinder motor. But it was impossible. His thoughts kept straying to what might be happening upstairs. He had heard such terrible things of what women suffered in childbirth and found himself imagining all of them. He wondered if his father had paced like this on the night of his birth or if one day he would wait for the birth of his own child. He remembered, with a sudden burst of pain, Sir Hector's desire for grandchildren, and wondered how he would have felt if it had been Celia who was upstairs. It was a foolish and sentimental thought, he knew, for he had told himself a hundred times that there could have been no happiness if she had chosen to live, that it would have been a doomed and bitter affair if they had married, but something very deep in him craved that it might be the truth that he was waiting for his own wife and child.

'A girl! Oh, such a lovely girl!' said Mrs Erskine, wrapping the squalling bundle in a towel. 'Oh, Jessie, she's so beautiful.'

Jessie was speechless, partly from exhaustion, partly from exaltation. She had been safely delivered after over ten hours of labour.

'Let me see her . . .' she managed to say.

Mrs Erskine did more than that and put her daughter into her arms. Never, never in my life will I forget this moment, thought Jessie, as she looked down at that tiny, crumpled face. In a moment she had laid her entire being at this child's disposal. What a journey, what a journey we are beginning together, you and I . . .

'Isn't she beautiful?'

'Oh, yes . . . yes. Oh, I can't find the words . . .'

Mrs Erskine kissed her and said, 'I know. I know exactly how you feel. Isn't it . . . isn't it simply . . .?' And she laughed at her own loss for words.

With some instinct she did not know she had, Jessie loosened the front of her nightgown and brought the child to her breast.

'That's good,' said the doctor. 'I can't think there'll be any problems here. But you mustn't feed for too long, Mrs Hamilton, you need a good night's sleep now.'

'I don't know if I could think of sleeping,' said Jessie. 'I'm tired, yes, but I couldn't sleep.'

'You'll sleep,' said Mrs Erskine. 'You'll be surprised.'

She was right. While the sheets on the bed were changed, Jessie sat on a day bed, wrapped in blankets, the miracle still in her arms, because she could not bear to relinquish her. But she found her eyes heavy with sleep and her head kept falling back. Gently, Mrs Erskine took the child from her and ushered her back into bed.

'She'll just be in the crib by you,' she said. 'So you mustn't worry. And I'll be here as well.'

Someone had brought in the crib – a beautiful hanging cradle which had the look of having once borne Ralph and Alix. It seemed, as Jessie watched her through drowsy eyes, that as Mrs Erskine laid the child in the crib, her smile was not just one of happiness for the moment, but was full of a thousand happy memories. As she drifted away into sleep, Jessie hoped that heritage would be passed to her and her daughter. My daughter. My only darling . . .

She awoke, she did not know when, and found she had a visitor, or rather that her daughter had a visitor. She opened her eyes to see Ralph Erskine crouched over the crib, staring at the sleeping child. She felt a lump in her throat, for she understood at once the rapture in his face but had hardly expected it from him. It should be Sholto there, she thought. Oh, where is he? For she longed to hold him in her arms and tell him the wonderful thing which had happened. Yet she could not imagine Sholto there, half kneeling as Ralph did, like a domestic pilgrim in shirt sleeves, his whole body set in such a curve of tenderness that he might have been the father. And in that moment he looked up, their eyes met, and it seemed to Jessie that for a second their souls merged in some inexplicable fashion, for she knew at once that her child had a protector, a second father even.

It was, of course, exactly what Sholto had hoped for, and the memory of his cynicism shamed her. She closed her eyes again to avoid Ralph's gaze. She knew, without a word being spoken, that the quality of friendship that he and his family had extended to them was infinitely more precious than the trappings of it – those invitations to dinner, those hoped for school fees – which Sholto set such store by. They had let her roots mingle with theirs, establishing a quiet, complex intimacy so that she felt she belonged amongst them, that they were her family. For was she not a witness to all their private domesticity and now a part of it herself?

She felt she had never known such calm happiness as she lay propped up on the pillows and watched Ralph wake his mother, who had fallen asleep in her vigil, with a gentle hand. It was as if she had seen it all before. She knew how Mrs Erskine would start, then smile, and then offer a mild reproach, so that it seemed she had turned to a favourite scene in a much-loved novel. But this book was quite unknown to her. She was as unfamiliar with novels as with these refined and peaceful moments of family life, and yet she felt it all embrace her like an old friend.

12

St Andrews, March 1901

Since they were obliged to sit in alphabetical order, Andrew found Alexandra was sitting a considerable distance away from him at the head of the row across the aisle. He could see she was sitting very neatly and purposefully, her feet crossed under the desk, her hands folded on top of it, waiting for the instruction to turn over the examination paper. The fellow behind her was a complete contrast, nervously rearranging his pens and pencils, glancing at his watch and wiping his presumably sweating palms on his trousers. Andrew knew that Alix was just as frightened, but her composure gave no indication of it. That was one of the things he admired immensely about her. Indeed, if the English paper they were about to embark upon had a question asking for a brief account of the admirable qualities of Alexandra Erskine, he would have had no difficulty in filling half a dozen foolscap sheets. He only hoped he could manage the same eloquence on Thackeray, Milton and Shakespeare as he could on the subject of her eyes, her hair, her courage, her levity, her moments of intense seriousness – in short her everything!

To have the object of his devotion seated within sight of him was perhaps not the best condition for taking an exam, an exam in which he had to do as well as possible in order to secure a bursary. Sir Hector had refused to offer a penny in support of what he termed his 'ungrateful folly' in wishing to be an engineer instead of an advocate. The situation was not hopeless as Mr Erskine had offered to sponsor him, but he felt he must at least win the burden of his fees. Mr Erskine had been too kind already.

Anxious to distract himself from Alexandra, he stared down at the pink, virginal blotting paper and prayed for reasonable questions. If this had been a mathematics paper he would not have been so worried but he had studied English little at school. It was somewhat despised at Amesbury where classics still reigned.

'You may begin,' said the invigilator.

For a moment Alix did not want to turn over the paper at all. For a moment she wanted to run out of that gloomy hall and never look at a book again. She felt so stuffed with facts and ideas that she could not imagine how she would begin to use them coherently.'It's not what you know – it's how you use it!' Miss Russell and Ralph seemed to chant in her ears, but she felt she would not manage it. She wanted to turn round and catch Andrew Lennox's eye. She felt his broad, disarming grin was exactly what she needed, but it was impossible. If she turned round, even a fraction, she felt she would instantly be accused of cheating by that formidable-looking academic with Dundreary whiskers. So she turned over the paper instead.

It was not so dreadful. In fact, it was almost a pleasant surprise. She found she could do most of the questions and she only had to attempt five of them. The first task was an essay on a choice of dull subjects, but she had been prepared for dullness. Ralph had told her how he had gone to great lengths on occasion to twist round some dreary title into something remotely interesting. 'But choose the dullest of the dull and then be ingenious,' he had advised. 'The others will choose the more interesting ones and then at least the examiner will see you are different.'

The dullest of the dull . . . she mused as she studied the titles. There was an outstanding candidate for that prize, question 1b: 'Helps and hindrances to study'. It seemed there were two approaches to such a subject. One, she imagined, would be Ralph's choice, a faintly humorous dissection of the trials of some poor scholar in the bosom of his family, distracted by domestic disasters, barrel organs in the street, a rickety chair or a draught under the door. Ralph could get away with it. He would stuff it with Greek quotations, but if I do it, it will seem facetious. So I shall be radical instead.

'A lady of my acquaintance,' she began, making a first black mark on the clean paper, 'related to me an incident from her youth. She was one of several children, but an only daughter, and instead of being spoilt, as often happens in such cases, was neglected instead as the boys were the general favourites. For their education not a penny was spared, although the family was by no means able to afford it. When they worked at their books, they were given all the luxury of a room to themselves with a fire and their own tea tray. Now this lady shared something of her brothers' studious habits and could often be found working alongside them. She innocently believed that what was right for them to do was right for her also, but one day her mother came in and exclaimed "Goodness, dear, have you nothing better to do?" This shocked my friend, who could not understand that what was seen as necessary for her brothers was positively unnecessary for her. To her it was a piece of faulty logic, but for her mother it was a deeply held conviction, for she proceeded, as the girl grew up, to put every obstacle in her way to prevent her obtaining even the slightest rudiments of an education. The bitterness which this provoked was very considerable, especially as my friend saw her brothers praised and rewarded for their every least effort; in short, helped where she was hindered . . .'

★ ★ ★

'Well, I'm glad that one's over,' said Andrew Lennox, stretching. 'How do you reckon you did?'

'I don't know, really,' said Alix. 'I found I had plenty to say, though.'

'That's a good sign,' said Andrew. 'Wasn't the paraphrase terrible?'

'Rather,' said Alix. 'But I'm sure you did all right.'

'I hope so.'

They walked across the quadrangle together, enjoying the sunlight and the brisk wind after the stillness of the examination hall.

'Where shall we go and eat our sandwiches?' asked Andrew. There was only an hour between the morning and afternoon papers so they had brought a picnic.

'By the cliffs,' said Alix, 'overlooking the Castle. And we can test each other on our history.'

There was a bench by the railings below, after which the cliffs dropped down to the sea. It was a wild morning, but they were warmly wrapped up and the weather was pleasantly stimulating. To the right of them was the red sandstone ruin of the Castle; to the left, the straggling grey remains of the Cathedral, both of which had impressed generations of tourists with the history embedded in the stone. But for Andrew and Alix, their mouths half full of beef sandwiches, the scenery was easily forgotten. In that afternoon they had history, geography and literature to plough through, and the recitation of the principal towns in Africa, the battles of the English Civil War, and the characteristics of Satan in *Paradise Lost*, were for the moment more absorbing. An innocent observer might have taken them for lovers, for they were sitting close together, each thinking to protect the other from the wind.

'All right then, Andrew, how are you on Canada?' said Alix. 'There's bound to be something on Canada, you know, because it was Africa last time. Name the principal cities.'

'Oh, goodness . . .' he said, staring at the sky as he tried to dredge his memory. 'Going from west to east we have

Vancouver, Edmonton, Calgary, Regina, Winnipeg, Toronto, Ottawa, Montreal and Quebec – yes?'

'Too easy, obviously. Which city belongs in which province?'

'Vancouver is British Columbia. Then there's Edmonton in Alberta as is Calgary, then Regina is in Saskatchewan, Winnipeg is Manitoba, Toronto and Ottawa are in Ontario, which leaves Quebec and Montreal – which of course are in Quebec! How's that?'

'What about Halifax, Nova Scotia?'

'That's simply pedantic, Alix,' said Andrew, smiling. 'I got all the others, didn't I?'

'Yes, so shall I spare you the mountain ranges and rivers?'

'You can remind me of them, since you know Canada so well.'

'I was hoping you'd remind me,' she laughed. 'I can remember the places but never the wretched rivers, unless they are the enormous ones like the St Lawrence seaway.'

'I think we might be struggling with the geography questions.'

'Well, it will be all right if we get Germany,' said Alix. 'I know all that backwards.'

'Anyone would think you'd done a hundred exams,' observed Andrew. 'You seem so confident.'

'Oh dear,' said Alix, worried suddenly. 'Do you mean I'm over-confident? Miss Russell warned me about that.'

'No, I meant it as a compliment,' he said. 'It takes guts to do what you've done.'

'I'm foolhardy, rather,' she said. 'I shall be back here in October to take these again, I'm sure.'

'Most likely we both shall,' he said and stared out to sea. 'But I hope not. I don't want to waste time, you know. I want to go here and I want to start this autumn – I've decided that and I want to stick by it. I know one shouldn't hope to get everything one wants but I can't helping wanting this very badly.'

'Yes, I know what you mean. But we aren't asking for something wicked, are we?' she reflected. 'It's only being greedy for life and ideas. I can't imagine that sort of impatience is wrong.'

'No, it can't be,' he said, 'but I think my impatience is to do with something else.'

'Oh, yes?' She had said it teasingly and then wished she had not, for he was looking rather intensely at her. 'Oh . . .'

'I'm going to have to say it, you know,' he said, addressing the sky and not her. 'I'm sorry, Alix, this is probably the worst moment to say what I want to say to you, but I can't go on much longer if I don't. This morning it took all the effort I had to concentrate on that paper – I was thinking about you so much. But in a funny way it almost helped me concentrate, because I knew that I had to do well to be with you, to be worthy of you . . . oh, hell, am I making any sense? I don't think I can be – I hardly make sense to myself these days . . .'

She had never heard such a torrent of words from him before. Her slight astonishment must have shown for he said, 'Oh, goodness – look, if you don't want me to go on, if I've said too much already, please tell me to shut up, Alix. I wouldn't want anything I say to be unwelcome.'

'No. No, please go on.'

That seemed to give him renewed courage and he seized both of her hands.

'Oh Alix, I didn't dare hope!' he exclaimed. 'You see – well, you must guess how I feel about you. You've knocked me between the eyes – oh God, what an expression, that's not what I mean – well, I do mean it, but it sounds too brutal. Oh dear,' he said, seeing she was smiling kindly at his confusion, 'I shall have to come to the point, shan't I?'

She nodded.

'Alix, I love you,' he said.

She looked up at his kind, frank face and wondered how she could answer this tribute. It was so unexpected and yet, from the way she felt startled into joy, she had a suspicion she had been waiting for this moment ever since she had known him. Her throat felt dry. She could not find the words, but only sat and smiled stupidly.

'Then you're not angry?'

She shook her head vehemently.

'Oh, thank God!' he said. 'There's something else I want you to understand. Just because I love you doesn't mean I want to trap you. I know how abhorrent that would be to you. Your life is only beginning – and so is mine – and I don't want to make you promise me things that you perhaps aren't ready to promise. I just want you to know that I'm prepared to wait for you as long as you like. It doesn't make any difference to me, because I want you on your terms, not mine. God knows, I'm not good enough for you, but it's the least I can do to hope to win you – but really that's for you to decide. And when you do, I promise I'll be as good a husband as I can, or go away and never darken your door again, if that's what you want.'

'Oh, Andrew, I should never want that!' she said, earnestly.

'I'm not asking you to decide a thing now. I'm just telling you what I feel, very selfishly, because I have to, though I think I've chosen the rottenest moment to do it. I hope I haven't upset you.'

'You haven't made me unhappy,' she said. 'Am I allowed to say that?'

'Of course,' he said. 'And if you fail the paper this afternoon, you shall know who to blame.'

'I shan't fail,' she said, getting up from the bench, her hands still in his. 'Do you know why?'

'Why?'

'Because you have just treated me with more honour and consideration than anyone in my life before. That has a way of making one feel very confident about oneself. I should not have thought that I deserved to be loved by someone as . . . as . . . remarkable as you, Andrew, and now I know I cannot disappoint you. I have to do well because of you.' And she bent forward and kissed him on the cheek, very briefly.

'No, it's you who are remarkable,' he murmured.

13

'About bloody time, Sholto!' exclaimed Ralph, jumping up from his seat.

'Calm down, Ralph, calm down,' he said, glancing around them as if afraid they might be overheard.

'I don't know how you can talk of calmness,' said Ralph. 'I've been waiting here over an hour – you're only the junior counsel, for God's sake, surely Sir Edward could spare you?'

'It doesn't look good,' said Sholto, pulling off his wig. 'Now what the hell is all this? Are we writing melodramas now, instead of lyric poetry?'

'You are beyond belief sometimes! Sholto, you did get all my telegrams – you must have got one or two of them – I sent at least a dozen.'

'Anyone would think you were my nagging wife, Ralph,' said Sholto calmly. 'Of course I got your telegrams. I am aware I am now a father. Sir Edward was so kind as to buy champagne at dinner last night.'

'Sholto, she could be dying! Don't think I've come here lightly.'

'Who, Ralph, the bairn or Jessie?' asked Sholto, with a coolness that made Ralph's flesh creep.

'Jessie, of course! Now get back in there and tell Sir Edward. If he doesn't let you go he's a bastard, and I'll come in and tell him so if necessary.'

'I can't possibly go now,' said Sholto. 'Things are in the most delicate balance in there. That man will hang unless . . .'

'And she might die, Sholto, you do understand what I'm saying?' Ralph interrupted fiercely. 'She's delirious, you know, and calling for you constantly. You simply must come back. We've wasted enough time already. I can't believe that I'm even having to argue with you about this.'

'Look, Ralph, Jessie is not going to die. She's as sturdy as an ox. It will take more than having a baby to kill her. I know.'

'And I suppose Sir Kenneth Moray's opinion counts for nothing with you?'

'Oh, your dear mother and her doctors,' smiled Sholto. 'I only hope he doesn't send the bill to me.'

'I ought to knock you down!'

'This isn't the school yard, Ralph, for goodness' sake. You'll distract the jurors.'

'What do I have to say to convince you?'

'I'm afraid there's nothing. Look, of course I will come when we have finished this case, but for now I am staying here. It will be better for her in the long run if I can make an impression on Sir Edward than dashing back to Edinburgh just to hold her hand because she has a touch of a temperature. I have a living to earn, remember. Unlike some of us, who have nothing better to do than interfere in other people's business.'

'This is not a temperature, Sholto, this is puerperal fever. It is touch and go. For your own sake, go and tell Sir Edward you have to leave. If she dies, you will never forgive yourself.'

'Don't presume to read my conscience for me, Erskine,' said Sholto.

At this moment the door swung open and the famous KC came out of the court. He stared at Ralph.

'What is going on, Hamilton? This had better be material – I've just had to ask for a half-hour adjournment. I need you to cross examine the brother.'

'No, sir, I'm afraid it isn't material,' said Sholto, with a sigh.

'I'm afraid Mr Hamilton won't be able to cross examine your witness, sir,' said Ralph. 'He was just coming back in to ask your permission to go back to Edinburgh. His wife is dangerously ill. He has to come back.'

The expression on Sholto's face as Ralph said this was the first comfort he had had in hours.

'What train were you intending to take?'

'There's one in an hour,' said Ralph.

'Well, you can take it, Hamilton, but you can examine Murdoch first. It will take your mind off things.'

And with that piece of pragmatism he swept back into the court with Sholto in his wake.

'I'm not going to die. I'm not, am I?' she asked in a hoarse whisper as Mrs Erskine bent over her to sponge her forehead with a damp cloth. It was painful to speak, for her throat was so dry, but she had to ask. She was so afraid, not for herself, but because she would be deserting Chloe.

'No, of course not, darling,' said Mrs Erskine. 'The worst is over now, I promise you.'

'They're sure? Really sure?'

'Yes, absolutely. But you won't get well quickly if you worry about terrible things like that. Would you like something to drink?'

She nodded and allowed Mrs Erskine to help her to sit up. It was really agony to do so, for it felt as if her limbs were being roasted over a slow fire while her joints were stiff as if stuck through with skewers. But although she felt faint and desperate, she could perceive that she was now at least more lucid than she had been. She had had some terrible visions, conjured up in the heat of her fever, and had been so scared that she had screamed aloud. Now she was only afraid of losing Chloe.

Ralph had suggested the name. She had never heard of it before but the moment he had said it, she knew it was right. That had been only six days ago – or was it seven? She could not be sure. The fever had made her lose count. But she had felt well then, marvellously so, until this thing had unleashed itself on her like a devil, out of nowhere. But she was glad she had named her baby. If I die, I have at least given her life and a name. That is enough . . .

But she wasn't going to die, Mrs Erskine had said so, and she repeated it to herself so that she might be convinced. She certainly felt she was better than she had been. Perhaps soon she would be allowed to see Chloe – but there again, she would not protest if she could not. There was no point exposing her to the danger.

Mrs Erskine handed her a glass of something. She pressed both shaking hands to the sides of the glass – it felt deliciously cool.

'Barley water,' said Mrs Erskine. 'Drink it all up now.'

It was sweet and cold and she drained the glass in a matter of moments. Just as she was handing it back to Mrs Erskine, the door burst open. She knew at once it was him. No one had burst into her room at Rothesay Terrace before.

'Darling!' she said, struggling to turn towards him. 'Oh, darling . . .' She found her eyes were filled with tears.

'Shush, Jessie,' said Mrs Erskine, gently pushing her back to the pillows. 'Stay still. You shouldn't exert yourself in the least.'

But she could not take her eyes off him, for he stood in the doorway, still in his hat and coat, his arms filled with flowers.

'Yes, that's right, you do what she says, Jessie,' he said, coming over.

'You can have ten minutes,' said Mrs Erskine to Sholto, 'but no more. Shall I take those?' she added, indicating the flowers.

'If you would,' he said, taking off his hat and putting it on the chair beside the bed. He perched on the edge of the bed. 'Oh, my dear, you do look as if you've been in the wars . . .'

'You might say that,' said Mrs Erskine, as she left the room.

'She isn't very pleased with me, is she?' he said. 'Thinks I'm a terrible husband, no doubt – but you understand, don't you, my sweet?' he said, and stroked her forehead. 'God, you're hot!' he exclaimed.

'Have you seen Chloe?' she asked.

'You sound as if you've been drinking whisky,' he said. 'No, I came straight up here.'

'She's beautiful,' said Jessie. 'Go and see her, please . . .'

'No, I've come to see you,' said Sholto, brushing back a lock of hair from her forehead. 'I've come dashing out of court to see you.'

'I wish you'd come earlier.'

'Now, Jessie, don't get reproachful. I couldn't just leave everything like that. But I promise you, when we have our first boy, I'll hire a private train to be back in time.'

'But . . . but . . .' She could not find the words she wanted, or the strength to speak. Instead she found herself assailed by bitter tears that were agony to shed.

'Now, now, don't upset yourself, Jess,' he said. 'What is there to cry about? Everything is going to be fine. I'm back now – there's no need to worry any more, is there?'

Part Three
1906

1

Coming out of the lecture hall into the quad, Alix could see that Drew Lennox was already waiting for her, a familiar figure, gaudy in his red academic gown against the grey stone of the walls. Alix pulled her own gown up round her shoulders. She felt the cold bite into her keenly and the bleak February weather was not the time for standing on the tradition which decreed that as a fourth-year student she should wear it dangling round her waist, as if utterly hardened to the harsh climate of St Andrew. Drew was impressively nonchalant as usual, more craggy in his height and breadth than the architecture, hatless so that his sandy-blond hair, somewhat in need of cropping, was disarranged by the wind; in short, a powerful figure despite the student shabbiness of his clothes (namely that terrible tweed jacket with the large dark stain caused by a leaking bottle of ink, and a navy fisherman's sweater that was fraying at the edges).

'Ah, he's here again – your most faithful servant,' said Isabella Cameron, with whom she had been sitting in the lecture. 'Well, I shall make myself scarce.'

'You don't have to, you know,' smiled Alix, waving at him as they walked over.

'I shouldn't want to intrude,' said Isabella, and turned off towards the gate which led into Butt's Wynd, leaving Alix walking towards him.

'Miss Cameron scuttled off very smartly,' said Drew. 'Have I offended her?'

'No, no – she wants to work a bit more.'

'On a Friday afternoon? Even I am not that keen.'

'Come on, Drew, you should be. It's only two months until the final exams, remember.'

'As if I need to be reminded,' he said. 'But you remember the old saying: All work and no play makes Jack a dull boy – so we are going for our usual walk. I need to get rid of the cobwebs, if I am going to make a start on that dreadful botany revision tonight.'

The botany was a required part of Andrew's BSc and was a great thorn in his side. At most of his work he was outstanding, but he maintained that botany was a closed book to him. Alix did not quite believe him.

'Where shall we go then?'

'To the pier,' he said decidedly.

The cliff path down to the pier was deserted, which was hardly surprising because the sky was leaden, and the sea and the air were in turmoil. But this was Drew's favourite walk. If Alix preferred a calm ramble amongst the Cathedral ruins or the pretty seclusion of the Lade Braes, he would always accept her choice, but she knew that he always liked the great stony grey pier which jutted out into the sea with such defiance. It was like walking into solitude, he always said.

That afternoon it was almost dangerous to walk along it. The tide was in, and some waves had broken across the lower side, flooding their path. Her shoes were sturdy enough but Drew gallantly lifted her over the worst puddles. That he lifted her with remarkable ease she knew well from dancing with him. In a turn in the Gay Gordons her feet scarcely touched the ground.

At the far end, they climbed the iron ladder and stood, leaning on the rail, gazing out into the monochrome distance. They did not say much, not from awkwardness but from the comfortable familiarity of being old friends who knew when silence was better than words. Instead they savoured the noise of the waves crashing below them and the wailing of the gulls.

After a while she turned back and looked up at the many towers of the town.

'I shall be sad to leave all this,' she said.

266

'Yes,' he said, turning also. 'It's been good, hasn't it?'

'Oh, yes, better than I could ever have expected.' It was true. What she had imagined university might be like did not correlate with the truth of it, but she had not been disappointed. She had not thought that there would have been so much fun and companionship, so much sheer good humour. Of course, there had been difficult times as well, moments of loneliness and frustration when she had thought no one understood her at all, but such black moods had usually been remedied by a long walk with Drew or an afternoon of idiotic gossip in a tea-shop with a girl friend.

'What will you do next?' he asked. 'Have you any idea?' It was a portentous question to which she had no ready answer. The thought of going home and resuming her life by her mother's side seemed impossible now, but she could not think what she could do instead.

'I don't know,' she said. 'Have you any ideas?'

'One, but I hardly like to ask it.'

'Why not? You know I shan't bite your head off if you do?'

'I know, but I don't want to force you, you know that – and besides, I couldn't really support you yet.'

'You wouldn't need to. Remember my trust fund.'

'I couldn't take that,' he said.

'Andrew, really! You're too proud,' she said. 'Surely marriage is about sharing.'

'So you do want me to ask you that?'

'Yes, I do,' she said.

'Then, Miss Erskine,' he said, with a grave, formal smile, 'would you do me the honour of becoming my wife?'

She studied him, savouring the moment.

'If you'll take my money, so we don't have to wait. If you'll let me share with you.'

'I can't refuse you anything,' he said. 'You're my only weakness – except you're all my strength.'

'Then, yes, Drew, I will marry you.'

He pulled her into his arms and kissed her, a warm-blooded, passionate kiss such as he had never given her before. She felt the strength of him as she had never done and pressed herself against him, her heart somersaulting with happiness.

'Oh, Drew, I do love you – I love you so much. I couldn't bear to be apart from you now.'

'We won't be, ever again. Oh God, Alix, you don't know how happy you've made me.'

'I do,' she said, 'I feel the same.'

'I bet you didn't walk to your political economy lecture thinking this was going to happen.'

'No, not specifically,' she said. 'But it was inevitable. If we separated now, we would be thwarting our destiny, wouldn't we? I think this was always meant to happen.'

'It doesn't sound the least bit logical, but I think I agree with you,' he said, and kissed her again. 'I should give you a ring, shouldn't I? All your friends will want to see one, won't they?'

'That doesn't matter, really.'

'But I want to give you something. Here.' He pulled off his silver signet ring from his little finger. 'It's probably a bit big for you – but we can get it altered. I'm afraid it isn't what you would call pretty, but it is quite old, you know. It belonged to my mother's father – that's the Nisbet crest on it.'

'Oh, Andrew, I couldn't – you always wear this. I don't want to take it away from you.'

'I only wear it from habit. And I want to give you something that has a meaning at least, not just some cheap piece from a shop. So put it on.'

She pulled off her left-hand glove and he slipped the ring on to her finger. It was slightly too large and felt curiously heavy.

'I must give you a new signet ring, then,' she said. 'With A, E and L intertwined on it perhaps?'

'What a good idea,' said Andrew. 'If you're going to take my name, why don't I take yours? Erskine-Lennox sounds rather fine, don't you think?'

'Oh, yes, it does,' said Alix, laughing. 'But you know what Ralph will say. He's always so scornful about people with double names.'

'I think I can live with that. And he'll have to lump it if he's going to be the best man, won't he?'

'How long have you been planning all this?' she giggled.

'Oh, just ruminating now and again,' he grinned. 'When the botany becomes impossible!'

Ralph arrived at Allansfield to find Philip Winterfield lighting a fire in the living hall. The place was filled with smoke and Ralph was seized with terrifying doubts as to the architect's competence. Had they spent all that money to restore and extend the house, only to find that the chimneys smoked?

Winterfield obviously read the anxiety on Ralph's face for he was quick to explain:

'It's quite deliberate – I'm smoking the plaster. I can't bear fresh white plaster. It would jar terribly with your furniture.'

'Do you always do this then?' Ralph asked, amazed.

'Oh, yes, quite often – if it's appropriate. And it is here, don't you think?'

'Yes, of course,' said Ralph, dazzled as usual by Winterfield's bizarre ways.

'And,' Winterfield went on, 'you may notice a few bits of chipped plaster here and there – that's quite deliberate as well. I shall get Jimmy to restore them, of course, but with less than his usual skill. It will add to the authenticity.'

'That's as good as faking!' said Ralph, amused. He felt he knew Winterfield well enough now to pass such a remark.

'Yes, I suppose it is,' said Winterfield. 'But I can live with my conscience about it. After all, authenticity was what you wanted, I recall. You wanted an old house, beautifully restored and your parents wanted all the modern conveniences. I think we have achieved the best compromise.'

'I think so too,' said Ralph, looking at the empty room through the fug of wet wood smoke. The living hall was partially panelled and faintly baronial in character with a large stone fireplace, but any sense of gloom was dispelled by three large French windows opening on to the terrace and looking out over the marvellous view across the gently rolling Fifeshire countryside. 'I love this place already, you know. I can't wait to get the furniture in. I've found another seventeenth-century Scottish oak chair, by the way – a real beauty, with a dolphin carved on the back splat. So now I've half a dozen really fine examples – to do justice to your table, of course.'

Winterfield had designed a special oak table for the centre of the living hall, with superb twisted legs and stretchers, which were not simply turned as usual, like sticks of barley sugar, but were carved out, as if two strands of wood had been twisted together, like the hair of a Renaissance madonna.

'No, I should imagine it will not be up to the quality of your pieces, Erskine,' said Winterfield. 'I must say, I am looking forward to seeing your collection in situ. It isn't often that good taste and the means to exercise it go together.'

'I suppose I'm fortunate to be able to indulge my passions,' reflected Ralph. He knew, however, that this was something of an understatement. If fate was now to deny him the opportunity to continue forming his collection, he knew he would be more than miserable. It had become a very important part of his life, more than a mere pastime, a constant solace. It had been gratifying to realize that the more he strived at his business, the more he was able to afford, and he spent his precious spare time scouring sale catalogues and antique shops for that next elusive item, be it a pair of Chinese ridge tiles or a forgotten portrait by Allan Ramsay; in short, whatever he fell in love with next. He knew he was perhaps too eclectic, too much of a dilettante to gain the respect of those truly obsessive men whom he came across in the salerooms from time to time, who collected only Japaneseware of a certain period or only Louis Quinze furniture. However, he had at least the satisfaction of exercising his own taste and discretion, and soon he would be able to unpack and arrange all his collection for the house was almost complete.

When his parents had begun to think about building a

place in the country, he had seized on the opportunity to make it a suitable setting for the collection. He did not wish it to languish forever in the lumber rooms and attics at Rothesay Terrace or, in the case of the larger items, to be packed up in a storage warehouse, like buried treasure lost amongst other people's brass bedsteads and sideboards. His parents had wrangled a little at his idea but had come to an amicable agreement when Ralph had found Allansfield, a compact estate midway between Dundee and Edinburgh, and not too far from the railway, with an old mansion house on it which was in such a parlous state that virtual rebuilding had been required. The setting, even when the place had been in ruins, had been enough to convince them that this was a suitable spot for their retirement, and Philip Winterfield had been called in, despite Mr Erskine's initial qualms about 'over-expensive English architects'.

'What will you be doing next?' Ralph asked him.

'A castle, would you believe!' laughed Winterfield, 'For Sir Richard Dorking – the haberdashery king?'

'Dorking's Dragon Brand?'

'Yes, that's the fellow. He has real delusions of grandeur. He wants a castle in Devonshire.'

'I'm sure it will be a masterpiece.'

'I shall do my best with it, but even I cannot help thinking that it is slightly half-witted of him to want battlements and portcullises and such. What is he trying to defend himself from, I wonder?'

'Dragons who resent being associated with knitted combinations, perhaps?' said Ralph, thinking of the fierce red dragon on the enamelled advertisements that seemed to be everywhere.

'I shouldn't be surprised,' said Winterfield. 'Oh, well, it will be amusing at least, but I'm sure it won't be as enjoyable as this has been. Yes, I feel this has been quite a successful project – one of the most agreeable pieces of work I've had in a long time. I wish all my clients were as co-operative as you, Erskine.'

'It would have been churlish for me not to have been,' said Ralph. 'I think we were lucky to get you.'

271

'No, it was an irresistible challenge. I've always loved Scottish architecture. It's so austere, so utterly individual – like the people, I suppose. It's a lesson in economy which leads to even greater elegance, I think. I make my articled pupils study the New Town in Edinburgh – that seems to me to be the very essence of classicism. Somewhere like Bath is sybaritic by comparison, corpulent even.'

It was pleasant to be given a personal lecture by so famous an architect as Philip Winterfield, a man who was generally too busy to give public lectures. He was a dynamic figure, touched with that same conviction in all that he did that Ralph knew from his own father – that same narrowness of purpose which bordered on the fanatical. It had been interesting to observe how awkward Robert Erskine and Philip Winterfield had been with one another, and how Ralph had quickly become the negotiator between them. It had not been the easiest process at times, and he had seen his father's patience wearing dangerously thin at some of Winterfield's extravagances; extravagances, which, had not Ralph been meeting half the building costs, he would probably not have tolerated. Ralph, of course, saw that they were not extravagances but those necessary elements which made Allansfield not just another modernized country house but a really inspiring piece of architecture which would, in years to come, he hoped, be regarded as one of Winterfield's most important works. The plasterwork, for example, which was now being so carefully mellowed by smoke, had held back the completion of the house by several months, because Winterfield had insisted they wait until a certain craftsman, Jim Macleod of Errol, was available.

The delay had annoyed Mr Erskine and even Ralph, impatient to be in, had been slightly vexed, but when he had seen the man's work – a wonderful re-creation of old Scottish plaster ceilings, with naive classical garlands of dripping vines – he understood at once Winterfield's obstinacy on the point. 'There's no point doing it, if you don't do it properly,' he had said, sounding curiously like Mr Erskine on the subject of ship building or steel mills.

They made a slow tour of the house, discussing the final details of the decoration, and Ralph would gladly have prolonged their agreeable conversation, but he was conscious that the time was slipping away, and if he was to get to St Andrews before the afternoon was out, he would have to tear himself away. For he wanted to see Alix before going on to Dundee. Seeing her would act as fortification for the ordeal of the evening which lay ahead of him.

'Yes, of course, don't let me keep you,' said Winterfield. 'I'm sorry if I've been wasting your time. I get rather carried away – you may have noticed that.'

'I find it just as fascinating,' said Ralph, 'but I have to drag myself away. But before you go back to Warwickshire, Mr Winterfield, you will come and dine with us?'

'Gladly,' said Winterfield, shaking his hand. 'Now, hadn't you better go?'

The driver of the four-wheeler which he had hired at Cupar did not look too pleased about being asked to drive to St Andrews on such a bleak afternoon, but when Ralph showed him a sovereign he complied, and managed to push the horses along more smartly than their appearance suggested. But the speed was pointless, for on arriving at the women's residence where Alix lodged, the porter informed him she was out. Mildly irritated, he scribbled a note for her and went to call on Andrew Lennox instead.

He too was out, but his landlady was more accommodating than the draconian porter at University Hall, who probably thought it his duty to repel all men from the gates of his Princess Ida-esque citadel. Mrs Mackenzie, obviously a treasure amongst landladies, brought him tea and lit the fire in Andrew's room, assuring Ralph that he would be back soon, because, she said, he was a gentleman 'very regular in his habits'. Ralph felt he could have guessed this from his room, which was frighteningly austere and very organized. That Andrew had a methodical, orderly mind, he knew, but he had not quite expected him to live like it. His clothes, which were usually very careless, suggested nothing of the neat severity of this room. The only indulgences, as far as Ralph could make out, were a pipe and a tin of tobacco and a small flask of inferior whisky. Ralph resolved to send him a decent bottle. He studied the bookshelf to find something to read, but it was all too earnest and scientific for his taste, and Ralph wondered how Andrew, sustained by such an arid intellectual diet, managed to be so interesting.

He sat unoccupied therefore and instead enjoyed the comfort of the fire and the hot, strong tea. It was agreeably peaceful in there, the soft glow of the lamp dispelling the gloom, and he savoured it, knowing that the weekend ahead would be a gruelling one. It was not that Archibald Ross and his large family were particularly high-spirited and exhausting, rather it was their Presbyterian propriety that Ralph was dreading. But he had to go and stay with them. The business that Ross, a jute grandee, brought them was too good to be able wriggle out of their hospitality.

'Hello, Ralph!' said Andrew, coming in. He looked as though he had been through the eye of a storm, but his face was lit up with such a grin that if Ralph had not known him better, he would have thought him simple-minded. 'This is very fortunate, very fortunate indeed,' he said. 'You're just the chap I need to see . . .' And he grabbed the flask of whisky and poured out two drams. 'You will have to drink it, I'm afraid,' he said, 'no matter what your doctor says. We've too good a reason to celebrate!'

'Oh, yes?' said Ralph, taking the glass. 'What might that be?'

Andrew took a swift gulp of his whisky, savoured it for a moment and said, 'She's said yes!'

'Alix? Good God – but that's wonderful!' said Ralph, knowing at once what he meant. He had known of Andrew's ambitions for some time and thoroughly approved of them. 'Yes, you're right, Drew, we must celebrate. No wonder she was out when I just called – you were with her. Goodness, I can't quite believe it. Well, congratulations, Andrew,' he said, getting up and shaking his hand. 'I can't imagine anything better. May you both drown in your own bliss.'

'We shall, we shall, just you wait and see,' said Andrew.

'It was incredible, Ralph. I was prepared for a battle, and she simply said yes, just as if she didn't need to think about it – I suppose, because she didn't need to think about it! Oh God, I never knew it would feel this good!' he exclaimed and finished off his glass. 'I don't know how I'm going to concentrate on anything now.'

'Damn it, I should take you out to dinner,' said Ralph, 'but I can't. Those dreadful Rosses are expecting me. But I promise we'll celebrate properly yet – I can't let this pass, can I?'

'Not if you're going to be my best man,' said Andrew. 'That is, if you'd to like to be?'

'I'd be honoured!' said Ralph. He had hardly expected that. Andrew had legions of friends and he was surprised that he should be singled out. 'Thank you, Andrew – I'll be glad to do it, if it's understood that I shall make a hash of the speech.'

'Oh, we'll excuse you that, if you like,' said Andrew, cheerfully. 'Besides, my father will give us all we need in the way of oratory!'

'Goodness, yes, he will, won't he?' said Ralph, remembering Sir Hector's dreary eloquence at the garden party all those years ago.

'I suppose one just has to grin and bear that sort of thing,' said Andrew. 'There will be compensations, I should imagine.'

'I should think so,' said Ralph.

It proved impossible to keep quiet about it, although Alix had resolved, as she climbed the stairs up to her third-floor room, that she would keep it a secret and would not rush around like a silly girl, as if getting married had been the only thing of importance in her life. But the moment she turned into the passageway and saw two of her neighbours standing in the corridor talking, she knew it was going to be very difficult to keep the happiness which had overwhelmed her from them.

'You're late tonight, Alix,' said Catherine Drummond. 'What have you been up to?'

'Oh, this and that.' She smiled, and tried to sound offhand.

'That means she's been out with Mr Lennox, doesn't it?' said Sally Forbes. 'Isabella said that he was waiting for you this afternoon – again.'

'Lucky, lucky girl,' said Catherine. 'Only the most handsome man in the university.'

'Oh, I don't think so. Have you seen that young Canadian that's just come to St Mary's – Mr Scott, I think his name is,' said Sally, evidently keen to be provocative.

Alix was unable to resist gratifying their curiosity and pulled off her left glove with a flourish. Sally caught her hand at once and exclaimed, seeing the silver signet on her ring finger, 'My goodness! Oh, Alix – you aren't, are you?'

'I'm afraid so. I gave in, at last.'

'Heavens,' said Catherine. 'I always thought you would have been the last person . . .'

'So did I,' said Alix, feeling very sweet and calm, 'but something just came over me!'

'It's called love, my darling,' said Sally. 'Oh this is blissfully romantic. Where did he propose then?'

'Don't ask that, Sal, that's private,' said Catherine.

'On the pier,' said Alix, as a throwaway remark as she crossed the passage and opened her own door.

'On the pier!' exclaimed Sally. 'Bliss, bliss and more bliss.'

'But what will you live on?' said Catherine, ever practical, following Alix into her room. 'I thought he hadn't a penny.'

'My money, of course,' said Alix, taking off her hat. 'We've decided it is going to be a modern marriage, not the old-fashioned enslavement of the wife by the husband, but a proper partnership.'

'How dreary,' said Sally, flinging herself on the bed. 'I'd happily be a slave to the likes of Andrew Lennox. Tell me, does he have any brothers?'

'Not any unmarried ones.'

'So what are his people like?' asked Catherine.

'Quite grand actually,' said Alix, 'although Andrew doesn't get on with them. His father's a baronet.'

'So you could be Lady Lennox one day?' said Sally.

'It's possible,' said Alix, 'but we're not going to be Mr and Mrs Lennox. He's going to take my name as I shall take his. We'll be the Erskine-Lennoxes.'

'That sounds grander than being Lady Lennox,' observed Sally.

'It's not supposed to be grand,' said Alix. 'It's supposed to sound even-handed, which is what we want to be.'

'Well, I hope all these modern notions haven't got to you so much that you want to deny your friends the pleasure of a good old-fashioned Scottish wedding,' said Catherine.

'I don't think so,' said Alix. 'We'll have dancing until the small hours, I promise.'

'Where will you marry then? In Edinburgh, I suppose?'

'I thought in the country, in my parents' new place, actually.'

'Oh lovely,' said Sally. 'Well, we had better start saving our pennies, Kate, if we are to manage a suitably impressive wedding present. After all, this is going to be quite the wedding of the year, isn't it? What will the papers say now? Scottish industrialist's only daughter weds scion of ancient family! – that's the sort of thing, isn't it?'

'Oh, I hope not,' said Alix. 'I don't want it in the papers, really.'

'You can't be shy about it, Alix. Weddings are a common property,' said Sally. 'They'll want your photograph in the *Tatler*.'

'Yes, gazing into space! Ugh!' She shuddered.

'Or looking down modestly into a bunch of flowers,' said Catherine, striking a pose.

'If you two carry on like this,' said Alix, laughing, 'I shall go and call the whole thing off.'

'No, no, don't do that,' pleaded Sally. 'What on earth will we do for conversation at dinner if you don't marry him?'

'Talking of which, we'd better get dressed hadn't we?' said Alix.

'You'd better wear your white silk dress tonight, Alix,' said Sally, heading towards the door. 'Don't you think, Kate? That would look suitably bridal?'

'Yes, it would show off that glowing complexion, wouldn't it?' said Catherine.

'Do you want a veil and bouquet as well?' retorted Alix.

'We can wait,' said Sally magnanimously. 'See you in half an hour or so then, Mrs Erskine-Lennox,' she added, with particular emphasis.

'Oh, shut up!' Alix shouted as they left, and then laughed in her solitude, partly at their ridiculous banter and partly from her own absolute happiness.

To sit in the Rosses' drawing room after dinner was to be in a waking nightmare. If he had had something to drink the scene might have been bearable, but Ralph's hosts were strictly teetotal and there had not been the comfort of a glass or two of claret to dull the perceptions. So everything was dazzlingly and painfully clear in that great cavernous room, which reminded him more of the crypt of a church in its gothic intensity, a crypt furnished with the worst drawing-room knick-knacks he had ever come across in his life. This combination was almost more than he could bear, and his discomfort was compounded by the fact that Mrs Ross's five unmarried daughters (all between the ages of twenty and thirty) were circling round him like carrion crows. It reminded him irresistibly of a brothel, except that brothels, where the whores paraded themselves to attract the attention of the customer, had at least intellectual honesty to their credit. The Misses Ross would have been outraged at that suggestion of man-hunting, but there was no doubt that they had been primed by their mama to be at their most winning when Mr Erskine came, because he was a young, wealthy and unmarried man who would be considered a very good catch.

If this is them at their most winning, I should hate to see them in a bad temper, he thought, as the eldest of them sidled up with her photograph album. She was about a year his senior, and not unattractive, but her manner was so insipid, so sweetly feminine, that he felt he was being drowned in cheap scent.

'I thought you might be interested to see our photographs

from Florence, Mr Erskine,' she said. 'Such a beautiful city, don't you think? So many wonderful subjects . . .'

'You must be a dedicated photographer, Miss Ross,' said Ralph, observing with dread the thickness of the album. 'But don't you think there's a danger in taking photographs or sketching in such a place as Florence? One is so busy doing the sketch or taking the plate, one forgets to *actually* look properly. I've found I've missed things when I've been sketching.'

'But if one takes a photograph, one can always look later, at one's leisure. Now, this is Santa Maria dei Populi . . . with my sisters Agnes and Gladys outside, as you can see. And these are the Baptistry doors, again with Gladys and Agnes . . .'

The photographs were diabolical, there was no other word for it. No one could have tried more successfully than Miss Ross to distort the beauties of Florence through the lens of a camera. The buildings of Florence were for her a fresh backdrop against which she could arrange the various members of her large family, in seemingly endless combinations, to take inept portraits of them. For they were invariably too far away to tell one from another or too close for a proper focus. Ralph found himself, as she turned each successive page, consumed by a tide of hysterical laughter which he repressed only with the greatest difficulty. He suffered actual physical pain when they reached on the final page, a photograph of the whole Ross tribe, taken in the Uffizi in front of Michelangelo's David, the family so arranged that the statue's genitals appeared to be growing out of Mrs Ross's sensible hat. This was almost too much for Ralph to bear and he was forced to clap his hand over his mouth and brace himself although there was nothing he could do about the tears which were creeping down his cheeks.

Fortunately he was saved. Miss Effie Ross, the youngest of them, seeing that her sister had monopolized him for too long and that it was now her turn, came marching up.

'Mr Erskine must be so bored,' said Effie.

'No, no, far from it,' said Ralph, swallowing the last of

his laughter. 'Very entertaining. You've really caught the spirit of the place, Miss Ross.'

'Why thank you, Mr Erskine,' she said, blessedly impervious to his irony.

'Do you play at all?' asked Effie, going to the piano.

'A little,' said Ralph, 'but I'm hopelessly out of practice.'

'That doesn't matter. Shall we try some duets?'

She was perhaps the liveliest of them all, having just turned twenty, and girlishness was appropriate to her. He could not help but be reminded of Celia, not in her looks, but there was something piquant about her manner which the others did not share.

'You'll probably put me to shame,' he said, as she opened a book of duets. 'I shall only be sight reading.'

'Well, the left hand isn't really important,' she said.

She played with a brilliance which surprised him. He had been expecting a pianistic version of Miss Ross's photographs, but found instead she had a real bravura touch. That she was well aware of this fact he also noticed, for the duet she had chosen had a particularly showy right-hand part, full of runs and leaps in a difficult key, so that he was only able to limp through his own share of the music. It scarcely mattered, for the music was not profound. What mattered of course, was that Effie had been able to show him what a clever pianist she was.

'Do you play any Bach at all?' he asked when they had finished. He wondered if her skill should not be directed to a more worthy cause.

'Oh, you like Bach, do you?' she said, in a voice which was pleasantly disparaging. 'I might have guessed. My teacher likes Bach – she makes me play it.'

'You don't like playing it?'

'Well, it's a bit dull, isn't it? I like a good tune.'

'There are good tunes in Bach, surely? And wonderful harmony.'

'Some of it is a bit painful,' she said. 'And it does go on and on, sometimes.'

'I can't persuade you to play me some, then?'

'Of course I'll play you some,' she said.

As he settled in his chair and she began on a fugue from 'The Well Tempered Clavier', he wondered to what lengths these girls would go to oblige him. Effie disliked Bach but she would willingly play it to him, simply because he had asked. Her desire to please was nauseating and spoilt the pleasure of the music. I would respect her more if she had played what she wanted, and not given in to me like that. God help these women – must they be so submissive? They will make themselves miserable by it. He thought of some of Alix's friends from St Andrews, whom she had brought home to stay in the vacation – bright, high-spirited girls who crackled like incandescent flames, full of laughter and fun, but also powerfully serious about what they were doing. Giving them the freedoms and responsibilities of which their mothers might only have dreamt, had not destroyed their womanly qualities, as some traditionalists maintained. No, they were more impressive for it, more beautiful for it, because they were not caged like Archibald Ross's daughters, but noble and independent, like a race of lionesses ruling over some African plain. Mr and Mrs Ross should be indicted for what they've done to these creatures, thought Ralph, watching these drawing-room prisoners in their frilled dresses, their faces plain with incomprehension as Effie pushed with mechanical precision through the exquisite complexities of a Bach fugue. And what can I do to help them, especially when I'm cruel enough to laugh at them, as one laughs at the animals in the zoo?

2

It was the first really warm day of spring and Jessie and Molly went round the house opening every window they could and taking down the winter curtains. When they had washed down the window frames and dusted the poles, they put up the bright new cretonne curtains which Jessie had only just finished making.

'Well, Mrs Hamilton,' said Molly, studying the effect of the apple green-and-white-striped curtains in the bay window of the drawing room. 'You'll have to keep the blinds down in here now, to keep the sun off the furniture, if that's all you're having in here in the way of curtains.'

'I know,' said Jessie, 'but I hate keeping the blinds down. Why have big windows if you can't let in the sun?'

'Whatever you say, Mrs Hamilton,' said Molly, shaking her head. She had strictly old-fashioned ideas about housekeeping, which made her excellent at her work, but she was never slow to show disapproval of Jessie's way of doing things. If Molly had been left entirely to her own devices, everything would have been covered with green baize and they would have eaten off tin plates: 'In case the good china should get broken.' She was better than an insurance policy in that respect.

Jessie had never imagined she would employ a servant, but after Chloe had been born, Mrs Erskine had found Molly and she had been with them ever since. Jessie was forced to admit she would not have been able to manage without her, for her other two daughters had followed in rapid succession to Chloe. Having three children, all under five, was demanding enough but she had a large house to keep in order now. Molly, for all her dreariness in some ways, had been invaluable, especially when they had moved to Colinton last autumn. In Marchmont Road domestic chaos was somehow less obvious than in this ordered suburb. The other matrons in Redford Road set formidable standards, standards which Jessie would happily have ignored but which Molly regarded as a challenge. Jessie did not really care if Chloe's pinafore was grubby when they walked down to the grocer's together, but Molly would always catch them on the doorstep brandishing a fresh one, sparkling clean and fragrant with starch.

Chloe had just celebrated her fourth birthday. Jessie had given a small party to mark the occasion, attended by Nancy and her children, Mrs Erskine, and the newly affianced Alix. She was glowing with happiness, not just at being engaged but also from having flown through her final examinations and getting a mysterious beast called an 'upper second' for her pains. The only mildly galling circumstance seemed to be that the prospective bridegroom had got a first, but that had not been enough to stop her taking on the role of children's entertainer for the afternoon. 'Getting some practice for when it's her turn, I shouldn't wonder,' Molly had muttered. She had also been thoroughly disappointed by Alix's unshowy engagement ring, and expressed the opinion that she should at least have got him to give her something with a wee bit of a stone on it, and went about shaking her head at Alix's antics with the children. When Chloe and Frank were having what could only be described as a screaming contest, she had said: 'One of them will be sick, Mrs Hamilton, just you wait and see.' She was right, but it wasn't Chloe or Frank but Joceline, Jessie's last born, who at eighteen months had no tolerance to orange jelly. The others survived the ordeal and it was reported to her later that the O'Haras, including Nancy, had slept soundly on the drive back to Edinburgh in Mrs Erskine's carriage. And fortunately Chloe, Flora and Joceline were equally obliging and sleepy so that all was quiet and orderly by the time Sholto got home.

Now that Sholto had passed thirty he had become intolerant of domestic disorder of any kind. It was one of the reasons they had moved to Colinton, to the white-harled modern house with its generous garden. It had been too easy for the children to invade his studious privacy in Marchmont Road. She wondered if it might have been different if one of them had been a boy; if then the children would have meant more to him than noisy expensive inconveniences who merited scant attention.

We might have a boy yet, thought Jessie, wandering into the garden where the girls were being suspiciously quiet. There was nothing to worry about, however. Chloe and Flora were quietly occupied in the sandbox, making castles with an old pie dish, while Joceline had fallen asleep on the rug and cushions spread on the lawn. 'I think I'll join you, Jo,' said Jessie, sitting down beside her. The curtains done, she was in no particular hurry to do anything else. The children's tea was organized and there was no bother about dinner because Sholto was away for two nights in Glasgow. She was at liberty, unless Molly came out with some inspiring suggestion for further spring cleaning. I shall refuse to go along with her, she decided, lifting the sleepy Joceline into her lap, and reclining on the cushions.

'There, are you comfortable, Jo?' There was no response, but no wriggling protest either and she stayed there, warm and heavy, her head resting on Jessie's chest so that she could stroke the soft dark hair. 'There's a good girl . . .' said Jessie, gazing at the sandbox in the distance. Alix had sent it. She had been reading some advanced book on child rearing which recommended them for some abstruse reason Jessie could not at once recall. The reasons did not matter, though. It was the idea which was so good, for it gave them a patch of seashore in their own garden. The next time we go to the sea, thought Jessie, we'll get some shells and some seaweed for it – although Molly won't like that! She laughed to herself at the thought of her face, and then closed her eyes, reassured that all was well.

Two nights away . . . she thought, not with misery but with quiet relief. For when he was there it was almost impossible for her to relax. He liked very much to be master in his own house. He seemed to take over the place with his domineering personality, barking at the girls if they crossed his path and complaining if everything was not just so. He liked his dinner at precisely eight o'clock, and after he liked his coffee served in his own little study. He only ever sat with Jessie in the drawing room if they had a guest, which was rarely. It was also necessary to creep about the house while he worked in the evenings, for he had become acutely sensitive to every noise. Screaming children aroused particular wrath. She had had to learn to handle him with kid gloves. Although she had fought back in the early days, it now seemed pointless. He was too stubborn to change now.

Stubborn, self-willed and indifferent! she thought, holding Joceline a little more closely for comfort, for the state of things between them grieved her. They had set out with such high hopes, and yet what had happened? They were locked in a game, a suburban, pretending game, where their neighbours saw them as a respectable couple, going to church on Sunday with their pretty daughters, and ostensibly very happy about it. But I'm not miserable – I don't have any right to be miserable. Just disappointed, that's all, and really, I shouldn't even be that, not with the girls and all this . . . For she loved the house when Sholto was not there. It was so clean and white, with all those vast windows which filled it with light so that there was not a gloomy corner in the place, not even the kitchen, which opened on to the garden. The garden – oh my wonderful half acre, she thought, for it was as absorbing as any child. She had great plans for its future. What things will I do with this garden! Already the crocuses and daffodils which she had planted last autumn had given a wonderful show.

If pacifying Sholto is the price I have to pay for this, she thought, then I must pay it. It is still better than being a servant. And we were happy once, weren't we? At least we had that.

'You look like an oriental princess,' said a voice. 'All you need here is a fountain and I'll think I've strayed into a seraglio.'

Startled, she sat up very quickly.

'Oh! Oh, it's you, Ralph! What a start you gave me. I was miles away . . .'

'In the land of lost content?'

'What?' She blinked, disturbed that he had captured her thoughts in a remark.

'The land of lost content – it's Housman, from "A Shropshire Lad". You should read it, it is excellent stuff:

> '. . . That is the land of lost content,
> I see it shining plain
> The happy highways where I went
> And cannot come again.'

It took a moment for her to absorb what he had said and then she answered, 'Yes, that *is* good.'

'I'll send you a copy,' he smiled.

At this point Joceline woke up and put such a miserable expression on her face that Jessie wondered if it were indeed true that babies could sense, by some strange resonance, their mother's moods.

'Oh what's the matter with you?' she said.

'She doesn't like Housman, obviously,' said Ralph, bending over her and lifting Jo from her lap. 'Well, what do you like, Jo?' he said, jiggling her a little, so that she smiled and gurgled.

'I don't think she has any opinions yet,' said Jessie, pleased by the easy way he had taken her. The girls had little enough fatherly attention. 'You will stay for tea?'

'I was hoping you'd say that,' said Ralph. 'I've just motored up from Garbridge, and the road was rather hot and dusty.'

'I'm glad you came this way. It's been a while, Ralph.'

'I know, I'm sorry – I don't seem to have much time to myself these days. It's the price one has to pay, I suppose,' he said, glancing around him. 'It really is very pleasant here, isn't it?'

'I shall get the garden better yet,' said Jessie. 'Chloe! Flora! Come here now – it's time to get washed for tea.'

When they got inside, Molly was horrified at the state of the children in front of a visitor and rushed them upstairs to the bathroom.

'Do you mind eating in here?' said Jessie, when they were left alone in the kitchen. 'Molly fears too much for the dining-room carpet to let them in there yet.'

'Of course I don't mind.'

Alone in the bathroom, hovering over a basin of steaming water, Ralph felt a rare sense of comfort. It was odd, for he had not liked the nondescript modern villa when he had first seen it. He had thought it commonplace, but now it seemed anything but that. Jessie had made the place entirely her own, over-riding what he knew to be Sholto's rather vulgar taste, with her own perfect good sense. Her natural aesthetic sense, quite untutored and so pure as a result, delighted him. Even in the bathroom one could see

286

it, from the great jug of blazing yellow daffodils on the window sill to the small oak cupboard with gothic panels. Forgetting for a moment the elegance that awaited him at Allansfield, he considered how pleasant it would be to come back home to such a place, to throw one's weary bones in a hot bath, smelling that clean, sweet smell that hung in the air and hearing the children's voices from the room below. Such ordinary comforts, which in the past he might have despised, now seemed as precious as anything in his collection.

When he came to put his shirt back on, he found his collar and cuffs were too dirty to use again, and deciding that Jessie was hardly the person to object to shirt sleeves or open necks, discarded them. He left his jacket and waistcoat on a chair on the landing and went downstairs, imagining idly how it might feel to be the man of such a house. I should have filled up these walls with pictures by now – but that would have spoilt the simplicity of it. But one or two really good things . . . and he wished he might send some to her. But Sholto might take that amiss.

In the kitchen the table had been laid for tea with a checked cloth and Jessie was sitting at one end, the window behind her, presiding over a large brown tea pot. There was a space at the other end, at which she indicated he was to sit.

'Is this Sholto's place?' he asked, diffident for a moment about taking it.

'Oh no, he never comes in here,' she said matter-of-factly.

He doesn't know what he's missing, thought Ralph, leaning back in his chair and sipping his tea. He had rarely seen Jessie look so charming as she did that afternoon, although it was hardly the grandeur of the setting or the elegance of her clothes which made it seem so. Rather, it was the absolute artlessness of it all, making everything beautiful despite itself. For behind her, on the broad window sill, was a bank of geranium plants in cheerful terracotta pots which had not been put there to make a display but because it was a good spot for them to winter in. Her clothes were also not for display but for comfortable practicality – a deep blue linen dress that had been washed so often it had faded and softened into something quite different, and an apron, trimmed only with the slightest bit of lace at the top of its deep pocket. He thought suddenly of the Ross girls and their ridiculous clothes, which they had seemed to change umpteen times a day as if just to demonstrate how wealthy their father was, and admired Jessie's simplicity all the more. It meant that three small children eating bread and jam were not an inconvenience to her but a pleasure.

He found as he observed Jessie that Chloe was observing him. She was sitting on a pile of cushions on a handsome old settle which stood with its back to the wall, along one side of the kitchen table. Carefully, between both hands, she held a cup of milk, but had forgotten it while she stared at Ralph.

'What do you find so interesting, Chloe?' he asked.

She thought for a moment, and said haltingly, 'Where's your beard? My daddy has a beard.'

'I decided not to grow one,' he said. 'It's a thing that men have a choice about, but I'm afraid you won't be able to have one.'

'Oh,' she said, disappointed. 'Really?'

'I'm afraid not. But you do look a lot like your father already, if that's any comfort.'

'Yes, doesn't she?' observed Jessie. 'Mind what you do with that cup, Chloe.'

'I don't like milk,' she said, and put down the cup, obviously determined not to drink any more. 'Why do I look like Daddy then?' she said.

Oh God! thought Ralph, unable to think of an answer. He appealed with a glance to Jessie. She, smiling at his confusion, said, 'Well, that's a difficult question, Chloe, but roughly, it's because it takes two people to make a baby and they give certain parts of themselves to the new baby – so you have some things that are from me, like the colour of your eyes, and something from Daddy, like the shape of your nose. It's like when you make a cake – you put different things in, that come from different places, and you get something new. But you can sometimes pick out the bits and pieces you put together in the first place.'

'What an excellent analogy,' said Ralph, impressed by her frankness. He had a suspicion had he asked his own mother such a question when he was that age she would have answered, 'Because God decided you should look like him.'

Chloe looked up at him.

'Is she right?' she said.

'Who's she, Chloe?' said Jessie.

'Is Mummy right?' Chloe corrected herself.

'Yes, indeed.'

This affirmation seemed to satisfy the child perfectly and nothing else was heard on the subject, for she was now intent on drinking her milk.

'More tea, Ralph?' said Jessie, her eyes alight with amusement still. The children had got down from the table now and had gone into the garden with the maid to run around for a while.

'Why are you laughing at me?' he said, not at all displeased that she was.

'I wish you could have seen your face,' she said.

'I'd forgotten children could be so direct.'

'You were lost for words, weren't you?'

'Certainly. But I think you did the right thing.'

'Good,' she smiled. 'Sholto wouldn't have, you know. But I can't think there's any point in covering things up. Ignorance is a dreadful thing. I've seen lots of girls come to grief because of it.'

'I'll drink to that!' he said, and pushed his tea cup over to her. 'Tell me, Jessie, are you still an ardent suffragist?'

'In spirit, but I don't really have the time. Those three keep me very busy.'

'Can't Molly mind them now and again?'

'I can't bring myself to do that. I always thought it was funny the way rich people let others bring up their children, as if they couldn't be bothered themselves. I should think your mother was quite exceptional in the amount of time she spent with you.'

'We still had a nurse though,' said Ralph, 'Nanny Evans.

She made me give a shilling I'd saved up to the African orphans – I really resented that. She was a tough woman. She would have made a good businessman.'

Jessie laughed and said, 'Yes, Sholto thought we should have a nurse. How we were supposed to pay her, I don't know, but he thought it would be the right thing.'

'He's very conventional isn't he? It surprises me – at one time he was so . . . wild.'

'He stands on his dignity too much these days,' said Jessie, with a trace of bitterness in her voice that surprised him. He looked at her searchingly for a moment, but she avoided his gaze and began to clear away the tea things. She paused for a moment and gazed out of the window. 'You wonder how they'll grow up sometimes,' she remarked, 'what they'll do with their lives.'

Ralph watched the children. Chloe was playing with a doll, while Flora was spinning round in circles, presumably trying to make herself dizzy. Joceline, less adventurously, was crawling across the rug, pushing a ball.

'Well, I can't imagine that they'll make a mess of them,' said Ralph. 'Not with you bringing them up so sensibly.'

'Oh, we all make messes,' she said with a sigh, 'no matter how sensible we think we are, don't we?'

'I suppose so – it's part of the human condition.'

'Unfortunately,' she said, with resignation, and went over to the sink. 'Why don't you go and play with them, Ralph?' she appealed. 'Sholto never does. It would be good for them.'

It transpired that Ralph was a born storyteller, a talent of which he had not been aware until he was requested to tell one. Jessie stood at the nursery door and watched him sitting there in the lamplight, with Chloe and Flora on either side, absolutely rapt, as he told the story of Theseus and the Minotaur, which she might have thought too strong for such small children but which they seemed utterly fascinated by. When it was over they demanded another, but Ralph told them to get into bed and imagine how it must have felt to be the Minotaur trapped in his labyrinth.

That was where the general sympathy lay, it seemed, not with the hero Theseus.

'Close your eyes now, and lie still and think,' he said softly, putting out the lamp.

'You'll give them terrible nightmares,' said Jessie, on the landing outside.

'Oh no, they're too upset for that,' he said lightly.

'I wish Sholto was like you with them,' she said, as they went downstairs. 'He simply isn't interested.'

'Perhaps when they're older?'

'Perhaps,' she said. 'Now the children are in bed, shall we have something to drink?'

They went into the drawing room which was looking particularly smart that evening. Molly had lit the lamps and had been so good as to leave the blinds up, so that the magnificent sunset was rolling down in front of the french windows.

'Oh, I'm so glad I came here today,' said Ralph, throwing himself into an armchair, as if it were his favourite. 'It's been wonderful.'

'After all that work I've made you do?'

'That wasn't work, that was pure pleasure. They are lovely children, Jessie. I envy you them.'

'You'll have your own one day,' she said. 'Gin and soda is it?'

'You don't forget anything, do you?'

If she had once thought him ill favoured, she now revised her opinion. It was not that she suddenly thought him wildly handsome, but that she saw in that craggy face, when he smiled, that he was wearing the course a good deal better than Sholto. He had also started to wear his hair back from his forehead which made him look a great deal more distinguished. In twenty years' time, she reckoned, he would not look fifty, whereas she was sure Sholto would.

'You should marry, Ralph, you know,' she said, handing him a drink and sitting down opposite.

He shook his head.

'No, that's quite an impossibility. What wife could bear

the hours I keep? Besides, there's no one I feel remotely . . .'

'I'm sorry, I shouldn't have said that . . .'

'It doesn't matter. I'm used to it. My mother says it all the time.'

'I can guess.'

Lucky the woman who gets you, Ralph Erskine, she thought, but she was not thinking of his money, for that seemed irrelevant as he sat there in braces and shirt sleeves, looking quite ordinary, as if he were only doing something very humble in life. It was his kindness, his warmth, his cheerfulness she was thinking of, for they were indications of a great capacity to love. She thought of how he had been with her children and imagined how he might love his own, and how he might love a wife, with a measureless generosity of spirit which would hold fast through every disaster. He had so much to give and yet he so willingly condemned himself to loneliness. Perhaps he's never recovered from that business with the Lennox girl . . . but what a shame, and what a damned waste of himself.

'Yes, she'd like nothing better than for me to settle down,' Ralph went on. 'But I am settled, in a way. At least – too settled to let anyone else in.'

'I can't imagine that if you loved someone you'd be so selfish,' said Jessie. 'You're not that sort of person.'

'Am I not?' he said, raising an eyebrow quizzically. 'I wish I could live up to your good opinion.'

'You do,' she said, leaning forward. 'You can't say these dreadful things about yourself. It doesn't rub.'

'Oh, dear Jessie, why aren't there more people in the world like you?' he said, reaching out and squeezing her hand briefly.

'I'm sure there are,' she said. 'I'm very ordinary.'

'If you are ordinary, Jessie, then you are a genius of ordinariness. I rather think you are extraordinary.'

His sincerity embarrassed her, partly because she felt unworthy of his words, and partly because it gratified her. His admiration was somehow terribly precious to her and she could not think how she could respond adequately.

'You're a good friend, Ralph,' she said, at length. 'A very good friend.'

'Yes, we're lucky aren't we? Real friendship, without complications, between a man and woman is so very rare . . .'

3

Whatever modern notions Alix might have held about marriage, it soon became clear that these could only be put into practice after the wedding because Mrs Erskine, determined to make the marriage of her only daughter memorable, presented her with a fait accompli. It was as if she had arranged a hundred weddings for she had a fixed opinion about every trivial thing concerned with them. At first Alix had thought of protesting, but when she saw how much pleasure making the arrangements was bringing her mother, she had not the heart to demur. And strangely enough, as the time drew nearer, she began to enjoy it as much, finding a surprising excitement in every frivolous trimming.

The ceremony, according to the old Scots tradition, was not to be held in a church, but in the large living hall at Allansfield which seemed a momentous way of marking the completion of the house and which had caused the architect to remark that had he known, he would have worked some appropriate symbolism into the plasterwork. But Alix felt it needed no further elaboration. She thought the room quite perfect as it was, for it seemed to blend the past and the present in a way which was very appropriate for a wedding. For were they not, when they made their vows, going to embark upon a fresh journey, fusing their two separate pasts into one common future?

And what will happen to us? she could not help wondering, not with fear but with excitement. She knew the basic structure of the rest of the year, of course: on Friday morning they would be married, and they would leave the next day from Aberdeen for a cruise around the Norwegian fjords. When they came back, Andrew would start work at Garbridge – Mr Erskine had made him a junior partner – and she would no doubt spend a certain amount of time arranging the little house in Saxe-Coburg Place for which they had just signed a long lease. But those facts, she felt, contained no indications of what it would really be like, how it would actually feel to be married to Andrew, to find him beside her in bed each morning when she woke up. Well, I shall know soon enough, she reflected, for it was the Wednesday afternoon before the wedding, and she was lying on her bed because her mother had told her to rest. In a while she would get up and put on her new tea gown – an exotic item that was part of her trousseau – and she would go downstairs to greet the guests who were about to arrive.

'Well,' said Sholto, folding up his newspaper and leaving it on the seat opposite, for the train was coming into Cupar station, 'I suppose this wedding business will have some compensations. At least the wine will be good if Ralph has anything to do with it – whatever his follies in some respects, he knows a decent drop when he sees it. And I should imagine the house will be quite luxurious. One can't really complain.'

'You don't like weddings, do you?' said Jessie, getting up.

'No, especially not society weddings,' said Sholto, yawning. 'Oh, don't look like that, Jessie, for God's sake.'

'Like what?' she said.

'So bloody disapproving.'

'It wasn't intentional. I'm just worried about the children.'

'You've only been away from them an hour,' said Sholto. 'Molly will keep them in line – better than you do, anyway.'

'Sholto, I don't think we'd better arrive at the Erskines' having an argument,' she said, taking her hat box down from the luggage rack. 'It is supposed to be a wedding we're going to.'

'Who is having an argument?' he said. 'Not me, I assure you.'

Jessie gritted her teeth and stared at the upholstery for a moment, trying to keep her temper reined in. It was the first time she had left the girls for more than an afternoon – they would be there until Saturday morning, and she was already missing them. Sholto had done little to make her feel better, for it was he who had insisted she leave them, although she had felt sure Mrs Erskine would gladly have found room for them.

She had wanted to be at Alix's wedding, but as things had turned out her pleasurable anticipation had been almost entirely destroyed. Leaving the children was one cause, and Sholto's bad grace another. For he disliked Alix and had given Jessie only a trifle to buy her a wedding present. 'What does she need with wedding presents? They should give them to us!' he had complained. And worst of all was the prospect of coming face to face with Mrs Lennox again, for as much as Andrew claimed he did not get on with his family, they could hardly be excluded from the festivities.

A motor had come to meet them at the station, which she recognized at once as Ralph's for it was the one he had driven to Colinton. It was a large, sleek-looking thing, surprisingly elegant for a machine, and the thought of riding in it made her decide she would enjoy herself. After all, it did not do to appear gloomy at a wedding, no matter how rotten one might feel. Sholto was less than polite. His face wore an expression of open disdain as they walked over to it.

'Good God, Ralph,' he said, 'I'm surprised you actually use these things.'

'Oh, I was a slow convert, but now I'm a convinced one,' said Ralph. 'Climb in.' And he held open the door for Jessie.

'You're not going to break our necks, are you?' she said, suddenly nervous.

'No, I promise.'

Jessie sat in the back and pulled down her veil, for she had heard that motoring had a way of throwing all the dirt of the road into one's face. Sholto sat in the front, presumably making cynical comments which she could not hear for the noise of the engine was quite considerable. But she could not imagine he was praising the wonders of Ralph's machine. That would have been uncharacteristic.

Driving along the winding road from Cupar to Allansfield, Jessie could understand why Ralph's business was doing so well. It was quite a thrilling thing to bowl along at such speed and in such style and she wondered if she would ever learn to drive such a beast. *I wish the girls were here – they would love this. It's far better than the train, or even a tram.* Trams were Chloe's favourite form of transport and Jessie was glad she had such economical tastes and could be lifted into paradise simply by being allowed to ride upstairs on one. *But if I had three hundred guineas, I should buy one of these, and learn to drive it – what jaunts we could all have then!* she decided, as they turned into the long driveway. *But I shall never have three hundred guineas of my own . . . nor a house like this. Goodness, isn't it beautiful!*

Nothing that Mrs Erskine or Ralph had said about the house had prepared her for the reality of it. It was quite the most perfect thing she had ever seen. It was not too grand or overpowering, but it was large enough to have very real dignity. They drove up to the entrance, which was sheltered by an arched loggia up which a diligent gardener had already begun to train a few climbers, one of which, a pale clematis, was already flowering. In a few years, it would be a magnificent sight.

Ralph brought the car to a standstill, and glanced over his shoulder at her.

'Well?' he asked.

She lifted up her veil and smiled.

'Perfect!'

'God, I'll never keep you satisfied now, Jessie,' said Sholto. 'How much did this lot cost?'

'Wait until you see inside,' said Ralph, ignoring Sholto.

To her surprise, Ralph offered her his arm and took her inside. Sholto followed a few paces behind them, looking determined not to be impressed. He was too jealous, she reckoned.

Jessie had no thought of jealousy, however, for how could one be jealous of something one could not possibly hope to have? It was a pointless activity and it was better to enjoy oneself instead, as if to be there was a privilege rather than a right.

Alix met them first. She came running down the handsome staircase to the side of the large entrance hall, dressed in a magnificent creation of white chiffon and lace, so that Jessie thought for a moment they had caught her trying on her wedding dress. It proved to be 'only' a tea gown. Only! thought Jessie, amused. It is going to be some wedding dress . . . On anyone else, the dress might have been overpowering, but Alix was so radiant that afternoon that she overpowered it, in fact overpowered everyone so that one could not help but stare at her. She was obviously at a fever pitch of excitement and happiness, which transformed her from being merely a pretty girl into someone indescribably beautiful.

In the drawing room Jessie found all she had been dreading, and Alix all that she hoped for, for the Lennoxes were there. They were not staying at Allansfield but with some friends nearby and this tea hour would be the last time that the bride and groom would see each other until their wedding day. So it was not surprising that Alix rushed up to Andrew, who jumped out of his chair the moment they came in. They kissed each other, rather briefly but with unmistakable passion, so that Jessie thought, No wonder she looks like that! This intimate informality dispensed with, they collected themselves and the business of introductions and hand shaking began.

The irony was almost too much for Jessie, who found that Sir Hector insisted on kissing her hand, saying that it was a pleasure to meet young Hamilton's wife at last. He had aged considerably, as had James Lennox who had grown florid in complexion, but Mrs Lennox appeared no different. Only her clothes seemed to have changed, for they were startlingly fashionable, but her face appeared to have been preserved as if in aspic, still astonishingly beautiful but without warmth. When they shook hands, their gloved hands touched so slightly that Jessie wondered if she was quite real. She made her think of the mechanical doll, Coppelia, described in one of Chloe's story books. It was quite a relief, for no sign of recognition flickered on that mask-like white face. I was stupid to worry, thought Jessie, sitting down beside Mrs Erskine. It has been a long time, after all . . .

'It's been too long, Mr Hamilton,' said Mrs Lennox.

'Yes, it has,' smiled Sholto, 'but I can see no evidence of time passing in you.'

'You're too kind,' she said. 'Isn't this a charming room?'

'I always think that rooms are made charming by their occupants.'

'Well, she will make a lovely bride,' said Mrs Lennox, indicating Alexandra Erskine.

'She's not the only handsome woman in the room,' said Sholto.

'Your wife is handsome,' she observed. 'But is that any surprise? I couldn't imagine that you would have married an ugly woman.'

'That would depend how much money she had,' said Sholto.

'You are shameless, Mr Hamilton, I do remember that.'

'I see no harm in being frank.'

'You are refreshingly direct.' She smiled, leaning back in her chair a little, so that more of her face, previously hidden under her hat, was now visible to him. It was a very pleasant sight. He did not need to flatter her. To tell her that she was pretty was to understate the matter and he found her manner coolly tantalizing. I should think she has a lover, reflected Sholto. She wouldn't stay faithful to James. She's too independent for that.

'So what have you been up to all these years?' said Mrs Lennox. 'I hear you made a great noise at the bar. My husband is always speaking of your successes.'

'I've had my share,' he said, 'although some people think of me as notorious.'

'Why? Because you defend those terrible criminals?'

'Well, because I get them off.'

'How clever you are. I'm sure they don't deserve you. They probably all deserve to be hanged.'

'Justice demands that even the devil should have an advocate,' said Sholto. 'Now there's a brief I should like. He really is a most maligned fellow.'

'I should like to see you do that,' she said.

'I shouldn't let you into the court,' he said. 'I shouldn't be playing to the jury, but to you.'

'Mr Hamilton, really . . .' she murmured, but there was no hint of a reproach in her voice. But she did get up from her chair and walk away to speak to someone else, which did not grieve him greatly for it gave him a chance to look at her superb figure. It was strange how he had not appreciated it before. Perhaps the fashion of five years ago had not shown it to such effect, but her gown that afternoon revealed as much as it concealed. There was something about the cut of the skirt, which was made in a glistening, soft stuff the colour of a glass of sweet sherry, which made the swing of her hips particularly obvious and which stirred in him all sorts of pleasant memories of past conquests.

When the Lennoxes had gone, everyone dispersed and Jessie found herself alone with Ralph.

'Come and see my library,' he said. 'I've been looking forward to showing it to you.'

'Why to me?' she asked, amused.

'Because you have excellent taste and you will appreciate it.'

'That's an order, is it?'

'Of course,' he laughed. 'It is my favourite room.'

'I think it would be hard to make up your mind in this house,' she said, as they walked through the living hall.

'I'm so glad you like it,' he said, pushing open a door. 'Voila! Ça va?'

'Ça va bien, Monsieur,' she said, looking around the room. 'C'est absolument parfait.'

'I didn't know you spoke French,' he said.

'Oh Monsieur Auguste made sure of that. I'm probably very rusty, though I have taught Chloe a bit.'

'Chloe sera très bien instruite, Madame.'

'Je l'éspère – oh, Ralph, this is ridiculous!'

'I like to speak French,' said Ralph. 'It's such a pleasant language. Not as beautiful as Italian, but it is so civilized, don't you think?'

'I don't know,' she said. 'How would I? Besides, aren't I supposed to be admiring your library?'

'Tell me what you think of it then,' he said.

She went further into the room and walked slowly round it, letting the details of it register with her.

'It feels so comfortable, doesn't it?' she said. 'I want to sit in that chair and never move.' There were two chairs by the fireside. 'Which is yours?'

'This one,' he said, sitting down in the one opposite that which she had indicated. 'Sit down then.'

'Why two chairs, Ralph?' she asked.

'So my friends can sit here,' he said, and leant back in his own chair, smiling, his hands folded under his chin, while she walked around again and looked at the pictures.

'Who are these ladies then?' she asked, indicating the three portraits which hung on the far wall, above the long half-height book case. 'They look as if they are all by the same person.'

'That's right – those are my Ramsays. Well, two of them are definitely by him, but the little one isn't so certainly his. It could be by a pupil, but I think it has all the marks of being by him. And I also bought it because it reminded me of you a little.'

'You did?' she said, astonished.

'Well, she does, doesn't she?' he said, perhaps a little embarrassed by his admission.

She looked again at the picture and saw that in a sense he was right. The hair and clothes were strange, but there was something about her eyes and expression which made Jessie shiver with recognition.

'Goodness!' she exclaimed. 'But who is she?'

'A Miss Hepburn from Inverness. Are there any Hepburns in your family?'

'I shouldn't think so,' she said with a nervous laugh, because she had not quite recovered from what he had said earlier.

'I'm sorry, I didn't mean to embarrass you,' he said. 'You've gone red, you know.'

'Oh God!' she exclaimed, glancing at him. 'Have I?'

'Yes, it's very pretty actually,' he said, and then turned away and picked up an ornament from the shelf, fingering it nervously. 'What do you think of this then?' he said quickly. 'I think these things are charming – they always make me laugh.'

It was a little metal sculpture of a cockerel, its feathers of brightly painted enamel highlighted in gold. The head of the cockerel was inclined to one side and it had such an absurd expression that she could not help laughing.

'Yes, it is funny, isn't it? The children would like it, though it's too good for a toy, I'm sure. Is it very old?'

'Eighteenth-century – it's Chinese cloisonné work. There's a little group of them here.'

'How lovely they are.'

'Yes, I was lucky to find those. They're very sought after, it seems. There's a man in London who has dozens of them. When he heard I'd got them, he wrote to me asking to buy them. He offered a good price.'

'I'm glad you didn't sell them.'

'So am I, they dispel my melancholy. And they're so pleasant to handle, don't you think? Very soothing.'

'Yes, very,' she said, relieved that they appeared to be talking normally again. That sudden plunge into deep waters had been frightening. She had felt almost out of control, rocked by his admission of affection, for that was how it had seemed. We're friends, she reassured herself, it's quite permissible for us to like each other, isn't it? If he had my photograph, I shouldn't be worried, should I?

'Ah, here you are,' said Mrs Erskine, coming in. 'Ralph, I hope you aren't boring Jessie with all your things.'

'No, I'm not the least bit bored,' said Jessie. 'They're all so lovely.'

'You see, Mother, I'm not the only one.'

'Don't feel you have to be polite to him,' said Mrs Erskine. 'He thinks far too much about his collection. It isn't healthy, really it isn't.'

'Would you rather I bet on the horses, Mother? A man must have a vice.'

'I don't agree,' she said, 'but I shan't argue with you now, Ralph. It's not a time for arguing, is it? Alix is having a last fitting for her dress, Jessie – she wants to know if you want to see it?'

'Oh, yes please,' she said. 'I should be honoured.'

'And I do have another, rather awful favour to ask you,' said Mrs Erskine. 'Tomorrow, would you come with me and check that the kitchen staff know what they are about? I'm sure I'll have forgotten to tell them everything.'

'Oh course, I'd be happy to,' said Jessie. 'Two heads are always better than one in these things.'

'That was exactly what I thought,' said Mrs Erskine.

He was sad to see her go. Although he had planned the room for solitude, her presence had lit up the interior in a way he had not predicted. Others might intrude upon him there, but she would always be welcome. When the door opened again, he hoped it was her returning. But it was not – it was Sholto.

He did not ask if he might come in, which needled Ralph, but walked in confidently, sitting down opposite him quite as if it were his room and Ralph had been waiting there for him, as a visitor awaits his host.

'Well, well,' Sholto said, reaching for his cigarette case. 'It's been a long time since we had a tête-à-tête, hasn't it? We don't seem to run into each other like we used to.'

'No, it seems not,' said Ralph. 'How's the bar these days?'

'Oh, nothing to complain about it,' he said, lighting up.

Ralph wished he had not, for the smell of cigarette smoke always made him feel slightly ill. 'I don't need to ask you how you're doing, do I? The evidence is all around me – yes, this is quite some style, Ralph. It's a damned long way from those digs we had in Tollcross, isn't it?'

'So is your house in Colinton.'

Sholto frowned and said, 'Ah yes, Colinton.'

'I think Jessie likes it there,' said Ralph.

'Well, she has funny ideas. It comes from having been a kitchen maid. But personally I can't see that the place has much to recommend it apart from a fast train into town. It is full of ministers and gossips and generally indifferent people. It would drive *you* insane, Ralph.'

Shocked by this disparaging remark about Jessie, he felt inclined to be combative.

'That isn't how it struck me. I thought it was rather charming, artistic even . . .'

'Artistic!' exclaimed Sholto, laughing. 'My God, Ralph, you never change, do you? You're still as daft as you were at seventeen.'

'I'm glad to hear it,' said Ralph. 'I should rather be old and foolish than old and pompous.'

This had no effect, of course, and Ralph got little satisfaction from saying it. Sholto, naturally unabashed, went over to the window, his hands thrust in his pockets, his cigarette disgustingly stuck in the corner of his mouth. Ralph stared at him, wondering how he could ever have been intimate with this man. Once they had lived hand in glove, but now he seemed nothing more than a disagreeable stranger.

'Any chance of a drink?' said Sholto. 'You used to keep a decent drop of whisky about the place, I remember.'

4

It was the first opportunity Jessie had had of seeing a society wedding at first hand, but she suspected that the ceremony she witnessed (or indeed the very lack of it) was not typical. It was true that all the expected elements were there – the white dress, the veil, the flowers, the silk hats, the champagne and bride cake – but the general effect was anything but conventional. Alix and Andrew were too striking a couple to be merely the pretty bride and handsome bridegroom that custom demanded. They were too fair and tall and self-possessed for that, and the sight of them together inspired awe rather than notions of sentimental romance. Jessie wished for a moment that Andrew's costume might have been as picturesque as Alix's, that he might wear boots with golden spurs, a sword at his hip, a gold circlet on his brow and a swathe of plaid about him so that he might resemble a Celtic nobleman of ancient times. For she, in a dress of silk brocade that was not white but the palest shade of gold, seemed as she came downstairs, her face covered in a long veil, to have stepped straight from the pages of a story book, and Jessie half expected that they should all kneel and do homage to her as the daughter of a king. But instead everyone stood in perfect silence and stared, for there was really nothing else one could do, while she lifted up her veil and smiled on her lover, as if she were seeing him for the first time.

They made their vows quietly but confidently, the ring was put on her finger and the minister pronounced them man and wife. Then, with a quick movement which surprised everyone Andrew had pulled his wife into his arms and kissed her very vigorously for a moment, as if he were sealing the contract they had just made. Jessie noticed that the minister, a dry-looking man despite his youthful appearance, seemed quite shocked at this, but Jessie could see nothing shocking in it and it moved her more than the words of the vows, for with that kiss Andrew seemed to affirm all his love and loyalty towards Alix. They will be happy, I'm sure of it, she thought.

While the register was signed a quiet hum of conversation broke out amongst the guests. Sholto, who sat beside her, drummed his fingers on his leg and looked less than impressed.

'Well, well, that's that,' he said. 'At least we escaped a sermon from the minister. I wonder how long we shall have to wait before we can get a drink. There is always such an infernal lot of waiting around at weddings.'

Jessie could not help but remember their wedding. There had been no flowers, no guests, no ministers, but there had been a bottle of champagne, which they had drunk in bed in the afternoon. There had been no waiting around on that morning. They had hopped out of the cab into the Register Office in Bruntsfield and had come out again, a scant quarter of an hour later, as man and wife. Then they had gone back to the empty flat and made love for the first time in their new brass bedstead. At the time she would not have not swapped that wedding for anything, for the wildness of their passion for each other seemed to strew metaphorical roses in their way. The haste of the thing, which now seemed indecorous and ill-considered, had been wonderfully exciting. She had not had a moment to think about what she was doing and she had done it, breathless, with the anticipation of living for the rest of her life in that state of euphoria which had characterised their brief affair at the Quarro.

She watched Mrs Lennox get up from her seat and go and kiss the bride. She was dressed so that no one in the room could fail to notice her, in an apricot-coloured silk dress that was ruched and tucked and trimmed in the most fantastic fashion. It seemed to drip with lace, like a bough heavily laden with blossom, and Jessie wondered how many hours of tedious work it had cost her dressmaker. For she made her own clothes now (after some careful instruction by Nancy O'Hara who had been trained by clever nuns) and knew the labour even the slightest trimming entailed. For the sake of one's eyes it was best to err on the side of simplicity – and had not Monsieur Auguste always advocated that simplicity in dress was true elegance? Would he have thought Mrs Lennox elegant? she asked herself, and watched how one or two male heads turned as Mrs Lennox moved across the room. She glanced to her side and saw that Sholto was also looking at her and that his expression of discontent had quite gone away.

'Have you seen the gardens here?' asked Olivia Lennox. 'They are very pleasant for such a modern house. I wonder how they managed it.'

'With money,' said Sholto, 'one can get anything done, I imagine.'

'Yes, I suppose so,' said Mrs Lennox. 'Shall we go and look at them then, Mr Hamilton?'

Her invitation was gratifying. A tête-à-tête in the garden with the prettiest woman there was an infinitely more pleasing prospect than continuing with bland small talk amongst the other guests. Weddings, he considered, were infuriating affairs, an utter waste of time at which one rarely even got decently fed and watered. Such a diversion was therefore extremely welcome.

'I should be honoured,' he said, and offered her his arm.

It seemed, as they walked down the steps from the terrace to the lawn, that it had been too long since he had enjoyed the pleasures of walking with an attractive woman whom he knew only slightly. A few years ago it had been a common enough thing with him. Indeed, he had been addicted to the experience; those subtle, enjoyable moments of pursuit when acquaintanceship slipped imperceptibly into intimacy. It was delightfully refreshing to rediscover it, and it made it seem almost like the first time he had ever done such a thing, for Olivia Lennox was in a somewhat different league from the ballet girls and barmaids who had been his conquests in his bachelor days, those arcadian, distant days . . .

Is it possible to recapture them? he wondered, as Mrs

Lennox put up her parasol with an enchantingly coquettish gesture. Perhaps . . . for she smiled at him now, and he felt a stab of something which he thought had died with him: an intense moment of energetic desire and not that simple passive admiration which he generally felt too lazy to do anything about. If he saw a pretty girl he might have thought of her while making love to his wife, to give the experience a little, very necessary piquancy. But Olivia Lennox had awoken his old lust with a smile and he wanted her with unsettling urgency.

She seemed to shimmer beside him as they walked along a herbaceous border, a fabulous vision of femininity, made essentially to be possessed by man, to be transported by love. If this were Paris, he thought, princes would pay handsomely just to sit beside her . . .

'What are you thinking, Mr Hamilton?' she said, smiling again.

'I was thinking,' he began and wondered how precise he should be, 'how pleasant it is to be away from the wedding party. I find these affairs rather vapid I must confess.'

'I quite agree,' said Mrs Lennox, sitting down on the bench which terminated the walk. 'They are not really adult entertainments, are they? And they are always so very predictable.'

She is not only beautiful, thought Sholto, but sensible as well!

'Yes, they express such a conventional, such a novelettish view of romance, don't you think?' he said. 'Such a pretence of love, when of course people really marry for convenience.'

'Perhaps,' she said. 'But in the case of my brother-in-law, who could not love a girl with so much money? It would be difficult, would it not?'

'He is lucky she is not ugly.'

'Very lucky. We were all astonished, you know. We never thought he would have such good sense.'

'He is set up for life now,' said Sholto. 'All the Erskines dote on him, I understand. I suppose he is the sort of fellow the old man should have liked as a son. I suspect he was

307

rather disconcerted by what he did produce!'

'You mean Ralph Erskine? I suppose he is a little odd.'

'Soft in the head,' said Sholto. 'I've known him for years so I can say that.'

'So you're not the great friends you once were?'

Sholto shook his head and said, 'No, we have nothing in common now. We pursue different pleasures. He collects Ming and I . . .'

'Yes, what are your pleasures, Mr Hamilton?'

'Can't you guess?'

'I suspect you are a connoisseur of women,' she said, with surprising but delightful directness.

'Let me put it this way,' said Sholto, 'I do appreciate a fine pair of eyes and a pretty hand.'

Her expression seemed to say: Yes, I know you appreciate me – for I know how lovely I am, but this lack of modesty did not annoy him. He detested false modesty.

Encouraged, he took her hand in his own and began gently to pull off her pale kid glove, loosening each finger in turn. She did not object in the least, but he had known she would not, for he sensed that her mind was running on the same course as his own: that they both tempted each other.

'Well, is it pretty?' she said, spreading out her fingers. He said nothing, but bent over and kissed her hand, thinking, Good God – what will it be like to undress this creature if I feel like this from merely taking off her glove?

'You flatter me too much,' she said. 'Perhaps I don't deserve such a tribute.'

'You deserve more than that,' he said. 'You know you do. You deserve a lover who will appreciate how infinitely precious you are.'

'You would like to be my lover, I think, Mr Hamilton.'

'I should, if that notion does not offend you.'

'No,' she smiled. 'I cannot say that it does. My life has been very dull lately.'

'Oh, my dear lady,' he said, very pleased with her answer, 'then we shall make some amusement for ourselves – some discreet, adult amusement. We shall have to arrange something soon, don't you think, because, you see, Mrs

Lennox, I am quite bouleversé!'

She inclined her head in a gesture of gracious assent.

'Ah, Mrs Lennox,' he said, 'you are the perfect antidote to a wedding.'

'You must call me Olivia now,' she said, adding another crown to Sholto's sudden happiness. 'And we shall meet very soon. I often run up to Edinburgh, you know . . .'

Going upstairs to change into their going away clothes, Alix discovered the first intimacy of married life. In the bedroom they found their clothes had been laid out together, and since they were not inclined to ring for a maid, Andrew helped her out of her dress. He was less efficient than a maid, undoing the hooks with hands that were clumsy and nervous but also tender, which suggested he was both afraid and eager to perform this intimate task for her. She was relieved to find he was not over confident. She would have been worried if he had known his way around a woman's dress, not because she would have been shocked at his having prior experience, but because then she would have been the only innocent. It was somehow less embarrassing (and they were embarrassed, in spite of themselves) that they were both equally ignorant and unpractised. No one could think the other a fool then. They could be equally foolish without fear of censure.

Her mother, of course, had not been forthcoming on the subject of marital relations, as she so delicately described them. Alix had decided, for a woman about to be married, that she was shockingly ignorant of the facts (which naturally had not been taught by the university) and had got Ralph, whom she knew would be honest, to explain the whole business to her. She had been quite relentless with him, believing she had as much right to know as any man, and little by little he had spelt out all the details, though not without much hesitation. It had become clear from this conversation that Ralph's romantic adventures had not been entirely chaste and he knew what he was talking about. Alix had nervously assumed that this would be the case with

Drew. But as they got changed, it was quite obvious it was not.

'I hope I haven't damaged it,' he said, as she stepped out of the silk brocade pool her skirt had formed on the floor. 'All those wretched little hooks.'

'No, it looks all right to me,' she said, examining the edge of the bodice. She noticed, glancing up, how he was staring at her, as if he had never seen a girl in her stays and drawers before – and perhaps he had not.

'You look pretty like that, Alix,' he commented.

'Do I?' she said. 'You were supposed to say that when I was in my wedding dress.'

'Well, that was very nice, but you look more yourself like that.'

'Perhaps I shouldn't bother getting dressed again,' she said, sitting down to take off her glacé kid slippers. 'But I might catch cold on the train and expire in your arms before we even get to Oslo.'

'That would be a shame,' he said. 'Perhaps you'd better get dressed again.'

'And you'd better start getting changed,' she said, for he had not even taken off his frock coat. 'Or we will miss our train.'

She realized that although she had seen Ralph in various states of undress, male underclothes were as unfamiliar to her as her own had been to him. She found the sight of him divested of shirt and trousers equally pleasing. It showed such a great deal more of him, and she saw for the first time his well-muscled legs, the existence of which she knew about (for she knew his strength) but which were now tangible and highly attractive.

'Perhaps we should all run around like naked savages,' she observed as he took off his vest. He stretched out his arms to her and she pressed herself against the warmth of his bare chest. 'Oh Drew, darling, I can't believe this has happened. It still feels like a dream. I can't believe we are actually married.'

'We're not,' he said, 'well, technically not. We have to consummate it first, you know.'

'Yes, I know,' she said, looking up at him.

'I wonder if we've enough time now,' he said, glancing at the clock.

'I wouldn't know,' said Alix. 'Would you?'

'No, but we won't know until we try, will we?'

'Of course not,' she said, and noticed that it was with considerably more confidence that he undid the laces of her stays.

Ralph was amused to note that it took the bride and groom quite a while to struggle into their going away clothes, for they vanished for a full three-quarters of an hour. When they came down again, their faces were flushed in a tell tale fashion, a fact which caused much whispering amongst the guests, whose cheeks were only reddened with wine.

Custom decreed that they should have a final drink and Andrew downed a dram while Alix, he noticed, drank two glasses of champagne almost as rapidly. Then they made for the door, probably eager to be alone again, and in a shower of rice and rose petals got into the carriage. Andrew, like a true gallant, lifted his wife into her place and provoked many cheers. And so they drove off into their new life, leaving the rest of them feeling a little purposeless.

Ralph found himself suddenly rather exhausted and did not go back into the house but walked round into the garden. It was permissible now to go off duty. He felt he had done his part as best man quite adequately.

The garden seemed quite empty, for tea was being served inside. He wandered about a little aimlessly, half happy with his solitude and half melancholy at it, for the wedding had emphasized his own bachelor state. One cannot avoid at weddings those jocular, well meant, but nevertheless cruel remarks, such as 'It will be your turn next, won't it?' and he had suffered a good deal from it. People seemed to think it quite criminal that he should stay single, and perhaps it was, for he felt the quiet pain of his loneliness then.

He turned into the old walled garden, which Philip Winterfield had insisted they kept quite intact. It was

311

certainly a charming place, full of roses and lavender with a small pool at the centre into which a green bronze fish spouted water. Next season, he resolved to have it stocked with water lilies. He turned a corner and saw at the end of one of the paths a woman kneeling, her back to him, her hat and gloves discarded on the grass behind her. He recognized the stuff of the dress and called out, 'Jessie! Are you all right?' To which she threw up her hands and exclaimed, 'Aargh! I knew I'd get caught.' And then she turned to him, laughing heartily, one hand extended. In the palm lay a small mess of leaves and soil.

'What are you doing?' he said, laughing also.

'Weeding!' she said triumphantly. 'I just happened to notice that someone had missed this little bit.'

'Jessie, my dear, this is a wedding not a weeding,' he said. 'You can spell, can't you?'

'Of course I can spell!' she said, and with mock indignation threatened to throw the clod of earth at him. 'Look, I know it may seem that I've gone quite mad, but I have a passion for weeding at the moment.'

'Pity the weeds,' said Ralph, sitting down on the grass beside her. 'Tell me, don't you think it is rather unjust to differentiate between weeds and plants which you want to grow? They are only doing the same thing.'

'The difference is that a garden plant will grow with moderation, but your common weed just wants to run amok. If I hadn't spotted this, you'd have had a serious outbreak of couch grass here,' she said, as she rooted out another of the enemy with considerable force. 'There! Oh, look at my hands. I must be mad, I suppose, but I had to run away. I was about to be left alone with that Lennox woman and I couldn't face it.'

'No, I should imagine not. She's just the same, isn't she? Still a tremendous siren.'

'So you think she is beautiful too?' smiled Jessie. 'I did notice how the men were all staring at her.'

'Well, she fulfils a very conventional ideal of beauty,' he said: 'But I personally don't find it very appealing. The only blonde I've ever cared for is Alix – or should I say Mrs

312

Erskine-Lennox as we shall all have to remember to call her now?'

'Now, she did look wonderful,' said Jessie.

'Yes, she did. Did you see them before they went away?'

'Oh, yes.'

'She really was glowing then. Do you suppose that they, er . . .?'

'I should think so. They are very much in love,' said Jessie. 'And why shouldn't they? That's an important part of marriage.'

'I suppose it is. But there's more to it than that, surely.'

'Yes, of course – if you're lucky,' she said and turned back to the flower bed. 'I think this will be all right now, so I ought to get back inside and start behaving again.'

'Here,' he said, giving her his handkerchief so she could wipe her hands.

'Thank you,' she said. She got up and strolled over to the fountain. He picked up her hat and gloves and followed, watching while she rinsed her hands under the jet of water. This simple action, performed so calmly and naturally, made him wish for a moment that he could be present as she went about her daily business, for he felt she would endow it all with the same uncomplicated grace, like those figures on Etruscan tombs who comb hair or pour water, making the ordinary into art itself.

'What are you staring at?' she said, wiping her hands dry on his handkerchief.

But he could not answer, overwhelmed for a moment by an inexplicable reserve, a thing which he did not usually feel in her presence. Instead, he held out her hat and gloves for her to take, smiling rather clumsily. She looked puzzled for a second and then, putting on her hat, said, 'We should go in, shouldn't we?'

He nodded and they walked back up to the house together without saying another word to each other, a very strange thing for them both.

Jessie was astonished to find when they went to bed that Sholto was in a very benign mood. He seemed to have enjoyed the wedding in spite of himself and at dinner that evening had been quite the life and soul of the party. He was particularly charming to the Lennoxes, so much so that Jessie feared they might be invited to the Quarro.

As they got ready for bed, Sholto's good humour continued. He actually sang to himself in the bathroom, an expression of jubilation usually only reserved for days when he won cases against all odds. But Jessie did not point out this inconsistency, but enjoyed his gaiety. It brought back happy memories and she felt delighted at this return of his old charm, which was as infectious as ever. I must do everything I can to encourage him to stay like this, she thought. Perhaps this might even be a fresh start for us . . .

She was not disappointed. As she sat at the dressing table in her nightgown, brushing her hair, he came and put his arms around her, something he had not done for many months. He slipped her nightgown from her and kissed her bare shoulders and back, pushing the cloth away until she sat there half naked. Their love making of late had been somewhat perfunctory, indulged in only to let Sholto release himself. But this was how they had made love when they had first known each other, a sensual, full-blooded, uninhibited affair, which brought her as much satisfaction as him. She had not realized until they lay naked together, caressing each other slowly but with intensity, how much she missed such love making. He seemed eager and happy to have her, and she felt she was being haunted by the past as he unlocked, with kisses, with a touch, the ghost of that summer at the Quarro.

5

'And I say we should strike! It's gone too damned far now – we have to show them we mean what we say, that we will act if they won't! It's the only damned way now, I tell ye!'

'You're a blethering fool, Anderson,' said Macdonald

sharply. 'You're no even thinking what it is you're saying. Do you want to ruin us all?'

'Aye, he does,' said Frazer. 'It doesn't matter to him. He doesn't have a wife and wains to think of. How are we to keep them on strike pay – if there's any to be had? Tell us that, Anderson.'

It was a night for short tempers. It was close and sultry in MacDonald's wretched kitchen parlour, as the three union men sat round the table without even a drink to take the edge off their dispute. There was no money to spare for whisky at a time like this.

'And how will you keep them if they lay us off as well?' retorted Hamish Anderson. 'If you've no hope of a job anywhere round here, because the men have not had the guts to show the bloody bosses that there will be all hell to pay if they don't start treating us right? Christ, Frazer, the time is long past that we could go to them, like damnable beggars, and ask them for favours. They don't listen to that, you know they don't. No, the only thing that Erskine will listen to is action! We could bring this place to a standstill if we put our backs into it – and his yard in the Clyde. They feel the same as us. It's the only way to show him that we mean business!'

'We cannot,' said MacDonald. 'It's too desperate a step. We cannot ask the men to strike. They're too afraid of Erskine and besides, what if he decides to sue the union, like that bastard at Taff Vale? Are you prepared to ruin the union, Anderson? I've put ten years' work into building up membership here, and I don't know if I'm prepared to risk that just because you're spoiling for a fight.'

'Good God, man!' exclaimed Hamish. 'How on God's earth do you expect anything to change here if you're too afraid to fight for it? What the devil did you join the union for if you weren't prepared to fight? Look, all it needs is a little courage – and you will be amazed at what we can do. If we all come together, if we can show him we're not afraid, that we can match his threats with our own, then we will be sure to succeed! I know it is dangerous, and desperate, but that is what the situation calls for, doesn't it? I want to give that man a taste of his own bloody medicine. I want him to feel the despair that those men he's laid off feel, the agony of those men injured by his bloody machines who can't afford to pay the doctor . . .'

'Save the oratory for the meeting, Anderson,' cut in MacDonald.

'So you will call a meeting?' said Hamish, eagerly.

'Aye, I suppose I'll have to. But it'll have to be a clear two-thirds majority, mind. If it's what the men want, then I must support them. But I warn you, Anderson, they may be less than keen.'

'We'll see about that,' said Hamish, getting up.

'Aye, we will,' said Frazer darkly, staring up at him, his eyes still hostile.

'Are you men finished with your politics?' said Mrs MacDonald, coming in from the other room. 'I thought you were going to wake the bairns with all your noise.'

'I'm just going, Mrs MacDonald,' said Hamish.

'The young eejit wants a strike, Annie,' said Frazer. She looked sourly at him, as well she might. It was always the wives who suffered most at such times, but such a look could not break his mood of resolution.

Hamish was glad Frazer did not follow him. It would be too easy to quarrel violently with him and a street brawl was the last thing they wanted.

He walked along the charmless streets of the town towards his own lodgings, brooding on what had just happened. He had been astonished and angered by Mac-Donald's reluctance to strike. It seemed the man was as content to keep the wretched status quo as any of the bosses! But at least he'd agreed to call a meeting and let a vote decide it. Hamish felt sure that the men would all see the necessity of extreme action. He had felt the current of anger when those men in the plate mill had been laid off halfway through their contracts with no hint of an apology or a penny of recompense. It had been scandalous, a crowning injustice on a heap of grievances which must now find redress! And they would fight – tooth and nail they would fight for decent wages, decent hours and security.

He crossed the bridge over the canal and looked towards Erskine's mill, which in the half light of a summer evening, with its great chimneys belching out smoke, looked as grim as any preacher's vision of hell. But, Hamish sourly reflected, you don't need to be a sinner to be sent here – just an ordinary man in search of a wage. He looked at the town which seemed to huddle at its foot, filthy, mean and dark, and thought: Christ, it shouldn't be like this! It damn' well shouldn't! And I will do something to change it. I'll fight to the death if I have to! It can't go on like this, it can't stay like this any longer!

He thrust his hands in his pockets and carried on over the bridge. At the end of the street he noticed that there was more activity about the pub than was usual, that people were standing outside, glasses in hands, in a manner which seemed deceptively festive.

'Hey there, Hamish!' one of them hailed him drunkenly.

'Hello, Jock,' he said. 'I didn't think your missus let you have enough to come down here on a week day.'

'It's free booze!' he exclaimed. 'Would you believe it?'

'What for? Has old Laing gone mad?' said Hamish. The landlord was not renowned for his generosity.

'Och no, lad,' said Jock, slapping him on the back and propelling him through the crowd at the door. The place was packed solid and an an overwhelming smell of sweat, whisky and tobacco assailed his nostrils.

'God! What is all this?' said Hamish.

'Free booze,' shouted Jock. 'To celebrate the weddin' of course!'

'Whose wedding?'

'Erskine's daughter. What will you have?' said Jock, pushing his way towards the bar. 'There's free grog all night to celebrate! Isn't that grand? Will you have a dram?'

'No, I damn' well shan't!' exclaimed Hamish, horrified. 'What the hell does that bastard think he's doing? Does he think he can bribe us?'

'Och, don't be such a damned fool,' said Jock. 'His daughter's just got married. Why shouldn't we toast the bonny bride, especially since he's paying for it?'

317

Hamish did not stay to answer him, but pushed his way out again, disgusted at how easily a man's loyalty could be bought.

Well, you shan't buy my damned loyalty, Robert Erskine! he resolved. Not for a thousand pounds am I going to let this thing go! I'll have war here and nothing less, just you wait and see!

'But are you sure, Sholto?' Jessie had said. 'Are you sure you don't mind?'

'Of course I don't mind,' he had said. 'Why on earth should I?'

Nothing, it seemed, could destroy Sholto's present good humour. When Mrs Erskine had asked Jessie to send for the girls and extend her stay at Allansfield, she had been afraid to tell Sholto. It would mean such a disruption to his domestic routine, a thing of which he was generally intolerant. She had therefore rehearsed various arguments to convince him that she could go away without his home life being plunged into chaos. She had expected to have to fight over each point and had begun her request hesitantly while they sat in bed, drinking that luxury of morning tea which was always served under the Erskines' roof. To her surprise he acquiesced at once. It was a great relief, for she had steeled herself for a disappointment, sure that he would not countenance such a defection on her part.

'Yes, of course you must stay on,' he said, getting out of bed. He put on his dressing gown and took his tea cup over to the window to study the view. 'I'd stay myself but I have a lot of important business to get through – a shame, really.' He did not sound too regretful. 'And of course I shall be able to manage without you for a week or two. You forget, my dear, there was a time when I managed as a bachelor.'

She did not venture: 'But you were not so fussy then . . .' because she had no wish to sour his pleasant mood. She felt, for a moment, she might almost miss him if this tolerant, happy atmosphere between them were to continue. Whatever had brought it on she could not guess, but it was foolish to look such gift horses in the mouth. Instead she decided she would enjoy it, knowing what a treat it would be for the girls to have a proper country holiday.

That morning at breakfast Sholto felt he might have embraced Mrs Erskine, his unwitting liberator. He could not have organized things better himself for an amorous intrigue than to have his wife and children invited for a long stay in the country. It was very fortuitous to have them off his hands at such a convenient time. Not, of course, that he would have let them get in the way while he pursued Olivia Lennox, but their absence from the Colinton house would make it considerably easier to arrange things.

While he sat at the table, opposite Ralph who seemed to have a small mountain of post to get through, his thoughts were not at all on the supposed business that he was returning to, although he like Ralph was catching the early train to Edinburgh. He felt quietly superior. Ralph's earnest, hard-working demeanour struck him as sanctimonious, as if he were trying to proclaim to the world what a decent, self-denying fellow he was. The truth was, of course, that he had no stomach for real life. Sholto considered Ralph had always been a coward as far as women were concerned – a state of affairs which time had only proved. For there was no shadow of interesting scandal about Ralph Erskine; not even, as far as Sholto knew, any discreet married woman to whom he resorted for sexual comfort. He had not even had the courage to marry. Instead he wore his work like a hair shirt and fondled his pretty little bronzes for comfort. What a poor, half life! thought Sholto contemptuously. If I had your money, I should live like a king . . .

Mrs Erskine came in and Sholto was not moved to embrace her as he had planned. She looked worried; indeed she seemed to tremble with worry, like a delicate branch in a storm.

'Ralph, will you come and help me,' she said, her voice almost indistinct with agitation.

'Mother, what is it?'

'It's your father – he seems to have had some sort of fit.

319

He can't move . . . I don't what it is at all.'

'We'd better get a doctor.'

'I've sent for one.'

'Can I help, Mrs Erskine?' said Sholto.

'If you would.'

Ralph and Sholto followed Mrs Erskine upstairs into Mr Erskine's dressing room. Ralph went in before him, and Sholto heard him gasp at what he saw. It was not a pleasant sight. Erskine, his face red and swollen, appeared to have collapsed while washing, and was now slumped against a chest of drawers, clutching a towel against his chest.

With difficulty, Sholto and Ralph got him up from the floor. He was a large-framed man, and heavier than his leanness might have suggested. He felt like a dead weight as they lifted him into bed. Mrs Erskine rushed about propping him up on pillows, while Ralph, half on his knees, grabbed his hands and muttered at his father, seemingly desperate to talk some life back into him. But Sholto could not feel very optimistic.

Outside in the passageway he met Jessie.

'What's happened?'

'It's Mr Erskine – he's had some sort of fit. Ralph and I have just had to heave him back into bed. It doesn't look very good.'

'Oh, goodness,' she said. 'Oh, how awful. A fit – what sort of fit?'

'I don't know – how should I?' he said. 'He can't move. He seems to have collapsed and he doesn't seem to be breathing very well.'

'Oh God, I hope it isn't serious.'

'I think it is,' said Sholto.

'I'll go and see if there's anything I can do,' said Jessie, going to the door.

As he watched her go, he found himself thinking of Olivia. He did not feel guilty about this, for he did not think that worry and guilt could help a sick man – only medicine could do that. If he is ill, Jessie will not stay on here, he thought. And that will be a damnable nuisance.

★ ★ ★

In the dinner break MacDonald called the meeting he had promised Hamish Anderson. Runners were sent about the works and at one o'clock a good crowd of union men had gathered in the waste land behind number two furnace shed. Some seemed a little annoyed at this encroachment on their brief dinner break, but most, as far as Hamish could read in their work-stained faces, seemed sensible that the time had come for such a meeting and that something of import was to be decided.

He proposed the motion to strike, standing in front of them all on a makeshift platform of old planks and barrels which sounded hollow beneath his boots in the way of wood in summer. The air was as dry as tinder and the atmosphere too, for his words fell like sparks amongst the crowd, lighting them with his own passionate anger. And although he felt despair that their situation had brought them to this terrible threshold, he was triumphant too, to feel that he was expressing the will of those men in front of him, those men who unlike him could not find the words. He was their mouthpiece, and he prayed silently, in the applause which followed his speech, that he could go on serving these men, speaking for them, for the rest of his life, so that they should never suffer in silence again. For he knew then that life had not destined him just to be a furnace man. His destiny lay with the struggle of the union, and he would take that path wherever it led, even to the House of Commons! For that was not impossible now – there were others who had got there and spoke in the very bastion of privilege for the working man.

Frazer, of course, spoke against the motion, effectively enough, but Hamish sensed in the silent, grave demeanour of the crowd that all were preparing to fight. They had reached the point of no return. When they voted, the motion was carried, with the single proviso that a final deputation should be sent to the management. Then, if no way of negotiation could be found, they would strike. When Sam Kennedy proposed that Hamish should form part of that deputation, he felt honoured and excited. It would be a grand thing to march up to Erskine's office with a real threat, a real piece of trouble to throw at his door!

The siren sounded and the men went back to work, all except Kennedy, MacDonald and Hamish who were bound for the offices.

'Annie won't thank me for losing an afternoon's pay,' said MacDonald, as they walked across the yard. 'But we must do what we must do.'

'At least it's summer,' said Kennedy. 'Better to strike in summer than in winter.'

The central offices had a measure of grandeur that the rest of the works lacked. They were built in crisp red sandstone with a mahogany double door attended by a scowling doorman.

'What is this?' he asked as they approached.

'Union business,' said Kennedy. 'You've no right to stop us.'

He did not stop them, but neither did he open the door to them and they walked into the hallway unescorted. A mosaic floor, marble columns, and a clerk greeted them.

'This is a deputation from the union,' said Sam Kennedy staunchly. 'We want to see Mr Erskine.'

'You don't have an appointment,' said the clerk.

'No, but we will wait here until he is able to see us,' said Kennedy.

'You'll wait a long time, then,' said the clerk. 'Mr Erskine hasn't come in today.'

'What's going on here, Shairp?' Another clerk, more smartly dressed, now appeared.

'They say they're from the union, Mr Tealing. They want to see Mr Erskine.'

'Mr Erskine is indisposed,' said Tealing, 'but Mr Ralph Erskine will be in shortly. I will ask him if he would be so good as to see you.'

'He *will* see us,' cut in Hamish, impatiently.

'Please take a seat,' said Tealing, only superficially polite.

They went and sat down on a wooden bench at the foot of the stairs. Hamish stared down at the green and blue mosaic of the floor and wondered if their request would ever reach the ears of Ralph Erskine. Tealing might be a devious operator.

There was a certain flurry of activity a few minutes later. A train drew up in the sidings opposite and Tealing, with attendant clerks, rushed to the door to greet the gaunt young man who soon came in. He was dressed in a crumpled white suit, a battered, bursting attaché case under one arm. He did not look quite as Hamish had pictured a young Erskine.

Tealing seemed to assault him with words and documents and they came across the hall very briskly, as if in great urgency. When he reached the foot of the stairs, Erskine glanced at them for a moment and looked enquiringly at Tealing.

'Union deputation, sir,' said Tealing. 'Shall I send them away?'

'No, no – send them up to my office. I'll see them after I've dealt with the Admiralty men.' And he sprinted on up the stairs, taking two steps at a time.

'Well, that's better than nothing,' said MacDonald.

'This way please, gentlemen.' Now that Ralph Erskine had agreed to see them, it seemed that the clerks had to show them some civility.

Erskine's office was grand enough to make Hamish feel combative. He thought of the conditions in the works and mentally compared them to this cool, immaculate room, its blinds down. As well you might . . . thought Hamish, as Erskine's secretary adjusted the slats of the blind to illuminate the large silver and crystal inkstand on the desk and the carved chair behind. He looked up to the fireplace behind, at the softly ticking clock on the mantelpiece and various photographs in silver frames. Above hung a brightly coloured poster of a motor car appearing through a cloud of dust, but his attention was drawn back to the photographs.

He got up from his chair and went over to the fireplace to study them more closely.

'They'll accuse you of thieving,' said MacDonald, as Hamish lifted one up. But he was not listening. Instead, five summers seemed to slip away and he was back in the candlelight of that bothy, smelling the sweet wood smoke and looking deep into those beautiful, faithless eyes again. So that's what became of her, he thought, this is the damned fellow she married for his money.

He could have hurled the photograph across the room such was the anger he felt. For it was a second betrayal to find that she was now part of a dynasty the very name of which he had come to detest. *And that bastard Erskine could buy her and I could not!* The injustice was as fresh and bitter as it had been that night in the woods, the night he had tried hard to forget but which now rose up to taunt him, as did all those enchanted nights which they had spent together, those lovely but ultimately loveless nights. Yet he could not harm the photograph but could only stare again at her, a slave once more to her beauty, as she gazed out so calmly at him, with leaves in her hair and about her neck, as if she were in the woods again, as wild and free as she had been then.

But she would not be like that now. She would be weighed down by his jewels, lost in his luxury, like those dreadful photographs of society beauties he had seen for sale in stationers' windows. He glanced again at the other photographs, looking for her in this disguise. But there was nothing except this one terrible but truthful portrait. He had never seen a photograph catch a spirit so.

'What's got into you?' said MacDonald.

He turned and looked at his union comrades, perched awkwardly on their chairs, anxious about the meeting to come. He put down the photograph, conscious suddenly that any feeling he might have had about their cause was now raised to fever pitch. He would fight to the death on this one now, for in it he could sense at last the sweet taste of revenge.

After two long hours of anxiety, Mr Erskine's condition improved radically. He could breathe almost normally again, and managed, albeit hesitantly, to insist that Ralph went to Garbridge to see the Admiralty men in his stead. This struck Ralph as quite typical and therefore extremely reassuring, for if he could still think of such things, the situation could not be as desperate as they had first feared. The doctor had diagnosed mild heart failure and had prescribed complete rest.

Ralph, therefore, found himself in the position he had always feared; he was now effectively head of the company, but in fact, he had no time to worry unduly about it. The sense of crisis brought out in him instincts he had not thought he possessed, and he reserved his anxiety for his father's condition.

The Admiralty meeting successfully concluded, he went off cheerfully to meet the union deputation. At the Mussel-burgh works, he had few problems with his small work-force. He was quite proud of how much he knew about his men. He felt he managed to appreciate them as individuals and help them when they were in need. In return they gave a certain amount of loyalty and hard work. He did not feel worried therefore about what a union deputation might lay before him. He felt quite confident that any problems could easily be solved.

He was surprised then by the look of hostility greeting him from one of them, the youngest of the three men waiting in his office. He would not shake hands and his eyes blazed with something highly unnerving, as if he were out for blood.

'Well, gentlemen, what can I do for you?' he asked, sitting down at his desk.

The eldest of them, MacDonald, began: 'It's about those men who were laid off last week, sir. We wrote to Mr Erskine pointing out that they were only halfway through their contracts, but I'm afraid he hasn't bothered to answer us.'

'How many men are we talking about?'

'Thirty hands, from the plate mill . . .'

'Oh, the plate mill – yes, I see,' said Ralph. Orders for steel plates were thin on the ground. The ship building trade was very slack that year.

'Do you see?' cut in Anderson, the young man. 'Do you really see?' His voice was taut with anger.

'Anderson, for God's sake, shut up,' muttered MacDonald.

'No, I'm damned if I will!' said Anderson, leaping up from his chair and facing Ralph across the desk, leaning on bunched fists. 'I'm going to tell this fine gentleman exactly why we've come here today. We've come to warn you, Erskine, to warn you for the last time that unless things start to change around here, we will bring this place to a standstill.'

The naked contempt in his eyes was enough to provoke the mildest of men, but Ralph knew he must remain calm. He took a deep breath and said: 'You're going to strike then?'

'Aye, and if you think you can get round being ruined by getting in blackleg labour, you can think again because there isn't a scab in this town low enough to take your filthy money.'

'We don't want to strike, sir,' said MacDonald. 'But we've no choice. We are all agreed.'

'What are the charges then?' said Ralph. 'I think we are entitled to know of what we are accused.'

'Oh aye, so you can throw them out with pretty arguments?' said Anderson. 'But there are no arguments to excuse what you and your kind have done!'

'What have we done?' said Ralph, impatient now with his aggressive oratory. 'How can I help you unless you tell me what it is that needs a remedy?'

The offer of help seemed to astonish him and he stepped back from the desk, looking at Ralph with suspicion.

'Aye, let's be reasonable,' said MacDonald. 'We want those men reinstated, sir, and an undertaking that there'll be no more laid off without proper recompense. If that's not done, I'm afraid we must strike.'

'That's all you want?' said Ralph.

MacDonald nodded but Anderson leant forward again and said, 'No, that's just the start of it.'

Ralph saw the despair on MacDonald's face. He evidently felt their suit was being destroyed by Anderson's hotheadedness. But Ralph, whatever his personal interests in the matter might be, could not help but think that this man was a great asset to them. He had the fanaticism that every cause needed. His absolute conviction was hard to ignore, difficult not to respect.

'Tell me the rest of it, then, Mr Anderson,' said Ralph.

'You won't want to hear it.'

'Perhaps not, but I have a feeling I must.'

'Anderson thinks he can change the world in a day,' said MacDonald emolliently. 'But we don't want war, only the chance for security. You understand that, don't you, sir?'

'Of course,' said Ralph. 'And I promise you, I will do all I can. But I don't have the authority to do this alone.'

'Then we've been wasting our breath here!' exploded Anderson.

Ignoring him, Ralph went on: 'If you can hold off your strike for a week, I will do all I can about this matter. You must understand that my father is not well.'

'Don't make excuses!' said Anderson. There was a shocked silence for a moment and it took all Ralph's self-control to prevent himself from retorting. But anger, no matter what the personal slight, could not be justified in such circumstances. One had to keep a grip on things.

'I cannot expect you to trust me,' he managed to say. 'I do appreciate that. You do not know me from a common criminal. But give me a week and I will do all I can on your behalf.'

'That sounds reasonable,' said MacDonald. 'But only a week mind. The men's patience is wearing thin.'

'I realize that. But please, try and persuade them.'

MacDonald and Kennedy got up from their seats, apparently satisfied.

'We'll get back to our work then, sir,' said Kennedy. 'Thank you for seeing us.'

'No, thank you for your time,' said Ralph. 'I'll make sure it isn't deducted from your pay.'

'Oh, what a fine gesture!' spat Anderson. 'Should we touch our caps to you? Is that what you would like?'

Ralph stared at him, unable to locate the source of this animosity. The man had a right to be aggrieved, but this

327

bitterness went far beyond that.

'Are you coming, Anderson?' said MacDonald.

'No, Erskine and I have some more business to see to,' he said.

'What the devil. . . ?' said Ralph, bewildered now as Anderson calmly sat down again as the others left. Ralph was left alone with him, suffocating in the tide of hatred which seemed to flow from him.

'How's your wife then?' said Anderson.

'My wife? What the hell is that to do with anything?' said Ralph.

'Your wife,' he repeated, pointing at the photographs on the chimney piece.

'I'm not married.'

'You're not married,' he said, the cocksure tone reduced somewhat. 'Then how have you got her picture?'

'Whose picture?'

'Cissy's picture,' said Anderson. 'I'd know her face in a thousand.'

'Cissy?' said Ralph, astonished. 'You don't mean . . .' and he twisted round to look at the photograph at which Anderson had been pointing. 'Celia? What the hell have you to do with Celia?' But asking the question acted as a trigger. He remembered sitting in the shade of a tree in the country outside Baden-Baden with Alix close by him, and hearing her exclaim: 'Hamish Anderson!' But the coincidence was too ridiculous. He shook his head, took down the photograph and put it in front of Anderson.

'I think you are mistaken,' he said. 'This is Miss Celia Lennox.'

'Aye,' said Anderson, 'Cissy Lennox. I often wondered who the bastard was she left me for. And now I know . . .'

'Are you trying to tell me,' said Ralph, somewhat incredulously, 'that you were . . . you were the . . .' He hesitated to say it. It was so absurd that he could hardly bring himself to say it. 'That you were the poacher?'

'She's told you about me then?' he said bitterly. 'I bet you had a right laugh at my expense. I'm surprised you didn't have me turned over to the magistrate. Perhaps you didn't

328

want to marry her when you found she was spoilt?' That idea appeared to give him some satisfaction. 'She deserves that, the heartless little bitch. So she didn't get her rich man after all?'

'No, she didn't. She did not marry me – in fact, she did not marry anyone.'

'That surprises me – a bonny creature like that. I'd have thought she'd have snared herself another man by now.'

'Hardly,' said Ralph. 'She's dead. She killed herself.'

'What?' He stared up at Ralph, his anger suddenly transformed into pain. 'When?'

'In 1900, in August.'

'Oh Christ, no . . .' he said. 'August? August the fifteenth or thereabouts?'

'How in God's name do you know that?' said Ralph.

But he did not answer, only stared into space, his face quite bleak. After a while, he said in a dry voice that was addressed only to himself: 'Then . . . then she did love me – and I let her go.'

He buried his face in his hands and sat hunched in such an attitude of despair that Ralph could not stay to watch it. Those tears were a private agony and Anderson would not thank his imagined enemy for watching them.

He scarcely knew how long Erskine was gone, but when he returned Hamish felt glad at the length of his absence. It had let him get himself together again. The shock of hearing her innocence when he had believed her guilty for so long, was almost too much for him.

Erskine was carrying two bottles of beer.

'Will you have one? If you can bear to break bread with me?'

'I can bear it,' he said, managing a grin. Erskine was perhaps more decent than many of his kind and now he knew he had lost Cissy as well, he felt there was a patch of common grief between them. 'I'm sorry. I think I spoke out of turn.'

'Don't worry,' said Erskine. 'I can understand your anger. She was too good a thing to lose, too lovely.'

329

'You asked me how I knew when she died,' said Hamish. 'It was just that August the fifteenth was the last time I ever saw her. She told me she was getting married – and I was angry, so bloody angry that I was like a brute with her. She didn't deserve that . . . but honest to God, I never thought she'd do something like that. I didn't think she could have such a thought in her.'

Erskine shook his head and stared again at the photograph.

'Why do you keep her picture then?' said Hamish.

'As a memento mori – in case I'm foolish enough to think of falling in love again. She reminds me to be on my guard against myself.'

'I've never found another like her,' said Hamish, surprised that this man, so different from himself, should have the same fear of love. He also, had not dared trust himself. 'I'm wedded to the union now.'

'A worthier cause, I'm sure,' said Erskine, putting down the photograph.

'How can you think that?' said Hamish.

'It isn't as simple as you believe. I do have a conscience.'

'You don't,' said Hamish. 'If you did, you wouldn't let your old man get away with what he does.'

'What does he do?'

'You don't know?'

'Not specifically. It isn't my company, you know. How can I know unless you tell me the facts? And I must have facts, because that is the only language my father understands.'

'You want facts,' said Hamish, draining down the last of his beer, 'I'll give you facts.'

6

Jessie sat alone in Ralph's library toying with a yellow-backed French novel and finding it well beyond her comprehension. Ralph had clearly read it several times for its pages were all cut and it had fallen open easily, sitting comfortably on her lap in a fashion which belied its obscurity. She wished she had the knowledge to conquer it, for the glimmers of meaning she had been able to wrestle from it suggested that a rich and interesting journey lay on the pages. The very title which had made her take it from the shelf, *La Chartreuse de Parme*, had seemed deliciously evocative in itself, suggesting the odour of liqueur and violets to her, as well as a romance set in Italy. But she had failed on that journey, not only because the language defeated her, but because it was not a night for quiet concentration.

Although it was now clear that Mr Erskine was not in the gravest danger, he was not recovered sufficiently for her to be able to throw herself entirely into a laborious attempt, with the aid of a dictionary, to chart Fabrizio's destiny. There was still plenty to worry about, even if Mrs Erskine was doing her utmost to appear as if this crisis worried her no more than if her husband was suffering from a cold. But Jessie could not help but think ominous thoughts as she sat there, staring vaguely at Ralph's empty chair. It was past eleven and he had not yet got back from Garbridge. What could be keeping him away? He ought to be back, she thought. The nights are always the most dangerous – what if something were to happen and he wasn't back?

She prayed that something would not, addressing that nebulous, unfocused deity which we all snatch at in times of trouble. She worried for the Erskines. They seemed ill prepared for such a blow. Mr Erskine had always been a hearty, strong man, who had scarcely ever suffered a day's

331

illness. He had seemed as surprised as them all by his own body's failure, aggravated by it even, as if it were some unreliable piece of machinery which he could not manage to mend himself.

When Jessie had suggested she should leave Allansfield, Mrs Erskine had taken her hand, gripped it rather fervently with both hers and said, 'No, no do not even think of it, my dear. And the girls are still to come. That is what my husband wants – everything must be quite normal for him. He does not want any *fuss*.'

Mrs Erskine, who fussed inordinately over Ralph's trifles of ill health, had, in real difficulties, an instinct to good sense which made her an excellent nurse. Jessie saw at once that normality would be exactly the thing for Mr Erskine. If he were to make the full recovery the doctor had promised, if he was to bear the enforced rest of an invalid, a difficult thing for such an active man, it could not be compounded by turning his house into a nursing home, where voices were unnaturally hushed and the routine of the sick room overturned every consideration. And she had read somewhere that children could sometimes have a salutary effect on invalids. Besides, it was not as if they would be under his feet. The house was large enough to hide a dozen children and muffle their noise. Perhaps something of that had gone into its planning, for Mr and Mrs Erskine undoubtedly expected grandchildren. When the housekeeper had shown Jessie the little knot of rooms on the third floor of the west wing where the girls and Molly were to sleep, she could see at once that these were intended for nurseries, even if they had not yet been formally named as such. Why else would the architect have put in that clever low window, but to give future young Erskines a good view of the gardens? Jessie wondered if that enchanting idea had come from Ralph or the architect. If it came from Ralph, he perhaps had more idea of marriage than he had admitted to.

She was a little surprised when the door opened behind her. She turned in her chair and saw Ralph standing in the doorway. She was about to smile a greeting at him, but something in his face stopped her. He did not seem to be looking at her but staring blankly ahead of him, lost in some very private and grave pattern of thought.

For a moment, she thought the worst had happened, that Mr Erskine had had a relapse and that Ralph had come in some time ago, but had been by his bedside, only to see him die.

'Ralph, are you . . .?'

He smiled now, but it was lack lustre, and he sighed. He rubbed his chin with his hand and came across the room, sinking heavily into his chair. He was obviously exhausted.

'Yes, I'm all right,' he said.

'You're very tired, I think,' she said. 'I'd better let you alone.' And she got up from her chair.

'No, Jessie,' he said, grabbing her arm as she began to go. 'Don't go, please. I don't want to be alone. I need to talk.'

'Of course,' she said, sitting down again.

'Thank God you're here,' he said, loosening his tie.

'Is there anything you want?'

'A large whisky,' he said. 'I know I should not, but I damn well need one. It's in the cupboard there, if your husband hasn't drunk it all!' It was the first glimmer of his characteristic humour and she felt relieved.

'That's better,' she said, taking out the bottle. 'You know there's nothing to worry about. When I last saw your father he was sleeping like a bairn.'

'It's not my father that I'm worried about,' he said.

'Oh,' said Jessie, a little surprised. His tone seemed almost callous. She handed him a glass of whisky and he drained the glass promptly. 'What have you been doing?'

'Watching the scales drop from my eyes . . . oh God, that's better. Will you join me?' he said, getting up and refilling his glass.

'What have you been up to?' she asked again.

He took another gulp of whisky and pressed the glass against his cheek as if contemplating what he was going to say.

'You know,' he said, and began to pace about the room like an orator commanding his platform. 'I've always prided myself on seeing. I've always been sure that I was observant,

333

that I could see clearly, that I could appreciate beauty when I saw it. *That's* always been my great vanity, hasn't it?' The question was rhetorical, and Jessie, confused, could not think how she should answer. She sat instead and listened. 'Look at all these lovely things I've found! How long have I been searching for all this? Ten years at least I've been collecting, peering so hard that I never saw what was right under my nose. I thought I had vision, but I've been blind – blind for the last thirty years, haven't I?'

'I don't know what you're talking about,' said Jessie. 'You're not making any sense.'

'No, because there isn't any sense to make. Not any more. It's all a damned, utter mess and I don't know what to do about it.'

'Now, Ralph, sit down and calm yourself.'

'I can't be calm, Jessie, I can't be! I'm so angry – with myself, with everything, with the world, with all the bloody injustice in it!'

'What has happened to you?' she asked, astonished by his vehemence.

'Let me ask you something, Jessie,' he said earnestly, squatting down in front of her chair. 'If I may?'

'Of course. What?'

'When you were young, what was it like? What was your family like? How did you live? How much did your father earn, for example?'

'About two pounds a week, if he was lucky. But what do you want to know that for, Ralph?'

'I'll explain later. Now, just tell me everything you can remember. Were you ever hungry?'

'Of course, children always are.'

'No, I mean hungry because there was no money for food?'

'Well, my mother didn't get much out of my father, but she took in washing. When she was in service she was in the laundry, so she had real skill at it. That saved us from being really poor, I think, because my father used to drink, but she got good money for her work. There were always folk worse off than us. We were lucky, I think. I remember,

334

there was a family round the corner who were always in a terrible state. They only had a room to live in – seven or eight of them, I think. One or two of the bairns died. You know, they probably starved, because he'd only got one leg and he couldn't find any work. My mother used to send me down there if we'd any leftovers. I used to hate going. I didn't like to see his stump.' The memory of that room, years distant now, came back with haunting freshness and made her shiver. 'God, yes, we were lucky.'

Ralph sighed heavily and sank from his haunches on to the floor, so that he sat at her feet.

'Are you going to explain what all this is about then?' she said, looking at him. 'You haven't gone soft in the head?'

'No, I don't think so,' he said, smiling a little. 'Well, I suppose I could be a little more lucid. The thing is, today has been rather eventful. Strangely so, almost. I can hardly make sense of it myself yet – so you'll have to bear with me?'

'Of course,' said Jessie.

'I met a man today,' he began, 'called Hamish Anderson. Whereby hangs another complicated tale, which I'll tell you some other time, I think. Well, this fellow Anderson is from the union, and he came with his comrades up to my office to tell me that they were proposing to strike unless certain men whom my father had laid off were put back to work. But Anderson, being a hot-head, could not resist drawing my attention to other things which I scarcely knew about. The thing simply isn't a question of men being laid off because of a slump, there is a whole powder keg of grievances behind it. Justified grievances, unfortunately,' he added grimly.

'You mean, they want more pay?'

'It's not as simple as that. Well, it is simple, in fundamental terms. What they are asking for is so little, I find it shocking that it has to be asked for at all. I had no conception that people could live such threadbare, mean, inhuman lives. Clean air, clean water, clean clothes, these things that I have scarcely ever thought of, are for them privileges, dreams to which they cannot dare to aspire. I'd never seen it before today. Intellectually, I thought I understood that poverty existed, but it had never actually touched me. But I saw it today, and I do not know what I am going to do about it.'

'Oh, Ralph . . . it's not something you can solve on your own.'

'But I must try,' he said. 'Anything else would be a gross abnegation of my duty. I must try and do something, but God knows what. Patronizing sovereigns left on the kitchen table as I did tonight are little better than bribery. That won't solve anything, will it?'

'Every little helps,' said Jessie. 'Whoever you gave the money to won't despise it, I can assure you of that.'

'Are you sure? I did not have to stay there, I just left them there with that token gesture and came back to my fine house. The smell of one place made me sick, I'm ashamed to say, but the children were sleeping through it because they didn't know any better. And I was so eager to get out of the place, because I thought I would vomit, but she, the mother, was begging me to take the best chair and have a cup of tea as if I'd just given her a fortune instead of three miserable sovereigns! I mean, what are three sovereigns to me when I spend a thousand guineas on a painting? I can't even be decently generous.'

'You are generous, Ralph,' she said. 'You're a good, kind man, remember that.'

'No, I'm tarred with the same brush as every wealthy man. My money comes at too high a cost. My luxuries, which I do not need, mean bandy-legged children and newspaper on the walls of miserable rooms! I cannot live with myself if it is at that cost. I always believed that my father was an equitable employer – that I was, for that matter – that our industries created wealth for all men. I did not realize how unjustly that wealth was distributed.'

'So what will you do?'

'I don't know, but something must change, mustn't it? You must see this more clearly than any of us. Doesn't it sicken you sometimes that I should live like this, while you remember those people who starved?'

'I judge people as people, Ralph. Their money is not

important. It's what they do, how they are, that matters. I could not despise your family, not for the world, when you have all been such friends to me. Bitterness is pointless, you know that.'

'You're right, of course,' he said, looking up at her. 'One must be constructive, practical. There must be things one can do, simple things, that will make a start at the rottenness. I do mean to do something, I promise you that, Jessie.'

'Why promise me?'

'Because you sit like a judge above me – the best sort of judge, wise and temperate and forgiving too, although forgiveness is scarcely deserved in my case. But I will try and deserve it.' As he spoke he took her hands in his and knelt in front of her, still staring up her.

'Oh, Ralph, there's no need for this . . .' She smiled, but could not help but be deeply moved. It would have been so easy for a man of his intelligence and position to construct a host of arguments to defend the system from which he profited. But Ralph, with the simplicity of a child, had thrown himself into the deepest waters; he had let the situation speak for itself and he was like Paul on the road to Damascus, struck with the light of the truth. She felt quite ashamed of herself, for she had done as little as he had to change things which she knew to be wrong, for she was sensible now she had some power, more than she could ever have had when just a servant. She sensed she had the power to influence Ralph, for he looked to her like an oracle. 'You're a brave man, Ralph Erskine,' she said. 'You mind me of my own duty.'

'I can't believe that,' he smiled. 'Oh, Jessie, how is it you are always able to put me back on an even keel? I can't think how I should manage without you these days.'

'So long as you don't take me for granted,' she said lightly.

'I shall try not to,' he said, and then surprised her by leaning forward and swiftly kissing her cheek. It was the lightest touch, but she found herself profoundly unnerved by it. For the moment he drew back she knew without understanding, that she had wanted more from him, that the moment had been too brief. She blinked and touched her cheek, as if her fingers could sense the spot of warmth created by his lips. She tried to tell herself that the kiss was meant solely in the spirit of friendship, but her body seemed determined to misinterpret the gesture. She felt herself invaded by sudden, nervous weakness and sank back on the cushion and stared at him, unable to take her eyes from him. In his face she read the same message that seemed to have conquered her own heart – a flashing signal of desire. With giddy, clouding perceptions she saw him come towards her again, or rather felt, for every nerve in her could sense the decreasing space between them and seemed to stretch out to greet him. But she could not move her arms to embrace him, they were stupefied and stuck to the arms of the chair.

She felt his hands on her shoulders, his fingers on the bare flesh revealed by the low collar of her evening blouse. He gripped her with an urgency which did not frighten her. And when his lips met hers, there was a violence in it, as if a fuse, lit long ago, had suddenly reached the charge. It was painful, raw passion, which she knew came not just from him, but from herself. She stretched up her face and neck to meet him, as eager and as unheeding of the consequences as any curious girl.

She felt his hand slip inside her blouse, sliding beneath the cotton of her chemise and touching the curve of a breast. It made her gasp with surprise but in a second he had withdrawn his hand, with a rough hasty movement. In another moment, he broke away completely and seemed to propel himself across the room to put some distance between them. She wanted desperately to stretch out her arms to him, to call him back to her embrace, but she saw him struggle to master himself, and knew she must do the same.

'You . . . you really must forgive me,' he stuttered, and then bolted from the room.

Forgive you? For what? Jessie asked herself.

7

Ralph did not see her again until late the following afternoon and then only at a distance, from his bedroom window as she played with her children on the lower lawn. It made a pretty picture, and he stood and watched them for some time, absently and inefficiently drying his face and hands, glad to see straight-legged, plump children. No doubt she is glad too, he thought, remembering what she had said of her own childhood. The scene formed itself into an icon in his mind of how things ought to be, for it was equally far from what he remembered of his own youth, with its starchy regimes, as from those wretched slum families he had seen in Garbridge. Jessie seemed to have got the thing right, and her life was not particularly grand or extravagant. Surely it might be possible to bring such a standard of living to more people? Did it really make sense to pay men so little that they could not afford to feed their families properly?

He watched her get up from the grass, waving her arms at her daughters, stretching them up to the sky in some game, but it seemed she might be doing it solely to display her elegant figure for his benefit. He knew, of course, that she had done nothing to tempt him. She had been quite blameless in her friendship, and yet he had been tempted, wildly so, and breaking away from that embrace had been almost impossible.

His weakness irritated him. It really was unthinkable to have done what he had done – she was a married woman for God's sake – and the circumstances were hardly appropriate! Perhaps I thought it might anaesthetize me – but really, it was the most mutton-headed thing to have done. Good God, what must she think of me now? he wondered. For had he not been trying to prove to her (and to himself) that his gross self-indulgence was over? And then what had he done but to seize her and maul her with his filthy hands, as

339

if he were the worst sort of libertine? She scarcely deserved such cavalier treatment and he could not help but think he had destroyed the quality of their friendship. For now she would know that he was an untrustworthy fellow who could not respect a woman's person, despite all the extravagant claims he might make.

What the devil made you do it? he asked himself but looking at her still, a white figure in the distance, he knew the answer too well. She was lovely and desirable and she was touched, by some miracle, with a strange ability to understand him as few people had ever understood him. Last night he had been weak and wretched, made miserable by all that he had seen, and he had come back to find her, almost it seemed, waiting for him to come back, precisely when he needed her to be there. She had listened to his ranting patiently, and when, like a priest, she had given him absolution with her kindly, violet eyes, the only way he could think to thank her was with a kiss, a kiss which in a moment changed into something very different from the gallant tribute he had intended.

He sat down on the seat below the window, determined not to look at her any more. He had quite enough to torture himself with already. He sprawled in the chair, feeling the exhaustion of his body dull his brain. He closed his eyes and attempted rational thought, but it proved an impossibility. He had a hundred important decisions to make if the radical reforms he had in mind were to begin, urgent decisions, but for the moment he was not lucid enough to make them.

There was a gentle knock on his door and Mrs Erskine came in. Ralph staggered out of his chair, only to meet with her insistence (too late, alas) that he was to stay where he was.

'How is he?' he asked.

'Still improving,' she said, 'but he's still very weak and tired. But he has been sleeping. Dr Kaimes was very encouraging.'

'Good – can I see him?'

'That's why I came to find you. He wants to know how

you've been getting on. You were so late back last night – have you been very busy?'

'I suppose I have,' he said.

'Oh, good,' she said. 'That is just what he will want to hear.'

'I'm not so sure about that,' said Ralph.

'Why?' she said. 'Is there something wrong?'

'Yes, you might say that.'

'Well,' she cut in, 'you must promise me, Ralph, you won't mention it to him. It will only worry him, and the last thing he needs now is to be bothered by trifles.'

'It's hardly a trifle.'

'Whatever it is, you mustn't mention it.'

'I shall have to. I need his consent about various things.'

'No, Ralph,' she said. 'I cannot let you. No matter how important it may seem to you, it really cannot be so important as making sure he is not troubled by anything unnecessary.'

'But there are things I must discuss with him,' said Ralph, irritated. 'He will expect it.'

'No,' she said again, firmly this time, as if he were a child. 'Really, Ralph, your insensitivity surprises me. Anyone would think you cared more for the state of the business than for your father's health. You of all people should understand that he must have complete and serene rest.'

'It isn't simply a question of business . . .' he began, but she interrupted him with a warning note in her voice.

'Ralph, how many times must I tell you?'

He let the matter drop. It was pointless to quarrel with her. He thought, for a moment, of attempting to explain why he must talk so seriously with his father, but he knew she would only hear the note of accusation in his voice. That could only make her more entrenched in her position. She would be scandalized that he could even let the possibility of reproach cross his mind at such a time. When it came to family matters, or their personal well-being, she was as blind and as fierce a fanatic for her cause as any Hamish Anderson. It was laudable, he supposed, and he knew he should be thankful for it when her devotion had dragged him back from hell in the past, but now the larger question seemed indisputably more important. It was the suffering of one measured against the suffering of God only knew how many. He could not begin to count them.

But when he followed Mrs Erskine to his father's room, he was at once overcome with remorse at his own callous utilitarianism. He had attempted to simplify an issue which of course was not simple. The world was not black and white, but was shrouded by a pall of grey confusion.

The room was only half lit, and smelt sweetly of some aromatic pastille which was being burnt to help Mr Erskine breathe. The atmosphere reminded Ralph of a Roman church, and his father, so still and propped up on a majestic pile of white pillows, was like some venerable cleric on his catafalque. At once he knew there could be no question of disturbing this peace, especially when he saw the pathetic look of pleasure which his father assumed when he realized who his visitor was.

'How . . . how . . . is . . . everything?' Mr Erskine forced himself to speak, his voice so breathless and hoarse that Ralph, who knew from his now mercifully rare asthma attacks what difficulty those words had cost, said at once: 'Everything's fine, Father.'

He saw the relief on his father's face and thought he heard a sigh from his mother who was lurking in the shadows, supervising the interview.

His father reached out with a gesture which intimated he wished to take Ralph's hand, a rare thing for he was not physically demonstrative. Ralph put out his hand and his father grasped it, as if for dear life.

'Good . . . good . . .' he struggled to say. 'I always knew you would not let me down.'

This referred to those many conversations between them, which Ralph, when younger, had sought actively to avoid but which Mr Erskine had seemed to relish (or so Ralph had maliciously decided); conversations at which Ralph had been made to feel a first-class reprobate, incapable of understanding, let alone appreciating, the importance of his destiny as heir to the Erskine industries. 'I will not live for ever – you have to learn to deal with responsibility now. I need to know that you will be *reliable*.' How Ralph had hated that at eighteen – that desperate destiny of reliability which flew in the face of all his romantic dreams. But he had learnt to live with it and had hoped he would not fail. And now, as a man of thirty, in the midst of the crisis which the pragmatic Mr Erskine had carefully prepared him for, Ralph heard finally the approbation which he knew he did not deserve and which, more importantly, he was not sure he even desired.

'I always knew you would not let me down.' The words seemed to hang in the air, as if they had been shouted and not whispered and Ralph knew the sadness of his own betrayal, his own necessary hypocrisy. It was true that the mantle had at last fallen over his shoulders, but he knew that he would not, indeed could not, wear it in the same way as his father had. He would not carry on as he was expected, because to do that would be to perpetuate a state of affairs which he now saw clearly was indefensible.

But why did I have to discover this now? thought Ralph. Why not earlier – then we could have fought it out and perhaps I could have made him understand. But why *now*, for God's sake, when my hands are tied and I can do and say nothing? You cannot offend a dying man, no matter what his sins are. For it struck Ralph as he sat there, his father still grasping his hand, that whatever the doctors might say, his father would soon die. This premonition bit coldly into him, like a fact in a newspaper column, and made him wretched, for even in his anger at what he had seen the previous day, he had not wished such a swift and terrible retribution upon his father. If he had cursed him, he had scarcely meant it to have such an effect. Perhaps, in the eyes of Hamish Anderson, there would be justice in it, but Ralph found this primitive cause and effect terrifying. A man, no matter how guilty, should always be entitled to a defence, but it seemed Mr Erskine would not have such an opportunity. Ralph could do nothing about it, gagged still by his mother's mysterious power, and he would have to sit and watch the man die, knowing that his memory would be spoilt for him because had never been able to ask 'Why?'

But perhaps, he reflected as his father closed his eyes and seemed to want to rest, it is no bad thing. He had remembered some case which Sholto had once related to him, in which when a man condemned for a particularly horrible murder had been permitted to speak in his defence he had proved himself to be a monster, who by his own admission felt absolutely no remorse and who left everyone in court with a distinct impression that hanging was too good for him. If his father was able to speak out, perhaps he would have no adequate excuse, and worse still, perhaps no remorse. That, Ralph felt, would be impossible to bear, and it made him easier about his silence, although he felt he had only assuaged his conscience with casuistry.

Jessie and Ralph found themselves dining alone together that night, and predictably enough it was not the most relaxing occasion. The dining room at Allansfield was a beautiful, serene room on a summer's night when there was no need to draw the curtains on the lovely view. There were flowers on the table and lighted candles, and with only two places set, it might have been the perfect spot for a romantic tête-à-tête for a honeymooning couple. But it was singularly inappropriate for Ralph and Jessie, who sat saying very little to each other, still haunted by the events of the previous evening.

Jessie raked her mind for suitable topics of conversation, but rejected every idea as soon as she had formed it. She did not wish to prattle on, although the silence unnerved her. Ralph had such an introspective air about him that she suspected he would not have heard a word she said, that she would only be making irritating noise, like the buzzing of an insect. Besides, why should they talk? What on earth was there to talk about? Surely it was just one of those things that was inexplicable and certainly best forgotten?

Best forgotten . . . damn it, how can I forget? she asked herself, looking at him across the table. She could do this at her leisure, because he was dissecting his meat with the ruthless precision of an anatomist and did not seem likely to look up from this absorbing task. If their eyes once met she could not imagine what might happen; in all the confusion, in all this embarrassed intimacy, she knew there were many unanswered questions which she had been too afraid to ask herself. Seeing him now, engaged in the prosaic business of eating, she observed him as if it were the first time they had met, with a cold, objective eye – or, at least, attempted to. There was an effort at self-denial in her noticing his hair was going thin on top and that his wrists were unpleasantly bony. She tried to tell herself that it meant nothing to her to have been kissed by him, that the experience had left her quite unmoved. But when, suddenly, he looked up and she saw an expression of tortured melancholy on his face, these denials were useless. Her heart went out to him in a powerful rush of feeling, a mixture of affection, desire and pity. In that moment, she felt she would have done anything for him.

But he seemed not to be able to read her face, or if he could, chose not to understand it, and his eyes were no longer upon her but on the view from the dining-room window which, as dusk descended gently into night, had become more beautiful than ever. She looked at it too, and realized, with great sadness in her heart, that this was the only sort of communion which they could permit themselves.

8

It was strange to be sitting at the head of the table. It gave Ralph a fresh perspective of the Garbridge boardroom which he had not anticipated. It was a room he had always considered dreary and austere when he had sat in his humbler place along the side of the table between Mackenzie, the chief engineer, and Ross, the plate sales manager. But sitting in his father's chair, a large, flamboyant carver, he realized how easy it was to dominate the table. He seemed to be on a metaphorical dais and that gave him a certain amount of much-needed confidence. He had approached this weekly management meeting with a certain dread. After all, he had some radical ideas to put in front of those sound men. At least, sound was how his father always referred to that elite half dozen. Ralph was not sure how sound they would prove in their loyalty to him.

It had taken his father some time to gather this pool of expertise. It had involved poaching from other firms and the treachery to their former employers had been well rewarded when their loyalty to the Erskine Steel Company had been proved. They commanded the highest salaries at Garbridge. Ralph knew them only slightly, for his parents were not intimate with them, despite the positions of great trust they held. Naturally they and their wives were entertained once or twice a year but that was the extent of it. But, if he did not know the nuances of their characters, he knew very well the mould from which they were all cast for it was the same mould as his father, except that they were not touched with entrepreneurial genius. They were all officers, it was true, but only Robert Erskine had the vision of a general. These men, as they came into the meeting (staring a little to see Ralph in the seat of authority) were capable lieutenants, skilled in execution of orders which they could never have formulated themselves.

Am I a general? Ralph asked himself, watching those solid bodies, each in their uniform black suit and high, stiff collar, take their places round the table. It was as if they all patronized the same tailor, so little variation was there between them. Ralph, in white linen and a turndown collar, knew that to them he represented certain dangerous tendencies in modern society. These men could not have understood the notion of dressing to be comfortable on what was a very warm day. Those black suits were symbolic, and were worn with the same reverence as priestly vestments. Encoded in the expensive but durable cloth were a hundred statements of opinion and belief. These men believed in God (as expressed through the Kirk, naturally); in the Empire and the absolute rightness of the social order. They were the sort of men who would not let their daughters read French novels and who liked paintings of jolly, carousing cardinals (framed engravings of which they hung in their dining rooms alongside Doré's angels). It was going to be difficult for him to communicate to such men that there was an urgent need for a radical revision of how the company was run. It would mean standing their world on its head.

The meeting began, predictably enough, with enquiries after his father's health. Ralph was able to reassure them of his continued improvement, but regrettably it would be many months before he returned to active service. In the interim, he and Mr Lennox (when he returned from his wedding journey) were acting company directors and the source of all authority. Ralph did not quite use this phrase, although he was tempted. It smacked too much of the divine right of kings.

This clarified, the managers began to present their weekly reports. Ralph listened to these dry recitations of facts and figures with some impatience. There was nothing said that he did not already know and there were some glaring omissions. Henry Castle, the plate mill manager, droned on about number two press being shut down for the present, but that new orders were imminent . . .

Ralph, his patience exhausted, cut in: 'I understand you've had to lay off some men because of this, Mr Castle.'

There was a certain surprise at this. Not even Robert Erskine interrupted the giving of the weekly reports.

Castle, looking most offended, said, 'Well, yes – it's not economical to keep them on in the circumstances.'

'Is it usual for men to be laid off halfway through their contracts?'

'It happens, Mr Erskine. There is a recession on, as you well know.'

'Oh, yes, of course I know. But how many men were laid off precisely?'

'Thirty or forty, I recall. We may need to do a little more pruning yet if things carry on as at present.'

'I don't think so,' said Ralph.

'Excuse me?' said Castle.

'There will be no more men laid off without my express permission.'

'Your father does not require that,' said Duncan, the works manager. 'He trusts us to do what is necessary.'

'I know, but this is a highly sensitive issue with the men just now. I have spoken with some of the union people about it and they are not at all happy . . .'

'You shouldn't believe what they say!' said Duncan.

'Distrust on both sides, it seems,' said Ralph. 'That's a dangerous state of affairs, don't you think, gentlemen?'

'I'd like to know what it is you are driving at,' said Castle. 'Those men had to be laid off – there was no more work for them.'

'And what do you think they are doing now?'

'There's plenty of work hereabouts.'

Ralph shook his head and said, 'Haven't you just told me there is a recession? Do you think we are the only ones suffering? Of course we are not – you all know that. Aren't they doing the same thing at Parkhead, at Colville's and at every forge in Lanarkshire? They are all laying men off. There is no work to spare for anyone. Those men are starving.'

'There's work for those who are not too idle to look.'

'They do look – they do nothing *but* look. I spoke to a man who had walked to Paisley but found nothing.'

'I think you are exaggerating,' said Duncan.

'I wish I was,' said Ralph.

'The trouble is,' said Mackerson, 'that these people have no sense of prudence. They do not know the meaning of thrift. They simply squander their money without a thought for the future.'

'How can you save on twenty-five shillings a week?' said Ralph bluntly.

'It's a question of good management, of self-denial,' said Mackerson. 'A few shillings put aside each week in the savings bank, and these people would not be throwing themselves on charity now.'

'And how do you clothe, feed and house your family on twenty shillings? I should like to see any of us try that,' said

348

Ralph. 'It isn't merely self-denial – it would be suicidal. Some of the women do try and save, it's true, but it means they starve themselves and the children so that the man of the household can have meat – that is, if they can afford that.'

'I don't see what this has to do with anything,' said Castle. 'This is a business, not a charity.'

'This is a question of vital importance to the business,' said Ralph. 'This is a matter of investment. Now, if I were to suggest to you we spent a large amount of capital on new plant, which would keep us ahead of our competitors, then you would be nodding in agreement. Then you would not stint a penny and that new machinery would be tended like a mistress, would it not? What I am proposing, indeed *all* that I am proposing is some capital investment in our workforce, because without them we have no business. They are as important to us as any machine, more so perhaps, and better paid, better fed, better housed and better contented workers will mean higher productivity. A starving man will not work as well as a well fed one. That is obvious, is it not?'

'I don't know where you have picked up all this socialistic nonsense, young man,' said Mackerson, leaning forward in his seat. He spoke like a schoolmaster. 'But I think it is a damnable shabby way to go on. Are you not content that your father is ill? Do you want to ruin him as well? Because that is what this sort of nonsense leads to. It doesn't make any sense!'

'And it doesn't make any sense to me that a working man should live in squalor and I do nothing about it,' said Ralph.

'I shall write to your father,' said Mackerson. 'I cannot stand by and let you do this to the company.'

'You do not have to. If you do not agree with company policy, I do not think you could, in your conscience, remain with the company,' said Ralph.

'Is that a threat?' stuttered Mackerson.

'Perhaps,' said Ralph, getting up and gathering his papers together, 'because I will brook no opposition on this. It is too important a matter. I will leave you to discuss it, gentlemen – I'm sure you will have plenty to discuss. Next week, I trust we shall all meet again, for a more constructive session. We shall have a lot of work to get through then, if we are going to drag this company into civilized profitability!'

9

By eight o'clock the throng of men at the east gate at Garbridge was substantial. Men coming off the night shift joined the picket and in the warm, clear morning air there was a marvellous mood of optimism. It was always better to be acting than waiting.

Hamish's anger turned to elation as he saw the crowd calmly blocking the great gate. This was a grand answer to all those broken promises! Between the great gateposts they were suspending a union banner, a splendid gaudy thing, defiantly colourful in the face of the dreary industrial landscape, and much like the men themselves, who were confident and cheerful despite everything. They were like an army waiting for a battle to begin, an army with a just cause, motivated by righteousness.

When I think of the time we wasted, he thought. We should never have given them the benefit of time. They've not deserved it. This is what they have deserved – confrontation! It is the only way!

He had been so sure that Ralph Erskine had been sincere. He had been convinced of it, and yet not one promise had been carried out, not one of those men called back to work. He had promised, given the sacred word of a gentlemen that he would have them reinstated, and yet that word was nothing but treachery. He had been so convincing. Hamish had thought he had been genuinely moved by what he had taken him to see, but it seemed that it was nothing but play acting. Or perhaps the man was a weakling, full of good intentions but unable to carry them out. Whatever the case was, he had proved himself very false, and Hamish, addressing the meeting the previous night, had had no difficulty in producing a stream of invective against him. He had made it clear that such hypocrisy was worse than any sin his father might have committed. They had cheered at that!

Jessie had been a little surprised when Ralph had asked her to go over to Garbridge with him that morning, but she was glad of it. Perhaps it meant that he was reconsidering the chilly distance he had put between them for the last few days. After all, it was foolish to ruin a good friendship for the sake of a moment of folly. He had great plans for his transformation of the company and seemed eager to share them with her.

They motored down, with Ralph's secretary John Shaw driving, while Ralph and Jessie sat in the back of the motor and talked, quite as if it were the old days again. That there could be no more to their intimacy than this did not grieve her now, for it was so much better than that quiet between them. She had not realized, until denied it, how much his conversation meant to her.

'I've been trying to trace all the landlords of these tenements,' he was saying, unfolding a map and spreading it on the seat between them. 'Not easy, really. They don't like to own up to rank exploitation. They don't manage the properties themselves. It's all done by unscrupulous agents who employ thugs to squeeze the rents out of the tenants. But I am trying to buy up as many as possible.'

'Then what will you do? Become a corrupt landlord yourself?'

'No, of course not.' He smiled. 'No, I intend to raze them to the ground and build proper houses.'

'They won't be able to afford the rent.'

'They will – they'll be very low.'

'How will you manage that?'

'By a housing trust. The chocolate man Cadbury has set up one in Birmingham. It's marvellous – every house with a garden, and low rents for all.'

'It sounds too good to be true,' said Jessie. 'Can it really work?'

'I hope so. The marvellous thing about a trust is it keeps me out of the management, so it isn't so paternalistic. With luck, they will feel the community belongs to them and not to their employers. That's the trouble with a lot of these factory housing schemes – they're too like tied cottages for rural labourers. The people are made to feel they must be grateful to have a roof over their head. You know the sort of thing. When everyone must tug their forelock to the squire.'

'Like at the Quarro?'

'Exactly.'

'How are you going to pay for all this?'

'There's plenty of money slopping around. It's just a question of gathering it up. There was a huge amount earmarked for cattle ranching in Texas, would you believe? Overseas investment is fashionable at the moment. I suppose it's easier to send the profits out of the country than reinvest them into the people who really made them.'

'I hope it works,' said Jessie. 'It would encourage other people.'

'I only wish I hadn't realized so late,' he said. 'There's so much to be done, isn't there?'

'Yes, but to try, surely that's the thing. And you are trying, splendidly.'

'Good – I'm glad you approve. Ah look, we're coming down into the town now. You can see what needs to be done. I should rebuild the whole place if I could.'

'I have a feeling you might just do that,' said Jessie.

At about ten o'clock, a lad came running down to the picket, breathless with excitement, to announce that there was a motor coming down towards them.

Hamish knew at once it must be Erskine. He was the only one of the management who had not yet arrived. The others had irritatingly slipped through, and could be seen standing at the boardroom window overlooking the east gate. But there was no way they were going to let Erskine pass, motor or no motor.

'Let's block the gate then, lads!' he shouted, ushering bodies to fill the space between the gate posts. 'We'll not let this one through!'

He scarcely needed to say it. The crowd surged forward, and jumping up on to the makeshift platform they had built by the gate, he could see the motor slow as the crowd engulfed it. He recognized that it was Erskine's car and shouted: 'That's the sleekit bastard! That's your man, lads – that's our traitor!'

Somebody took up the shout: 'Traitor! Traitor!' and in a moment it had become a chant, accompanied by the slow and deliberate stamping of feet. The noise, so disciplined and yet so raw, was electrifying, and Hamish had no qualms of conscience as the those nearest the motor began to beat the rhythm of the chant on its bonnet and hard top. Erskine was well caught now – there could be no more wriggling out for him.

John Shaw let the engine die and they sat there for several moments without speaking, as the crowd and their menacing shouts surrounded them. Faces stared in at them and hands beat hard against the glass. Jessie felt her throat constrict and her stomach lurch with fear. She closed her eyes to it, finding even if she looked directly ahead she could not avoid the leering faces of the men who had climbed onto the bonnet. One, a lad of about sixteen, had pressed his face to the glass and assumed such a look of malevolent ugliness that she felt she had strayed into a nightmare. But it was all too obvious this was no nightmare.

'Shall I try and push through them, Mr Erskine?' asked John Shaw.

'No, John, that's the last thing we should do,' said Ralph. He sounded calm, surprisingly so, but a glance to her side established he had gone pale. 'God in heaven – what can this be? I don't understand this in the least. I had better go and speak to them.'

'Ralph . . . surely . . .' She was afraid for him. 'That can't be wise.'

'No,' he said, with an air of resignation, 'but what else can I do? I think they want to speak to me.'

'Then I'll come with you,' she said impulsively. The thought of letting him go out there alone was horrible to her.

'You stay right here, Jessie. There's no knowing what might happen. I don't want you to get mixed up in this. I can't imagine what all this might be about but . . .' And before she could stop him he had slipped out into the crowd. They stepped back only a little to let him out and the chant collapsed into angry jeers. Then the crowd surged forward again, seeming to engulf him. She could just hear him saying: 'Let the car go through! There is a lady inside who has no part in this. Let it go through!'

His words seemed to have some effect and a path cleared before them. John Shaw quickly started up the engine and began to pull away.

'You can't leave him there!' she exclaimed. She turned round in her seat and peered out of the back window. But Ralph was lost in the crowd now. 'Stop the car – you can't leave him. God knows what will happen!'

'He won't thank me if you get hurt, Mrs Hamilton,' said John Shaw. 'This is no place for a lady.'

I'm no lady! thought Jessie, in indignant impotence as the car bore her away from him. And I'm damned if I'm going to let these thugs get away with it! For she had seen the violence in those men's eyes and it incensed her. Any fear she might have felt seemed to die away to be replaced by anger and the moment John Shaw stopped the car by the safety of the entrance to the offices, she climbed out and began to run back towards the gate.

'Mrs Hamilton!' he shouted, and she could hear he was running after her. 'Please come back. It's terribly dangerous!'

She ran faster, but found some fifteen yards away from the fringe of the crowd, he had caught her and seized her arm.

354

'Let me go!' she exclaimed.

'No, Mrs Hamilton, you mustn't!' he begged.

'If I don't, who will?' she said, struggling out of his restraining grasp. 'I can't sit by and let them do this to him!'

And she broke away finally and plunged herself into the depths of the crowd, blind with fury at the male folly of violence.

Ralph imagined he must be whispering, for he could not make himself heard, not even to himself. But his voice was hoarse – was it from fear or from shouting? It must be from fear, for if he were shouting they would hear him, they would understand him. He could not be speaking loudly enough.

'Traitor! Traitor! Traitor!' they were chanting again, spitting the words out at him, and he could find no way to break the chorus.

'Listen to me! Listen to me – let me explain, for God's sake! You don't understand!' But no matter how many times he shrieked it, they could not or would not hear him. It occurred to him that they would not let him speak his defence. They were resolved to condemn him and anything he did was futile. However this thing had happened (and he could not explain it to himself), he was a condemned man. He wondered which of them would strike the first blow.

He looked into their faces, glancing restlessly at them all, hoping he might find some saving grace of humanity in their eyes, some recognition that he deserved more justice than this. But did he? He no longer knew.

He wondered if they would kill him, as they came closer and closer to him. He could smell their hatred and he felt sweat trickling down his temples. Utterly defenceless now, as two of them seized his arms and pinioned him to the spot, he closed his eyes, too afraid to look at the face of his assailant. And strangely, as he did so, a message flashed across his mind, written in the cramped hand of the copybook: 'The road to Hell is paved with good intentions'.

Then the pain began . . . ★ ★ ★

For a moment she could do nothing, not only because the crowd prevented her from getting any closer but because shock had paralysed her. It was the most disgraceful, disgusting thing she had ever seen. Two great louts had Ralph by the arms while another, built like a prize fighter, laid into him, swinging back terrible brawny arms with vigour to increase the impact of the blows. But unlike any prize fighter, this man was going scrupulously for the head and there was already blood streaming from one side of Ralph's face.

Without quite knowing how or why she did it, Jessie lunged forward and broke through the ranks. She hurled herself at the man in the white heat of her fury and managed to push him aside momentarily. It was probably surprise that moved him more than anything, but at least it had stopped him hitting Ralph.

'What the hell?' he exclaimed. 'What are you doin', woman?'

'No, what are *you* about, you great savage?' she said. 'Have you taken leave of your senses or does this sort of thing amuse ye? What has he done to deserve this?'

'That sleekit bastard is just getting what he deserves. He promised us our jobs back and what has he done? Nothing!'

'You fools!' said Jessie. 'Let him go. He's done nothing of the sort. If you'd given him a chance to speak, you'd know that. But what do you do, you daft loons, you just lash out because it's the only thing you know. God, I pity your wives!'

She stopped, for the men had indeed released Ralph and he had slumped on to the dusty ground. His head was bent between his knees and he seemed to be having the greatest difficulty breathing.

'What have you done to him?' she said, sinking down beside him and cradling him in her arms.

'Christ, man, it does look bad,' said someone, and the moment that was said, they had ceased to be a crowd with a single destructive ideal and become again a mass of individuals with individual consciences. A gentler atmosphere of remorse seemed to cloud the air.

'Get a doctor then!' she said. 'Don't just stand there!'

'It's no like Anderson to lie to us,' said someone.

'Aye – perhaps he did get it wrong,' said another man.

'I . . . I did . . . tell them . . .' said Ralph in a hoarse whisper.

'Don't try and speak,' said Jessie.

But he shook his head and with a great effort wrenched out the words: 'I told them . . . but they . . . they ignored me. I know I should not have trusted them . . .'

'Who?' said a man, who had not spoken before and who now knelt down beside Ralph. 'Who?'

Ralph smiled weakly at the sight of this man.

'Is this your effort, Anderson?' he asked. 'Thank you very bloody much . . .'

'Christ, Erskine, I'm sorry. We thought . . . you see . . .'

'You could have let him explain,' said Jessie.

'Aye, I know,' he said. He sounded genuinely sorry. 'This has been the most damnable cock-up!'

'That's what comes of stirring people up, Anderson,' said an older bearded man, who had appeared with him. 'Don't say you weren't warned. This isn't going to do the union any good at all. If the papers get hold of it . . .'

'They won't, Mr Kennedy,' said Ralph, making a valiant effort to get to his feet, supported by Jessie and Hamish Anderson.

'Then you won't bring charges?' said Kennedy.

'No more of this,' said Jessie firmly. She could feel his remaining strength evaporate as he leaned on her. 'He needs attention. If you please, could we get through?'

The crowd had vanished, dispersed in all directions. The men were keen to put some distance between themselves and the violence which they had witnessed, in case they were suspected of an active part. Certainly Ralph's assailant had disappeared, phantom-like, probably anxious to be away from retribution.

Ralph sat in his father's leather armchair, while Jessie cleaned up his wounds. Although she performed each movement with the greatest delicacy, each gentle brushing of the dampened cloth made him wince and she wiped away his involuntary tears with the blood.

'There,' she said, stepping back. 'Almost done. It should just be bruises apart from that cut on your temple.'

'Thank God for that,' said Ralph. 'I thought my brains had been knocked out. Who was that fellow, Anderson?'

Hamish Anderson, who was standing by the window, said without turning to them, 'His name is Jackie Fortrose. Why, do you want to set the police on him?'

'No, you know I don't,' said Ralph, watching Jessie charge a swab with iodine. 'Oh, must you use that stuff, Jessie?'

'It'll only sting a little,' she said. 'You coward!' And at that they all laughed. 'They'll be wondering what we're about in here,' she remarked.

'Oh, doubtless Tealing has his ear pressed to the keyhole,' said Ralph. 'To report back to Mackerson, I don't doubt. I suspect he's the one at the root of this bloody business . . . ah, Jessie, no.' She was dabbing at the cut with the iodine, but she might have been rending it with a knife blade.

'Shush, it's all done,' she said.

'It looks like they have sent for the police,' observed Hamish Anderson.

'Damn it,' said Ralph. 'We shall just have to be uncooperative then.'

Jessie, shaking her head, went and sat down. He supposed that to her the situation would appear absurd. That he was willing to condone the violence of which he had been the victim, that he was willing to let his assailant get away with it, was perhaps, to a rational outsider, a trifle difficult to understand. But however much pain he might be in now, he had a sense that anger and revenge were pointless. There was too much at stake here. The violence and menace of the crowd was merely a symptom, and like a good medical man, he knew that the best cures must attack the causes of a disease. Ralph understood very well that the responsibility for those causes lay very firmly in his own camp.

'There's blood on your dress,' he observed. She glanced

down at her bodice. 'I'm sorry – will it be ruined?'

'It doesn't matter,' she said.

'You must let me replace it.'

'Don't be silly, Ralph,' she said.

'I feel I must do something.'

'For what, for heaven's sake?'

'You probably saved his life, Mrs Hamilton,' said Anderson.

'Nonsense,' she said. 'I just did what had to be done.'

'The words of a true heroine,' said Ralph.

'It wasn't that. It was common sense – and I was angry, very much so. In fact, I think I still am. I can't stand violence, you know. And I can't think how you let that happen,' she added in an accusing tone to Anderson.

'It isn't his fault,' said Ralph.

'Oh aye, and who else put the notion in their heads in the first place? Well, Mr Anderson?' she demanded angrily. 'Oh, I know I may be a daft woman, but it strikes me you lot are the halfwits in this. I don't understand you at all. I suppose I didn't have you down as a saint, Ralph Erskine. It takes a bit of getting used to.'

'I'm not a saint, Jessie,' he laughed. 'God forbid. It's just as you said a minute ago, when you were refusing to be a heroine. You did what had to be done, didn't you? Well, this is just the same. I have to swallow my bruised pride because there is too much at stake here.'

'I know,' she said, 'I know that. But I'm just angry that they did it to you, of all people. I hated to see them do it. No matter whether they had good cause or no, I can't forgive them as easily as you can. I like you too well for that, Ralph!'

She looked embarrassed at having spoken so freely, and swivelled round on the chair so that she avoided his direct gaze. Her face was flushed and her hair disarranged. In such circumstances it had been impossible for her to hide her raw emotions as she sat there in her crumpled, soiled dress, although she looked resolutely away from him. She had opened her heart to him as she had rushed through the crowd and pushed away his attacker. She had risked her neck for him and she had been at his side when it had really mattered. Crisis had suspended the normal rules, those suppressors of unacceptable feelings. She had given herself up to instinct and that had been to protect him. Now, he sensed her shutting it away again, because, as he well knew, there was no place for such complications between them. He had to remind himself, with a terrible wrench of self-control more painful than any physical torment that Fortrose might have unleashed upon him, that they were simply, and could only be, good friends.

'What on earth has been going on?' asked Mrs Erskine with some astonishment as they came into the hallway. She was standing at the foot of the stairs, rivetted there, it seemed, in surprise at the sight of them. It was true that Ralph and Jessie did not make the most elegant couple. Ralph's face was now a mixture of flaming red and black and some of his hair was, in places, still a little matted by blood, while his clothes were crumpled and grey with dust. Jessie, for her part, knew she looked far from respectable. Her hair was falling down and she had not bothered to put her hat and gloves back on, for the hat had been knocked out of shape and the gloves were past salvage. There was a tear in her skirt and her blouse was stained with blood. They must have looked frightful.

'Ralph – your face!' said his mother, horrified. 'Has there been an accident?'

'Of sorts, Mother,' he said, going forward. 'Would you mind terribly if we explained this all later? I think we are rather desperate to get cleaned up.'

'But you are all right?'

'Yes, we're fine, Mrs Erskine,' said Jessie. 'How is Mr Erskine?'

'Oh, a quiet day, thank God. Ralph – you must be in agony. You look as though someone has . . .'

'Later, Mother, I promise,' he said, patting her on the arm as he passed her on the foot of the stairs. 'And don't worry about me. Do you promise?'

She nodded, but shook her head the moment he had gone.

'Jessie dear, what has happened?'

'It is all rather difficult to explain . . .' she began, but suddenly Ralph's voice called out above them, 'Let her be, Mother. I will tell you the moment I'm out of the bath.'

'Well . . .' said Mrs Erskine. 'Run along then, dear. You do look rather the worse for wear.'

The bedroom Jessie had been given at Allansfield was luxuriously provided with a dressing room and a bathroom. Despite the warmth of the day a hot bath was a very welcome thought and she soon had the place filled with billows of steam and the scent of rose bath oil. It was a curiously sumptuous conclusion to such a tumultuous day and she was glad to lower herself into the water and attempt to forget about the events she had witnessed.

Of course it was not that easy. The state of relaxation produced by a bath also induces a speculative state of mind, and she was soon trying to make some sort of sense of all she had seen, and more importantly of what she had felt. For she had surprised herself with her own anger, with her own capacity for action and her own lack of fear. She had simply plunged into that crowd without a thought for the consequences. She could quite easily have come to the same fate as Ralph, if not worse, for those men had not looked to her to be great respecters of womankind. She knew she had been damned lucky and that she should not really have done as she had done. A sensible person would not have done it. But what did sense have to do with it? The whole situation had been senseless and perhaps being sensible in such cases was a fruitless activity. Only the ludicrous could work, as if she had out-absurded the absurdity – if such a thing were possible. For were not men supposed to dash to the assistance of women, and not the other way round? Should not she have fainted with horror instead of being angry? That would be the conventional idea of things, and she had turned it all on its head, driven by something so strong within her that she scarcely understood it.

Her mind fixed again, without her wanting it to, on the

361

sight of those great fists pounding at Ralph's face and neck, every blow making his body jerk as if it were nothing but a stuffed sack. She had almost felt those blows herself, and knew that she had not rushed in principally because of a hatred of injustice or violence, but because to hit him was to hit at her as well. She had admitted as much to him that afternoon and she wondered if such openness had been prudent. It was not that she was afraid of what he might do, how he might use her. She had no fears on that score, for she knew that he would behave only as he should. But she was afraid for herself, for she had suddenly made concrete a feeling that had hitherto been vague and easily ignored. It was as if she had got up at a revivalist meeting and confessed she had been saved, instead of letting confused and mysterious longings remain locked away. To have declared, so plainly, what she felt for him, that in short she felt a very great deal for him, was to watch the walls of the ordered life she had built round herself come tumbling down.

It was time to tell him, Ralph decided. He had waited long enough and he could no longer go on without telling him. He needed to know, and Ralph hoped he might have some good advice. He would know, for example, how to deal with Mackerson.

He paced up and down in the passageway getting up courage. A bath and a couple of brandies had made him feel a great deal better, and he was almost able to ignore the pain in his face.

His mother came out of the room and, seeing him there, shook her head.

'I can't let you go in,' she said. 'Not looking like that. It will distress him too much.'

'Look, Mother, I cannot go on lying like this, you must realize that. You know how bad things are now. I need his advice, damn it.'

'There's no need to swear, Ralph,' said Mrs Erskine. 'And no matter how bad things might be at Garbridge I will not have you ruining his recovery with them. It is your mess, after all, you must get out of it.'

'My mess! It's his mess as much as mine!' exclaimed Ralph.

'For goodness' sake, be quiet,' she said. 'If you wish to grumble, go and do it elsewhere. He is not to be disturbed – he's sleeping just now.'

'Mother,' he said, with some desperation, taking her hands, 'I don't know about you, but I got the impression from the doctor yesterday, that he was well on the mend. Last night he seemed perfectly calm and able to manage. Why cannot I speak to him? He will hate us both when he is better if I do not tell him about this now. You must see that it is very urgent.'

'Why do you think he is doing so well?' she retorted. 'Because he has had no distractions of any sort. What good do you think worrying will do him? It might well kill him, and then who will be to blame?'

'Oh, this is simply impossible!' said Ralph, and he would have said more except that the nurse suddenly came out on the landing.

'Mrs Erskine, if you please!' she said. 'I think . . .'

There was something in her expression that needed no further elucidation and they both rushed into the room behind her.

It was obvious at once that something was going very wrong. His sleep had broken and he was wheezing badly, just as he had done on the day of the first failure. He was trying to sit up, and at once seized Mrs Erskine's hand when she came to the bedside. He seemed to try and speak but there was nothing. There were tears of pain flooding down his cheeks and the breathing became less and less regular. His face seemed to swell and his expression took on a ghastly grimace. And then, his body slumped forward.

The nurse held his wrist for a few moments and took his pulse. She shook her head.

'I'm sorry,' she said. 'It seems to be over.'

'Oh, Robbie,' said his wife, very softly. 'Goodbye.' And she put her arms around him and laid him back on the pillows. She closed his eyes and knelt down by the bed, bending her head in prayer.

10

A full board and management meeting at Garbridge without the presence of Robert Erskine seemed to Andrew to be anomalous – but it was an anomaly to which everyone would have to become accustomed. Even though they had buried him yesterday, Andrew half expected him to appear and oust Ralph from his place. But this, of course, would not happen. Robert Erskine was no longer the head man at Garbridge.

His son, thin and stiff in black suit and high collar, his face still grotesque with bruises and his hair cropped with monkish severity, now stood at the head of the table, dividing his glance between the faces round its edge and the papers spread in front of him. Seated on either side were Mrs Erskine and Alix, the latter reminding Andrew of how little he liked to see his wife dressed in black.

The last time there had been such a meeting had been three months ago. It had been a very different occasion – distinctly light-hearted, for he and Alix had just announced their engagement and the meeting had been called to make him a junior partner in the business. Then there had been clauses which the solicitor had galloped through because they had dealt with the necessary provisions for the death of Mr Erskine, an event which they had all blithely thought very distant. He had not expected to find himself the deputy director of the company for many years, and yet now he sat at the foot of the table opposite Ralph, who was himself still only a young man. It would have been, perhaps, a less grave occasion if they had had the opportunity to grow some grey hairs between them and scatter a few grown-up children in the ranks of the shareholders.

Alix was leaning forward in her seat, resting her chin on

her black-gloved hands, drumming her fingers very discreetly. Andrew quite understood her impatience, for although she and her mother held a substantial number of shares, it had been so arranged that they had no real control over it. Mr Erskine had firmly believed that women had no place in business, and although Ralph had attempted to explain to him that it was unfair to give Andrew significant power but still to shackle Alix, he had not had any success. Andrew had agreed with him for he knew very well Alix's own views on the subject, but a stern look from Mr Erskine (a look which he had learnt as well as Ralph to interpret as warning of a storm) had silenced them both. Perhaps Ralph would do something about that now, for it had not taken Andrew long to realize on their return from Norway that Ralph had undergone some sort of dramatic philosophical upheaval and had decided that the company must be turned on its head. Garbridge seemed set for as much a transformation as it had witnessed when Robert Erskine had taken over the place in 1869. And Ralph's dynamic, although very different from Robert Erskine's and somewhat late in flourishing, was equally irresistible. One could see at once how in control of the situation he was.

'Well, I think we are all here now,' Ralph said, straightening up. It seemed he did not intend to sit down but addressed them standing, a little like the schoolmaster he had once admitted to Andrew he might have preferred to become. Indeed a black gown was all that was needed to complete this image, for in that austere room, flooded with early autumnal light, there was a beginning of term atmosphere. And it is a new term of sorts, reflected Andrew.

'The reason I have gathered you here today is probably very obvious,' he went on. He sounded unusually confident. 'There are certain formalities which must be got through, which Mr Frazer perhaps you will deal with in due course? But I should like to say a few words before we get to that, which I think are appropriate in the circumstances.' Some of the managers nodded and murmured 'hear, hear' at this but Ralph cut in, 'No, gentlemen, I am not going to speak an elegy. That was for yesterday and, as my father always said, today is business. Of course, we cannot ignore him completely. The reason we are all sitting here today, the fate of a great company in our hands, is because of Robert Erskine and what he did and what he was. Now, I should like to put to you all a question: what would be an adequate memorial to such a man? What could we possibly do that would be a worthy tribute to his memory? Well, it seems to me that we have two choices. One is very straightforward and very obvious: we continue to run this company exactly as he would have wished, going on as if he were still alive, constantly holding up as a model his way of doing things. In principal, this sounds very fine, doesn't it? It is respectful and very easy to accomplish, because at its heart lies nothing but complacency. It does not require any alteration, nor any strenuous work, nor rigorous self-examination, nor any risk.

'I know that all of you would agree with me that such complacency is the enemy of good business. That is why I see another way in which we could go on, a radical, innovative route which involves risks, and may make us look like cranks, but in the long term, I am convinced, will put us leagues ahead of our competitors. We have a new century ahead of us, and the solutions of 1875 will not do for 1905. I think any of you who knew my father at all, will understand that this is his philosophy. You know how he constantly struggled to introduce the most advanced and efficient manufacturing methods, to make the most innovative products, here and at Clydebank, even to the pits which supply our ore. You all know this and you applaud it, rightly so, but I think that this sort of innovation is no longer enough. We need a broader, more humane vision for this company, that will make us the leaders in our field. Because the changes that I am going to make, will not, I trust, be simply the conscience-salving gestures of a wealthy man, but positive steps designed to make good business sense. For too long the working man has been treated as an expendable element who ranks somewhere below machines

366

and raw materials in usefulness. And now those men are growing angry, and they will continue to grow angry until they have no use for us at all. The only way we will ensure their support is to support them! That means, as I am sure you know, pay and conditions which bear some just relationship to what they give to us, because now, I am ashamed to say, we are cheating them.' He paused here to let his audience contemplate his words. In fact the silence was charged with shock.

'You may think that this is not the time for such pronouncements, that I am being grossly disrespectful to my father's memory by wanting to change so much of what he had created. I understand this, but I ask you to look very clearly at the situation and say to yourselves: "Can we, with clear consciences, go on like this?" I can see what my father could not, or perhaps would not, but I accept that this blindness was not intentional. If one does not lift a stone, one cannot guess what might lurk beneath it. His eyes were fixed on a very different horizon, but I believe if he had known what I now know, he would have recommended exactly the same course of action. He would see that it it the only option we may legitimately pursue. Therefore, in memory of my father, I ask you all to give me your support to make these changes and bring about this new era for Erskine and Company.'

Andrew, moved and convinced by his words, leapt up from his seat and strode down the room, his hand extended.

'You have it, Ralph,' he said, and they shook hands.

'Bravo!' said Alix, smiling. Andrew was glad to see it, for it was the first time she had smiled in days. But he also saw her gulp, perhaps to suppress more tears and he put his arm round her shoulder. Her hand reached up and took his own, and he felt how admirably this simple gesture indicated the strength that lay between them. Apart they would have been a pair of useless weaklings, but together, man and wife now, they could face anything. Of course, this time was hard for them. Alix loved her father very passionately and it would be a long time before she properly accepted his loss. But life was not all simple tranquil happiness, and marriage

367

far more than vapid romance. If they were tested, he reasoned, then so be it, for he felt soberly confident that together there was much they could survive.

'Might I say a word?' said Mr Mackerson, getting up from his seat.

Ralph gestured that he had leave to do so.

'Your oratory is very impressive, Mr Erskine,' he said coolly, 'but it is oratory, none the less. You have not given us one shred of evidence that these high-minded schemes of yours will lead to anything but financial disaster for this company.'

'Did you say that to my father when he put in the Leviathan press?' said Ralph.

'Of course not. That was obviously going to be profitable.'

'You are speaking with hindsight. I remember quite distinctly my father saying that some of you thought he was mad to build it, that there could not possibly be a demand for such large steel plates.'

'I think your memory is deceiving you, Mr Erskine,' said Mackerson.

'Oh, is it?' said Ralph. 'Then perhaps you might remind me of something else, sir? Am I wrong in thinking that I sent you a note telling you to reinstate some thirty men who had been laid off from the plate mill? I think I did, didn't I?'

The question hung in the air. Everyone knew why Ralph stood there with a mask of bruises and a crooked nose.

'You did,' said Mackerson, but defiantly. 'But having considerably more experience than you in these matters and knowing what the full financial consequences would be, I decided to disregard your instruction. You see, Mrs Erskine, there are some of us who care to protect the value of the shares more than others.'

'That is not the issue here, Mackerson,' said Ralph, 'and you know it! Please note, for future reference, gentlemen, that if I give an instruction it is to be carried out, or if for some reason you cannot comply with it, you will at least have the courtesy to come to me and explain why you cannot. You are, Mr Mackerson, an employee of this company, and if you are to remain one, you must accept that my judgement and my authority are the same as my father's. If you cannot accept that . . .'

'No, I cannot!' exclaimed Mackerson. 'I cannot accept your numskull idealism, which will do nothing but destroy this company. Your father used to worry about you, Ralph Erskine. I think we can see now that it was not without good cause. It must have grieved him to think he must leave his company to an idiot!'

'Don't you dare to presume about my relationship with him!' exploded Ralph, bringing his flattened palm down on the table with such a crack that it must have hurt him considerably. But only anger registered on his face, the anger of a man pushed to the limit of his endurance. 'Good God, man! Haven't you understood a word I've been saying? It is no more my intention to ruin this company than . . .'

'It may not be your intention, but that is what the effect will be, I am convinced of it! No rational person would pursue such policies.'

'Then I should rather be thought irrational than immoral,' said Ralph. 'And if you think your taunts will make me change my mind, you are very much mistaken. I have decided what will be done, and if you disagree, you must resign. I could dismiss you here and now for gross negligence, but I should prefer it if you were to offer your resignation.'

'Because you are too gutless and weak-headed to fire me, no doubt!' snapped Mackerson.

'No, Mackerson,' said Mr Frazer, the company solicitor, 'that you cannot justify. Mr Erskine is giving you an opportunity to leave here with some dignity. What you did, for whatever reason, was very much less than could have been expected from a man of your position and experience. It could have had very grave consequences – and not that I am belittling your battle scars, Mr Erskine, but that situation was potentially explosive. It was only because of Mr Erskine's considerable bravery and his subsequent evenhandedness that we are not now in the midst of a serious strike. Would you have got out of that motor?'

'No, I would not have! You surprise me, Mr Frazer, I would have expected that you would see that business is no place for foolhardy attempts at heroism, but if that is the way you all want to go on, then I resign, quite freely. I have no wish to stay with a sinking ship.'

'Resignation accepted,' said Ralph, taking his seat for the first time at the meeting. As Mackerson gathered up his papers, Ralph leant back and said, with elaborate casualness: 'Has anyone else any comments?'

But the other managers stayed resolutely silent. They were perhaps not as willing to let their own security slip through their fingers for the sake of principle. They might not like Ralph or his new ideas, but he was an Erskine, and they knew what side their bread was buttered. They would be submissive to the new order.

When Mackerson had gone, they rushed through the other business, for the atmosphere was still rather awkward. Andrew found himself appointed acting works manager, a prospect which terrified him for vacation work in the engineering office at Garbridge had scarcely prepared him for such responsibility. However, he remembered how Mr Erskine had always shown confidence in his abilities and he hoped that this baptism of fire would not disgrace the old man's memory. After all, Mr Erskine had not just helped him financially. He had been a patron in the fullest sense of the term, and more of a father to him than his own father had ever been. It was, he realized, a responsibility for which he had been trained, in many subtle ways, as Ralph had also been trained in different things. If Ralph had no head for the technical side of things, he had seen that he had that visionary quality without which any business dies. Andrew knew he was a good engineer, but he also knew that he could not have imagined change on the scale Ralph was proposing. Ralph could grasp at the larger thing, reaching into the distance and snatching back the future to take them all into an entirely new phase. It was obvious at that meeting, for why else would a cautious, sober lawyer like

Mr Frazer have leapt to Ralph's defence, if he had not seen, so clearly, the genius of the man they were still mourning working powerfully anew in his son?

New responsibilities brought a new exhaustion, or so it seemed to Ralph as he sat later that night in his father's study at Rothesay Terrace, half stupefied by work and yet nowhere near completing it. As his father's executor, there was a formidable amount to get through, despite all the legal assistance and the good state in which his affairs had been left. The scale of the problem was daunting and he reckoned that the probate would take up months of his time, in addition to the work he had simply running Garbridge and all the other concerns.

He got up from his chair and stretched, noticing the tray of supper brought in by the maid several hours ago, which he had quite forgotten. There was little comfort in a pot of cold coffee but a glass of beer and beef sandwiches would keep him going a while longer. He poured himself a glass of beer and sipped it while studying himself (with some melancholy) in the glass above the chimney piece. The bruises showed no sign of abating and he still had the appearance of a renegade. His nose, he suspected, would never be the same again . . . and then he reprimanded himself for his self-indulgence. It was not a time to be staring at the mirror, like a vain school boy. It was not as if he had a handsome face to mourn, and if he did look, to put it bluntly, ugly enough to frighten a small child, it seemed appropriate to the new ascetic life to which he · must accustom himself.

He turned his attention to the great disorder of papers on the desk. He had seen that desk piled with papers before, of course, but his father always had some clever, methodical system which had kept chaos at bay, a system which Ralph in his bohemian days had been wont to despise. Now, he would have been glad to know the secret of it. But that, with so many other things, had gone to the grave with his father and he wished again he had bothered to listen and remember during those business lectures which his father had given him. He had been too pig-headed, too stuffed full of youthful arrogance and too vaingloriously stuck in the artistic clouds to think that he might have needed any advice, that what his father had said would one day be useful to him. The ghost of those interviews seemed to appear before him, and he could see himself defiantly sprawled in the armchair while his father leant earnestly across the desk and did his damndest to knock some sense into him. He had scarcely listened to a word of it, he was ashamed to remember and angry too, at his own stupidity. He should have sat and taken notes, just as he might have at some illuminating lecture on Virgil by a scholar he had admired. If I had done that, Mackerson would have had no reason to say what he did, damn him!

Although he was aware that the meeting had gone as he had wanted, it had left him drained. Was everything to cost him such effort? If only I was better prepared – and God knows, Father, you did try, didn't you? You, of all people, knew what I was in for!

He sat down in the armchair and attempted to take comfort in his old nervous habit of running his hand through his hair, but he could not. His mother had sent for a malicious barber on the morning of the funeral, and his head had been almost shaved, like that of a penitent. He had been too abstracted to stop it, and it now seemed like a grim symbol of his own remorse. There was nothing for it but to go back to the desk and start working again.

Ten years ago, he reckoned, it would have been easy for him to be irresponsible. He would have sold out without a qualm and roamed Europe, living extravagantly and in all likelihood making a very great fool of himself. But now he knew that he could no more escape this destiny than a man on the scaffold with a noose around his neck. It was inevitable, although the ties that kept him were not legal or physical, but something more potent. He knew now how much depended upon him, how many were looking to him for great things. He had made promises which he must keep and the thing was too important to be aborted by his own desire for a simple life. If this lonely, difficult life was to be the price, then he would have to pay it. It was no time for self-love.

He wished for a minute, standing by that desk and reluctant to sit at it again, that Jessie was still with them. But she had taken the children back to Colinton, anxious, he suspected, not to be in the way. Her innate tactfulness, always so admirable, now annoyed him, for he felt a real pang at her absence. She of all people knew how to put him in a better frame of mind. He contemplated motoring out to Colinton and rousing her from her bed, simply to talk to her. But he knew he must not. He would have to exercise restraint in that quarter, or it would only become complicated and painful. There was nowhere that such a relationship could go, except to foolish destruction, and he valued her friendship too much for that.

The door opened softly and his mother came in.

'Shouldn't you be in bed?' he asked.

'Shouldn't you?' she responded.

'That's impossible, I'm afraid.'

She went and sat by the fireside, where she had often sat in the past, quietly doing some piece of needlework while his father had worked. Tonight she had nothing to occupy her hands and simply folded them in her lap.

'Do you mind if I sit here?' she asked.

'No, of course not. But shouldn't you try and sleep?'

'I couldn't,' she said. 'It's too quiet. The bed is too empty. I'd much rather sit here.'

'Do you want a fire?'

'No, it's too close for that. Don't mind about me, Ralph. You carry on. I shan't disturb you.'

'Are you sure, Mother?'

'Quite sure,' she said and they lapsed into silence.

Ralph again picked up the document he had been working on. But concentration eluded him, and he soon looked up to watch her. She sat very calmly, gazing directly ahead of her, her black clothes emphasizing the peculiar blankness of her expression. Her blue eyes, for which his father had always said he married her, now seemed to pierce the stillness. Then Ralph saw, with enough misery of his own, that her expression dissolved, cast over by a sudden cloud of tears, provoked by some very private memory which he could not hope to share. He had scarcely considered the nature of his parents' marriage before. He had thought it affectionate but perhaps prosaic, yet now, he sensed the passion of it as she sat and cried. A tide of feeling seemed to flow from her, feeling which had once had a vessel, but which now found only a vacuum. There had been so much love between them, dear quiet love, the most precious sort, that only increases and deepens with time, but now that lovely thing lay broken at her feet.

'Mother . . .' he managed to say, thought his throat was half choked.

She turned and looked at him with such a countenance that he did not think he would ever forget it.

'Oh, Ralph . . .' she said, her voice deep and distorted by tears. 'Oh, my darling . . . say you'll never leave me . . . promise me you won't. You're all that I have left.'

'No, no, of course I won't . . .' he said, rushing over to her and putting his arms round her. She clung to him and cried into his shirt front, a vulnerable child demanding protection. He remembered all those times he had clung to her, and how she had sheltered him and dried his tears when he had been a child. They had, according to that strange equation which acts upon parents and children, come to the point where the old roles are exchanged, and Ralph knew that his inheritance was far more than the chilly phrases of his father's will had at first suggested.

11

'It strikes me,' said Alix, as they came out of the meeting, 'that we are simply not doing enough – don't you think, Jessie?'

'What do you have in mind, Alix?' she said warily. 'Do

374

you want to go to prison like Miss Pankhurst?'

'Well, perhaps nothing as extreme as that – but I don't know. It just seems to me that the Edinburgh Suffrage Society is so locked in its old ways of doing things that we are scarcely making any noise any more. As an organization, we've achieved nothing! I think I shall write to Mrs Pankhurst.'

'So you are going to defect?' said Jessie.

'And why not? I can't see the E.S.S. going anywhere. What are we doing for the General Election? Whispering apologetically in the ears of the Liberal candidates. Where will that get us?'

'A long way if we get a Liberal government, which I think is the way it's going.'

'I don't trust the Liberals,' said Alix. 'You are coming back for tea, aren't you? You don't have to rush back to Colinton?'

'No, Sholto is dining out tonight.'

'Good,' said Alix, 'I'm hoping to recruit you, you see.'

'To the Women's Social and Political Union? Well, I'm not sure . . .'

'Oh, come now, Jessie. It's obvious, surely, that a national party, organized like one of the large political parties, has to be the answer. All these regional societies with their drawing-room meetings are hopeless. There's no strength in that. We need a national organization, and that's what Mrs Pankhurst has set up. What happened at the Free Trade Hall was simply tremendous.'

A month ago in Manchester, Winston Churchill, the Liberal candidate, had opened his election campaign with a public meeting, in the course of which Christabel Pankhurst and Annie Kearney had raised a Votes for Women banner and demanded of Mr Churchill: 'If you are elected, will you do your best to make women's suffrage a government measure?' This had caused considerable commotion, but worse followed when Churchill would not answer them, for they began to chant: 'The question, the question! Answer the question.' As a result of this they were hustled out of the hall, Miss Pankhurst hurling abuse at a policeman in the process. Undeterred, they began to address the crowd which came streaming out of the hall in their wake, for which they were promptly arrested. They refused to pay their fines and were sent to Strangeways instead.

Sholto had said, when he had read this in his newspaper: 'Only a week! If I had been the magistrate, I should have sent them down for a month. But it does serve that turncoat Churchill right to have his meeting ruined by a pair of hyenas!' For Sholto could not forgive Churchill's defection from the Tories over the free trade question. Jessie had not been sure how she felt about the incident. It was courageous of them, she had to admit that, but the talk of crowds and commotion disturbed her. The events at Garbridge still haunted her and she wondered how easily such a situation could collapse into violence. Besides, would such sensational events really be beneficial to their aims? It seemed to play into the hands of the opposition. Sholto had not admired their courage – he had been contemptuous of it. But it would not be easy to convince Alix of that. As they walked back to her house in Saxe-Coburg Place, Jessie could tell that she had been inspired. Even her step was brisk and determined.

'I mean, for goodness sake, the E.S.S. doesn't produce so much as a broad sheet,' Alix was saying, as she reached for her latch key. 'One would think it was a secret society the way we go on. A Scottish suffrage paper – that would be a good thing, don't you think? If I set one up, Jessie, would you write for it?'

'About what?' said Jessie, as they went inside.

'Oh, I don't know just yet – but we'll think of something, won't we? Ah, Rose,' she said, addressing the maid who had come out into the hall to take their coats. 'Mrs Hamilton is joining me for tea. Is the stove lit in the drawing room?'

'Yes, Mrs Lennox,' said the maid. 'Well – I did light it an hour ago, just like the master showed me, but I'm not sure it took.'

'I'm sure it did,' said Alix. 'You just have to learn to trust that it works.' But the maid went away shaking her head.

The stove in question had been brought back by Andrew and Alix from their honeymoon. It was a large, rather elegant thing, faced with tiles, but the maid it seemed could not get used to it.

'You'd think she'd like it,' said Alix, as they went into the drawing room. 'It makes so little mess.'

'And it does keep the place warm!' said Jessie. 'Perhaps I should start saving for one.'

'Andrew wants to start up a business importing them,' said Alix, opening the door and throwing on a couple of logs from a basket. 'He's so like my father sometimes, it's uncanny – the way he gets excited over mechanical things like this. He's so very practical.'

'They say you're supposed to look for your father in the man you marry,' remarked Jessie.

'Then are men supposed to look for their mothers, I wonder?' said Alix.

They settled in their chairs by the stove ready for a long, comfortable conversation.

As Alix poured the tea, Jessie took in the details of Alix's drawing room, which still surprised her, although she had seen it several times now. Her taste in decor was like her opinions – somewhat advanced. The walls were painted lemon yellow with a stencilled pattern of lilies while the curtains were of rough grey frieze. This perhaps was not particularly outlandish, but the furniture was. Alix had no time for Ralph's careful accumulation of old pieces. She had gone straight to an art cabinet maker in Glasgow and got him to fit out the room. So there were chairs shaped like half barrels but finished in checker-board marquetry; there was a white-painted settle, with a canopy resting on tapered posts and heart shapes pierced in the back; there was a writing desk, supported only by dangerously slender legs but with locks and finger plates that were almost as large as the bureau doors, and most striking of all, there was scarcely any clutter. Even the vase of lilies on the bureau looked as though the designer had ordained them to be there, and only there. It was a very definite reaction to the fussy depths of Mrs Erskine's drawing room at Rothesay Terrace, where palms sprouted from every corner.

'Is that Ralph's wedding present?' said Jessie, indicating the large landscape over the chimney piece.

'Yes, that's the Corot,' said Alix. 'I dare say Ralph thinks it is the only tasteful thing here. He was horrified when he saw this room, but what do I care? I think it's lovely – so simple.' She began to pile her tea plate with slices of bread and butter. 'Please excuse me,' she said, 'I'm hungry all the time just lately. Do you suppose I could be pregnant? I seem to want to eat enough for two.'

'You could be,' said Jessie.

'Oh, I hope so,' she said.

'If you're expecting, how will you carry out all your grand schemes?' asked Jessie.

'I don't see that it should stop me,' said Alix, cutting herself a slice of cake.

'Your mother might,' said Jessie. 'Don't you think she might send you to bed for nine months, for fear of a miscarriage?'

'I hadn't thought of that – I suppose she might. Well, I shall just not tell her until it shows. That is, if it happens.'

'You really want a baby then?'

'Oh, yes! Desperately! I was surprised at myself, but it was odd – suddenly it was exactly what I wanted. Especially, with Father, and all that . . . well, you know, it seemed right suddenly. And Drew wants it too. Tell me, how exactly will I know?'

'Well, there are various things you can look out for. Your flowers will stop for one, you start getting morning sickness – although that doesn't happen just in the morning, I warn you – and, well, you'll find your breasts swell up a bit, the veins stick out.'

'Do they? I didn't know that. Goodness,' she said, and then added roguishly, 'I shall have to get Andrew to have a look out for that. He'll enjoy that!'

Jessie smiled cheerfully, as she was supposed to at this hint about their happy, uncomplicated love making, but it only made her think of her own circumstances. She would have to be careful herself, for Sholto, in the last few months, seemed to have found a fresh interest in their relations. She was not sure that she wanted another child. If he were trying to make her pregnant to get his long desired son, she did not think she should comply, for there were three girls already who got scant attention from him. Another girl would be received indifferently and a boy would be spoilt to excess, which would scarcely be fair on the girls. There were precautions they could use but she did not think Sholto would agree to that. Abstinence seemed the only option, but she found it difficult to turn him away. His love making was so skilled that it drugged her into more than compliance; it made her eager and restless for more. When they made love, all the petty annoyances of their life together seemed to melt away. He might not tell her that he loved her any more, but when he pressed against her in the darkness, she felt that the old flame between them had not died.

Yet, sitting here, well removed from temptation, she felt annoyed at her own weakness. She would curse her own self-indulgence if she became pregnant again. Unlike Alix she would watch for the signs fearfully and then, if they came, she would not know what to do. Another baby was more than she could cope with, and certainly more than they could afford.

'Penny for them?' said Alix.

'Oh, I'm sorry,' she said, realizing she had lapsed into thoughtful silence. 'I was miles away. Oh by the way, I meant to ask earlier, how is Ralph getting on in London? Have you heard from him?'

'I had a letter this morning – rather amusing, really,' said Alix getting up and going to her bureau. 'Here, I'm sure he won't mind if you read it.'

Jessie unfolded the letter. It was written on a sheet of foolscap, in dense black ink.

Dear Alix,

I thought you'd be interested to know how I got on chez the Webbs. They *are* just as extraordinary as everyone says! I started out badly by being wrongly dressed of course in white tie, to find the others in homespun, sandals, etc, except for Mrs Webb who is very handsome and I suspect gets her gowns from Paris. But that is her only self-indulgence. The house is terribly austere and not a drop of wine was served at dinner. As for the food – well, it was so badly cooked, that I almost ventured the impertinent remark that it was an extravagance to treat good food so ill, because most folk left theirs. A Scottish hostess would have been mortified to see her guests get up from the table so hungry, but Mrs Webb seems to think a state of semi-starvation promotes better talk. Perhaps, but if I am bidden here again, I shall dine before I dine, so to speak!

Enough of the externals – you will want to know who I met. Well, the famous G.B. Shaw was there and he is every bit as impressive as his work. I fear I did not impress him though. Perhaps that hungry look in my eye was too obvious, that burning desire for red meat and claret, which he of course never touches. Also, my stutter came back with a vengeance, but what can one expect in the presence of genius? Fortunately Mrs Webb seemed inclined to protect me from the worst of them. Perhaps she understood my position better, for her money is railway money. She seemed to believe, thank God, that my intentions were good, but even she could not resist lecturing me on the evils of paternalism. On the whole, I thought there was too much theorizing amongst them and no practical action. They are all too busy making reports and writing pamphlets to do anything. I suppose it is an important part of the process, but I found myself very impatient with it. At least I have the opportunity to do something, even if it is paternalistic. Writing a report about rickets will not get rid of rickets, will it? I suppose what I really want is some sort of benevolent despotism which actually gets things done! God knows, that's a dangerous thing, but there must be a way that checks on power can be built into the system. I suspect I have different ambitions. They want to change the entire world. I, cynically perhaps, feel that is simply not possible, but we must do the best we can, where we can. What shocking pragmatism, that is . . .

I shall be back on Monday, if Andrew can hold the fort until then (which I'm sure he can) and I shall be at Philip Winterfield's place in Warwickshire this weekend – an altogether less terrifying prospect than dinner with Mr and Mrs Sidney Webb!

'You should get Ralph to write for your paper,' said Jessie, laying down the letter.

'Yes, he does write well,' said Alix. 'He used to write the most incomprehensible poetry, you know, but I suppose he has had to learn to be very clear. It's funny,' she said, taking the letter back and glancing at it, 'this thing about action, about needing to act – we both feel it at the moment. I wonder why?'

'Perhaps because of your father,' said Jessie. 'The best cure for grief is doing something.'

'Yes, that could be it. And he would like that, I'm sure, to know that we were making ourselves useful in some way or other.'

Jessie lay in bed, later that night, unable to sleep. Sholto had not yet got back from his dinner and there really was no point sleeping – he would only wake her when he came in with his drunken clumsiness. Besides, she could not sleep. For some reason the words of Ralph's letter were haunting her, as if they had been written in all their intimate eloquence expressly for her. This, of course, was a ridiculous thought, but she could not help but think of everything in connection with him with a proprietorial air. It was as if now he belonged to her, but she was the only person to know it. She certainly did not wish that he should know this – or, to be more exact, she longed in the very depths of herself that he might know, but her active, careful, practical and daily self did not wish that he should know. It was too dangerous a fact to release. For the gap in the bed in which she now lay was waiting not for Ralph, but for its rightful occupant, Sholto, the man to whom she was not only legally bound, but caught up with by a hundred ties of common experience and gratitude. That neat pile of pillows, carefully plumped, with linen slips (because Sholto would not stand for cotton), were to support the head of a man from whom she could not possibly disentangle herself, no matter how much she might desire it.

She heard the noise of a motor taxi in the street and knew it must be Sholto. The neighbours would not be best pleased, for as she lit a candle she saw that it was two o'clock in the morning. She heard him fumble at the front door and then come staggering in, his boots cracking through the silence like gunshots. She propped herself up on her elbows and waited for him to come in.

He stood in the doorway for a moment, his overcoat draped over his shoulders. His face was very ruddy with wine, but there was not the usual exhaustion he generally wore after such occasions. His look, if anything, seemed to be one of exhilaration.

'Ah well,' he said, looking at her for a moment and then coming into the room. He flung his overcoat over a chair and sat down heavily on the bed.

'Ah well, what?' she asked, but he was too preoccupied in unlacing his boots to answer. In silence he undressed and got into bed beside her. He stretched out like an animal, seeming to relish the embrace of the sheets.

'Put out the candle, will you, Jessie?' he said, 'I'm absolutely exhausted.'

She was relieved that he did not want to make love. Indeed, he had turned away from her and was singularly remote, like a stranger in her bed. In a few minutes he was asleep, and Jessie lay beside him, quietly brooding on the

382

strange feeling she had had when they had last made love. It had made her feel rather guilty, as if she were doing it for all the wrong reasons. She felt as if she were being a traitor, not to Sholto, but to herself because, she realized, in the dark loneliness of that bed, it was not Sholto that she wanted any more.

Part Four

1911

1

'But I've told you, Livy darling,' said Sholto in an agonized whisper, 'I simply don't have that sort of money at the moment. If I had, of course I'd give it to you, but the fact is, my sweet, I don't.'

'Can't you help me at all?' said Olivia Lennox. 'I need it soon or that horrid woman says she will tell James. Surely you must know someone who would lend it to you. You must know someone.'

'I do, but my credit has run pretty thin with everyone. Oh, Livy, how on earth did you get yourself in such a mess? Seven hundred guineas is a lot of money to spend on tricking yourself out, even by your standards.'

'It isn't a dressmaker's bill,' she said. 'I've had a run of bad luck at cards.'

'At cards? I'd call that more than bad luck, I'd call that disastrous. What on earth were the stakes?'

'Oh, they weren't that high,' she said. 'It's just it mounted up over time. And now the woman is pressing me for it. She says she needs it soon. Oh, Sholto, what on earth am I to do? If she does tell James, I'm done for. He'll be furious. He's so strange these days, especially about money.'

'Isn't there something you could sell? Some jewellery, perhaps?'

'It's all locked away at the bank. The old miser won't even let me wear the stuff.'

This desperate conversation was taking place amongst the potted palms and lilies of the little conservatory which had been built over the balcony of Alix's back drawing room.

They were quite alone and unobserved, because everyone was happily occupied in the well-lighted rooms beyond. Andrew and Alix's parties had become quite celebrated. Sholto always enjoyed them because the wine was good and he knew he would always see Olivia. Tonight, the entertainment was particularly lavish because it had just been announced that Alix was expecting her first child.

'He said he'd give them to her,' Olivia went on, referring to her sister-in-law with considerable indignation. 'As if she needed jewellery! Just because she's going to have a wretched baby. I do so hope it is a girl. That will put James's nose thoroughly out joint. He's been rattling on about "the heir" ever since we heard. Such a bore. He's worse than his father, if that were possible!'

'Poor Livy,' said Sholto, putting his arm about her waist.

'Oh, Sholto,' she said, leaning on his shoulder, 'sometimes I'm so miserable. I hate being without you. Why don't we run away somewhere? What is there to stay for?'

'And live in shabby boarding houses for the rest of our lives? How the devil would we? I couldn't inflict that on you,' said Sholto. 'You would loathe such a life. You would not have your carriage or your title then, my Lady Lennox.'

'I know, but it is too awful sometimes.'

'My poor love, I know it is, but we must just bear it. And I'll see what I can do about the money. I can't promise anything – you mustn't expect miracles.'

'No, of course not.'

He got up from his chair and said, 'I suppose we should go back in.'

'You go first,' said Olivia.

He was always reluctant to leave her. Those few moments of comfortable intimacy, although their talk had been troubled, were for him as stimulating and as welcome as a glass of fine malt whisky. And as with a good malt, one glass was never quite enough.

He would have liked nothing better than to have produced that money for her, counting it out in crisp five-pound notes. He would have thrown in fifty guineas, if he could, for her to buy those little frivolities which she so much enjoyed, and which, by their sensuous grace, contributed much to his own pleasure: those lace-trimmed chemises; those crystal bottles of rose and violet perfume; those ravishing hats, which when they met occasionally for a discreet lunch, seemed to symbolize to him the whole gamut of female temptation with softly curling, shaking feathers, cascades of shining ribbons and wisps of gauze veiling which suggested so much and concealed so little. He had given her all he could, but it was never enough, and he always felt angered by the constraints on his own pocket. There was so much he would have liked to give her. She would have liked to live like a duchess, and it was as much as she deserved, for how could such a wonderful, beautiful creature be expected to live by the ordinary rules of commonplace economy?

At the far end of the drawing room he could see Alexandra Lennox wearing such a rope of pearls about her neck that his dear Livy would have killed for. They would have looked much finer on Livy, for on Alix they seemed an irrelevant appendage, as if they were only a string of beads. She could not possibly appreciate their worth, for she had never had to do without such things. For a moment, he tormented himself with a vision of those pearls lying across Olivia's naked and pale breasts. Damn it! he exclaimed to himself. It is so unfair that those wretched Erskines should have so much and live as if they had nothing! Their damned fastidious notions of taste! Now, if I had been born Ralph Erskine . . . That was a theme that had haunted him for years, ever since they had first met at the university. Then, as an impoverished son of the manse, he had been taken to dine for the first time at Rothesay Terrace. He had gone in gleeful expectation of a palace and a feast, but the quiet respectability had angered him then. It still did.

Alexandra Lennox was now talking to his wife, who in her shabby, old-fashioned evening dress piqued his pride still further. But he consoled himself that his money was better spent hanging pretty clothes on Olivia's back than on Jessie's. She had not the slightest idea of style, being still locked in a servant's mentality where serviceability was the sole god. He wondered how he could ever have thought her handsome, looking at her now in that neat, ungracious black silk, cut so modestly that only the slightest hint of her shoulders was displayed. He thought again of the diaphanous, foam-coloured gauze that Olivia had wrapped herself in that evening, and wished he might rush back into the conservatory and indulge himself with the sight of her, the sound, the very touch of her. But he could not, and stared again at his wife, while gulping down rapidly a glass of champagne. Sometimes it was impossible to believe she was his wife, although he woke up in the same bed as her each morning and there were those three children of their common flesh, those skittish, noisy creatures who were his daughters. Yet they were nothing to do with him, although they called him Daddy and presented to him on his birthdays a selection of strange, hand-crafted objects for which he was supposed to display his profound gratitude or risk Jessie's wrath. On all other matters she could be relied on to keep her temper, which was some strange sort of a blessing, for if she had been at all jealous or overbearing as some wives were, it would have been intolerable. As it was, she was an excellent housekeeper who knew her duty, which was as much as he could expect, or indeed desire, because he had quickly discovered that marriage and domesticity were not situations in which passion could thrive. A wife could never provide the excitement of a mistress, and legitimized love was to him about as interesting as organized religion. The whole of that side of his life was quite meaningless. That clean, white house in Colinton was not his home, but only where he slept, ate and put on clean clothes. Reality was to lie in Olivia's arms, well sated by passion, the curtains firmly drawn on the dreadful ordinariness of the outside world.

He glanced behind him, moved, he knew at once, by some mysterious prescience because he saw Olivia come out of the conservatory, that extraordinary dress shimmering slightly, her smile composed and very inscrutable. He felt quite floored by her magnificence and realized how much better the fashion of the day suited her than the other women, who stood no chance beside her. That high-waisted, svelte look with the cloth draped in a suggestive, classical manner might have been designed for her alone, for on everyone else it seemed ill proportioned. He noticed from the corner of his eye that a group of men by the conservatory door who had been talking very earnestly, broke off to stare at her, as if she were a great actress coming out onto the stage. Amongst them, he saw the distinctive figure of Ralph Erskine, thin, tall and craggy, like some great ugly bird in his dark evening coat. Sholto, with amusement, understood at once the look which he directed at Olivia, for it was revealing in a way which would have horrified the man himself, but in its unselfconsciousness, in its sheer unguardedness, lay its truth, and Sholto recognized all its signs. For he had felt them often enough himself. A beautiful woman could drive, like the truest arrow, straight into the heart of the most highly principled, scrupulous man, and he knew Erskine's vulnerability then, as he knew nothing else. It was scarcely surprising, he supposed, for no man could really live like a monk. It went too much against the grain.

Olivia nodded politely in his direction, for they could not possibly speak publicly together. Everyone thought that they were only acquaintances — how could they be anything else? But he would have to speak to her again later, if he could contrive it, to tell her that he had solved the problem of her gambling debts. For he had just spotted a quarry, a poor defenceless creature waiting for Olivia's pretty, little talons. Erskine was the softest target in the world! He would not notice a thousand guineas slipping through his socialistic finger tips!

Jessie noticed that Sholto was looking pleased with himself about something. She could not imagine what. She did not presume to guess what might be going on in his head any more and neither could she think that he might have anything to be pleased about. It had been a brittle, gloomy few months between them, the air always full of unspoken arguments, or at least with her own unspoken complaints.

The shabbiness of her life made her despair; the constant scrimping and saving on that pittance of housekeeping money grudgingly given, if at all. He taunted her with charges of extravagance and yet she nursed a secret and bitter conviction that he was the one guilty of that. For he spoke of five hundred guinea briefs, of great successes in court, of stacks of work which kept him so much away from home, and yet she never seemed to see a penny of the profit of all that labour.

Only moments ago she had been talking to, or rather had been talked at by Mrs MacIntosh, another advocate's wife. Mrs MacIntosh had enthused about the pleasures of a Swiss holiday, wearing a dress which spoke of comfortable prosperity. Jessie, as the woman blethered on, had been keenly conscious that her sole pair of evening gloves, which she had laboriously washed with white soap and milk to save the expense of a fresh pair, still looked tired in comparison with those suede, subtly-shaded gloves that Mrs MacIntosh was wearing; gloves chosen very carefully no doubt from the fragrant heaps in Jenner's to tone exactly with her pretty rose-coloured dress. What on earth does Sholto do with the money? she found herself asking, for there was no way in which she could balance the equation.

It was not that she wanted the money for herself. True, she would have enjoyed looking as smart as Mrs MacIntosh, but that was quite irrelevant when she thought of the real victims of this sorry, sordid business: their daughters. My daughters, my girls, she told herself with a touch of defiance, for Sholto did so little for them. But they were his daughters, and they were growing up with all the expectations with which his name and profession endowed them. Chloe, who was now almost as old as Jessie had been when she had first gone into service, talked of nothing just now but piano lessons and party dresses because that was what the little girls at the doctor's house, her friends, talked of. Such things (unobtainable luxuries to the young Jessie MacPherson) seemed to be the sacred rights of Miss Chloe Hamilton, advocate's daughter. The vanity of those party dresses it was perhaps prudent not to indulge, but to have to tell her there could be no music or dancing lessons for her, would be hard. Such things seemed important, but if Sholto was going to continue so tight-fistedly, there would be scarcely enough for winter clothes and ordinary schooling, let alone anything else.

You're a coward, Jessie, she told herself. And you know it. You should have all this out with him. You've gone on too long letting him trample on you because you were grateful to have a roof over your head. It's daft to go on like this – daft to make your own children suffer for your cowardice!

'Now, Jessie,' said Alix, breaking into her temporarily suspended consciousness, 'there's someone I want you to meet. My latest recruit . . .'

She had only been half listening to what Alix was saying. She had been bubbling with joyous excitement about her long desired pregnancy (the reason for this party, after all) and Jessie had been nodding and smiling, just as one is expected to do in such circumstances, but this sudden allusion to the suffrage cause jolted her back. It pricked her conscience again, for it made her remember that women must stand up for their rights – fight even – something in which she had been negligent in regard to Sholto. She saw in that instant that the battlefield which Alix had ridden across with such confidence over the last few years was not as clearly defined as she and her WSPU comrades might imagine. The struggle for political representation was a grand one, yes, but there were still a hundred, thousand, million private battles to be fought, inglorious skirmishes between men and women, between husbands and wives, between fathers and daughters, which must be painfully struggled through, in order that some sort of justice might prevail. The key to change lay not in the public meetings or in stunts involving unfortunate cabinet ministers, but in the smallest and most unremarkable acts of rebellion. Damn it, I shall give him a piece of my mind! thought Jessie, angry and ashamed at herself for espousing such high ideals and yet doing nothing about them, carrying on in ignorant submission out of fear. Yet, was that not the the greatest battle of all: the battle with oneself? For women were not raised to quarrel or revolt. She had been schooled in dutiful obedience all her life, and now she saw it served nothing but Sholto's own self-indulgent prejudices. She then realized that if she had struggled more when they had first married; if she had been less overwhelmed by his self-assurance; if she had had the courage to change him, as he had undoubtedly changed her, then there might be more between them now than that uncomfortable void which rendered their life together quite meaningless.

Alix's latest recruit was a young schoolmistress called Mary Chalmers, who, breathless with excitement, told Jessie how she was to assist Alix in editing *The Gude Cause*. This was the magazine which Alix had founded a few years ago. It came out quarterly, handsomely printed on cream laid paper, with broad margins and Celtic style woodcuts made by those lady artists who were also responsible for the embroidered banners which appeared at meetings and marches. It could scarcely, therefore, be described as a scurrilous political rag, but its appearance had provoked many outraged mutterings in prosperous drawing rooms when radical-minded ladies had introduced it into the more familiar pile of *Blackwoods* and *Tatlers*.

'Now Mary,' said Alix, 'perhaps you can achieve what I have been trying to do for years and persuade Mrs Hamilton to contribute something.'

'Perhaps, Alix, I might after all,' said Jessie, for it struck her she had at last found what she might say, though God only knew how she would manage to say it. She was not in the habit of expressing herself in the elegant prose used so effortlessly by *The Gude Cause*.

'But that's splendid!' exclaimed Alix. 'I knew you'd do it eventually, of course.'

'Did you?' said Jessie, mischievously.

'Well,' smiled Alix, and then added brightly, 'I really must leave you two now – I'm neglecting my other guests, aren't I?' And she patted Jessie's arm and laughed, 'Goodness, how slippery I can be!'

'I'm glad I haven't had to coerce you, Mrs Hamilton,'

said Mary Chalmers when Alix had gone. 'Tell me, what will you write about?'

They went and sat down. Jessie did not find it easy to put her rather confused, incoherent thoughts into words but Miss Chalmers was a sympathetic and encouraging listener, and soon they had the bones of a brief piece sketched out in Miss Chalmers's pocket book. She, a true professional, produced this practical item from her evening reticule where other women kept rachel papers and scented handkerchiefs.

'You'll have to forgive me, Miss Chalmers,' said Jessie. 'I can be very stupid over things like this. I didn't have much schooling when I was young.'

'Nonsense,' said Miss Chalmers with refreshing briskness. 'You've as much education as any of us. You've learnt your profession, just as I have.'

'I suspect I'm rather rusty on the finer points of that. Cooking for a family isn't exactly the same as a grand dinner every night.'

'Do you miss the work then?'

'A little, but there's a pleasure in all cooking really, if you take the trouble to do the simplest things well. That is important, I think.'

'Oh, yes, you are a professional!' said Miss Chalmers. 'That's just what I'd say about teaching, you know. One doesn't spend the entire time putting lofty ideas into the children's heads. Most of the time it's spelling and handwriting one has to worry about – it may seem dull, but it demands exactly the same vigilance and zeal.'

'Rice pudding or a bombe glacé?' said Jessie, and they laughed, comfortable together having found this unlikely common ground.

'Where do you work just now?' asked Jessie.

Miss Chalmers described the place. A small, private school in the south of Edinburgh, it was only just beginning, but it had ambitions. All the staff were graduates but they did not simply wish to imitate boys' schools.

'No,' Miss Chalmers explained, 'what the headmistress wants is a new sort of school, where the girls aren't forced

393

and drilled, because unlike boys they don't actually need that sort of discipline. This is a place where they can be thoroughly educated but still remain individuals. There's such a prejudice against educated women, isn't there – as if we were all monsters and harridans. What we want to show is that one can be well educated and still remain a lady.'

'I think my daughters would enjoy that. I think I would have. Goodness, when I think of my old dominie with his tawse . . .'

'Oh no, there's absolutely nothing like that!' said Miss Chalmers. 'That sounds horrid. Perhaps you should enter your girls, Mrs Hamilton. We do have a preparatory department.'

Jessie hesitated. The question of expense loomed large, but she resolved that she would fight for this if she fought for nothing else. If the girls were well schooled, they could easily be independent. Miss Chalmers seemed to read her thoughts and said, 'It isn't too expensive really. And I believe they make generous allowances for sisters. Shall I ask the headmistress to send you a prospectus?'

Sholto would be furious at such an idea. She could hear his disgusted indignation already, but she would not lie down and take it any more. If this school was the right thing for the girls they would have it, no matter what he said, even if she had to sell every stick of furniture they had to do it. She would shame him into providing for them as he should!

'Look, there's Mr Erskine,' remarked Mary Chalmers. 'You know him quite well, I suppose?'

'I've known him quite a while,' said Jessie, anxious to be noncommittal. She had only spoken to him very briefly that evening, before Alix had borne her away to someone else, and what she had seen of him disturbed her. He had not seemed himself at all. His manner had been one of brittle cheerfulness but now she saw a hollow, exhausted look in his eyes and there was about his shoulders a melancholy stoop as if he bore some great burden. Which of course he does, poor fellow . . . She wished she had some influence over him, for she had a strong sense he was in great danger, that he might crack apart at any moment. His unhappiness was tangible to her, and more than painful, because she knew there was nothing she could do about it. Beyond the safe shallows of their friendship there lay a whirlpool of deep and dangerous waters, and to speak frankly to him now would be to plunge into them. He was troubled enough. Her own emotional interference might help, but might as easily destroy. For that she could not bear to be responsible.

'He really is an extraordinary man,' said Mary Chalmers admiringly. Jessie glanced at her. She was staring across the room at him, quite unconcernedly, because she wished to look at what she loved. Jessie understood this the moment Mary Chalmers spoke of him. She knew the very tone of her voice because it echoed those private, little-spoken words deep in her own heart, those words which she was so afraid to acknowledge. Her desire for Ralph was like a deadly poison, strong but venomous because no possible good could come of it. Of that she must *always* remind herself.

Mary Chalmers had no need for such restraint. Her love was expressed without shame or anger. She was free to love him and free to hope her love might be returned. And perhaps, thought Jessie, slowly filling with misery, he might love her – he could, so easily. Mary Chalmers was intelligent, young and idealistic, not to mention very good-looking. In short, she was exactly the sort of young woman one might expect Ralph Erskine to choose as a wife. She would certainly not hesitate to accept such an offer.

Her eloquence was a torture for Jessie. Mary sat and sang a paean of praise to Ralph Erskine and then, when Jessie had heard all she could bear, bent her fair head a little towards Jessie and said, in a confidential, hesitant tone, 'I wonder, Mrs Hamilton, since you know the Erskines so well, if you don't happen to know if there is somebody in whom . . . he's . . .' She was unable to finish.

Jessie wished she could manage a charitable and reassuring smile. Instead, she said with some severity in her voice: 'Ralph Erskine is not a man to give away his heart very easily. He has been badly hurt in the past, you see.'

'Hurt? In what way? You mean, by a woman?' Mary Chalmers was full of concern.

'It was a long time ago,' said Jessie, 'but I know it has made him wary.'

She had hoped to discourage her but instead Miss Chalmers said, 'Oh, how very dreadful – the poor dear man! Surely he cannot believe that all of us are the same as that wicked creature? How on earth could anyone hurt him, Mrs Hamilton? I can't understand how anyone could think to do such a thing, can you?'

Jessie shook her head, unable to think of any adequate response to this. She was too afraid to speak, too terrified of losing him by giving some encouraging word to Miss Chalmers. But how on earth could she lose something which she did not even possess, something to which she did not even have the courage to stake her claim?

2

It was one of those winter mornings when it would have been better to stay in bed, her head stuck resolutely under the covers, ignoring the world outside. But such indulgence was not granted to Jessie who had a husband to feed, children to dispatch to school, and most dreadful of all a heap of damp ironing which could not be delegated to Molly because she, poor creature, was confined to bed with influenza. Doubtless they would all soon be struck down with it and she would have a whole houseful of invalids on her hands.

She had not yet tackled Sholto, despite all those brave promises she had made herself at the party the other night. She had not had a moment; even when she had him alone in the dining room that morning, he was too busy with bacon and eggs and boning up on his brief to listen to a word she might say. She could have confessed to every crime in the statute book that morning and he would not have raised an eyebrow. She stood there, a cup of coffee in her hand, prickling with irritation, wondering how much the brief was worth. It was obviously important but she had a firm conviction she would see nothing of the profits. She wondered if he realized that he was the only one eating bacon and eggs, that his children were making do on porridge in the kitchen next door? But the steely sky and leaden tattoo of rain on the window pane struck her into terrible, impotent silence and she watched from the porch helplessly as he dashed away to catch his train into Edinburgh.

She went back to the kitchen and found the girls quarrelling over empty porridge plates, taunting each other in that terrible 'yes you did – no I didn't' fashion, loved by children and loathed by their parents. It was, it seemed, a life and death struggle over a hair ribbon, a pale pink ribbon, so dirty and frayed that Jessie was compelled to confiscate it rather than let this shabby item give her a reputation for slovenliness amongst the eagle-eyed mothers who waited at the gate of the dame school the girls were then attending. Jessie had thought the board school a better idea, but Sholto, taking an unusual interest in the case, would not hear of it. He had even found the Misses Fairlee's precious little school, and entered them there without consulting her. Jessie was not at all convinced about the place. They seemed to learn little more than how to sit still, a quality in a woman which she knew would impress Sholto beyond anything.

'Minna Hogg always wears pink ribbons,' said Flora, full of resentment as Jessie retied her hair with serviceable brown ribbon.

'At least they're her ribbons to wear,' said Chloe, equally piqued. 'That was my ribbon, Mummy, you know that. Mrs Erskine gave it to me.'

'Well, I'm sure Mrs Erskine wouldn't want you wearing it in such a state.'

'I don't want to wear it,' said Chloe, 'I want it in my pocket. It feels nice – like your party dress.'

'What's the use of having a ribbon in your pocket?' said Flora, struggling free from Jessie's ministrations. Her hair was less than tidy but Jessie, glancing at the clock, saw she had no more time to waste on such niceties. She bundled them into their overcoats and galoshes and hurried them out, exhorting them to avoid puddles – an impossible request, she knew, because Jo, at eight, had the spirit of an explorer and could not resist stretches of uncharted water!

No sooner had she shut the door than she heard the faint but insistent tinkle of a handbell. It was Molly, feverish and fearful, craving reassurance. Jessie made up the fire and brought her a jug of barley water, fussing round her while the old woman lay muttering in her distress. Jessie sat and held her hand. It was the least she could do. She had good cause to feel very guilty about Molly. Her wages were four or five months in arrears. Molly, when well, had been generous on this subject, but as she lay there, her face flushed, her grey hair collapsing over the pillow, Jessie felt desperately wicked, as if not paying her had been enough to make her ill. If only I could give her the money now – and some more – that would make her feel more secure . . .

'You won't want me to go the workhouse, will you, Mrs Hamilton?' she said pathetically.

'Good God – of course not, Molly!' said Jessie. 'Don't you dare even think such a thing. You are part of this family now, and no one in this family is ever going to have to resort to that.'

Eventually she was calm enough to try to sleep again, and Jessie, having tucked the clothes about her, was able to get on with her business again.

The household chores seemed endless and exhausting and Jessie began to wonder if she was not coming down with Molly's flu after all. By the time she had got a pan of broth on the stove, her head was splitting with pain and she sat down abjectly on a kitchen chair, wishing she might be anywhere but in that wretched house on that wretched morning.

With time and a cup of tea, she was able to be philosophical, but the question of Molly's wages still tormented her.

What does become of the money? she asked herself. What does he do with it?

There was one way she could try to find out.

Sholto's study, as it was rather grandly named, was a small, square room with a west-facing window, wedged between the drawing room and dining room. When they had come here, he had had it expensively fitted up with glazed bookcases and a turkey carpet. The quality of these furnishings showed now. If perhaps the rest of the house was looking shabby, this sanctum, very particular to Sholto and smelling faintly of tobacco, had a sleek, well cared for look, as if nothing could possibly disarrange it. It irritated her. Like the man himself, there was nothing shabby about it. Although the rest of them might be in rags, there could be no question of Sholto going without his fine tailoring! On the back of the chair, tossed quite carelessly, was his smoking jacket, the sort of expensive, dandyish item which arrived without warning from time to time from his New Town tailor (to which Ralph had introduced him years ago, so God only knew how expensive it was). Usually, she would have carefully hung it up, brushing out the creases with wifely devotion, but today it incensed her, as did the whole room, from the rack of pipes to the crystal decanter of whisky, which always had to be full – and woe betide the person who forgot to attend to this important detail. She had been scolded about it enough times.

'No more!' she said aloud, and sat down at the desk, a thing, she realized she had never done before. In front of her, on the morocco blotter, was a pile of fresh white foolscap. She leant back in the chair, feeling her back crush that wretched jacket (she had always loathed it anyway), and stared at the window, with its little panel of painted glass. For a moment, she pictured herself writing her great article for Alix's magazine and almost picked up a pen in order to set her mark on all that enticing blank paper. But then she remembered why she had come in and pulled open the first drawer of his desk.

She was as systematic and as calm in her search as any police detective. Most of the drawers held little of interest: stationery, various notebooks and a quantity of obviously legal documents. There was nothing remotely connected with money: no bank books, no accounts ledgers, not even a solitary unpaid bill. That's because they are all in *my* desk, she thought grimly, and tugged at the deep bottom drawer. It was locked. This did not alarm her as she knew where he kept his keys – in the pocket of his smoking jacket. In a moment, she had turned the little brass key in the lock and was pulling open the bottom drawer.

It was heavy and well filled, but with what it was not obvious, because everything was hidden in various boxes. A pot of gold, perhaps, she thought eagerly, as she lifted out a cash box. She wondered why she had not thought of doing this long ago, especially when she opened the lid and found four five-pound notes and a small bag of gold sovereigns. *The devil!* she thought, astonished, and wanted to run upstairs at once and pour the sovereigns onto Molly's counterpane in a triumphant gesture. But this little cache of money hardly explained everything. She continued her search.

Next out of the drawer was a marbled box-file, the flap secured with a bow of crimson tape. She opened it and shook out the contents. One glimpse of a tradesman's fancy heading showed she had come across a cache of bills and receipts. She looked through these with mounting astonishment because she was unfolding bills from some of the smartest establishments in Edinburgh. There was a crate of wine from Elliot's of Leith; an evening gown from Madame Maurois of Frederick Street; two hats from MacMurdo's; a parasol from Jenner's; and numerous small receipts for gloves, bonbons, hampers, flowers . . . She looked at them all again, quite unable to believe what she read. But it was all very plain and as well as these, there was a little pile of handwritten receipts, simply annotated: "From S.G. Hamilton, received with thanks for use of premises, 5 guineas" – and annotated, " J.F. For use of premises". And more receipts for hats and gloves and dressmakers . . . what on earth? She scrabbled through them again, still utterly bewildered, and then the meaning of it dawned on her. It's a woman – he's having an affair! And she found herself inclined to laugh, perhaps rather hysterically, for it had never crossed her mind that he might do such a thing. Yet, judging by this, he had done and over a considerable period of time. The first 'premises' note was dated 1905!

'Good God!' She stopped laughing abruptly. That was almost six years. For six years he had been deceiving her and she had not had the wit to realize.

She pulled the drawer out of the desk and upended it on the rug so that everything fell out. She felt she wanted all the evidence out at once. She could not bear to have the truth seep out in dribs and drabs. She could not stand her ignorance any longer.

But then she wished she had not emptied the drawer. The first thing that caught her eye was an envelope addressed to him in a hand which she knew at once, not because she had seen it frequently, but because she remembered exactly the moment when she had first seen it. It had been on her first day at the Quarro, a crabbed, copy-book hand, here forming an address, but then a menu copied straight from Mrs Beeton. It was Olivia Lennox's handwriting.

She picked it up tentatively as if it might burn her. She held it for a moment and sank back onto her heels (for she had knelt down on the rug) as she took stock of what it was she was holding. Of course, she reasoned, it could be just some social note . . . but she knew in the pit of her stomach it was not. For it had fallen from a plump brown packet in which she feared there were dozens more.

Slowly she drew the letter out from the envelope and unfolded it. The solid white paper, headed with the embossed legend 'The Quarro, Peebleshire, NB', she recognized at once. The same mark had been stamped on the menu cards that she had written out for each evening's dinner.

'My darling', the letter began. Was it worth reading on? Was that one 'my darling' not all the evidence she needed? Nothing could have been more incriminating, but she read on because the words which fell under her eyes proved to be so startling that it was impossible to ignore them. This was by no means an ordinary love letter full of lover's protestations. It was more, far more than that. Its contents could only be described as obscene.

She scanned through it again, to check she had read it aright, but there was no doubt about it.

I miss you my love, I miss every part of you. At night I lie awake and I long to feel your naked body pressed against mine and to feel you inside me again. Nothing can satisfy me until I am with you again. I call out for you in my dreams, because you and our love making are the only thing I can dream of. I want you to kiss me, to kiss every part of me, especially my breasts, my buttocks and that part which you call the little forest . . . Am I making you excited, my love? Are you as restless as I am, Sholto? Are you hard now, as you always are when I do my special dance for you? Perhaps you should know that as I write I am slipping my hands up inside my skirts, just as you always do, because I am damp with desire, just at the thought of you . . .

Jessie threw down the letter, unable to read any more. It continued, densely written, for several more pages, presumably all in the same vein.

For a moment she could not think. She was numb with astonishment. She knew of course that everyone was capable of such thoughts, but to commit them so freely and with such obvious relish to paper! It seemed unimaginable, especially from a woman with Olivia Lennox's pretensions to gentility. The image of her writing such a letter at the elegant little desk in her boudoir at the Quarro made Jessie shudder, and for a moment she wished to do nothing more than shovel the letters on the fire, as if that could destroy the disturbing thoughts which they had awakened.

Yet nothing, she knew, could do that. The secret was out and very unpleasant it was too. There was no way in which she could reverse the discoveries of the last half hour. Her world had suddenly changed, and it was as if she had been deposited in an unknown and frightening landscape. She had believed she had known Sholto, or at least that she had the measure of him. She had trusted him and it seemed that

402

to give him such trust was to have been extremely foolish. She remembered her earliest doubts about him, doubts which in her passion for him, and then in her dependence upon him, she had ruthlessly suppressed. And, although she thought she no longer cared for him, that she had at least emotionally detached herself from him, she found herself bleeding at this well-hidden deceit as if she were still that silly girl, madly in love with him.

It made a nonsense of all the explanations she had so carefully devised for their unsatisfactory life together; explanations which were really excuses for his conduct. She had generally blamed herself in some way: for being too ignorant to interest him any longer or for being too greedy for his money. But now the cause of it all was devastatingly clear. It was his own duplicity which was to blame. He had had a mistress for six years and he had been keeping her in some style as if he had neither a wife let alone children who might be entitled to his support.

And what a mistress! Of all the women in the world he could have chosen, none could have been more galling than Olivia Lennox! It was hard not to believe that he had chosen her simply to wound Jessie all the more, although she knew that such a delusion was ridiculous. For a relationship that had lasted so long, she supposed there must be some real feeling between them, though to judge by that letter, it was hardly the sort of love which she could understand. What sort of love could go on so long in secret, deceiving everyone? They had, it seemed, had their cake and eaten it. Olivia Lennox had her title now (for Sir Hector had died two years ago) and was the mistress of the Quarro, while Sholto got all the domestic cosseting of any respectable, middle-class husband. Superficially that was how they had lived, but in secret they had indulged themselves at the expense of everybody else. They had wrapped themselves in lies, indeed wrapped everyone in their lies, and Jessie felt sickened by it. Sholto's conscience had not kept him awake at night, although she had been tortured in silent agony about Ralph.

She remembered with a mixture of fury and intense

sadness that night in the dining room at Allansfield, that moment when they had silently agreed that self-denial was their only choice. Now Ralph was scarcely the dear friend she had once claimed. He was as distant as a stranger and she feared she had lost him for good. There was no chance for them now. The flame of six years ago was burning very dim, if it had not been entirely extinguished by time and good behaviour.

Good behaviour – why had she bothered? Why had she not told Ralph that self-denial was pointless, that they should give in to their feelings and let their love live, no matter what the consequences might be? Fidelity to Sholto had been a pointless gesture, a hollow martyrdom, because that blackguard amusing his mistress, playing her obscene games, regarded the bonds of the life they shared together as meaningless. She had been little more to him than a superior servant who washed his shirts, cooked his meals, and worst of all satisfied his sexual demands when the glorious, beloved mistress was not at hand.

She felt dirty and used when she thought of that. She wrapped her arms around herself in a pathetic gesture, partly for comfort, partly for self-protection. Tears, she angrily discovered, were forcing themselves from her eyes, although she could not think why she must cry. She knew she did not love Sholto any more, she had realized that long ago and she had guessed that for some time he had not loved her. Yet cry she must, to mourn the final expiration of their marriage after a long and lingering illness.

She heard the door open and looked up to see Molly standing there, swathed in dressing gown and several shawls.

'You shouldn't be up,' she managed to say.

'I'm feeling much better, Mrs Hamilton. I was sleeping like a bairn and then I woke up and heard you crying. Is there aught I can do for you?'

'You can go back to your bed,' said Jessie. 'I don't want to have to bury you, Molly.'

'Och, you won't have to do that, Mrs Hamilton,' said Molly, placidly, quite her normal self again. 'I think we should be worrying about you, lass. What were you crying over like that? If it's money again, I tell ye, it doesn't matter . . .'

'No, it wasn't money,' said Jessie, getting slowly to her feet. She had no inclination to gather up the contents of that drawer. Sholto could find them when he got home and draw his own conclusions. 'Now, let's get you back by a fire, Molly.'

'I'll make us a pot of tea, mistress,' she said as they went into the kitchen. She seemed happier to be up and about again. Jessie found herself ushered into a seat by the fire.

'Oh, I'm glad to be on my legs again,' said Molly. 'I hate lying up there like a burden, not earning my keep.'

'Molly, you've more than done that,' protested Jessie.

The old woman sat down opposite and poured out the tea. She looked expectant.

'I suppose you want to know what it was I was crying about then?'

'Well,' said Molly, her characteristic acid humour now returned, 'I hope you've a good reason for waking me wi' all that bawling!'

'Was I bawling? I suppose I was. I was angry, Molly, about . . .'

'About the master?'

'Aye – how did you guess?'

Molly smiled sagely and said, 'Well, to tell you the truth, Mrs Hamilton, I've long thought he was no as good a husband and father as he could have been.'

'Then you won't be surprised when I tell you that he's been spending your wages and my housekeeping on a woman.'

'On a woman! Goodness me! Oh, Mrs Hamilton, but that's terrible!' And she put out a comforting hand. She went on with much head shaking, 'Oh, dear Lord, who ever would have thought it? What will ye do?'

'That, Molly, I wish I knew. But I don't. Where we go from here, I haven't the least idea.'

3

'You're dining out tonight then, dear?' said Mrs Erskine, coming into his dressing room as he was tying his white tie. 'That's good.'

'You wouldn't have said that ten years ago, Mother,' he observed.

'Here, let me do that,' she said, 'I can't bear to see you struggling with it.' And she reached up and finished tying his tie. 'There – much more respectable. Your father never could tie an evening tie properly either. Where are you going?'

'To James Lennox's, would you believe? I presume Alix and Drew will be there, at least I hope so. I can't imagine why they've invited me.'

'Perhaps they've some nice girl for you to meet,' she said.

'Oh, I don't think Olivia Lennox is the type to tolerate pretty rivals at her dinner table. Mind you, it would be difficult for anyone to outshine those sort of looks.'

'I've always thought she had a rather cold, hard look about her. Beautiful, yes, but only superficially.'

'You're very severe,' said Ralph, smiling. 'I bumped into her the other day, you know, and she seemed quite human – in fact, a good deal more personable than she has been in the past. I suspect I've probably misjudged the poor woman. It's probably pure relief on her part . . .'

'Relief about what?'

'About the heir. You remember how obsessed old Sir Hector was on that point, and I think James is just the same. She must have been under such pressure and felt an awful failure. Perhaps that made her so abrasive.'

'It's possible,' said Mrs Erskine. 'I'm sure she would be happier if she had children. So you think Alix's pregnancy might have made her more cheerful?'

'Well, that family thinks in rigidly dynastic terms. They

are worse than crowned heads. The succession is every-thing, and now it's assured, so to speak. You should have seen James the other night at Alix's. Anyone would have thought he was the father!'

'You're very charitable to her, Ralph,' said Mrs Erskine. 'More than I have been, I'm ashamed to realize. Perhaps we had better have them here to dine.'

'I don't think that'll be necessary,' he said. 'Everyone knows we don't entertain these days.'

'Perhaps we should start again,' she said. 'I should like some people to dinner. That nice young friend of Alix's, for example, Miss Chalmers . . .'

'Mother, you are transparent sometimes,' said Ralph.

'But you do like her?' she said.

'Yes, yes, of course I like her,' he said. 'I like a great many people, but that doesn't mean I want to marry them.'

'I'm not suggesting that. No, I just feel you should try and get to know her better and then decide. Yes, Ralph,' she said, reading his scowl of disapproval, 'I know how you dislike this subject, but I do think it is important. You must think of your future. A man in your position needs a wife, needs the comforts of a family. Mary Chalmers strikes me as just the sort of girl who would suit you very well.'

'Mother,' he said firmly, 'I've managed very well without a wife so far. Why do I suddenly need one now?'

'Oh, yes, you can manage now, my dear, because I am still alive, to make sure all your domestic whims are attended to. But I am not going to live forever, am I?'

'That's exactly what Father used to say, you know, when he wanted me to do something.'

'Yes, I know, and it generally worked, didn't it?'

'Generally, yes. But, Mother, I simply can't fall in love to order – you must realize that.'

'Of course. But you must get out of this habit of thinking of yourself as a crusty bachelor with no time for anything but your work. You are only thirty-six, remember. I'm not having my son become a dry old man before his time.'

'You don't think I've become that, surely?'

'No, not yet. But you might, unless you find yourself a

pretty young wife and some children in the next few years.'

I'm not having my son become a dry old man before his time. His mother's words lingered with him as he walked to the Lennoxes' house in Royal Circus. They prodded him painfully in the mental ribs, and their sharpness surprised him, just as, when he was a small boy, one of her fierce scoldings would surprise him. She did not utter such taunts lightly and he knew that behind her words lay a great seriousness of purpose, a well of deep concern.

He knew that he deserved such a prompting. He had become reclusive, in a sense. It was not that he did not go out. He was constantly out, living in hotels and restaurants, in public meetings and in boardrooms. He met a hundred people a month, shook a hundred hands and talked, it seemed, incessantly and earnestly about the various causes in which he had involved himself. But in all the talk, all the meetings, he realized there had been little real human contact. He seemed to have lost himself. Yes, he was a functionary, an organizer, an administrator, an executor of bold, brave schemes. This was the Ralph Erskine that went into the world, but he knew, as he walked through the New Town on that bleak November evening, that it was not the essence of himself.

But who the devil am I really? he asked himself. He knew he was no longer the posturing young bohemian who had lived drunkenly on aesthetic perceptions. He had discovered a colder, crueller world since then, but it had not made him entirely pragmatic. Yet he did not feel in balance, as some people he observed clearly were. He felt unpleasantly close to his mother's grim prediction already, as if he were a husk, the reality of himself desiccated in a fever of activity. And how does one get that part of oneself back? he asked himself. By marrying a girl like Mary Chalmers? Such a thing was easily enough accomplished, and doubtless it would be pleasant enough. It would allay some of his loneliness but there again, was not such a bland, comfortable approach the very height of self-indulgence? To marry out of convenience instead of from instinct would only confirm that he was indeed dried out and incapable of real passion. There was no way in which he could imagine being intoxicated or obsessed by a woman like Mary Chalmers. She was too calm, too sweetly rational, too subservient, to inspire anything but affectionate respect. Surely such feelings were not strong enough metal to forge a successful marriage?

This line of speculation had to be interrupted as he had now reached Royal Circus and needed a few moments to prepare himself for what would undoubtedly be an ordeal. He disliked large dinner parties as a rule, and he feared that James Lennox would honour all the irritating rituals without providing any of the necessary stimulation which made such occasions bearable. But stimulation in other than liquid form he could not expect to find at 16, Royal Circus, and he rang the doorbell expecting little else than a dull evening.

He was taken upstairs and shown, somewhat to his surprise, not into a front drawing room full of people nervously discovering what interesting, or otherwise, individuals their hostess had consigned to them as dinner companions, but into the relative intimacy of the back drawing room which was occupied, it appeared, by Olivia Lennox alone. As the maid opened the door, and before he was announced, he saw her for a moment standing in front of the fire, her hands resting on the mantle-shelf, so that the light of the fire illuminated her face and her partially bared shoulders as well as making a radiant halo of her magnificent golden hair. It seemed for once he had found her being entirely herself, lost in a moment of intense introspection, of which, Ralph was ashamed, to realize, he would not have thought her capable. But she is human, as human and as fallible as any of us, he told himself, throwing away the last remnants of any prejudice he might have held against her, suddenly interested to know what sort of a person really lay at her core.

'Mr Erskine, My Lady,' said the maid, but before the girl had opened her mouth, Olivia Lennox had returned to the present, had turned to Ralph and was coming towards him to shake his hand. She was dressed somewhat picturesquely (that was the only word he could find to describe her costume, which had a quaint eighteenth-century accent with its muslin fichu collar and the cherry red and white stripes of its silk). In this, and the warmth of her greeting, she seemed to him very different from the mannered beauty he had first met at the Quarro all those years ago. Maturity (he reckoned that they were roughly the same age) had given her an unexpected poise.

'Oh, Mr Erskine,' she said, 'how grand you look! I think my card has misled you. This is only a little dinner – I hope you don't mind? Black tie would have done just as well.'

'I'm relieved to hear that, to be frank,' he said. 'I must admit I'm not fond of large dinner parties. They spell death to real conversation, don't you think?'

'I'd heard that of you.' She smiled. 'Would you like a drink? I'm afraid that James and our other guest, Mr Phelps – perhaps you know him?' Ralph nodded. 'Well, they are playing billiards downstairs. Of course, we can join them if you wish, but I seem to remember that billiards, like large dinners, are not to your taste.'

'You have a good memory,' he said, surprised.

'Yes, it's much pleasanter to stay here, where the fire is going so well, isn't it?' she remarked, crossing the room. She picked up a silver tray set with a claret jug and glasses, and coming back to the fire, set it down on the hearth rug. She then sat down, rather gracefully, on a low stool and poured him out a glass of wine.

'Do sit down,' she said, when he had taken the glass.

'That's a handsome piece,' he said, noticing the claret jug. 'It looks like a Jacobite piece, judging by the engraving.'

'Oh, is that what those roses mean?' said Olivia. 'How interesting. You must excuse me, you see, Mr Erskine, but I was very ill educated.'

'You sound as if you regret it.'

'Of course, who wouldn't? A man of your culture and vision would appreciate that a good education is the best thing one can give to anyone.'

'I'm not so sure,' said Ralph, sinking back in the

410

armchair by the fire, that first embracing mouthful of claret beginning to work upon him. 'For all my so-called education, I am still a long way from the culture or vision which you too generously ascribe to me. Formal education gives one as much narrowness in some ways as it does scope . . .' But he broke off, conscious suddenly that such a topic, somewhat pompously discussed by himself, would easily bore her.

But instead she said, 'Why did you stop?'

'Because I would probably have become very tedious on the subject. It's one of my little bug-bears.'

'I know – and that is why I want to hear you on it. I read that piece you wrote, you see. I found it in a magazine at my brother-in-law's house. I was very impressed.'

The surprise must have shown on his face, because she laughed.

'Oh, Mr Erskine!' she exclaimed with amusement, 'I suppose it is a surprise to you that I should even have an opinion on such a thing. No doubt, when we first met, I struck you as a very stupid creature, which I was, but since then I've been trying very hard to improve myself.'

'Onward and upward, eh?' said Ralph.

'Yes, exactly,' she said. 'Now, I think Lady Aberdeen is a very remarkable person. I suppose you know her?'

'I've met her once,' he said, 'but I'm sure she'd be most impressed by your zeal. And I am sorry if I looked so surprised – it was very ill mannered of me.'

'Not at all,' she said. 'You know,' she resumed after a reflective little pause, 'I am rather glad you could come tonight. Even if I am stupid myself, I prefer the company of clever people. My husband, as you might imagine, is not the most stimulating companion.'

Of course, it was not polite to agree openly with such a statement, no matter how much truth there might be in it. But something about the way she said it demanded a smile of acknowledgement. He gulped down the rest of his wine and she promptly refilled his glass.

He wondered if James approved of his wife having such an extended tête-à-tête with him, for Olivia Lennox's

manner was not exactly restrained. It disturbed him somewhat but he could not help being amused by it, not in a
contemptuous way, but because she seemed to speak a
mixture of sense and nonsense, the effect of which could
only be described as piquant. He could not remember
afterwards exactly what they had spoken of (the greater part
of the contents of that claret jug on his empty stomach in
some way explained that) but he knew he had not been
bored or irritated. Only when James and Phelps came up
from their billiards and they went in to dinner, did he
realize what a beguiling three-quarters of an hour he had
just spent, without noticing how the minutes had passed.
Although there were only four of them at table, he found all
the dreary formality he had at first feared. Phelps, whom he
had known very slightly at the university, and who was now
in London in the Foreign Office, provided most of the talk:
an alarming mixture of xenophobia and high Toryism which
usually would have made Ralph extremely angry. But that
night, he found his will to fight had seeped away and let
Phelps continue unchallenged with all his sweeping asser-
tions. In fact, he scarcely listened to the man at all, for his
mind kept drifting back to that strange interlude with Olivia
Lennox, to the way she had sat on that low stool, looking up
at him, her face hauntingly beautiful in the firelight, the
goblet of her wineglass pressed to her cheek.

He glanced to his side and saw her again, and she smiled
at him and with a delicate gesture indicated the fruit and
nuts heaped on the epergne to which he was to help himself,
for they had reached the dessert. It was a gesture that he
could not have resisted, a triviality perhaps to any observer,
but it seemed to him full of significance, as if she were
offering far more to him than crystallized fruit and last
year's walnuts. This impression was irrational, he knew,
but although he ascribed it to the wine and his own devious
mind, he could not disabuse himself of it.

It was the lurid dream of a schoolboy and he woke with a
start, ashamed and surprised at himself, at his own commonplace, animalistic desire, which he had thought

(naively, it seemed) that he had conquered. His body was dissolved in sweat and he ached with lust, worse than any he had felt as a boy, for crackling through his brain went images of every intimate encounter he had ever had with a woman, all rolled out to shame him and tempt him further.

He crawled out of his bed, his head throbbing, his throat as dry as tinder.

You can't deny it, he said to himself as he lit the lamp. He stared at his disordered face in the looking glass above the washstand while he poured himself a glass of water. You've been got, well and truly snared – you are in lust with Olivia Lennox, you stupid old fool . . .

He thought of his mother calmly hoping he would fall in love with a nice girl like Mary Chalmers, and yet here he was on the brink of an obsession with Olivia Lennox, an enigmatic, married woman. Yes, he was on the brink, but for how long? He knew, as he splashed his face with cold water, that this was the point to withdraw, the moment for steely self-sacrifice, before any real damage was done. But he was no longer certain he was capable of such a sacrifice. He knew the signs too well in himself. He knew that this weakness, this sudden, violent desire, was so much at the root of him that the public, prudent side of his nature would not prevail. Damn it, he would not let it! He would not let that aridity rule him any longer. He was thirsty and he would drink, no matter what the consequences. What sort of a man lived the life he had been living? Such a tight-lipped, high-minded, castrated life that it was, in truth, no life at all.

Suddenly he was afraid that he had misread the signals, but the more he reflected upon the evening, the more he felt his instinct was correct. He could not explain it, of course, but was it not ungrateful to expect an explanation of such a wonderful gift? For it was wonderful that this thing should have happened, although he knew there might be agony in it; surely that agony was better than living a bloodless life?

'But what is it, Jessie?' asked Nancy. 'I know there's something wrong, I can tell. I've known you too long.'

'It isn't something I can talk about,' said Jessie. 'I'm not ready to talk about it.'

'So there is something?'

'Yes, but that's all I want to say about it. It's not that I don't trust you, Nancy, or your good judgement, but I can't talk about it. I'm not calm enough to make any sense.'

'Well, of course, if that's what you want,' said Nancy. 'But the minute you want to talk, I'm here, remember.'

'You're the best sort of friend, you know,' said Jessie, 'I knew you would understand.'

'I'm not sure that I do,' said Nancy, 'but if it is what you want, then I can't force you, can I? But I know myself that a trouble shared is a trouble halved – cliché though that may be, it does have a grain of truth in it.'

'Perhaps you should force me,' said Jessie.

'No, I'll just leave you to think a bit,' said Nancy, 'and I shall go upstairs and check on the children.'

Jessie, left alone in Nancy's kitchen, did not want to think. She had been thinking about it all too much but she still had not come to any clear conclusion. Molly's question 'What are you going to do?' still hung over her and had brought on more cowardice than courage. For in the end, she had panicked and packed away all those incriminating letters before Sholto's return home. Nor had she said anything when he had come home. She had been afraid she would use the wrong words and that he would twist the situation to his advantage as he had done so many times before. She had resolved, however, one thing: she would confront him only when she was ready, only when she was so well prepared, her arguments so well marshalled that he would not stand a chance. Besides, how could she confront him, unless she knew what she was going to do, unless she knew what she wanted?

She turned her attention to the task in hand. It was easier to concentrate on the ranks of petit fours and tiny savoury bonne-bouches that she and Nancy were preparing for the private view later that afternoon. In an hour or so, the first guests, Finn's wealthiest customers, would be coming to sip lapsang souchong or sherry, as their taste determined, and examine the collection of paintings which he and his assistants were still hanging downstairs. For Finn's little empire had grown since she had first known them, and now, next to the antique shop, was an elegant little gallery specializing in all sorts of painted treasure, both ancient and modern.

With fastidious pleasure, although it was a painstaking task, she picked up the piping bag filled with a coffee scented crème pâtissière and began to fill the minute puff pastry horns which she had made earlier that day. She had been at Nancy's since after breakfast, and while the girls enjoyed the rough and tumble with Nancy's children in their attic nursery, she had put her mind to the food for the private view. Nancy had been happy to let her take control and had behaved like the best and most subservient of kitchen maids. Now, displayed on a variety of silver salvers and antique porcelain platters (borrowed from the shop and probably too fine to be used) were the fruits of their labours: tiny mouthfuls of exquisite tastes. Jessie knew, without false modesty, that they were exquisite, for she had always excelled at this sort of thing. After all, she had not been trained so carefully by Monsieur Auguste only to roast mutton and make rice pudding, as if cooking for the servants' hall all her life. She had been trained for such occasions as this, to make frivolities, perhaps, but frivolities of such quality they could only stimulate the senses of those who ate them. Besides, it would be an insult to the artists to serve anything less. Meat paste sandwiches and shop bought sponge fingers would not do.

'Oh, those do look good,' said Nancy, coming in.
'Was everything all right in bedlam?'

'Seems to be. Bridy has them all in order – or as much in order as you can expect with that lot.' Bridy was Nancy's stalwart nursemaid, a bright-eyed farm girl imported from Galway who was a genius with children.

'It's good of you to have them, Nancy. It's about time Molly had some rest.'

'It's about time you had a rest,' said Nancy.

'Well, I'm almost done.'

'I have to say, it looks splendid! I never could have managed this myself.'

'I've enjoyed it – stops me worrying.'

'About whatever it is that's cutting you up inside? Oh Jessie, I wish you'd just give a hint – I might be able to help.'

'This is a help.'

'What, being my cook for a day? Oh, come on now!'

'It's true. I enjoy this sort of work. I know how you hate cooking, Nancy, but this is more than just cooking, isn't it? I feel contented doing this – not the drudge you feel you are when you've a pile of potatoes to peel.'

'You should do that the Irish way, Jessie, and boil them in their skins. They peel much easier after that!' Nancy laughed. 'Heavens, listen to me, giving you advice when you're being so clever with that piping bag. If that was me, it would have gone everywhere by now.'

'It's just practice,' said Jessie, putting down the piping bag. 'Now, just a little something else . . .' And deftly she stuck a half almond in the cream of each pastry.

'Now, I would never have thought of that!' exclaimed Nancy. 'You're a treasure, Jessie, you really are!'

They arranged a final plate and stacked the dirty dishes in the scullery. Those, Nancy declared, could wait. It was more important that they went upstairs to dress.

Nancy had made a new dress for the occasion, which in in its glossy sage green satin newness made Jessie more than faintly jealous as she unpacked the clothes she had brought with her. She had the sober grey tweed coat and skirt which she generally wore for church. It was a dull outfit, she conceded, but the only thing that had seemed smart enough for a private view. She looked at it, somewhat despairingly, laid out on Nancy's embroidered bedspread.

'Do you know,' Nancy said, 'I was just thinking the other day . . .' And she went to the wardrobe and pulled out a dress. 'Would this thing be any good to you? It really doesn't suit me at all, but I think it might match your eyes.'

It was a pretty silk tea dress, the colour of a mauve iris, trimmed with velvet of a slightly darker shade and embroidered with pansies.

'Yes, it would look better on you,' she went on, holding it up against Jessie.

Jessie went to the long cheval mirror, still holding the dress against her. It was a glorious thing. The silk was soft and supple beneath her fingers, the colour exotic but discreet.

'I couldn't possibly borrow this,' she said. 'It's far too good.'

'Then don't borrow it – keep it! Come on, put it on, Jessie. It's going to look wonderful, I know it.'

Nancy was remorseless and Jessie, feeling drab, was easily persuaded. The dress proved a good fit, and Jessie, seeing herself in the mirror, felt choked up with an odd mixture of happiness and sadness.

'Oh, Nancy, it is wonderful,' she said, and kissed her friend. 'Oh, I haven't felt so . . .'

'So pretty for ages? I know, there's nothing like a new dress to make you feel better, is there? Come on, let me do your hair.'

She pinned Jessie's hair into a loose, full chignon and wound a violet silk scarf through it.

'I've been longing to do that for ages,' said Nancy. 'God, it isn't often we get the chance to titivate ourselves, is it? You should always wear it like that. It's much less severe.'

'You'll have to show me how.'

There was a knock at the door and Finn came in.

'You look like sisters,' he remarked. 'Now what is it you want me to put on, Nan?'

Jessie excused herself from these sartorial consultations and went slowly downstairs, savouring the feel of her fine clothes. She went into the gallery and began to study the pictures while Stannie, Finn's gawkish young cousin who had come over to learn the trade, stared at her. Do I look a fright, or does he think I'm personable? she wondered.

'You're looking grand, Mrs Hamilton,' he said.

'So are you, Stannie,' she said. 'Is that the new suit then?' Nancy had primed her on this story. Stannie had lived all his life in hand-me-downs, so his first visit to a tailor (Finn had insisted he look respectable in the shop) had been a great event with him.

'Yes, it is. Do you think it makes me look older?' he asked. He was sixteen.

'Oh, yes, at least twenty,' smiled Jessie, and he grinned and adjusted the flower in his button hole.

'I think the food looks marvellous,' he went on, encouraged. 'But do you think there's enough there to feed the whole pack of them? I'm always so hungry about now.'

'Well,' she said, amused, 'I don't suppose they'll all be as hungry as you. If you go upstairs, you'll find there's a plate of rejects on the dresser. That might take the edge off your appetite.'

'I can't go now,' he said, 'Finn says I'm to wait here in case anyone comes early.' And he eyed the buffet table with longing. 'I suppose I'll just have to wait.'

'I'm afraid so,' said Jessie, anxious that her hard work should not be destroyed by one ravening adolescent. She returned to studying the paintings, only to be interrupted by Stannie again.

'Do you know?' he said. She turned and saw he was still staring at the food. 'I reckon you could make a fair living doing this sort of thing. I mean, it's not just anyone who can make these, is it? Have you ever thought of doing that, Mrs Hamilton, like Nancy sells some of her embroideries?'

'I don't think my husband would approve of me working,' she said automatically, but then the significance of what he had said dawned on her. 'But it is a good idea, Stannie. Thank you.'

'It's all right. May I just try one of these little ones then?'

'Why not?' she said, suddenly indulgent. If he had asked

her for the moon just then, she would have given it to him, for it seemed that with his artless suggestion, she had the seed of a solution to her problem. If there was some way she might earn her own living again, and support the girls without having to ask Sholto for a penny then . . . it might just be possible to leave him!

'Yes, that's a beauty, isn't it?' said Nancy, who she found was standing beside her. Jessie had hardly been looking at the pen and ink sketch in front of her. She was prey to a flurry of ideas: Leave Sholto! Leave Sholto – could you actually manage to do that?

'Yes,' she said, answering Nancy's question rather than her own.

'I really like Guardi,' said Nancy. 'It was Ralph who put me on to him, of course. I think Finn is hoping he'll buy this one. He doesn't have a Guardi, I think.'

'I thought Ralph didn't buy pictures any more.'

'Oh, he does, from time to time – if they are really good, like this one. I think he buys for some great museum in the future. Finn is sure he will give it all away some day.'

Jessie thought of the Ramsay portrait he had once bought because it resembled her, hanging on the impersonal walls of an art gallery. No one would know its story, how it remembered a sentimental friendship which had come to nothing. For that was how she felt she must regard things with Ralph now. She had heard nothing of these plans for an Erskine bequest. It was another depressing indication of the distance which now lay between them.

Soon, the gallery began to fill up, and it was amusing to see such a mixture of successful artists and grandee businessmen, many of Scotland's greatest names, gathering so pleasantly to be parted from their guineas. It was easy to see from Finn's expression that the show was going tremendously, and Jessie was also pleased to see that the refreshments, often disdained at such functions, were being set upon, as if everyone was sixteen and had an appetite like Stannie's. Perhaps she could make money doing something of that sort.

Her mind was pursuing these possibilities when the door

swung open to admit more guests. She glanced over to see who they were, and was surprised, if not shocked, by what she saw. It was Ralph, accompanied by Olivia Lennox, of all people, and although she was not exactly leaning on his arm, she seemed to Jessie indecently close to him.

The words of that letter ran through her mind, as she stood and stared at Olivia Lennox in all her magnificence. She had not expected to run into her husband's lover, but here she was as a decorative, but incongruous companion to Ralph. Jessie felt sick, because it was all too obvious that Ralph did not find her incongruous. She heard him say, when Finn had greeted them: 'Olivia, I don't think you know my friend O'Hara, do you?' The use of her Christian name seemed ominous and Jessie found herself turning away from them, repelled, especially by Ralph who appeared to her a travesty of himself. He looked exactly like the glossy plutocrat he had always said he despised, very sleekit in a frock coat and silk hat, and carrying, most extraordinarily, a silver-topped stick – an affectation he had railed against in the past. Olivia Lennox's costume was so stupendous that Jessie could find no words to describe it, but could think only of the bills in that box and wonder how many joints of meat and scuttles of coal she and her family had been deprived of by all that fur and silk velvet. Or perhaps Ralph paid for that one! she thought suddenly, unable to avoid this horrible conclusion. For she had glanced back and seen their heads bent together, deep in conversation over some picture, and had known it might well be true.

She could not stand to be there any longer and dashed into the cool disorder of the warehouse behind the shop. She could scarcely breathe any more, her lungs stuffed up with anger and misery. She wished she could forget what she had just seen. She wished she could stand and scream out all the anguish that devoured her, in some way exorcise it. She pressed her clenched fists to her face, and whispered with breath that would have melted iron. 'No . . . no . . . no!'

'Are you all right, Mrs Hamilton?'

420

She looked up and saw Stannie. He was eating his way through the plate of rejected petit-fours. When he had spoken his mouth had been full.

'Mrs Hamilton?' he repeated.

'Oh, Jessie, there you are,' said Nancy behind her. 'You'll never guess who Ralph has come in with . . .'

Jessie turned slowly and looked at her friend. The tears were streaming down her face now. She could not manage to speak, her face crumpling as the tears turned into sobs.

'Oh, Jessie, my darling . . .'

'Nancy . . . can we talk . . . please . . .'

'How is she?' said Finn, when Nancy came downstairs again.

'Sleeping,' said Nancy. 'She's exhausted.'

'It's disgraceful,' said Finn. 'Hamilton should be horse-whipped. I always thought he was a blackguard, but this is terrible. Did Jessie say who the woman was?'

'No, she wouldn't say, but I got the strong impression it's someone we know.'

'She should tell us, and someone should tell the creature, whoever she is, that her lover is starving a wife and children for the sake of her parasols. I shouldn't mind doing that, you know.'

'I know you wouldn't,' smiled Nancy, 'but I don't think it's what Jessie wants. She doesn't want this spread everywhere. You know how it is, Finn, people so often blame the wife for this sort of thing.'

'Yes, I suppose so,' he said, and got up from his seat wearily. 'God, I should be ecstatic at the moment. We sold a hell of a lot of stuff today, but when you hear something like that, it just makes you sick, doesn't it? Oh, poor Jessie, I just wish we could do something for her. I hope you told her that she and the girls are welcome here as long as they like.'

'I did,' said Nancy. 'You're not going out, Finn?' For he was pulling on his jacket.

'Just to see Ralph. He bought that Guardi after all. I thought I would take it round myself.'

'Why on earth now?'

'Well, I was just thinking about Jessie. Ralph would be the person to ask, wouldn't he? She'd be too proud, of course, but I know he would want to help, wouldn't he?'

'Yes, of course!' said Nancy. 'You're always so practical, darling.' And she kissed him and sent him into the night, the carefully wrapped Guardi tucked under his arm.

As he reached Rothesay Terrace, Finn thought he saw Ralph's motor pulling away, and wondered with annoyance if he had just missed him. But on ringing the bell he found that he was at home. Ralph himself opened the door, clad in a sumptuous dressing gown and seemingly nothing else, because Finn could not help noticing his bare feet.

'It's the servants' day off,' he explained, but Finn sensed he was vaguely embarrassed about something.

'And your mother's in the country?' he guessed.

'Yes, she'd be horrified to find me opening the door like this. Come up and have a drink.'

They went to Ralph's dressing room, which was still furnished as it had been ten years ago. The door to the bedroom was open and Finn glimpsed the unmade bed.

'Oh God – I haven't dragged you from your bed, have I?' he said. 'I'm sorry, is it so late?'

'No, no, you haven't. Don't worry,' said Ralph. 'It must have been a good show. Did it go on for long after we left?'

'Yes, a couple of hours.'

'Then I missed a lot. I'm sorry I had to go so early, but I'd promised to get Lady Lennox back in time for her dinner engagement. But I was in time to secure my Guardi . . .'

As Ralph unwrapped his new treasure, Finn sat back and found, as he nursed an excellent glass of malt, he was also nursing certain unkind suspicions about his old friend. For he found himself wondering if the car he had seen driving away had not indeed been Ralph's and whether the passenger (although only imperfectly glimpsed) had been a woman.

Well, I'll be damned, he thought, and then refused to believe that this alarming evidence meant what he feared it might. With any man other than Ralph, Finn could easily have assumed that he had just arrived at the close of some romantic interlude. The disordered bed, Ralph's state of undress, his ruffled hair and relaxed demeanour, were strong indications that something of that sort had just occurred. But Finn could not credit it, or rather he did not wish to credit it, for there was something sordid and underhand about it, that did not suit Ralph in the least. It pushed him too much into the camp of that scoundrel Sholto Hamilton. If only he had taken everyone's good advice and found himself a wife, thought Finn, then there wouldn't be any need for these sorts of goings-on.

'This is even better than I first thought,' said Ralph, looking up from the Guardi. 'Do you want a cheque now?'

One could hardly give a moral lecture to a man offering such prompt payment. So Finn took the cheque graciously.

'I'm glad you came,' said Ralph, sitting down on the fender seat. 'There are a couple of things I want to discuss with you. The private view was hardly the moment.'

'No,' said Finn. 'As a matter of fact, I didn't just come to bring the Guardi . . .'

'We don't see enough of each other these days, do we?' said Ralph. 'We meet like a committee, don't we? Shall I make out an agenda?'

'Don't bother – you can give me another whisky and you can start.'

'Very well,' he said, handing over the decanter. 'I've decided to expand the collection in a fresh direction.'

'Sounds interesting.'

'It is – you'll enjoy hunting down what I want, I'm sure.'

'What?'

'Jewellery – not just any old stuff, of course, but sixteenth-, seventeenth-century pieces. The rarer the better.'

'This is a new departure. Any reason why? Anyone would think you were going to get married.' He had meant to be suggestive and watched Ralph's expression closely.

'It's a question of balance. I feel it is what the collection needs. A little sparkle, don't you think?'

'Well, fine. It shouldn't be a problem, but you will be

'bidding against the likes of Fergusson, you know.'

'I think we can manage that. Do you know if there's anything good coming up?'

'There's a fine German piece up for auction in London next week. I could have a stab at that. It's a necklace; gold filigree perfume balls, cabochon rubies and some good enamels. Is that the sort of thing?'

'Is Fergusson after it?'

'More than probably.'

'Well, if it's up to his standards . . .'

'I have a photograph at the shop. I'll send Stannie round with it.'

'Don't worry. I trust your judgement.'

This recklessness was as uncharacteristic as the sudden interest in jewellery. Ralph had never bought much of that – only a few attractive but unspectacular pieces for his sister and mother. And who bought jewellery simply for a collection, except the obsessive Lord Fergusson, who bought nothing else? Finn knew, from long experience, that jewellery, of all the things he sold, was the one most inexplicably linked with human passions, be they innocent or otherwise.

Would Ralph's mysterious mistress be the recipient of that extraordinary German piece, over which Nancy had drooled innocently? It would be an act of extravagance, even in Erskine terms, because a piece given to a mistress was lost to a family in the the way jewellery given to a wife was not. Finn felt certain that this woman would not become Ralph's wife, as certain of that as he now was of her existence as his mistress. For Ralph, he felt sure, could not have married the sort of woman one spent an evening with when the servants were not there. Mrs Erskine would not have been able to cope with such a state of affairs. Perhaps this woman was not even available to marry – a thought which made Finn shudder slightly. Adultery was the last reckless game that he would have expected to find Ralph mixed up in. To find out that he had been frequenting gambling hells or opium dens might have been less shocking because Ralph had always been fastidious and honourable where women were concerned. At least, Finn had always imagined so.

'Now what was it you wanted to say to me?' said Ralph. He sat perched on the fender, a glowing fire behind him, in an attitude of aggressive nonchalance that Finn did not recognize in him at all. For a minute he did not know what to say, because to speak of Jessie's troubles to a man who was probably playing the same dirty game as her disreputable husband, would be perhaps to speak to deaf ears. Oh hell, Finn, he told himself, what are you thinking? The drink has got to you after all! You're turning the poor man into the devil himself, without a shred of real evidence.

'It's about Jessie Hamilton,' he said.

'What about her?'

'She's just found out that Sholto has been unfaithful to her. I suppose that isn't so much of a surprise, is it? We all knew what he was like. But she is absolutely devastated. She'd been trying to sort it out herself, but something snapped today and she's had a sort of breakdown. This affair – it's been going on for years, apparently, and the worst of it is, he's been spending all his money on her. Jessie and the girls have almost starved because of it.'

'Sholto always was a fool,' said Ralph.

'It's more than foolish – it's wicked!' exclaimed Finn. 'You should see the state Jessie's in! And the silly girl won't tell us who this woman is.'

'Probably a barmaid or some such.'

'A barmaid kitted up from the most expensive shops in town. He probably keeps her in a little flat as well! I can't understand it, can you? Jessie's such a fine good woman – why on earth would he want to look elsewhere?'

'Love isn't always as simple as it seems to you and Nancy,' said Ralph. 'We are not all as fortunate as you.'

'Surely you don't condone what he's done?' said Finn, astonished. 'And I thought you counted Jessie as a friend.'

'I do, a very dear one,' said Ralph, 'but I don't think that condemnation will help her. It's a terrible thing to be betrayed – I know that. What she needs is our help.'

'Of course she does – why else do you think I'm here?'

'I don't suppose she'd take any money directly, would she?'

'No, she's too proud for that. But we should help her to leave him somehow, I think. Nancy thinks she shouldn't go back to him, that he's wearing her out. God, what a blood-sucker that man is!'

'Well, we must think what can be done. Obviously, whatever she needs, I'll give her. I couldn't do less, could I?'

Finn left feeling that he had been monstrously unjust to Ralph.

Lying to Finn had not been easy, although he had done it with a superficial accomplishment that might have suggested that such dishonesty was commonplace with him. But it had hurt, to sit and be bland and noncommittal, while Finn eyed him with such suspicion. He could read that much on his face. Yet how could he possibly begin to explain to Finn, who was so respectably uxorious, who had never so much as glanced at another woman since he had married Nancy and whose whole upbringing had convinced him that adultery was the most unpardonable of sins? Just to hear him on the subject of Sholto's defections was enough to make Ralph stop his tongue. He could not have stood to hear Finn's own cold, moral disapproval, sense his undoubted disappointment and watch a wall rise between them, destroying their former intimacy. But I've begun to build that wall myself, thought Ralph, flinging himself into an armchair when Finn had gone. I should have told the truth – but, damnation, do I want to tell the truth? Won't that destroy everything?

In fact, he was not at all sure whether he had the words to describe, let alone explain, this strange thing which had happened to him. It defied words as it had defied his imagination to predict it. No one could understand what he did not yet comprehend himself, and to speak of it in the chilly light of Finn's morality would be to give up its secret power. That he was not prepared to do. How could he, when he felt alive for the first time in years? When he felt

426

that he had come out of the shadows into such startling clear light that he was half blinded by its intensity. He felt like a boy again, drunk on every perception, so that he could scarcely concentrate on anything. She hovered in his consciousness, transforming everything he did into a sensual experience. Even in the grim orderliness of his office, the snow white blotting paper made him think of her flesh, naked against white linen sheets, and the columns of figures before his eyes would dissolve into weird hieroglyphics which told the legend of this strange love affair. He was a man possessed, he knew, but he could no more relinquish her than his own soul.

For since that moment, just over a week ago, when their friendly acquaintance had slipped into a dangerous intimacy, he had known that he could do nothing less than give her the passion and devotion which she so fervently demanded of him. She had cried, tears of real frustration, when she had told him of her wretched, hollow life with James Lennox, and he had been moved by more than pity to comfort her. Then she had seemed to throw herself against him in a gesture of such angry desperation that it opened all the floodgates. His longing and hers fused into an explosion of pure physicality which no one could have stopped.

He refused to feel guilty. He would not permit this drunken happiness he felt to be destroyed by scruples which, he was sure, were only the product of an over-censorious society. There was too much that was marvellous in this affair for it to be judged by ordinary standards. It was a 'grande passion', which owed nothing to common bonds. It could not be compared with Sholto's extra-marital philanderings, conducted very grubbily no doubt. There was a depth of feeling between Olivia and himself, although it was scarcely expressed, which he felt with great certainty. And this, for him, justified everything.

5

'But how can I not go back to him?' said Jessie. 'I can't see that I have any choice.'

'I shan't tell you again,' said Nancy, 'you're staying here. This is your home now, for as long as you like.'

'Nancy, I simply can't do that. I can't get under your feet like this. It isn't fair. I can't even bring you a penny to pay for our keep.'

'If you had the money, I shouldn't take it,' said Nancy. 'Oh, you're too proud, aren't you? Stupidly proud, I think, even to contemplate going back to Colinton and that man . . .'

'But what else can I do? If I'm with him, the law says he has to keep me and the children, doesn't it?'

'How can you even think of that – after all he's done?'

'Because even the pittance he gave me was better than being penniless. I don't want to have to live hand to mouth and send my girls out to work. I don't want them to suffer what I suffered. Nancy, it's the worst thing in the world growing up and knowing you're a burden to someone, believe me. I know, I saw it every day in my mother's eyes until I went. She couldn't wait to be rid of me.'

'If Finn and I have anything to do with this, you will not be living hand to mouth.'

'But we can't go on like this. I can't simply stay here. I have to find some way to support myself, don't I?'

'At least you see you can't go back to him,' said Nancy.

'Yes, I suppose so. But, Nancy, what will I do?'

'What you need is a little business of your own.'

'But you need savings for that.'

'Usually, yes, but remember, you have wealthy friends.'

'The Erskines – but Nancy, I couldn't possibly . . .'

'Why not? Ralph has a half share in the gallery, you know. He thinks it is a good investment. Now if you could convince him that your business had good prospects – well, where is your difficulty?'

'Yes . . . yes,' said Jessie, who had not thought of it that way before, 'I suppose it would be all right.'

'That's the spirit,' said Nancy. She glanced up at the kitchen clock and exclaimed, 'Is that the time? Father MacNeil will be here in a minute and I bet that Frankie hasn't learnt a word of his catechism.'

'I'll get out of your way, then. I'll take the girls out for a walk.'

It was one of those sparkling mornings that often occur in the few weeks before Christmas; very bright, cold and exhilarating. Jessie and the girls made their way down to St Bernard's Well and the pretty path which runs alongside the Water of Leith there. After giving strict injunctions to them not to go near the water, Jessie sat down on a bench in a sunny spot while the girls bowled their hoops and skipped with that fierce childish concentration which belies such simple activities. She was reluctant to tell them that their ordered life was about to undergo a profound change. At present, they thought they were just visiting, as indeed did Sholto. They had exchanged brief notes; hers had been as calm as possible, his quite indifferent. She wondered if she would ever have the courage to tell him to his face she was leaving him, or would she merely creep away with her boxes, like a coward.

'Excuse me, Madame, but I think . . .' A shadow had loomed over her, blocking out the sun, but if that was surprising, it was not as startling as the voice which accompanied it. She knew it at once, although she had not heard it for many years. She looked up and saw she had not been wrong.

'Monsieur Auguste!' she exclaimed, jumping to her feet.

'I was right – I knew it! There was something . . . and it was you, my little MacPherson. Que de bizarre!'

'Yes, yes, isn't it?' she said. They shook hands with embarrassed spontaneity and he clasped both his around her own with earnestness. She saw how he had aged, though it made him more grand than before. If once he had struck her as aristocratic, he was now imperial, with his white hair. His girth was still splendid and was encased in a smart overcoat that was made quite clearly of cashmere.

'You are looking so well,' she said delightedly.

'I wish I could say the same of you, ma chère MacPherson,' he said gravely. 'Perhaps you have been ill?'

'Not exactly,' she said. 'But what are you doing here? I thought you had gone to London to be properly appreciated.'

'Oh, I have been there. But I find I am at a crossroads just now. I cannot quite decide what I must do. I have come here to attend a funeral – do you remember Mr Ross?'

'Of course, how could I forget?' He had been the frighteningly authoritarian butler at Randolph Crescent. 'So he's died? What a shame. He wasn't that old, was he?'

'He was sixty-five and about to faire la retraite. It is very sad, is it not?'

'Was he married?'

'Fortunately not. These things are much worse when there is a grieving widow to console. Ah, well. May I join you?' he said, indicating the bench. 'We have much to talk about, I think.'

They sat down together and Jessie was convinced that this strange, chance meeting was more significant than the externals might imply. An observer would see perhaps nothing more than a teacher and a pupil meeting again after some years and indulging in all the pleasant memories of their former association, but Jessie knew at once, instinctively, that it could be nothing so simple. They had been brought together by the mysterious forces of fate, no less. This was an idea at which she would have laughed ordinarily, but that morning, by St Bernard's Well, she was convinced of it, as is any zealot of the articles of his faith. That he felt it too she was sure, for they wasted no time on inessentials and in minutes had unfolded to each other the complex disappointments of their respective lives.

It seemed he had not come back to Edinburgh out of any great affection or respect for the late Mr Ross, but because his own darling mother had died in the South of France the year before and he had not been able to reach her in time. He now felt, after this, that the only way he could make amends was to give the dead all the honour and ceremony which his mother (such a good daughter of the Church) had been wont to give them. So a bleak journey to Edinburgh in the depths of winter to attend a gloomy, shabby Presbyterian funeral had been a sort penance for him.

'So I do not bury Ross, but I bury her again – do you understand?'

'Yes, I do.'

'Yes, you would. You always did – you were the only one of them who ever understood properly.'

'You're forgetting the times I was stupid,' Jessie smiled.

'Oh, that was only over little things,' he said, 'never over what was important.'

'Then I am probably a disappointment to you now,' she said. 'Giving everything up because I thought I was in love.'

'You were in love,' said Monsieur Auguste. 'You could not have acted with insincerity, I know that. No, what happened was that there was no one to remind you that love does not always last.'

'I wish you had been there. I should not have made such a mess of things then.'

'Is it really such a mess?' he said. 'You have three charming girls to your credit – and at least now you see that your husband is no good, and know you cannot go back to him. You have a great opportunity here, I think, to start again.'

'I do?'

'But of course. You are still young, ma chérie. In my opinion, there is absolutely no question as to what you should do.'

'What?'

'Well, in Paris, or Nice, or Lyons, a woman in your position is not despised. She is quite able to look after herself. She would do exactly what my dear maman did when Papa died – she would open a restaurant.'

'A restaurant?' said Jessie.

'Oh, you British! You have no idea, have you? Not one of

431

those dreadful chop houses, or a railway buffet, or those places in hotels that claim to be restaurants, but a respectable establishment where a man can take his wife and children to dine. Why must they all believe here that the only place one can eat well is at home?'

'A restaurant in Edinburgh?' she said, still incredulous at this audacious suggestion.

'I do not see why not. There are such places in London now. I have a friend with such a place and he does very well for himself. I think you could manage such a place admirably.'

'Well . . .' But she was quite speechless. Only an hour ago, Nancy had been saying she should have a 'nice little business', and here was Monsieur Auguste suggesting much the same thing but more specifically. 'A restaurant . . .'

'You seem bouleversée – it is not such a wild notion, is it? If I were twenty years younger, I would do the same.'

'You would?' she said, and then, like disparate ingredients coming together to form a beautifully flavoured sauce, the idea at last formed in her mind and became a reality which she might reach out and grasp for herself. A plan unfolded like a clean, starched napkin before her: yes, she would ask Ralph for help. That would not be against her principles, because what Finn could do, she could do also. She felt convinced that she could create a very successful business, one which even the redoubtable Mr Erskine senior would happily have invested in, because sitting beside her on that park bench, looking lonely and unloved, and like her at a crossroads, was the key to that success: Monsieur Auguste.

'All right,' she said, with some resolution, for she was vowing to herself as much as to him. 'I think I could do that, you know. But I'll make one condition, Monsieur.'

'What's that?'

'That you'll come and work for me.'

For a moment he looked astonished, and then so happy she was afraid he was going to cry.

'Ma chère, I knew I was right to come here. I think I came half hoping I might find you again.'

Nancy, always hospitable, and no doubt intrigued by all
Jessie's stories about him, welcomed Monsieur Auguste into
the house in Raeburn Place like a long lost relative. Only
she could have been so unabashed as to invite him to stay for
a luncheon of such simplicity that anyone who did not know
him as well as Jessie, might have suggested he decline. For
Jessie knew that in Nancy's lunches, meatless because it was
Friday and the priest was staying also, there was a simple
perfection that Monsieur Auguste would appreciate.

In that sunny dining room, filled with noisy children and
the not inconsiderable bulk of Monsieur Auguste and
Father MacNeil, Jessie felt happier than she had done for
months. Steaming plates of champ and fresh-baked soda
bread could have been nectar for the gods to judge by the
relish with which they were eaten. Nancy was soon explaining in pretty broken French the business of boiling potatoes
in their skins and steaming them dry in a tea-towel, and
Monsieur Auguste was listening contentedly, like a man
who after many years has found a family. Jessie resolved,
with a spontaneous rush of generosity, that she would
accord him all the affection and care she owed to her own
father, but which she had never been able to give. It was an
easy gift, for he had given her so much in the past – given
her not just her education, but an identity and consciousness. And, as if that had not been enough, he had appeared
now, when she had been lost and purposeless, to throw her
a rope and pull her back to shore. At fifteen, he had begun
her life for her. Now, at past thirty, he made it afresh.

6

It was almost lunch time, and Ralph, working his way
through the pile of papers which always awaited him on his
twice-weekly visits to the motor works in Musselburgh, was
extremely pleased to be interrupted by the office boy

announcing that there was a lady to see him. It was unlike Olivia to do something so audacious, and yet was it not entirely in keeping with the recklessness of their affair? Doubtless (or at least so he hoped) she had been overcome with that sudden longing to see him which he knew so well in respect to his own desire. She was a creature of such fierce passions that he wondered that such a thing had not happened before.

He glanced about the office. It was hardly the most propitious place for such an encounter. But there again, what did surroundings matter with them? He only knew that when he was with her, he was in an enchanted realm.

He put down the paper he had been studying and leant against the front of his desk, his arms folded, waiting for the agreeable moment when she would come in and dazzle him again with her presence. The chocolate-coloured paint and frosted glass of the door were, for a moment, more exciting than any great crimson and gold theatre curtain that concealed from the eyes of the audience an illusory kingdom, for what would appear was, in this case, no stage fantasy, but a wonderful reality in his otherwise prosaic life.

It swung open, its hinge creaking, and Ralph, in that sudden, sharp moment of disappointment, wished he had bothered to ask the boy the identity of his caller and saved himself those few seconds of misguided expectation.

'Jessie! Well – goodness . . .' was all he could find to say.

His transparent surprise was not lost on her, it seemed, for she smiled and said, 'Yes, yes, I know I shouldn't really be here, Ralph, interrupting you at your work, but I need to speak to you about something, and I thought this was the best way I could catch you. I've brought you some luncheon.'

'Who could refuse that?' he said, recovering himself and relieving her of the basket which she held. 'Goodness, what is there in here? A whole feast?'

'Not quite,' she said. 'Now, where shall I set it out?'

There was a small deal table in the corner of the room, and in a moment she had pulled it out and covered it with a starched white cloth. With the same quiet efficiency, she unpacked the picnic; wine glasses, bread basket, napkins and all, so that he found himself laughing at this incongruous elegance in that most functional of rooms.

'Don't laugh,' she said, although she looked amused herself. 'It isn't supposed to be funny.'

'It isn't, I assure you,' he said. 'It's delightful!' He meant it. Although she was not Olivia yielding to him with hot-breathed ardour, he knew he could never find Jessie's company irksome, and watching her now setting out that table was irresistibly calming.

'Wine as well,' he said. 'You put me to shame. We don't even have a corkscrew here.'

'Don't worry, I've brought one.' And he watched with amazement as she uncorked with a deft and effortless motion an interesting-looking slender green bottle which she had unveiled from its hessian wrapping as if it were very precious. 'Gewurztraminer – I hope you like it.'

'Yes, yes. Oh, come on, Jessie, what is all this?' He was impatient to know what this extraordinary business was about. She seemed such a long way from the woman whom Finn had described as near hysterical at her husband's defection. She was calm, and terrifically determined about something.

'After we've eaten,' she said, and indicated he was to sit down. Like a dutiful child with his nurse, he sat down and ate as he was bid, but such food never reached the normal run of nurseries. It was sublime, staggeringly so.

Firstly, there was a small Dunbar crab, dressed very simply (and not spoilt by a wash of mayonnaise), served with tiny brown rolls which tasted like Nancy O'Hara's famous soda bread, but which had been plaited into unrecognizable elegance. This was followed by a galantine of guinea fowl which in no way resembled the usual run of galantines with their stringy meat and gutta-percha aspic. No, the meat was succulent and surrounded by a delicate, wine-scented jelly, as sensually rich as the orange and endive salad which accompanied it was tart and refreshing. To end this symphony (and this was how his ecstatic palate must think of it, for it was too exquisite for ordinary compliments) were three tiny tartlets: one with frangipani, one with brandied Smyrna raisins, and one lemon, in taste like an exclamation mark. This was not to mention a noble piece of Stilton, hand baked Bath Oliver biscuits and a dish of crystallized fruit perfect enough to sit in a jeweller's window.

'Now,' she said, refusing the Stilton of which he could not resist taking more, 'is there anywhere you know of in Edinburgh where we could eat like this?'

'No, unfortunately,' he said, his mouth enthusiastically full of Stilton.

She smiled and said, 'Then do you think people would pay good money to dine at such a place, like they do in London or Paris?'

'I can't think why not – if the food were as good as this. Why, what are you driving at?'

'This is why I've come to see you,' she said. 'I've made a decision, you see. I'm going to leave Sholto and I have to support myself, don't I? So I thought I'd set up my own business, a restaurant.'

'And you want me to lend you some capital? Gladly . . .'

'No, you must understand, I don't want you to lend me anything just because it's me and you think I need help, do you see? No, I'll only let you help me if you really believe you will get some sort of return on your money. I'm not a charity case. At least, I should rather not be one. I'd do this thing on my own if I could, but you have to be realistic in business, don't you?'

'Methinks the lady doth protest too much,' said Ralph. 'Believe me Jessie, there is no shame in asking for a loan in business. It's how the thing works. How do you think my father would have built up Garbridge, if he hadn't sold his soul to a bank for a few years? And I'm glad you've come to me first, not just because I should have hated the thought of a bank bleeding the interest out of you, but because it is a wonderful idea and I should want to be in on it whatever.'

'You do? Really?' she said. 'Are you sure? You're not just saying this to be kind?'

'Haven't I just eaten like one of the gods? You saw

yourself how greedy I was. Jessie, I think it is the most splendid idea, and it is exactly what you ought to do. I only wish I had thought of it myself, but then my father always said I didn't have enough imagination to be a true entrepreneur. But you have thought of it, and I'm convinced it will be a success. Now, have you seen any possible premises yet?'

'Well, there is a place to let in Frederick Street, but I don't know for how much.'

'It'll be exorbitant, I'm sure, but we can knock them down. That's the right part of town, certainly.'

There was a knock at the door, and the office boy came in with the two o'clock post. At the top of the pile lay a lavender-coloured envelope, addressed in that newly familiar hand. This small token of Olivia seemed to flood the place with memories of her, and Ralph was unable to resist picking it up, desperate to touch the paper which she had so recently touched herself.

It had all been going so well, like a dream in fact, until the boy brought in the post and deposited amongst the remains of that most successful luncheon, a pale blue-grey envelope, addressed in a hand which was distinctive because it was painfully etched on her memory as if by an engraver's needle.

Ralph Erskine Esq., written just as Sholto Hamilton Esq. had been written. The 'Esq.' was unmistakable.

What was worse was the way Ralph had at once picked it up, and was rubbing it between his thumb and forefinger, caressing it, fondling it almost. She could not help wondering if the letter contained the same disturbing indecencies as those in the letters to Sholto. His impulse to touch it had obviously been very strong, as if the letter was the woman herself. She feared his mind might be racing over what the contents might be, over what erotic excitement might be found there.

Oh, but not you, Ralph, not you as well! she thought in agony. Not you of all men – but you are a man, damn you, and as weak and as foolish as the rest . . . but why her? Why that terrible creature, why always her?

She wished she had the courage to tell him what she knew, and tell him what an addle-brained, wicked fool he was being, but her courage had deserted her. It had cost her so much to come here in the first place, and ask for his help, that to make a further onslaught seemed impossible. Besides, how could one tell a man who had generously offered to help you, and had quite accepted your terms into the bargain, that he was being a fool? Even with such an old friend, such a thing went quite against the grain. And, after all, was he such an old friend any more? Was there not a great deal of chilly distance between them, despite that illusory hour of pleasant companionship which they had enjoyed over lunch? That now seemed to her a little bubble of insubstantiality, although they still sat where they had been sitting, and the remains of the food (which had perhaps created the spell more than anything else) were still spread out in front of them. That bubble of enchantment (and it had been enchanting – she could not deny the pleasure she had felt in having him to herself) had been pricked and exploded by nothing more or less than a lavender blue envelope, addressed in a hand which obviously meant something quite different to each of them.

Of course, what Olivia Lennox might be to him in reality she could not know. She had no hard evidence to say that things between them were anything but entirely proper. She had only the clawing pain of instinct in her guts and the dry, bitter taste of jealousy in her throat, knowing that Olivia Lennox, of all women, should have so easily taken that which Jessie had so scrupulously denied herself. It would have taken but a few steps for Ralph and herself to become lovers that traumatic summer at Allansfield, but they had held themselves in check, exactly as they ought, until whatever mysterious thing there was between them had quite evaporated. At the time, it had seemed absolutely the correct thing to do, but now, as this blood-sucking female leeched away firstly what she had once loved, and now, worst of all, the man she still loved, Jessie wondered if there was any reason for caution and duty. There was, it appeared, no profit in it.

'Well . . . I should leave you to your letters,' she said springing up from her seat, anxious to soothe away her agitation with activity.

She was aware her voice sounded nervous and strange, for he glanced up at her and said, 'Jessie, is everything all right?'

In fact, he did more, and reached out and put his hand over hers. She pulled it away swiftly. She did not wish to be touched by him and his concern for her suddenly made her very angry. She felt sure it could not be sincere, and to see him reduced to ordinary, glib insincerity like the rest of them, hurt her more than she could possible have imagined.

'Of course!' she said as brightly as she could. 'Why should I not be? I am very well sorted out, as you can see.'

'You always were exceptionally brave,' he said, and the compliment, which previously she might have enjoyed, made her wince. She turned away briskly so that he should not see the displeasure on her face.

'My dear,' he said, getting up, 'there is something wrong, isn't there? You know you shouldn't suffer things in silence – it's dangerous. God knows, you must have been through hell with Sholto, but please don't make a martyr of yourself. I'd always hoped we were friends enough to talk . . .'

'Oh, for God's sake, Ralph, don't speak so!' she snapped, losing control. 'All these sleekit words, I canna bear it! You sound just like Sholto!'

This seemed to astonish him into silence and she saw that familiar rueful expression settle over him.

'Look, I didn't mean that,' she said, feeling she had perhaps overstepped the mark. 'I suppose I should be straight with you, shouldn't I?'

'About what?'

'About . . . about . . . about that woman!' She could not quite manage to say her name and pointed to the letter. 'She's not what she seems, Ralph. Believe me, I know it. You might think the world of her now, but she'll cut you up into little pieces and throw you away! I know!'

439

'Jessie, what on earth are you talking about?'

'Olivia Lennox, of course! Look, I don't know how deep you're in this, but I can't stand by without warning you. She's a scheming, heartless . . .'

He laughed, a hollow laugh which made her wish to hit him and bring him to his senses. She knew then he was in deep with her.

He said, as if vastly amused, 'How the devil have you got such a wild notion into your head? Olivia Lennox – good God! Perhaps you should write purple romances, Jessie, instead of opening a restaurant.'

'Ralph, for goodness' sake, stop lying! It doesn't damn well suit you,' she said fiercely, throwing the last few things into the picnic basket. 'If you don't choose to say what's going on, that's your business, but I can't stand by and not warn you. I couldn't not say it – be careful, for God's sake.'

And she snatched up her cloak and gloves and left him.

If lying to Finn had been difficult, this had been worse, far worse, for he had realized how desperately he wanted to confide in her. Had she not always understood him so well? But the lies had come so easily to him – the incredulous amusement, the unconcerned expression – while she, her eyes blazing, had spat out grim prophecies. She had seen straight through him. It had been pointless lying, but lie he must. He was trapped in a prison of deception which he rightly despised but within those walls lay a room containing all the earth's treasure, which so dazzled and drugged him, he could not find the energy to escape.

How on earth does she know? he wondered, remembering how she had pointed at Olivia's note. He picked it up again, and opened it. It contained but one sheet of paper, with only a few words written upon it.

'Dearest R. Not this Thursday, simply not possible. Nor next week, too dangerous. It will have to be next year. Will write later, but no more letters from you, my sweet, not safe at present. J. v. funny. Mille regrets, your O.'

She'll cut you up in little pieces and throw you away!

Histrionic nonsense, thought Ralph, choking back his

disappointment as he read the letter. Broken engagements are part of the game, surely? One can't take too many risks.

Yet, as he settled at his desk for the afternoon's work, he could not help feeling that Jessie's words had perhaps a speck of uncomfortable truth in them. She would be the last person to make up such things and there was a note of passion in her voice, in her anger, which suggested he was perhaps in very real danger. But what on earth could he do? He could not give her up, he could not. He needed her too badly. She had invaded him and held his being in captivity. Without her, he knew he would be half dead again, and that he could not face, not yet.

7

Jessie, who had been convinced that she had ruined any chance of obtaining Ralph's help, was surprised to get a long letter from him, quite as if nothing except business had passed between them at Musselburgh. This both relieved and angered her: the former because she had realized that she wanted the restaurant to succeed above anything else; the latter because it seemed her words had made no impression upon him, that he was beyond the powers of reason in respect to Olivia Lennox. No matter how many times she told herself that it was none of her business what he did, she could not rid herself of the uncomfortable conviction that he was heading for disaster, which she was unable to save him from. It was her deepest instinct to protect him, exactly as she had done that day at Garbridge, but then she had been able to act, to help him, while now he had slipped beyond her reach like a wilful child who will not be protected any more.

She was glad then that when they went to look over some premises in Frederick Street, Monsieur Auguste came with them. It prevented any repetition of her ridiculous outburst at Musselburgh.

The house, it soon became clear, was ideal for their purposes, give or take some alterations which Ralph and Monsieur Auguste dismissed so confidently as 'mere trifles', that she almost believed them, although she was certain nothing could be accomplished that easily. The basement, still divided into the maze of service rooms typical of a New Town house, was to be the scene of most of the alterations. The kitchen was not large or modern enough for the number of covers they were to provide (she had quickly learnt the correct terms) and so walls were to be knocked down and new gas stoves installed. Monsieur Auguste was now dismissive of coal and Jessie could not help but think gas would create a wonderful saving of menial labour – how marvellous to banish coal dust and soot from the kitchen for good! There would also be a gas geyser put in the scullery to provide endless hot water, and a nondescript shed in the back court would make an excellent boiler house so that the eating rooms upstairs would be properly heated. There was unanimous agreement between them all that the thing should be done handsomely, and Ralph, who had after all a great industrial complex at his command, took the technicalities quite in his stride. But he was most impressive with the bumptious house agent and managed, there and then, to get fifty guineas knocked off the annual rent.

While Monsieur Auguste continued to look over the kitchen, Jessie and Ralph went over the rest of the house. It looked drab and empty in the winter light, but Jessie found it did not take much effort to imagine how it would look properly fitted up. The two street-level rooms would be the public dining rooms, while the first-floor drawing room, with three windows overlooking the street, was ideal for private parties. Behind it was the traditional breakfast room, still with its walnut-stained half panelling.

Seeing it, Ralph said, at once, echoing her own thoughts: 'Your office, I think?' She nodded. 'Yes, I can see you in here.' He spoke with all the old warmth and affection, and she felt her heart twist at it. How inexplicable it all was, that now he should be able to be the normal, kindly man she had always so admired, and yet he would probably leave them to give himself up to lunacy, to find whatever strange comfort he did in Olivia Lennox's greedy arms. Why on earth had she chosen him, of all men? Could she possibly love him, or was Ralph only the duped victim of her wiles: wiles, which Jessie imagined had effectively snared James Lennox. But Ralph was not such a fool, or at least Jessie hoped he was not. After all, Sholto was no fool either, and he was caught in the same trap. Did that harpy use them all the same, and if so, why? What pleasure could she find in it? Jessie, although she struggled to understand (perhaps to diminish the sting of her own, very keen jealousy), could find no pattern in it. *Can she possibly love him, as I love him?*

This question rang in her mind as they stood together in that empty room. He looked singularly distant again, and perhaps he was thinking of her. *I wish he had not lied to me,* she thought. *If he had told me, tried to explain, then perhaps I could bear this better.*

Suddenly she despaired of the whole, ridiculous situation and particularly of her own foolish obsession with the matter. She decided she had better concentrate on the matter in hand. After all, was it not sheer stupidity on her part to waste energy on Ralph's entanglements when she could have no legitimate claim on him? Although she might be estranged from Sholto, she was still married to him. *For heaven's sake, Jessie, ignore it all. Let the man make his own mistakes if he must, and enjoy your independence. Love is a game for fools, you ought to have realized that by now!*

So she marched out of the office (she could already think of it as that) and on to the landing, her shoes ringing on the bare, polished boards. She pushed open the grand double doors to the drawing room and strode in, mentally taking possession of the place long before she had signed the lease. It was a splendid room, perfect for the purpose. She pushed up the sashes and pulled out the shutters, checking that everything was as it should be. She tapped on the walls for damp and ran her fingers over the pretty carved fireplaces in case the scrolls and leaves were coming loose with age. They were not, and she permitted herself a moment of fantasy, predicting the room on some evening in the future: a large, well-dressed party around the table, flowers and candles everywhere, the buzz of lively conversation in the air, while she stood discreetly in a corner, not in the black sateen of a servant but in the black silk of la patronne, supervising every detail so perfectly that the place would soon become a legend.

'Fleur de lys,' she said aloud, for she had suddenly noticed that the flowers in the frieze were stylized lilies. It was a wonderful name, exactly what she had been searching for, and she knew that to name a thing was to make a fantasy real. Thus, as she said it, the restaurant became a concrete, inevitable, and most marvellous episode in her destiny.

'The Fleur de Lys – what do you think of that for a name?'

Ralph followed her after a few minutes into the drawing room and found her lost in a sort of rapture. He was not able to respond at once, for those few moments alone had cast him into unexpected melancholy, as if clouds were obscuring the sun. He had had a terrible sense of foreboding, quite inexplicable and equally difficult to shake off. He had tried to dismiss it as merely physiological, for he had shaken with cold for a second, and had quickly gone to rejoin Jessie so that he would be distracted by the matter in hand. But her obvious happiness at having found the name, a very good name at which he should have liked to have been pleased, only stopped his tongue.

'You don't like it?' she said, misinterpreting his silence.

He got a grip on himself and said, 'Yes, of course . . . forgive me, Jessie, a goose just walked over my grave. I wasn't quite ready for that. But it is a good name.'

'Are you all right?'

'Oh, yes – it was just one of those silly things,' he shrugged it off. 'Now, what colour do you think in here?'

'Yellow,' she said, very decidedly. 'The colour of a tarte au citron.'

It struck him, in that moment, that this business was one to which Jessie had been born, and that the rest of her life

444

had been merely a preparation for it. She knew by some instinct exactly what was required. Although she had never been to any of the great restaurants of Paris or Brussels, her vision embraced them. He wished he might take her to some of them and watch her artlessly pick up on their faults and suggest improvements which sprang from her God-given good sense about food and how it should be served. To have fresh, yellow walls in the private room of a restaurant, indeed in any dining room, was almost inconceivably audacious, and yet the rightness of it, for that room, was obvious. Philip Winterfield would have embraced her for it, and indeed he felt half-tempted to himself, for as she stood there she seemed the embodiment of all that was physically, intellectually and emotionally desirable.

But he checked himself, partly because he felt at once guilty for finding her so attractive when he had sworn blindly to himself that it was Olivia whom he loved and it was to Olivia he owed his loyalty. But that was only a superficial cause of his restraint, for he knew at the root of it lay a sense that Jessie was now, as she made careful notes in her pocket book, a creature independent of the foolish and transitory desires of men. She had left Sholto and become a person entirely her own. She could not be subjected to the normal code of wanting and taking. She had broken the code, and stood alone and triumphant, a brilliant future ahead of her. For he was sure that whatever money he put up would be as nothing compared to the genius Jessie invested in the place. That was a thing which could not easily be violated, especially by one such as himself.

8

One last time, thought Jessie, taking the latch key from her bag and putting it into the lock of the door to the house in Colinton. She remembered the first time she had unlocked that door and walked into the bare whiteness of the hall. It had seemed like a clean slate then, a place where they would put the domestic inconveniences of Marchmont Road behind them and perhaps find less to annoy each other. Or so she had hoped. I lived on hope then, didn't I? she said to herself, like a fool.

The house now seemed as strange to her as it had done that first time. Although she had not formally deserted it, she had made the mental break some time ago. It was no longer her home and she was a little surprised at her own disloyalty to that which she had once held precious. She stood in the hall looking at the once familiar objects which furnished it: the hideous umbrella stand; the rickety hall chair with the Duke of Hamilton's crest (a source of great pride to Sholto); and hanging above it, rather incongruously, a framed cover of the *Police Gazette* showing the trial of the Clackmannanshire Strangler at which Sholto had been a junior counsel for the first time. These things, which she had always suspected were slightly dubious, now filled her with antipathy. How on earth had she stood them so long? How had she been so blind? The answer, of course, was depressingly simple. She had been blind in the same way to all Sholto's faults, wilfully so, as if she had some earnest need deliberately to deceive herself.

'Is that you, Mrs Hamilton?' Molly came out of the kitchen. 'Oh, it is, thank goodness. I thought for a minute you were the master.'

'Why?' said Jessie, alarmed. 'Are you expecting him?'

'Well, he did say he'd be back for tea which could be any time, couldn't it?'

'But you're all packed up?'

'Oh, yes, it's all done, Mrs Hamilton.'

'Well, the carrier and his lads are just outside,' said Jessie. 'They'd better get going at once. I don't want Mr Hamilton catching us flitting.'

'No, no,' said Molly and bustled out to instruct the removal men.

While they banged boxes downstairs Jessie went into the drawing room and sat down at her desk. She had meant to have a letter ready to leave for him, but every attempt had ended up in the wastepaper basket. She thought she had better try now.

But words still eluded her. Instead, the past, ghost-like, hung around her, and she sat and remembered a thousand foolish things that had happened in that green and white drawing room. She remembered, for example, when the minister's wife had called for the first time. She had been a most condescending creature until Mrs Erskine had arrived (most fortuitously) with a great basket of cyclamen as a house-warming present. Or, less happily, there had been the time when she had heard that her mother had died, and she had sat alone there while the children played outside and been racked with guilt at never having managed to love her. Then another sunny afternoon came to mind, when Ralph Erskine had been there, sitting in braces and shirtsleeves like the man of the house, drinking gin and soda. Now, she realized, such a state of affairs was as impossible as ever it had been for her to be close to her mother. Although they had been working closely together over the last few weeks, she sensed an impenetrable reserve in him which had not been there in the summer of 1906.

She took out a piece of writing paper and wondered again what she could say to Sholto. It was almost pointless to try, for there was nothing left to say. It would have been easy to pour curses down on his head but it would have smacked of jealousy. She was not jealous, and neither was she angry any more. She felt strangely detached, as if there had never been anything between them. The past was suddenly a vacuum, perhaps because she was anxious to forget it. She did not like to remind herself of her own shameful compromise, her own foolish dependence upon him.

Molly put her head round the door and said, 'It's all loaded now, Mrs Hamilton.'

'You go on with them then, Molly,' she said. 'I'll take the train.'

'But what if he comes back?'

'I'd rather he did,' she said, getting up from the desk. 'I think it's about time I gave him a piece of my mind.'

'Well, Mrs Hamilton, if you're sure . . .' She sounded doubtful.

'Oh, don't worry, Molly,' said Jessie. 'I think he'll be glad to be rid of us.'

From the window of the girls' bedroom, Jessie watched the carrier's van rumble off. It was oddly tidy in there, as Molly had packed up their toys and books and had taken down the paper alphabet frieze which had enlivened one wall. Jo had especially requested that it be brought to Frederick Street. It was fortunate that Jo and Flora had quite accepted the changes in their lives but Chloe had been unimpressed even by the prospect of her own bedroom. She had not openly complained at her exile from Colinton, but Jessie feared she might when she understood that it was permanent. She would probably think it a gross injustice to be uprooted from what she knew; from friends and a certain social position to a more ambiguous life above a restaurant run by her mother. In terms of Colinton mores, of which she had shown herself to be an eager and clever student, it was distinctly irregular. Chloe was also inexplicably attached to Sholto – or perhaps not so inexplicably, for as Nancy had shrewdly pointed out, Chloe did not really *know* Sholto. To her, he was a remote, glamorous figure who achieved great things in Edinburgh and who occasionally (very occasionally) descended from his Olympian heights to bestow shillings and bags of sweets before vanishing again.

Jessie knew that this was the real reason she was waiting to see him, although she would quite happily never have seen Sholto again. She knew that she had some responsibility towards her daughters. He was, after all, their father, and however inadequate he might be, they had a right to claim him as such and he to claim them if he so wished. It would have been pleasanter to make a clean break, but on this point she felt she must be scrupulous. She would tell him he was welcome to see them when he liked, even if he did not deserve such magnanimity. But she could not deny their right to him. She did not want them to grow up resenting her for keeping him from them. If he chose not to see them, they could draw their own conclusions and then she would at least be exempt from any blame in the matter.

She walked around the house for some time. It was cold and empty now, despite all the furniture still being here, because the meaning of the place had gone. It had been a stage for the girls, for the little dramas of their childhood, and now they had gone to a new theatre to act a new play – that of growing up into young women. Only the props remained here.

She could scarcely bear to look at her own bedroom. It was as immaculate as ever, for Molly was a fastidious housekeeper. The bed looked pristine, as if no one had ever slept in it, let alone made love or borne children in it. Yet all these she had done, and at one time she had thought she might die in it. She would not, but Sholto might, she supposed.

She closed the door quickly and began to go downstairs because she had heard the front door being unlocked. She stopped halfway because she was suddenly terrified.

'Molly!' he shouted. 'I want a large pot of coffee, and sharpish!' And she saw him fling his hat and coat on to the hall chair and then go into the study. 'Molly!' he shouted again, coming back into the hall. 'Why on earth haven't you lit the fire? Haven't I told you a dozen times . . .' and he went towards the kitchen door, presumably to continue the harangue.

'She's not there,' said Jessie, finding her courage and coming downstairs. She stood on the bottom step, steadying herself with her hand on the newel post.

There was a little pause.

'Oh, it's you,' he said acidly. 'I thought you weren't coming back until next week. Well, since you are here, and Molly evidently isn't, perhaps you would be good enough to make me some coffee. I've had a gruelling afternoon – that damned Sheriff Montcurrie has it in for me, I'm convinced of it.'

'No,' she said, 'I won't.'

'What?'

'I am not going to make coffee for you, and neither is Molly. She's left.'

'Damn the woman! Well, get someone else – one of those agencies . . .'

'I think you had better organize that,' she said. 'It's not my responsibility any more.'

'What on earth are you talking about? Of course it is.'

She shook her head and came down from the final step.

'Not any more,' she said, and pulled from her finger the gold band of her wedding ring and the little pearl ring he had given her at the Quarro. 'Here, these are yours, I think.'

He did not reach out and take them, so she balanced them on the edge of the umbrella stand.

'Aren't you going to say anything?' she said, surprised by his impassivity.

'A gesture like that scarcely requires any comment,' he said, reaching out and taking the rings. 'I can interpret its meaning well enough, and if you think I am going to pander to your vanity by begging you to stay, well, you are mistaken. But I don't think you want that, do you?'

'No,' she said, 'I want my freedom for myself, not because I'm angry with you and I want to make you suffer. Although I was, and I did, I don't now. I just want to be rid of a sham, that's all.'

At this he smiled that too familiar, cynical smile.

'The whole world is constructed of shams, Jessie,' he said. 'Can't you see that yet? Or does your servant-girl mentality still cherish naive notions of goodness and honesty? Such things don't exist, I assure you.'

'But you pretended they did, when it suited you, didn't you?'

'Yes, in the same way this sham, as you now call it,' he said, gesturing about the hall, 'suited you perfectly didn't it? It was more than you could ever have hoped for, and far more than you deserved. Yes, it was good enough for you until something better came along. Perhaps I misjudged you, Jessie, I'd have never have thought you were that ambitious.'

'What do you mean?' she said, angry now.

'What I mean, madam, is that you can give up any hope

of being Mrs Ralph Erskine. For one thing, I am not going
to give you a divorce, and if I did, I know he wouldn't touch
a divorced woman – well, not in an honourable way.
Besides, you shouldn't delude yourself that he is interested
in you. He isn't – I know it for a fact. It's only because of his
ridiculous, chivalrous, socialistic loon-headedness that he is
helping you set up your blessed business.'

'How the devil did you find out about that?'

'How do I know? My sweet, I am omniscient! When I
heard about Erskine's latest venture, it did not take me long
to put two and two together. You've always been soft on
him, haven't you? And here you are handing back your
rings. It won't do you any good. He's not interested.'

'Do you really think that is why I am leaving you?' she
said, incensed. 'Is that really what you think?'

'Well, as the French don't quite put it: "Cherchez
l'homme".'

'Ralph Erskine is nothing to me,' she said, with all the
defiance she could muster. 'He's a friend and nothing
more.' He seemed inclined to laugh at that. 'A thing which
you could certainly not understand,' she went on. 'It's all or
nothing with you, Sholto, isn't it? It's either lust or
contempt, and nothing in between!'

'Oh, we are back to the novelette notions, are we? Come
now, do you honestly expect me to believe in this saintly
friendship of yours? I know how the land lies. You're in
love with him, you have been for years – don't even try and
deny it. You thought the only way to get him was to leave
me, didn't you? Though God only knows what you see in
him. But I suppose all that money is quite a powerful
aphrodisiac.'

'Don't judge everyone by your own standards, Sholto.'

'I admit, of course,' he went on with astonishing placid-
ity, 'I too was attracted by the money at first. I wanted to
know people who would have money and influence. Ralph,
I was sure, would have both. I could foresee a great future
for him, and for myself as his friend. But, my God, he has
come to nothing, hasn't he? When one thinks what he might
have done – he could be in the cabinet by now, instead of

which he still lives with that shrew of a mother and dabbles in charity like a maiden aunt!'

Sholto's greatest weapon against her had always been words, and now he talked, calmly and indifferently, as if to a third party. Certainly, he did not seem concerned about her, or anything she might say. He had decided his line of argument and was, in effect, unassailable. As he stood and poured out this well-phrased venom, she thought of those times in the past when she had quite hopelessly tried to argue with him, to steel her poor reasoning against his brilliantly sharp, court-room wit. But she had always failed and he had always succeeded in overturning her words, filling her with doubt about her stance on the matter. She had never been able to make him see her point of view, even when she had compromised wildly simply to bring him a shade closer to some middle ground of understanding. Now, she realized that such exploits on her part had been doomed even before she had opened her mouth. He would never see how she felt or why she acted in such a way, because to do so would be to open up a chink in the massive armour of his self-importance. His self-love was too monstrous for him to see another's opinion. It was this blindness which had, no doubt, accounted for his great success as a barrister, but she saw that as a man it made him woefully inadequate.

'Be quiet, Sholto!' she said. 'I won't listen to a word more!' She decided she would no longer waste her breath trying to make him see why she was leaving him. He would never understand it. He was incapable of it. 'I've heard enough out of you to last me the rest of my life, and that's too much. I don't care what you think of me. It isn't important. I'm going and there's an end to it. I only came today to tell you I was going and that you can see the girls when you like, if you can be bothered!'

She could not resist that final jab and having tossed her latch key at his feet, walked out of the house and into the street, a free woman at last.

9

'And there's something else, Mr O'Hara,' said Dundonald, 'if you can spare a moment more . . .'

Finn could not really. He had a train to catch and was under strict instructions from Nancy not to be late because they were expected in Frederick Street at seven o'clock prompt, for the opening of the Fleur de Lys. However, there was something in Dundonald's manner, a sudden lowering of the voice, which suggested that he was worried about something. Worry was not a quality which Finn generally associated with the smooth, frock-coated Dundonald, who, in the elegant fastness of his jewellery shop in the West End of Glasgow, was well shored up against the problems of the world. But it seemed that not even he was immune.

'Perhaps we'd better go into the back,' he said, when Finn had nodded his assent. For they had been standing at the counter while Finn had appraised one or two antique pieces which had come Dundonald's way. He did not care to deal in such stuff and often hoped to sell items on to Finn. But there had been nothing very interesting and they had been put away again. Now, as he followed Dundonald into the back of the shop, Finn realized that those unremarkable mourning rings and Russian silver bangles were only a pretext. Perhaps Dundonald had something extraordinary stashed away, and Finn felt a prickle of excitement at the possibility of a bargain. He knew that Dundonald was ignorant of that side of the market, and that, with luck, he might get whatever it was for a good price.

'To tell you the truth,' said Dundonald, unlocking his safe, 'I really don't know what to think about this. I rather fear . . . well, let's see what you say.'

And he put a dark blue leather case on the table, a Dundonald's case, distinctive with gold tooling.

'Oh, that isn't the case it came in,' he said, undoing the catch and lifting the lid. 'It was in a dreadful, shabby old box when the gentleman brought it in, so you can imagine my surprise when I saw that inside . . .'

Finn could, quite easily, because the sight of the contents had put him into a mild state of shock. It was not because of the exquisite beauty of what he saw, which was a finely wrought gold necklace with filigree perfume balls, cabochon rubies and exquisite enamels, but because he had seen this lovely piece before. It was the late-sixteenth-century Bavarian masterpiece he had bought for Ralph a month ago, supposedly for his collection.

'Where did you get this?' he asked.

'As I said – a gentleman came into the shop and asked what I would give him for it. He said he wouldn't take less than six hundred guineas, but I could see it was worth far more than that, of course. But he was happy with seven hundred.'

'Did he give his name?'

'Oh, yes – that's why I didn't think anything more of it. It seemed perfectly in order, but then when he'd gone, I began to worry that it might be . . . well – you know – why else would he let it go for so little?'

'What name did he give?'

'Hamilton.'

'Hamilton? Are you sure of that?'

'Quite sure.'

'Can you remember what he looked like?'

'It is stolen, isn't it?' said Dundonald, with sudden dread. 'I shall be ruined . . .'

'No, no, I don't think it is,' said Finn. 'What did he look like?'

'Well, dressed like a gentleman: a beard, dark hair, I think. One would call him good-looking, I suppose. Certainly, he didn't seem suspicious. He even left a card, now I think of it.'

'May I see it?'

'Yes, of course. So you know this piece, Mr O'Hara?'

'Yes, I do. I bought it at Sotheby's before Christmas.'

'For this Hamilton fellow?'

'No, not for him.'

'Then how did he get hold of it, if he didn't steal it?'

'I don't think he's the type to steal anything,' said Finn, 'though he's scoundrel enough in other respects.'

'Let me see, where did I put his card? Ah, yes, with the old box, I think. I'll just go into the store and fetch it for you.'

When Dundonald was gone, Finn lifted out the necklace, anxious to make sure it was the same piece. He had not been mistaken, although he wished he had been. It threw up too many confusing questions. Why on earth would Ralph give the necklace to Sholto Hamilton and ask him to dispose of it at a third of the price he had paid for it? If that was what had happened, it made no sense at all. Ralph was too good a businessman for one thing, and he had been too pleased with the piece to want to dispose of it so cavalierly. 'Yes, yes, this is just the right sort of thing, Finn!' he had exclaimed. 'It's perfect, in fact!'

Perfect for what? Finn had wondered. To sit in a display case or to decorate the white neck of some pretty woman? He remembered all the suspicions he had had the evening after the private view, the suspicions which his better nature had been able to dismiss, but which now seemed the only thing which would explain the inexplicable. Perhaps Ralph had given it to his mistress as a Christmas present, and she had disposed of it with Sholto Hamilton's help. Then might she not be the same woman whom Sholto had been keeping instead of looking after Jessie and the girls, as he should? And who might she be? 'Someone we know' Nancy had said, and his mind flicked back to the private view: 'I don't think you know my old friend O'Hara, do you, Olivia?' Ralph had said, and even then, the use of her Christian name had struck him as odd.

'Here we are,' said Dundonald, putting down the box. Finn recognized its shabby, cracked leather. 'Sholto Hamilton, Advocate, 12 Great King Street, Edinburgh.' Is that your man?'

'It is – that's his business address.'

'Thank goodness. So it isn't stolen?'

'I think not.'

'You can't know how pleased I am to hear that. It has almost ruined New Year for me. I have been so worried that I had made the most foolish mistake – but it was so beautiful, and at that price, who could refuse? I was dazzled by it.'

Finn, as he ran through the rain to Glasgow Central Station, wished he felt the same sense of relief, but he could not, having unwittingly stumbled on a viper's nest. He would have to tell Ralph, there was no doubt about that, but oh God, what an awful task that would be!

Nothing, nowhere in Edinburgh, can match this . . . Jessie told herself, walking round the public dining room of the Fleur de Lys in the early evening of January 15th, 1912: that auspicious date which at one time she had thought would either not arrive, or would creep up on them all unseen when they were not ready. For the last few weeks had been so busy that she had scarcely had a moment to herself, and although half of her sensed them fleeing past too quickly, her other, child-like self, longed for them to pass so she would know soon how it would feel to be properly the proprietor of the Fleur de Lys. She did not believe it yet, and she knew she would not until she had seen empty plates sent back to the scullery; until she had heard approving comments from the diners; indeed, until she had counted out the first change onto one of the little silver trays she had bought for the presentation of the bill. Then, when she held their money between her fingers, and only then would she begin to believe it. Then, thank goodness, she could begin to repay the awful debts which would probably take a lifetime but which would be worth it, because at that moment, as she adjusted the flowers in one of the vases, she had a sense of what a wonderful thing it was to be at the helm of such a business, to be in control at last of all her world. Such a feeling, she knew, was rarely granted to a woman.

In a neat line by the door stood her small but impressive

regiment of waiters: three handsome and courtly Italians who had worked in some grand restaurant in Lucca until hard times had forced them to Scotland. Fortunately they had been over long enough to have a good grasp of English (albeit curiously laced with Scots) and they knew the form, or at least Franco, the eldest of them, did. The other two, Guiseppe and Fabrizio, were related to him (cousins or brothers, Jessie had not been able to determine which) and obeyed Franco slavishly. She was their lieutenant, he the sergeant.

'You all look very smart,' she said, which they did in their new suits, their hair slick with macassar oil.

'Grazie, Signora,' said Franco, bowing slightly. 'We 'ope that everything go well for you tonight.' And he produced from behind his back a small but pretty boutonnière.

'Oh, but you shouldn't have . . .' she said, surprised and very touched by this unexpected gesture. 'But thank you – it's lovely.'

'Flora tell us you like roses best, Signora,' said Guiseppe. The two young men had surprised Jessie with their affectionate patience with the girls. Only Chloe had thought it beneath her dignity to play with them. Indeed, she could not understand why Jessie had decreed everyone should eat together in the basement servants' hall. It was perhaps eccentric, but Jessie thought it better for esprit de corps that they did so, as if they were a family, all about the same table, and Molly especially loved the company. She, in fact, had ceased to be a mere nursemaid and had made herself indispensable. She was all too willing to help in the most menial chores. Jessie had two strong-armed dailies to clean and wash up, but Molly would not be denied her part. She took a special pride in the linen and displayed a hitherto unknown talent for folding the starched napkins into a variety of complex shapes. She had learnt this in her first place in a big house in the highlands, and had never forgotten it, although she'd had little chance to display it subsequently. She had instructed Franco in this difficult art and now all the napkins were settled into a fantastic flourish called the water lily. No wonder Chloe is is miffed, thought

Jessie, Molly doesn't goffer her pinafores so beautifully these days . . . and then she felt guilty for belittling Chloe's evident annoyance with the whole situation. She had explained it enough times but Chloe had responded sulkily, demanded to know why she couldn't have stayed behind with Sholto at Colinton. How on earth could Jessie tell her that her father would not want her there, that he simply did not care? She would not understand. Oh, bother you, Chloe, she thought, of this thorn in her side, you may not see it now, but when you are older you will. But she hated all the same submitting her to that age-old autocracy of parents which makes us all convinced (or at least we attempt to convince ourselves) that we know what is best for our children.

She looked around the dining room again as Fabrizio went from table to table, lighting the candles with a taper. Soon the room was softened by the gentle glow of candle-light and the furnishings she had planned so carefully came into their own. In that shaded light, the soft French grey of the walls was wonderfully delicate and the toile de Jouy curtains and the pretty tapestry on the chairs looked pleasantly antiquated. 'It will look like the parlour in an old Norman manor,' Ralph had said. She did not know whether it would or not. She only knew that it worked, that she had created a discreet and elegant background for Monsieur Auguste's food.

Satisfied with the dining room, she went downstairs to the kitchens, which had none of the same serenity. If the dining room was where Franco's subtle charm reigned, here Monsieur Auguste's flamboyant perfectionism set the key note. The place was alive with sound and smell: the crashing of pans on to the flames (which for a non-professional is alarming, but for Jessie as reassuring as the sound of iron on the anvil to a smith); a most delicious scent of stock made from duck bones, being reduced with red wine and juniper berries to make Monsieur's incomparable sauce pastorale. These then first assaulted her senses, like the main theme of a symphony, but as she stood a moment longer, other sights and sounds, more subtle but equally

458

pleasant, registered with her: a great heap of diced carrots glowing orange against a copper colander; the sizzle of onions sautéing; the elusive tang of fennel in the air; and as delicate as the sound of a flute above the orchestra, the pale cream colour and gentle smell of the crème de la grand'tante – a simple but wonderful cauliflower soup which Jessie had made herself. She had chosen to do soup and pâtisserie as most of the work could be done in advance, leaving her free to supervise the restaurant while Monsieur Auguste and the two kitchen maids tackled the entrées and the vegetables.

'Ah, Jessie – what do you think of this?' said Monsieur Auguste, summoning her with a gesture of the tasting spoon. She tested the sauce, flattered he had asked for her opinion.

'Fine,' she said, after a moment, 'but don't you usually have a little more bay in than that?'

'You never forget anything, do you!' he laughed.

'Then you were only testing me, you old rogue!' she exclaimed as he dropped in the little bunch of bay leaves. 'And I thought you actually trusted my judgement.'

'I do,' he said with sincerity. 'Would I be here if I did not? I can see that here you will have an établissement du premier rang.'

'Only because you are here,' she said.

'Non, non, a good chef is only part of it. It is the ambiance, you understand – you have done that. It will be irresistible, you'll see. You will be as famous in Edinburgh as the Mère Filoux in Lyons.'

The jangling of the street bell interrupted this little tribute.

'But it is only half-past,' said Jessie, alarmed.

'That will be your protector, Monsieur Erskine,' remarked Auguste, returning his attention to the sauce.

'What?' said Jessie, bemused by this description. 'You don't think that he's . . .'

'Of course, I forgot,' said Monsieur Auguste blandly, 'this *is* Edinburgh. Now, you had better go and receive, had you not?'

Jessie ran upstairs, still disturbed by this throwaway

remark. If Monsieur Auguste had suspected that Ralph was her protector – which term, for all its obliqueness, implied a great deal – then how many people had drawn the same conclusion? She began to worry that some undesirable taint might already be endangering her respectable establishment. After all, as Auguste had said, this was Edinburgh and not Paris where such a state of affairs would scarcely be remarked upon. In Edinburgh it would be considered shocking, if it were believed. It was unconventional enough in Edinburgh for a woman to set up in business on her own.

But reaching the hall and seeing Ralph accompanied by his mother, sister and brother-in-law, all her fears vanished. Nothing could give more of a sanction of respectability than Mrs Erskine, her arms full of hot-house flowers, anxious to kiss Jessie and wish her all success. It might have taken Mrs Erskine a while to accept Jessie's defection from Colinton, but now that she had, she was a loyal supporter. Alix had brought a copy of *The Gude Cause* which contained a glowing account of the Fleur de Lys as yet another example of woman's activity in every sphere of life, with the inevitable conclusion that it was criminally unjust to deny such self-evidently useful members of society their political rights. She also promised that a suffragist party would be dining downstairs. This made Jessie slightly uneasy as suffragettes, as the press had now dubbed them, were enjoying much notoriety at the time. Mrs Erskine, for one, had confided that she was greatly relieved that Alix was pregnant and thus 'hors de combat' as she feared that otherwise her committed daughter might have been encouraged into some terrible scrapes. But the doctor had banned public meetings and Alix's passionate vitriol was confined to journalism.

They went upstairs to the private dining room where Chloe, Flora and Joceline were waiting, carefully supervised by Molly who was anxious that none of the immaculate furnishings should come to grief. Because it was a special occasion they were dining with the adults, something which made Flora and Jo a trifle diffident, but Chloe, Jessie was relieved to see, had risen to the event. She was sitting very neatly in one of the window seats, carefully smoothing the silk of her new dress, and seemed pleased by the grandeur of her surroundings. She looked even more pleased when Mrs Erskine commented on how grown up she was looking.

'Well, how do you like it here, Miss Hamilton?' asked Andrew gallantly, and made her blush. She stared up at him admiringly, but was speechless.

'Do you think Chloe is old enough for a glass of champagne?' said Ralph, who was opening a bottle.

The pop of the cork made Jo shriek and cower behind Jessie's skirts.

'Surely you're not afraid of that, Jo?' said Ralph. 'That is one of the most marvellous sounds known to man. It leads to the most delicious of drinks.'

'Ralph, really,' murmured Mrs Erskine.

'Oh, a little champagne never hurt anyone.'

'Is it like ginger beer?' asked Flora, watching him pour out a glass.

'Better than ginger beer,' he said.

'Can I have some?' she said bluntly.

'May I have some please, Mr Erskine, is what you should say, Flora,' said Chloe tartly, coming up to them.

'For that you shall have a glass of champagne,' said Ralph, amused. He handed her the first glass, which Chloe, much to Jessie's delight, took straight up to Mrs Erskine. She smiled approvingly at this.

'If it is sweet,' Mrs Erskine said, 'then I don't suppose there can be any harm in it, can there, Jessie?'

'Better to be used to it now than be giddy at eighteen,' remarked Alix. 'But I'll just have an Apollinarius, thanks.'

'What's that?' asked Jo.

'Fizzy water. You'll like the champagne better.'

'Well then, just half a glass each,' said Jessie. 'And the same for me, Ralph. I have to keep my wits about me.'

'We should have a toast,' said Andrew, 'before you are too busy to be toasted.'

'Yes, a toast, definitely,' said Alix, getting up slowly.

'Oh, don't get up, for goodness' sake,' protested Jessie.

'Och, I can stand for a toast. Come on then, Drew.'

'Well then, ladies and gentleman, will you raise your glasses and drink in honour of the gallant lady of this fine establishment. I give you, Jessie Hamilton!'

Their warm goodwill embraced her. She even felt Chloe's forgiveness. She had that comfortable sense that, having travelled for long miles, she had finally reached her destination – a destination, which, when she had begun her journey, she could not even have guessed at.

If you give a creature wings, you cannot expect her not to use them, reflected Ralph as he savoured the last mouthful of his 'Canard à la pastorale'. It seemed too rustic a name for a dish of such subtle richness. It had made Finn exclaim: 'By God, how do they do this!' at the first mouthful, and then everyone had been strangely quiet, preferring to eat the duck with due reverence than make trivial conversation. Even the children, he noticed, who might have found it too complex, were carefully cleaning their plates with forkfuls of pommes dauphinoise, and he had been moved to imitate this gesture of natural greediness.

Jessie, who had not sat down with them, had come in to see how they had been getting on, and had stood in the doorway, smiling at them as they so clearly relished every mouthful. She came forward and gathered up the empty plates, in a manner that was not in the least servant-like but merely an extension of her hospitality. He was reminded how she had seemed when they had looked over the premises, how strikingly independent she had been, so entirely an entity in her own right. Now, as she walked around the table with much graciousness, smiling and laughing with her enraptured guests, that independence seemed to hang about her like an aura. He felt he might touch it, as he might touch the crisp frills of her elegant but still functional apron. But as much as it might be tangible, it was a barrier which only those closest to her might violate. For Joceline, who so much resembled her, could reach out and claim a kiss from her mother. That closeness, which he understood from his family, he envied, and it seemed he had once had a right to claim it from her. She had been nearer to him once. He had seen her vulnerable and ill after the birth of Chloe – how on earth had time put such a wall between them?

A sorbet arrived, and he found her at his elbow. He felt startled by his own sudden longing which confused him, making him feel guilty in regard to Olivia. He had made her promises, promises he was bound to keep, and yet nothing could stop this sudden mental infidelity. As Jessie was about to take away her hand which had laid the sorbet glass in his place, he could not resist laying his own across her wrist where it extended from a neat frilled cuff. She looked at him quizzically, and he thought he sensed a reproach and at once took his hand away. A moment later she was gone and he felt bereft and foolish, for as on that occasion when he had kissed her, he was again the victim of his own self-indulgence – that passion for self-pleasuring that drove him above all others. But he would not taint her with it, not Jessie Hamilton whom he respected too well. He was a poor enough piece of stuff, as his own behaviour of late amply demonstrated. He could not deny that for all the pleasure he got from this wild affair of his with Olivia, there always remained a sordid residue, like the sediment in a bottle of claret which has not been properly decanted: a bitter aftertaste which ruined the remembrance of the rest of the bottle.

He glanced again at Jessie, and watched with creeping despair as the wings of her newfound freedom carried her further away from him. His money had bought this splendid goddess her deliverance, but he wished he might have enslaved her with it. But he knew he could not. It was not only wicked, but impossible. Sholto had tried and failed. She was not to be caught by ordinary men.

'What are you dreaming about, Ralph?' asked Nancy. 'Your sorbet is melting away.'

'Oh, nothing,' he said offhandedly. He saw that Finn frowned and looked away. Ralph had noticed he looked troubled that evening, for he had been almost aggressively charming, as if he were anxiously concealing some

463

disturbing thought. Ralph made a mental note to tackle him about it.

He was quite gratified then, when the party was on its way upstairs to Jessie's somewhat humbler drawing room, Finn caught his arm and said, 'Could I have a word in private, do you think, old man?'

Ralph was flattered that he should think of turning to him.

'Of course,' he said. 'If there's something wrong, you know I'll do anything I can . . .'

'Oh God,' interrupted Finn with vehemence, 'you are a fine one to talk! No, there's nothing wrong with me, you fool. It's you that I'm worried about.' He sounded exhausted and at the limit of his patience. 'I'll come to the point, shall I? You're not going to like what I'm going to say but I've got to say it.'

He sounds like Jessie, that afternoon at Musselburgh, thought Ralph, and began to feel uneasy.

They sat down at the foot of the stairs and Finn took out his pipe, in need of its calming solace.

'I don't know where to start.'

'Have a go,' said Ralph, trying to sound calm and cheerful.

'Perhaps you should start,' said Finn. 'And would you stop acting like an innocent, for one thing? Look, did you give that Bavarian necklace to your mistress?'

'What!' Ralph almost choked at the directness of the question. He thought of denial but only for a moment. Finn's face advised him that it was worthless to lie any longer. 'Christ . . . am I so transparent?'

'Well,' sighed Finn, 'it's just that I've been putting two and two together. You see, this afternoon, that piece turned up at Dundonald's, the jeweller in Glasgow.'

'What? Are you sure? Have you seen it?'

'Absolutely sure. I could not be mistaken about a thing like that, could I? Dundonald bought it for seven hundred guineas from our old friend . . .'

'Olivia Lennox?' Ralph said slowly, and with regret. He knew now that the end he had always feared had come. But then Finn said, with surprise, 'No – Sholto Hamilton.' He went on, as if thinking aloud: 'Then those two cooked this thing up between them? I didn't think . . . but I did guess she was Sholto's woman, this mistress of yours. But . . .' He now sounded as astonished as Ralph. 'It's that Lennox woman, is it? No wonder Jessie wouldn't tell us! Christ, what a bitch she must be!'

'A very lovely bitch,' Ralph managed to say. 'You can't help thinking that, can you? I mean, any man would do the same, wouldn't he? Wouldn't you, if a creature that beautiful flung herself at you, told you she loved you – wouldn't you be just the same, for all your bloody good intentions?'

'Calm down, Ralph, for God's sake. Of course I don't blame you. I just think you should get yourself out of this bloody mess. What a damned pair of vultures! What did she say to make you give her that thing anyway?'

'Do you really want to know?' said Ralph, getting up. 'Aren't you content to have solved this little mystery or do you want all the sordid details, so you can see what a damned fool I've been? Well, no, Finn – give me credit for a little pride, won't you?' He stopped in the middle of this tirade for Jessie was coming upstairs. She had taken off her apron and in her black dress looked like a prophetess.

'You were right,' he said to her. 'You all saw it, didn't you? You all saw what I damn' well couldn't! I couldn't see her for what she was, could I? Well, why not? Why can't I be like the rest of you, clear-sighted enough to see what's worth having? Eh?'

He did not stop to hear any answer, but stormed past her, and through the restaurant full of contented diners, into the street, to expend his rage into the black January night.

10

They had arranged to meet the next day. After quite a few broken appointments (the reason for which Ralph saw quite clearly now), Olivia had finally agreed to meet him by the Scott Monument in Princes Street Gardens. He went at the time they had decided, not yet sure whether he would attempt to wring her neck or ask a policeman to arrest her on a charge of fraud. He still felt violently angry and could not say how he would behave, but beneath the anger lay a desperate hope that Jessie and Finn were wrong, that she was as true as she said, and as innocent.

She arrived a little late, as usual. Before, he had found this extraordinarily exciting, this breathless lack of punctuality, but now he could see it was contrived, an artful, whorish trick to ensnare him. She was dressed extravagantly, with a white fur hat and collar in the manner of the Ballet Russe.

'We can't stay here,' she said, glancing around. 'I've just seen . . .'

'Spare me this,' he said, dispassionately. 'Please.' He even managed a touch of mockery.

'Ralph?' she said.

'Sit down,' he said. 'You and I have to talk.'

'I really don't think we should sit here.'

'Why? You won't catch cold in all that.'

He brushed a gloved finger across the luxuriant fur of her collar, and knew if he had not been wearing gloves he would not have been able to touch it, for the fur which looked so beautiful, and so expensive, was made repellent by its wearer. He forced himself to touch it for the same reason he had kept the appointment. He wanted the thing ended cleanly, however painful it might be. He felt that only cowardice was served by staying away, and if he was able to indict himself upon most moral counts, of that at least he would be innocent.

'You know why,' said Olivia. 'We don't want to be seen, do we? We want to keep our little secret a secret, don't we?'

She spoke so archly that he felt his temper slip.

'Christ, woman, I am not a child! You can stop all your tricks, right now. I have had enough!'

'Ralph, my dear, what is it?' She sounded incredulous, but it was the studied incredulity of an actress. He could see that now.

'You know perfectly well.'

'My dear, I've really no idea what you are talking about!' she said, laughing. He had spoken like that, lied to his friends in that same brittle, amused tone. She had dragged him down to that level and he felt his own rottenness more than he saw hers. She was amoral and she had no conscience to torture her. These were not tricks to her, but the very grammar of her life. He was the monkey who had played the tricks, he was the fool.

'There's no point reproaching you, is there?' he said. 'There isn't a thing I can say or do to make you feel you've done anything shabby, is there? But I'm going to say it all the same, because if I don't, I will go to my grave regretting that I never gave you a piece of my mind, that I never told you what a heartless, scheming bitch you are!'

He half shouted this and she took alarm.

'Ralph, for goodness' sake – people are staring!'

'Let them! It's no bloody secret, is it? It seems that the whole of Edinburgh knows what a damned fool you have made of me – you and Sholto Hamilton! Christ, what an unholy alliance! Why the hell didn't you just ask me for money, woman? Couldn't you even be that honest?'

'I'm not staying here to be insulted,' she began with such a horrible show of mock-prudery that, as she half rose from her seat, Ralph pulled her down again with some force.

'You are going to stay, whether you like what you hear or not! Have you been seeing Sholto Hamilton all the time that we've been together?'

'What if I have? What is it to you?'

'I know about the necklace. I know what you've done. It's turned up in Glasgow, sold to a jeweller who knew a unique piece when he saw it. But I suppose you two didn't think it was anything in particular, did you?'

'You chose to give me that,' she said. 'What I did with it is my own affair.'

'So you did give it him to sell?'

'What if I did? What business is it of yours?'

'Oh, for God's sake, Olivia, stop being so obtuse. I gave you that in good faith . . . because . . .' He could not bring himself to finish.

'Because you thought I loved you?' she said coolly. 'Ha, then you *are* a fool. Sholto said you were.'

'So you admit it?'

'Admit what? Selling that hideous necklace – of course! What else could I do with such a thing? I could scarcely wear it, could I? Besides, I needed money – urgently. And as for loving you, well, I never said that, did I? I understood we had an arrangement.'

'What the hell do you mean by that?'

'Now it is you who is being obtuse,' she said. 'You know as well as I do that love had nothing to do with it. Or did you just fool yourself to salve your precious conscience? You wouldn't have had the courage to go to a whore, would you? Although that was what you wanted me for, wasn't it? You can't deny that.'

For a moment he was silenced. Her cold frankness on this point was unexpected and gave her the upper hand.

'Can you?' she said, getting up. This time he did not attempt to restrain her. He had no defence to this charge. It was exactly the thing with which he had been scourging himself all the previous night.

'I thought not,' she said. She looked down at him with utter contempt and he felt annihilated. 'Oh, Sholto *will* be amused when I tell him this.'

He could only think of hurling obscene abuse at her and Sholto, upbraiding this whore and pimp to the entirety of Princes Street Gardens. But he could not. It was pointless. The dreadful rush of his anger and humiliation would be wasted. Nothing could move her but money.

With great self-control, he got up and faced her.

'By the way,' he managed to say, 'you made a bad loss on that piece. It was worth double that at least.' He thought he saw a flicker of annoyance on her face, which stopped his own plunging spirits from descending any further into self-pity.

'Oh, really?' she said.

'Really.' He managed a smile, raised his hat and turned away, setting off very briskly in the direction of the Cafe Royal. The matter was best left there. There was, after all, nothing more to be said.

Andrew was waiting for him, deep in a newspaper. They often met there on Saturday for lunch before catching the afternoon train to Allansfield.

'You're early,' he said, folding up the paper. 'Success?'

Andrew assumed he had been doing business.

'I think so,' said Ralph, glad to see a friendly face. 'Right then, Ian,' he said, addressing the waiter, who knew them well. 'Two halves of dry champagne and some smoked salmon, please.'

'What are we celebrating?' said Andrew, for they usually had claret.

'The liberation of your foolish brother-in-law from the clutches of a vile woman.' He did not know how he managed to be so jaunty, but he felt he must be.

'Good God, Ralph!' said Andrew with some surprise. 'I had no idea that you were . . .'

'Having an affair? Yes, rather stupidly, I have been. I should have been better staying at home with the accounts. God, is there no hope for me?'

'She'll come along eventually,' said Andrew.

'Now come on, Drew, don't threaten me with the blessed Mary Chalmers, please.'

'Oh no, I don't mean her. I was thinking of some person as yet unknown, that you don't expect to meet. It's strange, I was just remembering when I first set eyes on Alix.'

'At Celia's funeral . . .'

'Yes, all that time ago.'

'It feels like yesterday, the state I'm in – ah, Ian, good man,' he said, as the waiter appeared with the silver tankards of champagne.

'Do you want to talk about it?' asked Andrew.

Ralph took a first comforting swig of champagne.

'No, I'm past the age of that sort of self-indulgence. I'm a fool, and there's an end to it. I can't possibly go mad these days, can I? How the devil would the company manage?'

But as the day wore on, he found these stoic high spirits increasingly hard to maintain, especially in the face of his cheerful relations. Alix's baby chose that evening, of all evenings, to kick for the first time and Ralph found it took all his strength to muster sufficient enthusiasm. His mother noticed him attacking the whisky and reproached him for it. He snapped back at her and then retreated to his library, hearing as he went Mrs Erskine saying plaintively: 'Oh, Ralph, what is the matter with you tonight?'

She had, it seemed, been about to pursue him to his lair, but Andrew had murmured something and he had not been interrupted.

But later Andrew came in and sat opposite, chewing on his pipe, tactfully quiet while Ralph in a morose and alcoholic state turned over in his mind, again and again, the pages of recent memory.

'You're a lucky beggar, Drew,' he said, at length.

'I know,' Drew replied, not with smugness, but with real gratitude. He was so tranquilly happy in his approaching fatherhood that Ralph felt he could not disturb him with sordid details; no matter how much he might wish to confess and no matter how willing Andrew might be to listen.

'Why don't you turn in, Drew?' he asked. 'I'm very poor company, as you can see. Why don't you go and listen to your heir kicking poor Alix?'

'No, I can't go to bed yet – not until she's asleep. She can never get to sleep these days with me threshing around like a brute. So I give her a chance and come up later.'

It was an artless torture, as the whole evening had been in its simple way, to hear these details of a comfortable, shared life. It was impossible not to feel jealous and to sense again the full burden of his own magnificent folly. Andrew's life was so ordered and happy, but dynamic when necessary – in fact, just like the man himself. For a moment Ralph seemed to step back from himself and saw two men sitting by a fireside, saw them with ruthless objectivity. One, it was easy to see, was honourable and trustworthy, as he was fair-haired and handsome. He was the sort of chap to whom one would gladly marry one's daughter, or entrust one's investments. The other, dark, dishevelled and half stupefied with the whisky that his doctors had forbidden to him for years, was a less straightforward case. One would, Ralph was ashamed to realize, perhaps hesitate to lend five pounds to such a man. It's a good thing I have private means, he reflected wryly, and struggled to his feet, anxious to use this scrap of humour to good effect, to make him do something other than sit there in a self-pitying stupor until the end of time.

He crossed the room to his writing desk and began to leaf through the papers carefully arranged by his secretary for his attention that weekend. He remembered how he had been distracted by his daydreams of late, how figures had blurred into visions of her voluptuous limbs, and wondered how much time, not to say money, he had wasted in journeying up that particular blind alley. He was surprised he could think of it so dispassionately, like a bad investment, or rather like a gamble on some beautiful but as yet untried race horse. The odds had always been stacked against him, and yet, like a hardened gambler, he had entirely believed in his own good luck. He had believed in her love, believed in his own, but that, it seemed, was as false as hers, because he felt no desire to see her again. His desire had collapsed as swiftly as it had arrived, and he was not even angry with her any more, but only with himself for ever permitting such a thing to happen. It was not a mistake that Andrew or his father would have made. They would have seen her for what she was – a touch ruthlessly, perhaps, but it was necessary ruthlessness for it kept them clear-sighted.

It had been the same with Sholto Hamilton. Mr Erskine had never trusted him and had never understood their friendship. Ralph saw now that much the same things that had once drawn him to Sholto, had drawn him into Olivia's arms. It was quite easy to believe they had formed some dreadful conspiracy – they were so very much alike: the same sensual recklessness; the same amorality (which to Ralph was a forbidden but tempting drug); the same blind indifference to anyone else in the face of their own ambitions; and the same almost devilish charm. Like stones in the pockets of a man overboard, these things had dragged him down, and he had been powerless against them. There was nothing in his upbringing which had prepared him for such people, and their very weakness gave them a hold over him. He understood them too well to despise them as he should. He had been like a curious child who, anxious to understand the nature of fire, had come too close and got burnt.

He found himself sighing aloud and Andrew looked across at him, an enquiring and sympathetic expression on his face. Ralph could not answer that glance. Instead, making a fierce mental resolution to close this particular subject, he fixed his attention on the paper he held in his hand and said, 'Have you seen these estimates for the Admiralty contract, Drew? Surely these figures can't be right? They seem absurdly low. Who compiled them?'

Drew got up to look at them, and Ralph sensed his brother-in-law's relief that it was not an emotional outpouring he must deal with but merely the vagaries of some accountant.

11

In front of him, spread out across the desk with a weight at each corner, were the plans for the new Erskine shipyard on the Clyde. It was a bold scheme, Andrew's particular

472

brainchild, and Ralph, although not skilled in the interpretation of such complex, technical drawings, was conscious enough of its quality to indulge in a moment of pure satisfaction that the scheme had at last got this far. They needed to gain the edge again, especially with Harland and Wolff stealing all the thunder lately with their monster liner, and this scheme of Drew's, even if it was not as attention grabbing as the *Titanic* in Belfast Docks awaiting her maiden voyage, would show the merchant lines, with whom Erskine's did most of their business, that the march of progress was not entirely confined to luxury ships.

This new yard would be the most efficient and up to date in Europe. It would cut months off the process of building ships without sacrificing an ounce of quality. Andrew, with his ruthless devotion to detail and practicality, had been studying the processes of ship building for months, watching every craft at work, from the welders to the fitters, and seeing where time and energy was wasted. For there was no doubt that the process as it stood now was profligate with muscle, especially with the muscle of skilled men who were being needlessly wearied and distracted by unnecessary physical labour. A trained craftsman, they had decided, should not need to sweat like a navvy – it was as ridiculous as making a solicitor copy out all his legal papers. The unions had been wary at first, of course, but Ralph and Andrew had been frank as to what they were trying to achieve. And the men liked Andrew, and soon trusted him absolutely, going out of their way to help him with the project. It had been a model of staff–management relations and Ralph looked forward to the day, which would undoubtedly come, when their competitors would stand and stare, amazed to see that 'young Erskine's lunatic socialist notions' had produced such a miracle of capitalistic efficiency as that new yard on the Clyde.

He knew he had a great deal to thank Andrew for in this. Andrew, so much the product of Robert Erskine's training, might so easily have refused to see Ralph's point of view. But he had, and had done more. With his calm, logical mind he had developed it, so that sometimes Ralph was left standing, amazed by his originality. This yard was one such idea – a great crackle of inspiration, months of really hard work, and voilà: a blue print spread out on Ralph's desk, humbly requesting his approval.

'My approval!' said Ralph aloud, but to himself for he was alone. 'My gratitude is more like it. Perhaps you should be sitting here, Andrew.'

But Andrew was not a man for offices or account books or administration. His spirit would have been stifled by such things whereas Ralph, who had once taken such pleasure in translating Latin iambics into Greek, had found the same quiet amusement in the methodical mysteries of bureaucracy. Thus the work was equitably divided between them, and they had the pleasure of knowing that their partnership was a true one, created by more than the legal documents which recorded it.

He pored over the blueprint again, dazzled by its detail, and found himself, for the first time in a month, feeling immensely calm and happy. He had been bitter and angry inside for so long now that this fresh sensation assaulted him with its novelty. He was very surprised that he should feel so; that his emotional wretchedness, which he had been nursing like a malignant tumour, should choose to depart so suddenly, like an unreliable servant leaving without notice. But now, gazing at the elaborate beauty of those functional but intricate lines, he found he did not care. He did not forgive, but he realized that the whole, sordid business did not matter. Wretched introspection and self-torture had been an indulgence on his part, a poisonous wine to which he had easily become addicted. Yet now, he had woken up, oddly clear-headed, free of the past, enjoying the moment. For spring had come, even to Garbridge: there was this spring-like scheme in front of him, a bud which would soon blossom, and there were, he realized, several sweet-scented hyacinths now blooming along his office window sill. These incongruous intruders had arrived the week before, bought by his mother at a meeting of the Garbridge Gardeners' Institute (of which she was honorary president). She had left the then uninteresting green spikes in their terracotta pots with the hope they would 'cheer the place up a little', by which she meant that they might cheer him up. Now the spikes had brought forth lilac, white and pink plumes and a scent that was too exotic for Garbridge.

He was just wondering if there was not room for more cheerful vegetation about the place, and whether the recreation ground and bowling green could not be extended and more trees planted, when he was interrupted. This did not surprise or annoy him. He was in fact slightly surprised he had not been disturbed for so long. Garbridge did not usually favour the contemplative life.

'Well, then, John, what have we got this morning?' he said, aware he sounded cheerful and relaxed as his secretary came in. A second later he was aware that John Shaw was not. 'Is there something wrong?'

'You'd better come at once, sir,' said John Shaw, twitching with anxiety. 'There's been an accident.'

He did not need to say any more. That one word 'accident' was enough to pull Ralph out of his chair and propel him towards the door.

'Where?' he asked, as they walked smartly downstairs.

'Cogging mill . . . it's . . .' He seemed to hesitate.

'Come now, John, this is no time for . . .' said Ralph, and so John Shaw interrupted him.

'It's Mr Lennox, sir!'

He almost thought he had not heard it, that the swish of the glass doors opening had distorted what he heard, and so he went on briskly to ask if Lennox had not been the name mentioned.

'You do understand, sir?' said John Shaw. Ralph looked into his face – it was bleached and afraid. John had always admired Andrew.

In that moment he did understand and began to run towards the cogging mill, not noticing that a path cleared before him, oblivious to the powerful current of shock that charged the air.

Entering the huge shed, dark and hot, illuminated by the opening furnaces and the flash of molten steel beneath the giant rollers, he could not at once see anything. He stopped in his tracks, terrified to go on, to find anything, for he knew in his bones something more than dreadful had happened and for a moment could not face the truth.

'Over here!' The voice he knew at once. It was Vincent Douglas, the medical officer. But it was not Ralph he was summoning but a stretcher party coming up behind him with terrible haste. He remembered ordering that stretcher with Andrew – they had made a great many tasteless jokes in the process, hoping it should never be used. He felt his gorge rise, sick with terror. He wanted to turn and go, but he knew he must follow them. Andrew really needed him now.

The little huddle broke away at the sight of him and the stretcher bearers. But Ralph only saw Andrew, collapsed like some great statue on the dirty floor, a Greek god toppled by barbarians. His face, that mild, handsome face, was contorted by pain and there was a rush of blood from his mouth and temple. His chest rose and fell violently, and he gulped at the air like a drowning man.

Ralph squatted beside him, and grabbed his hand. Drew clasped him fervently and seemed to smile. My God, how can he? thought Ralph. He seemed to be trying to speak, and although Ralph at first urged him to conserve his strength, Andrew's persistence silenced him. He had to speak, Ralph realized, before it was too late.

'T . . . te . . . t . . .' The breathlessness made it impossible, but Andrew, screwing up his face, made the most valiant effort. 'A . . . A . . .' And then his voice failed completely; indeed, his whole body collapsed from tension into inertia. The doctor bent over him and listened to his chest and then checked a pulse. Ralph stared across at him, utterly bewildered, and watched as Douglas shook his head slowly, answering the unspoken question. And then Ralph saw the men standing about them slowly take off their caps to honour the dead.

'What happened?' he asked again, for he was getting no answers. They were anxious to spare his feelings, he suspected. 'God damn it, tell me!'

'It seems,' said John Shaw, nervously stirring his coffee, 'at least, what I can gather is, that there was a loose bolt in the gantry and the chain at the front had been removed. Apparently, Mr Lennox was going along it briskly – you know how he does. I mean,' he corrected himself, 'how he did, and that section of the gantry gave under his weight.'

'And he fell sixty feet?' said Ralph, turning to Dr Douglas.

'Yes,' said Douglas, 'so that one of his ribs punctured his lungs.'

'Go on,' said Ralph.

'Are you sure, sir?' said John Shaw.

'I have to know, I have to!' said Ralph, steadfastly. He was not sure why, only that he must learn all the dreadful details. 'So the actual cause of death was?'

'A collapsed lung and severe internal bleeding.'

'Thank you,' said Ralph, and noted the facts down. He wanted to see the sequence of events on paper. Perhaps then he could make sense of it, see a pattern in it. But the words dissolved in front of him, and he could see only Andrew lying on the dirty floor, senselessly dead.

He shook his head and screwed up the piece of paper, wishing he could screw up the image in his mind. He wished he had never seen it, had never left his office where he had been in such a tranquil state only that morning, only an hour ago.

But it was a lifetime ago. He felt the age in his bones, felt all the savage sadness of the world press down upon him while the devil, who called himself God and ruled the world, laughed long and hard at this fresh injustice. The wicked senselessness of this could only have been conceived by a supernatural being. It was too evil to have been ordained by the mere workings of chance. Chance would not have loosened a rusty bolt and sent to his death a fine young man whose wife was expecting his child. Chance would have been more merciful.

Then why? Ralph appealed silently to this unknown Devil-God to whom he had never prayed before, and in whom he had never believed, but in whom he fervently believed now that he wanted a scapegoat. It proved the wickedness of God to him, for a truly just God would have sent Ralph along that gantry to stab his lungs with a broken rib. If a man should have died at Garbridge it should have been him, the feckless idiot who could leave nothing behind except his own folly, and not Andrew, not wise, loving Andrew, who had everything to lose and left so many grieving. It could not simply be chance, such a thing.

He reached out and took up his cup of coffee. He sipped it and found it sticky with sugar and foul-tasting. That happened when people died, he noticed banally. One found one's drinks laced with sugar. God only knew why they did it, but he had seen the doctor shovelling sugar into his cup.

He looked at the two men across his desk, Douglas and John Shaw. They were silent, but he felt the waves of their sympathy and it destroyed him. He felt sapped and wanted to break down, to scream like a child and weep like a woman, long and bitterly. But he had a sense that he could not. That was not allowed any more. He had to carry on. He could not give way to the chaos that his guts wished to wrench up and destroy him with. In the past he had done that and clung to others to support him. But now he had to be the pillar, the rock of strength for them all. They needed him and his strength, all of it. He had to sacrifice his own grief to the comfort of others.

He put down the cup of coffee and said to Douglas, his voice dry with control, 'I know you're not my sister's physician, Douglas, but I wonder if you can predict how she is going to react to this. I imagine that there is a risk to the child involved.'

He went with his mother to Saxe-Coburg Street directly after lunch. He changed, because there was blood on his clothes, but his mother did not go into black. She did not want to alarm Alix unduly. Mrs Erskine had taken it well. She had cried a little, and then mastered herself, at once concerned for Alix and the baby. They, after all, were the real victims of this.

As they drove over, they decided Ralph should break the

news because he had been with Andrew at the last.

Alix was resting upstairs and Ralph went up directly, leaving his mother to explain to the servants. One, he observed, she sent to fetch her doctor.

He had not been in the habit of going into his sister's bedroom since her marriage, and wondered if the simple fact of his appearing there would alarm her. But she seemed pleased he had come to see her.

The room was furnished for comfort, unlike the drawing room downstairs, and in its banal way struck Ralph as very pleasant. There were flowers about the place – more hyacinths – and Alix was stretched on a large chintz-covered sofa, dressed only in her nightgown, a light rug across her knees.

'I've been so lazy today,' she said, when he bent to kiss her. 'But they say seven months is tiring, so I'm allowed to be lazy, I think.'

'Yes, I think so,' he said, caressing her warm hand for a moment. 'My dear . . .' he began, but could not continue. She was so serene and beautiful in that moment. Her cheeks were lightly flushed for the tiled stove was blasting out heat (he could feel it on his back); the broad, ruffled collar of her nightgown was hanging loose to reveal the curve of swollen, milk-filled breasts and below this, under a sweep of white lawn, was the bulge of her child, large but not ungainly, and such that he wanted to touch it and sense the life inside.

'Have you come to tell me your troubles, Ralph?' she asked. 'You should, you know. Drew and I have been so worried about you. We always used to talk in the past, didn't we?'

'I'm not here for that, I'm afraid,' he said, sitting down beside her.

That 'I'm afraid' seemed to change her mood. She caught its disturbed inflection and stared at him intently for a moment.

'You are going to tell me something terrible,' she said. He had looked away from her, unable to bear her gaze, ashamed of what he must unleash on her.

'Yes,' he said. 'It's Drew . . .'

'He's dead, isn't he?' she cut in. 'You wouldn't be sitting here like this if he wasn't, would you? I can tell, I can feel it.'

'Yes, he's dead.' The words were brutally straight but Alix loathed euphemisms. 'He was killed this morning at Garbridge. A gantry collapsed and he fell sixty feet and punctured his lungs with a broken rib.'

After a minute she said, 'I'm glad you've been straight with me.'

'I was there when he died. He tried to speak, to say something, but he couldn't.'

'Was he in pain?'

'I'm afraid he was, but it was quick. He died very quickly, about fifteen minutes or so after the fall.'

'He always wanted to die in his bed . . . I suppose we all do,' said Alix, and he felt her shake and twitch as the truth sank in. 'Dear God, no!' she exclaimed. 'No, no, no!'

He tried to embrace her but she refused it. In a moment she had gone from a dreadful calm to a worse anger. She kicked off the rug and got to her feet, almost sprang up, regardless of her seven month burden. He tried to take her hand again, to make her sit, but she would not be restrained.

'Why? Why?' she exploded, throwing up her hands and walking away from him. 'Why in God's name?' She began to pace up and down. 'What have we done? Where's the justice in this? Are we supposed to be miserable? Who is punishing us, Ralph, who? What have we done?'

'Alix, I think you should sit down and . . . and . . .'

'And have a cup of tea!' she interrupted vehemently. 'For God's sake, Ralph! Don't sit there so grave and good. Aren't you angry, for Christ's sake?'

'Yes, but I have to think of you and the child. It's what Drew would have wanted. You have to try and be calm . . .'

'How on earth can I be that, Ralph?' she said, stopping her pacing. 'You of all people should know, you must know how . . . how . . .' She fought back her tears.

'Alix, you must cry,' he said, going over to her. 'Anger won't help. Tears will.'

'No!' she said, pushing him away. 'Don't you dare tell me what to do, how to behave – get out!'

'Alix, are you sure?'

'Get out!' she ordered. 'And don't come back!'

'I will be just outside,' he said.

He sat at the top of the stairs, exhausted. His mother came up.

'You shouldn't have left her,' she said.

'She kicked me out. She wants to be alone.'

'She shouldn't be alone.'

'It's what she wants, Mother.'

'She will not know what she wants,' said Mrs Erskine, going to the door and tapping on it. 'Alix, my dear?'

The door opened slowly and Ralph turned to see her standing in the doorway, her face still full of fury. She looked at each of them in turn and said, 'Do you think we are cursed? Is that why we must suffer like this?'

'My dear, it is as God wills,' said Mrs Erskine.

'No!' said Alix, with absolute contempt. 'No, no, no!' And Ralph saw her raise her hand as if she were about to strike out in her anger. But she did not lower her hand in a blow. It fell, it seemed to Ralph, with its own force, because suddenly she had bent double and shrieked out with pain.

12

It seemed to Alix that she had been lying there for many weeks, although she knew it had been only a few days. But time had lost sense of itself in the muffled room where the blinds were kept down, and the horses in the street outside walked over cobbles shrouded in straw. Perhaps there was black crêpe on the door knocker because she was dead as well, and lying like this because she was a corpse. She might as well be one.

But she was not. As she turned her head a little and looked across the room to the fireplace she saw the handsome tiled stove standing in front of it, gleaming slightly in the dull light. Andrew's stove . . .

She heard the door open but did not turn to see who it was. Often people came in and did things quietly, without speaking a word to her. But this visitor spoke.

'Alix?'

Ralph, her brother. She felt herself smile.

'Hello,' she said. Her voice was feeble, as if she had never used it before.

She heard him walk around the room and then saw him standing over her. His clothes were very black, but he carried a great bunch of coloured flowers.

'The men at the works sent these for you,' he said, laying them down near her. She could smell it now; the unmistakable scent of lilac – such as Drew had once gathered for her one May morning at St Andrews. She closed her eyes and drowned in the smell, remembering the moment. It had been so early, about five, but the sun had been high and bright. Everything had seemed unimaginably perfect – and then she had walked back to Hall for breakfast and there on the lawn, on the sun-lit green grass, lay a white bird gored to death. Now, that seemed like a terrible omen.

'Am I alive?' she said, wondering if the lilac was not to decorate her coffin.

'Yes, thank God, you are.' He smiled and bent and kissed her, a chaste, brotherly kiss. She remembered the kisses Andrew had given her, the kisses and the lovemaking they had had in this very bed in which she now lay, alone.

'I'm alone,' she said to Ralph.

'You have me, and there's Mother.' But she shook her head. He could not know what she meant. He had never been married. He could not know the private world between them, created in all those nocturnal conversations, in the warmth of each other's arms, under the embrace of the blankets. He could not know how empty that bed felt, after she had fought so long to keep his great legs out of her territory. She would give anything now to have him appropriate all the covers and fling a sleepy arm across her pillow.

Ralph looked sadly down at her, his hands in his pockets.

Now she would be like him, perpetually lonely and melancholy. If he could not understand what she had lost, she now understood what he had endured.

'I've arranged for the baby to be buried with Drew,' he said. 'If that's what you want.'

'Yes. Yes, I do.'

Her little boy. He had lived only an hour. He was too weak and too tiny to live, they said.

Ralph reached out and stroked her forehead. She saw there were tears in his eyes and felt them in her own. She had not cried yet, not in sadness, only in pain. His cool fingers touched her forehead and then moved to wipe away that first tear.

'My dear,' he said so softly that he might have been speaking to himself. 'Whatever shall we do?'

She did not know. She did not think she would ever know.

Part Five

1

August, 1912

The day was as hot and dry as a roasting oven, and Jessie, standing as inconspicuously as she could in the crowd, wondered why she had agreed to come. Her free time was precious enough these days and she would rather have spent it with the girls or even idling over a book, but Alix had been insistent. She had hauled Jessie's conscience over the coals, taunting her with accusations of cowardice and complacency, with such ruthlessness that in the end Jessie had agreed to come. She had sensed that if she had not, Alix would have become impossible.

They had to make allowances, of course, and they all had, but there was no doubt that Alix's strident suffragism was not only disturbing but downright annoying. If she had been keen before, now she was fanatical and Jessie had always mistrusted fanatics, religious or otherwise. She believed in the same cause, actively supported it indeed, but she could not comprehend Alix's dangerous passion. It was destroying her. She was no longer the same woman.

So here they were in Leith outside the gates of a stocking factory in the hour between the change of shifts when the girls and women whom the place chiefly employed were going away or coming to their work. Alix and one or two other WSPU members were standing on a makeshift platform, a 'Votes for Women' banner hanging behind them and propaganda posters nailed to the front. Others attempted to sell knots of white, purple and green ribbons (the WSPU colours) and copies of *The Vote* to women in the crowd who, Jessie suspected, had not the money to spare for such things. Alix was the most striking figure amongst them, dressed in a dazzling white linen dress emblazoned by a silk shoulder sash in the WSPU colours, her broad white straw hat trimmed with violets. She had never put on black for Andrew, saying he would have hated her to do so. She spoke with animation, and had great presence, but Jessie could not help thinking that what she said was self-destructive madness.

'Sisters,' she was saying, 'the time has long since passed when petitions and processions might help us. We have tried time and time again to persuade the government by force of numbers, by spectacle, by oratory – and it has come to nothing. We are still slaves! Yes, slaves! We are still condemned to injustice despite all our efforts. We can, therefore, no longer be merely protesters calling for change. It is not enough. One cannot fight with a shout – no matter how loud – one must fight with a sword! For we are at war now! They have declared war upon our just cause. When Marion Dunlop was imprisoned for merely reminding this most forgetful government that the Bill of Rights permits *all* citizens to petition their king, she was denied the rights of a political prisoner and treated like a common criminal. This is not justice, this is war! And so we must respond with war!'

There was a burst of applause at this point, but Jessie did not join in. Alix was being deliberately misleading. Marion Dunlop had reminded the government of the Bill of Rights by painting them on the wall of St Stephen's Hall at Westminster. It really was unfair of Alix to misrepresent this to a crowd of silly girls who had only stopped to giggle at the suffragettes. Her rhetoric was too irresistible. Jessie could see that her charisma was affecting some of the girls. They were staring ardently up at her.

'So, sisters, you must be asking yourselves what you can do to help win this war – and please don't feel that your efforts would be wasted. An army needs privates as much as generals, if not more so. What should you do then? You should join the WSPU – the Women's Social and Political

Union – which is the only national suffrage organization that counts, the only organization which is doing something, that understands the situation as it is. The others who claim to be helping this cause are doing no such thing. They have no sense of the urgency of this cause, that the battle is upon us *now*! And the WSPU is the only suffrage society absolutely committed to the improvement of the lot of the working woman. Come to us, lasses, come to us, and we will liberate ourselves! And we will not come meekly, our heads bowed to beg for what is ours by right! No, we will come with fire and the sword and make them beg for mercy for withholding our liberty! Join us now, sisters, and you will be part of it. Your names will go down into glory as the women who changed the world!'

She finished by throwing open her arms in a gesture of welcome to any new recruits, and evidently encouraged by the cheering, actually helped one girl up on to the platform as if she were a saved soul at a revivalist meeting.

Jessie found it all too easy to resist the enthusiasm of the moment and shuffled from foot to foot, wishing she might slip away. She wanted nothing to do with such extreme opinions, they could only do more harm than good, but loyalty to Alix kept her there. She had been through so much, suffered so terribly, that Jessie could not desert her because of politics. But try as she might, Jessie could not help but feel the awkwardness this difference imposed upon them. She was angry, despite herself, to see Alix with her rolling rhetoric capturing the hearts and minds of girls who had not been taught to resist such appeals.

She watched with some alarm as a police constable made his way through the crowd. If Alix were to be arrested . . .

'Have you finished now, ladies? Any more folk here and this would have been unlawful assembly.'

'There are no laws for those who have no votes, Constable,' said Alix, smartly. 'But we are finished now, and I thank you for your restraint. Perhaps you are sympathetic. Here, accept a copy of our magazine with my compliments. If it does not interest you, your wife might like to look at it.'

He took it a little grudgingly and said, 'Well, that's as

maybe, missus. If you could all just move on now, please . . .'

'Yes, of course!' said Alix, beginning to take down the banner.

This show of obedience to the police relieved Jessie greatly. Perhaps Alix had only been speaking metaphorically.

They walked back to Alix's motor together, carrying the various banners and pamphlets. The motor was permanently decorated with a 'Votes for Women' placard and was even painted green. She drove the car herself now, although when Andrew was alive they had kept a chauffeur. But much of Alix's obedience to convention had gone with Andrew. Alone, she was proving herself very radical.

'You really should join us, Jessie,' she said. Her tone was emollient now. She was obviously pleased by the way the meeting had gone. 'I'm sure if you had spoken, we would have got a dozen more names on the list.'

'I don't know about that . . .' said Jessie.

'I simply don't see why you don't commit yourself,' said Alix, with a touch of exasperation, as she crank-started the engine.

'I am committed,' said Jessie, when Alix had settled into the driver's seat.

'That is not what I mean by commitment. What is the point of believing in a thing if you will not stand up and fight for it? There is no point, is there?'

'I don't think there is any point in breaking the law.'

'There are no laws for those who have no votes,' she said, glibly repeating what she had said earlier like a dogma.

Jessie sighed quietly as they drove away. It was difficult to argue with her. She had a dismissive line for everything.

'I don't think you should encourage girls like that to break the law.'

'Why not?'

'Because they don't know any better. They haven't had enough schooling to decide the issue for themselves. They take what you say as gospel because you can talk like a preacher.'

'Better that I get them than a preacher. A preacher won't change their wretched lives.'

'Will you, really?'

'How can you doubt it? Really, Jessie, sometimes I despair of you.'

'I think you'll ruin a few of them if you are not careful. They would be better joining their trades unions.'

'The unions have done nothing for the cause.'

'There is more to this than the vote, Alix.'

'No, the vote is the key. You can't ignore that. If we don't have the vote, we have nothing. We cannot let men control legislation directed at us.'

'It won't change everything. It's not a magic spell. There are working men with votes who still starve. The vote on its own won't help those girls. Better pay will, education will, better hours will, not just the vote.'

'And those things will never come without it – and I am sick to death of this pussy footing around because we are afraid of losing the moral high ground. We have that so securely that no matter what we do, we are still a just cause.'

'I can't agree with that.'

'Well, that is your loss,' said Alix sharply. 'If you can't join us, then you will be the one who must answer to your own cowardice. You'll be the one who must answer your daughters when they ask you what you did.'

'Alix, what has got into you?' Jessie could not help exclaiming. That last barb had been too much to take. 'To talk as if this is war – it's madness!'

'It seems perfectly straightforward to me.'

To Jessie's infinite relief they had got to Frederick Street, and she jumped out of the car with only the briefest of farewells. Alix drove off very smartly, as if she were on a charger, galloping across the battlefield.

Jessie went into the Fleur de Lys feeling rattled, wondering if militant stones might soon come flying through her own windows. She climbed the stairs wearily and met Chloe on the landing.

'Did you have a nice time with Mrs Lennox?' she asked politely.

489

'Nice is not exactly the word I would choose,' said Jessie. 'What have you been up to?'

'Helping Monsieur with the preserves.'

'Oh, thank you, Chloe, that will have been useful.'

'I didn't mind. He let me eat the squashed ones.'

'Then you won't want any supper?'

'I didn't have that many. Monsieur ate quite a lot.'

Although Jessie had always hated jam making, which inevitably came in the fiercest heat of the summer when the fruit was at its sweetest, she would have preferred it to that afternoon and the quarrel with Alix. She felt guilty for quarrelling with her. She should, she knew, have kept her opinions to herself, but she had found that when provoked she had opinions as strongly held as Alix's. It was a point on which neither of them could or would give; a depressing thing, considering that they were supposed to be working to the same end.

They went into the sitting room and Jessie found the rest of her family having tea. She called them family, although Monsieur Auguste, Molly and the two kitchen girls who lived in were not relations, because that was how it felt.

'A dozen bottles of raspberry done today, Mrs Hamilton,' said Molly, as she came in. 'And I have to say that French way of doing it is just as good . . .'

Jessie smiled a little abstractedly. She was thinking of Alix alone in her house in Saxe-Coburg Street. How could she possibly have have been angry with Alix? She should have been more sympathetic. For it struck her coming back to the Fleur de Lys, which was her home and full of people she cared for, that she had no need of battles or causes. She had purpose enough, more than enough, with a business to run and children to raise. Alix had only a void because everything she had loved and hoped for had been destroyed. No wonder she needed a cause, no wonder she dreamt of action: because there was nothing else for her but raging emptiness.

'Will you take tea, ma chère?' asked Monsieur Auguste.

'In a minute, please,' she said, her conscience prompted. 'I have to telephone someone first.'

She went to the telephone in her office and asked the operator to get her Alix's number.

'Alix? Hello – it's Jessie.'

'Hello! Have you changed your mind then?'

'No, but I think I should apologize. I was a bit sharp with you. I'm sorry, I wasn't thinking. I wondered, would you like to come and eat with us tonight?'

'Thanks, but I can't. I've got a committee meeting.'

'Oh, I see. Perhaps another time?'

'Yes, perhaps,' said Alix. 'Goodbye then.'

The coolness in her voice was unmistakable. She no longer wished to know, let alone compromise. She only consorted with her fellow militants and candidates for martyrdom.

2

Hamish Anderson hesitated on the doorstep. Although he had never cared much for conventional morality, which in his opinion generally covered a bleeding sore of hypocrisy, he could not help but feel awkward calling on a young widow at such a time of night. But nine o'clock was what she had said in that typical lordly Erskine fashion (so irritatingly compelling), and he had had to come, although it was quite absurd that he should be there. What on earth, after all, could she want to see him about?

They had met at a Labour Party meeting at which she had spoken, offering the WSPU's support for any Labour candidates at the next election. It had been surprising to see her there. He had always thought that women of her class went into purdah when their husbands died, enjoying the extravagance of mourning clothes and an expensive show of grief which no working woman could afford. She had not even been dressed in black and her seriousness impressed him. In fact, it was difficult not to be impressed by her. She was a handsome quean: tall, slender and determined-looking. He had been quite pleased when after the meeting she had come up to speak to him. Although he had met her once or twice at Garbridge, he was surprised she should remember him.

'Mr Anderson, isn't it?' she said, putting out her hand to him. 'I wondered if I might find you here. My brother tells me you are hoping to be adopted as a candidate.'

'Yes, but I am not that hopeful,' he said. 'There are better men for the job than I.'

'That won't get you anywhere.' She smiled. 'For what it is worth, you have my support.'

'I'm sure it's worth a great deal. That was a fine speech, Mrs Lennox. Perhaps you should be our candidate.'

'Ah – if only,' she said. 'Well, our time will come, Mr Anderson.'

Hamish wondered if she was simply fantastically brave or if she had not loved her husband. He decided on the former, suspecting that if it had been the latter, she would have made more of a show of grief.

'We must talk properly, you know,' she had said, and had told him to come and see her at Saxe-Coburg Street in a few days' time. Without knowing why, he had agreed.

Now he stood there hesitating, his hand on the bell, drawn there he was afraid to admit by motives other than socialism. When a pretty woman issued such an invitation what lonely man could have refused it? In this he knew he was no better than anyone else.

He had no opportunity to break the appointment because the door opened before him and he was faced by three women obviously about to leave. Behind them in the hall he could see Alexandra Lennox, like the flame of a candle in a white dress and he felt his bowels turn over at the sight of such incandescent beauty. He felt elated and then sickened. He had no right to feel like that about a woman who had so recently belonged to another man.

The other women, clearly suffragists, with their 'Votes for Women' badges and pamphlets under their arms, were soon on their way, and they were alone together, she on the threshold and he still on the doorstep.

'Well, Mr Anderson?' she said.

He followed her into the house. It struck him as clean and handsome, smelling sweetly of furniture polish.

'We'll go in here,' she said, and took him into what was clearly the dining room, except that it had, by the look of it, just been used for a meeting of some kind. She sat down at the head of the table and indicated that he was to do the same.

'Cigarette?' she asked, and having taken one herself, pushed the box towards him.

For a while they were silent, enjoying the quiet relief of a cigarette. He wondered if he should speak but she seemed quite happy to be silent, which relieved him because he could not think what to say.

'I suppose you are wondering why I've asked you here today,' she said eventually.

'Well, yes . . .' he admitted.

'It must seem a little strange to you, I suppose,' she said, getting up and beginning to walk back and forth.

'Well, it's not what I expected,' he began.

'Did you expect yards of crêpe and black-edged hand-kerchiefs?' she asked, and then without permitting him to answer, continued, 'Yes, I imagine you would. But, frankly, I detest that sort of thing – and so did he.'

'I can believe that,' said Hamish. 'He didn't strike me as a slave to convention. I mean, a man in his position, well . . .'

'Could so easily be like my brother?' She smiled. 'All convention and paternalism? No, he wasn't like that, not in the least. Oh,' she added with a warm burst of enthusiasm, 'I knew I was right to ask you here.'

'But why have you asked me?'

'I want your opinion on something.'

'My opinion?' He could not help smiling. 'What does Mrs Lennox want with my humble opinion?'

'You should stop being so modest,' she said. 'It will get you nowhere. I am asking you because I hear good things of you, excellent things – that you are committed and devoted to your work.'

'Well,' he said, 'I've always believed that I was wedded to socialism.'

'Then you can see the thing clearly. You know exactly what needs to be done.'

'I can't say that I am short of ideas.'

'So you will give me an honest opinion?'

'If I can. But I cannot promise that it'll be what you want to hear.'

'Oh, don't misread me, please, Mr Anderson. I'm not how I seem. For all this,' she said, gesturing about her, 'I want to stand the world on its head. I'm not just like my brother with his model housing and his workers' institutes.'

'He has done good work, Mrs Lennox,' said Hamish.

'Yes, yes, but you and I know that isn't enough.'

'Rome wasn't built in a day . . .'

'Please!' she exclaimed. 'Don't let us descend to clichés.'

'You think I'm too pragmatic, don't you?' he said, vaguely amused. 'But, Mrs Lennox, you must realize that politics is a practical business. You canna change the world without getting your hands a little dirty. Perhaps your brother has gone about things in the spirit of old-fashioned paternalism, but you can't deny that there's far less injustice and misery at Garbridge than there was. That's why I left. There was nothing left for me to do there. You can't just dismiss his work like that.'

'You are very fair,' she said. 'But I still say it's not enough. It's one little flower bed on the wasteland. I know I shall not be content until the whole of that wasteland is green and bright with flowers! And that cannot come from above – it must come from below, from the people themselves.'

'You want a revolution, Mrs Lennox.'

'Of course. Don't you?'

'Yes, but . . .'

'Now, Mr Anderson, don't "yes, but" me!' she said, not angrily, but with a persuasive charm which he found unsettling. 'I have not asked you here to be a "Yes, but" man.'

'You've asked for my opinion,' he said, unable to let this

pass, no matter how winningly it might be put. 'But perhaps you have already decided what you want to hear. You don't want opinions, but confirmation.'

'Perhaps. Very well then – shall we see if that is the case? I wanted to ask you, as someone absolutely committed to fundamental social change, to what lengths you would be prepared to go to achieve that end.'

He whistled softly, a little staggered by the question.

'What have you got in mind?' he asked, unable to keep the astonishment from his voice. 'Are you going the same way as Mrs Pankhurst and her troops?'

'Well, shall we say I have been called to the colours.'

'Christ!' he could not help exclaiming. Her coolness was extraordinary. 'And will you . . .?'

'Will I act? I can't tell you that, can I? Unless I can trust you.'

'You can,' he said. 'But then, why do you want to know whether I think it is right or not? Surely you must have decided already.'

'I have,' she said. 'But I need to know whether we have your support. Will women be the only ones able to take this ultimate step for their liberation?'

'Obviously, I can't speak for the party,' said Hamish. 'But for myself, I would say, act. It's a very powerful thing for a woman to do. It says more than a thousand petitions for a woman to . . .'

'To take up the sword? Yes, it is powerful, isn't it? So you are not such a pragmatist, after all.'

'I am,' he said. 'I can see the use of this. You could disrupt the whole nation if you put your minds to it. In fact, I've often thought, if I had the ear of your Mrs Pankhurst, I should tell her to call a general strike. If the women downed tools, it would make a damnable mess.'

'Yes!' she said. 'You men would all starve! I will mention it to her. No one could ignore us then.'

They talked for hours, enveloping themselves in a fug of cigarette smoke and throwing about wild notions, drunk on idealism. She was a true visionary, and more than that because she was prepared to do more than dream. She intended to act, by God, she would act and kick away every remaining shackle of her conventional life. 'I was a prisoner,' she said, 'a happy prisoner, but when the walls fell down I saw what a wicked, rotten place the world really was. And what could I do? Sit and cry – no, I could not! I could not waste myself on that. So I have given myself to my work, just as you have.'

'They can't take that away from you, can they?'

'No,' she said. 'They can't, thank God! If they could, life would be meaningless. There is no life without this struggle.'

When she said that he had wanted to kiss her, not like a woman, but like a comrade, to show that he recognized and understood exactly what she said. Love had cheated them both and would not come again. There could only be comradeship; a forging of two souls in the fire of a common cause. That night he sensed they had made such a pact between them. They would never claim each other emotionally, but spiritually they were as one. How this could be, he could not understand. He only knew when he finally rose to say good night that it was so.

'You will come again?' she asked.

'Surely,' he said, and walked back to Fountainbridge, reeling.

3

September, 1912

The brick, carefully wrapped in brown paper, looked quite innocuous, like a parcel of books perhaps, a three-volume novel for the lady's holiday amusement. Alix had put this package into a light Japanese basket with long handles and walked down the Scores swinging it gently, smiling charmingly at anyone she happened to recognize. Even some gentlemen whom she did not recognize tipped their hats to her, because she had dressed with special care for this important occasion. The écru lace dress with soft violet-coloured trimmings and that somewhat large but undeniably dashing hat were perhaps too smart for St Andrews, even at the height of the holiday season. Tweeds, white flannel and boaters were more the thing, but Alix, decorously veiled in Brussels point lace, was there to make a point. No vicious journalist could portray her as a hysterical, unwomanly harpy in a tweed tailor-made. They would have to see her as she knew she was – and she could not fail to be aware of those admiring glances – an elegant, beautiful woman, who nevertheless . . .

Who nevertheless is about to . . . She smiled to herself, relishing the joke of it. It was wonderful what she planned to do. She had been ecstatic when she thought of it, and now, standing at the corner of the foot of the Scores, by the red sandstone pile of the Grand Hotel, she knew she had not been wrong. Her quarry lay before her, a hive of activity, just as she had known it would be at that time of year. There was a cluster of expensive motors parked there. One could smell the money, smell the privilege and smell the power. Alix, because she had been brought up with these things, could recognize them at once. The Royal and Ancient clubhouse was a bastion of all these things at that moment, and Alix knew that inside that stunted Greek Temple devoted to the god of Golf, one might find more MPs than one could ever hope for during a late night reading of a Fisheries Bill in the House. She knew, in that moment, how Guy Fawkes must have felt on November 4th, laying his charge. This was a God given opportunity and it was not to be wasted.

She strolled across the road towards the clubhouse and passed groups of men in flat caps and ridiculously broad breeches who were standing around smoking. She was pleased to notice that her arrival caused some of them to throw away their expensive cigars. What foolish chivalry! She would soon show them.

She stopped at the white picket fence that edged the clubhouse terrace overlooking the eighteenth green. On the green a man who looked suspiciously like Lord Fergusson was attempting, with little success, to sink a putt. How splendid! she thought. I shall enjoy putting him off his game!

'Can you see all right?' said a man beside her, moving so that she could have a better view.

'Oh, perfectly, thank you,' she said, glancing at him because she had felt him look her over. He looked like a stuffy young Englishman, an officer on leave perhaps.

Lord Fergusson, for it was he, had at last sunk his putt.

'Oh, well done, sir!' exclaimed the man beside her, and clapped, as did some others. Disgusted by this show of obsequiousness, she decided he must be part of Fergusson's house party at Rossie Park, a vulgar place where she and Andrew had once had to endure a weekend.

Now, Alix, now! she told herself, for Fergusson was coming towards them. In a moment he would recognize her and speak to her. Then it would be too late. Now!

She steeled herself, for suddenly her resolve was wavering. She glanced again at Fergusson and his ugly face, which for a moment summed up everything she detested and convinced her again. She turned away from the green and faced the plate glass windows of the clubhouse.

Inside, like gold fish in a tank, sat her prey, lounging in armchairs, drinking and smoking, blissfully unaware of what was about to happen. Gently she swung her basket, taking the handles in both hands to improve her aim. She swung it with more violence, feeling the weight of the brick beginning to give the thing its own momentum. It felt suddenly like an animal which must be released, and running forward two or three steps she let it go. It soared away, no longer a brick but a wonderful projectile instead, especially engineered, she felt, to collide with and destroy that acreage of smug plate glass which faced her.

For a second or two time seemed suspended as she watched her brick fly towards the window, and then, when at last it touched it, the normal clock sprang back into action. All was noise and confusion. At first it was difficult to see exactly how much damage she had done, but soon she saw the men in the clubhouse cowering and gibbering like monkeys in the zoo. They looked very thoroughly upset and she realized that she was laughing.

She turned and found herself facing a sea of faces. Some of them were white with shock, others red with rage. Lord Fergusson's was irresistibly apoplectic.

'Votes for women, my lord!' she said to him, and sank into a deep curtsey, a great actress acknowledging her bewildered audience.

Ralph, when he was driving over to St Andrews, summoned by an irate Lord Fergusson, had wanted to be angry with her. He had been quite prepared to be, but found, as the policeman unlocked the door of her cell, that any coherent expression of indignation he might have planned, simply collapsed. That grim passageway, smelling of sweat and God-only-knew-what, with its grey walls and bare bulbs, was enough to make him feel guilty without having done anything and he imagined she would be quite distraught. The humiliation of being locked up in such a place would be reproach enough. He could not heap on any further injury.

So he followed the constable into the cell, prepared to find her in tears, prepared to comfort her. He expected she might throw herself into his arms in the relief of seeing a friendly face and the means of her liberation from this awful place. After all, he had just arranged for her bail.

But she did not. She did not even turn to see who had come in.

Oddly, she was standing in the middle of the cell, facing the small window set high in the wall, which was only an apology for a window because it let in very little light. She had taken off her hat and gloves, and these pieces of discarded elegance lay incongruously on the Spartan wooden bench which he imagined would often serve as a bed. She was standing with her arms folded, and he saw her scratch at her temple as they came in, presumably a nervous impulse from being deprived of cigarettes. She had begun to smoke very heavily since Drew's death. He felt the tension in the air, felt the strangeness between them which had been growing more and more apparent over the last few months.

Although he recognized everything about this woman, from the style of dress to the way that her pale hair was arranged, he found he scarcely recognized Alix, his sister. And when he said, 'Alix, it's me . . .' he wondered if she would answer to that name any more.

'You can go home now, Mrs Lennox,' said the constable.

'Why?' she said, turning at last. 'Surely you can't drop the charges?'

'Oh no, I'm afraid we can't do that – but we can't keep you here overnight, and the magistrate can't see you until tomorrow. This isn't a place for a lady.'

'Is it not?' she said, quizzically. 'Well, Ralph, how much did that cost you, I wonder?'

He was so astonished by this question, so harshly put, that he could not think what to say for a moment.

'It is extraordinary what money can do,' she went on, picking up her hat from the bench. 'Well, I suppose you want to take me home now and scold me.'

'For God's sake, Alix, this isn't a game!' he exclaimed.

'Oh, I know that,' she said, calmly. 'You don't have a cigarette do you, Constable?'

He produced a crumpled packet of some cheap brand. She frowned at the sight of them and declined. Alix only smoked expensive Turkish cigarettes. The constable looked relieved, as if he would not have been able to cope with the business of lighting a cigarette for such a grand lady. Ralph suspected his hands would have shaken. He looked out of his depth. As out of his depth as I am, and she's my sister! he thought ruefully.

'Well, let's go then,' he said, anxious to be away from the place.

They drove back to Allansfield in silence. Ralph refrained from issuing a barrage of questions, because he feared the answers would make him so angry that he might lose control of the car. Her silence was provocative enough, and when finally they walked across the lawn at Allansfield to where their mother was sitting, he knew that his tolerance could not last much longer. Her manner had destroyed in him the will to understand.

Mrs Erskine was lounging calmly under an awning, while the tea things were set up. It was an innocent scene, beautifully ordered, and certainly not one for dreadful revelations. She smiled and waved as they approached.

'Ah, everyone back for tea, how nice,' she said. 'What have you been doing, my dears?'

This artless question was the spark which lit the explosion. For as she spoke, Alix threw herself into one of the basket chairs with a look of such petulance that Ralph could not hold his tongue any longer.

'You might well ask!' he snapped, glaring at Alix. 'Would you like to know, Mother, what damnable mess I have had to sort out this afternoon?'

'Ralph!' Mrs Erskine began to protest, but Alix cut in, 'I might have known you wouldn't understand!'

'Understand? How on earth do you expect me to understand? I am not a bloody anarchist!'

'No, you wouldn't have the guts to be,' said Alix. 'Such a wretched conformist as you. So spineless!'

'I would say breaking the law like that is pretty spineless, Alix. Where's the courage in throwing a brick through a window? Any fool could do that. Only a fool could do it, come to think of it.'

'What on earth is this?' exclaimed Mrs Erskine. 'What is going on?'

'Alix has been clever enough to get herself arrested this afternoon, for throwing a brick through the R and A windows.'

'Surely not?' said Mrs Erskine, turning to her daughter for confirmation.

'He's right, Mother,' she said lightly. 'I did it for the cause.'

'For the cause . . . for your silly Votes for Women? Oh, Alix, I don't . . . I don't know what to say.'

'Then don't say anything,' said Alix. 'I don't think anything further needs to be said.'

'Do you think I'm going to drop this, just because you've

501

got it into your stupid head, Alix, that this was a justified thing to do?' said Ralph, exasperated. 'I am going to keep on at you until you see what a ridiculous thing it is to have done.'

'Nothing you say will change my mind, Ralph,' said Alix. 'I have made up my mind on this issue, just as you have in your own dogmatic way.'

'I may be dogmatic,' he said, 'but I know I am right. What you did was not only criminal but the most foolish, wicked, damaging thing. You have put back the cause twenty years!'

'Be quiet!' she shouted. 'What right have you to preach to me? What right? I should have been better throwing that brick at you, Ralph, because for all your liberal notions, you are really as bad, if not worse, than all of them. At least they are not hypocrites. How dare you say what is good or not good for our cause? You say you support women, and then the moment they do things which offend your oppressive notions of womanliness, you are horrified. If you really supported us, you would be rejoicing today! You would be throwing bricks yourself.'

'For God's sake, Alix, how can you be so naive? How can you possibly believe that such actions can help the cause? It's blindingly obvious to me that . . .'

'Because you see nothing,' she interrupted. 'You cannot see the scale of this, or rather you will not, because it frightens you. You can't see that this is an act of war, can you?'

'An act of war? Oh, for heaven's sake . . .'

'Dismiss it if you like, but at your peril. I'm telling you, Ralph, this is just the start, so you had better get used to it. Women all over this country will declare war, and will not make peace until we are given our freedom. This is a just cause, and we will do what is necessary in that cause!'

'You could easily have hurt someone this afternoon.'

'Oh, what a tragedy,' she said, with sarcasm. 'That's part of war, isn't it? Anyway, after centuries of oppression and injustice against women, of rape and beatings, what right have you, as a man, to ask me to worry about spilling a little

502

blood? Aren't we entitled to a little revenge? Or is that another privilege denied to us?'

'Alix, you don't know what you're saying.'

'I do, I assure you I do. More than you will ever know. You can't feel this anger, Ralph, you cannot, because you are a man.'

'I wish you would get off the platform for a moment, Alix,' he said. 'All these damned speeches . . . can't we talk rationally about this?'

'There's nothing to discuss,' she said, getting up from her chair. 'You'll have to excuse me, Mother, but I'll have tea sent up to my room. I want to prepare what I'm going to say to the magistrate tomorrow.'

'No, Alix, no speeches then,' said Ralph, managing to muster some authority. 'That I will not have. You will plead guilty and pay the fine, and that will be an end to this.'

'What a bully you are, Ralph! It's a good thing you are not married, you would make life miserable for a wife.'

'Promise me, Alix, please . . .'

'Oh, from bullying to begging!' she said. 'Well, just you understand this, Ralph. I shall do exactly as I choose over this. I will not take your orders!'

'Alix . . .' He attempted to make her stay by reaching out and taking her arm as she passed him, but she wrestled out of this and, having given him a look of utter contempt, went briskly back into the house.

'Oh God!' he exclaimed to the skies, and then looking down at his mother, who was no longer lounging in her chair but sitting bolt upright, her hands grasping the arms, her face white with shock, he felt wretched. 'I'm sorry, Mother, that was really unforgivable. I shouldn't have let go like that . . .'

'Why is she doing this?' she said, in a tone of absolute bewilderment. 'Why, Ralph? I don't understand this at all.' She sounded close to tears.

He could offer no words of consolation. He had hated the sound of his own voice in that argument, that arrogant, bullying tone which he would have despised in another man. But he could not understand her, and his dumb

503

confusion had come out as hectoring anger, the whine of a petty schoolmaster exasperated more by his own situation than the irksome pupil.

'What shall we do?' said Mrs Erskine.

'I don't really know. I suppose we can't do anything. She has made up her mind to do this and . . .'

'But some of those women have been going to prison,' said Mrs Erskine. 'And refusing to eat. Do you think that's what she wants?'

'Martyrdom?' The word seemed portentous, but apt. She had been talking like a fanatic. 'Perhaps.'

'You must do something to stop this, Ralph,' said Mrs Erskine, very suddenly and with great decision. 'It has to stop here. It can't go any further. Alix doesn't know what she is doing. You have to protect her.'

'I can only try, Mother.'

'Well, you must. You are the only one she will listen to, I'm convinced of it. Why don't you go and talk to her now?'

'I think I'd better let us cool our heels a little,' he said. 'I don't want to lose my temper again. It wouldn't help.'

'No, you're right, it wouldn't. Perhaps before dinner? You will try, won't you, Ralph?'

'Of course, Mother, but I can't make any promises. You saw what she was like. It wasn't Alix at all, and I don't know how to deal with this new person yet, do I?'

Alix, dressing for dinner, was not surprised to hear a knock at her door. It was the time her mother had always chosen for those little talks which were in truth scoldings and were usually enough to put one quite off dinner. She expected it would be her mother, but then, when Ralph came in, knew that she had sent him in her stead. He stood so awkwardly in the doorway, his hands deep in the pockets of his dinner jacket, a half apologetic, lame smile on his face, that she knew he was not there through choice.

'Well?' she said. 'Have you come to give me a lecture?'

'No, just a quiet talk, if you don't mind.'

'No, of course not,' she said. 'So long as it is quiet and

504

you don't start laying down the law.'

'It will be,' he said. 'Can I come in?'

'Of course.'

He sat down on the ottoman at the end of the bed, still rather ill at ease.

'So what did you want to say?' she asked.

'I was going to make a suggestion, actually,'

'Oh?'

'Yes, you know how Father always used to say how he solved problems . . .'

She wanted to point out that there was in fact no problem, but his tone was reasonable and it seemed only fair to let him state his point of view.

'How?' she asked.

'By turning the thing on its head and trying to find a positive solution.'

'Yes, I see, but I don't see what you are driving at.'

'Well, I was thinking that you obviously feel you need to do something with your life now that . . . that . . . Drew's gone, and that the suffrage campaign is just something to fill an awful hole.'

'What do you want me to do?' she said, astonished. 'Get married again, just to fill a hole?'

'Oh God, no, that's not what I meant. I was thinking you could help me. You could work at Garbridge. I'd make you a real partner. I mean, since you own so much stock these days, you might as well actually control it. It would be carrying on what Andrew did and I think you'd be splendid at it – a real asset to the company.'

She could not help smiling.

'I am in earnest, Alix,' he said. 'I should very much like you to come and work with me.'

'Yes, I can see that,' she said. 'But, Ralph, you've missed the point completely, haven't you? You are trying to stop me campaigning, fighting for what I believe in, and not all the jewels in the world could dissuade me from that. I have given myself to this cause. I don't need to fill any gaps, I have found my life again. There is no problem that needs solving – well, there is, but it's your problem and not mine.

You must accept what I am, what I believe in and what I must do.'

'But, Alix, just think what you could do at Garbridge. The power you would have, the influence . . .'

'The influence! That has always been thrown at women to sweeten them. They may have influence but no real power. Besides, I don't want this thing for myself – I want it for all women. Helping you run Garbridge will change nothing for ordinary women.'

'And throwing bricks will?'

'Yes, I believe so.'

'Then God help civilization!' he said, with some bitterness.

'Ralph, I wish you could see it,' she said. 'If we had the support of men like you . . .'

'You will not have it. I can't condone this, Alix. Not for the best cause in the world could I condone it. Perhaps it is only bricks now, but once the principle of violence is accepted, you are heading for atrocities.'

'There are times when one must accept that,' she said. 'It is the grimmest step, I know, but one which must be taken. I have taken it now, and I cannot turn back.'

'I wish to God you could, Alix.'

She could not be immune to his agony. She knew well that he was bleeding and felt that he was her first casualty. In a sense she had thrown the brick at him, and she saw for the first time, as he sat there, his whole, gangling frame racked by distress, that this war of hers was not the clean game that the glorious oratory suggested. The pain and dirt had to be faced. The sacrifice was larger than she could have guessed, but she was still resolved, if not more so. To quit now would be cowardice and cowardice had never achieved anything.

4

It was half-past one in the morning and Jessie was at last locking up. It had been a busy night with high takings and she had the satisfaction of knowing that however tired she might feel, there would not be an empty table for the rest of the week. They were fully booked, a state of affairs that was becoming increasingly common. Edinburgh had been busy since August, full of people stopping en route to the highlands to buy tweeds and shooting sticks. Such people, staying at the Balmoral and the Caledonian, the like of which Jessie had never seen before, even in Erskine circles, seemed to have taken over the Fleur de Lys. The place had been full of braying laughter and incomprehensible slang, pronounced in strange, strangled accents. They seemed to enjoy themselves famously (that was one of their words) and tipped handsomely, as well as ordering, it seemed to Jessie, gallons of champagne. It made her wonder what it must be like to own a restaurant in London; profitable, she imagined, if these people were in any way typical.

As she was inspecting the state of the flowers (noting that fresh ones would be needed the next day in the public rooms as well as the special arrangements for the birthday party in the private room) she heard the door rattle and then the bell jangle, because whoever it was had discovered that the door was locked. With some annoyance she went to the door, because she did not relish interruptions at such a time of night. Who on earth would come calling this late?

She unbolted the door and looked out. She was surprised to see no one standing there and then irritated to see a hunched figure sitting at the foot of the steps. It was obviously some drunkard mistaking her restaurant for a pub.

'Get away with you!' she said. 'Get to your bed, man!'

But he turned very slowly to face her and she saw, as the

lamp revealed his features, that it was Ralph, his face set in a grimace of absolute pain. He was not drunk, it was clear, but ill.

'Oh, my God!' she exclaimed, and rushed forward.

'I'm sorry,' he gasped, 'I couldn't . . .'

'Shush,' she said, putting her arm round him and helping him to his feet. His body felt rigid and heavy and she could see the sweat beading his temples.

'Let's get you inside,' she said.

When they got into the Fleur de Lys, he doubled up again the moment he sat down.

'I'd better get a doctor,' she said.

He shook his head.

'No point,' he wheezed. 'Give me a minute, and I'll be all right . . .'

It was difficult to believe him, but dutifully she waited, sitting beside him, wishing there was something she could do. After what seemed an eternity he straightened up again and threw back his head, gulping air and sighing, his face relaxed with relief.

'Thank God that's over,' he said at length, wrenching loose his collar and tie.

'Yes,' said Jessie. 'What on earth was it? Something you ate?'

'No, it's my ulcer,' he said. 'Over the last few weeks it has been playing up a bit.'

'That seems more than playing up,' she observed. 'Have you been to a doctor about it?'

'Doctors are useless,' he said. 'It's simpler to put up with it. Besides, I've better things to worry about these days than the odd stomach cramp!'

'I wouldn't call that the odd stomach cramp,' she said. 'Ralph, you really ought to see someone.'

'Yes, yes, I know . . .' he said wearily. 'You're right, of course, but frankly I don't seem to have had a minute to myself. I've just wasted an entire evening at a committee meeting for the Infirmary Fund at which nothing was decided except to have another damned meeting —' He broke off with a sigh. 'I'm sorry,' he said, 'you don't deserve this grousing of mine, not when I've banged on your door at such a godless hour.'

'No, no, it doesn't matter,' she said. 'What are friends for?'

'I sometimes think I presume on you too much, Jessie.'

'You can never do that,' she said with sincerity, pleased that he could still think of her as his confidante.

He smiled briefly at this, but then his countenance lapsed again into a troubled frown. Then he yawned.

'You should be in your bed,' she said.

'I know, but I can't bear it. I never sleep these days.'

'Ah, well, I can help you there,' she said. 'Camomile tea – one of Monsieur Auguste's tricks. I'll go and make you some.'

To her surprise he insisted on following her downstairs into the now cool and calm kitchen. In the bright, unshaded electric light she could see just how worn and haggard he looked, and it distressed her. She tried to concentrate on the business of making the tea, but kept glancing back at him as he sat so very awkwardly on that kitchen stool. At one point he looked up at her with a look she knew well from her own children, a look of sheer helplessness, desperate in its appeal. He would not ask her for help, but every inch of his body suggested that he needed it.

'My dear . . .' she could not help saying it as she looked down at him, halting in the action of warming the pot. She wanted to throw her arms around him and hold him, without saying a word but putting all her eloquence into the simplicity of an embrace. But she did not; she could not, whether from a fear of being rebuffed or from some silly lip service to convention which said that women should not do such things, she did not know, but she could not.

'Yes?' he said.

'You really should rest.' It was a commonplace and not at all what she wanted to say to him but, aware that she was on a cliff edge, she suddenly baulked at stepping over. She thought of the recklessness with which she had thrown herself into Sholto's arms, merely because he had appealed to her, merely because she had been dazzled by him. With

Ralph, of course, it was scarcely a question of being dazzled, blinded by a brilliant surface. She could claim that to some extent she knew him – and yet (and was it this which held her back?) she was no longer certain that she did know him. Had he not only months ago fallen wildly in love with Olivia Lennox, an action which to her was as unfathomable as the deepest ocean? Perhaps she was a fool to think she could understand the complexities of such a man as Ralph Erskine. She could no longer be sure that he would react as she expected, or more to the point, as she wanted him to do.

She disliked her cynical caution a great deal and tried to call it prudence. But it stuck in her throat, although she knew there was no other way in which she could act. There were a thousand good reasons, and a thousand rules which she was still afraid to disobey and which shaped her life. She was powerless in spite of herself, in spite of the longing she felt.

'Well, I am going to the country,' he remarked, 'but I don't suppose it will be much of a rest cure. I've been invited to the Quarro.'

'What!' She could not conceal her astonishment and almost slopped boiling water everywhere. She turned sharply and said, 'Why?'

'James wants to see me about Drew's will. I don't want to go, naturally, but he was very insistent.'

'Naturally,' she said tartly. She had realized she did not believe him. She could not stop herself thinking that Olivia was the reason. She knew he had broken with her, but perhaps he wanted to heal the rift. If not that, then why? The business of the will sounded like an excuse. She had been right. She did not know him, not in the least.

And then, to her surprise, she saw him smile.

'Oh, I know what you are thinking,' he said.

'You do?' she said, with what she hoped was a bland, sweet expression, as if she were astonished by his cleverness.

'Yes, and you've nothing to fear. This old fool has quite

come to his senses in that quarter. Didn't I tell you, you were right?'

'Yes, yes . . . but . . .' she said, half relieved, half alarmed at this sudden frankness. 'But it's never easy to break from people, is it?' she finally blurted out. 'Besides, what is it to me what you do? I'm not your keeper, Ralph, am I?'

'Perhaps you should be. You have a great deal more sense than I. If I had taken your advice . . .'

'People would think it very odd that someone like you should take my advice. Shouldn't it be the other way round?'

'What nonsense you talk sometimes,' he said, 'for a person of such good sense.'

'Well, that just proves I'm a fool, doesn't it?' she retorted, and then angry that they were talking in riddles, said, quite frankly, 'You were right – I could only think that you wanted to go because of her.'

'I would rather stay away because of her.'

'Are you sure?' She was surprised at the boldness of her question but she wanted to satisfy herself, subdue her own jealousy. 'It's very easy to forgive people you think you love. I know – I've done it enough times myself. Oh, I know I am being presumptuous and interfering but I just want to be certain. I like you too well to see you fall into her hands again.'

'To be honest,' he said, 'I don't know why I am going. I just feel I must, for some strange reason. But it isn't to see Olivia Lennox, it isn't to fall in love with her again, I promise you, Jessie. You see, I can't love like that now. I've realized that love is not a game that I should play. I was fool enough to forget that with Olivia.'

His quiet bitterness frightened her. It was as if he had shut a door in her face.

'It's something to which I have had to resign myself,' he went on baldly, as if he were speaking of doing without tobacco.

'I don't believe you!' she said fiercely, unable to hold her tongue in the face of such self-abnegation. 'You might as

511

well say you must do without water!' And then conscious she had overstepped the mark, turned her attention to stirring the pot.

'You surprise me,' he said. 'I hadn't thought of you as sentimental. I would have thought that after Sholto . . .'

'That I'd be as afraid of love as you are?' she cut in.

'So you think I am a coward?'

'No, not exactly. It's just that you've thrown the baby out with the dirty bath water – and it's a damned waste.'

'But it never works for me. I always wade into disaster.'

'You talk like an old man, as if you are half dead.'

'Well, it's how I feel these days.'

'Oh God, man,' she said, kneeling in front of him and taking his hand, moved to knock this foolish desperation out of him. 'You're no done yet, for all your troubles.' She could not resist brushing her hand across his forehead. 'There'll be good times yet, I promise you – all the happiness you want will come.'

'But when?' he said. 'How bloody long must I wait? How much pain does there have to be? Oh God, Jessie, I know I'm selfish, and weak and a fool, and that I shouldn't complain, but sometimes I feel so close . . . so close to breaking in two. These last months, I don't know how I've gone on . . .'

'Because you are a fine, brave, strong man,' she said, squeezing his hands. 'Because you are a better man than you give yourself credit for. Now listen, Ralph, I won't have this silly doing yourself down – do you hear me?' It was the sort of tone she might have used with one of the girls and she saw it made him smile, and felt herself smile also.

'Sorry, Mama,' he said, and added, 'You're right – self-pity is a desperate thing. I promise to abjure it.'

'That's the spirit. Now, do you want this tea I've been promising you?'

They talked over a great many things that night: Drew's death; Sholto and Olivia; Alix's politics – all anguished topics, but they were calm and rational over the camomile tea. When he rose at last to go, he kissed her on the cheek and thanked her for her friendship.

'No, Ralph,' she could not help saying, 'thank you.' For she had the happy sense that he had at last come back to her.

5

'You're in the red chamber, sir,' said Mr Maxwell, the butler, who was obviously very pleased to see him. 'Just like the last time.'

Ralph had not forgotten the room and wondered if it was really a kindness to be returned to it. It had been twelve summers since he had last been there and nothing had changed. The house had kept that stillness, that scent of sweet polish and of quiet decay about it, and he half expected, half wished, that Alix and Celia would run out dressed as girls still, laughing at some private joke. It would be a fine thing to have the past in one's grasp again, to have another chance not to make the same mistakes. However, looking about his gloomy quarters with the musty, red-brown hangings and those gruesome engravings, he was forced to conclude that being the sort of man he was, he would probably act in exactly the same way. After all, was not his very awkwardness at having to be there the result of the same foolish self-indulgence which had sent him chasing after Celia? It seemed he had learnt nothing from the past, as with deliberate slowness he washed and made himself ready to go downstairs to the drawing room.

Fixing on a fresh pair of cuffs, he went to the window and stared out at the dank pleasure ground, dreary despite the autumn colours, because there had been a grey mist in the air all day. He recalled how that view had once enchanted him, with the sparkling surface of the canal under a high July sun and the velvet green of the turf. Now it made him shudder, not just with cold (although there was a noticeable draught from the window frame) but from the recollection of himself, enslaved first by Celia, who stood like a ghost in

513

that mist, and then by Olivia, who, worse than any ghost, waited to receive him downstairs with a mocking smile.

Courage, mon brave! he told himself with a grim smile and shrugged on his jacket again; a sober black item, aridly formal in cut, which he felt sure his younger self would have despised him for. But such clothes suited his mood. If he was not older and wiser, he was at least older and penitent.

He went out on to the landing and was just in the act of pulling his door to when he heard a voice ring out a few paces behind him.

'Well, well – it is you, Erskine! What a surprise this is! Quite like old times, eh?'

Ralph did not wish to turn and look, hoping for a moment that this distinctive voice was simply a figment of his imagination. It was awful to think that to crown all the embarrassment, all the awkwardness of this damned weekend, *he* should be there!

But he did manage to turn, some semblance of civility on his face and in his voice, as he said, 'Yes, it is quite a surprise! How are you, Hamilton?'

They had long since ceased to use each other's Christian names.

'Nothing to complain of,' Sholto said with a smile in which Ralph could read barely concealed contempt. 'I am relishing my freedom, if truth be told.'

'I can imagine,' said Ralph, but restrained himself from remarking that Sholto had never given up one iota of his freedom during his marriage. He did not want to start a brawl, after all. In fact, he decided that the only way that he would survive that weekend was to retreat behind a veneer of politeness. It was a way of proceeding he would usually detest. He liked plain speaking and honesty, but here he saw they would not do at all. It was better to lie and let it pass. There were too many nasty secrets for any sort of revelation. Even the slightest hint, the vaguest spark, could lead to a monstrous explosion and Ralph decided he was not going to be responsible for that.

So he went downstairs with Sholto Hamilton, ostensibly as a slight acquaintance, pleased (more or less) to find him there. They talked of politics, in a vague way, of the rumblings in Ulster, without any real opinions being expressed although they each knew that one was a fervent Unionist and the other a passionate Home-ruler.

The drawing room was just the same, despite the absence of the frail Miss Lennox and the florid Sir Hector. Their places, which Ralph remembered, had been left unoccupied, but whether this was from respect or repulsion, he had no idea. Olivia was just as she had been the first time he had ever seen her: languid on her little pink-covered chaise; the hem of her tea gown slipping off her ankles; her smile as artful and as inscrutable as ever. At least now he knew to whom this little display of charm was directed and glanced at Sholto to see if he was moved by it. It seemed not. He kissed her hand with some gallantry but that was all. They were accomplished performers, it appeared, for James Lennox looked blandly on, his stupid face (there was no other word for it) entirely unperturbed.

Ralph accepted the offer of whisky instead of tea, partly for dutch courage and partly because he could not bear to watch Olivia at her tea ceremony. He had seen it too recently but in very different surroundings. They had spent a night in Glasgow together in a hotel – it had been the night he had given her the necklace. With painful clarity he remembered watching her pour out his tea the following morning, dressed only in the flimsiest silk wrapper, her hair falling about her shoulders. Now, watching despite himself, he saw the same gestures, done to enchant rather than to pour out the tea. He thought suddenly of Jessie and her pot of camomile tea where there had been no such ceremony but the utmost simplicity. It had been a commonplace enough thing, but in that moment he would have seized all that ordinariness, all that everyday orderliness no matter how banal it might be, because of its fundamental sanity. He felt overwhelmed with longing for the bare, bald electric light of that functional kitchen, where Jessie had stood, tea pot in hand, transparent with concern for him. At least in his life there was something left: that deep yet simple friendship between them. If he were to have a religion it would be

Jessie Hamilton. Of all the people he had ever met, she alone inspired that mixture of intense awe and tender devotion one was supposed to find for one's god.

He glanced at the clock and began to calculate how many hours he must remain there. It would not be polite to leave until after luncheon on Sunday and it was only five o'clock on Friday now. Already the conversation had dried up and only Sholto, who talked for a living, was making any effort, for which Ralph supposed he should be grateful. He was making Olivia laugh in a girlish fashion, as if she felt guilty at being amused by his vague suggestion of some very slight impropriety. It was a whorish trick and it sickened him to listen to it.

Glass in hand, he made his way to the other end of the drawing room where James Lennox was sprawled vacantly in an armchair, the whisky decanter within easy reach. He decided he might as well get on with the business in hand.

'What was it about Andrew's will that was bothering you?' he asked, sitting down. 'It struck me as all very straightforward.'

James frowned slightly and reached for the whisky.

'Let's not talk about that just now, shall we? There's plenty of time for that. Won't you join me in another?'

'Thank you, but no.'

'As you like,' he said, pouring for himself. He sipped it and then glanced towards Olivia. 'Ain't she charming, Erskine, my little Livy? Most beautiful filly I ever saw. I've never seen anyone to match her, you know.'

For a moment Ralph thought he detected some irony in these words, but dismissed this as a creation of his own guilty conscience. He could not imagine that James Lennox would be capable of such subtlety.

It had become clear at dinner the previous night that rough shooting was the diversion for that Saturday morning. Ralph, no sportsman and certainly no shot, was coerced reluctantly, but refused to carry a gun. He would watch and not participate. Sholto, he was amused to see, was delighted with the suggestion and showed a surprising familiarity with the weapon with which James presented him. From what Sholto had said when they had been younger, Ralph had always imagined that he had pursued such sport illegally, in the company of more dubious members of his father's flock, snitching grouse and pheasant from the Perthshire moors by more devious means than the blast of a shotgun. Now he was the perfect laird, his tweeds as expensive and as rough as James's. It was left to Ralph to feel like a cit, without a game bag or a gun crooked over his arm. However he was glad to be free of these encumbrances and followed a few yards behind them as they crunched into Quarro woods talking ostentatiously of the great bags of yesteryear.

He had forgotten the dense complexity of those woods, how they were riddled with burns and their paths blocked by fallen trees. As they made their way through them, their noisy footsteps raising birds, James's spaniel barking with excitement, he thought of Celia going silently through these same woods, sure-footed in the moonlight as they were clumsy in bright sunshine. He had never seen her there, of course. He only knew what Alix and Hamish Anderson had told him of it, but he could imagine it vividly, even as James and Sholto raised their guns to take the first shots. He looked up into the clear blue autumnal sky and watched a bird soar and wheel away from them, free for only a moment until a blast of gun fire brought it tumbling down. Like Celia . . . Like Andrew . . . he could not help thinking, and his blood ran cold at this act of senseless destruction.

He looked away into the empty parts of the woods through which they had just come, trying to calm himself, for he felt sick and disgusted, not just by the death of the bird, but at all the pointless loss and misery of the world against which he was utterly powerless. It was a moment of absolute despair, and he staggered a little in it, gasping for breath as his spirits plummeted. He knew in that moment if he had been carrying a gun he should gladly have turned it on himself.

He leant against a tree, pressing his hands against the rough bark, trying to feel and capture the inexpressible

517

essence of life which lurked inside; doing anything to restore the will to carry on within him. He found he was looking at James and Sholto again. They were advancing and more birds were taking flight. He watched Sholto take aim, forced himself to do it; indeed, to try and overcome this thing by facing the worst.

The partridge was still in the cover of the trees and Sholto squared up to it. Several shots were fired but Ralph did not see the bird fall. For a second he was relieved – until he saw Sholto keel over backwards.

He turned slowly and saw James, a smoking revolver gripped between his hands so firmly that Ralph could see the tautness in the shining leather of his gloves.

'One down,' said James, turning to face him. 'And one to go!'

And then the life which Ralph would so gladly have tossed away only a moment ago returned to him with a vengeance. He knew he was an unarmed man faced by a lunatic with a revolver who had just calmly killed one man and seemed to want to kill him as well. He knew that the odds were stacked impossibly against him but an instinct to survive, so powerful and so primitive that he would not have thought himself capable of it, had gripped him. He did not feel afraid, or if he did, it was a fresh sort of fear which prompted action and not cowardice.

'This will get you nowhere,' he said. 'Nowhere. You know that, James. What is the point? Think, man.'

'Be quiet!' he barked, with a little flourish of the gun. 'No one touches my wife, do you understand? No one! He did – and he's dead. You did, and I'll kill you too.'

'No, you won't. You won't kill me, James Lennox,' said Ralph. 'You'll put down that gun. You won't have the guts to kill a man who's looking you in the eyes.' And he stepped forward, fixing on James's face with all his concentration, hoping he could hold him in a glance.

'You had her, you bastard!' shrieked James, and fired.

Ralph found he was lying on his face, the smell of earth and dead leaves assailing him. He was aware that he had been shot, but he was also aware that he was still alive. He felt a sharp pain in his ankle and then a far worse explosion in his left shoulder, which had been numb and was now livid with pain. He wanted to clasp his hand over it, but scarcely dared move. Gingerly he looked up and saw James running away, crashing rather, through the undergrowth, vanishing into the most secret depths of the woods.

He thinks I'm dead, he thought with triumph, despite everything. But I'm not. At least not yet.

He rolled carefully on to one side and found the reason for his salvation. In stepping forward he had caught his foot in a tree root. That had made him fall and not a bullet in his chest. With infinite relief, he managed to get up on to his knees, realizing that there was blood pouring out of the top of his arm. He groped for his handkerchief and made a very clumsy tourniquet, pulling it as tightly as he could bear. He was glad to see that James had quite disappeared now. He knew he must get back to the house as quickly as possible.

He glanced towards Sholto and saw his body twitch. There was some life left there, thank God. He might have wished Sholto dead as heartily as James on occasion, but now he could only think of getting him back alive. Ralph limped over and found he was scarcely conscious. He was also impossibly heavy, but Ralph managed to half drag him to his feet, his arm around Sholto's waist while Sholto's arm settled around his neck with a death-like grip as if he wanted to take Ralph with him to oblivion.

But oblivion Ralph would not have, and staggered with his unwieldy burden through those tortuous woods, driven on by he knew not what. At length, and at what length – at least eternity it seemed – they emerged at the end of the great lawn with the canal stretching out interminably ahead of them, measuring the agonizing distance which they still must travel.

A gardener's boy assiduously raking leaves stopped in his tracks and stared as they came towards him.

'For God's sake!' exclaimed Ralph, hoarsely, and the boy scurried away to fetch help (or so Ralph prayed, and that the lad was not a hopeless simpleton). They laboured on a while until the door at the top of the steps opened with a crack and people ran out.

Ralph, exhausted, laid Sholto down upon the damp grass. He was scarcely breathing and his chest was nothing but a mass of blood. Ralph saw Olivia running out of the house towards them, running despite her ridiculous hobble skirt. He sat there on the grass, dazed and in pain, and saw her fling herself on the ground beside Sholto and gather him into her arms. His head fell back and in an instant it was clear he was dead. She held him still and covered his face in kisses, stroking him with feverish hands, her entire body consumed in the sudden tragedy of leave-taking.

Ralph turned away, nursing his own wound, conscious that for all the tricks and all the deceits, this was love of the truest, fiercest kind. Olivia, her face distorted with tears, her hands stained with Sholto's blood, looked more noble and more beautiful than he had ever seen her before. She was almost worth killing for.

In the heart of the woods, stopping to catch his breath, James Lennox realized what he had done. No jury would excuse him and he was forced to choose between the noose and the bullet. For the sake of his name, and for Olivia's, he chose the bullet.

They found his body an hour or so later, his spaniel licking his face.

6

Olivia Lennox stood nearest to the grave, a waist-length black veil covering her face, yards of crêpe on her skirts, and as a final detail, as if she had just stepped from the pages of some mourning warehouse catalogue, she clasped in her black-gloved hand a handkerchief with a deep black border. Jessie, standing some little distance away, her hands resting on Chloe's trembling shoulders, could not help wondering if she had worn this rig-out for James's funeral. That display of widow's weeds would have been more appropriate in the tiny Episcopalian burial ground in Quarro Village than beside the Hamilton family vault in the kirkyard at Longnithrie in Perthshire. She was after all Lady Lennox, and not Mrs Hamilton. Jessie supposed she should be at the graveside performing that particular role, but she could not manage to act the grieving widow. She was only there under sufferance because Chloe had been intent on going. One could not forbid a child to attend its father's funeral, and one could not let her go alone, no matter how it stuck in the throat to be there. Watching Olivia Lennox drop red roses into the grave did not help matters.

Chloe was clutching a small bunch of flowers, carefully tied up but wilting a little now after the long journey from Edinburgh. She glanced up to Jessie as if to ask if this was her moment to throw them in. Jessie nodded and Chloe made her way forward. The small crowd parted a little to let her pass and it seemed to Jessie that this small tribute was far more moving than any of the pompous funeral rites which Olivia Lennox had arranged. It was as if she was throwing her innocence into the grave, and Jessie felt that her daughter returned to her sadly, full of the heavy realization that her father had not been perfect. Her devotion to him had died, as Jessie's had so long ago. With Olivia Lennox being so conspicuous, it had been difficult for her to remain ignorant. She guessed at once that this strange woman, lording over all, making such an exhibition of herself, was not simply a friend. Chloe knew the meaning of those widow's weeds as well as anyone, and it was equally obvious that her mother was not wearing them.

Olivia was the only mourner she recognized. The others appeared to be locals, some who perhaps had known Sholto as a boy and others whom she suspected liked nothing better than the entertainment of a good funeral. There was entertainment enough for them here. They had all supposed that Olivia was the wife, and then to see the strange child at the back of the crowd push through and throw flowers into the grave — well, Jessie could read the expressions on their faces and knew very well what they were thinking of by-blows and scandal. This funeral would cause much whispering in Longnithrie about the old minister's son.

It really was typical of Olivia Lennox to behave in such a way. It was in such poor taste, as Sholto would have said. Jessie wondered what he would have thought of his funeral. He would have enjoyed the obsequious elegy of the minister, which spoke of him in such glowing terms that Jessie wondered if she had come to the right funeral. But no one ever seemed able to speak ill of the dead, no matter how unpleasant they might have been in life.

The majority of the mourners shuffled away, leaving Olivia standing by the grave, statuesque and impressive, despite everything. Chloe turned and demanded an embrace from Jessie. She was crying suddenly and clung tightly.

'Why couldn't everything have stayed the same?' she sobbed. 'Why not?' She buried her face in Jessie's coat, while Jessie attempted to think of some honest but comforting answer. She did not succeed, but there would have been no time to give it to Chloe because Olivia Lennox was coming towards them. Chloe must have felt Jessie stiffen because she let go and turned to see Olivia's approach. She glanced up, panic-stricken, her face sticky with tears.

Olivia seemed to look them over with a cool, callous eye, just as she had once looked Jessie over in the boudoir at the Quarro. It spoke of utter contempt and Jessie felt all the old annoyance flare up in her. She had come there charitably, prepared to let Olivia have her vulgar show of grief, but now all such thoughts vanished. She only wished to settle an old, old score.

'Good morning,' she said, with all the calm disdain she could manage. 'Thank you so much for arranging everything. I think Sholto would have been most pleased by it. It really is very kind of you.'

This seemed to astonish Olivia Lennox into silence. Perhaps she had been expecting her to be outraged. I will not stoop to that though, thought Jessie.

'He was a wonderful man,' said Olivia very pointedly to Chloe. 'A wonderful man. If you ever meet a man one-tenth as good, you will be happy, my dear. Such men are rare.'

'Oh, yes,' said Jessie, with some irony, 'very rare.'

'Don't you listen to what your mother says,' went on Olivia. 'She is only bitter because she lost him. Who wouldn't be?'

'What are you saying?' burst out Chloe. 'Who are you to say such things? What do you know about him?'

'More than you could ever know, and far more than your poor silly mother could possibly understand.'

'I may be ignorant, Olivia Lennox,' said Jessie, unable to let this pass, 'but I am not a fraud.'

'What an extraordinary accusation!'

'Just the plain truth. You loved Sholto because you are the same as he was. You lie and you charm your way everywhere. You've never been honest in your life, woman, not to your husband, nor to your people, nor even to yourself.'

'How dare you!'

'You can't talk to me like a servant now. I'm not anyone's to be ordered around, especially not by Sholto's damned mistress. Why don't you face it, Olivia? You are nothing but a sham! You use people, but I'm damned if I am going to stay here and let you use my daughter as you use everybody else! Come along, Chloe, shall we go?'

And then, in one of those marvellous moments of family loyalty, Chloe, who might have resented being dragged away, said with great dignity, 'Yes, Mother, I think we should. I don't want to stay here any longer!'

They walked away arm in arm, Jessie cheering silently.

'You were damn' lucky, you know,' said Dr Blake. 'Each time I look at this, I can't help thinking it.'

'Do you think I don't know?' said Ralph, cheerfully. 'It's doing well, is it?'

'Fine, absolutely fine,' said Blake, studying the wound. 'You'll be able to stop having it dressed so frequently in a few days' time, I should imagine.'

'Excellent,' said Ralph. 'I shall be glad to get back to work.'

'Ah, I didn't say that,' said Blake.

'Well, I didn't mean at once – a week or two more should be sufficient rest, don't you think?'

'Hardly,' said Blake.

'But the wound will be healed by then. You've said so yourself.'

'That is hardly the point, Erskine. You are generally very run down, let me tell you. If you actually tried to do something you would be putting yourself in grave danger.'

'Of what?' said Ralph, dismissively. 'What could be worse than what I have been through? I feel fine. Surprisingly well, in fact.'

But the doctor shook his head and began to bandage up the fresh dressing.

'That is a false state of euphoria,' he said gravely. 'The wound might have healed – and that it has, so quickly, given the state of the rest of you, is little short of a miracle. But miracles don't happen very often – you can't rely on them. What you can rely on is that if a man with your medical history carries on the way you have been – with overwork, late nights, and hard drinking – he is more than likely heading for disaster.'

'Really, isn't that just slightly alarmist?'

'Look, Erskine, I do know the facts. You've told me about the stomach cramps and the insomnia. I've seen you myself in the grip of a migraine, and there isn't a soul in the house who doesn't know that you are halfway to being a laudanum addict.'

'I think you are exaggerating there . . .'

'I don't. And if you've got any sense, which I think you have, despite the shocking way you've been going on, you'll realize that this has got to stop or you are not going to see forty.'

'Are you quite sure?' said Ralph, after a moment's silence. Blake's bluntness had shocked him.

'I wouldn't joke about such a serious matter, would I?'

Ralph sank back on to his pillows. He was used to the

warnings of doctors but this one had been delivered with startling directness. Perhaps only now, when he had been within a hair's-breadth of death, could he understand what such a warning meant.

'Is there a chance for me?' he managed to say.

'Yes, a very good one if you take my advice now.'

'Which is?'

'Absolute rest for at least three months – abroad if possible. Exercise, good plain food, and definitely no work.'

'But three months! That's impossible,' interjected Ralph. 'I cannot possibly drop everything like that. You must see that it is absolutely out of the question . . .'

'Make it possible, Erskine,' said Blake grimly, packing up his bag.

Ralph was left alone feeling somewhat helpless. He could not begin to think how he might relinquish all his responsibilities and sat for some minutes twitching at the sheets, feeling he should not be idling in bed but kept there in impotent terror. It had, after all, been a stern warning and Blake was not a nannyish, warm flannel sort of doctor. That was why Ralph had chosen him rather than the molly-coddling variety which his mother was wont to set great store by. George Blake was a plain-speaking Yorkshireman, with guts enough to practise and succeed in Edinburgh where generally only Scots medicos could prosper. Ralph had always trusted his judgement in the past and he had no reason not to trust it now – except that it was impossible to act on his advice. How could he possibly leave now?

It had been over two weeks since that awful business at the Quarro and he had spent most of it in bed, at first under chloroform when they took out the bullet, and then in a state of worried exhaustion in which he had been constantly interrupted by police inspectors asking searching questions and nurses changing the dressing with brisk but agonizing regularity. Only at night, kept awake by the pain and by the night-light which the nurse had insisted upon, had he time to reflect on what had happened. Both Sholto and James had been buried. It did not take much to imagine James lying in the woods, a bullet through his head, the dog licking at his face, frozen into that look of manic grief and rage which he had worn when he had turned his gun towards Ralph. He thought that look would never leave him and wondered how he could have misread James so, how he could not have seen in him the depth of passion to commit such an act. But I never could judge character, he had been forced to conclude ruefully.

Presently his mother came in, carrying a letter.

'George Blake wants me to go abroad,' he said.

'I know,' she said.

'Well, how can I?'

'More easily than you think,' she said, taking the letter out of its envelope. 'John Shaw just gave me this.'

'Is John here?' said Ralph. 'I must see him. There are some things I must discuss with him.'

'No, you may not see him,' she said firmly. 'No work, remember?' She unfolded the letter. 'This is from Monsieur Maurois, the company agent in Paris. He's found us a charming house in the Loire. Listen – the château de St Florimonde aux Champs, seventeenth-century manoir set in extensive demesne. Beautiful situation, twenty rooms, usual offices. Excellent resident staff, etc., etc. What do you think of that, then?'

'It sounds idyllic, but that's hardly the point, is it? I can't go.'

'You really must learn to trust your people, Ralph,' she said. 'I've been discussing this with John Shaw and it seems that with a little adjustment they will manage quite well in your absence. You will need to appoint a deputy, of course – actually, I think John might do very well for that. Your father always thought he had great potential.'

Ralph could not help laughing at this show of efficiency.

'Perhaps I should leave you to run it all, Mother.'

'Nonsense. I'm just an old woman, Ralph. Besides, I'm rather looking forward to a winter away. The Loire is supposed to be very mild, and I for one can do without a Scottish winter now and again.'

'Of course. Have you told Alix about this scheme of yours then?'

She frowned slightly.

'I haven't seen her this week,' she admitted. 'When she was sure you were all right she went dashing off to some conference or other. It's very thoughtless of her, really it is.'

'You mustn't worry over us both,' said Ralph.

'Oh, I don't, I assure you,' she said, with a little fierceness. 'Alix always wanted her independence, didn't she? Well, she may have it if she likes. I just hope she doesn't do anything foolish. But I don't think we could stop her – could we?'

'Unfortunately not,' said Ralph, wishing that there was not this additional burden upon her. An invalid fool for a son was enough trouble without a daughter with criminal intentions.

Jessie had seized a quiet half hour to do her accounts. She had rather neglected this of late, what with the funeral and sorting out the girls – and not least sorting out herself. She had thought no residue of feeling remained within her towards Sholto, but as in the days after the funeral she turned the events at the Quarro over in her mind and realized he was gone, she found herself profoundly shocked. It was the manner of his death that had caused this. He had not been knocked down by some indiscriminate disease but someone had willed that he should die and had pulled the trigger on him. No one, she had reasoned, quite deserved that, not even the blackest of sinners. And she found she had cried once over it, though she had not been at all sure why – whether from grief at the passing of that particular chapter of her life, or whether from sheer relief when she had realized that Ralph might so easily have suffered the same fate. Then she did not know what she would have done.

She heard the bell ring and went herself to answer it. Callers were rare at the front door in the middle of the morning. It was Mrs Erskine's footman and she went down the steps to the brougham to invite Mrs Erskine in herself. With that old-fashioned elegance which distinguished her, Mrs Erskine did not care to use a motor in town.

'I hope this isn't an awkward time, my dear,' she said, as Jessie handed her from the carriage.

'You are a welcome distraction,' said Jessie. 'I was just doing the accounts.'

She took Mrs Erskine up to her office which was none too tidy at that moment for the table was littered with bills and Flora's artistic attempts. She hastily removed a basket of darning from the best chair and settled Mrs Erskine in it.

'How is Ralph this morning?'

'Oh, very well – improving all the time, I'm pleased to say,' said Mrs Erskine, glancing around her as if such workaday surroundings were quite strange to her. 'And you, my dear, how are you managing?'

'Oh, quite well – but Chloe is still miserable from the funeral. I wish she hadn't insisted on going.'

'Some children can be very independent-minded,' said Mrs Erskine, with a sigh which presumably alluded to Alix. 'It is something one must learn to live with, I suppose, even though one cannot bear to see them inflicting pain upon themselves.'

'Oh, does it not get any better?' Jessie could not help saying, moved by this heartfelt admission.

'Oh, my dear, don't you fret too,' said Mrs Erskine with a brave smile. 'As I say, one learns to bear it, I think. Besides, your girls are very sensible. They have such a sensible mother.' She reached out and took one of Flora's colourful little sketches from the table. 'Is this Flora's? I thought so. She is rather clever with her pencil, isn't she? Perhaps she will be a painter.'

'She wants to dance with the Ballet Russe at the moment, though goodness knows where she gets such notions from in Edinburgh!'

'It is rather a progressive school,' observed Mrs Erskine in a mischievous tone which made them both laugh. 'Oh, Jessie, it is pleasant to escape here. I have been so busy over Ralph and it tires me these days – not that I would rather not do it, you understand, but sometimes it is such an effort. Actually, it is about him that I have come to see you.'

'Well, if there is anything I can do, you know you only have to ask.'

'As a matter of fact, you can. You see, the doctor has ordered that Ralph should winter abroad and I've taken a simply lovely house in the Loire from October which should be just the thing. Oh, my dear, I don't quite know how to ask you this – it is such a dreadful imposition.' Jessie began to wonder what awful favour was to be requested of her. Mrs Erskine went on, 'I know how busy, how involved you are here, but I think it would be so splendid, not just for me, which is of course terribly selfish, but for Ralph. It would do him such good.'

'What would, Mrs Erskine?' said Jessie, gently.

'Oh dear, I am not making myself very clear, am I?' she said with a slight laugh. 'I'm asking if you and the girls would like to come to France with us.'

'Us? To go to France with you?' She was so astonished that she could not help repeating what Mrs Erskine had said.

'Of course, I don't expect you to be able to give me an answer at once. You must think very carefully and decide for yourself.'

'I don't need to think about it,' she said, very quickly, aware she was being rash. But the idea had caught her and she was enchanted. 'I should be glad to come with you. How could I possibly refuse such an offer?'

'Now are you sure?' said Mrs Erskine, perhaps a little alarmed at the recklessness of her reply. 'If you are only coming because you think you ought, out of some loyalty to us, which we do not merit . . .'

'Oh no, it wouldn't be a duty, Mrs Erskine, it would be a pleasure, an absolute pleasure. I have dreamed for years of going to France, and to go with such dear friends, well . . .' She found she was speechless and the only thing she could manage to do was to kiss Mrs Erskine.

Only when she had gone, did Jessie realize quite how impetuous she had been. She had not considered the girls' schooling or the Fleur de Lys for a moment. However, she soon reasoned that a winter in France would be education enough for anyone and felt a certain confidence that the restaurant could manage quite well without her. Monsieur Auguste of course knew the form, and they had a new assistant cook, Maggie Phillips, who had come from a large house in Lancashire. Between them they were more than able.

She was a little ashamed of her disloyalty, but a higher loyalty had claimed her. The thought of spending so much time in Ralph's company, the possibility of their old intimacy being renewed, was too much of a temptation for her to resist.

7

November, 1912. Victoria Station

'Are you sure you won't change your mind, Alix?' said Mrs Erskine.

'Mother dear, we've been through this before,' she said, somewhat exasperated. The boat train was due to leave in a few minutes and Alix did not have a ticket, let alone any luggage, and yet Mrs Erskine seemed to imagine that even at this late hour she would and could yield to impulse and climb on board with them. 'It simply isn't possible, you know that.'

'But Ralph has made it possible, and Jessie – why not you, my dear? What is there to keep you in London all winter when your family want you, when they need you to be with them?'

'Mama, this is hardly the moment for emotional blackmail! You don't need me, and as for saying I have no business to be in London – well, you know exactly why I must stay here. My work is too important, you must see that. It comes before everything else.'

'Before your family? Really, Alix, I can't believe that I'm hearing you say this. You know what Ralph has been

530

through, what we all have been through – you must see where your duty lies . . .'

'I know quite well where my duty lies, thank you!' said Alix sharply, and then added in a conciliatory tone, 'Oh, please, Mother, not now! You'll miss your train.'

'Hear, hear!' said Ralph who had appeared at the carriage doorway. 'You shouldn't be quarrelling now, either of you.'

'I was not quarrelling,' said Mrs Erskine pointedly, at which Alix saw Ralph suppress a smile and glance at her in that old way of his which seemed to take them all back to the school room. This tiny moment of conspiracy startled her. It was strange that however much might change, these old alliances and relationships should persist, no matter what. For a minute or two she was dumbfounded by the strength with which they still held her, and found herself staring at her shoes, wishing that it *was* possible for her to climb on to that train and live again in the simplicity of her past where love came uncomplicated and unclouded. It was suddenly heartless to let them go without her, with her mother so frail and grey-haired now, her face pained with rejection and Ralph making such an effort to be cheerful, his arm still resting in its black silk sling.

Impulsively, she grasped her mother's hands.

'Now you mustn't worry about me, you mustn't,' she said.

'How can I not worry?' said Mrs Erskine. 'If you were with me, then . . .'

'No, Mother.'

'Alix can always change her mind,' said Ralph tactfully, but she was not sure whether this did not imply some sort of order when he added, 'Couldn't you?'

'I can't make any promises,' she said, 'but I will try and visit if I can.'

The relief in their faces over this barely adequate compromise made her feel guilty. That they were prepared to accept such a slight undertaking from her, an undertaking which in fact exerted no real obligation upon her, was shaming, but she had to accept that this was how it must be. She had not the slightest intention of coming out to France to visit them but she had had to say that she might to make sure that they went. If she had not indulged in this nasty little deception, she could imagine that her mother might call the whole journey off at the last minute. It was better to let them go, with a feeble hope, than have them stay. Nothing could have been better for her purposes than their decision to go abroad that winter, for the last thing she wanted was the family interference which had ruined her enterprise at St Andrews. There, Ralph had effectively silenced her protest, and it had galled her greatly, not because of what he had done, which she could easily have predicted, but because of her own foolishness in acting in a place where she was so well known. It had been all too evident that the law could excuse Mrs Andrew Lennox whom they all pitied. She was convinced that this would not be the case elsewhere if she were to go to work more anonymously. She did not want such sympathy and excuses. They were not the terms of her war.

'Now you must go,' said Alix, observing that the guard was going along closing the doors of the train. She kissed her mother and threw her arms about Ralph for an instant, pressing his bad arm by accident and making him wince.

'Be careful, darling,' he murmured as he bent to kiss her forehead. That surprised her. She had half expected 'Be good', which would have hurt, but 'Be careful' implied a level of acceptance which she would not have thought possible with him.

'Don't worry, I know what I'm doing,' she said. He nodded and gave a grim little smile which she knew must have cost him much effort. He climbed back on to the train and shut the door, pulling down the window. They said nothing more for the engine had begun to let out a tremendous hiss of steam which would have drowned any words. She glanced at her mother and Jessie who were at the window of one of the compartments and waved and smiled at them, and then turned back to Ralph, filled suddenly with a terrible fear which swept round her like an ice-cold blast of wind. That smile of his, which summed up the most herculean act of tolerance, had floored her and she was ashamed of all the wicked things she had thought and said of him. He was as good a man as any and she had no right to despise him because they thought differently. He did not despise her. He never could – such a thing was not in him, and she was weak with fear she might lose him, just as she had lost Drew. For she had had an awful presentiment that they might never see one another again. After all, his health had never been good . . .

As the train pulled out, she ran alongside for a few yards and called out, 'And you be careful, Ralph, do you mind me!'

She saw him grin at this and he blew her a kiss and waved, looking just like a boy who is going off on his summer holiday.

Hamish sat in the dark in the flat in Kensington feeling stifled. He had never felt quite like it before, but the whole place felt vilely oppressive. It was not just the flat, which was replete with furnishings, but as if the whole city was pressing down upon his chest, squashing the life out of him. He could find no energy, although he was desperate to go out for a drink. But he imagined that Alix would not be pleased to come back and find him absent, or drunk. Where was she anyway? She had been out for hours, and here he was cooped up in this dreadful place, waiting for her like a dog.

He did not want to light the lamps, because he felt to sit and look at all the stuff which surrounded him would only remind him that he was there, like a fool, and not in Edinburgh. Why the devil had he agreed to come with her? What on earth was he, Hamish Anderson, a crude, low-born Scot, doing in this suffocatingly genteel flat in Kensington, waiting for a woman to return, a woman whom he had not even kissed but who was keeping him now like a mistress. He could not understand how he had let it happen, and yet he had, and quite willingly.

He knew why, of course, but hated to admit it, because it made him feel feeble-minded. But when he was with her he could not see straight. She could turn him upside down with a single word. She had him caught in a net – not the usual net of feminine tricks, but a net woven out of some passionate magic which he could not understand. She did not make love to him; indeed, she treated him almost as if he were not a man at all, as if there were no difference between them, but for all this evenhandedness, he sensed that something far darker lay between them. He felt it so strongly himself that he knew she must feel it too. Why else would they be together like this unless some force greater than all the ideas which superficially had made them comrades were dragging them together? And how long would it be before they would have to acknowledge this, before all the trappings of distance fell away? Would it be here in the strange secrecy of this vile flat which she had so unthinkingly asked him to share with her, a plan to which he, equally unthinking, had been happy to agree? This thing between them, as yet unspoken, had little to do with thinking. It drove them both and it would drive them further yet, he feared.

Why did he fear it? Why did he sit there in the dark, wanting her to come back and yet afraid to see her again? No man ought to be afraid of passion, he knew, and yet he was deeply troubled. It seemed all wrong, just as it had seemed all wrong to sleep with Cissy in the old bothy. Yet he could not have prevented that, and he could not prevent this. He had to let it happen although every minute he was alone he was tortured, first by Celia's face and then by that of her handsome brother, Alix's dead husband. It was scarcely decent, and yet what did he care about decency? Why did he have to feel so guilty about loving her, for that was what it amounted to, he could not deny that, when his rational mind told him that the objections he threw up were only the remnants of outmoded morals and mores. The fact she was a lady, a nine-month widow at that, should have meant nothing to him, but he could not muster that level of rationality. He was tortured by it, and yet could not help himself from loving her.

He heard her key in the lock and felt relieved. When he was with her, when he saw her lovely face, all the self-torture fell away. Just to look at her and hear her talk was justification enough.

She switched on a light in the hallway and then came into the room. She called it the drawing room – he, never having lived in such a room before, had no name for it.

'You're all in the dark,' she said.

'I was thinking. It's easier in the dark.'

'Yes, you're right. But may I put the light on now?'

Her kindly question astonished him. He had not expected her to defer to him like that.

'Of course. It's night out there.'

She reached out and switched on one of the table lamps – an extraordinary thing; its base a writhing nude female in bronze, its shade frilly pink silk, like whorish underwear.

He saw she was carrying various packages which she dumped unceremoniously on a chair opposite him.

'You're very late.'

'I know, I'm sorry. I had an idea, you see, just as I was coming out of the station. So I had to sort it out.'

'What idea?'

'About justice, actually,' she said, pulling up her veil and taking off her hat. 'Shall we have some tea and then I'll tell you?'

'All right. Do you want me to make it?'

'Would you?' she said, smiling. 'That gas ring terrifies me.'

She had hardly ever made tea for herself, still less cooked a meal.

'I can make cocoa all right,' she said, following him into the tiny kitchen. 'We used to make that at St Andrews.'

'Seems we've got it all the wrong way round,' he said, filling the kettle.

'Why should it be wrong? Most men of my class wouldn't know what to do in a kitchen.'

'And mine,' said Hamish. 'I've only learnt because I've lived alone. My brothers don't know a thing. They have wives to scrub and cook for them.'

'Tell me about your family.'

'There isn't much to tell,' he said. 'They're all in

535

Peebleshire still, refusing to join a union or even look much beyond their own front door.'

'You must have been a changeling.'

'A bastard more like. My mother wasn't exactly faithful, I don't think, and my father, if he was my father, made me feel pretty unwelcome.'

'Who would you have liked for a father?' she asked.

'You want me to say something snobbish, don't you?' he said, with a grin. 'You want to catch me.'

'What do you mean?'

'Well, perhaps the Hamish Anderson you're seeing is less the great socialist, and more the social climber? Perhaps I'm as bad as I think I am. Why else would I be here?'

'Because you want to be?'

'Aye, but why?'

'I can't tell you that. But I'm glad you came. I don't like to be alone. I can talk to you. You make me feel right.'

'Aye, I suppose that's about it. But, Christ, what am I to do now I'm here?'

'Take those courses at the LSE. The more you learn now, the better a politician you'll be. I'm going to get you into the House if it's the last thing I do.'

'I don't know . . .'

'Always so doubtful of yourself! Why? You are a brilliant man, Hamish, you must realize that. You've come so far . . .'

'From so little,' he interrupted, bitterly.

'And what is wrong with that?' she said. 'I always thought it was a virtue.'

'Self-help as taught by the dreadful Samuel Smiles? But I haven't even done that, have I? I shouldn't have got anywhere without your family. I haven't done anything on my own account.'

'That's just your monstrous pride, Hamish,' she laughed. 'You want to be responsible for changing the world single-handed. You're so like me. We can't bear that fundamental principle of positive co-operation, although that is how we should live. Working together is bound to be more effective.'

'Working together for what?' he said. 'I think I'm losing sight of it all. It's getting too easy. Your money makes everything so easy.'

'And you said you were pragmatic!' she said. 'I think you are more idealistic than I am.'

'Well, I came into this thing with a hungry belly, Alix, you have to understand that. That struggle – if I forget that, I lose myself. And look at all this . . .' He gestured round the little kitchen so stuffed with china and tins and things: things which he had never had in such quantity before. 'I canna live with all this. It chokes me up.'

'I know, I know,' she said, and laid a soft hand on his arm.

'How can you?'

'I can try and understand. I can, can't I? There is hope for me, isn't there?'

'Hope? I should think so,' he said, managing a smile. 'You're strong enough and brave enough to do anything. It's me I'm afraid for.'

'Then don't be, please,' she said, her hand still on his arm. 'Your conscience will never leave you, I'm sure of it. There are some things one can never forget. You will always be who you are, despite everything. Because you are strong, wonderfully strong.'

They were standing close now, and he felt the breath of her words against him, the very warmth of them. He stared at her ardent face, strongly illuminated by the bare electric bulb above them, and felt quite broken down by it. He could not resist any longer and bent that little distance to kiss her on the lips. She did not seem surprised but neither was she eager. He felt instead that she yielded with such delicate grace, giving herself to him in the gentle inclination of her face so that there was no awful submission of woman to man in it. He drew away for an instant and looked at her again. She smiled crookedly, and he saw the glint of a tear in her eye.

'I'm sorry,' he managed to say.

'Don't be,' she said, laying her other hand on his arm so that he could not help but clasp her elbows in a half embrace. 'He wouldn't have wanted me to be alone.'

He was so profoundly asleep that Alix was able to slip out of bed without his even stirring. That was just like Drew, and yet he was so different. He lay curled in bed like some wild animal, when Drew had always spread out across the bed without any shred of inhibition. There was something nervous about Hamish's sleep, no matter how deep it might be.

Going to the window and standing behind the curtains to look out on a dank November Kensington night, the street absolutely silent except for scurrying leaves in the wind, she was astonished at her own calmness. For the first time she had been able to think clearly about Andrew, remember him without agony but with pleasure. She had made love to another man, a seemingly inconceivable thing, and could for the first time accept that he had gone. It was not that Hamish had replaced him in her heart, she knew that could never happen, but that she understood the thing now. At last she knew that he was not coming back.

She supposed she ought to be sad, but she was relieved if anything. For months she had lived with that secret hope, of hearing him come into a room behind her, of turning and seeing him again, just as he had always been. Time and time again, she had reached out in the darkness of her bed and hoped to find him under the covers. But he had never come and she had been exhausted by the pain of disappointment, punishing her at every moment of weakness. Now, finding another man in her bed, a man who had kissed her and made love with equal passion but who was not his replacement, she knew she could remember calmly, without having to wish and pray and hope, always in vain. Andrew was gone. He would not come back, but she would always have him deep in the heart of her and could begin to be thankful for the life they had lived together. There was no need to resent fate any longer.

She turned back into the room and looked at Hamish hunched under the covers. His clothes were scattered on the floor, his strange working man's clothes, coarse and horrid.

He had never had anything new in his life, he had said. It seemed oddly appropriate that she should love such a man now, it was in keeping with her new life. Her arcadia was over, when Andrew had been enough. Such perfect happiness could not come again, but that did not mean there could not be affection, passion, love even. One made the best in the wicked world of realities.

Now he stirred and sleepily reached out for her. Finding her gone, he awoke slowly and stared across at her, his bonny face caught in the shaft of lamplight coming in from the street. 'He's so handsome . . .' Celia had said. 'So handsome I could die for him!'

Alix wondered what weakness in her had drawn her to him. The same weakness, perhaps, which had made her want to climb on that train with Ralph and her mother, that same weakness which had frightened her into thinking Ralph might die. She strove to control these things but they conquered her again and again. And now Hamish, with his puzzled, sleepy face, dragged her down into an emotional life which she both needed and did not need. For her work demanded she cut herself off from all this. She needed to be alone, and yet how unbearable it was to be alone. She could not be the ascetic that her conscience demanded she should be. For all her attempts to strip away herself, she still had a very great deal to sacrifice in the name of her ideals, almost enough to make her think twice.

'Did I do wrong?' he asked.

'No, you didn't,' she said, coming back to him, drawn by his outstretched arms. He held her very tightly for a moment, as if he were afraid he might lose her.

But perhaps I have, she thought, and then feeling the warmth of his lips on her cheek could not agonize any longer, caught up again in the oblivion of their passion.

8

'Well, what do you think?' she said, coming out of the bedroom.

Hamish was surprised. He had expected her to come out of the room sporting some piece of expensive finery, but she was standing before him wearing a long drab coat the colour of dung and a brown hat modestly trimmed with only a band of black velvet.

'Well?' she said again, and then smiled, obviously reading the look of incomprehension on his face.

'Well, I'm no expert on fashion,' he began, 'but I can see . . .'

'That it isn't the sort of thing I usually wear? Yes, isn't it awful? This thing is more like a blanket than a coat but it is just perfect for what I want.'

'Which is?'

'It's a disguise,' she said, unbuttoning the coat to reveal a black skirt and a cheap blouse. 'These are not my clothes, but those of Mary-Ann Scott.'

'And who might she be?'

'She's no one. She doesn't exist. Well, she didn't until yesterday when I went shopping for her. Do you think it works? I think she's a clerk – or perhaps a board school teacher. I must decide.'

'What the devil is this all about?' he asked.

'I want to be incognito. If I'm going to act, I don't want to be recognized. That was the trouble the last time.'

'What are you going to do?'

'I can't tell you, you know that,' she said, taking off the hat and fingering it. 'I really never knew you could get such horrid stuff. I dread to think how much the people who made these got paid. It was all astonishingly cheap, worryingly so.'

'What are you going to do?' he asked again, suddenly filled with concern.

'Don't ask that,' she said. 'Anyone would think you were worried.'

'I think I am. I don't understand all this,' he said, grabbing at her sleeve. 'This play-acting. It's not a game, you know.'

'I know that, Hamish, believe me,' she said, very earnestly. 'And this is not play-acting. I want to prove something with this. You know as well as I do, if not more than I do, that there are two laws in this country – one for the rich and one for the poor. As Alexandra Erskine-Lennox I was excused, but no one will excuse a little nobody like Mary-Ann Scott. They cannot possibly sympathize with her.'

'But what are you going to do?'

'I can't say, can I?' she said. 'And you mustn't worry, Hamish – goodness, you are the last person I thought I should have to say that to.'

'Perhaps, but things are different now.'

'They are not,' she said, rejecting him slightly when he tried to put his arms around her. 'Well, perhaps things are different between us, but the cause is no different, I still believe in that. Nothing can ever change that now. I have made a commitment to it.'

'But I don't . . .' he tried to protest. She put a finger on his lips.

'Shush, let's not worry about it. If you accept me, Hamish, you accept all this. You can do that, can't you?'

He wished he could answer with a confident 'yes' but uncertainty had gripped him. He was suddenly very afraid for her, afraid of losing her, although he had himself told her that to act so bravely for her cause was admirable. He had found it admirable then, but now, having been her lover for a week, it was less clear-cut. He knew her too well now, knew that she would not fail to go to the limit, to martyrdom if necessary, and that terrified him. He had only just found her, only just understood that he could love again, and yet it seemed more than possible that it could all be destroyed.

'Oh, damn it,' he said, and pushed her away from him, steeling himself to separation. 'Alix, I don't know what's happening here. It's all wrong.'

'The world is all wrong,' she said. 'Until we change that . . .'

'Don't you ever think of anything but politics?' he said, exasperated. 'What about us, what about the future?'

'The future will take care of itself,' she said. 'It is the present that matters.'

'Oh, Christ . . . I wish I could be as determined as you,' he said, wandering across the room. 'Everything is upside down for me now. I should never have come with you.'

'Regret is foolish.'

'I don't regret it, that's the thing,' he said. 'This has been the most marvellous week of my life. I never knew I had such feeling in me, Alix, but now I can only think of you and me, and being together. I love you, you do understand that?'

'Yes, and I love you. But there are some things which love cannot change. I have to go to Liverpool today, I have to be Mary-Ann Scott, I have to do this thing. Nothing, not all the adoration in the world, will stop me. If you love me, Hamish, you'll let me go.'

'I couldn't stop you,' he said ruefully. 'But you won't stop me missing you, hurting for you, Alix.'

'Oh God, no, I couldn't because I shall be missing you too, don't you see? But I can't stay. In this case my duty is more important than my selfish desire. There hasn't been a thing in the world worth getting, if it wasn't got without a little pain.'

'That's a sick argument,' he said, and then repented of his bluntness, seeing her face. He saw the courage in it, but realized that it was true courage, because she had so much to lose. She was making a great effort for what she believed in. 'Oh Alix, love, I'm sorry,' he said. 'I just don't want you to go.'

'I don't want to,' she said, 'but I have to. Please understand that.'

'I do,' he said with reluctance. 'Are you going soon?'

'I'm catching a ten o'clock train,' she said. 'I don't know when I will be back.'

'No, of course not. Be careful, won't you?'

'You sound just like Ralph.' She smiled. 'Of course I will be. And you be good and go to your lectures . . .'

'I feel a right fool there,' he said, attempting to inject some humour into the moment, 'I can't bloody write fast enough.'

'You'll learn soon,' she said. 'There's some money in the kitchen drawer.'

'Aren't I supposed to say that to you?' he said, and she smiled and put on her ugly felt hat.

'I have to go now.'

They kissed goodbye, and he held her very tightly for a moment, trying to capture the essence of her to keep during their separation. He wished he knew when she would be back so that he could count the days. He stood in the window and watched her walk away down the street towards the Underground station. Mary-Ann Scott could not, of course, afford to take a cab to Euston.

Travelling third class was for Alix, like her new clothes, an uncomfortable novelty. In the pursuit of absolute authenticity she had even bought a new set of underwear: rough flannel combinations; a pair of standard-sized washing stays (so very different from the expensive French stays she usually wore which were made to measure); and black merino stockings with the clumsiest garters to hold them up. Her chemise and petticoat were trimmed with coarse machinemade lace, with clumsy inserts of openwork which the shop walker had been very proud to point out. Alix could not think why. This combination of badly made, ill-fitting clothes with the barely upholstered banquettes of the third-class carriage was more of an object lesson in the conditions of the majority of women than a hundred pamphlets and reports. By the time they reached Liverpool, she was feeling exhausted and insignificant with her shins well kicked and smoke blown in her face. There were coal smuts on her cheap gloves – Mary-Jane's hopeless attempt at gentility – and as she climbed off the train, no porter rushed to attend to her luggage. This was to be truly incognito.

Since she had no luggage, but only a handbag, of such ugliness as she would never usually have consented to use, she had no need to feel aggrieved that porters did not demand to help her and passed swiftly to the main entrance to the station where she and her fellow soldier had arranged to meet.

'Good grief, Alix, is that really you?'

'Mary-Ann,' said Alix, amused by Catherine Phillips' astonishment.

'I didn't think you were serious about this.'

'Well, I am, deadly. It will make a marvellous point, don't you think? Where have we been assigned to go?'

'One of the smartest shopping streets. Perhaps you are not dressed for it, Mary-Ann?'

'I'll be your maid, ma'am,' said Alix, in a thick Scots accent.

'You'll never keep that up,' said Catherine.

'I bet you a guinea I do.'

'I shall expect to be paid when we get out of Walton Gaol.'

Catherine was an old hand. She had been in prison before.

'Very good, ma'am,' said Alix with deference, and followed her new mistress into Liverpool.

They were dazzled by the number of plate glass windows from which they must choose. They walked up and down the street several times, affecting to be nothing but innocent shoppers, so that they could choose the best target. In the end they selected one with a large display of products from the empire, which was complete with photographs of the King Emperor, Union Jacks, bunting and colour lithographs of various natives slaving for the good of the empire.

'This man is obviously a Tory,' said Alix. 'Why don't we

have a go at all five windows? There isn't a policeman in sight.'

Catherine nodded, and they reached into their bags.

For a moment Alix hesitated, struck into sudden cowardice by the memory of Hamish's bewildered, anxious face. The stakes were now so very much higher than they had been at St Andrews; now she was making a real sacrifice. There would be no one to rescue her. The fate which she had wished for would be inevitable now, and for a moment she could find no glory in it, only fear. She could almost have run away had she not looked back at the window she intended to break, at that smug display of conventional values. Yes, it would have to go and the thing would have to run its course. She was too far along the path to turn back at that late hour.

She managed to throw three stones, with good aim. Catherine seemed to manage four or five. There was a wonderful mess of glass but they had little time to appreciate their handiwork. Within a matter of moments she found herself being very roughly manhandled by a policeman who almost pushed her to the ground. She struggled as he pulled back her arms behind her, incensed that she should be treated so.

'I will come, Constable,' she said, fiercely.

'Huh!' he said, unbelieving, and handcuffed her.

It seemed that the police station was very far away, although it was really not a great distance, but it was turned into a via dolorosa as they walked along, or rather the policeman walked her along, a common criminal on show to all the public. There were outraged faces to pass. Women whispered behind gloved hands, men jeered and laughed, while most agonizingly of all, a small boy who reminded her of pictures she had seen of Drew as a boy, stared at her, a piercing gaze full of silent reproach.

She was deposited in a police cell which smelt of vomit. The door crashed behind her and she heard someone say:'We can get these up before the magistrates this afternoon. Sir Jeffrey Field is on the bench today, isn't he? He always sends these damned women down.'

'Mary-Ann Scott, I sentence you to thirty days' hard labour in the third division,' said the magistrate.

It had taken him only three or four minutes to reach his verdict. The police report effectively damned her. She felt a strange surge of triumph on hearing him, his voice thick with disapproval. It had worked. She had got the sort of sentence which Alexandra Lennox would never have received. Catherine Phillips, well spoken and well dressed, despite past offences had got the same, but in the second division. It was a marvellous travesty of justice! So just before she was hustled away from the dock, she shouted out in the most raucous Scots voice she could manage 'Votes for Women!' and saw one of the court reporters take down her flourish in a notebook.

Although he hardly expected her back that night, Hamish could not help hoping she might be. He sat by the fire, with a torturous book on economics open but unattended, waiting to hear her key in the lock. He wanted her so passionately, like a boy in the keenness of his desire. Suddenly he loathed the business that was keeping her away from him. What on earth had she been going to do, disguised as a shabby clerkess? She had been deliberately looking for trouble, wanting to break the law for the glory of martyrdom. The suffragettes who went to prison sported little medals, like gallant soldiers. She believed she was at war and nothing could stop her fighting.

He sat there, trapped by his love for her. He knew it was gutless of him. If he had had any real courage he would have done the same, fought with her, alongside her, instead of wanting to keep her imprisoned within his arms, enslaved with his kisses. He knew he was as bad as all the men she wanted to fight. He in effect was one of them, and the hardest to fight of all because she loved him. That he knew, he could see it in her face, he had seen the pain of it when she had torn herself away from him that morning. By Christ, she was brave, wonderfully brave, but that could not take the longing away.

Where was she? he wondered. What was she doing? Perhaps she had already got to prison, just as she had desired. The thought of that made him feel physically sick. Prisons were no place for the likes of her. She was too beautiful, too fragile for such a place. How could she possibly bear it, especially if she had decided to go on hunger strike like those other brave, mad women? He had seen the forcible feeding posters – there was a pile of such propaganda lying on the table and it made him furious to think that anyone might touch her roughly, let alone push her around and force tubes down her throat and nose.

I can't stay here, he thought, springing out of his chair. I can't stay and do these damned classes. Not if she's suffering, not if she's in pain. I'm going to Liverpool. I can't bear to be so far away from her.

'Name?' asked the wardress, in a bored voice. It was not surprising she was bored. There had been a great queue of women before they got to Alix, a motley group of suffragettes, prostitutes and simple drunkards who were holding themselves up by leaning against the white-tiled wall against which they had been made to line up after coming out of the Black Maria.

'Mary-Ann Scott,' she remembered to say.

'Age?'

'Twenty-nine.'

'Religion?'

'Church of Scotland.' This was purely nominal, of course, but this did not seem the time or the place for expounding religious doubts.

'Place of birth?'

'Edinburgh.'

'Next!' said the wardress and dismissed her with a wave of the hand. But Alix had something more to say. She had been briefed that this was the moment to make the situation clear.

'I think you should know that I will refuse all food and will not obey any prison rules. I am sorry if this gives you trouble, and will try to give as little inconvenience as possible, but my fast is against the government and I will fight them with my life, not hurting anyone else if possible.'

The wardress did not say anything. She had doubtless heard it all before. She simply waved again to dismiss Alix in the direction of a row of cubicles. Here she stood and waited for a few minutes until another wardress took her to a room with two other officers.

'Will you undress?' asked one. Alix shook her head and they began to loosen her clothes. She did not resist although she wanted to. The indignity of being stripped was enormous, but she tried to console herself that that was what all of them were doing. In the end she managed to convince herself it was a relief to be divested of Mary-Ann Scott's awful clothing, especially those crippling stays.

She allowed herself to be propelled into the bath cubicle, which was a stall in a row, called by the old hands the cowshed. This amusing description enabled her to get through the next humiliation without breaking down. She imagined herself simply an unfortunate piece of cattle being washed down before being taken to market, and made no protest at the vile scummy surface of the bath water or the rough and painful way the wardress scrubbed at her back. In fact she began almost to enjoy this passive resistance, for she could sense the irritated boredom of the wardresses as they attempted to get her dry on a coarse towel which had been made in order not to absorb any moisture. For a moment or two she contemplated attempting to talk them round into joining the movement, asking them to refuse to deal with suffrage prisoners, but something in their grim masks restrained her. In the next cowshed one of the drunken women was howling unrestrainedly, as if it were the end of the world.

They dressed her in her prison clothes – clothes far stranger than those worn by Mary-Ann Scott. For underwear there was a coarse cotton chemise striped red and white, which ran down to her knees; a pair of knee-length drawers in the same stuff; a pair of stays that had to be laced up rather than closed with metal hooks and which were so unyielding to the actual form of her body that Alix wondered if this was not some feminine version of a ball and chain; and to finish this wonderful ensemble, a thick cotton petticoat pleated on to its waistband with such generosity it stuck out, almost like a crinoline. Then came a dress in brown serge, a cap and apron in checked holland cloth, a pair of short but warm woollen stockings and a checked duster which was apparently to be used as a handkerchief. All these items were marked with arrows. A large basket yielded a pair of uncomfortable boots and Alix was at last transformed, by no doing of her own, into the prisoner Scott.

She was returned to a cubicle, not unlike a cupboard with a bench, to await the doctor. The medical examination proved to be very cursory – merely a few questions as to whether she might be infectious or pregnant – and she was left alone again to await the transfer to her cell.

She sat down on the bench, leaning back against the wall, grateful for a few quiet moments to herself. She realized then she was utterly exhausted and very hungry. She had had nothing to eat since breakfast, except for a sandwich on the train. I should have eaten more last night, she thought. I should have fed myself up a bit. But last night food had not seemed very important. She had gone to bed rather early, with Hamish . . .

Hamish . . . She could not help thinking of him, thinking of how they had made love the night before. Suddenly she felt as faint with desire for him as she did for a solid meal. She could be lying comfortably in his arms now, sated with passion (her stomach full as well), and yet here she was, sitting in a cupboard, waiting to be locked in some miserable cell, with very little to look forward to except the glory of resistance.

The door of the cupboard opened and the wardress told her to get up. A pair of sheets was thrust into her arms and she followed the woman, feeling somewhat dazed by the long passageways and many doors. Eventually they reached her cell. My cell for the next month, thought Alix, unable to envisage it without despair now. The door crashed shut behind her and she was alone, with nothing but the small compass of those four walls to look at. For a moment she was really afraid, for now it had actually sunk in what she was doing, that this was not the end of it but only the beginning. There was much worse to come. The ordeal of the last few hours would soon seem insignificant.

9

After two days, two male officers arrived to take Alix to see the governor. As she waited outside the office she was made to stand up against a wall with hot water pipes running up it. The warmth on her back was delicious, the first real comfort she had had in those days.

'Now then, Scott,' said the governor, looking up blandly from the papers on his desk, 'I hear you are refusing to do your work.'

'I refuse to obey any prison rules,' she said stoutly, though she wished she might steady herself against the front of his desk. She felt very fragile.

'Do not answer unless you are asked a question, Scott,' he said sharply. 'I also hear that you have defaced your cell with various slogans and broken the shade of the lamp. You are also refusing food. Is that correct?'

'Yes.'

'Ten days in a special cell,' he said, and dismissed her.

She was taken downstairs, a little sad to be exiled from the cell which she had decorated carefully with her slate pencil. Slate pencils were probably forbidden in the special cells. She would imagine the wall daubed with 'Votes for Women' instead. Or perhaps she could call out – but her voice, she soon found, had grown weak. Defiance was exhausting. There remained only weak resistance.

She curled up on the planked bed and made herself as comfortable as she could, which was not very comfortable, but tucking her legs up to her chest gave her some semblance of security. She closed her eyes, hoping to sleep.

Sleep was the best she could hope for, but she felt too tired for it. Her brain would not settle and the terrible dryness of her throat assaulted her far more than the grinding of her stomach. The hunger she could bear, but for some water . . . some water . . .

But to drink was as bad as to eat and she would not give in. She had, she told herself sternly, lived in privilege and luxury all her life. This was only a small thing to bear and the end was great. She must bear it. But she could not help thinking of strawberries and the wonderful grapes they had eaten in Baden Baden that autumn when Ralph was sent for his cure. They were the finest grapes she had ever tasted but Ralph had not been able to touch them at first. She remembered how frail and feeble he had become, how his face had gone white, his cheeks hollowed out, how his expression had become haggard and old. Will I look like that? she wondered.

Time began to lose any meaning when she arrived in that special cell. She slept intermittently, but could not tell for how long. She was not sure what time of day it was. Occasionally a wardress came in and told her to slop out or brought bread and water which she always refused, although the act of refusal was heroically difficult and she longed to seize the bread and gnaw at it, like some wild animal. She could sense the smell of the bread, a rich earthy smell for it was made with brown flour, and could imagine just how it must taste, and that the water would taste as clear as if it were from some sparkling burn in the mountains.

A man came in who called himself the senior medical officer and asked her when she had last eaten.

'Tuesday morning,' she said. 'I think.'

'That's four days ago. That is too long. I shall have to feed you.'

Could it only be Friday? Had she only been there three whole days? It felt like a lifetime had passed. Only three days and a whole twenty-seven left to endure . . .

The doctor returned an hour or so later (at least she reckoned it was an hour or so). He was accompanied by five wardresses who carried the feeding equipment. The cell seemed stuffed with people, and she lay still, crouched on the bed, mortally terrified by this grim phalanx of faces above her. She knew what they were going to do to her. She had read all the propaganda, she had met people who had endured this, who had survived it, but none of this could comfort her. She felt rigid with terror, especially as they all moved slowly and with deliberate menace into positions where they could hold her down. Two of the women took her arms, the other two her legs, and they pulled her flat on the bed. The doctor then stooped over her, crushing down her knees with his bulk. He dangled the tube in front of her eyes and she clenched her teeth together, keeping her mouth tight shut. He attempted to force the tube between her lips, but using all her strength she kept it out. It was the only point of resistance she had left for they had the rest of her severely overpowered.

He looked annoyed and said, 'We shall have to use a gag. Now there is a wooden one or a steel one. The steel is very painful, and I should not like to have to use it, but if you continue to resist, I shall have no other choice.'

He tried with the wooden one, but only for a moment or two. The sadist, thought Alix, suddenly clutching onto this thought to keep her going. The bastard wants to hurt me! That somehow made it easier when he forced the gag between her teeth, with all the strength of a burglar forcing a lock with a crow bar. She was desperate not to give way, but he succeeded and then screwed open the gag so wide that she thought her cheeks would rip open.

'There,' he said, with some satisfaction, and picked up the tube.

Now she was quite defenceless. There was nothing she could do to stop them pushing that wretched tube down her throat. It seemed to scrape down the sides of her gullet more like a thorny branch than a smooth rubber tube, and it made her choke, her body shuddering with each suppressed cough. But then came the worst of it. She saw the food being poured in and then felt it hit her gullet but in an instant it rose again and she was violently sick all over the doctor. Still they kept pouring, although she continued to vomit. Eventually they pulled out the tube and released her from the gag. The doctor, his expression absolutely contemptuous, slapped her across the cheek but this indignity she scarcely noticed. She was panting from relief at being released from those terrible constraints.

She discovered as she lay there that she was soaking wet, a mixture of food and vomit, some of which had soaked her own hair. She could not move, but could only lie crouched in that foetal position, her body racked with pain. The wardresses informed her it was too late to get a change of clothes as the office was shut, and departed. They were busy, it seemed, for a few minutes later, from the next cell, she could clearly hear the same torture being repeated on someone else. For the first time since she had come, she found that she was crying.

Searching through Alix's address book, Hamish had found various addresses in Liverpool, and so was standing at the door of a large suburban villa while the maid fetched her mistress.

'Miss Phillips?' he said tentatively.

'No,' said the woman, 'I'm afraid my daughter is not at home. As you do not appear to know her, what do you want here?'

'I'm looking for Mrs Lennox. Do you know her, perhaps? I thought you might know where she is.'

'Mrs Lennox? Oh . . .' She seemed reluctant to say anything else. 'What have you to do with Mrs Lennox?' she said disparagingly, for even if Hamish was wearing his best (and only) suit and looking moderately respectable, it was evidently not respectable enough for the likes of Mrs Phillips.

'I'm a friend. I need to know where she is. Can you help me? Please, Mrs Phillips?' he added, with a touch of a plea in his voice.

'I do not know where Mrs Lennox is at present,' she said.

'Well, perhaps you know about Mary-Ann Scott then?'

he asked. At this name, she looked surprised. 'Oh, so you know her, do you?'

'I think you had better come in for a minute,' said Mrs Phillips.

She took him into a stuffy little sitting room – he was obviously not good enough for the drawing room – and did not ask him to sit down. She was probably concerned about the neighbours, for it was clear that she was concealing something.

'I may as well get to the point,' she said. 'My daughter was arrested in the company of a Mary-Ann Scott. I was at the court. She was sent down for a month, I think.'

'I see,' said Hamish. 'Which prison, do you know?'

'Walton Gaol. What has this woman to do with Mrs Lennox?'

'She *is* Mrs Lennox,' said Hamish.

'No, surely not? I've met Alexandra – seen her with my own eyes. Surely I would have recognized her . . .'

'She was well disguised,' said Hamish.

'Why on earth?' exclaimed Mrs Phillips. 'Oh, these women – I simply don't understand it. Really, I don't. I've had to resign myself to Catherine's antics, but there are times . . .' She broke off suddenly and stared at him intently. 'You are not from the press, are you?'

'No, ma'am,' he said, 'I'm not. My name's Anderson, and I'm very sorry to have come to you like this. I didn't know where she was, you see, and I had to find out. I have to see her.'

'There isn't much chance of that,' said Mrs Phillips. 'I have been up to Walton every day this week and spoken to the governor, but he will not let me see my daughter. It is disgraceful. If he will not let me see Catherine, I cannot think a mere friend will be allowed to see Mrs Lennox.'

'Who's to say that Mary-Ann Scott hasn't got a brother?' he said, with a slight smile at the thought of his joining this grave masquerade. But Mrs Phillips did not look very impressed.

'Sometimes,' she said, with a slight sigh, 'I think the whole world has gone mad, Mr Anderson.'

Mrs Phillips was right. There was no chance of being allowed to see her. Hamish did not manage to get to the governor's office, even as Hamish Scott. He was treated with scant respect by those whom he did see, who evidently regarded the brother of a third division criminal as likely to be a criminal himself. The situation was not helped by his own hostility to such places – he had spent several nights in police cells in his boyhood – and he knew very well the contempt with which the law treated anyone who it could not clearly see was worthy of preferential treatment. It was this, he supposed, that Alix was attempting to prove, but it angered him dreadfully that she should be treated as a nobody. He wished to God that they had seen through her disguise, had seen that she was too precious, too fine to be subjected to the usual rigour of the law. He knew this was a nonsense, that he was a fool to wish for injustice when he had fought all his life for the opposite, but his love for her had turned him into a fool. Yes, but a glorious fool who acted for nothing else but love, forgetting everything he had ever held dear because now he believed that he had found the most precious thing in the world. Every principle and ideal could be thrown away, because of her. She justified anything.

He stood outside the gates of the prison and felt his heart sink. He was entirely impotent. He could not help her, could not see her, although that was what he most desired in all the world. God only knew what she might be suffering in there and he could do nothing more than stand outside, powerless and angry, his soul sold for her and no reward. But nothing would make him go away.

In a terraced street near the prison, he spotted a sign for lodgings. They were more than he could ordinarily afford, but Alix had left a hundred pounds for his expenses. It was nothing to her, but a fortune to him and it had wounded his pride at first to take it. But he was beyond pride now. He only wanted to be near her. Lifting the lace curtain in the plain little bedroom at the back of the house, he could see the prison.

'No, I'm afraid it's not the prettiest view,' said the landlady.

'It's all I want to see,' he said, turning round. 'I'll take the room.'

Alix decided to attempt to clean her cell. It would probably take hours, she felt so weak, but it was better that she should attempt to clean it than that poor dab of a creature they had sent in after she had been fed. Imprisonment was enough punishment, and to make prisoners clean up the mess made by others seemed unjust. That woman, in fact little more than a girl, was in for soliciting, she had murmured. She had been kind, and had washed Alix's face for her. Alix resolved that she should not suffer the indignity of cleaning up for her again.

They had fed her twice since then, with the same result. She had felt near to choking and had been violently sick and was now left in considerable pain. Every joint in her body seemed at its last ebb, and when she had gone to fill the pails with water at slopping out, it had been difficult to move. However, she knew she must keep moving, although wanting to lie on the bed all day and slip into unconsciousness.

Getting down on to her hands and knees, she knew that the task of cleaning would be fairly futile. The floor was dirty, not only with her own vomit, but with accumulated dust. A scrubbing brush was not equal to the task, but she slopped a little water around and attempted to get some of the rubbish up. She tried to scrub at it vigorously, as she had seen housemaids cleaning the front step, but watched with creeping despair as the water washed all into a sea of mud, some of which was soon soaked up by the bulky hem of her serge skirt.

'Oh, damn it,' she whispered, realizing the futility of it. She leant forward, resting on the brush, and stared down at the vile floor. 'I should rather die.' She was ashamed of her own cowardice, and of the tears which she could not help shedding. It seemed, as she squatted there miserably on the floor, her hair falling around her, wild and knotted now

556

from food and her own vomit, that she was at the very nadir of her life. This was not life, but exile from life. There was no point living like this. But escape was closed to her. The cells were carefully bereft of anything with which one might kill oneself. Memories of the past, which should have fortified her, could do nothing but taunt her with her present wretchedness. 'Look what you have thrown away, look what you could be doing, you stupid fool! You could be so happy, and yet you have brought all this on yourself! Give up, Alix, give up!'

It would be so easy to give up. It would be so easy. Hadn't she done enough for the cause? Surely everyone would understand if she gave up now? It would be entirely forgivable. So the devils spoke to her, and she almost answered 'Yes', but heard a rattle of keys in the door. One of the male officers was standing there, his expression grimly unsympathetic, and in his face she seemed to see summed up all the oppression and all the contempt which she had set out to fight.

'Get up, Scott!'

She struggled to get up. It was very difficult as her bones seemed to have set into that squat. As she managed to straighten, she moved her foot slightly, but slipped and found herself tumbling down to the floor again, having lost her balance. Her face fell flat into the mess. She would have stayed there and wept at her own indignity, had she not heard the officer laugh. How dare he! With all the strength she could muster, she got to her feet again and drew herself up as tall as she could.

'How dare you laugh at me!' she said imperiously. The man looked startled. 'How dare you!' He was obviously not used to prisoners speaking back.

'Don't speak out of turn, woman!' he snapped back, but he was obviously rattled. It had been Alix Lennox speaking, not Mary-Ann Scott.

Hamish, after over a week of desperation, decided to tell the truth. That surely would make them listen. He loitered in the prison forecourt just as the governor emerged, and grabbed the man by the arm before he had a chance to climb into the four-wheeler that was waiting for him.

'What do you want?' he said, attempting to shake Hamish off. 'Let me go, man, or I'll have you arrested.'

There was a look in his eyes which suggested he thought he was being molested by an aggrieved former prisoner.

'I want to talk to you about Mary-Ann Scott.'

'Who?'

'Christ!' Hamish could not help exclaiming. 'She's one of your prisoners. I think you should know something about her.'

'Don't tell me – she's innocent?' he said with an acid smile.

'You should know who she really is,' said Hamish. 'She is not Mary-Ann Scott, it's a false name. She is Alexandra Erskine-Lennox.'

'Mrs Lennox?' said the governor. '*The* Mrs Lennox?'

'Yes.'

'Good God!'

It was agreeable to see how surprised and then how immediately distressed the man was. Alexandra was well known from her association with the Pankhursts. She had appeared many times on the platform with them.

'I thought you might be interested to know,' said Hamish.

'Yes, thank you,' he said, without gratitude. 'Well, I must go.' And he climbed into the four-wheeler and drove off smartly.

How many times had they done this to her now? She had lost count. She had thought she might grow used to it, but every time the fear and pain seemed worse. She could not sleep for fear of it, and the doctor's face had grown to be that of the devil for her as he sat across her knees, his awful bulk crushing them down, so that she could not move.

'Right then, Scott,' he said, forcing in the gag. She was weaker now and resisted less. She could no longer grit her teeth or shout out her resistance, but her body proclaimed it. Her throat and stomach would not take that tube. In their pain they shouted it, in each bout of vomiting they made it clear that she would not submit to this.

'Bovril and brandy today,' he said. 'Perhaps that will stay down better.'

He had given her this mixture the other day. The brandy had warmed her for a while and then she had been left in a state of unnatural cold as if the blood had stopped flowing round her body. She had believed that she was near death then. Yet her body seemed determined that she should live.

He pushed the tube in, provoking that intense sharp pain again. She felt how difficult it was to breathe, her chest rising and falling sharply. She wondered how she would get enough air for her lungs and felt the nausea come, even before the food. Soon she was shaking and retching. It had never been so bad before. She felt she was drowning and saw the faces above her lose focus, as if swirling mist had come between her and them. The food came rushing down the tube and into her, as hot and as deadly as molten steel. It was absolute poison to her. She resisted it with all the little strength in her body.

She realized that she was about to lose consciousness, felt she was on the blink of oblivion at last. Dimly, as she fell away from them, she heard someone else come through the cell door and say, 'Well, well, if it isn't Mrs Lennox.'

'You are to be released on medical grounds,' they said.

She had come round in the prison hospital and noticed at once that she was being treated differently. She was no longer Scott, to be dealt with contemptuously. Her clothes were returned to her and she was allowed to have a bath. She collected her other possessions, signed for them, and wandered out into the fresh air, the first she had had for days. She could scarcely move her legs, but she was determined to walk to freedom as fast as she could.

It was late in the afternoon, she discovered, and winter dusk had covered everything. The wind stung her face and she felt as weak as a reed in a storm. She wondered what she was going to do. She felt too feeble to get very far, and she had only a small amount of money on her. But suddenly she was aware of someone running over to her, running with great vigorous strides, a fine tall young man, his face wild with joy.

'Oh, thank God!' Hamish exclaimed. 'Thank God!'

He folded her in his arms, and Alix, who had forgotten tenderness and warmth and human compassion, felt overwhelmed. She buried her face in his coat, heard his heart beat, felt his warm hands stroking her. Her legs gave way. He alone was holding her up.

10

It was strange, Jessie thought, standing at the window, how quickly people could accustom themselves to a new place. They had been at St Florimonde aux Champs for only a few weeks now, but already a domestic pattern of unfailing regularity had established itself. She felt she had lived there a hundred weeks already, or even a hundred years.

The château was not as grand as its name suggested. It was, in fact, an overgrown farmhouse with only a single, round tower to give it pretensions to nobility. But there was room enough for all of them and in every room there were vast stone fireplaces, made to burn vinewood in, grand enough for any castle.

Below the window, Ralph, in his shirtsleeves, was giving Chloe a riding lesson while Jo and Flora, hardened by Scottish winters, were sitting on the large stone mounting block, basking in the brilliant winter sunshine like a pair of lizards. Soon it would be Flora's turn to ride and Jo would scowl with jealousy because she was still too small for the pony (but Ralph, the day before, had thrilled her by taking her up in front of him on his bay mare and trotting round the forecourt). Beyond the forecourt and the jardin-anglais, as the small park was called, lay the gentle darkness of the woods which surrounded the property, still coloured soft brown with fallen leaves. There she would walk later with the children, through the wonderful scrunching litter of autumn, capturing a wonderful abundance of glossy horse chestnuts, which it seemed French children had no use for. Then they would go back to their lessons with Miss Baird, the governess, and Ralph would come back from his ride and sit in the petit salon immersed in a book for an hour or two. Jessie would sit there too, perhaps also with a book, but more often in delicious indolence, savouring the joy of sitting and thinking. She had never had such free time on her hands before, for all her domestic chores were taken from her by the charming and diligent French servants, and the children, growing independent now and fond of their kindly old governess (who had once taught Alix and Ralph), relied on her less. She had unexpected liberty here. At first she had worried that she would not be able to fill her time, but already over a week had slipped through her fingers and she had scarcely noticed the time passing. But she had noticed a great deal else.

It was as if her senses had been unlocked in that first experience of a foreign place. She felt she perceived everything with extraordinary clarity; from seeing the strangely elegant cracks in the ochre-painted plaster of the dining room, to smelling the rich, earthy scent which lingered in the woods; from the delicate taste of the beurre blanc which Genviève had served with pike, to the peculiar, depressed sound of the bell in the village church. These, and a myriad of other, tiny, seemingly insignificant things, she realized were a sort of treasure for her. She looked as if there were rubies and pearls strewn about her. Each experience was as precious, if not more so, because she saw their uniqueness. They belonged and could only belong to her, because she alone had gathered them and stamped them with her own consciousness, linking them into all her past experiences to make some fabulous chain in her imagination which would be with her as long as memory served her. Even then she suspected that these were not things one could forget. They were not the names and dates so easily mislaid, but shreds of life, with all the vigour that implied.

She pushed open the casement and leant her elbows on

the window sill, enjoying a moment of maternal pride to see
Chloe managing the pony at a trot, with not a trace of
concern on her face. She seemed to have a natural ability
with horses which Jessie could not understand, being
nervous of them herself. She would soon be galloping off
into the woods with Ralph.

He saw her at the window and waved and smiled up at her
in a way she scarcely recognized. There was nothing
guarded or melancholic about it. It was exactly the frank,
free smile of a man who had nothing to care about in the
world; as if he had, in coming here, shed a skin of
responsibility (just as she had, she supposed) and become
light-hearted, boyish even. He seemed almost a different
person, a new person who was doubly attractive to her.

She could not deny *that*, although it made her sigh to
think she could not express it, not yet at least. For she had
begun to think she would have to give him some indication
of what she felt. To see him every day, to be on such
terms of intimacy with him, had only strengthened the
conviction of her desire. If living with Sholto had stripped
the illusion of his charm from him, living so closely with
Ralph did nothing but confirm what she had known for
years. She could see no signs of a domestic tyrant, but only a
brilliant, intelligent man who had not let his public success
destroy his essential gentleness. It was perhaps that above
all other things which she admired most in him. It was rare
enough in a man, for many would have thought it a
weakness, but Jessie could only see it as a strength.

She watched him help Flora mount the pony, and dispel
her nervousness with a few careful words (for Flora had
none of Chloe's aggressive self-confidence). She saw her
daughter smile as she became used to the movement of the
animal, and saw Ralph, who held the bridle, glancing back
with solicitude to see that all was well. It was odd how easily
children accepted Ralph and yet older, supposedly wiser
people found him so difficult. It was hard to forget Sholto's
absolute scorn, for example. But there again, it was easy to
see how such subtlety of character would have been wasted
on Sholto.

I should tell him. I should, she thought, but she knew she was too afraid to speak although not because she was afraid of him and what he might say. She knew that any rebuttal would be put with exquisite tact. She was afraid of breaking the spell of this lovely place by speaking. Was it really necessary to speak, when she had almost all she could desire? She had his company every day and his innocent affection. What more should she possibly want? Surely it was only greed and selfishness that made her feel she must unburden her uncomfortable feelings on to him, feelings which must alter their relationship for the worse if they were not reciprocated. He would start to avoid her in order to avoid fanning any unnecessary flames. The thought of such a quiet rejection was enough to stop her tongue. No, I will not, not unless he comes to me. He must break the silence! she resolved. That was what she dreamt of, like a yearning girl she dreamt it – that the kiss he had given her so long ago might not be simply a distant memory but a portent of something that would come. That he would once again throw himself into her arms and lay his soul bare at her feet.

And why could that not happen here, in this enchanted place? Why not here, where wayside shrines to the Virgin spoke of an ancient and mysterious faith? Could she not trust in the sheer will of love and learn patience for a little while longer? She felt sure that here such patience might well be rewarded.

Ralph rode back through the woods, conscious of, and perhaps slightly guilty about, the sense of deep contentment which had come over him. The château was all that he had ever dreamt a house in the depths of France should be. It had been miraculous that his mother had chanced on a place that so exactly suited his temperament. He had been surprised, indeed, that she had not settled on some hideous villa at Cannes but on this miraculous place, lost in the forest. If he were to have chosen a place to abandon his responsibilities for a few months, he could not have chosen better.

The house came into sight again, its friendly grey-gold stone welcoming him. He could smell the vine smoke in the air and breathed it in deeply, his body well exercised, his brain well rested. He had thought it would be difficult to cast aside the horrors at the Quarro and his worries about Alix, but he had shrugged them off and given himself up to that wonderful selfishness that was only permitted to invalids.

He dismounted in the stable yard and walked back to the house at a leisurely pace, his hands thrust in his pockets, thinking of the excellent coffee which would be waiting for him, in a swirling rococo silver pot, and the dish of palmier biscuits. There was the re-reading of the *Chronicles of Barsetshire*, interspersed with *Madame Bovary* (after all this was France) to divert him until luncheon and then, when Genviève had done her worst (which was her best) and had stuffed them all senseless with wonderful food, they would all go out and walk in the jardin-anglais.

He went into the entrance hall and found a suitcase and attaché case at the foot of the stairs, the attaché case stamped with the initials J.S.

'John, you're early!' he exclaimed, going into the grand salon and seeing his secretary sitting by the fire with his mother and Jessie. He had been expected the following day.

'I'm afraid so, Mr Erskine,' he said.

'Don't apologize – you'll be glad you did come early, when you realize what a wonderful place this is.'

'You are certainly looking very well, sir,' he said, with a smile. 'And you'll be pleased to know there are only a very few things requiring your attention.'

'Everything's going smoothly then?'

'Perfectly. In fact, I think business is going well for everyone. I took the liberty of telephoning Monsieur Auguste before I left Edinburgh, Mrs Hamilton, and apparently there isn't a cover to be had there without a week's notice.'

'Perhaps we should just leave them to it, Jessie?' remarked Ralph.

'Yes, we're obviously superfluous,' she said. 'Coffee?'

'Of course,' he said, throwing himself into the armchair opposite John Shaw. 'A good journey then?'

'The crossing was fine. Oh, and I've brought you the London papers. No *Scotsman*, I'm afraid, Mrs Erskine.'

'I'm getting to like *Le Figaro*,' she said.

When they had finished coffee, the children came down ready for their walk, and Jessie got up to go with them.

'Might I come with you?' asked John Shaw. 'I'm in need of exercise after all that time on the train.'

'Of course.' She smiled. 'Ralph, will you come?'

'I'm rather tired just now,' he said, unavoidably stifling a yawn. 'I rode further this morning than usual.'

'Yes, Ralph, you mustn't overdo it,' said Mrs Erskine.

He settled in the petit salon, pulling one of the bergère chairs into the window recess to catch more sunlight. Stretching his long legs across an upholstered stool, he found himself so indolent that he scarcely attended to the page in front of him, but kept glancing idly out of the window to the jardin-anglais where Jessie and John Shaw were walking, apparently deep in conversation. What can they find to say to each other? he wondered, and noticed through the door to the grand salon that his mother was observing them also.

She must have sensed he was looking at her, for she turned and came towards him.

'They make an excellent couple,' she said. 'A good man like that would be just the thing for Jessie and the girls, don't you think, Ralph?'

The question caught him quite off guard.

'Jessie and John?' he could not help exclaiming. 'Mother, I really don't think . . .'

'Oh, I know it hasn't been that long since Hamilton died, but that marriage was long dead before she was widowed,' she went on. 'I think they would deal excellently together.'

'You do?' he said, getting up and watching them again. They stood in profile now, John with his arms folded and Jessie saying something with extravagant gestures which was making him laugh. It disturbed him, but he cast it off by saying, 'You're just match-making, Mother.'

'Perhaps,' she admitted. 'But I can't think Jessie will stay unmarried for very long. She's too attractive. She will have plenty of offers, I'm sure. She has her future to think of as well. Those girls need a father – she knows that.'

Ralph tried to dismiss this as one of his mother's wild fancies but he could not. He stared again at John Shaw, convinced now that the man was flirting with her and was she not responding? They had known each other for some time, and now she was free, who was to stop him pressing his suit? Perhaps, he had, like Ralph, admired her from a distance. Ralph found, to his shame, that this thought appalled him. He had for so long been accustomed to take Jessie for granted as his own object of private devotion. It was obvious, of course, that other men would admire her, but he could not help realizing that this made him feel aggrieved, as if she had in some way been unfaithful to him. Naturally she was quite innocent of that, but no one could deny that she was clearly enjoying John Shaw's company a great deal. And he could not deny that he felt the green ghost of jealousy creep over him.

It was pleasant to have a visitor to the château and Jessie had not realized what good company John Shaw was. But anyone whom Ralph had worked so closely with for so long would have to be of the same turn of mind. He had himself said, as they walked in the garden before lunch, that Ralph as much as anything had been responsible for his education, always throwing books and ideas in his way. That was a feeling she knew well herself and it was agreeable to talk to someone who admired him as much as she did. There was in fact a great deal of common ground between them. His background had not been dissimilar, although his parents had been slightly less feckless and more prosperous than hers. But he had felt cheated of his education – he even confessed that at one time he had hoped to become a minister: 'But Mr Erskine soon cured me of that. He set me reading Hume, would you believe?'

She had been happy to let him talk, to tell her about his early days at Garbridge, remembering when Ralph had first come to work there in his summer vacations.

'He was a revelation to me,' he said. 'I couldn't imagine how he could be Mr Erskine's son. He was so different, so agin everything at Garbridge, and always getting in trouble for it. We used to feel sorry for him, I'm ashamed to say, in a very contemptuous way. But he's proved himself a hundred times over – in many ways, he's done more than his father.'

'I don't think he'd let you say that to his face.'

'No, but that's the feeling. God, the place is strange without him – the same down in Musselburgh . . .'

'Like an army without a general.'

'Aye, that's it, Mrs Hamilton. That was a close thing, that business at the Quarro. It would have been a disaster for the company if he had . . .'

'Yes, I can imagine,' she cut in. She did not like to think what a close shave it had been. 'Well, give him two or three months here and he'll be back to you in full working order, just like a Thistle engine.'

'I should think so,' he said. 'Now, where have those bairns of yours got to?'

'Oh, they always disappear into the woods. They'll be all right.'

'I think we should go and find them. They might want someone to help them climb the trees.'

'Do you like children, Mr Shaw?'

'I love them. I've a stack of nephews and nieces.'

'I wonder you haven't got married.'

'Oh, I never met the right woman,' he said, but added with a grin, 'but you never know, there's plenty of time, isn't there?' And with that he strode off into the woods.

11

'John Shaw has achieved a miracle, you know,' Jessie remarked a few days later.

'He has?' said Ralph. 'Regarding what?'

'Regarding arithmetic. He has finally managed to convince Flora that long division is not some devilish trick invented by dominies to torture innocent children, but actually of some practical use.'

'Good God,' he said without enthusiasm.

'Ah, well, perhaps he never converted you,' she went on cheerfully. 'He did remark that you were not the world's finest mathematician.'

'That's an understatement,' said Ralph. 'It took me far longer than Flora to understand long division. I must have been at least twenty-two before I finally grasped it. I always detested the way things would not divide up equally. It offended my aesthetic sense not to have a neat division of the parts.'

'Two apples for me, and two apples for you – that sort of thing?'

'Yes, that exactly,' he said, and found himself thinking how pretty she looked that morning. She was resting her hands lightly on the top rail of a handsome high-backed chair in a way that showed off her figure to great advantage. Dressed as ever with extreme simplicity, in a walking skirt in Black Watch plaid, with a long navy knitted jacket, she was superficially without airs, but he could not help detecting in her manner, in the line of her very body, some element of display. She was conscious of her attractiveness, it seemed. It must be all those damned compliments that John Shaw has been ladling over her, he thought irritably, for he had become as perverse as Leontes, seeing flirtation in every conversation. Yet he could not bring himself to say anything, although every time he saw them together, which seemed to be all the time, he felt his own desire quicken and kindle inside him. He would not speak to her of it, for he feared a terrible put down, a sudden announcement of an engagement. 'She will not stay unmarried long,' his mother had said. 'She is so attractive.'

'Penny for them?' she said, seeing that they had lapsed into silence. It was on the tip of his tongue to ask what she might feel about John Shaw, but suddenly the sound of a motor coming noisily up the avenue distracted them.

'Who can that be?' he asked, getting up from his seat.

'It's the station taxi,' she said. 'I wonder who it is.'

They went out into the forecourt to wait for it. As it turned a little, he glimpsed a woman's face.

'Good heavens!' he exclaimed. 'It's Alix . . .'

But more surprises were to come when the taxi stopped, and from the far door Hamish Anderson leapt out.

'I couldn't think what else to do,' he said. He looked flustered to say the least. 'I had to get her away.'

If Erskine was shocked that Anderson was his sister's escort, he was too polite to show it. He reserved his shock for Alix's appearance as she climbed carefully out of the car, supported tenderly by Hamish. She was still very frail, and he feared making her travel had made her worse. He saw Ralph and Jessie Hamilton blench at the sight of her, but she managed a gallant smile and said, 'Well, I said I would try and come. Won't Mother be pleased, Ralph?'

'What on earth has happened to you, Alix?' he said, rushing forward. 'You look like a ghost.'

'I nearly was,' she said. 'But we Erskines are tougher than that, aren't we?'

'I think we'd better get you inside,' said Jessie Hamilton.

They went into the house, which seemed very old and shabby to Hamish, but in a large parlour there was a great fire blazing which made the place look a great deal more cheerful. Alix sank gratefully into an armchair by the fireplace.

'You should be in your bed,' said Ralph. 'What's wrong with you? Why on earth didn't you wire us?'

'His Majesty's prisons do not permit one to send telegrams, Ralph,' she said.

'What! You've been in prison?'

'I have been in prison, yes, but I have not submitted.'

'You've not been on hunger strike, have you?' said Jessie Hamilton, horrified. 'But, Alix . . .'

'You know my views, Jessie,' she said simply.

'I'll go and fetch your mother,' said Jessie. 'She will be pleased to see you.'

'She won't,' said Ralph Erskine bluntly. 'Not in this state. Good God, for how long?'

'Not now, Ralph,' she said, leaning back. 'I can't bear too many questions . . . please?'

'Oh, Alix . . .' he said, his voice thick with distress. 'Why on earth . . .'

'I think she should sleep,' said Hamish.

'Yes, of course. I'll go and sort something out.'

In a few moments Mrs Erskine appeared in a great state of agitation. She threw her arms around her daughter, thanked Hamish profusely for bringing her there and bore her off upstairs, issuing a stream of orders to just about everyone. Hamish was left alone with Ralph Erskine.

'You look pretty tired yourself, Anderson,' Ralph said, offering him a chair.

'It was a hellish journey,' he said. 'She is still in a lot of pain.'

'What on earth have they done to her?'

'She was forcibly fed.'

'Oh God, no!' Ralph turned away.

'You see, she was in disguise. She pretended to be a clerkess called Mary-Ann Scott so that they shouldn't treat her favourably. She was a third division prisoner.'

'So they treated her like a common criminal – it's bloody disgraceful!'

'I managed to tell the governor who she was. I had to get her out of there. I couldn't bear the thought of it.' He knew his voice had betrayed too much.

'I'm glad you were able to help her,' Ralph said. 'Really, Hamish, you do turn up at extraordinary moments,' he added, as if he were trying to salvage something cheerful.

'Aye, I suppose I do. I suppose it all looks a bit odd to you, us travelling together and all that.'

'No, it doesn't matter. What matters is that she's here now, and that she's safe.'

'Yes, thank God,' he was able to agree.

'Of course I shall come down for dinner,' said Alix, shortly after waking up. 'Are we dressing here? I can't account for the state of my clothes. Hamish packed them and he is no lady's maid.'

'You let Mr Anderson pack for you?' said Mrs Erskine, glancing at Jessie.

'Yes – who else was going to do it? I could scarcely lift my arms at that point. I simply lay like an idiot on the sofa while he did everything. He even made me mutton broth.'

'Goodness,' said Jessie. 'He sounds a useful person.'

'A knight in shining armour, obviously,' said Mrs Erskine. 'I didn't know that you had become such friends.' This remark was offered in a mildly interrogative tone and made Jessie smile. She expected Alix to make some evasive answer, for it was all too clear how things stood between them, but instead she said with extraordinary bluntness, 'Yes, and if you want to make sure that I carry on getting better, you had better have his things brought in here. I can't sleep alone these days.'

'Alix! Really . . .'

'I need him, Mother,' she said simply. 'I have nightmares.'

This left Mrs Erskine bereft of words and Jessie could not help wondering at Alix's lack of tact. After a few moments Mrs Erskine, having collected her thoughts, said, 'Alix, you may be ill, you may have suffered a great deal, but if you think that that can alter the fundamental laws of morality . . .'

'They don't exist,' interjected Alix. 'You only think they do.'

'This is my house, Alix, and while you are under my roof I will not have anything as disgraceful as you and Mr

571

Anderson playing at being man and wife. Think what sort of an example that would be to the children.'

'I think that is for Jessie to decide, Mother. You have no right to interfere. She doesn't, does she, Jessie?'

She was a little annoyed to find herself dragged into this dispute. It was going to be difficult to disentangle herself without offending one of them. It was true she had no personal objection to their being lovers, and she did not think it would be such a pernicious thing for the girls to see that the world did not in fact operate under a simple and universal set of rules. But this was Mrs Erskine's roof, and her beliefs were to be respected. If only Alix had not been so blunt – there was no doubt, since it was a large house, that they could have carried on without Mrs Erskine being offended. She need have known nothing, but Jessie suspected that Alix would have found such subterfuge indefensible. Like her mother, she lived by very high principles. It was unfortunate that in all their idealism there was very little common ground.

'Well, Jessie?' asked Mrs Erskine.

She took a deep breath and said, 'I really don't think I should say. I like you both too much to take sides.'

'Oh, Jessie, really!' exclaimed Alix. 'How lukewarm you are sometimes. Surely you agree that conventional morality is really a stranglehold upon women? That the sooner we are out with it, the better.'

'No,' said Mrs Erskine, who had obviously decided to answer for her, 'of course she doesn't agree with you. She is simply being tactful for your sake, although you scarcely deserve such consideration the way you go on!'

'Be careful what you say, Mother,' said Alix sourly. 'You may give me a relapse.'

'Oh, Alexandra, you are impossible!' said Mrs Erskine, throwing up her hands. 'Come along, Jessie, I think we had better go and dress.'

Jessie was glad to reach the solitude of her room and forget about the quarrel while getting ready for dinner. That had been the most awkward thing about staying with the Erskines – they could not contemplate the thought of eating dinner without a change of clothes. It was easy enough for Ralph and John Shaw, of course, but for the women the case was more complicated. Jessie had no smart evening clothes to speak of, only a few dinner blouses, and it had been galling to notice that Miss Baird had a more extensive selection of these items. But this had recently been remedied. She had gone to visit Saumur with Mrs Erskine, and they had both been astonished by the quality and smartness of the clothes for sale there. It had made Mrs Erskine regret that she had no need of such things, and then perhaps seeing the look of longing in Jessie's eyes as she gazed at a dinner dress in mulberry crêpe-de-chine, had said, 'But there is someone who does need a few fresh things, I think.'

Whereupon Jessie had been marched into various shops and kitted out very splendidly, despite protesting loudly against this embarrassing generosity. Mrs Erskine had said, 'I did use to enjoy choosing clothes for Alix, but I am not allowed to do that now, of course, so you must submit to my indulgence like a good girl, Jessie.'

So now she had three magnificent dinner dresses to choose from: a blue and cream striped silk, with a high, tight waist; a silver grey gauze with marcasite trimmings; and the wonderful mulberry crêpe-de-chine. She chose the latter, and when she was dressed in this finery, went to see the girls.

After a chapter of *The Wind in the Willows*, Jo had fallen asleep and Flora was quite settled. Chloe, being the eldest, did not go to bed until later and was sitting in the next room catching up on her correspondence. She was writing to a school friend on a piece of blue Erskine and Company letter paper.

'Who gave you that?' asked Jessie.

'Mr Shaw,' she said, carefully dipping her pen into the inkwell.

'Barbara will think you have gone to Lanarkshire.'

'Not if she looks at the postmark.'

'True,' observed Jessie.

Chloe looked up at her and said, after a moment's

573

deliberation, 'Mother, do you like Mr Shaw?'

This put her on the spot.

'Well,' she said, as blandly as she could, 'of course I like him . . .'

'He likes you, you know,' put in Chloe.

'Did he say that?'

'Well, I wouldn't make it up, would I?'

'No, of course not. I'm just rather surprised, that's all.'

'Because it means he wants to marry you?'

'You are wise beyond your years, Chloe.' She smiled. 'It might mean that, or it might mean nothing.'

'Oh, it can't mean nothing,' said Chloe, 'or he wouldn't have said it, would he?'

'Good point,' said Jessie. 'Well, thank you for warning me, Chloe.'

'So you don't like him?'

'I do like him, but I wouldn't marry him.' It was best to be frank. Chloe was too bright to be easily duped.

'Oh, good,' she said, and returned to her letter.

'Does that mean you don't like him?' asked Jessie mischievously.

'Oh, no,' said Chloe coolly, 'I like him, but I wouldn't marry him.'

Jessie, highly amused, said, 'Oh, well, I'm glad we agree on that. Good night then, darling.'

'Good night, Mother,' she said, glancing up as Jessie went to the door. 'But I wouldn't mind if you married Ralph, you know.'

It was on the tip of her tongue to say 'Neither would I!' but although she felt she could be honest about what she might feel for John Shaw, she could not be clear about Ralph. So she said instead, 'That's because you have expensive tastes, my dear.'

'Perhaps,' admitted Chloe. 'Hadn't you better be going down now? You'll be late for dinner.'

'Aren't I supposed to say things like that to you?' said Jessie as her parting shot, and blew her daughter a kiss.

In the grand salon she found John Shaw chatting politely with Mrs Erskine and Miss Baird. He had his back to her and did not see her come in, but when she announced herself, she noticed, as perhaps she had not done before, how he leapt out of his chair at the sight of her. He smiled broadly and said, with complete sincerity, 'Oh, Mrs Hamilton, how bonny you look tonight!'

Dear God, he is falling in love with me, she thought, for the way he looked at her in that moment was unmistakable and to her annoyance it, as much as the compliment, had made her blush. She was embarrassed that she should have provoked such a show of devotion.

'Ah, here we all are,' said Ralph, coming in. 'Yes, she does look handsome, John.'

She started and turned, her face still crimson, and saw, just as she had seen John's ardour, that Ralph had read the situation and was not amused. The tone of his voice had made that clear. In fact he was obviously so rattled that he then walked straight past her, as if she were not even there.

He's jealous! thought Jessie, turning back to look at him. There must have been an enquiring expression on her face, because he raised an eyebrow to her, as if to say: 'Well, what? Surely you should be answering the questions!' She sat down in a slight daze, troubled by the sudden frost in the air. She had never felt the breath of his anger upon her before, but now it was all too evident, especially when Shaw came and sat beside her. Heavens, if he is jealous, if he is angry with John for flirting with me, then it must be that he loves me . . . What else could explain such a show of ill temper that was so unlike him? He was obviously stirred up to the very core to behave like that, stirred up about her. Yet he had not said a word about it. If he felt so strongly for her, as she was convinced now that he did, then what on earth was keeping him quiet? She was angry herself now – it was a shabby way to learn of his regard, through a show of petty jealousy. Damn you, Ralph, she found herself thinking. This is not what I wanted! And in this spirit of pique, she did not move away when John Shaw inched a little closer to her on the sofa. She was keenly aware that Ralph was watching the space between them like a hawk.

Fortunately the arrival of Alix and Hamish created a

spectacular diversion. Dressed in an ivory silk dress of superb simplicity, with a gold-embroidered gauze scarf tossed carelessly about her shoulders, her beauty had never seemed to Jessie quite so magnificent or so forbidding. There was still an ashen quality to her face, and her hair, very plainly and smoothly put up, had an almost metallic look. She was more like a statue than a human being, and the sight of her silenced them all. Hamish hovered at her elbow, looking as harried and as ill rested as before. But he was obviously wildly in love with her. His every gesture betrayed it.

As they went in to dinner, Jessie sensed the complex currents running between them all. What should have been a happy family dinner was going to be nothing of the sort, she was sure. There was an oppressive atmosphere in the room which one could have sliced with a knife. Jessie could sense the soft whisper of Mrs Erskine's disapproval, the quiet insistent beat of John Shaw's creeping love, the high clear note of Alix's idealism, the throb of Hamish Anderson's manic, confused passion, and most discordant of all in this symphony of tension, like the squeak of a rusty hinge, was Ralph's jealousy. He sat at the head of the table, glowering at her, smiling a thin-lipped smile which she loathed!

And what wretched noise are you making, Jessie? she demanded of herself, feeling that her nerves were being pummelled in a meat pounder. An angry noise, like the low rumbling at the start of a storm . . .

She was angry at all of them, and most particularly at herself, for forgetting simplicity and behaving badly, for letting unpleasant emotions take over when they should have been sitting there amiably, enjoying that wonderful food. Genviève had obviously put her entire artistry into the Porc aux Pruneaux, and yet no one seemed to bother to acknowledge this, choosing instead to make brittle, somewhat pointless conversation. Jessie was beginning to wonder how much more of it she could bear when Alix remarked, with all the blitheness of a lunatic throwing dynamite on to a fire, 'Do you know, I am surprised that we are the only nation to campaign so vociferously for women's rights. I think that our French sisters must be particularly oppressed.'

It was the first time that anyone had actually mentioned the suffrage question, and Jessie had the distinct sense that the remark had been directed at her.

'Perhaps they do not feel oppressed,' said John Shaw, gamely.

'Perhaps,' said Alix, thoughtfully, 'but I rather think it is something dreadful in the feminine character which makes them natural cowards. So many women are slaves to convention and that is the lowest form of cowardice, naturally. Now, if there were some way of motivating women out of that trough of cowardice, then there would be no end to what might be achieved, would there?'

'Oh, for God's sake, Alix!' said Ralph tetchily. And reaching for the decanter, went on, 'Not this, now – please!'

'I don't think you can dismiss all women as cowards, Alix,' said Jessie, mettled now for a fight. 'It hardly shows you to be their champion if you despise them all so.'

'I don't despise them. I despise their attitudes, which are largely produced by men. It has been in their interest to make women spineless.'

'But, Alix, don't you think women are brave despite all that? They bear children, they make lives and homes for themselves despite dreadful odds . . .'

'And you think that is enough? To go on enduring, until the end of the world, making the best of a bad job. That's pragmatism, isn't it? I think it's shoddy behaviour, frankly.'

'It isn't shoddy if you've only a few shillings,' said Jessie, hotly.

'All right, let us excuse the poverty-stricken,' Alix said magnanimously. 'What about those middle-class women who have enough money to feed themselves and their children – the women who waste their lives on trivial things? How do we get them to fight for us?'

'By showing we are serious and responsible,' said Jessie.

'Yes?'

'Look, Alix, I know what you are trying to get me to say, but I won't fight with you over this.'

'I wasn't suggesting a fight, Jessie,' she said, 'I just want you to reconsider the question.'

'Oh, you do, do you?' said Jessie, reining in her temper with difficulty. 'Do you not think I have considered it? Of course I have, and very carefully. But I decided one thing and you another. Can't you let it rest at that?'

Alix shook her head.

'No, I can't. Because you are wrong, because you are not doing your duty as an intelligent woman with convictions. This is war, Jessie, we need every soldier we can get!'

There was a shocked silence. Jessie, who could scarcely believe she was being subjected to such a harangue, felt her temper snap.

'Don't you talk to me about war and duty!' she exclaimed. 'Don't think you can frighten me with words like that. It is not a war – at least it damn' well shouldn't be! It is only a war because the militants have turned a peaceful campaign into war. And you should know, as a woman, Alix, because it's in your bones, that no good ever comes of war.'

'And what good came of that peaceful campaign?' retorted Alix.

'A great deal more if we had only been patient! It makes me furious to think how many years the cause has been put back by little escapades like yours. We had public respect and sympathy until people started throwing stones!'

'Oh, don't preach patience, for God's sake! Patience only brings oppression. It is just an excuse, isn't it, Jessie? It is still cowardice, and you know it! Why else would you be quarrelling with me like this if you weren't ashamed of yourself?'

'If that's what you think,' said Jessie, getting up from her seat and throwing her napkin on the table, 'then I won't bother!' And she marched smartly out of the dining room.

When she had gone, Ralph noticed John Shaw slipping out of his seat.

'I'd better see if she is all right,' he said.

'No,' said Ralph, forestalling him, 'I shall.'

As he left, he paused by Alix's chair and leant for a moment on the back of it.

'If you ever speak to her like that again,' he said, with some menace, 'you'll have to answer to me for it!'

He found her in the petit salon, staring at the dying embers in the fireplace.

'Jessie?' he said tentatively.

'Oh, it's you,' she said, not turning. 'What do you want? To drag me back in there, I suppose, to apologize.'

'Good God, no! Alix's behaviour was dreadful. I came to see if you were all right.'

'Oh, I'm fine,' she said, with sarcasm. 'I can cope with being called a coward now and again, can't I? I suppose I can because I am one.'

'What nonsense,' he said. 'You are the bravest creature I know. Braver than Alix, for all her antics. That is easy to do, but to stand up for oneself is not so easy.'

'No, it isn't, is it?' she said and turned to look at him. She regarded him quizzically.

'You seem very bruised,' he said.

'Are you surprised?' she said.

'No, no, of course not. What Alix said was . . .'

'Oh, it isn't just Alix!' she blurted out. 'You know it isn't. I've seen you, Ralph. I've seen you, all this week and especially tonight. I can forgive Alix – I will do when I've calmed down, but you – to behave like that. It was so damnably petty, Ralph, growling every time poor John Shaw got within twenty yards of me!'

He was frightened by this outburst. He did not know how he should interpret it. He had a terrible feeling that it meant that she did like John a great deal and that she felt he was interfering.

'I'm sorry, I didn't mean to presume . . .'

'You didn't mean to presume!' she exploded.

'I'm sorry,' he said again, his heart plunging with the sense he was about to lose her. It was unbearable, but he would prefer to know the worst now rather than later. 'Of course, if you care for John, then I wouldn't wish . . .'

'If I care for John?' she said, astonished.

'Well, you do, don't you? Or at least you will, soon . . .'

'Listen, Ralph, I don't care for John any more than for a straw in the wind. I care for *you*, you idiot, and a great deal more than that!' She spoke fiercely, and then turned away and muttered, 'Damn, I wasn't going to say that . . .'

'Are you telling me you love me?' he managed to say, after a moment.

'Yes,' she said.

'Oh, good God . . .' he said. He was quite unable to think how to react to this admission. He stood there in silence, staring at her. This seemed to alarm her, and she said in an anguished voice, 'I knew I shouldn't have said it! You weren't jealous, were you? That was just my stupid imagination, wasn't it?'

'No! No, it wasn't,' he said, beginning to grab at the whirling thoughts inside his brain. 'That was jealousy – but I've only just realized it was. I couldn't understand why, but it was driving me mad to see you together. I can understand why, now. My God, this is so . . . extraordinary. I've felt for you something so powerful, for so long now, but I didn't dare think that it would be what you wanted of me. I didn't think it possible you could want a fool like me. But then, you're not a goddess, are you?' he finished, putting his hands on her shoulders.

'No, unfortunately not,' she said.

'I don't want a goddess,' he said. 'You see, I thought you *were* and that I couldn't possibly be good enough for you, that it would be an insult to love you like a woman. And yet here you are, and you love me . . . even when I have been such a damnable idiot.'

'Perhaps I was the idiot,' she said, looking up at him. 'I never dared to say anything. I was a coward, just like Alix said, I suppose. I was so afraid of ruining everything. I wanted you as a friend, and I thought that if we were lovers that would be destroyed. So I had to shut myself away, so you wouldn't see it – and you think I've been cold and untouchable . . .'

'No, never that,' he said. 'There hasn't been a day gone by that I haven't thought of you. You've been my conscience, and God knows, I have needed one. And there hasn't been a day gone past that I haven't wanted you near me. I see that now. All that longing, it was for you . . .'

A calm fell between them, a calm of deep understanding, like an untroubled ocean, as they stood silently together by that dying fire, joined physically only by his hands resting gently on her shoulders. Past and present whirled about them, but they were, in their own space, entirely untroubled. They had at last found each other.

He bent and kissed her.

Suddenly to be held by him made her feel faint, as if the force of his embrace had knocked the air out of her lungs. The moment of calm had passed and she was confronted by the power of her own desire, awakened by that first kiss. For a moment it frightened her for it was so overwhelming that she felt she had no shred of control left, that she could only give herself utterly. But then, when she looked into his eyes and recognized the same look of terrified eagerness in them, she was able to yield to herself. Reserve was meaningless. There was nothing to do but to give in entirely.

Like children they ran upstairs, hand in hand, in breathless silence. He pushed open the heavy oak door of his tower bedroom, and as if he could wait no longer, kissed her again with such force as they stood on the threshold that they seemed to fall into the room. She had never been into his room before and yet it seemed to have been waiting all its life for them to come into it together. The air was softly warm, the light comfortably dim and the tapestried walls enfolded them, to make them more forgetful of the world outside. It was the bridal chamber of a hundred virginal dreams.

But this was no dream, thank God! She knew that well enough as she fell under him on to the bed, feeling the bony weight of him against her, feeling his hands swiftly disarranging her clothes, his warm tender fingers running over her like small flurries of molten lava. She was powerless now, drowning slowly as he touched her, as he unfurled her body from its rose petal layers of crêpe-de-chine, until she lay naked before him, stretched out, every nerve singing with anticipation.

She watched with excited amusement as he stripped off his own clothes, a process delayed by his bending to kiss her or to caress her breasts. She saw his body revealed for the first time; not a god-like physique but the lean, almost ramshackle frame of a mere mortal. But she would not have had it any other way. Those long shanks and unlovely jutting bones were as handsome to her as those of any Greek god, because in their rickety way they enclosed what she loved so dearly, the very soul and heart of Ralph Erskine.

For a second he seemed embarrassed by the look of himself, but she smiled and stretched her arms out to him, feeling tears start in her eyes at the look of relief in his face. With a simple gesture she had said all that needed to be said: it was him that she wanted and for no other reason than that it was him, in all his plain awkwardness.

He lay on top of her, and they shuddered together at the pleasure of that first contact of bare flesh against bare flesh. She raised her knees and guided him into her, unable to wait any longer for this ultimate union. He came in gently but with strength, and they lay locked together, feeling that strange welding of their bodies, as if they were now indissoluble and that although they might separate physically, from that moment their souls could not: they were at last one.

Slowly, they made love, and each time he thrust into her, she felt a deep, warming pleasure as if she were slowly drowning in some miraculous sea. She cried out at each breaking wave and stretched up so that he might reach into her more deeply. All the time he looked down at her with such a face of quiet, grave ecstasy that she felt they might die at the moment of final consummation and never need regret it. This was enough for any man or woman.

And then the storm broke within her and in her utter astonishment at the force of it, she clung on to him and cried out, 'Oh Ralph, my love!' He quickened his movements and with sudden violence he was with her, being washed by the same extraordinary tide of feeling.

Then they slept, cradling each other, her hand laid in his, to wake to the morning of a new life, a life together.

12

Alix sighed deeply and twitched the newspaper in her lap.

'What are we doing here?' she exclaimed to Hamish. 'What?'

He looked up from his book.

'Oh, look at you,' she went on, with some annoyance. 'You are as bad as the rest of them. Sunk into idleness! What are you reading?'

'*Pride and Prejudice*,' he said.

'*Pride and Prejudice*? Good God, what has the world come to when you are driven to reading novels – you, Hamish, of all people? You should be ashamed of yourself.'

'I was quite enjoying myself, actually. I never had a chance to read like this in my life before. Don't despise it.'

'This is the land of the lotus eaters, really,' she said with another sigh. 'I wish we hadn't come, Hamish. It was ridiculous.'

'You wouldn't be feeling so well if we hadn't. This is the best place for you at the moment.'

'Do you think so?' she said. 'I feel more of a prisoner here than I did in Walton Gaol.'

'Oh, come on, Alix, you can't say that.'

'It's true, I tell you. At least there I was acting, making a protest – but here I am, in the depths of nowhere, throttled by my family and by you! That's far worse. There's still so much to be done.'

'Haven't you done enough, love?' he said, laying down his book and taking her hand.

She removed her hand sharply, and said, 'One can never do enough. What a half-hearted thing to say! What on earth has happened to you, Hamish? If I'd known you were going to be like this, I shouldn't have . . .'

'Got involved?' he interrupted, nettled by this. 'Do you regret it now, then?'

'No, no, of course not . . . it's just that I thought you understood, Hamish. I thought you understood what I was about.'

'I do, but I'm not sure that I can agree with it any more. Things have changed now, Alix. I love you and I want to look after you.'

'You can love me, Hamish, all you like, but I won't be looked after. I'm not a child.'

'For God's sake, you act like one!' he exclaimed. 'I can't love you without wanting to look after you. Its part and parcel of love for me.'

'So much for your progressiveness. What about personal freedom?'

'I may have preached a lot before, Alix, but now I can't practise that. There's too much at stake. When you were away I went half mad . . .'

'You should learn to control this possessiveness. It's too primitive,' she said, getting up as if to put some distance between them. She stood at the window and he could see that she was almost trembling with impatience.

'I can't stay here a day longer,' she said. 'I really can't.'

'I think we should. You're not better yet,' he said, getting up. He was anxious to mollify her now, persuade her to stay, because going back would only mean further separation and despite all her perversity at that moment, the thought of that he could not bear. He stood behind her and put his arms around her and was pleased that she did not reject him.

'Oh, look at them,' she said. On the muddy, winter-stained lawn below Jessie, Ralph and the girls were playing French cricket.

'They make quite a family,' said Hamish.

'So you think he will marry her?'

'I think they are in love,' he said. 'And he'd be a fool not

584

to marry her. She's a fine woman, Jessie Hamilton.'

She turned and looked at him searchingly.

'What makes you say that? Because she isn't a militant, perhaps?'

'Not that, but I did agree with what she said the other night.'

'You turncoat,' she said, with quiet contempt.

'If I was mistaken before, then . . .'

'Oh, don't make excuses, Hamish,' she said, twisting out of his arms, 'I can't bear it.'

He leant back against the window embrasure, folding his arms and wondering how much longer this torture would continue. He had thought that in France, away from the heat, she would change her mind, she would see that she had done enough, but it had done nothing. She was like a wounded lion, locked in a cage, a cage which he knew he had made, but which he could not bear to unmake. He could not bear to set her free and lose her.

She was going towards the door and he suddenly felt desperate.

'Alix,' he said, 'just one minute.'

'Yes?' she asked impatiently.

'Why . . . why don't we get married?'

She looked at him for a moment, an expression of incredulity on her face. Then, with a forced smile, she raised her hands and brought them down in a damningly negative gesture.

'Oh no, Hamish, no, not that . . . please.'

'Why not?' he said, angry now. 'Why not, Alix, give me one good reason why not?'

'You fool!' she exclaimed. 'You see nothing, do you? Only an idiot would have asked me that. I didn't think you would be such a one.'

'What is wrong with asking that? I love you, Alix, and I want you as my wife. I don't care what the world says about it, I think we should be together.'

'No!' she said. 'Don't you see, I need my freedom.'

'You can't have love and freedom!'

'Then I choose freedom, Hamish, freedom every time. I

won't be suffocated by you, even if it is with the best of intentions.'

'Alix . . .'

'No more!' she said, and left him alone.

She had hated being so rough with him, but he had an obstinacy which could only be broken by brutality. It was better to finish the thing. There was no place in her life for idle romantic hopes any more. Marriage to Hamish might be very pleasant but it did nothing, it changed nothing, and there was still too much to do, more to do than she had ever expected before she had gone to prison. There were too many sins crying out for vengeance. It was a harsh road, but that was the only way that her conscience would permit her to go.

She went upstairs and began to hunt for a suitcase.

'Where is Alix?' said Mrs Erskine, as they gathered for dinner.

'Resting, I think,' said Jessie Hamilton.

'Oh, good,' said Mrs Erskine. 'Really, it is such a relief to have her here, isn't it? You'd better have Genviève take her some dinner up, Jessie dear.'

'Yes, I'll go and tell her now.'

Hamish wished he could share their cheerfulness. He had not seen Alix since their argument. He had avoided her, not yet feeling strong enough for a second bout. It was extraordinary that she should make such mincemeat of him, but he was really powerless against her. He wished he could manage a little coolness, a little contempt even, but he knew if he saw her, he would beg her to stay, like some whining whelp of a boy. Any humiliation would be worth it to keep her in his arms.

Jessie came back from the kitchen a few minutes later, looking somewhat troubled.

Ralph Erskine said at once, 'Jessie?'

'She's gone,' said Jessie.

'What?' said Mrs Erskine.

'Gone – Alix has gone. She told François to drive her to the station while we were all walking this afternoon. She took a bag with her apparently. Geneviève thought we all knew . . .'

'We ought to go after her, don't you think, Hamish?' said Ralph. 'She's not well enough to travel alone.'

'I don't think there is any point,' he said, at length. 'She didn't want to stay.'

'Do you mean you knew she was going?' said Mrs Erskine.

'No, I didn't think she would go today. But I suppose it makes sense she wouldn't linger . . .' He broke off and looked round him. They were all looking anxiously at him. 'I asked her to marry me,' and added with a bitter laugh, 'I think that was the straw which broke the camel's back.'

'What do you mean?' said Mrs Erskine.

'I mean . . . I mean . . .' He could not find the words.

'What?' said Mrs Erskine again.

'Mother, not now,' said Ralph. 'I think we ought to go after her, Hamish. There's a nine o'clock train to Paris.'

'She could be over the Channel by now,' said Jessie.

'She might have stayed in Paris.'

'They have safe houses, you know,' remarked Hamish. 'The militants. She could go underground. She doesn't want to be found. She made that very clear.'

'We ought to try.'

'I'm telling you, Ralph, there's no point. She will do what she wants. Not you, nor I, nor anyone can stop her. I wish I could, I wish that more than anything, but I know her. If she wants her freedom, I shall let her have it. It's the only thing I can do for her, it's all she wants from me. Her freedom.'

13

It had been remarkably easy to get in. Alix found she was surprised. She had expected them to lock up the place a great deal more securely, but a door with a half panel of glass had proved to be her only obstacle. With the calm ease of a practised housebreaker she pulled on her heavy gauntlet gloves, picked up her hammer and smashed the panel. There was no need to worry about making a noise. There were no houses within earshot of the little station at Leuchars Junction. She put her hand through the hole and pulled back the bolt. The door swung open and she was in.

She had been in that little booking hall many times, changing trains from St Andrews to Edinburgh. On one side was the ticket office, on the other the waiting room where she had often sheltered in bleak weather. She walked in with her various packages, feeling like a passenger with her luggage. But no one would be waiting there when she had finished.

It had been an exciting time planning this raid, part of a co-ordinated attack which she had dreamed up when travelling back from France. On that night, December 10th, 1912, three Scottish railway stations would be blown up for the cause. No one would be hurt, of course, they had made certain of that. Only deserted stations through which no night train ran had been chosen. It had taken two days of hard work with Bradshaw's Guide to work them out, but she had had nothing else to do when she had been hiding out in Margot Carmichael's flat in Glasgow.

Excitement pumped through her now as she lit the small lantern she had brought with her. The chaos this would cause would be magnificent. Three railway stations tonight, and then tram depots, post offices, harbours . . . the possibilities were endless and they would all be pursued until the government finally gave in. With care she began to unpack the bombs.

They had two, just to make sure. If one failed, the other was sure to go off – and if they both went off, so much the better! They were not entirely sure of their reliability, but Annie Histon, an intrepid chemist from Bishopriggs, had done her best, pretending to be making fireworks in the garden shed.

She put one of the bombs on a bench in the waiting room and took the other into the booking hall. Seized by a desire to make the roof go up she decided to roost the bomb in the rafters and managed to find a step ladder in a store cupboard. Carefully she balanced it across the beam, allowing the fuse to dangle down.

'Excellent!' she said, and went to collect the other fuse. The fuses were fifty yards long, which would put the protective distance of a field and a stone wall between her and the station. She put the knapsack which had contained the bombs on her back and began to unravel the fuses, backing slowly and carefully out of the door so that she would not dislodge the bomb in the rafters. She crossed the platform and, crouching down, swung off the edge to reach the tracks. In a moment she was scrambling up the embankment on the other side. The rest was easy.

She reached the wall, pleased with what she had done. She sat down and lit a cigarette which she felt she deserved. All that remained for her to do was to light the fuses and then away back to the crossroads where a car was waiting.

Light the fuse and retire . . . She wanted to stay and watch it go up, she wanted to see the fruition of all her hard work. Finishing her cigarette, she decided that she would stay. She struck a match, took a deep breath, bent and lit the two paraffin-soaked fuses.

They crackled away across the dark ploughed field, two tiny specks of light. Her heart was thumping. Soon, oh so soon – and the sky would be lit up by fire and the ground would shake with the force of the charge. It would be a glorious, powerful thing, the most eloquent statement they had yet made of their resolution, of their unshakable conviction. Soon!

She seemed to be waiting an eternity. Crouched by the wall, smelling the dank earth, she began to wonder if something had gone wrong. Perhaps the fuses had gone out, extinguished by a gust of wind or damp puddle in the field. It had certainly been muddy. The hem of her skirt was sodden with the stuff.

'Damn!' she said, peering over the wall into the obstinate darkness. 'Something should have happened by now.'

She was suddenly seized by angry impatience. Afraid of

failing – she did not want her wonderful explosion to degenerate into a damp squib – she decided to take a calculated risk. She would check the first twenty-five yards of the fuse, relighting if necessary.

She stumbled across the field, staring down at the ground, picking out the lines of the fuse with the lantern. All seemed to be well – so why had the bomb not gone off? Reckless now, she got closer and closer to the station. Something had to be wrong with both bombs, she reasoned, climbing on to the platform again . . .

Jack MacInnes, the signalman, was half asleep in his chair by the stove. They were expecting a special train through at three in the morning, and so he had to be on duty, despite its being a bitterly cold night. Still he consoled himself with the thought that a job on the railways was still one of the best a man could have, brewed up a pot of tea and lulled himself asleep, vaguely ruminating on what vegetables he would grow that spring . . .

An almighty explosion cleaved the still night air, shaking the signal box and shattering the glass. French beans and cabbages forgotten, a terrified MacInnes staggered out to see the station engulfed in flames. He began to run along the track, convinced he had seen a body lying there.

He was not wrong. On the Dundee side, amongst a pile of bricks and debris, lay a woman. Regardless of the fire, he dashed forward and began to drag her away. When they got twenty yards (and he always thanked God afterwards that he had not been a cripple and she just a bag of bones) there was another tremendous explosion which threw him flat on his face. He glanced at the woman beside him. She seemed half dead already, her lovely face illuminated by the light of the blaze.

'Christ!' he murmured. He recognized her. 'It's that Mrs Lennox.'

14

The journey back was hell. There was no other word for it, even when they were only a few hours from Fife. Mrs Erskine's face seemed to Jessie to say it all: it was white, drawn and silent, as she sat rigidly in the corner of the compartment, exercising iron self-control so that she would not give way to the despair which was slowly eating them all up. 'We must be cheerful – we must pray and be cheerful,' she had said, and had managed it until London. But at London there had been frantic telephone calls and more bad news: a further operation necessary but the best specialist not available – time of the essence – situation critical . . . in fact a terrible litany which Ralph had returned to them with. Mrs Erskine had given up being cheerful then, but she had not ceased to pray. Her bible was on her lap and she had, from time to time, sifted through it for comfort as that so-called express train dragged them slowly north. Sometimes she would mutter through a psalm and then stare across at Jessie with such terrible fear in her eyes that Jessie had scarcely been able to look at her. It was like looking at the face of death.

Jessie stared out of the window into the thickening dusk and saw Ralph's reflection as he stood in the corridor, his arms resting on the rail across the window. Hamish Anderson was standing beside him, smoking. She wished Ralph might turn to her so that she might smile or, because she did not think she could manage a smile, at least make some tiny gesture of encouragement, of support, to show that she was at his disposal and that he did not need to bear this dreadful thing alone. But he did not move and she felt the deep pain of his aloneness which she knew she could alleviate but which he would not permit her to. And this terrible distress at losing him when they had been so close, this was worse than all the rest. If only he were not so proud, if only he could see that I am strong, that I can take this burden from him, she thought, racked by the realization he believed he must suffer alone. He does not need to spare me . . .

At length he did move and came into the compartment, saying nothing but sighing heavily as he sat down. He reached out and took his mother's hand but still stared across at Jessie, bleakly, blankly. She saw Mrs Erskine clutch his hand, grasp it as if for dear life, and found she had to look away.

'I'll go and see how the girls are,' she said, getting up. To her surprise, he reached out and stopped her.

'Don't be long,' he said.

'No, of course not.'

He got up with her and stood very close to her. He took both her hands and pressed his forehead against hers.

'I need you,' he whispered. 'Do you understand?'

'Oh, yes. Yes, of course,' she said, and briefly touched his cheek. 'I'll not be a moment.'

He dismissed her with a grim smile and she went into the corridor, flooded with extraordinary relief. Whatever happened now, she felt they could face it together.

She came face to face with Hamish Anderson. He must have witnessed that moment of intimacy for she saw the envy in his face. But it was not covetous, unpleasant envy. It was regret, the look of a man who was coming to terms with the most bitter loss of all.

Half an hour later the train crawled into Cupar. They seemed to alight in a tumble, into brisk evening air. Ralph, Mrs Erskine and Hamish were to go directly to the cottage hospital where they had taken Alix, while Jessie was going with the girls to Allansfield. As she was about to get into the second motor, Ralph came running up and said, 'Perhaps you had better come now.'

She shook her head and said, with all the optimism she could muster, 'There'll be plenty of time when she's stronger.'

'Of course,' he said, and managed to smile. 'Good night then.' He kissed her very briefly and went back to the other car.

★ ★ ★

The atmosphere at the cottage hospital was electric. Ralph knew, the moment he crossed the threshold, that all the hopes he had constructed had been idle. There was no mistaking the gravity of the situation.

They were taken directly to her. She was, the doctor explained, slipping in and out of consciousness, and they could not yet tell if the operation had been successful. It was a critical time.

He saw at once that she was dying. He felt it in his very marrow, felt the insistent tattoo of despair beating on his heart, telling him that there was no more time, that it was almost over; that she was dying. He saw this in his mother and Hamish knew it too. Their distress, a mother's and a lover's, was almost palpable and it pressed down upon him, another dreadful burden.

Then he looked down at her lying on that narrow white bed. Her hair had been shaved away and most of her head was wrapped in bandages. Her face was bruised and cut. He was glad that the sheet covered the rest of her. He could not bear to see any more of her beauty destroyed.

His mother began to cry, her hope extinguished at such a sight. Hamish crouched by the bed and murmured, 'No, no, no . . .' and Ralph, at the foot, gripped the iron rail and felt it was impossible for him to survive this last terrible injustice. He was destroyed now.

She moved a little and seemed to try to speak. He saw her recognize him, and some faint hope returned to him. It was still Alix there. There were still a few minutes left.

'Oh, you are all here . . .' she said. She spoke almost inaudibly and it was clearly very painful for her to do so.

'My dear, my darling, please don't,' said Mrs Erskine.

'No, I will,' she said, with some faint glimmer of her old obstinacy. 'I must.' She turned her head with obvious agony to look at Hamish. 'Oh, my love . . . I'm so sorry.'

'I understand,' he said. 'I do understand.' And he kissed her very gently on the lips. 'Goodbye, my darling.'

'Goodbye,' she said.

'Oh, Alix, Alix . . .' blurted out Mrs Erskine, suddenly. 'You mustn't.'

'I'm sorry,' she said again, and with all the effort in the world it seemed, stretched out her hand to touch her mother's cheek. Ralph, unable to watch, buried his face in his hands.

'Oh, Ralph . . .' he heard her say, and looked up. There was no more. Her head had fallen back on the pillow. She was gone.

Jessie sat alone in the living hall at Allansfield, waiting for them to come back. She hoped that they would not, because that would mean there was good news, but she waited for their return, nonetheless, steeling herself against the worst. She knew she must be prepared, she must know what to say, what to do in order to help him. He had said he needed her and she did not want to prove unworthy of that cri-de-coeur.

At last, at about nine o'clock, came the sound of the motor. She sat frozen in her chair, knowing that this was the end. But now that it had come, she could not face it. I must be strong. For his sake, I must be. But all she could find was weakness and terrible grief. Poor brave, heroic Alix, to end like this . . . It was all wrong.

The door opened and she half rose from her chair, waiting for them to come through to the living hall, the room where, she could not help remembering, Alix had been married.

Ralph came in alone. She stared enquiringly at him and he shook his head slowly, turned away and began to climb upstairs.

For a moment she did not know what to do. She felt the tears running down her face, half for Alix and half for Ralph. He had walked away from her. If he felt he could not turn to her now, then what future had they? With rising panic she followed him upstairs. She could not let him suffer this dreadful thing alone.

She had expected him to go towards his room, but instead he went to the door of the room in which Flora and Jo always slept. He pushed it open very gently and she saw his

594

figure outlined by the night-light. Jessie, quite transfixed, stood a little distance away and watched in silence as he went softly into the room. The children did not stir as he kissed them and murmured good night.

Then he turned, and having carefully shut the door, came towards her.

'I wanted,' he said, his voice dry, 'to make sure there was still life left . . .' but he could say no more. His tears overcame him and he clung to her with desperate strength, pouring out his agony for many bitter minutes.

And then he said, 'Let's be married soon, love, I can't go on without you.'

Epilogue

May, 1913

Hamish squatted down beside the grave in the spring sunshine and put the irises with the other flowers which already enlivened the simple green turf and plain grey headstone. There was a mass of white lilac and daffodils, presumably from the grounds at Allansfield, as well as several small posies of violets tied with suffragette ribbons. Alix's friends had not forgotten her. But then, how could anyone forget her?

He eased himself back on to his haunches and sat down beside her, calmed by the sunny quiet of the old kirkyard. It was good to be in the country. It was a world he could understand. Had the grave been in some vast city necropolis, he did not think he could have managed such tranquillity. There she would have been lost amongst numberless graves, stretching out in ordered regularity like the dreary suburbs where their occupants had lived. There was no peace in such places, but here, where thrushes hopped upon old table graves and where over the wall there stretched a green sea of springing corn, he could believe in a sort of redemption. She was feeding the earth and that pleased him, because that morning, despite everything, the earth *was* sweet.

He gave the stone one last caress, felt how the sun had warmed it, and suddenly, bending over the grave, the scent of the lilac filled his nostrils, almost drowning him with its intensity. For a moment that scent seemed to be the very essence of her, like her own dear warm breath upon his cheek. Before, such a thing would have made him cry and beg the fates to bring her back to him, but that morning it did not. It told him only to rest easy, to remember now only the happiness that they had snatched together. She was safe in oblivion now, free from terrible choices and duties. She had lived bravely and for that he should be thankful. He need not be angry any more.

He broke a sprig from the lilac and put it into his button hole. He laughed to think of Hamish Anderson succumbing to such a bourgeois notion as a buttonhole, but he was no longer so ardent in his hatred. He no longer demanded revolution but hoped instead for reconciliation. Some of his old comrades thought that he had lost his faith but he knew it was only his fanaticism that he had cast aside. He still believed that the world must be changed.

Slowly he walked back across the fields towards Allansfield, enjoying the exercise and the stimulation to his appetite which it brought. This was necessary because it was Ralph's birthday and his wife would let no one else cook his birthday dinner – no, luncheon, he corrected himself, with a smile. Mrs Erskine would look askance if he got that wrong. She was, Ralph had remarked, 'Quite incorrigible', but Hamish had the suspicion that Mrs Erskine was more of a revolutionary than any of them, for all her preoccupation with trivial niceties. She had, after all, accepted Jessie as her daughter-in-law with joy, and even treated him as a sort of honorary relative. That, for a woman of her background, took courage, and for that reason Hamish was at pains to remember his manners in her presence. She deserved that much at least.

He stood and looked at Allansfield for a moment. It was

really not a pretentious house, only a very beautiful one. Ralph could have built a vulgar palace if he had wanted, and had chosen this instead. Hamish was not sure that if he had been in Ralph's shoes he would have exercised the same restraint.

He walked on further into the gardens and found the master of the house in the little summer house which caught the best of the sun and of the view.

'Ah, Hamish,' he called out. 'The very person I wanted to see.'

'What are you doing out here?'

'I've been banished,' he said, with a smile. 'But that's no bad thing as this is an excellent place to work.'

'Just work, eh?' said Hamish, indicating the bottle of wine sitting in its silver bucket.

'It is my birthday. A man needs some consolation as he creeps towards forty. Will you join me? It's a rather nice Pouilly Fumé.'

'That means nothing to me,' said Hamish. 'But you shouldn't drink alone.'

'And you shouldn't listen to my mother. Sit down,' he said, clearing a pile of papers from the other basket chair. 'I'm glad you came along. I've been sorting out the probate and I think I've had rather a good idea.'

'Alix's money, you mean?'

'Yes. There is a hell of a lot more than we thought. I've only just discovered that she was heir to the Lennox property by default. It wasn't entailed, surprisingly.'

'You mean then that she owns,' he corrected himself, 'owned the Quarro?'

'Well, I own it now, since she left everything to me.'

'What about Olivia Lennox?'

'Disinherited by her husband. I was going to offer her the use of the house for her lifetime, actually.'

'How do you manage to be so bloody magnanimous?' asked Hamish, with astonishment.

'She didn't want it though,' Ralph went on, ignoring this interjection. 'She settled for an annuity – it will pay for the gin, it seems. John Shaw found her in Brighton, of all places, making a great deal of being a baronet's widow!' He laughed. 'So I have a country house at my disposal. I don't suppose you want it?'

'Good God, no!' said Hamish. 'Surely you know me better than that?'

'I didn't honestly think you would want it, but I thought I had better ask, just in case. But I have got a much better idea. Alix's capital was very substantial . . .'

'I don't want any of her money either,' cut in Hamish, 'I've told you that before.'

'I know,' said Ralph, 'I'm not proposing to give you any. What I was going to say was that there's enough capital to set up a really effective charitable trust – not one of those namby-pamby things that can only provide hot dinners for six old fishermen in Piteenweem – you know the sort I mean. No, this would be able to give, at its discretion, really substantial sums to worthwhile projects and organizations.'

'For example?'

'Oh, well, to get more women into Higher Education, perhaps, or housing schemes, workers' education, play-grounds, sports fields – whatever, in fact, you decide is valuable and appropriate.'

'That *I* decide?'

'Well, I was going to suggest that you should be the chief trustee.'

'And not you?'

'Goodness, no. I don't have the time for one thing. This would be a full-time job, you understand.'

'So I could choose where the money went?'

'Yes, providing the other trustees . . .'

'Didn't disagree?' interrupted Hamish. 'I see. And who are the others to be then?'

'Well, you have to have a lawyer and an accountant, but they can only throw their weight around on financial and legal matters. They won't be able to object to what you do, unless you propose to abduct the funds or invest in some-thing that will damage the capital value of the trust.'

'So I'd have an almost free hand?'

'Yes, if you can find some like-minded souls to be the

other two trustees. Actually, I thought that Jessie might be rather good at this sort of thing. She hates to be idle, and now that the restaurant looks after itself . . . She needs something . . .' He seemed to hesitate to suggest this. 'But, of course, that may not be an independent enough choice for you.'

'I should think Jessie is independent enough for anyone,' grinned Hamish. 'She is so very clear-sighted.'

'I think so,' said Ralph, with a smile. He filled up their glasses and said, 'I know it isn't precisely what Alix would have done with it, but it is better that the money should be put to work.'

'And the Quarro?'

'That's for the trustees to decide. The capital value is enormous, so you could sell it. But it is a handsome place, there might be some better use for it.' He sipped his wine. 'Funny to think of it. When I first saw that place I wanted it for my own. And now it is . . .'

'You'd rather it were razed to the ground?'

'No, not that. It is a beautiful place and I think houses are not so easily haunted as we imagine. I think it is capable of regeneration.'

'Aye, I'll drink to that,' said Hamish, his mind teeming with possibilities. 'And I will be your trustee.'

'Not my trustee,' Ralph corrected, 'Alexandra's.' He raised his glass. 'To regeneration, then!'

The dining room was looking splendid, even if she had stripped the garden bare to do it. Chloe and Flora had been most helpful, arranging flowers and making garlands of ivy and ribbons, and Jo, who was still too clumsy for such fine work, had made a good effort at putting out the cutlery. It did her no harm to do such things occasionally, although Lizzie the housemaid did it ordinarily. Jessie did not want her daughters to be spoilt by the luxury of their new life. It would make them appreciate the startling sums of money which Ralph had insisted on settling on them for when they came of age.

Lizzie came in from the pantry with a tray of sparkling

599

glasses. She looked a little astonished at the transformation of the room into a bower, and said, 'Oh, it does look lovely in here, Mrs Erskine. But are you sure the master will like this?'

'If he doesn't, I'll box his ears,' said Jessie, pinning a final garland to the hem of the tablecloth. 'You can put the blinds up now, Chloe – and perhaps open the window too. It is awfully warm in here.'

'Look, Mother, Ralph and Hamish are coming up from the summer house. It must be time.'

'It is,' said Jo, staring at the clock.

Jessie helped Lizzie to put out the last glasses and took off her apron. She went to the mirror and checked her hair, wondering if the slight bulge below the high waist of her apple green silk dress was visible enough for Ralph to have noticed. It was perhaps wicked of her not to have said anything yet as she was almost four months gone. But she would tell him today. It was the best sort of birthday present.

They came into the living hall just as Hamish and Ralph were coming up to the french windows. Mrs Erskine put down her embroidery and declared herself very satisfied at her step-grand-daughters' appearance and hoped that Ralph would notice their smart new dresses. She also glanced at Jessie, who saw from her sudden stare that *the* new dress was as revealing as she had hoped.

'My dear . . .' whispered Mrs Erskine. 'You are, aren't you?'

Jessie nodded and would have told her not to say another word more just yet, had not Ralph come in and stood behind her, putting his arms about her waist and his hands most pointedly on her swelling stomach.

'Oh, you did know!' she could not help exclaiming. 'You have ruined your birthday surprise, you know!'

'You wanted me to guess, didn't you?' he retorted, turning her to face him.

'Yes,' was all she was able to say because he began to kiss her vigorously.

'Ralph, really . . .' remarked Mrs Erskine, evidently

embarrassed by this public show of affection.

He released Jessie gently, and smiling said:

> ' "There's naught but care on ev'ry han',
> In ev'ry hour that passes, O!
> What signifies the life o'man
> An' twere na for the lasses, O!" '

'I didn't know you liked Burns, Ralph,' Jessie said, astonished. 'You never mentioned it.

'Did I not?' he said absently, in that way she so liked in him. 'Perhaps not. Well, shall we go in to luncheon? I want to see if your hollandaise is equal to this Pouilly Fumé.'

'It will be,' said Jessie, not the least offended, and took her husband's arm and led him into the garlanded dining room. She saw the pleasure in his eyes when he saw it.

' "Auld nature swears the lovely dears," ' he said, resuming with Burns:

> ' "Her noblest work she classes, O.
> Her 'prentice han' she tried on man,
> An' then she made the lasses, O!" '

'Do you think that?' asked Jessie, laughing.

'Yes,' he said, 'I think I do.' And took her to her place at the head of the table.